"*The Magicians and Mrs. Quent* by Galen Beckett is a charming and mannered fantasy confection with a darker core of gothic romance wrapped around a mystery. Fans of any of these will enjoy it. Readers who enjoy all these genres will find it a banquet."
—ROBIN HOBB, author of *The Dragon Keeper*

"*The Magicians and Mrs. Quent* is a charming and accomplished debut, sure to delight fantasy aficionados and lovers of gothic romance alike."
—JACQUELINE CAREY, author of *Kushiel's Mercy*

"*The Magicians and Mrs. Quent* combines the sense and sensibility of Miss Austen with the sweep and romantic passion of the Miss Brontës in a fantastical feast of delights. From the moment I encountered the resourceful and charming Miss Ivoleyn Lockwell, I was eager to follow her from the fashionable streets of the city to her new employment as governess at lonely Heathcrest Hall on the windswept and rugged moorlands. In Altania, Galen Beckett has created a fascinating and engaging world where the formalities and courtesies of polite society conceal the emergence of a dark and ancient force that threatens to destabilize the kingdom and destroy everything that Ivy holds dear."
—SARAH ASH, author of *Flight into Darkness*

"An enchanting blend of Victorian melodrama, Edwardian comedy of manners, and magic, a trip into an alternate universe in which top-hatted gentlemen dabble in magic and young women of great spirit are as beleaguered by their lack of dowry as they are by the evil villains. The characters are convincing, the plot vertiginous, and the danger bone-chilling."
—DELIA SHERMAN, author of *The Porcelain Dove*

"I loved reading this piquant page-turner of a retro-modernist fantasy novel. But it's more than just a rattling good time. Like its characters, it is not merely devastatingly clever, but has a heart and a soul."
—ELLEN KUSHNER, author of *The Privilege of the Sword*

"Wonderful! Jane Austen meets high fantasy. Just a delightful story in a parallel world of magic and adventure."
—BARB AND J. C. HENDEE, authors of the Noble Dead saga

# The Magicians and Mrs. Quent

# The Magicians and Mrs. Quent

## GALEN BECKETT

BALLANTINE BOOKS, NEW YORK

2009 Spectra Trade Paperback Edition

Copyright © 2008 by Mark Anthony

Published in the United States by Spectra, an imprint of The Random House Publishing Group, a division of Random House, Inc., New York.

SPECTRA and the portrayal of a boxed "s" are trademarks of Random House, Inc.

Originally published in hardcover in the United States by Spectra, an imprint of The Random House Publishing Group, a division of Random House, Inc., in 2008.

Library of Congress Cataloging-in-Publication Data
The magicians and mrs. Quent / Galen M. Beckett.
p.   cm.
ISBN: 978-0-553-59255-9 (trade pbk.)
I. Title.

PS3602.E27 M34 2008            2007041394
813'.6—dc22

Printed in the United States of America

www.ballantinebooks.com

9  8  7  6  5  4  3  2  1

Text design by Carol Malcolm Russo

For Jane,
Oscar, and Charles.

# The Magicians and Mrs. Quent

# BOOK ONE

## Invarel

# CHAPTER ONE

$\mathcal{I}$T WAS GENERALLY held knowledge among the people who lived on Whitward Street that the eldest of the three Miss Lockwells had a peculiar habit of reading while walking.

So often was she observed engaged in this activity that, while the practice was unusual—and therefore not altogether admirable—people had become accustomed to it. On almost any fine day she might be seen striding past the brick houses that stood along the street as upright as magistrates, a volume in her hands and her attention absorbed by the pages before her. No one bothered to wave or call out in greeting as she passed; they had learned long ago there was no point in it when she had a book with her.

And Miss Lockwell always had *some* book about her, be it small or large or thin or fat, with gilt-edged pages or a cracked leather cover or letters writ in gold down the spine. When they saw her coming, people stepped out of her path. Or, if the charitable thought occurred, positioned themselves in front of loose cobbles, lampposts, or other hazards so she would be forced to go around them, which she did without breaking her stride. Or taking her eyes off her book.

For many years the Lockwells had dwelled at a solid, respectable address in Gauldren's Heights, which was itself a solid, respectable district in the Grand City of Invarel: home to lawyers, well-to-do tradesmen, and those members of the gentry who could not afford to live along the more fashionable lanes of the New Quarter (or who had not yet pauperized themselves attempting to do so). Their house was not far Uphill, of course; the Lockwell fortune was too small for that. But neither was it too far Downhill; the Lockwell name was too old for *that*.

The house was tall, if not particularly wide, with four floors and a gabled attic, and it had a pleasing if somewhat old-fashioned aspect when viewed off the street, from which it was desirably removed by a small gated garden. Something was always blooming there, and wisteria coiled around the bars of the fence, so that passers-by were always greeted by a fulsome array of colors and scents.

If the Lockwells themselves were not quite as respectable as the address at which they lived, they were all the same charitably regarded by their neighbors. All three of the sisters had grown into beauties (though the eldest Miss Lockwell was considered to be the prettiest). And the people of Whitward Street could have only respect for Mrs. Lockwell, who had been forced to do for her daughters with so little assistance, as Mr. Lockwell had long been confined to the house by illness.

That the Lockwells never threw parties or gave dinners had to be allowed, given Mr. Lockwell's condition. And if the three Misses Lockwell never attended masques or went for tours about the city in a four-in-hand, leaning out the windows of the carriage and waving their fans at young gentlemen, then Mrs. Lockwell should only be commended for not favoring fashion over finance. Considering their lack of fortune, her daughters would have to marry for security, not attachment, and would do well to take whatever they might get, no matter how old or how dull.

Less easy for the good people of Whitward Street to excuse were the muffled sounds that might be heard from the street at odd hours or the flickering lights that could sometimes be seen in one of the upper windows. But it was rumored Mr. Lockwell had been something of a magician once, so perhaps such things were only to be expected. And if from time to time, in the lingering twilight before a greatnight, a pair of men arrived at the front gate, dressed in dark hats and dark capes, then the neighbors never made mention of it, for Mrs. Lockwell always turned the strangers away.

Besides, such occurrences had become less frequent over time and had not happened at all in recent years. What was more, after a long period of being held in low regard, the study of magick was coming into fashion again, particularly among the sons of lords; and if the magnates aspired to a thing, it would not be long before the lesser classes followed suit.

All the same, there was something peculiar about the house on Whitward Street, just as there was something peculiar about the bookish habits of the eldest Miss Lockwell. Thus, while people regarded both of them well enough, people also tended to leave well enough alone.

❦

𝒮T WAS LATE in the hot gold afternoon of a long day—not quite a greatday, but a lumenal of over thirty hours—and as she often did, Miss Ivy Lockwell walked along Whitward Street with her nose in a book. She maneuvered around a puddle without lifting her gaze, then stopped just in time to avoid a certain trampling as a delivery cart hurtled from a side lane. Ivy turned a page, then, when the way was clear, adjusted the basket of apples that hung from the crook of her elbow, stepped over the deposits made by the horses, and continued along the street.

A group of boys stood on a corner, hawking copies of *The Comet* and *The Swift Arrow* freshly printed with the week's politics and scandals. As Ivy passed by, a gust of wind rushed down the street. The boys let out shouts of "Hey there!" and "Hold on now!" while a number of broadsheets peeled off the stacks and went flying away. It was as if the headlines—intended to agitate the reader—had instead animated the papers they were printed on, propelling them to rebellious action. Fueled by the change in the wind, the broadsheets winged along the street toward the center of the city, and some traveled so far that they did not come to rest until they were plastered against the very doors of Assembly, wherein the laws of Altania were debated and set down. Several magnates, upon leaving those halls, met the papers with some distaste, unable as they were to avoid reading the prominent headline: LORDS MAKE A FOOL OF OUR KING AGAIN.

The boys clutched for their papers and Ivy for her bonnet. A thunderstorm was coming, as they commonly did on long afternoons. It was the heat that caused them, her father had told her once, building up during the protracted hours of sunlight until the air was moist and oppressive, full of restless energy that only thunder and lightning could release.

Ivy quickened her pace; it would not do to let rain hit the pages. Shutting the book, she hurried through the gate, up the steps, and into the front hall of the house.

"Please take this to the kitchen, Wilbern," Ivy said as a gray-haired man in an overlarge suit shuffled into the hall. She handed him the basket. "And let Mrs. Murch know I'll have a cup of tea in the parlor."

Ivy started up the stairs, anxious to continue reading. She had just begun a chapter about the famous magician Slade Vordigan, who seventy years ago had conjured an army of shadows at the battle of Selburn Howe, thus helping the king to win the day and driving the Old Usurper back to the sea, banishing him from the shores of Altania. However, by the time she reached the top of the staircase, Mrs. Lockwell was waiting for her.

"Really, Ivy, I don't know how you expect to catch a gentleman's eyes when your own are always on a book!" her mother exclaimed. Mrs. Lockwell seldom said anything she didn't feel was worth exclaiming.

Ivy tucked the book under her arm. "I gave the apples to Wilbern. They were a halfpenny apiece. The grocer said supply was short due to the state of the roads, which have grown thick with robbers. Though given the price he charged, I might have done better to deal with a highwayman directly."

"I was watching out the window," Mrs. Lockwell said, following Ivy into the parlor. "Do you know you walked right past Mr. Gadwick? You could have greeted him—you are acquainted, after all; there would have been no impropriety. He might have invited you to his house for tea. Only you didn't give him so much as a glance. What do you say to that?"

"I'd say that I'm lucky for my book," Ivy said, setting the volume on a table. "For Mr. Gadwick has a large number of dogs, each of which he enjoys speaking about in exhaustive detail. And the only time we were ever received at his house, as you'll recall, he made Lily sit on a footstool because one of his whiphounds was lying on the sofa and 'must not be disturbed.'"

"He's a gentleman! Gentlemen often keep dogs."

"He has his servants carry them on damp days when he's out with them for a stroll. One for each dog."

"Well, we should be so fortunate to have that many servants. I'd have them carry everything up and down all these dreadful stairs. I'm beginning to think this house has grown taller over the years. Some days it seems I can hardly catch my breath." Mrs. Lockwell was a plump woman, though still handsome. "And you know how I have to follow Cassity to make certain she's not skulking about instead of working. Besides," she went on, back to exclaiming now, "I've heard it said that Mr. Gadwick has over two thousand regals a year!"

Ivy sat in a horsehair chair. "I wonder if Mrs. Murch knows to peel the apples before they're boiled," she said, at which point Mrs. Lockwell forgot all about Mr. Gadwick and, fearing the ruination of the sauce for that night's supper, hastened from the parlor.

Finding herself alone—save for a tortoiseshell cat that lazed on a windowsill—Ivy picked up her book and resumed reading. Soon she rose from her chair and began pacing the length of the parlor, book in hand. The cat hopped down from the windowsill and followed her paces. Outside the window the storm blew past, and the day faded in its wake. However, the twilight would last for hours, as it always did at the end of a long lumenal.

It was not a noise that let her know she was no longer alone but rather a change in the air, and a sensation of being watched.

"Hello, Lily," she said, not looking up from the book.

"But I didn't make a sound!" came an exasperated reply. "How could you know I was here?"

"It's an eldritch power. Elder sisters always know when their younger siblings are creeping up on them."

"No they don't. Rose is two years older than me, and she never knows when I'm sneaking up behind her. I could be wearing bells and it wouldn't matter. But you always know."

"Make that *eldest* sisters, then." Ivy looked up as Lily flounced into the room. She was trying to scowl but wasn't doing a very good job of it. Lily had a soft oval face and a pink mouth that seemed designed only for laughing.

"So why were you spying on me?"

"I was waiting to see if you'd run into a wall."

"You would have been waiting a very long time, then. I never run into walls."

Lily drooped onto one of the sofas. "I suppose not. But you *should* run into them, walking and reading at the same time as you do. Why do you bother?"

This question startled Ivy; she wasn't certain she knew the answer. "There's so much to learn. I suppose I don't want to waste a moment. So if I can read while I'm out on my errands, so much the better. Besides, walking helps me to think."

Only that wasn't entirely right. When she was reading, Ivy could feel herself filling up with jittery energy, just as the air had that afternoon when the storm was gathering. Walking was her way to release it, her lightning and thunder.

"Mother says there are so many books in this house it could drive a person mad. She says they used to multiply like mice and that Father was always reading five at once."

Ivy smiled again. "Yes, he was. I can't picture him without a book in his hands. And another in his pocket."

"But he doesn't read anymore. He just gets books out and scatters them around." Lily plucked at the ribbons on her dress. "Do you think Mother is right? Do you think it was too many books that made Father mad?"

"Lily!"

Ivy intended to utter a firm reprimand, but at that moment Rose appeared in the doorway. Rose was biting her lower lip, concentrating on the tray in her hands as she advanced slowly into the parlor.

"Look, we brought you your tea," Lily said. "Mrs. Murch had forgotten all about it, as Mother wouldn't stop talking to her. Something about eels or peels, I couldn't tell which. But I saw it sitting on the sideboard, and Mrs. Murch said it was for you. We aren't having eels for supper, are we?"

Ivy set down her book and hurried forward, taking the tray from her sister and setting it down. "Thank you, Rose."

Rose was seventeen and the tallest of the three sisters, though she was younger than Ivy by five years. Of course, even Lily was taller than Ivy now, and she was only fifteen. Ivy poured a cup of the tea and took a sip. It was stone cold.

"Is it good?" Rose said.

Ivy smiled. "It's lovely. Thank you."

Rose smiled too, then sat at the pianoforte. She never pressed the keys, but she liked to run her fingers up and down the keyboard, touching first only the black keys, then only the white.

"Here, Rose, I'll play for us," Lily said, rising from the sofa and parading to the pianoforte. She alighted on the bench, scooting Rose to one side, and opened a book of music. "You can turn for me."

Rose shook her head. "I won't know when to turn."

"I'll make a signal when I'm ready. Like this." Lily gave a grand nod, as a queen might when greeting a courtier, then placed her hands on the keys. A brooding music filled the parlor. Their mother complained that Lily only ever played gloomy songs, and Ivy would not argue that her youngest sister had a proclivity for rumbling and dissonant pieces. However, even Mrs. Lockwell had to admit that Lily's skill was great.

Rose tilted her head, staring at the keys, fascinated by the music—so much so that, when Lily reached the end of a page and her flamboyant nod resulted in no noticeable effect, she was forced to give her sister a nudge. Rose hastily turned the page, and the music continued.

To that portentous accompaniment, Ivy picked up her book and resumed her reading. And soon her pacing. In Ivy's experience, books about magicians always went into great detail about *what* the magicians did but never *how* they did it. This book was different. After recounting the events of the battle of Selburn Howe, the author went on to describe the means Slade Vordigan used to conjure the shadow army, which the narrator claimed to have witnessed firsthand. Her pace quickening, Ivy read the account again.

"Oh!" she said, and the music stopped.

Ivy bent down, rubbing her smarting shin. She had struck one of the drawers of the secretary, which someone—Cassity, likely—had left pulled out. She shut the drawer and sat at the table in the center of the parlor.

"What are you up to?" Lily said, turning around on the bench.

"Nothing," Ivy said. "Keep playing." She opened the book before her, making certain she had the sequence correct and sounding out the strange words in her mind.

"You *are* up to something," Lily said, moving to the table.

"I need a candle," Ivy murmured, not realizing she had spoken the words aloud until Rose set a silver candlestick on the table. The candle was burned halfway, which was exactly what the spell called for.

She was supposed to use the dust from a crushed carbuncle to draw runes of binding around the candle, but she had no idea where to acquire such a substance. However, Cassity had neglected to clean the parlor, and Ivy settled for drawing the symbols with a finger in the dust on the table. She supposed that wouldn't be as good, but she didn't want to conjure an entire army anyway, just a small bit of shadow.

Lily sat at the table. "What do you think you're doing?"

"Magick," Ivy said.

"But you can't do magick!" Lily's eyes grew large. "Can you?"

"Yes, I can," Ivy said, checking to make sure she had copied the runes precisely. "At least I *think* so. I've been reading about it for some time now, and I'm ready to try something myself."

"The candle isn't lit," Rose said.

Ivy smiled at her. "It's not supposed to be. It's extinguished as a sympathetic representation of darkness. I'm going to summon a bit of shadow to me."

"But you *can't* do magick," Lily said again. "Not if you hope to marry a gentleman. Everyone knows it's dreadful wicked for a woman to work spells." She lowered her voice ominously. "They burn witches, you know."

Ivy gave her a stern look. "Lily! You shouldn't say awful things."

"Why shouldn't I say them when they're true? They *do* burn witches, in Greenly Circle."

"Nonsense," Ivy chided her, conscious of Rose's worried expression. "There hasn't been a witch in Greenly Circle in two hundred years. And even if there was, a magician is not the same thing as a witch." Ivy laid a hand on the open book. "The magicians fought the witches long ago, during the time of the Risings."

When Ivy was a girl, Mr. Lockwell had told her stories about the Risings. Long ago, the island of Altania had been covered by the Wyrdwood: a primeval forest tangled with green shadows. For eons its rule was complete—until the day ships landed on the shore of Altania, bringing men who wielded iron and fire. They cut down the Wyrdwood and burned it to make room for their settlements.

Some accounts told that the Wyrdwood fought back against the invaders and that many men were lost within its dim groves. One of Ivy's favorite tales as a child recounted how a great chieftain rode into a valley only to find a forest where his army had been encamped the day before. According to those stories, it was the witches who had awakened the power of the wood and compelled it to rise up. However, in time more and more trees fell, and at last the Wyrdwood's fury was quelled by Altania's first great magician, Gauldren. From that day on, the music of axes rang out freely.

At least, that was what the histories told. In these modern times, only a few ragged patches of the Wyrdwood remained. Ivy had never seen any of them herself, as most were far out in the country.

"Besides," Ivy went on, "our own father is a magician, and he's not wicked, is he? And it can't be wicked for me to do what he did."

"Yes, it can," Lily said. "There are lots of things that men are free to do that women get in all sorts of trouble if they so much as try. Like act onstage in a play."

Ivy hesitated. It was true that all of the magicians she had read about were men, and most of them lords at that, descended from one of the seven Old Houses (though a few gentlemen practiced the arcane arts, as her father once had). However, magick wasn't like acting in a play. By its nature it was occult, a thing done in secret, away from prying eyes. Ivy would never do anything that might bring discredit upon her family. But how could there be even the appearance of impropriety if no one but her sisters saw her?

Resolved, she fixed her eyes on the book. "Don't speak," she said. "The incantation must not be interrupted once it's begun."

Before there could be any more protest, she began to recite the unfamiliar words on the page before her. Rose's mouth hung agape in silent amazement, and though Lily squirmed in her seat, Ivy's warning must have sounded suitably dire, for she made no more protests.

The words were harder to speak than Ivy had supposed. Her tongue seemed thick and heavy, as if she had just eaten a mouthful of honey. The language of magick was older than humankind itself, or at least that was what a book she had read once claimed.

She spoke the final words. A silence descended over the parlor, and it seemed to Ivy that a gloom seeped through the windows and pressed from all around. In the gray light, something dark and sleek darted across the room.

"I see a shadow!" Rose gasped.

Ivy shivered. Had the spell worked?

"It's only Miss Mew," Lily said, reaching under the table and picking up the little tortoiseshell cat. True to her name, the cat let out a noise of protest. Her fur was a mixture of cream and caramel and deep brown, but in the gloom it seemed darker.

"Was Mew chasing the shadow?" Rose said.

Lily rolled her eyes. "No, silly, she *is* the shadow."

Rose smiled at Ivy. "Then the spell worked, for Miss Mew ran straight to you, Ivy."

The cat squirmed from Lily's arms and walked across the table, touching its nose to the runes drawn in the dust and smearing them with its paws.

Ivy did her best to disguise her disappointment and gave her youngest sister an arch look. "Well, it appears you're right. It seems I can't do magick after all. There is no need to suppress your gloating."

Lily rose from her chair, then moved around to press her cheek against Ivy's. "I'll go down to the kitchen to see if Mother needs any help distracting Mrs. Murch. Come, Rose, you can help."

"I'm sure she can do that quite well enough on her own," Ivy said, but Lily was already bounding from the parlor, Rose in tow.

Ivy shut the book and wiped away the remainder of the runes with her hand. Perhaps Lily was right. Perhaps magick was something only for men. Just as so many things in the world were.

Miss Mew let out a plaintive sound and nudged her nose against Ivy's dusty hands.

"I have no sympathy for you," Ivy said with a laugh, scratching the cat's ears. "You're allowed to make your own livelihood. You may hunt mice with the tomcats whenever you wish, while we must . . ." Her mirth faded to gray, like the sky outside the window. "While we must sit here and wait for the Mr. Gadwicks of the world to stop paying attention to their hounds for a moment and look at us instead. Two thousand regals indeed! I would take a husband with far less income, as long as he had far fewer dogs."

Not that she had any prospect of marrying a gentleman like Mr. Gadwick. While the Lockwell name might be old enough to warrant such a match, it was far from rich enough. They could barely afford to keep the house here on Whitward Street, let alone grant a generous portion to a would-be suitor. However, that was something her mother had a tendency to forget. Lately she had been filling Lily's head with the notion that each of the sisters would marry a well-off gentleman, or even—if they were very lucky and made themselves very charming—a baronet. Ivy knew *that* was unlikely. They would do well to win the attention of far more humble suitors, if they won any at all.

🜚

$\mathcal{S}$OMETIME LATER, WILBERN limped into the parlor to light the candles; outside the window, the long twilight finally gave way to night. Ivy shut her book; reading by candlelight made her eyes ache. Besides, candles were too expensive to waste. According to stories Mrs. Murch had heard, the Crown was buying up great quantities of them, hoarding them for some unknown purpose, and driving up the cost. Ivy waited for Wilbern to leave, extinguished all but one of the tapers, then went upstairs to return the book to the shelf where she had gotten it.

Ivy had just reached the third landing when she heard a thudding noise from above. She halted, gripping the banister. The sound was repeated once, then twice.

"Ivy!"

She glanced down the stairs. Lily was on the landing below her.

"What was that sound?" Lily said in an exaggerated whisper, such as an actor might use onstage in a critical scene.

"I believe it's Father."

Lily nodded. "That's what I thought. It was very loud, and Rose isn't *that* clumsy. You'd better go to him, Ivy. You're the only one who can make him calm again."

"That's not true."

"It is so. You know it is. Even Mother says it."

Ivy started to protest, but then another thud emanated from above.

"Please!" Lily implored. "Do it before Mother hears. You know how upset she gets."

Tucking the book under her arm, Ivy turned and dashed up the stairs. She made a quick survey of the fourth floor, but all the rooms were empty, so she ran around back to the servants' stairs and up the steps to the attic.

It took her eyes a moment to adjust, for the only illumination came from the streetlamps below. She moved forward, stumbling as her foot struck something. It was a book. She bent down to pick it up and saw more books scattering the floor.

Another thud. She hurried to the far end of the attic and around a tall bookcase. Mr. Lockwell stood on the other side, muttering as he ran his hands over the volumes that crowded the shelf.

"I can't find it," he said. His blue felt waistcoat was askew, and his white hair was a cloud about his head.

"It's all right, Father," Ivy said, touching his arm. "I'm here."

She might have struck him, given his reaction. Mr. Lockwell recoiled from her, mouth agape and eyes wild.

Ivy gripped his wrist. "It's me, Father. It's Ivy. Do you see?"

He tried to pull away, but the motion was weak, and she did not let go. Finally he shuddered, and the feverish glint of terror faded from his eyes. He turned back to the bookshelf, pushing his spectacles up his nose. "It's here somewhere, but I can't find it."

"What can't you find?" she said, even though she had asked the same question a hundred times before. "What are you searching for, Father?"

He pulled a book off the shelf and let it drop to the floor without looking at it.

Ivy took a breath. "I'll get a light."

She ran down to the third floor and found on the landing a lamp Wilbern had lit, then hurried back up the stairs, so that by the time she reached the attic she was panting. Mr. Lockwell was on his hands and knees now, picking through the books. She lit candles all around— light always seemed to help him—then pulled him to his feet.

"It's not here," he said, scowling.

She smoothed his hair with a hand. Years ago it had been dark and thick, just like Mother's and Rose's and Lily's; Ivy was the only one in the family who had light hair and eyes. Then, almost overnight, Mr.

Lockwell's hair had gone from black to white. That had been years ago, when Ivy was younger than Lily was now. Her father had not left the upper floors of the house since.

"Come, Father. Show me your globe." She gave his arm a tug, and he followed as a child might, feet shuffling against the floor.

In a corner, on a carved stand with clawed feet, rested the globe. It was a fabulous artifact, larger than Ivy could put her arms around, fashioned from various spheres wrought of crystal and silver and lacquered wood. Some of the spheres were arranged concentrically, one nested inside the other, while smaller orbs were mounted on arms and could be swung around the whole.

While most globes depicted the world, this one was different; it depicted the heavens instead. The spheres represented the celestial orbs, which held the sun, moon, and stars in a substrate of crystalline aether, along with the eleven wandering planets, each of which was named for a figure from ancient Tharosian mythology. Inside the globe was a profusion of gears and pulleys, and the stand offered knobs that could be used to turn the spheres in different directions.

It was like some fantastical clock. Indeed, from what Ivy had read, the movements of the heavens *were* like the workings of a great clock. Each of the celestial spheres spun at a certain rate, moving about the others in whirling revolutions and subtle epicycles. It was by studying these patterns that men of science were able to predict the length of days and nights and when eclipses and other heavenly events would occur.

"Yes, very good," Mr. Lockwell said, growing excited as he turned the various knobs with trembling hands. "I can use this to calculate when the conjunction will occur. I must set Dalatair to retrograde, and Anares must be in phase with Loerus . . ."

While her father worked the globe, Ivy began picking up books. Some of them were about magick, but other volumes discussed Tharosian philosophy, or the taxonomy of snails, or the making of mechanical engines; a few were books of poetry, and there was even what appeared to be one of Lily's romances (the only kind of book her youngest sister would bother to open), which had somehow found its way up here—no doubt by means of Cassity and her haphazard methods of straightening.

A metallic sound interrupted her, and she looked up to see Mr. Lockwell's hands slip from the globe's knobs and levers. Two of the smaller, outermost orbs had collided. Now they were lodged against each other, so that the knobs would not turn.

Ivy rose and went to her father. She moved the two orbs apart, freeing them, and replaced her father's hands on the knobs, but they slipped off again, falling to his sides. His lips moved, but no sound escaped them.

A heaviness came over her, a sensation of oppression, as if she could feel the night outside weighing down on the roof and straining to creep inside the windows, through cracks in the ceiling, pressing on the very air so that she could hardly draw a breath. It was like what she had felt in the parlor when she tried to work the incantation, only the feeling was more distinct now. It was as if the darkness wanted to suffocate her, or rather, it was as if it wanted to *replace* her, wanted to consume everything she was.

*You're tired and dusty from putting away the books, that's all,* she admonished herself.

Only it wasn't just that she was tired. Because maybe it didn't matter how many books she read. No number of them would ever be enough, not if Lily was right. Not if a woman could never do magick.

She took Mr. Lockwell's hand and gazed into his eyes, willing him to look back at her with affection and intelligence as he did when she was a child. He stared as if he did not see her and instead looked on some far-off place.

"Tell me, Father," she said, tightening her grip on his hand. "Please, tell me what spell will help you. All you have to do is show me the right book, and I will find a way to work the magick. I will!"

Mr. Lockwell's lips continued to move, but he made no answer that she could hear. Lily might be the only one indecorous enough to say that it was too many books that had made Mr. Lockwell like this, but she was not the only one to think it. Mrs. Lockwell would not speak of it—and even Lily had prudence enough not to press their mother on the matter—but they all knew the truth of it.

They all knew he had been doing magick when he went mad.

A sob rose up in her, but Ivy suppressed it. She would not give up, not if she had to read every book in this attic a dozen times over. Her father had been a respected doctor and a man of science; when she was a girl, he had taught her that any problem might be solved if one applied sound logic and diligent investigation. It stood to reason that if it was magick that had altered him, then it was magick that would set him right again. The answer was there, somewhere in the books; it had to be.

"I can see them," Mr. Lockwell said suddenly, his voice hoarse, but whether with fear or excitement she could not say. "I can see them through the door!"

"Who do you see, Father?" she said, but she expected no answer and received none. He was tired, she could tell by the droop of his shoulders and the way he followed her—docile as a lamb—as she took his hand and led him downstairs to his room. She sat him in a chair; Wilbern would come soon to make him ready for bed. Ivy kissed his brow, then went back up to the attic to finish putting away the books.

At last the only book that remained was the misplaced romance. Ivy had not seen this one before; Lily must have brought it into the house. It was entitled *The Sundering of Vaelus and Cyrenth* and appeared to be a retelling of the Tharosian myth of ill-fated lovers, whom the gods cast into the sky for a crime they did not commit, dooming them to never meet again. It seemed just the sort of gloomy fare Lily would favor. Ivy blew out the candles, retrieved the lamp, and carried the book down to the third floor to the room she shared with Lily. She put it on the shelf beneath the window, then reached up to draw the curtains against the night.

Her hands froze. The window looked out over Whitward Street, in the direction of Downhill. The street, so busy earlier, was dark and empty now. Then, as she leaned closer to the glass, they stepped into the circle of light beneath a streetlamp, reappearing to view. She could not see their faces, for they wore dark hats with broad brims. Black capes billowed out behind them, shadows summoned in their wake.

A thrill passed through her as the men paused before the front gate. Ivy could imagine black-gloved hands reaching out, taking the latch, raising it. The figures passed through the gate, and she lost sight of them, for she could not see directly into the yard below.

Ivy rushed from the room and down the stairs. As she reached the first landing, a breath of night air wafted up, and voices rose with it. They were deep and sonorous, and she halted, listening. While she could not make out the words they spoke, there was a questioning tone in them. They wanted something.

Before Ivy could wonder what it might be, she heard her mother exclaim, "And good night to you!" Then came the sound of the front door shutting. Ivy raced down the last steps.

"There you are," Mrs. Lockwell said as Ivy reached the front hall. "Supper is nearly ready, though I must say it was nearly ruined instead. Mrs. Murch was on the verge of putting peppercorns in the sauce rather than cloves. Cassity had mixed up the jars!"

Ivy looked past her mother, but the front door was closed, and there was no sign of the dark-caped visitors. "Father is in his room," she said. "I'll ask Wilbern to bring up a plate for him. Are Lily and Rose downstairs?"

"Lily already fetched Rose to the dining room," Mrs. Lockwell said. She started toward the stairs, then paused with a sigh. "*He* was the one who started calling you by those names, you know. Ivy, Rose, and Lily." Her voice, usually pitched at a volume that could be heard two floors away, had gone low. "I always wanted to call you by your proper names—Ivoleyn and Roslend and Liliauda. Names suited for proper young women. But Mr. Lockwell said you were all so beautiful you were like a garden."

Mrs. Lockwell turned her gaze on Ivy, and it was filled with affection. "*His* garden, he called you. And I daresay you're all beautiful enough, though Lily tends to sway this way and that in whichever wind is blowing, and I fear our Rose is a tender bud that will never quite unfurl. And then there's you, my dear Ivy." Mrs. Lockwell took her eldest daughter's hands in her own. "It's you who binds us all together. Without you, I fear we should all fall apart. Or go to seed, more likely!"

These words left Ivy without a reply. She couldn't imagine *she* was the one who held them all together; she only did what a daughter should. And it wasn't nearly enough.

Yet perhaps there were others who could help her—others who knew her father and who knew far more about magick than she did. Perhaps, if she could speak to them, they could tell her what she had to do. Her eyes strayed to the front door.

"Who was that calling, Mother? Were they . . . acquaintances of Father's?"

Mrs. Lockwell's eyes, so warm a moment ago, turned cool, and she pulled her hands back. "They had the wrong house," she said. For a moment she appeared uncertain, even frightened. It seemed she wanted to look back at the door, only she held herself from doing so.

"Come, Ivy!" The strange moment had passed, and Mrs. Lockwell was back to exclaiming as she started up the steps. "We had best hurry. I fear what Mrs. Murch might try next if I'm not there."

Ivy didn't move. *I can see them through the door,* her father had said. A longing came over her to fling the door open, to go out into the night. To go searching for *them.*

Only where would she look? She hadn't the faintest idea. Leaving the door shut, Ivy turned and followed her mother up the stairs.

# CHAPTER TWO

"J HAVE JUST HEARD the most terrible rumor, Mr. Rafferdy,"
Lady Marsdel said, her voice rising above the hum of conversation in
the parlor. "I demand that you offer your assistance at once in establishing its complete lack of merit."

A hush fell over the room, and for a moment the only sound was the
swish of playing cards being set down. Mr. Dashton Rafferdy turned
from the window through which he had been watching the moon rise
above the fine houses of the New Quarter. Few of those houses were
finer than the one he stood in at present, and the parlor was of such
ample dimensions that it was necessary to take a number of steps across
the room to address the speaker in something less than a shout.

"Most rumors lack merit, your ladyship," he said with a bow.
"That's what makes them irresistible."

"Then it is not true you have made plans to leave the city?"

"Is that what you heard? Then this rumor you speak of is a rare
specimen, for it is perfectly true. I will be departing Invarel at dawn."

*And may tonight be a greatnight,* he added to himself. Rafferdy had
no idea how long this night was to be; he seldom consulted an almanac. What did it matter when the streetlamps were always lit and
the taverns always open? But the longer the umbral tonight, the better it would please him; he was going to need time to drink enough.

"I am vexed that you will not refute this gossip, Mr. Rafferdy."
Lady Marsdel gave her fan a flutter; its lacquered blades were painted
with exotic birds and scenes of Murghese palaces. "It is ill of you to
defy me. The dullness of these gatherings will be greatly increased by
your absence."

"I cannot imagine that to be possible," he said sincerely.

"This is a transgression," she went on, "that will go far beyond my
ability to forgive. I will write to my cousin tomorrow and tell him of
your objectionable behavior, Mr. Rafferdy. I am certain he will order
you back to the city at once."

"Then I am just as certain your disappointment is assured," he replied. "For it is at Lord Rafferdy's command that I must leave Invarel. He sent a letter, calling me home to Asterlane."

"And am I to believe you a dutiful son?"

"If you believe nothing else, your ladyship."

"I believe many things, Mr. Rafferdy. And one of them is that young gentlemen in this day and age cannot be counted upon for anything."

"I must disagree," Lord Baydon said. He sat on the sofa next to her ladyship, all chins and mustaches and good cheer. "I find young gentlemen these days to be very reliable. Indeed, my own son always does precisely the contrary of anything I ask him. There is nothing in the world more constant."

Rafferdy laughed with delight. "Did you hear that, your ladyship? We young gentlemen are not nearly so unreliable as you believe."

Lady Marsdel subjected him to a scathing look, then waved him away with a flick of her fan. Playing cards were returned to their owners' hands, and the drone of conversation filled the parlor again.

"I think you handled that very well, Mr. Rafferdy," Mrs. Baydon said as he approached. She sat at a large table, fitting together a puzzle. Across from her, Mr. Baydon perused the latest issue of *The Comet.*

"Do you think so?"

"Indeed. As a rule, my husband's aunt does not accept *no* as an answer."

"Nor, I'm afraid, does my father."

"Then you should consider yourself fortunate to have found an escape from such a predicament."

"You mean as a rabbit escapes a snare by gnawing off its own leg?"

Mrs. Baydon smiled up at him. "Really, Mr. Rafferdy, surely it's not so bad as *that.* You seem, at a glance, to possess all your limbs."

"Check again after my return from Asterlane," he said, and sat down at the table.

Mrs. Baydon fit a piece into her puzzle, and Mr. Baydon continued to be absorbed by the news in *The Comet.* Though Rafferdy seldom looked at them himself, the weekly broadsheets were immensely popular in the city. Men might be observed reading them in every tavern, coffeehouse, and private club. While those of the higher classes favored *The Comet* or *The Messenger,* simpler folk were more likely to be seen reading *The Fox* or *The Swift Arrow.* As far as Rafferdy could tell, the only difference was that in the former the king was excoriated along with the worst of the criminals, while in the latter His Majesty was lionized with them.

Rafferdy slipped a hand inside his coat pocket, touching the letter he had received from his father earlier that day. He did so gingerly, as one might probe a recently acquired cut or bruise, desiring to gauge its severity without exciting further discomfort.

As a habit, he kept his correspondence with Lord Rafferdy to areas of discourse well-explored by sons and fathers for generations; that is, Rafferdy wrote requesting funds, and his father wrote back with a bank note as well as stern advice concerning the business of managing one's finances. The advice was discarded immediately, and the money not long after, in clothing shops, taverns, and gambling houses. However, Rafferdy had had a good run at dice of late and had not been compelled to write his father for many weeks. Which made Lord Rafferdy's letter every bit as unwelcome as it was unbidden. For what reason could Rafferdy be wanted at Asterlane?

He must have sighed without meaning to, for Mrs. Baydon looked up from her puzzle.

"Are you very bored, then, Mr. Rafferdy?"

He leaned back in his chair. "I haven't decided yet. I've heard that appearing uninterested in everything is the latest mode. Tell me, do you think I would appear more fashionable if I were bored?"

"You always look fashionable, Mr. Rafferdy."

"Well, then I must be bored."

Mr. Baydon glanced over the edge of his broadsheet. "As well you should be, Rafferdy. Socials at Lady Marsdel's house have all the appeal of a streetlamp at night."

"And how is that?"

"They're bound to attract every brainless, fluttery thing in the vicinity." The broadsheet was raised again. The headline read, CROWN REFUSES TO FORTIFY OUTLAND GARRISONS.

Mrs. Baydon fit another piece into the puzzle: a painting of a verdant garden. "That's not true at all, Mr. Baydon. The guest list is very exclusive. Only thirty-two are invited to attend on any particular occasion. And it's said everybody wishes to be invited to parties at Lady Marsdel's."

"Which is precisely the reason why I don't," Rafferdy said. "If everybody wants a thing, then it's a sure sign it's awful."

"Really? Then why did you come tonight?"

"To help you find this." Rafferdy picked up a piece and set it into the puzzle.

Mrs. Baydon clapped her hands, her face aglow; she was a lively young woman and always looked prettiest when animated. "I've been searching for that piece for the last hour. I must have stared at it a hundred times. Whatever will we do without you, Mr. Rafferdy? Lady Marsdel is right; everything will seem dreary when you're gone. You *will* come back to us soon, won't you?"

"Like a moth fluttering to a streetlamp, no doubt. I hope to return before the beginning of the month."

Mr. Baydon emitted a grumble as he turned another page; all that could be seen of him were the furrows in his forehead and a thicket of curly brown hair.

"Why do you read those broadsheets, Mr. Baydon?" his wife asked. "You know they always make you frown."

Rafferdy took the liberty of answering her. "But, Mrs. Baydon, that's precisely the reason he reads them. Here in the Grand City, a gentleman's life is so filled with ease and luxury that annoyance is prized as a novelty, and thus becomes a form of amusement."

"Is that so, Mr. Rafferdy?"

"I swear to it."

"Then your level of amusement is likely to increase, for here comes Mrs. Chisingdon, no doubt in search of a fourth hand to complete a table. You do enjoy playing parlor games, don't you?"

"Nearly as much as I enjoy donning my most expensive coat and strolling St. Galmuth's Square where all the pigeons fly." And he excused himself, departing just in time to pretend not to hear Mrs. Chisingdon calling his name.

He retreated into the study and there discovered a number of men who, like him, were refugees from the parlor. They were drinking brandy and discussing the ills of the monarchy and agreeing that only Assembly was wise enough to lead Altania in these trying times; they were, in other words, avid readers of *The Comet*.

Still, they were preferable—if only just so—to a table of Mrs. Chisingdons and an endless game of Queen's Court. Rafferdy claimed an empty chair on the edge of the room, declined the tobacco box a servant offered him, accepted the brandy, and pretended to find a globe of the world fascinating.

There was a general complaint in the room that the making of business had grown risky of late. The Outland counties were all but lawless, with the king doing nothing about it; the roads were unsafe. And how many ships, laden with gold and chocolate, had been dashed to bits by capricious winds on their way back from the New Lands? True, trade with the Murgh Empire was profitable. *Very* profitable, several men were quick to say. Even so, there were whispers of an ill wind that might one day blow west across the sea. Yes, there had been peace for over fifty years with the empire, but who knew when *that* might change?

There was, in sum, an overall want of stability, a deficit of that most precious predictability upon which both civilization and business relied. Nor was there any hope that the king would do anything about it. Rothard's will was as weak as his constitution, though all agreed his daughter, Princess Layle, was a modest young woman, sensible and not given to frivolous displays. The only hope was that she would be married to a man of good sense who would do what King Rothard had not: namely, rely upon the wiser heads of Assembly in determining the best course for Altania. Regardless of the man, marry she must, and before her father's health failed. That a woman should rule Altania on her own was, of course, unthinkable.

"It seemed to go well enough for Queen Elsadore all those centuries ago," Rafferdy said, looking up from the globe. "Grant you, I'm no historian. But there is a rather enormous statue of her in front of the Citadel."

"And a shame it was ever erected!" exclaimed Sir Earnsley, a high-colored old fellow who wore a gray flannel waistcoat despite the balmy evening. He was a baronet—that is, a member of the gentry, and not a far step up from a country squire. Lady Marsdel must have been positively frantic to get to thirty-two that night. "What sort of signal does it send to the young ladies of our nation to have *her* lauded so? Queen Elsadore never took a husband."

"I believe that, upon her ascension to the throne, she claimed she was married to Altania," said Mr. Harclint. He was a nephew of Lady Marsdel—not that this was at all special, as her ladyship seemed to have a multitude of nephews. This one had the usual receding chin and watery eyes.

"No, not married to Altania," Sir Earnsley said darkly. "She said she was married to the *land* of Altania. We all know what that means. It is wrong for her likeness to stand in such a place of respect."

"Just so, Sir Earnsley," Rafferdy said, "for I gather she did nothing at all, save to turn back endless hordes of Murghs who wished to overrun our fair island, thus preserving the sovereignty of our nation and the identity of the Altanian people forevermore. I agree, *that's* hardly worth commemorating."

Earnsley glowered but said nothing more on the topic, and after that the conversation turned to a proposal put forth by Lord Farrolbrook, which, if passed by both halls of Assembly, would require the king to seek approval before commissioning new ships for the royal navy. At present, the king could order new ships at his whim. As the government must pay its debts, Assembly was forced to levy new taxes to pay for the ships whether it approved of their being built or not. This, it was agreed, offered another example of the monarchy's unwarranted powers and habitual irresponsibility.

"Your father sits in the Hall of Magnates, Mr. Rafferdy, does he not?" Mr. Harclint asked.

Rafferdy set down his empty brandy glass. "Yes, Lord Rafferdy holds a seat in the Upper Hall, though circumstances have not allowed him to attend Assembly of late."

"Tell us, then, what is Lord Rafferdy's opinion on the New Act for Rationality in the Commission of Naval Vessels?"

"I have no idea. You'll have to ask him when you see him next."

This resulted in a moment of blinking on the part of the questioner. "Well, what about you, Mr. Rafferdy? What is *your* opinion?"

"How can that be of any relevance? I neither sit in the Hall of Magnates nor have a vote on such proposals."

"Yes, but we would know what you *think* about it."

"Even when it can have no significance?"

"Of course it has significance," interjected Sir Earnsley. "A man's opinions are everything. They tell you what he stands for, why he acts as he does, and who he is."

"I don't have opinions," Rafferdy said pleasantly.

Mr. Harclint let out a high-pitched laugh. "Now you're being willfully perverse, Mr. Rafferdy. *Everybody* has opinions."

"I don't. Or if I find I'm developing one, I remove it from my mind as quickly as possible, as one might have a surgeon draw a bad tooth."

"What sort of nonsense is that?" Sir Earnsley said with a bristling of brows. "It sounds like the sort of prattle a philosopher would spout. You're not at university, are you, Mr. Rafferdy?"

"Not anymore. It made my clothes smell of books."

"Good. I don't approve of this current custom of young gentlemen attending university and getting their heads filled with outlandish notions. The universities are nothing but breeding grounds for agitators and anarchists—that is to say, men who lack proper opinions. In my day, once a man knew how to read and cipher, the only things he needed to learn were what his own common sense taught him."

*Which meant he learned nothing at all,* Rafferdy was going to add cheerfully. Before he could, another spoke instead.

"And how should a young gentleman learn about magick, Sir Earnsley, if he does not attend university?"

At first Rafferdy could not locate the speaker. Only when the other moved did he become aware of a gentleman whose name he did not know sitting in the corner of the study. The lamplight ventured into that area of the room only reluctantly, and Rafferdy could discern little more than the sharp lines of a sallow face and the glint of dark eyes.

"How should they learn about magick?" the old baronet answered, scowling. "I'd rather they teach young men philosophy, or foster them in the courts of Murgh princes for their education, than instruct them in such foolishness."

"But it isn't foolishness, sir," Mr. Harclint protested, making what seemed a great effort to raise his voice in passion. "Surely Lord Farrolbrook is no fool. Everyone expects him to sit on the front benches in the Hall of Magnates one day soon, and it's said he's a magician of superior ability."

"More likely he is a superior charlatan," Earnsley replied. "You'll more likely find a hog with wings than an honest man who claims he can perform magick."

"You cast aside the notion of magick very easily, sir," said the dark-eyed man in the corner. With his long limbs and black attire, he gave the impression of a coiled spider. "Yet, were it not for magick, we would not sit here now bewailing the weak rule of King Rothard but rather the harsh rule of the Old Usurper's grandson. For without magick, the battle of Selburn Howe would have been lost."

Earnsley shifted his bulk in his chair. "No one in this room was born then, myself included. Who's to say what really happened on the field at Selburn Howe?"

"What happened there has not been forgotten where I come from," the dark-eyed man said. He pressed the tips of long fingers together before him. "I have heard you all say that winds of trouble blow. And I would say that you are right, and also that other winds stir, the likes of which have not been felt in a long age. The time may come sooner than you think when Altania has need of a great magician again. When that happens, I can only hope she will have one to call upon."

Mr. Harclint took up the cause for magick then, proclaiming there was no force at work today that had more potential for aiding progress and industry or for furthering the general advancement of Altanian civilization. "As for the coming of our next great magician, I warrant we may have to look no further than Lord Farrolbrook. His powers are extraordinary, and it's said he can trace his lineage all the way back to Myrrgon himself."

Rafferdy laughed. "I find it fascinating," he said, "now that studying magick has come back into fashion, that so many sons of lords have suddenly discovered they can trace their ancestry back to Myrrgon or Xandrus or Gauldren the Great."

Mr. Harclint worked his wan features into a vaguely indignant look. "Lord Farrolbrook has a ring that proves his descent, one bearing the crest of House Myrrgon."

"What a marvelous relic," Rafferdy said. "Perhaps I'll buy a similar bauble from an old gypsy the next time I venture to the Beggar's Fair. Then I, too, can follow the latest style and claim descent from one of the seven Old Houses. How about you, Sir Earnsley? Will you accompany me?"

The old baronet crossed his arms and settled back in his chair. "I am quite certain there is no trace of magick in *my* lineage."

"Of that, sir, I have no doubt," Rafferdy said with a bow.

After that, the conversation turned to other topics, and Rafferdy went back to spinning the globe. However, from time to time he was aware of a pair of dark eyes gazing at him from the far corner of the study, and he began to wonder if he knew the tall man in the corner. Though how that could be, Rafferdy could not say. He was sure he had never seen the fellow at Lady Marsdel's before; meeting someone interesting at one of her socials was such a rare occurrence that Rafferdy would certainly have remembered it.

He was just on the verge of rising from his chair to see if the parlor was still being prowled by Mrs. Chisingdon when the conversation in the study turned to the matter of enclosure and its many merits. Rafferdy stiffened and kept his seat.

Enclosure had first become the fashion in the counties closest to Invarel a generation ago. Lords no longer allowed their tenants to wander freely through lands that were part of their demesne but instead erected walls to keep people out. At first, the walls were raised only around limited areas: an earl's favorite hunting grove, perhaps, or the hills that formed the view from a baronet's dining hall. However, as time went on, the pace of enclosure increased, and more and more lands were shut off, until the countryside around Invarel had become a veritable labyrinth of high stone walls: one from which the common people could find no escape. Instead, they were forced to contain themselves in ever smaller areas and to scrape ever more meager livings from the ever more squalid tenant villages where their lot required them to live.

It was, in other words, a great success.

In recent decades the practice of enclosure had begun to spread outward from the lands closest to Invarel. If it kept going apace, soon there would be hardly an inch of countryside in the central counties that didn't have a wall around it.

"Every lord with any sense at all has enclosed his lands by now," Sir Earnsley declaimed, summing up the general mood of the room.

"My father hasn't," Rafferdy said.

He might well have confessed he was the secret son of the Usurper for the looks that pronouncement won him.

"Well, he ought to do so at once," Mr. Harclint said, blinking his watery eyes.

"And why should he? If there is an area in his lands he wishes none to trespass, he may simply post a sign in the village."

Mr. Harclint took a pinch of tobacco. "Walls and nooses are greatly superior to notices and rules for keeping unwanted folk out," he said with a delicate snuffle. "I'm sure even the Outland lords and earls will learn that fact soon enough. After all, they have only to look at the wonders enclosure has worked here in the central counties."

Rafferdy did not remember rising from his chair, but there he was all of a sudden, standing in the midst of the others. A warmth infused him so that his cheeks glowed, but it was not from the brandy.

"Indeed, the number of starving has doubled, at the very least," he said, "now that in lean times common folk can't hunt a rabbit or gather an acorn on lands that have been public territory for time out of mind. Happily, such folk can be hanged by their necks at Barrowgate the moment hunger and desperation drive them to go over the walls and they are caught in the act. So the problem presents its own cure, getting rid of the starving just as efficiently as it creates them. A wonder indeed!"

Without waiting for a reply, Rafferdy bowed and turned to depart the study. As he went, he was again aware of a pair of dark eyes watching him. But whether they shone with mirth or derision—or with some other feeling—he did not stop to consider.

In the parlor, he searched for Mr. and Mrs. Baydon in hopes of bidding them a surreptitious good night, but his plan was thwarted when he discerned them sitting near to Lord Baydon and Lady Marsdel. He attempted to go in the other direction; however, he was too late to avoid the flick of her ladyship's fan and was compelled to approach.

"Where have you been hiding yourself, Mr. Rafferdy?" Lady Marsdel said. "There has been no sign of you for at least an hour."

"I saw him exit the study," Lord Baydon said.

"The study? So you have been avoiding me, have you?"

"No more than the stars could avoid the moon, your ladyship."

She gave him a look of flint. "Do not attempt to make light with me, Mr. Rafferdy. If you think because I am old that my mind is no longer sharp, then you are mistaken."

Rafferdy addressed her with all seriousness. "Your ladyship, I may be one of those inconstant and undependable young gentlemen you spoke of; it is, I confess, my ambition to be exactly such. But there is one thing upon which you may depend: I know very well that you are a force that must never be underestimated."

This elicited a dry laugh. "You are transparent to me, Mr. Rafferdy. You would deflect my ire with your appealing manner. By confessing your poor behavior in so charming a fashion, you hope to win forgiveness for it. Such methods work with meek young ladies, I have no doubt. But I am neither young nor meek, and so I will say this: a man can hide behind his charms for only so long. Someday that mask must fall aside, Mr. Rafferdy. And you should take great care how you act now; otherwise, you might not like the face it reveals when it does."

It was rare that Rafferdy was at a loss for words. Yet at that moment they eluded him, and he found himself blinking like a regular Mr. Harclint.

"Do stop staring like that, Mr. Rafferdy," Lady Marsdel declared. "You look positively witless, and it's for your wit that your presence is required at these affairs. Besides, I have decided to forgive your infraction. This once. But you must give me your promise to return as soon as possible."

This assurance was willingly given. With matters resolved to her satisfaction, Lady Marsdel folded her fan and retired from the parlor. Her brother followed suit, and as he went, Lord Baydon cheerfully commended the room to the younger people.

Now that Lady Marsdel had retired, it was safe to depart, and not a moment too soon; no doubt Eldyn Garritt was already at the Sword and Leaf and two cups ahead of him. He went to Mr. and Mrs. Baydon to bid them a good night. Mr. Baydon snored in his chair, his broadsheet over his face, while Mrs. Baydon conversed with a man in an ill-fitting black suit—or, rather, the fellow was directing all the vigor of his conversation at her, and she was braced in her chair, enduring its brunt.

"Mr. Rafferdy!" she said, fixing a wild look upon him. "You *must* come here and meet one of Lady Marsdel's guests. I insist!"

Rafferdy had encountered more than enough of her ladyship's guests, but the fellow had already turned around in his chair and was beaming at him. He was not much older than Rafferdy, but rather bald and doughy in both figure and feature. Reluctantly, Rafferdy sat down next to Mrs. Baydon. Her companion's name, he learned, was Mr. Wyble.

"Mr. Wyble is a lawyer, Mr. Rafferdy. He lives in Lowpark." Mrs. Baydon clutched his arm. "You know, between Gauldren's Heights and Waterside."

He extricated himself from her grasp. "Thank you, Mrs. Baydon, you needn't draw me a map. I know Lowpark." That is, he knew he would never have cause to set foot in that part of the city, as it was home to neither seamy taverns, fine clothiers, nor any other thing of interest to him.

"And how do you come to know Lady Marsdel?" he asked out of real curiosity.

"Know her? Oh, I cannot claim to *know* her, Mr. Rafferdy. What an honor and delight it must be to be able to say one *knew* her ladyship! However, I had the recent pleasure of serving her in a minor capacity, representing her cause on a small matter of business before the court."

"Mr. Wyble is too modest," Mrs. Baydon said. "I gather he saved my husband's aunt a considerable sum of money."

His face grew red. "Her ladyship's case could have been argued by anyone. That she was in the right would have been clear to any rational mind."

"Indeed, argued by anyone?" Rafferdy said. "Yet it was you who came to represent her case? How so?"

"I was recommended to her by someone in her acquaintance." He placed a hand on his lapel. "I do not think I give myself undue credit to say I have something of a reputation. All the same, it was a kind act. Just as it was kind of her ladyship to invite me tonight. Was it not too kind of her?"

Rafferdy smiled. "Far too kind."

"Indeed, so it was! But I cannot say I was not pleased to receive the invitation. I am of an age—as I am sure you understand, as you appear to be of much the same age yourself, Mr. Rafferdy—when it is desirable, I should say even expected, to expand one's circle of acquaintance. For one can never know when and where one might encounter a suitable lady who would be amenable to entering into a mutually beneficial arrangement."

"I take it you mean you seek to marry, Mr. Wyble."

"Does not every respectable man? I have not yet been fortunate in the regard. However, my success in the endeavor is assured, for I am certain that winning the favor of an eligible lady is in no way different from winning a case before the bench."

A fine line marked Mrs. Baydon's brow. "Truly, you think so?"

"I know it for a fact," Mr. Wyble said. "My theory on the matter is quite well developed and my reasoning irrefutable. Once an appropriate aim has been decided upon, I must only present clear evidence and argue my case with force and logic, and a judgment in my favor is certain."

Rafferdy did his best to affect a serious expression. "Tell me, Mr. Wyble, have you won many cases?"

"A good many—very many, if I do say."

"And in the course of your work have you convicted many criminals?"

"Yes, some. A fair number, in fact."

"I see," Rafferdy said. "Then to win your case would be like sentencing the lady in question to a lifelong term with you."

"Precisely!" Mr. Wyble tilted his head. "That is to say, I had not thought of it in that manner. But I concede there is perhaps *some* similarity, though I think this sentence would be more happily received. Indeed, I am sure of it. But I must say, what I've heard about you is correct, Mr. Rafferdy. It was my hope to make your acquaintance tonight. I was told I should meet nobody more clever than *you*."

Mrs. Baydon gave Rafferdy an arch look. "Indeed, our Mr. Rafferdy is sometimes too clever for his own good."

"Nonsense," Rafferdy said. "No one can be too clever for his own good, only for other people's." He rose from his chair.

"But you aren't going already, are you?" Mr. Wyble said.

"I have business I must attend to."

Mrs. Baydon frowned up at him. "Business? At this hour?"

Mr. Wyble stood as well. "I had hoped we would have time to sit and converse, Mr. Rafferdy. It is so rare I encounter another mind sharp enough to engage my own. I would have come to speak with you earlier, but I was having the most delightful time playing cards with Mrs. Chisingdon. Have you met her? I'd be happy to introduce you."

Rafferdy demurred on the plea his business could not wait. Mr. Wyble asked for a promise that they would continue their conversation another day, and Rafferdy granted it willingly, for nothing was easier to give away than a thing that had no worth. He made his farewell, and Mrs. Baydon rose from her seat, claiming it was her duty to see him out.

"Do return to us soon as you promised," she said as they reached the door. "And be safe on your journey. I have heard such frightful things about the roads of late!"

"I'll be going with the mail, which is always accompanied by a pair of the king's redcrests. Besides, I'm far less concerned about encountering a highwayman than I am Mr. Wyble!"

He gave Mrs. Baydon's hand a warm clasp, then called for his hat and cloak and was out the door into the soft night. The streetlamps blazed along the Promenade, and the lights of the Old City glittered beneath the Citadel, a mirror to the stars.

Several carriages were waiting in the street. One of Lady Marsdel's men let out a whistle, summoning the nearest one, and Rafferdy climbed in. As he settled himself on the bench, he saw a tall figure in a black coat walking down the steps of the house.

"Excuse me," he said to the servant, "but do you know that gentleman coming out just now?"

The servant scratched his chin. "Him? Why, that would be Mr. Bennick. He used to come around often enough, but that was years ago. I haven't seen him since Lord Marsdel passed on, not until this very night. I suppose he's been in the west county all this time."

"In Torland, you mean?"

"Aye, that's where his grandfather was from. A man by the name of Vordigan. It's said Mr. Bennick owns the estate now."

"Vordigan, you say? Then Mr. Bennick inherited through his mother somehow?" That would certainly be unusual.

"Nay, he didn't inherit through father nor mother." The servant grinned in answer to Rafferdy's look of puzzlement. "Mr. Bennick may have gotten his father's looks, but he didn't get his name, if you know what I mean. The word is his half brother got deep in debt to Mr. Bennick and was forced to sell the estate to him to settle the debt, then he died not long after that. So Mr. Bennick got his father's land in the end."

Yet still not the Vordigan name. All the same, this explained Mr. Bennick's interest in the famed magician. The tall figure in black reached the street, but rather than taking a carriage he turned and was swallowed by the gloom of a side lane. Someone interesting indeed.

The servant shut the carriage door. "Tell me," Rafferdy said through the window, "how long is the night to be?"

"It's to be a middle umbral, sir," the servant replied. "Eleven hours from dusk 'til dawn. Where shall I tell the driver to take you, sir?"

"To the Sword and Leaf, in the Old City."

The servant raised his eyebrows, but he relayed the direction to the driver, and the carriage started down the broad curve of the Promenade. Rafferdy leaned back against the seat. So the night was to be eleven hours long? Good. Very good.

That left more than enough time for him to get properly drunk before beginning the journey home to Asterlane.

## CHAPTER THREE

ELDYN HID IN the shadows.

He held his breath, standing in the corner where the fuller's abutted the brewery. The drab air that threaded its way through the cramped lane spun around him, forming a gray veil. Just as his lungs started to burn, the one who hunted him rounded a bend, head sidling back and forth, jaw jutted forward. He pressed himself deeper into the corner.

His hunter stopped not five paces from him and let out a huff. "Well, blight me, I swear I saw him come down this way just a moment ago. Now, where has that Mr. Garritt gotten to?"

The woman turned, and for a moment her eyes were directed at his hiding place. She was of an age with him, twenty-four perhaps, and would have been passably pretty if her face were better scrubbed and her dress not so plain. However, neither soap nor ribbons could have improved her unrefined manner.

At last she turned away and rambled down the lane, the hem of her gown mopping up the gutters. He breathed in, and so starved were his lungs that even the river air—dank with the exhalations of tanneries and fish markets—seemed wholesome.

As he stepped into the lane, Eldyn offered up a silent prayer to St. Andelthy, patron to artists and the wrongfully condemned. He was grateful to have escaped another encounter with Miss Delina Walpert—though it had been a close thing. Fortunately, some instinct or premonition of doom had caused him to glance over his shoulder just in time to see her turn a corner. There had been only a moment to nip into the shadows. But, as so many times in the past, within their folds he had found blessed sanctuary.

Eldyn couldn't remember when he had learned to hide in shadows.

Even as a child he had found it a natural thing, simple as a thought. He would use the trick when his father came home drunk, which he did often enough, his hand heavy and aching to hit something—usually his son, since his wives seldom endured for long. Eldyn would creep into the shadows under a staircase or behind a cupboard and wrap the darkness around him like a blanket while his father raged and bellowed, bruising wood and shattering crockery as substitutes for flesh and bone.

"Where do you get yourself to, boy?" his father would say when he woke from his stupor. He would be quiet then, sitting at the table with a bowl of gruel, but the fury would still shine in his eyes, along with a crafty light. "I wasn't so blind as that from drink. Where did you hide yourself last night when I wanted you? She taught you some trick, didn't she? That witch, your mother. She was a sibyl, I know she was. That was why no other man would have her."

Those words never made sense to Eldyn. If she had known the trick, wouldn't she have hidden herself away as well? Instead, he had stood beside her bed, a child of seven years, holding her cold hand, watching her white face: the only thing in the world that had ever smiled at him up to that point. But she would never smile again.

Leaving shadow and memory behind, Eldyn walked up the lane and quickly turned onto a busy thoroughfare, lest Miss Walpert see him on her way back to the inn. He did not know what he had done to win her affection; surely it was through no interested looks or flattering comments on his part. One day he intended to find a wife and start a family, but those things would have to wait until he had succeeded in restoring the Garritt family name and fortune—both of which his father had squandered.

Besides, Eldyn's wife, when he did take one, would not be a Miss Walpert. Once the Garritts had been gentlemen of worth and respect; Eldyn's grandfather had once sat in the Hall of Magnates. While his father had cast the family reputation into the gutter, Eldyn was determined to raise it up again. When he did, he would find himself a proper wife, perhaps a daughter of well-to-do gentry. He must not reach too high too quickly, he knew that, but his children could expect to fare better and would see the restoration of the Garritt name completed. And once he was married, he would find a respectable husband for Sashie; a baronet would be a good match. No lord or magnate would have her, of course. But she was exceedingly pretty. A gentleman would be glad to take her, provided Eldyn could offer an acceptable dowry, and would keep her in comfort, if perhaps not always in style.

As for Miss Walpert, Eldyn would make every effort to avoid her, for while she was an annoyance, and dull, and had a snorting laugh, she was a good-hearted thing, and he did not want to upset her. Or her father, who kept the inn where Eldyn and Sashie had made their home these last three months.

It occurred to him that perhaps the best solution was to move their lodgings to another inn. However, the Golden Loom was the best he could afford; while it stood in an unsavory part of the city, it was decent and well-kept, and he didn't want to make Sashie move again so soon. These had been hard times for her; she had been his father's favorite, the child of his last wife, and she wasn't as accustomed to want as Eldyn was. Besides, she liked living at the Golden Loom. She had told him so just yesterday, and he couldn't remember the last time his sister had said she was pleased about something.

Eldyn walked up a steep way and passed through the Lowgate, avoiding the eyes of the king's men who stood on either side of the arch in their blue coats and red-crested caps. He made his way through the contorted streets of the Old City, past the bell towers of St. Galmuth's, beneath the shadow of the Citadel, and toward the sober gray edifices of the university.

Though the brief morning was passing quickly, he took a detour along a lane down which he had spied the sign of a moneylender. Most moneylenders kept offices on Marble Street, but there were a few of them in the Old City, and this was one he had not yet tried. He paused outside the door to straighten his gray coat. He kept it scrupulously clean, though it was starting to get threadbare at the elbows. Eldyn entered the office, waited several minutes to see a clerk, sat at the ink-stained table when beckoned, then presented his request for a loan of a hundred regals.

"What is the purpose of this loan?" the clerk asked, taking a sheet of paper from a drawer. His lace cuffs had evidently served to wipe his pen when no other blotter was at hand. A circle of gray fringed his bald pate.

"It is for an investment in a business venture," Eldyn said, uttering the words in as firm a voice as he could manage. His father had always complained that he spoke like a priest.

The clerk scribbled on the paper. "What sort of business venture?"

"I intend to buy shares in a trading company that is preparing a voyage to the New Lands."

The clerk could not possibly think poorly of this use for the money. Trading companies were being formed at a rapid pace, now that the routes east across the sea had been charted, and many men had made quick fortunes upon the return of ships they had invested in.

"And what have you to secure your loan?"

"I would secure it with my name."

The clerk set down his pen and looked up. "I cannot sell a name if you default upon the note."

Eldyn moistened his lips. "My name, then, and the shares of the trading company."

The pen returned to the clerk's hand. "And this name of such great worth is . . . ?"

"Garritt."

The clerk pulled a ledger from a drawer and thumbed through it with smudged fingers. "Mr. Vandimeer Garritt?" he asked, his finger on the page before him.

"No, I am Eldyn Garritt. Vandimeer was my father."

The finger tapped against the page. "Your father has a debt with us."

Beneath the table, Eldyn clutched his knees. He was starting to believe his father had debts at every lending house in the city. "My father's accounts were settled when his estate was sold."

The clerk peered at the ledger. "So I see. The account was settled, as you say—but only in part."

"That was the agreement reached between my father's creditors and the magistrate at the debtor's court. It was decided his estate would be sold and the proceeds divided as the settlement for all outstanding sums."

"And so he ends up paying no more than fifty pennies for every regal he owes. It appears your father has gotten off quite easily."

"Gotten off easily?" Eldyn swallowed an incredulous laugh. "I should think not. He has been deprived of everything he had and ever will have. He is dead, sir—he has lost his life."

"And what trouble is it for him to lose a thing of so little worth, when my accounts are down forty regals?" The clerk slammed the book shut. "Good day to you, Mr. Garritt."

Eldyn showed himself out to the street, then stood on the edge of the gutter, his cheeks hot. He had presented his request for a loan to a dozen moneylenders, and all had refused him. Eldyn's father might be dead, but Vandimeer Garritt still haunted him, tormenting him from beyond the grave as relentlessly as he had when alive.

A four-in-hand—glossy black with gilded trim—clattered by, and Eldyn had to jump back to avoid the muck its wheels splashed up from the gutter. He watched the carriage race up the street. There was so much wealth in Invarel, and he asked for only the smallest part of it for himself: a pittance, a seed from which he might grow his hopes, that he might have a chance to earn back what his father had gambled and drunk and whored away.

However, if he was not able to secure a loan soon, those hopes would be dashed. The trading company that had approached him as a possible investor was already preparing for its voyage. And more, he was running out of money for day-to-day expenses. When he was a boy, his mother had hidden away a number of trinkets and jewels so that his father could not sell them for his gambling debts. Vandimeer had all but torn apart the house looking for them, but only Eldyn had known where they were concealed, for he had watched from the shadows as she hid them in a hollow in the wall. He had recovered them the night before they departed the house at Bramberly, which his father was forced to give over to tenants for the income, and had kept them secret ever since.

Until recently. Over the last year he had sold the jewels one by one, making the proceeds from each sale last as long as possible. However, all he had left now was a single brooch of carnelian and a pair of pearl earrings. The lot might fetch fifteen regals, twenty at most. A few more months, and even lodgings at the Golden Loom would be beyond his means; he and Sashie would be on the street.

Only Eldyn would not allow that to happen. It didn't matter if a dozen lenders had refused him; all he had to do was convince one to write him the note. Not that it would be easy. While the affluent had all the money, Eldyn had learned that no one was less willing to part with his coin than a rich man. Well, except for Dashton Rafferdy.

Then again, Rafferdy's family would not have remained rich for long if Lord Rafferdy didn't strictly limit his son's allowance. Rafferdy would pay anyone's tavern bill; the idea of someone going without their drink was a notion he could not bear, most likely because he could not bear going without his own. As a consequence, the one wealthy friend Eldyn possessed in the world had empty pockets as often as full.

Despite his grim mood, Eldyn smiled at this irony, and he found himself wondering how Rafferdy was faring back at Asterlane. He had not been in good spirits when Eldyn saw him at the Sword and Leaf just before the half month. While he had not alluded to the reason he had been summoned home, clearly it was a meeting Rafferdy had not anticipated with joy. He had gotten so deep into his cups that night that Eldyn had been forced to drag him out into the street in the wan light of dawn and heave him into the back of a carriage.

What sort of condition he had arrived in, Eldyn could only imagine. The moon was nearly to its darkest, and Rafferdy would likely be returning to the city soon. When he did, no doubt he would regale Eldyn with the story of the whole sordid affair.

Cheered by this thought, Eldyn stepped over the gutter and put the moneylender's office behind him.

❧

𝕿HE SUN WAS already above the towers of the Citadel by the time Eldyn arrived at Mrs. Haddon's coffeehouse in Covenant Cross.

Given its proximity to the university, Mrs. Haddon's was always populated with students. Young men crammed around the tables, talking noisily, filled with the hot energy of ideas and the brew they drank. However, their conversations tended not so much toward rhetoric and mathematics as toward philosophy and gambling and, especially, politics.

Eldyn's plan was only to see which of his former schoolmates were hanging about and to find out how they were faring now that the new term was under way. He did not intend to loiter, for he dared not buy more than a single coffee. Even so, at ten pennies a cup, it was more than he could afford. However, Mrs. Haddon was so elated to see him after a long absence from her establishment that she cackled like a hen and pinched his cheek and told him he should have as many cups as he liked that day and not pay a thing. For, as she said, "The sight of your cherub's face, Mr. Garritt, is payment enough for me."

This comment provoked laughter all around. Mrs. Haddon was old enough to be a mother to any of them; her white wig was frizzy as a dandelion gone to seed, and her cheeks were painted like a Murghese teapot, which was not inappropriate, as her shape recalled a teapot as well.

After disentangling himself from Mrs. Haddon, Eldyn noticed a group of Gauldren men sitting at the table nearest the window. He had been introduced to some of them before, as they were classmates of Rafferdy's. However, they ignored his glances and instead talked intently—and rather loudly—of astral conjunctions and runes of power. It was only at Gauldren's College that the subject of magick was currently taught, which was why it had become fashionable for the sons of lords to attend that particular college, which was consequently too expensive for anybody else.

Eldyn passed their table and instead—having noticed several hands waving vigorously from across the coffeehouse—made his way to a table in a cozy corner near the fire. At the table sat several of his classmates from St. Berndyn's College. Or former classmates, as Eldyn had not been able to afford that term's tuition. They found a chair for him, and he sat, grateful for the heat; the day was chilly, as short days after long nights often were.

As he sipped his coffee, savoring the flavor of it, he asked his old companions about which classes they were attending and what their professors had discussed. However, as usual, they were less inclined to talk about their studies than the news in the latest issue of *The Fox*.

"It's criminal, that's what it is," Curren Talinger said, thumping the table so that they all had to grasp their cups and saucers to keep them from flying off. "It's positively criminal what they're doing."

Eldyn shook his head; he hadn't read the broadsheets in several days. "What *who* is doing?"

"The criminals, I should imagine," Orris Jaimsley replied with a bent grin. "They're usually the ones who perpetrate the crimes."

"Oh, they're criminals, all right," Talinger went on, clearly in a mood for oration. His red hair belied his Westland heritage. That and his temper: the table received another blow from a meaty fist that seemed better suited to a workman than a student of philosophy. "They'd make the king crawl on his belly and beg just to build a ship to defend Altania's shores. But the swine are running things now, and we have only ourselves to blame for it. We're the ones who put them on top."

"I don't remember voting for a Sir Hogg or a Mr. Porkly in the last election," Eldyn said, returning Jaimsley's grin.

"I think he's referring to members of Assembly," Dalby Warrett said, as usual not getting the joke.

"Then he's insulted swine everywhere," Jaimsley proclaimed. He was a gangly young man who more than made up for his homely looks with an appealing wit. No one was more popular at St. Berndyn's.

"Really, Talinger, do you think this new act is so bad as all that?" Warrett said when their mirth had subsided. He had a face that, while well wrought, was too placid to be handsome; he was forever attempting to throw water on Talinger's fires. "The Hall of Magnates has committed worse crimes than this of late. Besides, Assembly has always held the kingdom's purse strings."

"Held them?" Talinger shook his head. "More like clutched them tight and knotted them shut, while at the same time slitting a hole in the bottom of the purse. They build walls around their manors to protect them, but they won't let the king build a ship to protect our country."

"Protect our country from what?" Jaimsley said with a roll of his eyes. "There's been peace with the Murgh Empire for half a century. And even if they decided to invade tomorrow, do you really think you could trust our king to keep Altania safe?"

Talinger had to concede the point. "Maybe not King Rothard. He was already weak before he got ill. He never should have given up so much ground to Assembly. But if we had a strong king, a rightful king . . ."

Jaimsley gave him a sharp look. "What are you saying?"

"All I'm saying is . . ." Even Talinger had the sense to lower his voice, noisy as the coffeehouse was. "All I'm saying is that if *Somebody* was ever to come back to Altania, he would put an end to these sorts of problems. You can bet *Somebody* would stop the magnates from raiding Altania's coffers and leaving nothing for the common folk, and you can bet he would put Assembly in its place. And if the princess married *Somebody,* then no one could complain the crown wasn't rightfully his."

Warrett's cup clattered against his saucer, and Eldyn cast a glance over his shoulder. What Talinger had said was dangerously close to treason, and the Gray Conclave had spies everywhere.

"Oh, dry your breeches, Warrett," Talinger said. "I didn't speak a name. Even if the Black Dog's men are sniffing about, there's nothing they can do. All I said was *Somebody.*"

Yes. And Eldyn, just like everyone else, knew that *Somebody* meant not just anybody but rather Huntley Morden—grandson of the Old Usurper, Bandley Morden—who rumor told dwelled in the court of a Murghese prince, waiting for the right wind to blow him and the fleet of ships he was building east across the sea to the shores of Altania so he might seize the throne his grandfather had failed to win. Given these times, Eldyn was not so certain as Talinger that one of Lord Valhaine's agents, if he had overheard, would have sat there and done nothing. Men had been jailed for as much and hung for little more.

However, nothing did happen, and after a moment Warrett retrieved his cup, giving Talinger a dark look. "Whatever you might think of the king, Talinger, you cannot truly believe Princess Layle would willingly marry her father's sworn enemy."

"What do you want with a king anyway, Talinger?" Jaimsley said more lightly. "Are you so keen to be told what to do? If so, you need only to look there."

Jaimsley gestured toward the wall behind them. Warrett and especially Talinger glared at the piece of paper tacked to the wall, and Eldyn could not blame them. The Rules of Citizenship had gone up in every public place in the city by order of the Black Dog himself, Lord Valhaine. They listed all the things a good citizen of Altania was to do and not do. Among its myriad lines, the rules stated when people could gather, and where, and in what numbers. Rule Six said that anyone hearing treasonous talk should report it to a magistrate at once. Rule Fourteen stated that one was not to insult the king, the princess, or Assembly in public.

Eldyn was pretty certain they had all violated *that* particular rule.

Breaking any of the rules was a punishable crime. Tearing the rules down was one too. Whether that crime got you a fine, a night in jail, or an appointment with the noose at Barrowgate all depended on how foul a mood the judge was in, how large a bribe you could pay, and whether your grandfather had marched under the Arringhart stag or the Morden hawk.

"That's what a king does, Talinger," Jaimsley said with a serious look. "He can't help it. It's in his blood. So if you're intent on having a monarch, be sure to take special note of Rule Twenty-four. It tells you when you can wipe your arse."

Talinger's face reddened another shade. "Better a just king telling you what to do than a bunch of greedy lords."

"And I say we'd be better off without either king or Assembly," Jaimsley said, balancing a spoon on his finger. "Perhaps, if we're lucky, one will do away with the other, and Altania will be rid of the scourge of both."

"And who would rule us then?" Talinger said with a snort.

"Why, we would rule ourselves." Jaimsley gestured around the table. "The people would rule Altania."

Perhaps it was only the effects of too much coffee, but these words filled Eldyn with a peculiar exhilaration. What if it did not matter that one was a lord or of the gentry or the lowest of the commons? What if a man's fate wasn't decided by who his father was, but was rather something he could choose for himself?

"I would start by tossing all the magnates in the pits beneath the Citadel," Warrett declared, his usually tranquil manner replaced by a certain vehemence. "Throw away the keys and let them rot in there with the other rats, that's what I say."

"Now, that's the spirit," Jaimsley said with a laugh. "We don't need them to make decisions for us. The people can decide for themselves what's best for Altania."

"But can they?" Eldyn said, realizing only after the fact that he had spoken the words. His excitement had faded. "Can common people really be counted upon to make decisions about important matters? What if they choose unwisely?"

Jaimsley gave him a sharp look. "But that's not possible, Garritt. If something is truly the will of the people of Altania, then it cannot possibly be wrong. It is only when the desires of the people are supplanted by the greed of the magnates that ill arises."

While Jaimsley's words made sense, somehow Eldyn could not feel the same certainty. He remembered once, years ago, when his father took him to see a hanging at Barrowgate. Eldyn had been no more than five or six; why his father had wished him to see such a spectacle, he couldn't say. Perhaps it was out of simple cruelty.

He remembered how his father had hoisted him up on his shoulders so that Eldyn could see the black walls of Barrowgate. Who the men on the scaffold were he did not know, but the crowd shouted and jeered at them as if they were beasts. Except, after a while, it was the crowd that seemed to be comprised of beasts. Men threw stones and old women howled, while children danced about and vendors sold sweets and cups of grog from carts, as if it were a festival. There was a hunger in the air, and if one man had dared to get up and claim that one of the condemned was in fact innocent and should be spared, Eldyn was sure the crowd would have dragged him down and torn him apart with their hands.

As they waited for the execution, his father had bought him a treacle tart—which was strange, as his father never bought him sweets or presents. But he did that day, and he urged Eldyn to eat it, which he did, even though it made his stomach sick.

"Cheer," his father told him. "Cheer when they pull the lever."

Then the trapdoor on the scaffold was dropped, and the prisoners fell. However, the hangman had tied the ropes too long, and when the men stopped falling, their necks broke, killing them. The crowd hissed and swore at being denied the spectacle of a slow death; then they turned away, going back to their lives as cobblers or washing women or grocers.

Eldyn wondered—were these the same people who would decide the fate of Altania in the absence of king and Assembly? His stomach felt sour, as it had that day long ago. But it was only too much of Mrs. Haddon's strong coffee. He glanced out the window and saw that dusk was gathering; the short day was nearly done. He stood and bid his companions farewell.

"You will be back at university next term, won't you, Garritt?" Talinger asked as Eldyn put on his coat. "We need that pretty cherub's face of yours to attract the girls when we go out drinking."

"Of course I'll be back," he said, doing his best to sound confident. "I'm preoccupied with business right now, that's all. It should be concluded soon. Until then, you'll just have to make do with Jaimsley's wit."

"Then saints help us all," Talinger said.

And the three were already back to discussing the doings of king and Assembly by the time Eldyn turned from the table.

🍂

HE WALKED PAST the old church of St. Adaris on his way back to the Golden Loom.

Eldyn knew he shouldn't have come here; the church was out of the way, and he had told Sashie he would be back by afternoon. Now the brief day was done, and twilight settled like ash over the city. Besides, he had not set foot inside a church in years. There was nothing for him within those walls.

But he wanted to see the angel again.

Like so many of the old churches in Invarel, the chapel of St. Adaris had seen better days. It glowered at the end of a squalid lane on the far side of Durrow Street. It was a hulking edifice, its walls streaked with soot and bird droppings.

Eldyn gripped the bars of the fence that bounded the churchyard. The statue of a beautiful youth glowed amid the gravestones in the moonlight. He was naked save for a ribbon of cloth that swirled about him; his wrists were bound behind his back, and steel arrows pierced his flesh. Dark tears streamed from the weathered hollows of his eyes.

The statue was not really that of an angel. It was only years after he first saw it as a boy that Eldyn learned it was meant to depict St. Andelthy, who was martyred for his faith fourteen centuries ago: shot full of arrows by the barbarians who inhabited Altania when civilized men first set foot upon its shores, bringing the word of God with them. Maybe it was his silent prayer to St. Andelthy earlier that day that had made him think of the statue, or perhaps it was the thoughts of the past that had haunted him of late. Eldyn wasn't certain. All he knew was that he had wanted to look upon it again, and here he was.

Why his father had brought him past this place long ago, Eldyn couldn't remember. Certainly it hadn't been to hear the priests speak; as far as he knew, his father never willingly crossed the threshold of a church in his life. More likely he had come here to see one of his dodgy acquaintances, someone to whom he owed a gambling debt, or who owed him. He would often drag Eldyn along on such encounters, perhaps with the thought that men were less apt to be violent with a child about. However, more than once Eldyn had seen his father come out of some back room with his jaw dripping red and his grin less a tooth than it had possessed upon entering.

"Come, boy," he'd say, grabbing Eldyn by the scruff of the neck and shoving him out the door. "Don't you cry now, or I'll give you something to truly weep for later." And with that he would spit blood onto the street, head for the nearest tavern, and drink until he ran out of money. After he was thrown out into the gutter, Eldyn would have to lead him staggering back to whatever dank house they were letting at the time.

It was on one such occasion that they passed by the church of St. Adaris and Eldyn spied the statue. That time his father left him outside while he called on his business associate—some men, Eldyn had learned by then, had no qualms at all about doing violence when a child was watching—and he stood for an hour, staring through the iron fence. A holly tree grew behind the statue, and a pair of branches spread out like dark green wings. Eldyn supposed that was what had made him think the statue was an angel.

As he gazed at it, he wondered who would shoot so beautiful a creature, why it hadn't spread its wings and flown away, and whether it wept because it hurt or—and Eldyn still didn't know why this thought had occurred to him—if it wept for the men who had shot the arrows.

The statue wasn't truly weeping, of course. It was rainwater dirtied by soot, running from the timeworn pits of the statue's eyes, that had made the black trails down its marble cheeks.

All the same, the statue still held some of that same magick it had for him as a child. Yet it was altered as well, just as Eldyn himself was altered. Despite the black tears, despite the arrows that pierced his side, the expression on the angel's face no longer seemed one of pain to him but rather one of ecstasy. The ribbon of cloth, so delicately wrought in stone, flowed about his body, clinging between the legs, obscuring but not completely hiding the fullness there.

A noise disturbed him from his trance, and a wedge of dirty yellow light cut across the churchyard. A door had opened in the side of the church. Even as Eldyn watched, one of the priests came out, wearing a black cassock and carrying a basket in his arms. Likely the basket contained the leavings from the night's meal in the refectory and was bound for the poor box in the alley behind the church.

As the priest drew closer, Eldyn saw that he was not old, as Eldyn had expected for some reason, but was instead a young man. His hair was blond and curling, and his face smooth and not so unlike the angel's. Eldyn must have taken a step back from the fence, for the priest halted and peered at the shadowed street.

"Who's there?" he called out.

Eldyn turned, ready to hurry back down the lane.

"You need not fear, friend. The church is open to all. If you wish for God's blessing, you have only to enter and ask for it."

Though he did not know why—he had nothing to say to a priest— Eldyn turned back. He had never attended church as a boy. But a few times, on those occasions when Vandimeer had brought him into the Old City only to abandon him, he had slipped inside the doors of St. Galmuth's and watched from the niche of some nameless saint while the priests performed their rituals.

He could not understand the words they spoke, chanted as they were in high Tharosian, but it seemed to him the sounds that soared up among the arches were somehow beyond words: purer, truer—a language that spoke not to the mind but to the heart. Most of all he had loved the pageantry. He loved the scent of the incense, the vestments of gold and white and scarlet, the candles, and the silver font on the altar. He loved the way the priests moved: slowly, deliberately, as if even the slightest flick of a finger carried meaning.

When he was sixteen, he told his father he wished to enter the priesthood. That had earned him a laugh and the back of a hand across his mouth. "No son of mine will ever be a priest," his father said. "I'd sooner break your neck than give you over to those simpering prats. Get that idea out of your head, boy. You'll follow me to the pits of the Abyss, you will—if I don't send you there first."

He had never asked his father about it again, and in time Eldyn had forgotten about his wish to enter the priesthood. But now, as he stood there in the gathering dusk, the forgotten desires came back to him. Was that why he had come here? He longed to breathe in the incense again, to touch the cool water in the font, to let it wash away the taint upon him.

Eldyn stepped from the shadows. The young priest appeared startled, but only for a moment; then he smiled, and so beautiful did the expression render him that he seemed a statue himself. Eldyn opened his mouth to speak, but at that moment another figure appeared in the doorway.

"What are you doing, Brother Dercent?" This one was short and squat, and his voice was coarse. "Are you talking to someone out there? Who is it?"

Whatever magick had gripped Eldyn was dispelled. What had he been thinking? A peaceful life within the walls of a church was closed to him. Even if the priesthood would accept one as old as he, he had not the funds to pay the required endowment. Besides, who would take care of Sashie? Eldyn shrank back from the fence. The younger priest seemed about to speak, but the newcomer was faster.

"Has one of them come again from Durrow Street to mock us? You should have called for me at once." The priest hurried down the steps and pushed past the younger man, the one called Dercent. He shook a fat fist in Eldyn's direction. "I see you lurking there in the shadows. They cannot conceal you from the light of God. Begone, daemon. By all the saints, I command you. Go back to your houses of sin and trouble us no more!"

A shame welled up in Eldyn, as it had earlier that day outside the moneylender's office. Surely the elder priest had mistaken him for someone—something—he was not. All the same, the full force of those words fell upon him, and as if there was power in that invocation, as if he were indeed a wicked thing deserving to be cast out, Eldyn found himself retreating.

"That's right," the elder priest called after him. "You have no power here, fiend. Begone!"

Folding the shadows around himself, Eldyn turned away from the priests and the angel and slunk into the night.

# CHAPTER FOUR

**H**ALF A MONTH had gone by since the unexpected visitors appeared at the door of the house on Whitward Street. Though each twilight Ivy looked out the window, she never saw a pair of tall men in dark capes walking up the street, and no one called at their front gate.

A few times she considered asking her mother about the men. Then she remembered the fearful look she had seen in Mrs. Lockwell's eyes that night and held her tongue. Nor could she ask Mr. Lockwell. He never answered her questions, and the one time she did mention that some men had come to the door, he grew agitated, snatching books from the shelves in the attic and tearing out their pages, and it took her over an hour to calm him.

Just after the turn of the month, there came a series of particularly long nights interspersed by brief days. The weather grew chilly with so little sun to warm the world, and a mist rolled out of the west. By the fourth such night—an umbral of twenty-two hours—it grew so cold that the rain turned to snow, and when dawn finally came it found all of Invarel glazed with white.

They kept to the parlor on the second floor as much as possible so they would not have to heat the upper stories, save for Mr. Lockwell's room. Since it was too cold to be out of doors, they found what activities they could within. There were linens to mend, and Lily's charity basket had languished in a corner for so long that Miss Mew had taken it for a bed. Ivy urged Lily to remove the cat and pull out the basket of half-finished shirts so she might complete some of her work.

"Mighty Loerus!" Lily exclaimed as she pricked her finger for the third time that day. She had copied the bad habit of swearing by extinct Tharosian gods from a romance she had read in which the hero did the same. "It's so dark in here I can't see what I'm doing. Did you misread the almanac, Ivy? I thought you said nightfall was hours off."

"It's the fog that makes it so dim," Ivy said, peering at her own sewing in the wan light. "But tonight is to be a long umbral and tomorrow short again, so we'd best sew as much as we can while we have any sun at all."

"We could light candles," Lily said.

"Candles are for night, not day."

"Well, it's nearly dark as night, so I think we should light some."

"Not when they cost as much as they do. Move closer to the window, and you'll be able to see better."

"It's too cold by the window."

"You can share my lap blanket. Now, come here and sit down."

With much dragging of feet, Lily did so, plopping her basket down beside her. "I don't know who would want to wear these ugly shirts anyway."

"There are many who will be grateful to have new garments, however simple," Ivy said. "Not everyone in the city is so fortunate as we are. Besides, Rose's shirts aren't ugly at all. They're quite handsome."

Rose looked up from her work and smiled at Ivy. No matter how dark the room, her needle always set neat, even stitches in the cloth. "I always have light when you're near, Ivy," she said.

Ivy smiled back at her, then bent her head over her sewing. Before long Lily let out a sigh, crumpled her shirt back into the charity basket, and went to the pianoforte, where she commenced practicing all her most dolorous chords.

Mrs. Lockwell entered a short while later, huffing for breath after coming up the stairs. "Oh, it's so dark in here!" she exclaimed. "I can hardly see my hand if I wave it before my face. Light a candle, Lily. Or two or three. And put more wood on the fire, Ivy. We shall freeze to death!"

Lily gave Ivy a smug look, then flounced about the parlor, lighting candles. Ivy said nothing and did as her mother asked.

After that, their work proceeded more easily, with more laughter and fewer needle pricks, and Ivy tried not to think of the extra cost of the wood and candles. She decided a little tea would be a welcome reward for their work—Lily had finally been coerced into finishing a shirt—and went down to the kitchen to prepare a pot.

As she started up the stairs, she heard the bell at the front gate ring; the post had come. Ivy wrapped her shawl around her shoulders, braving the bitter air to retrieve the post from the box, then hurried up to the warmth of the parlor.

"Here's the tea," she said, setting the tray on the table. "And the post as well."

Lily leaped up from the bench at the pianoforte. "Is there anything addressed to me?"

She always seemed to think there would be a letter for her, though from whom it might come, Ivy couldn't imagine. The cold had been so shocking, Ivy hadn't taken time to look at the post. She picked it up from the tray. There were two letters, neither of them for Lily.

"There's one here for Father," she said in surprise.

Ivy held up the letter. The address was written in a formal—if rather cramped—hand and was sealed with a circle of red wax. Before Ivy could turn the letter over and read the sender's name, Mrs. Lockwell plucked it from her grasp.

"I'll take that," she said, and without looking at it tucked the letter into the pocket of her apron. "Now, pour the tea, Lily, before it turns to ice."

"Who is the other letter from?" Rose asked.

Ivy tried not to think of the letter her mother had whisked away and picked up the other. "It's from our cousin, Mr. Wyble," she said.

"A letter from Mr. Wyble?" Mrs. Lockwell said in a tone that might have frosted the windowpanes if they hadn't been already. "What an unexpected pleasure. Usually he chooses to inflict himself upon us in person."

Lily giggled but clapped a hand to her mouth at a sharp look from Ivy. "Would you like to read it, Mother?" Ivy said, holding out the letter, but Mrs. Lockwell shook her head.

"You read it to us, Ivoleyn. My eyes are too poor for this light. And perhaps his words will be improved coming from your lips."

Ivy doubted that would be the case, but she did her best to inject a note of enthusiasm into her voice as she held the letter close to a candle and read aloud. It was written in an overlarge and effusive hand, which, though a strain on the eye, meant the letter was thankfully not very long despite its several pages.

"*To my beloved Aunt Lockwell and my cherished cousins,*" Ivy read, "*submitted with most felicitous greetings and a fervent wish for your continued happiness and well-being.*"

"I hardly think he wishes for *my* continued well-being," Mrs. Lockwell exclaimed. "For the longer I continue to be well, the longer this house will continue to not be *his*."

Ivy chose to ignore this comment and kept reading.

"*I regret that I was unable to pay you a visit this month past, as is my usual custom. My occupation, as you know, requires my fullest attention. I must always be at my law books, for it is my duty to know of every regulation and statute there is. Indeed, there is no rule too minor, obscure, or dull that I will not spend hours and hours reading all that there is about it.*"

"And then spend hours and hours telling us about it," Lily said with a groan.

Ivy cast her a sharp look, though she had to admit, Mr. Wyble *did* have a tendency to expound at length upon legal philosophy when he visited.

"*While my schedule would have permitted me to pay you a visit around the middle of the month, another opportunity was presented to me, which, I am sure once the particulars are heard, you must judge was the wisest investment of my time. Recently I had the good fortune to be of service to Lady Marsdel, a most noble personage of the highest degree. In her extreme—dare I say, almost overpowering—generosity, she invited me to an affair at her house in the New Quarter. There I was happy to make the acquaintance of many remarkable and important persons.*"

"More important persons than us, it seems," Mrs. Lockwell said with a frown as she poured a cup of tea.

Despite his profession of affection for his aunt and cousins, it was clear that going to a party had been more important to Mr. Wyble than visiting family. Not that Ivy felt they should complain, and certainly Lily would speak the praises of anything that kept Mr. Wyble away. She glanced over the next few pages and saw that there was a great deal about the affair at Lady Marsdel's. Ivy decided it judicious to offer a brief summary and get to the end of the letter.

"It seems the party at Lady Marsdel's offered much amusement," she said, turning to the last page. *"And in close, it is my intention to visit you this month—if other obligations allow—and when I come I hope to bring with me a delightful new friend whose acquaintance I made at Lady Marsdel's and whose introduction I am certain you would enjoy as much as I have. Until then, I am yours in every regard. Mr. Balfineus Wyble."*

Ivy set down the letter and saw that Lily wore a horrified expression.

"An acquaintance of Mr. Wyble's!" she exclaimed in a fair imitation of one of their mother's outbursts. "How awful! Can you imagine what a friend of Mr. Wyble's must be like?"

Ivy smiled. "I confess, I am *more* confounded by the fact that Mr. Wyble can have a friend at all."

At last, their mirth subsided to a point where they could resume their sewing, while Mrs. Lockwell went downstairs to see what Mrs. Murch was doing now that might put the edibility of their supper at peril.

"It was kind of our cousin to write," Ivy said, extinguishing several of the candles as soon as their mother left the room. She meant what she said; a kind deed must always be appreciated, no matter what one thought of the doer. "I am glad he has made some acquaintances he admires."

Lily clipped a thread with her teeth. "And I hope he admires them so much that he spends all his time with them and never comes to call on us again!"

$\mathcal{D}$ESPITE MRS. LOCKWELL'S fears, disaster was somehow once again averted, and Mrs. Murch's supper was excellent, though it was a close call, for the salt and sugar jars had mysteriously been swapped—no doubt by an act of Cassity's. As a result, they had nearly dined upon candied beef and salt-crusted plums.

After supper, Ivy went up to her father's room. Mr. Lockwell sat in a chair by the window, dressed in the same suit of gray wool that Wilbern always put him in. He made no sound or motion as she entered but rather sat rigid, staring through the glass into the night. Ivy knelt beside his chair and smoothed his shock of white hair, which seemed to grow tangled no matter how still he sat, as if it had a life and will of its own.

"What is it you see out there, Father?" she asked cheerfully.

His hand was limp in hers, and his eyes were as dark as the window glass. Ivy rose, kissed his brow, and left the room, shutting the door quietly behind her.

She went up to the attic to see if Mr. Lockwell had pulled out any books again. However, everything was in place, though she did notice that her father must have been working the celestial globe, for the two outermost spheres were lodged against each other again. It pained her to see this, for as a man of science her father had well understood the workings of the heavens, and he would have known that the furthest two planets never appeared next to each other in the sky.

When she was a girl, her father had delighted in giving her riddles and puzzles to solve. *Use your wits, Ivy,* he would tell her. *Any problem can be solved through the application of sound reasoning.* Despite this advice, she often became frustrated when trying to solve one of her father's riddles. At such times he would give her a hint or a small clue—something to spark her imagination and help her arrive at an answer. But there would be no hint to help her with *this* puzzle.

She touched the arms on which the balls were mounted, listening to the whir of gears from deep within the globe as she moved them apart. Then she went downstairs.

She found Wilbern in the kitchen, finishing a late supper with Mrs. Murch, and let him know her father was ready for bed. Mrs. Lockwell had already retired, complaining that "If I am this weary when the days are brief, I hardly know how I'll make it through even a middle lumenal when we next have longer days!"

It was the darkness, Ivy told her; it made them all dull.

Yawning, Ivy climbed the stairs to the bedroom on the third floor that she shared with Lily. They had given Rose the other room on that floor to have for her own, as she had a tendency to get up in the middle of the night for hours at a time.

Exactly what Rose did while the rest of them slept, Ivy wasn't certain, though sometimes she heard soft singing coming from Rose's bedroom, and Ivy knew she often wandered about the house in her robe, passing silently from room to room. More than once Ivy had dreamed an angel was watching over her, only to wake and see Rose standing above her bed, smiling down at her. Ivy would smile in return, then she would shut her eyes and go back to sleep. Nothing ill could come into their house unnoticed, not when Rose was keeping watch.

Ivy slipped into the bedroom, not wanting to wake Lily if she was already asleep. However, that was far from the case: Lily sat up in her bed, bathed in candlelight, her wide eyes transfixed on the book that rested on her knees.

"It's time to blow out the candles," Ivy said after she had changed into her nightgown.

"But you can't!" Lily cried, turning another page with greedy fingers. "Lord Vauntly has shut Anabel up in a tower, and he's going to marry her at dawn, even though she despises him and loves only Sir Brandier and would rather dash herself on the rocks below the tower than let Lord Vauntly take her hand in his."

"I hardly think *that* would do Sir Brandier a service," Ivy said. "Besides, it's going to be a long umbral tonight. Dawn is many hours off yet, which means Anabel has plenty of time to find a hidden door or send a secret message." She blew out the candles, and night took the room.

Ivy always found it a little unsettling: the sudden termination of the rule of light, and the swift and complete supremacy of darkness in its place. However, the darkness was not entirely victorious, for a thin trickle of moonlight seeped between the clouds through the window.

"I don't want to go to sleep now," Lily complained. "Why do we have to go to bed?"

"Because it is night."

"Well, I think if the day is short we should be able to stay up later. Besides, it's to be a long umbral—you said so yourself—which means it will still be night when we get up. So what difference can it make?"

"The difference is that you will be very tired when you get up if you don't go to sleep."

"But I'm not at all tired *now*."

Despite this claim, she was asleep long before Ivy, who lay awake in her bed, staring into the darkness and wondering who would write a letter to Father and why.

It had been many years since Mr. Lockwell had spoken to anyone outside the household. Who could have cause to write him, and concerning what business? While Ivy had no evidence to suggest such a conclusion, she couldn't help thinking that the author of the letter was perhaps one of the men in dark capes who had come to the door a half month ago. And if that was the case, what was it the two magicians (for she was certain that was what they were) wanted from Father?

All of her questions would be answered if she could just get a look at the letter. However, where Mrs. Lockwell had put it Ivy did not know, nor did she think it prudent to ask; her mother had not seemed interested in discussing the letter. Ivy did her best to put the matter out of her mind and tried to follow Lily into slumber.

*E*IGHT HOURS LATER, though it was still pitch-black outside, the denizens of the house on Whitward Street rose from their beds and lit candles and lamps to carve a waking day out of the middle of the long night.

Long umbrals were always hard, especially after several of them in a row. Ivy always felt a sense of *wrongness* getting up in the middle of the night, but like everyone else in Altania, they had no choice. They couldn't very well sleep for twenty-seven hours straight. Though by the great yawns she cracked over her tea and toast, Lily might have made a go of it.

After breakfast, Ivy went into the parlor and, by the light of a single candle, reviewed the household ledger.

The room was frigid, but she wrapped a shawl around her shoulders instead of building up the fire. She sat at the secretary, taking demands and receipts from the various drawers in which Mrs. Lockwell had hidden them and entering them in the ledger. By the time she made the final tally, her hand was so stiff that she could hardly dip the pen and write the figures. When she saw her breath fog on the air, even Ivy could no longer make a case for conserving wood in the name of frugality and went to the hearth to stir the coals and add a few sticks.

As the flames leaped up, she held out her hands, rubbing them to life. Despite the cheerful light, her mood was dark. As usual, their receipts for the month had barely covered their expenditures, leaving them with only a tiny sum to save against a long night. And it was only due to Ivy's constant vigilance that they had even that much left over.

"But we *must* have at least a few fine things!" Mrs. Lockwell would exclaim as she made a fuss over some porcelain bauble or fancy bit of cloth in an Uphill shop. "After all, we have a fine house."

Perhaps *too* fine, Ivy often thought. Other than a small sum Ivy had managed to accumulate through economizing, their only asset was a modest income paid to Mr. Lockwell as a return on some past investments, which just covered their expenses.

However, those returns would last only so long as Mr. Lockwell lived, and love did not make Ivy so blind that she could not see how frail her father was. Without Mr. Lockwell's income, small as it was, they would not be able to keep the house on Whitward Street. Indeed, they could barely afford to keep it as it was.

"Perhaps we should let Mr. Wyble have this house sooner rather than later," Ivy said to the flames.

The house on Whitward Street was already entailed to Mr. Wyble; it would go to him upon Mrs. Lockwell's death rather than to any of his three cousins. However, as Mrs. Lockwell was not yet fifty, he would likely have to wait a long time for the house to be his—a fact that, on occasion, elicited some degree of impatience on his part.

That impatience could be turned to their advantage. Their cousin was much better off than his appearance might suggest, Ivy knew. He had confided in her once that he had been hoarding a tidy sum against the day he would be married and would need to start a household. So far he had had little success in finding a wife, but no doubt his prospects would be significantly better living as a gentleman in Gauldren's Heights than as a lawyer from Lowpark. Mrs. Lockwell could sell her interest in the house and its contents to him for a sizable amount, and with that money they might return to the old house on Durrow Street and live there comfortably.

Ivy had only faint memories of the house in which she had spent her youngest years. Her recollections of the house on Durrow Street were indistinct images of tall staircases, narrow windows, and shadowed nooks.

She had been very small when they lived there, so it was small things she remembered: the clock over the mantelpiece that showed whether it was light or dark outside, and if the moon was up, and how full it was; the coatrack in the front hall, with its brass hooks shaped like eagle talons; and the newel posts at the ends of the banisters, their knobs carved to look like eyes, their lids shut in sleep.

It had been, in sum, a magician's house. As such, Mr. Lockwell's young bride had hardly found it to her liking, what with it being old and dark and located in a part of the Old City rather less seemly than the daughter of a gentleman might be expected to consider acceptable. For a time, Mrs. Lockwell had been content enough (or patient enough) to accept her husband's peculiar abode as well as his peculiar pastime. However, by the time she had a small daughter and another on the way, she had grown more vociferous in her criticisms of the house on Durrow Street, and at her urging Mr. Lockwell moved their household to Whitward Street.

From time to time her father had returned to the house on Durrow Street in the course of his work as a magician. But as the years passed and sufficient quantities of his books and materials were transferred to their new home, his visits there decreased in frequency. Then they ceased altogether with the onset of his illness. The old house was shut up now, and Ivy had not seen it since the day they left it.

Her hands sufficiently warmed, Ivy banked the coals, then went downstairs to see if Mrs. Murch needed her to go to the market. For outside the window, despite the dark and cold, the streetlamps along Whitward Street were lit and many people were out, going about their usual business even though it was the middle of the night.

THEY HAD PASSED twelve hours awake in the dark when they gathered for a meal. Afterward they retired to their bedrooms to conserve candles, though Ivy found it difficult to sleep, as she always did when lying down for the second time in the course of a long umbral. For hours she stared into the gloom, listening to Lily's soft breathing, and tried not to think of the figures in the household ledger, or the old house on Durrow Street, or the letter that had come for her father.

She must have fallen into a fitful slumber, for when she opened her eyes she saw pale gold sun spilling through the window. Finally, day had come. Nor was it to be a short lumenal but rather a day with hours enough to melt the snow and warm the air. A day with plenty of light for reading.

Ivy dressed hurriedly. She made an attempt to rouse Lily, but the only response was a groan that emanated from deep beneath the bedcovers. Giving up, Ivy went downstairs. If she could finish the tasks that required her attention as quickly as possible, it would leave more time for perusing books from her father's library.

Mrs. Lockwell was still readying herself for the day—a task that could not be rushed—and Rose was in her room singing softly, so Ivy fixed a cup of tea in the kitchen and toasted a piece of bread on the stove. As Ivy took her little breakfast and Mrs. Murch made up a list for market, Wilbern carried in an armful of wood—his boots leaving puddles on the floor, to Mrs. Murch's dismay, for the frost was already beginning to melt.

It was discovered they were out of onions. Though the box had seemed full, upon opening it Mrs. Murch saw that Cassity had filled it with potatoes; in turn, the box for potatoes contained only a broken crock and some string. So onions were added to the list, which Ivy took, and putting on her bonnet and cape, she went out.

By the time she returned, the frost was melted in the garden and the day was growing fine. However, Ivy's thoughts were not of going on a stroll but rather of sitting in a sunlit corner and reading book after book. She deposited her basket in the kitchen and hurried up the stairs.

On the third landing, she came upon Mrs. Murch leading her father toward his room. Ivy asked if he had been taking out books again, but Mrs. Murch replied that she had found him standing at the window "as quiet as a lamb." Ivy promised she would come to visit him later, then climbed the last steps to the attic.

She moved among the shelves but was unable to settle upon just one book to read, so she took out three, then started for the stairs, intending to go down to the parlor. However, as she passed near the celestial globe, she noticed that the two outermost orbs—the two that she had so carefully moved apart—once again abutted each other. Her father must have been working the globe again.

Ivy might have simply left the globe out of order, but it was not in her nature. As she touched the orbs, the morning light glinted upon them, catching the letters engraved there. One orb was labeled *Cyrenth* and the other *Vaelus,* those being the names of the two furthest planets, which were also the two smallest and the only two that were never in conjunction in the heavens. She moved them apart again. Yet why did those names ring in her mind?

Ivy remembered the book she had found in the attic, the romance entitled *The Sundering of Vaelus and Cyrenth.* She had assumed it belonged to Lily, that Cassity had brought it up to the attic by mistake.

Again she looked at the globe. As a child, her father had taught her how the eleven planets were named after mythical figures of ancient Tharos. Like so many myths, the story of Vaelus and Cyrenth attempted to explain something the Tharosians had observed around them. In this case, the myth told the tale of two lovers whom the gods forced apart as punishment for a crime of which they were wrongly condemned. According to the myth, that was why the two planets never met in the sky—because it was the doom of the two lovers never to meet again for all eternity. It was a story her father had known well. Yet three times now she had found the globe arranged so that Vaelus and Cyrenth were next to each other.

Ivy was moving before she fully realized what she was doing. She dashed down two flights to the third floor, hurrying to the room she shared with Lily. The book was still on the shelf under the window where she had placed it. She took it out, ran a hand over the cover, then opened it.

There was writing on the overleaf. *To my dearest Ivy,* it read, *On the occasion of her thirteenth birthday. For now this is but a story, and one I hope you will enjoy. However, one day you will learn that behind a myth can lie a greater truth. I hope you will seek it out.*

It was signed by her father.

For a moment Ivy felt her heart was no longer beating. Reading the inscription was like hearing a beloved voice from the past. He must have acquired this book for her as a present, had even inscribed it, but he had never had the chance to give it to her. The affliction had come upon him just before her thirteenth birthday, and the book had been lost among her father's things all these years, until the day when he pulled it out by chance.

Her heart was beating again. No, it wasn't chance that he had taken this book out. Just as it wasn't chance that three times she had found the celestial globe configured in an impossible position. He was trying to tell her something in the only way he could, she was sure of it. But what?

Again she read the inscription. *He's telling you to seek out the truth. So do it.* But what truth? And where was she supposed to find it? It was a riddle, she realized, like the ones he always used to give her. The key to solving a riddle was looking for meanings other than those on the surface. He had told her where to find the truth. She was to look for it in a myth. *This* myth, perhaps. Which meant she had to read the book.

Ivy sat on the bed and opened the book. But even as she read the first lines, something prickled in the back of her mind. No, this was not right. She was not applying logic properly. Again she looked at the inscription. It did not say the truth was *in* a myth.

Hands trembling, she opened the back cover of the book, examining it. The endpaper was blank, but it seemed thick compared to that inside the front cover, and one corner of it curled up. Ivy hesitated—harming a book in any way was against her most basic nature—then gripped the loose corner.

The endpaper peeled away easily from the cover board, and a folded slip of paper fell into her lap. A laugh escaped her. Of course. *Behind a myth can lie a greater truth.*

Ivy picked up the slip of paper, unfolding it, and recognized her father's thin, elegant hand as she read the words upon it.

> *When twelve who wander stand as one*
> *Through the door the dark will come.*
> *The key will be revealed in turn—*
> *Unlock the way and you shall learn.*

Despite the sunlight that streamed through the window, a chill came over her. The poem made her think of how she had felt that night in the attic, when the darkness seemed to press down, creeping in through the cracks and windows, wanting to suffocate all light, all life.

But it wasn't just a poem. It was another riddle; Ivy was certain of it. Yet she was also certain that this one would not be solved so easily as the first. She was supposed to find a key. Only to what? And what would she learn when she found it?

Ivy didn't have the answer to that. However, there was one thing she did know. Mr. Lockwell must have known what was going to happen to him. Why else would he have left a message like this for her, only days—perhaps mere hours—before his mind was stolen from him? Only the affliction . . . It must have come upon him sooner than even he had expected, and he had never given her the book for her birthday present.

Now she had finally found it, but to what end? Ivy doubted that would be an easy question to answer. It was clear he had not meant her to find this riddle as a child but rather later, when she was older, when she could properly understand.

When she could help him.

A thrill passed through Ivy, a bright spark that burned away the cold. That was the answer. He had known that one day she would be old enough to understand. Old enough to help him. And she *would* help him. The answer was right here before her. All she had to do was understand it.

*Unlock the way and you shall learn.*

Ivy folded the paper, tucked it back into the book, and rose. There was no time to waste; she had reading to do.

## CHAPTER FIVE

ON THE MORNING of the first long lumenal since his return to Invarel, Mr. Dashton Rafferdy took a late breakfast with Mr. and Mrs. Baydon at Lord Baydon's house.

Like many fashionable young gentlemen, he had much in common with a beggar who, for lack of better means, must go from door to door scrounging for a bite. In similar fashion, as he did not keep a cook, Rafferdy was required to proceed from acquaintance to acquaintance in order to procure his meals. Even as he was dining at one house, he was always considering whom he might call on next—

whether it had been too soon since the last time, and if they had gotten a better cook.

Happily, Mr. and Mrs. Baydon seemed not to have wearied of his frequent companionship. A note sent early in the morning to Vallant Street was enough to win Rafferdy an invitation, and as soon as he rose and had his coffee and was dressed—that is to say, after the sun had been up for four hours—he called for his carriage and went directly to Lord Baydon's house, just off the Promenade.

They had only just started their repast when Mrs. Baydon set down a piece of toast she had barely nibbled and turned toward Rafferdy. "Have you heard the news?" she said, eyes aglow. "There is to be a masque at Viscount Argendy's. I learned it from Mrs. Darlend just yesterday."

"I would hardly call that news," Mr. Baydon said from behind the stiff wall of his broadsheet. It was a copy of *The Messenger* this morning.

"But it *is* news," Mrs. Baydon said, her forehead creasing in a pretty frown. "The viscount's masques are famous for their extravagance."

"I was always given to understand it was their absurdity they were famous for," Mr. Baydon said. "Unless you find men dressed as songbirds dangling about on wires to be a matter of delight. Though I warrant there might be some small amusement in the proceedings should the wires prove faulty and fail to hold."

"It's to be held at the viscount's home on the night of the full moon," Mrs. Baydon went on, undeterred. "I've heard that the centerpiece of the masque will be performed by the finest troupe of illusionists in the city. Please, Mr. Rafferdy, say you'll attend with us."

"That will be quite impossible," Mr. Baydon said before Rafferdy could fashion a reply.

"Nonsense. Mr. Rafferdy has just returned from Asterlane. Surely his father would not recall him so soon."

"It's quite impossible," Mr. Baydon reiterated, "because whether Mr. Rafferdy is in the city or not, he cannot attend the masque with us as we will not be attending ourselves."

"Not attending?" Mrs. Baydon gave the raised broadsheet a cross look. "But, Mr. Baydon, can we not at least consider it?"

"I already have," he said, and turned a page.

She cast a rueful look at Rafferdy. "I've heard the Siltheri weave enchantments out of air and light that are beautiful beyond description. You can picture anything at all—a mountain or a castle—and they can conjure it with a wave of the hand. I've often asked when I might be allowed to attend one of their performances, only I have ever been denied this pleasure for reasons that are beyond me."

Mr. Baydon lowered his broadsheet. His expression was stern but not ungentle. "The reasons are *not* beyond you, Mrs. Baydon. Lord Baydon has forbidden any in his household to venture to the theaters on Durrow Street. It is only on a solid foundation of real progress and industry that the future of Altania can be secured, not witchery and illusion. How could my father face his peers in the Hall of Magnates if it was known a member of his own family habituated a place of such questionable repute?"

"But Viscount Argendy's house is not on Durrow Street."

"The viscount's good reputation is his own to preserve or discard as he sees fit," Mr. Baydon said, and the broadsheet was raised once more.

"I fear I wouldn't be able to attend anyway," Rafferdy said, putting another cake on his plate. "I'm already in danger of falling from your aunt's good graces. I had better not compound the situation by appearing to support the viscount's disreputable plans."

Mrs. Baydon sighed several times, but she did not bring up the subject of the masque again—for which Rafferdy was grateful. While in her innocence she might imagine illusionists conjuring castles and rainbows, he knew the plays put on by the Siltheri were not always limited to such wholesome topics. There was a reason respectable men did not venture to the theaters on Durrow Street. At least not without a hat pulled low and a pocketful of coins to buy a carriage driver's silence. As for a woman who attended the plays—she might be called many things, but *lady* would not be one of them.

"You still haven't told us about your trip to Asterlane," Mrs. Baydon said as they took a final cup of coffee. "How was it?"

"Unremarkable," Rafferdy said, though *dreadful* would have been a more accurate term. Indeed, the visit had gone exactly as he had dreaded.

He had hardly arrived at Asterlane, head aching from a night at tavern compounded by eight hours of jostling in a coach, before Lord Rafferdy asked to see him. His father had been in the library, his foot propped up on a stool. Upon entering, Rafferdy was immediately— and without any consideration for his need to rest after such a long journey—delivered a typical lecture on the need to take on more responsibility now that he was a man, to put aside foolish pursuits, and to turn his attention toward settling down.

*There will be a time when I can no longer perform my obligations and duties,* his father told him. *When that time comes, you must be ready.*

Rafferdy had only the vaguest idea of what his father's obligations and duties actually were; in fact, he had made a point of *not* knowing. That he worked on matters at Assembly, Rafferdy knew. Also that he saw to the affairs of his estate, and was often writing missives and reports, and met frequently with various agents of the government who did Rafferdy knew not what but who always gave a salute to the king upon their departure.

While his father had been somewhat more grim than usual, this topic of conversation had been nothing out of the ordinary—certainly nothing warranting a summons home. It wasn't until he prepared to depart that Lord Rafferdy at last broached the topic Rafferdy had dreaded for so long. Still, why had his father insisted on his returning to Asterlane to give him that news? A letter would have more than sufficed.

"Surely, Mr. Rafferdy, your time in Asterlane cannot have been *entirely* unremarkable," Mrs. Baydon said. "Did you not have the pleasure of making a new acquaintance while you were there?"

Rafferdy gave her a sharp look. "As a matter of fact, I did. Lord Everaud was visiting at Asterlane, and I made the acquaintance of his eldest daughter. But I wonder how you should know such a fact."

"I am not without my abilities," Mrs. Baydon said.

"Gossiping with other young women being chief among them," Mr. Baydon added, lowering the paper. "You should be warned, Rafferdy, that Mrs. Baydon and Miss Everaud have recently become fast friends and will no doubt do everything they can to entrap you in some scheme of their concoction, as two silly young women acting in concert must always try to do."

"She is very beautiful, isn't she?" Mrs. Baydon said brightly.

Rafferdy only smiled. He suspected he had better heed Mr. Baydon's warning and proceed with care. Men far more clever than he had been caught in snares laid by women far less clever than Mrs. Baydon. Propriety might prevent women from visiting the theaters of Durrow Street, but like so many charming young ladies, Mrs. Baydon still found a way to craft her own small spells of illusion.

"Indeed, Miss Everaud is very pretty," Rafferdy said, though he could not remember what she looked like or anything she had done or said while he was there. However, he thought she *must* have been pretty. If she had been otherwise, he surely would have remembered *that.*

"What was your favorite thing about meeting her?"

"It would be quite impossible for me to choose," Rafferdy said. Fortunately, his answer seemed to satisfy Mrs. Baydon, and she sipped her coffee with a pleased expression.

Rafferdy mused awhile over his own cup. This conversation had done much to cast a new light on his visit to Asterlane. It wasn't just for the purpose of admonishing him to behave more responsibly that his father had summoned him home—or to give him the news about his plans for the estate at Asterlane. No, Lord Rafferdy had had other intentions in mind. Nor could Miss Everaud's presence there be ascribed to chance. A snare had been laid for him indeed, only its purpose was not to clamp an iron band around his foot but rather a gold band about his finger.

Rafferdy took his leave of the Baydons, then returned to his house near Warwent Square. This was a neighborhood nestled between the New Quarter and the Old City. It was neither so splendid as one nor so shabby as the other, and given its convenient proximity to the houses of the wealthy as well as houses of drinking and gambling, it was the favored choice of many young gentlemen.

Lord Rafferdy did own a house in the city, not far from Lady Marsdel's abode, but he was seldom in Invarel, due to his infirmity. Rafferdy might have dwelled there, but Warwent Square suited him better, and on this one matter he and his father agreed. The house in the New Quarter was much more expensive to operate, requiring a staff of at least eight. In contrast, at his current residence Rafferdy kept but a single man to serve and dress him, and he took every opportunity to remind his father how much money he was saving the family by choosing to dwell at Warwent Square.

❧

HE SPENT THE rest of the morning in the parlor, responding to the heap of letters that had grown on the table. There were invitations to dinners and parties and dances, and he took much care in choosing which he would turn down (very many) and which he would accept (very few).

By the time the sun reached its zenith, Rafferdy was ready to venture out, having spent an hour choosing what to wear and another making himself presentable. He paused to write a note to Eldyn Garritt, telling him to be at the Sword and Leaf after sunset, then he was out the door.

He told his driver to bring the cabriolet and put down the calash top, for there was no threat of rain. It was now midday, and according to the driver (who, unlike Rafferdy, was no stranger to an almanac), the sun would not set on the long lumenal for another thirteen hours. Thus there was time for all sorts of amusing pursuits, followed by a rest, so that Rafferdy could wake as the day ended and be refreshed for the night's various activities.

He began by taking a dinner at his club, where he lingered for a time in a comfortable chair, enjoying a pinch of tobacco and pretending to read a copy of *The Comet*. On the front page was a particularly captivating image of Princess Sahafina. The daughter of a wealthy Murghese prince, she had recently made a journey to Invarel and while there had captured the fancy of the city with her beauty and exotic customs.

The image of the princess was not a typical illustration but rather an impression. From what Rafferdy understood, there were some illusionists who could hold an engraving plate in their hands and concentrate upon it, working an enchantment so that what they imagined in their minds appeared on the plate, rendered with an accuracy that caused the subject to appear clearer than in the most skillful painting.

Once he tired of the club, he instructed his driver to take him to Marmount Street, where the finest clothiers resided. By the time he returned to his carriage, the sun was well on its descent toward the towers of the Citadel, and he had been fitted for two pairs of trousers, a coat, and several shirts.

A pleasant weariness had settled over him, and he decided a cup of chocolate was in order. The best chocolate houses in the city were in Covenant Cross. However, just as he leaned forward to tell the driver to go in that direction, his attention was caught by a figure in black walking with long strides along Marmount Street.

The man cast a glance over his shoulder, and a jolt of surprise coursed through Rafferdy. A moment later the other vanished into the dimness of a side lane. Surprise gave way to curiosity, and Rafferdy found himself wondering what sort of place a man such as Mr. Bennick might frequent.

A compulsion to discover what Mr. Bennick was doing seized Rafferdy. Why he wanted to know he couldn't say, except that it seemed a diverting entertainment, and of all the people he had ever met at Lady Marsdel's, Mr. Bennick was the only one he had found intriguing.

Mr. Bennick had vanished from sight. The lane was too narrow for the cabriolet to follow, but Rafferdy knew that it led toward Coronet Street, and so he directed the driver to take him around the block.

Sure enough, as the cabriolet turned the corner onto Coronet Street, Rafferdy glimpsed a tall form in black. However, he had no sooner caught sight of Mr. Bennick than the other man crossed the busy thoroughfare and, with another look over his shoulder, started down a stair. Rafferdy was not certain where the stair led, so he asked the driver, who said if he remembered right it let out on the edge of Greenly Circle.

That was ill news. Greenly Circle was in a part of the Old City where several streets came together. From there Mr. Bennick might proceed almost anywhere. Finding himself well amused by the thrill of the chase, he ordered the driver to proceed to Greenly Circle by the most direct route.

This proved a difficult feat, for the New Quarter was situated upon a heights, and the driver was forced to descend to the Old City, then navigate a labyrinth of twisting ways before at last proceeding along King's Street and down into Greenly Circle.

At once noise and odor overwhelmed Rafferdy. The booths of flower sellers and butchers and fishmongers crowded against one another in the shadow of the Citadel as tradesmen, servants, goodwives, and boys hawking broadsheets jostled between. On the steps of a fountain, a pair of mummers juggled torches, sometimes pausing to lay the flaming ends against their tongues while the crowd gasped as if the two were Siltheri illusionists rather than common street players, their rough faces smeared with greasepaint, their callused hands blackened beyond feeling.

Rafferdy had the driver make a circuit three times, and each time it took ten minutes for the vehicle to maneuver through the crowd. At last Rafferdy was forced to admit defeat at his little game; he had seen no sign of Mr. Bennick. With both his curiosity and craving for chocolate gone, he instructed the driver to turn toward home.

This was easier said than done, as a cart carrying apples had turned over and spilled its contents, and the result was a crowd of children, women, men, and horses all vying for the fruit. After much cracking of his whip, the driver was able to guide the cabriolet into a side street where it only just fit.

In contrast to the raucous circle, the lane was all but deserted. Only a murky light filtered down between buildings that leaned overhead. As the carriage started down the lane, a door opened ahead, and a man stepped out.

He was tall and wore black.

Before Rafferdy could even think to call out, the man pulled his hat low, then started up a stair between two buildings and was lost to sight. Once again he had gone a way where a carriage could not pass. Nor would there be any tracking him in the maze of the Old City.

Rafferdy had found him only to lose him for good; there was no way to know where he had been going.

Except Rafferdy *did* know. For this had to be the place that Mr. Bennick had come. Why else had he gone into that building? A sign hung over the door. Rafferdy couldn't read it in the dim light, but there was a picture painted on it in faded silver: a single eye that stared through the gloom. Directing the driver to wait, he left the cabriolet and approached the door. It looked to be some sort of shop, though what manner of goods it sold he couldn't say; the objects beyond the grimy window were impossible to make out. Having come this far, he opened the door and entered.

At once he reconsidered this action. A musty odor perfused the air, calling to mind a library gone to mold. Indeed, the shelves all around were crammed with books, and more books were stacked on tables and heaped on the floor. Few looked to have been printed in Rafferdy's lifetime, given their cracked leather covers and the tarnished gilt on their spines. Other objects were scattered among the books: polished stones, brass candlestick holders, copper braziers, glass vials, and jars in which various objects floated—shapes unfathomable in the dirty light that seeped through the windows.

In all, the shop was in such a disheveled state that Rafferdy wondered why anyone would set foot in it, let alone a gentleman like Mr. Bennick. Hoping to learn something of his quarry, Rafferdy picked up a book.

"That one is not for beginners, you know. Do not blame me when you lose a finger. Or an entire hand, more the likely. The fellow I acquired it from had one made of silver. It was rather handsome, I grant you, but somewhat less useful than the appendage it replaced."

Rafferdy dropped the book. He turned toward the sound of the voice and saw a little man waddle from behind a counter piled so high with flotsam and jetsam it had rendered him invisible.

"You've come for a ring, I suppose," the man said. His voice had a wet, croaking quality to it, as if his throat was perpetually in need of clearing. "Well, the term has begun, so I haven't as many as I did last month. Every young gentleman seems to want one these days. It's the fashion, or so I've been told. The fashion! As if power were a fancy coat like the one you're wearing—a thing you might don for a party and take off again when you were done. But I suppose you're no different, so come here, and we'll see what I have that fits. And do not think it will be cheap."

Rafferdy hesitated, then edged his way between the various tables to the counter, where the little man had opened a drawer. He was roundish, with pale skin, bulbous eyes, and limp hair combed tight against his skull. In all, he made Rafferdy think of some preternaturally large toad.

"Actually," Rafferdy said, "I was wondering if I might ask you a question about . . . about someone."

"These aren't easy to come by, you know," the shopkeeper said, rummaging through the drawer, which contained a collection of ornate rings. "They appear on the market only rarely, and there are precious few left who can make them." He picked one up—a thick silver ring with a lurid green gem—peered at it for a moment, then gave Rafferdy a speculative look. "So which House are you?"

"Pardon me?" Rafferdy said.

The man scowled behind dusty spectacles. "You'll not get far in your research if you're really that dull. Which of the seven Old Houses are you a scion of?"

At last, things became clear to Rafferdy.

"I'm quite sure I'm not a scion of any of them," he said with a laugh. "Magick is far from an affectation of mine. I am comfortable in my certainty that I cannot claim descent from any of the Old Houses."

"I wouldn't be so sure if I were you. A gentleman has a better chance than anyone of being able to trace a line back to one of the seven. Of course, not every son who gets his father's name gets his father's blood. And there are chimney sweeps and lamplighters who are the spitting images of portraits hanging in grand manors. But you . . ." He peered at Rafferdy over the rims of his spectacles. "You have a likely look about you. Here, try this one."

He handed Rafferdy the ring with the green gem. It was heavier than Rafferdy would have thought, and cold. He had no intention of purchasing such an ugly piece of jewelry, but it seemed that trying it on was the quickest way to be done with this exercise and get on to making his inquiry. The ring was overlarge, so he put it on his right middle finger.

Or tried to, that is. The ring had not reached the first knuckle of his finger when he felt a curious resistance. It was more than large enough to accommodate his finger, but even with great force Rafferdy could not manage to push it down.

"So not Baltharel, then," the little man said with a sniff. "Well, that's no surprise. There are few left who are descended of *that* House, though it was once one of the greatest." He took the ring back and handed Rafferdy another.

This one was of gold and bore a row of seven red stones, as well as elaborate designs and tiny symbols carved outside and inside the band. It was thick and heavy like the other ring, and even gaudier. This time Rafferdy attempted to place it on the fourth finger of his right hand. Just as before, he could not get the ring past the first knuckle no matter how hard he pushed, even though it was more than large enough.

The shopkeeper clucked his tongue. "There are some who might be disappointed not to be able to wear *that* ring. It bears the crest of Myrrgon. Of all the Old Houses, none has given Altania more of its greatest magicians, and these days no ring I have would win you more praise and admiring looks than this one. But there's no use fretting about it. This one's not for you." He snatched the ring back.

Rafferdy hardly knew what to think of all this, except to wonder if maybe he had just been insulted. The little man dug through the drawer of rings, at times picking one up, studying it a moment, glancing at Rafferdy, then putting it back. "I doubt it would be Xandrus," he would mutter as he sorted through the rings, or, "Oh, I should think not Vordigan!" Just when Rafferdy was ready to put a stop to this, the little man plucked a ring from the corner of the drawer and held it toward Rafferdy.

"Try this one."

The ring was rather plain compared to the others; the silver band bore only a single stone, bluish in color, as well as a line of thinly etched runes around the circumference. Rafferdy was growing rather perturbed by then, so he fairly snatched the ring from the shopkeeper and jammed it onto his right hand.

The ring slid on smoothly and easily, fitting snugly but not too tightly around the base of his fourth finger. Rafferdy stared at it.

"Well, that's rare enough," the shopkeeper said, and clapped pudgy hands. "I must say, I am rather surprised. I almost always pick the correct House on the first or second try, and I really wouldn't have thought it would be *this*. But Gauldren it is; there can be no doubt of it. I suppose you should consider yourself fortunate. Many would give much to have a claim to *that* name—Gauldren the Great, who quelled the wrath of the Wyrdwood and made all of Altania safe for the establishment of civilization. Without doubt it is the most revered and respected of the seven Old Houses. But the most powerful?" He shook his head and let out a gurgling laugh. "No, I wouldn't say that."

Rafferdy had no idea how to respond. Had the man just played some trick on him? He raised his hand and looked at the ring; the cloudy blue gem had a faint sheen to it despite the dim light of the shop.

"What is your name?" the little man asked.

"Rafferdy," he said, studying the ring. "Dashton Rafferdy."

The shopkeeper opened a massive book on the counter and flipped through its pages. "Would that be the north country Rafferdys or the Rafferdys of County Engeldon?"

"Engeldon." He gave the shopkeeper a look. "And you are . . . ?"

"I am Adabrayus Mundy, purveyor of magickal books and arcane objects." The squat little man bowed.

"Well, Mr. Mundy, here is your ring back," he said, taking off the silver ring and setting it on the counter.

"But do you not wish to purchase it, Mr. Rafferdy? I am certain we can agree upon a . . . fair price."

"The price does not matter, as I would not wear such a hideous thing were it given away free," Rafferdy said. Besides, he was increasingly certain the shopkeeper had indeed played a ruse upon him, one intended to dupe him into thinking the ring was special and buying it. "But as I have indulged you in trying it on, I hope you will return the favor by answering a question. The man who was in here before me—do you know him?"

"Mr. Bennick? Yes, I know him." He gave Rafferdy a sly look. "And do you know him as well?"

"I have made his acquaintance," Rafferdy said, though this was not entirely true. "Tell me, does Mr. Bennick . . . Is he something of a magician, then?"

"Well, he is a scion of House Vordigan." Mr. Mundy licked his fingertips and flipped through the book. "Throughout the ages it was always the least of the Houses—until recent years, that is, when it gave Altania its last great magician. You have no doubt heard of Slade Vordigan."

"Yes, I heard the tale, like every child," Rafferdy said with growing annoyance. "How Slade Vordigan stood on a hill at Selburn Howe, waved his hands, and mumbled some nonsense, which served to drive the Old Usurper back to the sea, no doubt by confounding him with absurdity, thus winning the day for king and country."

"A tale, you call it," Mr. Mundy said. "But is it not King Rothard who sits upon the throne rather than Huntley Morden? Here we are, the Vordigan crest." He tapped a page that bore an engraving of a serpent devouring its own tail. "Mr. Bennick is Slade Vordigan's grandson. In his youth he was a very promising magician. He is no lord in name, but few lords can best him. Or could, at least. He does not practice these days."

"Really? And if he does not do magick, why was he here in your shop?"

Mr. Mundy closed the book with a *boom.* "My customers expect and receive complete discretion, Mr. Rafferdy."

Rafferdy stepped back from the cloud of dust conjured by the shutting of the book. He had learned all he could—and had endured more than he could tolerate—from this toadlike little man. "Thank you for your time, Mr. Mundy," he said, and made his way to the door.

"Do come back when you change your mind about the ring!" the shopkeeper called after him.

"Thank you, but I'm quite sure I won't," Rafferdy said, and closed the door behind him.

Rafferdy made his way down the dank lane back to the carriage, absently rubbing his right hand as he went. He was suddenly weary and instructed his driver to take him back to Warwent Square.

Rafferdy leaned back in the seat. So Mr. Bennick fancied himself some sort of magician—or had at one time, at any rate. It could not be surprising, given his comments that night at Lady Marsdel's. All the same, Rafferdy found himself disappointed. He had not thought a man of such keen mind would be seduced by such a silly fashion. Perhaps Mr. Bennick was neither so intelligent nor so intriguing as he had thought.

Constrained by the tangled lanes, the carriage had no choice but to escape the Old City by the Hillgate and make its way around through the streets of Gauldren's Heights. This part of Invarel was populated by gentry and well-to-do professionals, and its streets were lined with sturdy houses of brick and stone. It was a decent and entirely respectable neighborhood—that is, of no interest to Rafferdy.

They were nearly to the edge of the Heights when they found the street ahead of them blocked by a hack cab with a broken wheel. While its driver tried to effect a repair, the hapless passenger—a man dressed in an ill-fitting black suit—stood to one side.

Rafferdy instructed his driver to go around, but as the cabriolet passed the broken-down hack, an astonishing thing happened: the passenger standing in the street waved and called out Rafferdy's name in a cheerful, rather high-pitched voice.

"Shall I stop, sir?" the driver asked, turning around in his box.

Rafferdy's first thought was to tell the driver to whip the horses into a gallop. However, it was too late; he had been recognized. If he tried to flee now, Lady Marsdel would surely hear of it, and he had no desire to earn another scolding. Instead, he directed the driver to pull up in front of the hack cab, and its passenger hurried over to the cabriolet.

"I say, good day, Mr. Rafferdy!"

Rafferdy managed a pained smile. "Good day, Mr. Wyble."

"What marvelous fortune that you should happen upon me at this moment," the laywer exclaimed. "What a remarkable and happy occurrence! But I say, I would never have thought to find *you* in this part of the city."

"Yet here I am," Rafferdy said. There was an awkward pause, and he could hardly bring himself to say the words that must follow next. However, at last he managed to utter them. "Are you in need of assistance, Mr. Wyble?"

"Oh, indeed! Indeed I am, Mr. Rafferdy, if you would be so kind. As you can see, I am utterly stranded."

As was Rafferdy. But there was nothing for it, and he soon found himself sitting next to Mr. Wyble as the cabriolet continued through the streets of Gauldren's Heights.

The lawyer clutched his hat to keep it from flying off his head and affected a broad smile. "Well, out of misfortune comes opportunity, as wise men say."

"How so?" Rafferdy asked.

"I mean now is the perfect chance for us to engage in our postponed conversation, Mr. Rafferdy."

"So it is," Rafferdy said. "In fact, I imagine it can in no way be avoided." And he settled back in the seat, bracing himself for the long ride to Mr. Wyble's destination.

# CHAPTER SIX

ELDYN WATCHED THE two men in gray coats depart the inn, then sighed into his half-empty cup of ale. His conversation with Mr. Sarvinge and Mr. Grealing, though brief, had filled him at once with new hope and new dread. His opportunity was not yet lost, as he had feared, but it soon would be if he was not able to acquire a hundred regals. And Eldyn's pockets were as empty as ever.

"What did those men want with you?" Sashie asked, alighting on a chair across from him.

Eldyn looked up in surprise. The inn's public room was not a proper place for an unaccompanied young woman, and he had told her she was never to come down here without his permission—though that was a rule, he had to admit, he had not been able to strictly enforce.

"Is it money they want?"

Eldyn fidgeted with the cup. So far he had not told Sashie of his plan to earn back the Garritt family fortune; he did not want to worry her about their situation. However, the look in his sister's blue eyes was earnest and trusting, and he could not lie to her, not like their father had. How often had he promised her fancy dresses and pretty baubles, only to leave her crying once he drank and gambled the money away?

"It is not a debt I have with them, Sashie. You need not fear that. Rather, I wish to make an investment in their trading company, an investment that would serve to better our circumstances."

She laughed at this; it was a music he adored above all others. "But, sweet brother, you *have* improved our circumstances. How can we fare better than to dwell here at the Golden Loom?"

Eldyn could not help smiling at her enthusiasm, even as it perplexed him. The inn was well kept, but like Eldyn's coat it was growing shabby. And while the clientele were generally respectable folk, that was not entirely the case, as must be for an inn down in Waterside.

"I would do much to improve our lot, Sashie. I would get us a house to live in, with servants to keep it, and our own carriage to drive about the city. I would be a gentleman and go back to university. And I would buy you dresses and jewels, so you might attend a party in the grandest house in the New Quarter and command the attention of all eyes there." He leaned across the table and took her hands in his. "I would see us happy."

"But, dear brother, I *am* happy. Indeed, it is impossible that any of those things you speak of could make me any happier than I already am."

She cast a look over her shoulder, across the public room toward the bar. A man stood there, speaking while others gathered around, listening and laughing. The spectators were some of the inn's less savory denizens: their clothes thickly patched, their grins gap-toothed and yellow. A woman leaned over the bar toward the man, her face over-painted and her bosom nearly spilling out of her frock as she howled with laughter.

The speaker might have been taken for a young gentleman of worth hanging about a seamier section of the city for a thrill. He was tall, with a lion's mane of gold hair, and was by any measure very hand-some. His coat of russet velvet was superior to anything Eldyn had ever owned. Rings glittered on both of his hands.

The man went by the name of Westen, though whether that was his given name, his family name, or simply an affectation, Eldyn did not know. What Eldyn did know was that, despite his fine looks and fine clothes, he was no gentleman, and none of the rich things he wore had been gotten by forthright or respectable means, for the fellow was known to be a notorious highwayman. This was not a matter of rumor or idle speculation, as Westen had brazenly admitted to it on more than one occasion, and some of his exploits had been so audacious as to be the subject of articles in *The Fox*.

Even now he was regaling his listeners with some tale of his shad-owy deeds. Eldyn could not catch the details from across the room, but the gist was clear when Westen made a little play, his hands flying up and his mouth forming a circle of surprise as he mimicked some hapless traveler whom he had accosted on the road and whom, at the point of a pistol, he had bereaved of all valuables.

The onlookers laughed, the coarse music of their mirth ringing out over the inn. Eldyn might have been tempted to call for a king's man, but he knew there was no point. Though Westen enjoyed telling tales of his criminal doings, he was ever scrupulous to avoid mention of any details that might link him to a particular incident, and it was said he did his work in disguise, his face covered by a mask, so that none of his victims might recognize him.

During their first weeks at the Golden Loom, Westen had come in only rarely. However, before long the highwayman had started to show up at the inn with increasing frequency, and now Eldyn thought he be-gan to have an inkling why. As Sashie gazed at Westen across the room, her pretty face alight, the highwayman paused in his storytelling to smile and nod in her direction. At this, Sashie snatched her hands back from Eldyn and drew a silk handkerchief from the sleeve of her dress; she let out a sigh as she clutched it in both hands.

"I do not recognize that handkerchief, Sashie. It looks very rich." She resisted turning her head toward the bar, but her smile was enough to tell him his suspicion was correct. "Did Westen give it to you?"

At once a stricken look came over her face. "Please, sweet brother, don't take it!" She pressed the handkerchief to her breast. "You mustn't take it away from me. He said it is a token and that I must hold on to it. He said that only if his . . . only if one who thinks well of him holds on to it and keeps it close will he be warded from harm when he is on the road. If I give it up, he will be placed in grave peril."

*It is you who are placed in peril by holding it,* Eldyn wished to tell her, but such was the anguish in her expression that he could not bring himself to utter such hard words. Instead, he said, "If he is in danger on the road, it is because he brings it on himself, Sashie. You must know that."

Only it was clear she did not. Sashie was but eighteen and a guileless thing; she could not understand how it was that Westen acquired all his clothes and rings. To her he was simply handsome and tall and marked by wealth—all things she naturally responded to.

No, Eldyn could not blame her. He was the one who had brought her to the Golden Loom, and it was his fault for not seeing what was happening sooner.

"You know you must give it to me," Eldyn said as gently as he could. "A young lady cannot accept a gift from a man with whom she has no proper association."

"But we *live* here," Sashie said, tears forming in her eyes. "And this is where I met him. What association can be more proper than that?"

"You know it is not proper," Eldyn scolded softly. "Else you should not have kept it a secret from me. A young lady deserves and requires the society of gentlemen, Sashie, not scoundrels."

"He is no scoundrel!" she said, but her weeping had all but stolen away her voice, and hardly a sound came out, a fact for which Eldyn was grateful. Slowly, and taking the greatest care so as not to cause her hurt, he opened her fingers and took the handkerchief from her. He tucked it into his coat pocket.

"I shall see that it is returned to him," he said, "so that he might give it to another who is better able to bear it for him."

Sashie said nothing. She only slumped in her chair and stared at her empty hands.

Eldyn hated this. But it had to be done now, before it went any further. A man like Westen, given his occupation, could have no compunction about ruining an innocent young woman. In one awful, selfish act, he could remove all hopes Eldyn had for finding Sashie a husband and giving her a happy life. He could steal away her future, just as he stole gold from his victims, and reduce her not only to poverty but to the life of a slattern. She might not understand now, but she would thank him for this later.

"You should return to our chambers," Eldyn said. "I will speak to Mr. Walpert and see that supper is sent up."

She rose without a word, her face cast down, and ascended the stairs from the public room. Eldyn finished his cup of ale, then looked toward the bar. However, Westen was gone. Eldyn would have to return his handkerchief to him later.

Happily, there were better things to anticipate. His conversation with Mr. Sarvinge and Mr. Grealing had left him with new hope, if new urgency as well. That he had met the two outside a moneylender's office on Marble Street that first time was surely a stroke of providence.

Eldyn had been at the moneylender's to settle a dispute regarding a debt of his father's, though it had taken several distressing hours. Anxious to be away from the place, he had rushed out of the lending house—and collided directly with Mr. Sarvinge, knocking a bundle of papers from his hands.

With a profusion of apologies, Eldyn helped Mr. Sarvinge and his associate, Mr. Grealing, gather the papers that had scattered on the street. As this was done, Eldyn could not help noticing a number of handbills advertising for investors in a trading company to the New Lands. Once the papers were retrieved, he invited the two men to a nearby tavern, buying them a drink as amends for his rudeness, and he listened as they described their business venture—how the trading company was to be formed, what goods it expected to carry back from the New Lands, and how it expected to bring its charter members a tenfold increase on their investment.

One drink turned to three, and it was not long before Eldyn became certain he had found the means to earn back some of the fortune his father had squandered. To their credit, Mr. Sarvinge and Mr. Grealing never so much as suggested that Eldyn should invest in their company. However, by the time they departed the tavern, after a fourth and a fifth drink, Eldyn broached the matter himself and announced he was determined to be an investor in their company. Such was the solicitous manner of the two men that, despite the way he had accosted them earlier, they assured him they would hold a set of shares for him as long as possible, and they parted on the most agreeable of terms.

Gaining the required hundred regals had so far proven more difficult than Eldyn had expected. However, Mr. Sarvinge and Mr. Grealing had brought good news with them today, at least from Eldyn's perspective. The approval of the trading company's charter had been delayed by the Ministry of Imports; due to the great number of New Lands charters being requested these days, the ministry was reviewing each application more scrupulously to be assured it met the highest standards.

There was no cause for concern, as Mr. Sarvinge had been assured that the charter for his and Mr. Grealing's company would receive the ministry's stamp shortly. While this delay was frustrating for the other investors, it now appeared that the expected returns would in fact be fifteen times the initial investment, and no one could complain about *that*.

Eldyn was fortunate that there yet remained a few shares in the trading company, due to the untimely death of one of the initial investors. While Mr. Sarvinge and Mr. Grealing promised to hold the available shares for Eldyn, he could not impose too long on their kindness; he had to purchase the shares, and soon. But where was he to gain the hundred regals?

As pressing as this question was, an even more immediate concern impinged upon him as he saw Miss Delina Walpert emerge from the inn's back salon. Her frock was even drabber than usual, and the pale green ribbon she wore about her throat lent her face a sickly cast; he supposed she had donned it in an effort to make herself pretty, though simply combing her hair would have done far more toward that end.

Eldyn rose from the table, retreated into the shadows beneath the stairs, and gathered the darkness around himself. There was a tense moment as she passed near, her shoes clomping against the floorboards, but her gaze never turned his way, and after that she passed out the inn's front door. Eldyn let out a relieved breath, then went to find Mr. Walpert and order his and Sashie's supper.

❦

TWO HOURS LATER Eldyn brushed his only coat, put on his second-best shirt and trousers, and polished his boots with a rag he had obtained from one of the inn's maids with a few kind words. He had no hat so instead tied his hair behind his neck with a black ribbon.

He told Sashie he was leaving, received only the tersest of replies through the door to her room, and, knowing he would get nothing more, departed their chambers. On the street, Eldyn looked for a hack cab to hire, then thought better of it; it was not so far to the Sword and Leaf that he could not walk, and it was better to save what little coin he had for a drink or two in case Rafferdy's pockets were empty that night.

It was not very far to the tavern, but neither was it safe to walk there alone after nightfall. If times were difficult in the country—where, according to the broadsheets, the number of men without a scrap of land to farm grew every day—then times were harder still in the city, for it was to the city that all those who could not make a livelihood in the country came. And saints help them if they could not find work here, which few enough of them did, for no one else would help them. The poorhouses were overflowing and the churches exhausted of charity, with only the gibbet at Barrowgate doing anything to reduce the population of the indigent—and at this task it worked tirelessly. However, despite its industry, its labors were not enough to reap the prolific crop of destitute that grew by the day.

Keeping to lighted ways when he could, and folding the shadows around himself when he couldn't, Eldyn made it to the Sword and Leaf unmolested. The carved sign above the door depicted a silver sword piercing a curling green leaf. It was said that, long ago, the Sword and Leaf had been a favored haunt of magicians. However, the only magick he had ever witnessed there were the usual spells of bliss and forgetfulness conjured by drink.

Inside, Eldyn found his friend seated in a paneled booth that provided privacy on three sides yet afforded a view of the rest of the tavern on the fourth. Rafferdy was smoking something from a hookah pipe and had already had at least one drink, given the empty glass on the table.

"I started without you," Rafferdy said, the words accompanied by a puff of spicy smoke.

"For which I can in no way blame you," Eldyn said, not minding in the least. If Rafferdy was already at it, then it meant he had money tonight. "But, I say, you have a more determined air about you than usual. Is it your purpose this evening to drive all senses from your skull with the greatest efficiency possible?"

"It was a long and trying day."

"How so?"

"I have no intention of speaking about it," Rafferdy said, by which Eldyn took him to mean he had no intention of speaking about it until he had imbibed a sufficient amount of drink and had inhaled a sufficient amount of smoke. Toward that end, Eldyn signaled the bartender.

"So why did your father recall you to Asterlane?" Eldyn said when a bottle of whiskey and two cups had been delivered. "You never told me before you left."

"That's because I didn't know before I left. The dear old man hadn't the courtesy to tell me in his letter."

"Perhaps that's because he thought if you did know, you wouldn't come at all."

"You're right in that," Rafferdy said, and quaffed half his whiskey in a swallow. "I am sure I would have refused him if I had been granted foresight of what was to be."

"No, you wouldn't have," Eldyn said.

Rafferdy sighed. He was in no way a homely man, but he was only really good-looking when he was smiling, which fortunately was much of the time. However, at the moment he wore a morose expression.

"No, I suppose I wouldn't have refused him. Though on occasion I like to think that I might."

Eldyn had sometimes thought the same thing. Even with Vandimeer dead, it was no easy thing to step out from under the shadow of his father. He finished his own whiskey and refilled both their cups. "So what was it your father summoned you home for?"

"I thought it was because I left university," Rafferdy said.

The bottle clattered against the table as Eldyn fumbled it. "What do you mean you've left university?"

"Didn't I mention it?" Rafferdy said, his glum expression replaced by a sly smile. Rafferdy always waited to deliver news when it would have the most dramatic effect.

"No, you didn't mention it, as you know perfectly well."

"But you must have noticed I haven't been hanging about the colleges or the coffeehouses."

"You hate the coffeehouses," Eldyn said. "What was it you told me? *Beer might make a smart man dull, but coffee is worse because it can delude a dull man into thinking he's sharp.* Besides, there's no way I might have noticed you weren't hanging about the university. You know I wasn't able to . . . that I didn't go back to university this term myself."

By the look on his face, this was a fact Rafferdy had forgotten. "I'm sorry, Garritt. It slipped my mind."

"As does everything not related to clothes or gambling or your own appearance in a mirror."

Rafferdy was not a selfish or unkind man; he was quite the opposite, really. But like many the son of a lord, a life of privilege had trained him to be generally preoccupied with himself before others, and he had a habit of assuming everyone had the same choices he did.

"You liked university, didn't you?" Rafferdy said, topping off their glasses. "My father thought it important that I go, but I found it a load of rubbish. Half the professors were drunks, and the other half were mad. The only useful thing any of them taught me was that I had better clean my teeth if I don't want to have a frightening smile when I'm forty. But I should have known *you* would like it, Garritt. You have a perverse way of enjoying things that are dreadful and disdaining anything that is marvelous. I've seen you sit in a musty corner, happy as can be reading some dreary old book, and frown when a pretty young woman passed by and waved her fan at you, as if it were the most unwelcome of distractions."

"I *did* like it," Eldyn said, and he left it there for a moment, for how could he explain to Rafferdy, to whom it had all meant so little, how to him it had meant so much? At university, he felt as if he was making something of himself—something better. At last he said, "Sometimes I still go to the coffeehouses. I was at Mrs. Haddon's the other day. I saw Talinger there, and Jaimsley and Warrett."

"Be wary of those troublemakers, Garritt. Especially Curren Talinger. The gap between discussing politics and proposing treason is not so great as you might think, not these days."

"But it's only talk," Eldyn said, even though the same concerns had occurred to him. "It can't harm anyone."

Rafferdy shook his head. "That's where you're wrong. Why do you think my own speech is always so silly and worthless? I've not your brains by half, but I'm not witless either. I speak this way because I know how perilous speech can be. Look there if you think I'm wrong." He nodded to the copy of the Rules of Citizenship posted on the tavern wall. "A word is all it takes to put a man in prison, or to seize his property, or to end his life. A saber might be stopped by a shield. A bullet might be dodged by a stroke of luck. But you can't dodge a word. If one is flung at you, it will hit its mark unerringly. No, Garritt, there's nothing in the world more dangerous than talk."

Eldyn frowned. These were unusually somber words from his usually cheerful companion. "By the saints, Rafferdy, what happened to you in Asterlane?"

"I suspect my father wishes me to marry."

"Really, Rafferdy, what's so unexpected about that? Your father has always urged you to take on more responsibility."

"It was different this time," Rafferdy said, fidgeting with his empty glass. "He's getting old. And he's not well. He can hardly bear the journey to the city anymore."

Eldyn lowered his voice. "But you always knew this must happen."

"Must it?" Rafferdy said, reaching for the bottle.

As so often, Rafferdy was an enigma to Eldyn. Sometimes he wondered why they were friends at all. They dwelled in different worlds—a fact that Rafferdy sometimes forgot but that Eldyn never did. If they had not known each other from boyhood, they would certainly never have formed an association now. However, their grandfathers—both scions of well-to-do houses—had been devoted friends, and while

Rafferdy's father had risen as far as Eldyn's own had fallen, and the two men had held nothing but disdain for each other, their sons had been given the opportunity to form a close friendship while their grandfathers yet lived.

However, at the moment Eldyn's friend confounded him. "I don't understand, Rafferdy. I've often heard you complain about your father's decisions and practices. Well, one day *you* will be Lord Rafferdy. That will be your chance to do things as you see fit, to make yourself into something." He leaned over the table. "Don't you want to *be* something, Rafferdy?"

"Yes," Rafferdy said. "I want to be utterly harmless." And he raised his glass and drained it.

"What are you talking about? You're to be a magnate."

"And I have seen what magnates do, Garritt. Despite what you might have heard me say, I believe my father is a good man. Yet even he has . . ." Rafferdy looked away. "It is a terrible thing to be lord over another man, Garritt. To be the master of his fate. Only God should have that power."

"Better to be lord over another man than to be lorded over, to have your fate rest in another's hands," Eldyn said, unable to keep a bitter note from his voice. "But I said it once, and I say it again. What happened at Asterlane? What did your father say to you?"

"He told me he is enclosing his lands," Rafferdy said. And after that they drank their whiskey in silence.

At some point while they sat there, a rather large group spilled into the tavern and took over the booth opposite their own. They were mostly men, but a few women were with them—though which were dressed more lavishly or outlandishly was hard to say. As a whole, they offered such a profusion of velvet, lace, and brocade—in every variety of hue from crimson to cerulean to the deepest violet—as to make a flock of peacocks appear drab. The men and women alike wore powdered wigs and powdered faces, pale contrast to their rouged lips and cheeks.

The newcomers called out for drink, and laughed, and sang in high voices. It was a beautiful music but forlorn as well, and for some reason it made Eldyn think of exotic birds locked in filigree cages. From time to time a flash of light issued from the booth across the tavern, catching the corner of Eldyn's eye. However, each time he turned he saw nothing save mouths open in laughter, and a tangle of white arms and long white necks.

"You must forgive me, Garritt," Rafferdy said, looking up from his cup, which was empty once again. "I'm dreadful company tonight. I should never have dragged you out. But you're here, and the damage is done, so tell me—what of you? How have you been occupying yourself since you're not in university this term?"

A burst of trilling laughter rang out across the tavern; Eldyn made an effort not to turn and look. "Would that I had something of great interest to report. I'm working on a few business ventures, that's all. I have a hope they will do me and my sister well."

Eldyn described in general terms how he intended to invest in a trading company to the New Lands. However, Rafferdy was not paying attention, and it was just as well. For some reason, describing his dealings with Mr. Sarvinge and Mr. Grealing left him uncomfortable; perhaps it was only that he did not want Rafferdy to know how great his need was. In truth, he feared Rafferdy would insist on helping him raise the necessary funds, and he did not wish to be indebted to a friend. Not that it was likely that Rafferdy had ten regals to spare, let alone a hundred. He was not Lord Rafferdy yet.

"I'll go get us more to drink," Eldyn said, picking up the empty whiskey bottle.

He went to the bar and handed off the empty bottle. As he waited for it to be refilled, he heard a sound behind him. It was soft amid the clamor of the tavern, like the voice of a dove.

Turning, Eldyn saw one of the women from the peculiar group. She sat in a chair apart from the others, dressed in a high-necked gown the color of apricots. Her face was a thing of perfect beauty, flawlessly white, framed by snowy ringlets of hair, her lips and cheeks painted on just so. Something was cradled in her cupped hands.

Eldyn approached. A warm scent rose from her. She smiled and opened her hands. On her palms rested a tiny bird. It was like no creature he had ever seen, for its feathers were pure silver, tinged with gold at the wingtips. Its beak was gold as well, and its eyes tiny sapphires. At first he thought it a clever facsimile wrought of metal, but then he saw its wings stir and its throat flutter as the soft music emanated from it.

The woman held the bird higher, and Eldyn reached out a finger to stroke it. However, even as he touched it, the bird vanished in a flash of white light. Eldyn let out a gasp, and mocking laughter fell from the woman's red lips. Resting on her hand where the bird had been was a silver disk, like some sort of coin. She held it out toward him. Eldyn hesitated, then took it.

"Your whiskey, sir," said a voice behind him, and Eldyn stumbled around. He took the bottle, shoved the silver coin into his pocket, and, without another look at the woman, hurried back to his table.

"Be careful, Garritt," Rafferdy said. His glum look was gone, and he wore an amused expression now. "They are not what they seem."

"What do you mean?" Eldyn said, too startled to say anything else.

Rafferdy arched an eyebrow. "You really don't know? Haven't you ever been to one of their plays?"

Eldyn made an effort to hold his hand steady as he poured whiskey. "Plays?"

"They are Siltheri, Garritt. Illusionists."

Eldyn looked up from his pouring. Of course—their outlandish clothes and wigs were costumes. They were players, come into the tavern after a performance at some theater.

Rafferdy took his whiskey. "Just because one looks to be a lady on the outside doesn't mean there's not something very unladylike hiding underneath that dress. As they say, if you see an angel on Durrow Street, it's sure to be a devil beneath. Or didn't you know that all Siltheri are men?"

Eldyn's cheeks glowed with shame, and he was grateful for the dim light. In recent years, the theaters of the illusionists had grown in popularity, if not so much in respectability. Not that Eldyn had ever attended any plays, for want of money. However, he knew that Rafferdy was right, that onstage all roles—both male and female—were played by men, as it was against the law for a woman to work in such a vocation. And if from time to time an illusionist was found floating in the River Anbyrn, it barely earned a mention in the broadsheets. For such things were only to be expected from time to time with men who did such things and who lived such lives.

"I'm sorry, Garritt, I shouldn't laugh," Rafferdy said, then proceeded to do just that. "But the look on your face is quite priceless. I've never seen you so addled."

Eldyn glowered. Rafferdy was having far too much fun with this. The bird had been an illusion, nothing more.

Yet its beauty had been real. It had moved Eldyn just as true beauty did. And that it had vanished did not lessen its worth in any way, for all beauty was fleeting. For some reason he thought of the church of St. Adaris, and the statue of the angel in the churchyard, and the priest who had shouted at him.

*Has one of them come again from Durrow Street to mock us?* the priest had said to the younger man. And at Eldyn he had shouted, *Begone, daemon. Go back to your houses of sin and trouble us no more!*

The illusionists must have come to the church before. Why they had done so, Eldyn could not say. But the older priest must have mistaken Eldyn for one of the Siltheri, half-hiding in the shadows.

"You're thinking something, Garritt," Rafferdy said, eyeing him. "I know that look."

Eldyn could not have explained it if he wanted to. "I was thinking you have yet to tell me what happened to you today," he said, changing the subject back to Rafferdy—a topic his friend could always be easily persuaded to speak about. "What made it so very trying?"

Rafferdy glanced at his hands, as he had done several times that night, and at first Eldyn thought he was going to say something about them, but instead he looked up and said, "I'm afraid I have gotten myself in a most disagreeable situation I can't get out of."

"*You,* Rafferdy?" Eldyn said, incredulous, and amused as well. "You've been caught in a trap your golden tongue can't free you from? I can hardly wait to hear the details!"

Eldyn listened with ever-increasing enjoyment as Rafferdy described what had happened: how at Lady Marsdel's he had made the unlikely acquaintance of a lawyer named Mr. Wyble; how he had happened upon this Mr. Wyble in Gauldren's Heights, stranded by a broken carriage wheel; and how he had been forced to take Mr. Wyble back to his accommodations in Lowpark. On the way, Rafferdy had been subjected to conversation of the most tiresome sort, and had been so bored he had hardly heard a word, and had contributed nothing himself to the discourse save for nodding and saying, *Yes, yes, of course,* at periodic intervals.

Unfortunately for Rafferdy, one of those absentminded declarations had come right after Mr. Wyble asked if Rafferdy wished to accompany him on a visit to some acquaintances of his. Rafferdy had realized his error too late, and Mr. Wyble had been so delighted that there had been no opportunity to rescind the acceptance.

"So who are these acquaintances of your Lowpark lawyer, the ones you are to see on the first of the month?" Eldyn said, having difficulty speaking through his mirth.

"They are his cousins," Rafferdy said with a scowl. "Three young ladies. Can you imagine what they must be like, being *his* relations? And they are of the gentry!"

"Yes, I'm sure they're quite hideous," Eldyn said merrily. "But tell me, Rafferdy, what in the name of all that's holy were *you* doing in Gauldren's Heights? It's hardly a place I'd expect to find you."

"You must come with me," Rafferdy said. He grabbed Eldyn's arm across the table. "When I go with him to visit his cousins, you must come with me, Garritt."

"Why is that?" Eldyn said, taken aback.

"You're far handsomer than I," Rafferdy said, "which means they'll look at you."

Eldyn laughed. "Not when they discover who is the son of a magnate, Rafferdy. Then all their gazes shall be for *you*. I am quite sure they'll think God above has sent them a miracle, and they'll be trying to get a proposal of marriage out of you before the tea gets cold."

However, Rafferdy would not let go of his arm until Eldyn swore that he would accompany him on his unwanted social call next month. So it seemed Eldyn was caught in his own little trap, and as he shook his head and sipped his whiskey he thought Rafferdy was right after all.

There really was nothing more dangerous than words.

# CHAPTER SEVEN

$\mathcal{S}$OONER THAN ANY of the denizens of the house on Whitward Street might have wished for, the beginning of the new month arrived, and the visit of Mr. Wyble and his acquaintances along with it.

The new moon had come just before the rapid dawn, according to the almanac, and the first day after Darkeve was to be a short lumenal of only seven hours and twenty-three minutes, to be followed by an umbral of middle duration—which meant, if nothing else could be hoped for, the guests would not be tempted by a long afternoon to linger over tea.

"They're coming, I can see them coming!" Lily cried from her perch by the parlor window. For the past hour she had been kneeling on a chair, a hand across her brow like a lookout atop the mast of a ship in the royal navy. Lily had been reading romances concerning sailors of late.

"A carriage is stopping in the street," Lily went on. "It's black and very stylish and is drawn by the most beautiful horses. It cannot be Wyble's. There are three of them getting out. I cannot tell what they look like from here, but one is shorter than the others, and thick about the middle, so it must be our cousin. Now they've left the carriage and are coming to the gate. I must say, they walk very well—the two who are with him, I mean."

"Quick, everyone!" Mrs. Lockwell exclaimed. "We must be ready for them. Hurry now, there isn't a moment to waste!"

Despite their mother's admonition of urgency, there was nothing for any of them to do, as every possible preparation had already been made in advance of the visit. The parlor was dusted, the windows polished, and the best lace set out. Mrs. Murch had been given instructions on how to prepare and deliver the tea. Even Cassity had been accounted for and at present was under strict watch, helping Mrs. Murch put the finishing touches on the sandwiches.

As they were already dressed, and their hair combed, and ribbons done and redone, they could do nothing but regard their mother, who was driven to the edge of despair by their inaction, even though it was beyond her to give utterance to what they *should* be doing.

"Ivy, put away that book!" Mrs. Lockwell said, triumphant at finding something that yet needed to be done. "And, Lily, take that chair back to the table. Look lively, everyone. We must show him how content and pleasantly engaged we are and how we suffer no want of additional society."

Ivy did not say that she might look more convincingly engaged in a pleasant activity *with* the book in hand than without it. Instead, she closed the volume she had been reading and rose, intending to take it to the shelf in the corner, then reconsidered. Mr. Wyble had a tendency to pry when he was visiting, examining everything in the house as if making an inventory of its worth. The book concerned a topic that might not be deemed entirely appropriate for a young lady, involving as it did legends of pagan origin, for she was still trying to determine the meaning of her father's riddle.

So far she was at a loss. She had read the riddle a dozen times over, backward as well as forward, and had even looked for patterns by taking only the first letters, or the last, or every other one, and rearranging them.

She had begun to wonder if the meaning had something to do with the planets. After all, the book she had found the riddle in concerned the story of two of the planets, and the ancient Tharosian word for *planet* and *wanderer* was the same. However, after much thought she was forced to dismiss that idea. There were only eleven planets, not twelve—a fact of which her father would have been well aware.

Ivy started for the stairs, intending to take the book to the attic, but just then a knock sounded at the front door, propelling Mrs.

Lockwell to even greater heights of anxiety. Ivy tucked the book beneath a cushion on the sofa and went to help Lily with the heavy chair.

The door opened below, and the sound of Wilbern's greeting echoed up the stairs. With frantic motions, Mrs. Lockwell directed her daughters to arrange themselves about the parlor. Rose was baffled by their mother's gestures and only stared until Ivy took her hand and led her to the sofa, while Lily sat at the pianoforte and Mrs. Lockwell plopped into a chair, cheeks glowing.

"Thank you, Wilbern," came their cousin's overloud voice. "Are they in the parlor, then? There is no need to escort us. I will show my company up, for I know the way. Indeed, I always feel very at home here."

"He acts as if the house is already his!" Mrs. Lockwell muttered, a bit louder than was prudent.

Footsteps sounded on the stairs.

"Play, Lily!" Mrs. Lockwell whispered. "Play something cheerful!"

Lily commenced playing, and of course the piece was low and dolorous. Before Mrs. Lockwell could direct her to play something else, the gentlemen were arrived at the entrance to the parlor, and they found the Lockwell women thus engaged: Mrs. Lockwell red-faced and leaning forward in her chair, Lily pounding away at the keys of the lowest register, Rose sitting transfixed on the edge of the sofa, and Ivy doing her best to appear happily occupied with absolutely nothing in her hands.

There was a moment when all was frozen, then Mrs. Lockwell rose and affected a convivial smile (an expression that faltered only for a moment, when she was forced to wave for Lily to stop her performance). With great solicitude she greeted Mr. Wyble. He in turn presented his two acquaintances, Mr. Rafferdy and Mr. Garritt.

Whatever their flaws must be—and they must be significant, to be associated with Mr. Wyble—their looks were not to be counted among them, as both men made fine figures in their suits. True, Mr. Rafferdy's attire, while darker and more simple, was also more rich, and he was the taller. However, it was the case for Mr. Rafferdy that his attire added to his appearance, for his face, upon closer inspection, was open and pleasing but not really handsome, while Mr. Garritt was a striking man—so much so that what he wore was quickly forgotten. His face suggested the bust of some Tharosian hero, framed by a tumble of dark hair much too long for current fashion, of which Ivy—if handed a pair of scissors—would not have shorn off an inch.

Mr. Wyble greeted his cousins then, a lengthy proceeding involving in each instance at least a half-dozen declarations of exultation at the meeting. Always deeming it best to cleave to the truth, Ivy said in return that he was always welcome here, and she and Rose curtsied. However, Lily's greeting comprised no more than a muttered, "Hello, cousin."

There was no time for Ivy to prompt Lily to do more, as by then Mrs. Lockwell was already hovering near the sofa, unable any longer to restrain herself from introducing her daughters to the newcomers. Her eye was shrewd in such matters, and no doubt she had noted that, of the two young men, one was exceedingly handsome and the other exceedingly well dressed and that both appeared to be gentlemen of some degree.

The introductions were made—a bit floridly, for their mother presented each of them with a grand wave of the arm, as if this were a ballroom rather than their little parlor, which, accommodating nearly twice its usual population, suddenly seemed cramped. Ivy gave each of their hands a firm shake, but Rose could only be compelled to grant them each a nod. In contrast, none of Lily's reticence at greeting Mr. Wyble was in evidence as she clasped their hands heartily, lingering particularly long upon Mr. Garritt's, and when he attempted to pull it back, he did not find himself immediately able to do so.

They sat, though not without some false starts. "Do try the sofa, Mr. Rafferdy," Mrs. Lockwell said. "The center is the most comfortable part, I'm sure." And "I think you'll find that chair to your liking, Mr. Garritt—no, no, not *that* one—yes, the one near the pianoforte." There was even a whispered "Not *there,* Rose!" which was of course audible to everybody in the room.

Finally everyone was settled according to Mrs. Lockwell's satisfaction, if not to their own. Mr. Rafferdy sat on the sofa between Ivy and Rose, while Mr. Garritt was situated in a horsehair chair that was more notable for being near the pianoforte than for being comfortable. Lily had alighted on the pianoforte bench. Mr. Wyble was relegated to the periphery of the room near Mrs. Lockwell, though he seemed oblivious to any slight, and he beamed as if bearing witness to some utterly delightful scene.

What followed next, in fact, was an extended moment of fright. It was Mrs. Lockwell's place to begin the conversation, but evidently she had not thought past making the seating arrangements, and though she was usually loquacious, words were suddenly beyond her ability. Mr. Rafferdy shifted on the sofa next to Ivy, and Mr. Garritt cleared his throat as if he was about to say something, only he didn't. The clock on the mantel ticked away the seconds. Mr. Wyble smiled.

They were saved by the arrival of the tea.

Ivy helped Mrs. Murch set the heavy tray on the table. She took the opportunity to make a survey of its contents and was relieved to note that the sugar bowl indeed contained sugar, and that there were lemons and spoons. However, the odor rising from the sandwiches confirmed that they were filled not with butter but rather with neat little slices of soap. She covered the plate with a napkin and gave it back to Mrs. Murch. The biscuits would have to do.

"Mr. Wyble, why have you never told us you went about with companions of such great distinction as Mr. Rafferdy and Mr. Garritt?" Mrs. Lockwell exclaimed once tea had been served. "Surely they are remarkable."

Ivy swallowed her tea. "As you'll recall, Mother, Mr. Wyble has only recently had the pleasure of making the acquaintance of Mr. Rafferdy."

"You're quite correct, cousin," Mr. Wyble said. "I had the good fortune to meet Mr. Rafferdy at the house of Lady Marsdel last month. And hardly a brief lumenal had passed before I wrote to tell you of my overwhelming pleasure at meeting so excellent a gentleman."

"Indeed, we have never known you to keep news of your own good fortune to yourself," Ivy said. "You have ever been generous in that regard."

Mr. Wyble nodded. "Why should I spare news of such grand happenings from those who can have so little excitement in their own necessarily sedate lives? If I can impart a hint of what such affairs are like, even a fraction of the joy and pleasure I experienced myself, then it is a gift I am glad to give."

"And one that happily costs you little," Ivy noted. "Yet you have been ungenerous in one regard, cousin, for prior to this you have not shared news of your acquaintance with Mr. Garritt."

"In my defense, I could not have told you of that acquaintance!" Mr. Wyble declared. "For I have only just made it this very day. It was Mr. Rafferdy who designed to bring him, and I must say I am elated he was able to come."

"As are we!" Lily said, a bit too robustly.

Ivy found this a curious revelation. She could understand what had caused her cousin to seek the acquaintance of a lord's son; Mr. Wyble had ever been drawn to the grand, the gilded, and the glorious, and liked nothing more than to bask in its glow, no matter that such a light might serve to illuminate his own ordinary nature. But how the relationship was reciprocated she had difficulty imagining, unless it was simply that gentlemen like Mr. Rafferdy and Mr. Garritt needed to be admired by those lesser than themselves in order to continue to feel superior. In which case they were men of the most shallow concerns and superficial tastes.

She turned to Mr. Rafferdy. "We would much like to hear about your initial meeting with our cousin. I'm sure the party at Lady Marsdel's was an impressive affair."

Mr. Rafferdy shifted on the sofa next to her, and a grimace crossed his face. "So Mr. Wyble tells me," he said, which was hardly the gush of praise she had expected.

Mr. Wyble, however, more than made up for Mr. Rafferdy's reticence and for several minutes regaled them with every possible detail he could recall from the night at Lady Marsdel's, from the size of the house to the number of the servants to "the very lovely little spoons upon the tea table, each one possessing a handle carved in the most unique and delightful way, and so ornate as to render ordinary silver spoons such as these you have here dull, even austere."

"Yet I find they stir the tea remarkably well," Mr. Garritt said, which won him a brilliant smile from Lily.

"What of you, Mr. Rafferdy?" Ivy asked. "Do you not share Mr. Wyble's appreciation for the fineness of spoons?"

"Although I have known him but a short while," Mr. Rafferdy said, "I have become certain that Mr. Wyble, above all other men, has an acute and keenly developed appreciation for the most minute and trivial of details. Such is the nature of his appreciation that it varies inversely with the importance of a thing. That is, the more insignificant the detail, the more our Mr. Wyble pays attention to it."

"Indeed, indeed!" Mr. Wyble said, clapping his hands. "I have often observed that I notice things others remain quite oblivious to. But it is only natural that, as a man of law, I should do so. Even the most important case can turn on the smallest, most tedious fact."

Ivy was astonished. Mr. Rafferdy seemed to be having some amusement at Mr. Wyble's expense. But were not the two of them friends?

"If it is the most minute of things that demands my cousin's attention," she said, "what is it that captures *yours,* Mr. Rafferdy?"

"Very little, I confess. If Mr. Wyble's interest is held rapt by the tiniest of matters, I am quite his opposite in that even the grandest of things cannot maintain a grip on *mine.*"

Again he grimaced, then he reached beneath the sofa cushion and extracted the book Ivy had been reading. She felt a thrill of panic— the title *Pagan Tales of the Occult* was wrought in gilt on the cover—

but he set it on the floor without glancing at it, sighed as he settled into the sofa, and resumed sipping his tea.

"Rafferdy excels at being bored," Mr. Garritt said.

"Oh, how delightful that must be!" Mrs. Lockwell exclaimed. "I say, I should be very glad to be bored of fine things. For it can only mean you have everything you could possibly wish for and that you never waste a moment's thought fretting over some thing you must but cannot have. I say, you must be exceedingly content, Mr. Rafferdy!"

For a moment an expression of discomfort passed once again over Mr. Rafferdy's face. But the book had been removed, and perhaps it was only that his tea had gone cold. Ivy used the moment of distraction to nudge the book beneath the sofa with her foot.

"My friend does me a disservice," Mr. Rafferdy said at last, with a pointed glance at Mr. Garritt.

"How so?" the other young man said. "You know it is uncommon for you to be engaged in something with true interest."

"Yes, but that is not because I am easy to bore. Rather, I am exceedingly difficult to amuse."

These words brought a sudden agitation upon Ivy. *They* had not asked Mr. Rafferdy to visit here; yet he seemed to imply, almost to accuse, that they were somehow remiss in providing *him* with sufficient entertainment. That he was a man of frivolous nature and poor judgment she had assumed, given his association with Mr. Wyble, but this showed a level of callowness that she had not expected.

"Then a monumental task has been set before us today," she said, "and one that I fear is beyond our ability to achieve success in. For if all the grand sights and wondrous diversions to which a gentleman must surely be accustomed cannot engross you, Mr. Rafferdy, I am certain it will be impossible for the simple, even mundane pleasures at our disposal to do so. I would offer you a biscuit or suggest that Lily play a piece on the pianoforte, but perhaps it is better to admit defeat immediately rather than subject you to such rude delights. If you decided to ask your leave at this moment, I can only imagine its being granted."

Ivy found herself out of breath and waited for his expression of shock or his declaration of affront. She was assured of his rising quickly, and calling for his hat, and making his immediate departure with his friend Mr. Garritt. However, when at last he responded, it was not with words.

Rather, he laughed as if he had just heard the most amusing story, and he was forced to set down his teacup to keep from spilling it. Mr.

Garritt was laughing as well, though more at his friend than anything else.

"I knew you would find the eldest Miss Lockwell to be particularly engaging," Mr. Wyble said. However, given the uncertain look on his face, he was as perplexed as Ivy was concerning the source of Mr. Rafferdy's sudden mirth. Speech had fled her; she could do nothing but gape at Mr. Rafferdy, and she noticed that he was really quite good-looking when he smiled.

As no one seemed to know what to do next, Mrs. Lockwell took up Ivy's idea and called for Lily to play, and this suggestion was greeted with universal approval.

Ivy was grateful for the temporary suspension of conversation. Mr. Rafferdy's response had confounded her; neither he nor Mr. Garritt were what she might have expected in a friend of Mr. Wyble's. Both of them watched Lily, who was summoning the most doleful music out of the pianoforte: a dark and rumbling piece, which she no doubt fancied especially mature.

To his credit, Mr. Garritt listened intently. He seemed genuinely affected by the music. However, Mr. Rafferdy, while initially adopting a grave expression, was soon doing everything he could to conceal his rising mirth. He held his teacup before his mouth, and when that was in danger of shaking too much, he set it down and took out his handkerchief. The more she watched him, the more Ivy felt absurd laughter rising in her own breast, and she was on the verge of releasing it against her will when at last, with a flourish, Lily finished the piece.

They all clapped, none louder than Mr. Wyble, who proclaimed the composition quite ominous and said that it reminded him of the firm and unforgiving hand of justice.

This comment elicited a gasp of horror from Lily.

"It is a romantic piece, Mr. Wyble," Mr. Garritt said seriously, and Lily shot him a grateful look. "Though I will grant you, there is a sorrow to it."

"But is not the ability to feel sorrow intimately related to the ability to feel love?" Lily said. "For if you are insensible to the one, surely you must never feel the other."

"I believe it is so!" Mr. Garritt said, leaning forward in his chair, animation lending his visage, if possible, even greater charms. "To understand joy, one must be able to experience sadness as well. Indeed, there are times when the two are so mingled as to be indiscernible. Sometimes, when I awake in the middle of a long night and hear the bells of St. Galmuth's, I think that there is no lonelier sound in all the world, no music more forlorn and desolate, and none more beautiful."

Lily gave an emphatic nod. "I have heard them too," she said, rather breathlessly.

"Well, I am filled with an incomparable sorrow myself at this very moment," Mr. Rafferdy said after a long moment of silence.

"And why is that?" Ivy said, suddenly concerned.

"Because my teacup is empty, and the biscuits are all gone."

And this time it was Ivy who laughed.

MR. WYBLE'S ACQUAINTANCES lingered far longer into the afternoon than Ivy would have ever expected. More tea was fetched, and biscuits, and a tray of sandwiches that were actually edible. Lily asked if Mr. Garritt had ever been to the theaters, and when he replied that it was Mr. Rafferdy who more often attended plays, Lily plied him with a multitude of questions about what attending the theater was like, and what people wore, and how the actors looked upon the stage.

Much to Mr. Rafferdy's credit, he indulged Lily with answers to all her questions, and when she made the very impertinent suggestion that they all read from a play that very moment, he was the first to agree to the scheme.

Sitting there in the parlor, they read through the first act of *Alitha and Antelidon*. Lily was Alitha, of course, and she assigned the other parts to her liking, so that Mr. Garritt was the noble Antelidon, Mr. Rafferdy arrogant King Daelos, and Ivy was both Queen Selenda and the doomed seeress Ephalee. Rose could not be compelled to take a part, though she agreed to strike a spoon against a cup when the direction called for the toll of a bell offstage, and Mrs. Lockwell wished only to be the audience. When Mr. Wyble asked what his part was to be, Lily assigned him the role of the courier and assured him the part was crucial, despite his sudden death in the middle of Scene One.

They passed around the book of Tharosian drama, each reading their part in turn. By the time the end of Act One was reached, and Alitha thought Antelidon perished, when in truth he lived, though the caprice of the gods had left him bereft of memory, the afternoon was fading outside. As Mr. Garritt spoke his final lines, beseeching Loerus to reveal who he really was, Rose watched so raptly that she quite forgot her cue until Lily nudged her, upon which she struck the cup, heralding the return of the king and the end of the act.

A feeling of oppression came over Ivy. But it was only the sadness of the play, she told herself, and the failing daylight. For a moment none of them was willing to break the silence, as if a spell had been cast by the ancient words they had spoken. Then a shadow sprang up, landing on the open book on Mr. Garritt's lap, giving them all a start. It was Miss Mew, of course, craving attention. Lily made an attempt to retrieve her, but only succeeded in chasing the cat onto the back of the sofa, which she raced across until deciding that Mr. Rafferdy's shoulder would form an excellent perch.

"I am so sorry, Mr. Rafferdy!" Ivy exclaimed, snatching up the cat.

"It's quite all right," he said, though she noted he did make a quick examination of his coat.

"She's very beautiful," Mr. Garritt said, petting the cat while Ivy held her. "What is her name?"

Mr. Rafferdy looked at him. "And how do you know it's a *her*?"

"Tortoiseshell cats are always *hers*," the young man said with a laugh. "Didn't you know that, Rafferdy?"

"We never had cats at my father's house," Mr. Rafferdy said, though the words sounded wistful rather than scornful. He hesitated, then scratched Miss Mew behind the ears. "Where did you come by her?"

"Mrs. Murch brought her into the house," Ivy said. "She was the only tortoiseshell in the litter, and so the only lady cat. I've always found it interesting that a certain trait—the color of the fur, in this instance—can be determined by whether a cat is male or female. I keep meaning to perform some research to see if there are any other traits similarly linked."

At this Mr. Rafferdy gave her a curious look, and Mrs. Lockwell leaped from her chair. "You must forgive her, Mr. Rafferdy. Mr. Lockwell is a man of science, and I fear he filled my daughter's head, when she was younger, with some peculiar notions."

"There is no need to apologize, madam, it's fascinating," Mr. Rafferdy said, at which Mr. Garritt gave him a startled look. "And is Mr. Lockwell about today?"

Mrs. Lockwell sank back into her chair, raising a hand to her throat.

"I'm afraid my father is indisposed," Ivy said. "Please accept his regrets for not being able to come down to meet you."

"Of course," Mr. Rafferdy said, and the matter was dropped.

After that the visitors begged their leave, for the day was nearly done, and the Miss Lockwells bid the young men and their cousin farewell, asking them to return again whenever they liked; and if the invitation was more warmly extended to the former than the latter, no one made notice of it. Mr. Garritt shook each of their hands, and Mr. Rafferdy followed suit.

"It was a pleasure to meet you, Miss Lockwell, Miss Lily," Mr. Rafferdy said to each of them. "And you as well, Miss Rose."

"It feels like you've been holding lightning," Rose said as Mr. Rafferdy took her hand in his.

It was clear he did not know what to make of her words—none of them did, as sometimes was the case with Rose—so instead he smiled and nodded. Then the three visitors were down the stairs, and the front door opened and shut, leaving the women to themselves in a parlor that suddenly felt large and empty and dim.

It was Mrs. Lockwell who found her voice first. "Did you see how well they presented themselves and how terribly handsome they were?" she said, as if the rest of them had not been in the parlor for the last several hours. "Who would have thought our own Mr. Wyble would have acquaintances of such quality!"

"It is no mystery to me that he sought *them* out," Ivy said. "Our cousin has ever been drawn to those whom he perceives to be superior. But that *they* should find a reason to reciprocate his interest I find to be something of a mystery."

"It is no mystery at all!" Mrs. Lockwell said. "That they can derive much from Mr. Wyble's companionship I doubt, as do you. But he had only to mention that he had three cousins, all exceedingly beautiful, and all of an age to consider marriage, and *their* interest in his friendship was assured. For neither of *them* yet wears a ring on his finger."

"Do you think they will call on us again, Mother?" Lily said. She was flitting about the parlor. "I thought Mr. Garritt was unbearably handsome. Do you not think he made for a perfect Antelidon? He understood—*really* understood—what the role meant."

"Yes, he was excellent," Mrs. Lockwell agreed. "It would be impossible for a young man to present himself better. Though I thought Mr. Rafferdy did very well at his part too."

"On the contrary, he could hardly keep himself from laughing during the most serious passages," Ivy said. "Though I thought he was very indulgent of all of us."

"Oh, yes!" Mrs. Lockwell exclaimed. "Exceedingly indulgent!"

"Well, Ivy can have Mr. Rafferdy, then," Lily said, "and I shall take Mr. Garritt. He has the soul of a poet."

"And likely the pocketbook of one as well," Ivy said.

Mrs. Lockwell gave her a shocked look. "Whatever do you mean?"

At several times during the visit, Ivy had come close enough to Mr. Garritt to notice that, while his clothes were impeccably kept and suited his figure very well, they were neither so new nor so fashionable as Mr. Rafferdy's attire. Also, each time Lily had asked a question about what exclusive parties or lavish affairs the two had attended, Mr. Garritt always referred the inquiries to Mr. Rafferdy. Ivy could only presume it was because he had few experiences of his own to relate.

As for Mr. Rafferdy, while he had appeared to genuinely enjoy himself during the course of the visit, it could only be due to the novelty of the situation, being so far from what he was used to. Nor could he be expected to find continued pleasure in the simple entertainments offered in the houses of the gentry.

Ivy related these observations with great care and delicacy to her mother and sister, not wishing to upset their sensibilities. Still, the reaction she encountered was one of astonishment.

"What are you implying, Ivy?" Mrs. Lockwell said, quite agitated. "Are you trying to tell me that you think these two were not as fine a pair of gentlemen as any young woman could hope to encounter in this city? For if you are, I will not hear of it!"

"Nor will I!" cried Lily.

Ivy took in a breath to steady herself. "I am only saying that it would be prudent not to base too many hopes and expectations on a single meeting. Especially because I think it clear that, while both Mr. Rafferdy and Mr. Garritt are gentlemen of quality and worth, they do not both possess each characteristic in the same proportions. That is to say, I think it very clear that the one is far too rich to marry any of us, and the other far too poor. Besides," Ivy went on more lightly now, "there were only two of them, which meant there was not one for our dear Rose."

Rose smiled and took Ivy's hand. "But I don't mind, Ivy. I'll come live with you and Mr. Rafferdy."

"There!" Mrs. Lockwell said. "As always, it is Rose who sees the simplest truths. In no way could she ever want for anything if her sisters were well situated. I should never worry about Rose if you and Lily were married."

A chill came over Ivy. But it was only the coming of night that caused her to shiver; the short day was all but spent outside, and she moved to light a few candles. All the while Lily continued to speak in an animated manner, though one would think from her talk that there had been only one man, by the name of Garritt, in the parlor that day. Mrs. Lockwell was hardly less enthusiastic, and even Rose could be heard laughing and clapping her hands.

Ivy smiled at their lively conversation, but her smile kept waver-

ing, just like the candles she lit. Did she, too, feel some unseen movement of cold air that stole past shut windows and closed doors? As she
set a candle on the secretary, she noticed several new receipts and demands her mother had stashed in a teacup. Ivy took them out, and a
sigh escaped her. "Perhaps we should just let Mr. Wyble take this
house and be done with it."

It was only after a moment that Ivy realized the room had gone
quiet. She turned to see her sisters and mother staring at her.

"What are you talking about, Ivy?" Lily said with a frown. "Are
you mad? Why in the world would we give our house to Mr. Wyble?"

Ivy smoothed the papers in her hand. "I did not say we should *give*
this house to him. Rather, we might . . . that is, Mother might sell her
interest in it to him. I know he has a rather large sum saved away, and
I have no doubt he would be willing to part with a good deal of it to
win the right of dwelling in this house early. And with the proceeds,
we would have income enough to live very well for years to come."

Rose's expression was suddenly worried; she sat on the sofa and
petted Miss Mew.

"But where should *we* live?" Lily said. "You don't expect us to
move to Lowpark, do you? Mr. Garritt would never come visit us
*there*."

Ivy started to reply, but Mrs. Lockwell was quicker. Her usually
cheerful face became hard, as it had that night when the two men in
dark capes came to the door. "I know what Ivy is thinking. She is seeking ways to economize. But our need is not *that* great. And even if it
were, I would not hear of what I know she is proposing. When we left
that house, I told Mr. Lockwell that I would never return there, and I
will keep my word."

Ivy knew it was not prudent, but the topic had been broached, and
she might never have another chance to speak of it. "I am only saying
that the house on Durrow Street is not entailed to anybody. It is Father's outright."

"Durrow Street?" Lily said, and it was clear she suddenly did not
know what to think, and so she said again, "Durrow Street!" And she
sat down on the sofa next to Rose.

Before her mother could interject, Ivy finished her thoughts. "The
house on Durrow Street is Father's, and when . . . and in any event it
will always be in our family. With the income earned from granting
this house to our cousin, we could, if we lived modestly, dwell there as
long as we wished and never have any fear of real want or need."

Lily was still visibly struggling with this idea. No doubt the notion
of giving anything to Mr. Wyble was unthinkable for her, yet the name

Durrow Street held particular enchantment, for it was on Durrow Street that the city's theaters were to be found. At last she said, "If we need income, why do we not sell Father's house?" Money, it had evidently been decided, was more likely than proximity to grant access to wonders such as theaters. "We could sell the house on Durrow Street and live very well *here*, I am sure."

And where should they live when they were spinsters and this house belonged to Mr. Wyble? However, Ivy did not voice this thought, and there were other constraints on that course of action. "The house on Durrow Street is Father's alone," she said. "Only he could make a decision to sell it."

They all knew such a decision was beyond his ability.

Before Ivy could press her argument, Mrs. Lockwell stood. Her cheeks had a high color to them. "I will endure no more speech on this subject, Ivoleyn! Durrow Street is not a place where respectable families dwell. There is nothing for us in that old house. It is a horrid place, fit only for the likes of *them*." She waved a hand at the darkened windows. "And they should go *there,* rather than show up on our doorstep, when they come for—"

The color drained from Mrs. Lockwell's face, and she sank down into the chair.

"Mother, what is wrong?" Lily cried, rushing to Mrs. Lockwell's side. Rose hurried after, a frightened look on her face, and Ivy as well. They patted Mrs. Lockwell's hand, and fanned her to help her breathe, and brought her water to sip.

Soon her color returned, and she said she had felt faint for a moment, but the moment had passed, and she was perfectly well now, so they could stop their fussing. She waved them away and stood again, for she needed to see what Mrs. Murch was doing in the kitchen, having developed a sudden certainty that something was amiss with the supper. Lily departed as well, humming the song she had played on the pianoforte earlier, though somehow she made it sound not doleful but light and cheerful.

"Is there someone out there?" Rose said, and Ivy realized she had been staring out the window into the night.

The words of the riddle came to Ivy's mind, unbidden. *When twelve who wander stand as one, through the door the dark will come. . . .*

"No, dearest," Ivy said, sitting down on the sofa and helping Rose to pet Miss Mew.

However, she could sense the darkness slinking in through the window, as if the sash were raised and the gloom a living thing, and she knew the words she had spoken were false. There *was* someone out there. *They* were out there, the magicians who had come here looking for her father. Looking for something. Yet Ivy was now certain that, whatever it was they wanted, they would not find it in *this* house. And if she wished to gain their aid—in helping Mr. Lockwell, or in deciphering his riddle—then she must go to where she was more likely to find them.

She sat with Rose in the parlor, passing the time quietly. An hour later Mrs. Lockwell called everyone to supper, and by then Ivy had formulated her plan. There was only one thing to do.

As soon as possible, she must go to Durrow Street.

# CHAPTER EIGHT

*E*LDYN'S MEETING WITH Mr. Sarvinge and Mr. Grealing was not so heartening as on the previous occasion.

He met them at Mrs. Haddon's coffeehouse in Covenant Cross, in request to a note he received at the Golden Loom. Their manner remained polite, yet he could feel a sort of unseen lightning crackling back and forth on the air while the coffee he had bought them with the scant coins in his pocket grew cold. There was a sharpness to their words that—however courteous—gave everything they said an urgent tone.

They had gone out of their way to accommodate the peculiar demands of his schedule, they informed him. Now the ship was ready to sail for the New Lands, and he had left them in an awkward position. In order to hold a place for him, they had put off other investors. It was an unfortunate situation; there was nothing else that could be done to resolve it. They must have the money he had promised them. If he did not deliver a hundred regals to them by sunset of the next day, they would be forced—regretfully, of course—to spread word among all men of business in the city that Mr. Eldyn Garritt could not be relied upon; no one would enter a contract with him ever after. Both of them despised the idea of doing this, yet there would be no choice. It would—rather, it *must*—be done.

"You know we hold you in the highest esteem, Mr. Garritt," said Mr. Sarvinge as he rose from the table. He was long-limbed and thin as a whip, with a long face, a blade-thin nose, and long black hair that draped over very thin shoulders.

"Indeed, the highest esteem," said Mr. Grealing, who was short and in every manner soft and round where his companion was lean and angular, and who bore a single patch of hair atop his round, soft head. "We know you will not disappoint us, Mr. Garritt."

They smiled and bowed, they gave him sharp looks, they smiled again, and the two departed, leaving their coffee cups untouched. For a time Eldyn could do nothing but sit at the table and tremble as if he was chilled to the bone, though the atmosphere in Mrs. Haddon's was, as always, close and stuffy and boisterous.

What was he to do? He fretted over this question again and again. But there was nothing to do; he was ruined, and his sister with him. Mr. Walpert would evict them from the inn, and Sashie would be forced to live on the streets. She would become a servant, a slattern. Or far worse. A vision came to him of her lying in a dank lane in Waterside, her once-pretty face dirty and slack, insensible to what the coarse men who passed by did with her, save whether they put another bottle of gin in her hand.

He dug the palms of his hands into his eyes, trying to grind away the unspeakable vision.

"Hello there, Garritt!" a voice called out. "Quit staring at your cup and come over and join us!"

Eldyn looked up. Orris Jaimsley, Curren Talinger, and Dalby Warrett sat at a table across the crowded shop. As usual, Talinger was banging a fist on the table, expounding upon some treatise or another, while Warrett grabbed for their cups to keep them from flying.

Jaimsley waved a skinny arm. "Talinger still seems to think we need a king for some reason," he called out. "Nor will he listen to me. I need you to come talk some reason to him, Garritt."

Had he been more in his right mind, Eldyn might have flinched at so brazen an advertisement. Only days ago, in *The Fox,* Eldyn had read how the White Lady had accused the proprietor of a tavern not five hundred paces from this spot of harboring conspirators against the Crown. *The Fox* had decried this as a falsehood and another example of the injustice rampant in Altania. All the same, the man had been swiftly convicted by the Gray Conclave—which had the luxury of convening its own courts—and the broadsheets might as well have been printed in the tavernkeeper's blood. Next week, in Barrowgate, he would hang.

Jaimsley gave him another wave. Eldyn granted him only a shallow nod, then headed for the door. He caught a puzzled look from his friend, then he was outside, into the coolness of the early twilight. The day had been short, the umbral was to be even briefer, and tomorrow would be a lumenal of no more than middling duration. The next sunset would come all too quickly. In a few hours, hope would be at an end.

*But it is not yet,* he told himself. The brisk air revived him after the torpid atmosphere of the coffeehouse. *There has to be a way.* But where could he get a hundred regals?

Once more he considered asking Rafferdy, but as quickly dismissed the notion. It was highly unlikely his friend would have such a sum about him. There was only one possibility Eldyn could think of. He reached into his coat pocket, touching the carnelian brooch and the pearl earrings—the last of his mother's jewels. He had taken them from their hiding place at the inn that morning with the intent of selling them, for he was running low on funds to pay Mr. Walpert. They were worth far less than a hundred regals, but if he could fetch a good price for them, he might be able to offer the money to Mr. Sarvinge and Mr. Grealing as a token of his good faith. Surely if he did that they would give him more time; they were honorable men.

Eldyn quickened his pace, hurrying to reach Gold Row before the shops closed.

❧

AN HOUR LATER found him walking the streets of the Old City. Shadows gathered around him, soft, unbidden. Earlier, Eldyn had gone to every shop on the row, showing the brooch and earrings, and the best price he had been offered for the lot was five regals.

Five regals! It was an insult. No, it was a crime. The jewels were the last things in the world he had of his mother, save for the memory of her face, her gentle touch. When he was a boy, her hands had been like a balm against his face, soothing the scrapes and bruises his father gave him.

He fingered the coins in his pocket. Five regals. That was all he had left of her now. It would do nothing to help his cause with Sarvinge and Grealing. Such a small sum could be only an affront to them. It was hardly enough to keep him and Sashie at the inn for another month.

A ghostly face appeared in the darkness. Eldyn stopped and looked up. Behind iron bars, an angel hovered in the gloom, dark tears streaking his pale, beautiful face. Only it wasn't an angel. It was just the statue of St. Andelthy. Eldyn's feet had led him again to the old chapel of St. Adaris, at the end of its narrow lane in the Old City.

He gripped the bars and peered through, but the churchyard beyond was empty and silent. There was no sign of the priests.

Eldyn reached into his pocket and took out a coin: not one of the regals from the sale of his mother's jewels but rather a circle of silver. One side depicted the moon as a smiling face, while the other showed a similarly humanized sun, framed with a radiant mane yet stern of expression. He spun the coin in his hand and saw the faces in alternation: moon, sun, moon. Yet never both faces at once, just like in the sky above.

Why the illusionist at the Sword and Leaf had given him the coin, and what it was for, Eldyn did not know. He might as well cast it into the gutter. The coin would not pay his way at the inn or buy an investment in the trading company. It was a thing of beauty: worthless.

He slipped the coin into his pocket with care and continued on his way to the Golden Loom, leaving the darkened church behind.

Another message was waiting for him at the inn, this one from Dashton Rafferdy. His friend thirsted for drink only slightly more than he did for company. Eldyn went upstairs to check on Sashie, but even as he opened the door to their little rooms, the door to *hers* slammed shut, nor could he elicit any answer from her through its wooden panels.

How long she would refuse to speak to him he did not know, but he was growing weary of this behavior. Couldn't she see that what he had done had been for her benefit?

*And how exactly have you benefited her?* He looked around at the cramped room, with its rickety chairs and the hard bench where he made his periodic attempts at sleeping.

He glanced again at Rafferdy's note, then leaned his head against the door to her bedchamber. "If you do not need me tonight, dearest, then I will go out for the evening." He caught the sound of the bed creaking; she had thrown herself upon it. She had heard him.

Eldyn brushed his coat—though in some places there was little coat left to brush—then returned downstairs. The scent of food wafted from the kitchens. His stomach uttered a noisy complaint; he had not eaten anything that day. He ordered a meal to be sent up for Sashie, but forwent anything for himself. He had already spent too much on the coffee.

Distracted as he was, Eldyn did not see Miss Walpert until he neared the door. By then it was too late, for she was coming in from the public room, a basket in hand, and there was no way to duck beneath the stairs before she saw him.

"Why, Mr. Garritt, there you are!" Miss Walpert exclaimed, and at once was upon him. She reached a hand up to her bonnet but succeeded only in making it more crooked yet. "Every time I look for you, you aren't there, but somewhere else. I should hardly think you lived at my father's inn anymore for how seldom I see you."

He made some soft, useless reply, then started toward the door.

"You are always in such a hurry to fly away, Mr. Garritt. I'd think you were a kind of bird if I didn't know otherwise." She laughed, a sound not unlike what a horse might produce. He gave a tight smile and moved again toward the door, but she said, "You have not eaten! Papa told me to send a meal up to your rooms, but just one, and Miss Garritt is there, I know she is, and so I thought to myself, Mr. Garritt can in no way have eaten properly, it is not possible, and he is so thin, so awfully thin. I've often said to myself, I could thread him and sew stitches with him, he's that thin."

Miss Walpert was herself somewhat plump, having a tendency to sample from whatever plates she was bringing from the kitchen.

Eldyn could not help but be touched by so genuine a concern, however crudely expressed. "Thank you, Miss Walpert, but I am well." He adjusted his coat, which indeed had grown looser of late. "I am going out. I shall find something later."

"You won't, though," she said. "You'll be thinner when I see you next, and one day I won't see you at all. You'll step in a crack in the street and slip right through, and no one will ever know what became of you." She fumbled with the basket and pulled out half a small loaf. "Here, Mr. Garritt." She pushed the bread into his hands. "Go on, now, let me see you take a bite. Right this moment."

He hesitated, but the bread smelled good, and she was watching him. Eldyn took a bite; the juices flowed in his mouth, and his stomach let out a triumphant roar. Now that he had tasted food, it was beyond him to stop; he took several bites, gulping each down.

God in Eternum, was he some mangy animal scrounging in the street? He willed himself to lower the bread, to slip the remainder in his pocket. "I will pay you for this."

She shook her head. "But you needn't. You could have all the bread you wished and never pay for a thing. Your sister too. My father says his knees do him no good. He says he wishes there was a young man about, one to help him with things around the inn. You wouldn't have to be so thin, Mr. Garritt. You wouldn't have to fly like a bird no more." She smiled, a lopsided and yellow-toothed expression; even so, for all its flaws, it might have seemed a kindly gesture, save for the hunger in it—a hunger as fierce as any Eldyn had felt while consuming the bread, and one just as unsatisfied.

"Good night, Miss Walpert," he stuttered, and before she could speak again, he was out the door.

He hurried down the lane, not knowing if she followed, wrapping the shadows around him just in case.

*You could have all the bread you wished and never pay for a thing.*

Yes, he understood now. He could ease his own kind of famishing, and Delina Walpert hers. Mr. Walpert would gain the son he never had. It would not be such an awful existence. It would be far from the life of a gentleman, to be sure. He would have no fine clothes, no fine house or fine carriage. The work would be tedious, and endless, but not without its securities and comforts. Mr. Walpert appeared well fed; he smiled at times. And Sashie would be provided for. A life of work at the inn would quickly fade the flower of her beauty; she would become drab. No bright world of masques and balls would await her; no baronet would sweep her away. But nor would she be reduced to dwelling in gin alleys. It would not be such a terrible thing—it would *not*.

Like a dark bird, he flew on through the night.

The sign of the Sword and Leaf flickered in the grimy light of a streetlamp. A large fellow stood watch in the doorway, arms crossed, for it was after nightfall. "Pardon me," Eldyn said when the man did not open the way.

"Who's there?" the big fellow said, squinting into the gloom. "Show yourself." He made the sign against ghosts and curses, two fingers splayed before his heart.

The shadows—Eldyn had forgotten to release them. He did so now, casting them off like a cloak, and made a motion as if stepping into the pale circle beneath the streetlamp. The big fellow gave him a startled look, then shook his head and opened the door.

"Damnable Siltheri," he muttered as Eldyn passed through.

These words sent a shiver up Eldyn's back. He thought of the band of illusionists he had seen the last time he was here, recalling their shimmering attire, their pale necks. Surely he could not be mistaken for one of *them*. Nor were they inside the tavern this night. However, Rafferdy was, waving at him from his place in the corner, and Eldyn went to join him.

Rafferdy seemed in a fine mood. He laughed and announced he was delighted to see Eldyn, and now they could order punch. He signaled a man, who delivered them a crock, two cups, lumps of sugar, spoons, and a lemon. The fellow held out a hand.

"Garritt, you wouldn't mind paying our bill this time, would you?" Rafferdy nodded toward the man.

Eldyn winced. What sort of cruel fate was it that Rafferdy's pockets should be empty and his own full? God mocked him. But then he smiled despite himself, as if comprehending the divine joke. The money he had gotten today could not buy him a future; it might as well buy them a drink. He pulled a coin out.

"A regal!" Rafferdy said, eyes alight. "Our amusement is assured tonight."

"I thought *your* amusement was always assured," Eldyn said. The punch was sweet and strong.

"Only because I go to great lengths to assure it. Amusement is a challenging business, Garritt. If one does not concentrate, if one lets up even for a moment, the risk of suffering something boring or tedious is immediate and dire. As you are no doubt well aware, given your glum looks. What's the matter? How is that business of yours going?"

There was no use speaking of it. "I am still working to arrange things," he said, and downed the contents of his cup. "But what of you, Rafferdy? You seem in fine spirits. What has propelled you to such great heights?"

"Propelled? No, it is rather that nothing has weighed me down. The natural progression of my spirit is ever upward, even as yours is always directed down. But let us see who will tug the harder tonight, Garritt. By God, I would drag you up if I could." And he refilled Eldyn's cup.

"So you've seen her again," Eldyn said with a laugh, feeling a heady warmth from the spirits. "Miss Lockwell."

"It was a chance encounter, over on Warden Street."

Eldyn raised an eyebrow. "A chance encounter? After your driving halfway across the city and lying in wait, you mean?"

"As I've learned at dice, sometimes it helps to give chance a nudge when no one is looking."

"And as I've learned, you're a pauper tonight," Eldyn said, refilling Rafferdy's cup. "No doubt from losing at gambling. I'd think you'd be more careful."

"What was there to be careful of? I simply spied Miss Lockwell and her sisters as they left a shop, greeted them, much to their obvious delight, and walked with them awhile. You should have joined me, Garritt. They are all three pleasing to look at."

Eldyn shrugged. "Perhaps, though I cannot say I find them so fetching as you do. The youngest is lively, it is true. And I warrant you, there *is* something about the eldest. I can't quite describe it. She is pretty, I suppose. And she carries herself well, though she is too short to be a beauty. And did you notice her freckles? Does she never wear a bonnet?"

Rafferdy said he had indeed noticed Miss Lockwell's freckles. He did not seem to find them properly abhorrent.

Eldyn would be the first to admit that their visit at the house on Whitward Street had gone better than he had feared. It had been long since Eldyn had known any society besides that of his sister and Rafferdy, and he had found the Lockwells engaging. The middle sister was too mild, of course, and their mother too loud. But he enjoyed discussing plays with the youngest sister, and there could be no faulting either the wit or the manners of the eldest.

"Well, it hardly matters how fetching they are," Eldyn said. "They are beneath you, Rafferdy."

"Indeed!" Rafferdy said with a laugh. "Their connections are hopelessly inferior, at least to one in my situation. And what society they keep—their cousin is a lawyer with all the manners of a leech. They are completely beneath me. And I can assure you, Miss Lockwell is very aware of this fact."

"Is she?" Eldyn said over his cup. "Has she said this to you?"

"No, of course not. It would be uncouth to be so direct. But she is clever. She has so much as said it in a dozen subtle ways. I have no fear of untoward attachments on her part. No one is more sensitive of the gulf between us than she."

"If that is so, then do you not think that your encounters with her might cause her distress?"

This idea was unfathomable to Rafferdy. "I enjoy her wit, as she does mine. There is a freshness about her speech—a way of being sharp without being cutting—that I never will encounter at a party in the New Quarter. She is utterly without affectation. Given that affectation is all I have, I naturally find her fascinating. Besides, they may be beneath *me,* but for you, Garritt . . ."

"As for me, I fear I am beneath *them,*" Eldyn said, and quaffed his punch.

"Nonsense! Not *beneath* you. You are the grandson of a magnate, after all. And you're not so broke as you'd like me to think. I saw your pocketful of money. Either of the younger two would do well to catch you."

Eldyn did not bother to argue. That a marriage between him and any one of the Lockwell sisters could result in anything but misery was impossible. When both sides wanted for money, a match was doomed.

Besides, there was already one he might marry to assure himself a living. He felt the lump of bread in his pocket. His stomach had gone sour; he should eat more. Instead, he filled their punch cups again, and after that they put all their attention into getting drunk.

THE BRIEF UMBRAL was nearly done when he returned to the Golden Loom. As he stumbled through the streets of the Old City, he had forgotten to gather the shadows around him, and he had nearly been parted from what remained of his money by a group of men in ragged clothes who appeared from behind one of the buttresses of St. Galmuth's. However, fear had cleared his mind, and with an instinct as natural to him as drawing a breath, he had spun the darkness into a concealing garment and had darted down a dark lane, losing the robbers.

By the time he reached the inn, the clarity imparted by a brush with peril had faded, leaving his head dull and throbbing from too much rum. He nodded to the doorkeeper, then headed for the stairs, wanting only to go to his room, to throw himself in a chair and not move, not even think—that is, to enjoy the blissful, insensible hours of a drunken stupor. However, before he could start up the stairwell, a tall form stepped from a doorway.

"You have something of mine," the other said in a deep voice. "You have had it for days, and yet you have not returned it to me. Did you think to keep it for yourself?"

Eldyn gripped the newel post. A man stepped into the circle of tarnished light cast by a lamp that hung from the ceiling. He was tall and broad, clad in a coat of russet velvet. His lion's mane of hair was loose about his shoulders.

"You have something of mine," Westen said again, prowling closer.

At first, in a mad thought, Eldyn thought he was speaking of Sashie. Then his foggy mind recalled the handkerchief tucked into his coat pocket. He fumbled for it, pulled it out, and the half-eaten hunk of bread came with it, tumbling to the floor.

"My apologies," Eldyn said, fighting to keep his voice steady. "I would have returned this to you sooner. However, I have not seen you about of late. Yet now that you are here, you must take it back." He held out the silk cloth and cursed himself for the way it betrayed the trembling of his hand.

Westen did not reach for the handkerchief. Instead, he took another step nearer. "I do not give a token of myself lightly. I give it only to one who will keep it in good faith. It is a spell of sorts, a charm, one that protects me in my work. Always the spell has kept me safe on the road. Yet I have been much harried by the king's redcrests of late. At first I did not suspect the reason—until *she* told me that you had taken it from her."

A spark of anger ignited in Eldyn's chest. "I fear that you made a mistake. It was—it *is*—impossible for my sister to keep it in any sort of faith. If you had hoped to elicit any protections in granting it to her, you did so in vain."

Again Eldyn held out the cloth, but the highwayman did not take it. His tawny eyes were still on Eldyn, and Eldyn could feel a power radiating from him: the aura of a man who was strong, and handsome, and rich, and who knew it. All at once a grin spread across Westen's clean-shaven face. It was a perilous expression. The spark in Eldyn's chest collapsed to a cinder.

"Perhaps you are right," the highwayman said. "Perhaps I did give it to the wrong keeper after all." And with that he took the handkerchief.

The sweat cooled on Eldyn's brow. He turned to ascend the stairs.

"I understand you need regals, Garritt."

Eldyn's fingers tightened on the railing.

"The sum of a hundred regals, to be exact."

Eldyn turned from the stairs. "How can you know that?" However, even as he said this, he understood. Westen must have eavesdropped on one of his conversations with Mr. Sarvinge and Mr. Grealing. "You have been spying on me."

The highwayman shrugged. "I can give you the gold you need."

Despite his tiredness and dread, Eldyn laughed. "Give? You would *give* it to me? I should think not. You are not much one for giving but rather *taking,* are you not? Would that I had a mask and pistol, Mr. Westen, if that is indeed your name. For then I could elicit your charity just as you do of those you waylay on the roads."

"Do not think you know me," Westen answered, his voice low. "Though I will grant you, there is some truth to your words. And you are right. I offer no gift. For I want something in return."

Fear was gone, as was weariness. For all his present uncertainty, there were some things that caused Eldyn no doubt. "If you think I would sell my sister to the likes of you, think again."

The highwayman laughed. "So you *would* sell her, you mean, but only to the right man. How like a true gentleman, who thinks nothing of love but only of money, and who, from his female kin, would gladly steal any hope of the former in order to gain the latter. For what is marriage but whoremongering for the wealthy? And they say I'm a thief."

Eldyn's cheeks burned, and his hands became fists. "I would do anything to assure her happiness."

"Would you, Garritt? I am curious: what exactly would you do in order to assure your sister's future?" Westen reached inside his jacket and took out a leather purse. It was heavy, by the way he held it. "I have it here, Garritt—a hundred regals. Is that not what you need to make what you dream come to pass?"

Eldyn licked his lips. A few hours ago, in this very spot, he had taken bread from Miss Walpert. Now he felt a different sort of hunger. He meant to tell Westen to sod off, to turn away and march up the stairs.

Instead, he said, "What do you want?" The highwayman smiled, led him to the corner, and spoke in the lowest of voices.

The thing was not difficult, and that was what first let Eldyn know it was wrong. There was a village at Hayrick Cross, three miles north of the city. There was a blacksmith's shop in the village. There was a man in the shop with red hair. Eldyn was to ask the man for nine nails and to pay him with three pennies. After buying the nails, he should go to the public house in the village. He should order an ale. He should take a quarter hour to drink it, no more, no less. Once finished, he should go to the old well east of the village. He should look for a loose stone in the rim and pry it up. Under the stone would be a slip of paper. On the paper would be a word. He was to memorize the word, then tear up the paper and throw it in the well.

Upon returning to Invarel, he was to read *The Fox* every day it was published, particularly the advertisements on the last page. When he saw an advertisement listing pewter candlesticks, silver snuffboxes, and gold thimbles for sale, he was to go to the street printed in the advertisement but not to the house number. Instead, the address he must go to could be derived from the number of candlesticks, snuffboxes, and thimbles listed in the advertisement. Once there, he should knock. A man would ask him his name. He should give it as Mr. _____, with the surname being the word he had read on the paper at the well.

The man would give him a leather tube. The tube would contain a letter at one end and a reservoir of ink at the other. Eldyn was not to look at the letter. He was to put the tube in a cloth sack with the nine nails he had bought and travel to Hayrick Cross that night, arriving precisely halfway through the umbral, no matter how long or short the night was. He was to wait by the well until the red-haired man from the blacksmith's shop arrived. He was to tell the man he did not need the nails and to give him the sack. If anyone else arrived at the well, or if anyone else was with the red-haired man, or if anyone accosted him on the road there—especially an agent of the king or a servant of the Gray Conclave—he was to turn one end of the tube, which would release the ink, letting it spill into the other chamber and blotting out the message written on the paper.

Once this business was done, he was to go back to Invarel. He was to look for more advertisements in *The Fox*. If he saw one, he was to go to the address (remembering how to decipher it) and get another leather tube. If a week passed and he saw no advertisement, his work was done and his hundred regals earned. That was it. That was all he had to do. There was nothing else.

As he spoke, Westen had pressed Eldyn into the corner, blocking his escape with an arm braced against the wall.

"It is mischief you wish me to work," Eldyn said, keeping his voice low. "And treason as well, I warrant. What messages could be passed back and forth in such an ungodly manner save those that seek to harm the Crown?"

"So you are a king's man?"

"I am not a criminal."

"And what deed, if it be just, can ever truly be called a crime? How can it be stealing to take something that was already stolen and give it back to its rightful owner?"

"You call it justice, robbing people on the road? I don't care who you give the money to. I don't care if you give it all away—which I am certain you do not. I still call it thievery." He broke free of the highwayman. Except he had the feeling it was Westen who let him go, that if the taller man had wanted it, Eldyn would still be pinned in place.

"You will change your mind."

Eldyn halted on the stairs, but he did not turn around.

"I know what your dear sister has spoken about you. And I've watched you. You are like me, Garritt, whether you know it or not. We both want to be something more than we are."

No, he was wrong. They were nothing alike. Eldyn hurried up the stairs, into his rooms, and locked the door behind him.

❧

THE BRIEF DAY was already half over when he awoke. Sunset was five hours away. He was glad. It would be a blessing to have this done with. Once his fate was decided, there would be nothing more to worry about.

He washed his face, ran a razor over his cheeks, and combed and tied back his hair. He polished his boots and brushed his coat, gently, so as not to cause more distress to the poor garment. Soon he would have a new coat. Not fine like this one had been once, but not threadbare either. A simple coat, and warm.

The door to Sashie's little room was closed. He knocked. "Please come out, dearest," he crooned, but he heard only a shuffling of steps. He sighed. She would forgive him soon.

*And when will that be? The moment you tell her that you have assured her future working as a servant in the very inn where her happiness was ruined? Is that when you can expect her to forgive you?*

There was nothing for it; he went downstairs.

He saw the innkeeper just heading into the back salon. Good, that would give him a private place to make his proposal. He gathered his will, then headed for the dining room to ask Mr. Walpert for his daughter's hand.

His boot kicked something as he went, and he looked down. On the floor lay a hunk of half-eaten bread. Flies danced upon it in a merry feast. A moment ago he had been ravenous, but now his stomach clenched.

"Is there something you need, Mr. Garritt?"

He looked up. The innkeeper stood before him, smiling, a kindness in his rheumy eyes.

Eldyn took a breath. "I wanted to—"

Then Eldyn saw him, past the innkeeper's shoulder, through the door into the public room. He leaned against the bar, regaling a group of coarse men and painted women with some tale of his exploits.

"Yes, Mr. Garritt?" The innkeeper cocked his head.

Eldyn swallowed. "I just wanted a cup of tea, that's all."

"But of course! Anything for our young Mr. Garritt. Sit yourself down, and I'll bring it to you myself!"

Sickness flooded Eldyn, but only for a moment. Then he felt a strange sensation come over him. It was like the lifting of a weight, like the release of a vise's pressure. He went to sit in a corner of the public room and soon was sipping his tea. He did not look at the bar.

Just as he finished his tea, he heard the sound of boots behind him. A leather purse landed with a *thud* on the table.

"You begin tonight," said a low voice in his ear.

Eldyn reached out and took the purse. There was a soft laugh, then the sound of boots walking away. Eldyn weighed the purse in his hand. It was heavier than he'd imagined. He tucked it inside his coat, then rose and hurried to the door. He had just four hours to find Mr. Sarvinge and Mr. Grealing.

And after that, time to work.

# CHAPTER NINE

THAT A CHANGE had come over Dashton Rafferdy was soon apparent to his intimate acquaintances. It was a fact noted at Lord Baydon's city house over breakfast and expounded upon in Lady Marsdel's parlor during evening conversations. The languid air about him had all but dissipated; mirrors no longer seemed to occupy him so fully; and some mornings he had been seen out and about the city no more than an hour after dawn. All agreed that he looked unusually well.

As the month since his return to town progressed, there was much speculation among his acquaintances as to what had so energized their usually languid Mr. Rafferdy. Lord Baydon suggested it was a suddenly realized interest in business, and he pressed Rafferdy to tell him what sort of propositions and futures he was considering.

That the young man's thoughts were indeed consumed with future propositions, Lady Marsdel appeared convinced. She expressed concern that the dealings be equitable, resulting in no undue enrichment on the opposite side and no unwarranted impoverishment on Rafferdy's own. Her niece, however, allayed her fears. Mrs. Baydon was certain Mr. Rafferdy's new vitality stemmed from a meeting he had made recently and that it was a connection of the highest quality—one that could bring only great profit to both parties involved. When Lord Baydon asked who this respectable business partner was, Mrs. Baydon only smiled and deferred to Mr. Rafferdy, saying that such information was for him to divulge.

Rafferdy never denied nor confirmed these various suppositions. He was content to let the others divert themselves. For his part, he knew that any change that had come upon him had nothing to do with a matter of business, nor, despite all of Mrs. Baydon's intimations, with the matter of Lord Everaud's daughter.

Miss Everaud had written to him on several occasions since his return from Asterlane. He had responded to her twice to fulfill the obligation placed upon him by his father's friendship with Lord Everaud, but that was all. As for business, Rafferdy neither had a head for such matters nor wished to develop one, as he often said, on the fear it might alter his hat size.

Besides, Rafferdy was not convinced he *had* changed. For how could one be changed by feeling *more* one's self? And he saw no need to discover any particular reason for such an occurrence. If he felt like rising earlier, walking farther, and laughing more often than usual, it was only because it amused him to do so at the moment, and when it ceased to do so, no doubt he would return to his usual ways.

"It seems to me that people are too interested in seeking out causation," Rafferdy announced one morning over breakfast at the Baydon house, after nearly a month of this sort of speculation.

"What do you mean?" Mrs. Baydon asked over toast.

Rafferdy stirred his coffee. "I mean that people seem determined to find the reason why things are as they are. What causes the stars to spin one way and not the other, why tall hats are fashionable and short hats are not, how there can be so many afflicted with poverty when the wealthy constantly want for novel ways to spend their fortunes. To me, it is all a great waste of effort that could better be spent looking in shops or going for a drive along the Promenade and noting how poorly dressed everyone is compared to oneself."

Mr. Baydon lowered his broadsheet. "But it is to be expected, even desired, that people wonder about such things, Rafferdy," he said with a scowl. "You speak of the movements of the stars, and here in *The Messenger* today is a story of a new celestial body that has been glimpsed for the very first time by means of ocular lenses. What sort of object it might be is unknown, but you can be assured that, now it has been discovered, men of science will seek to learn all that can be learned about it. They will not rest in their examinations until there is not the slightest whit of mystery left to it and it becomes like the most familiar old thing we have known forever."

"I am no scientist," Rafferdy said. "And I would dread to live in a world devoid of even one whit of mystery. However, it seems to me that sometimes—or perhaps, I might venture, most of the time—occurrences have no cause at all. New stars appear and old ones vanish. Short hats become popular again. Things are as they are, and do as they please, for absolutely no reason at all."

"Certainly *you* do as you please, Mr. Rafferdy," Mrs. Baydon said with a laugh.

"No," he answered her, "I do what pleases *me*. And others would do well to follow suit. I am sure people would be far gladder if they simply stopped searching for all the causes of their unhappiness." He rose from his seat. "Now, speaking of causes, you've caused me to be late, for I meant to leave a quarter hour ago. I must be off."

"Where are you going in such a hurry?" said Lord Baydon. He had joined them for breakfast that morning, though he had participated little in their discussions, as he claimed he seldom had any idea what young people were talking about. "Is it some matter of business?"

When Rafferdy said it was not, Mrs. Baydon said, "I can guess where he is off to. He is going to visit his new acquaintances. It turns out our Mr. Rafferdy has befriended three daughters of gentry."

"How curious!" exclaimed Lord Baydon.

"To be sure," Mrs. Baydon said. "I would have thought it quite out of character for the previous version of our friend. But the new Mr. Rafferdy shows evidence of a disinterested, even charitable nature."

"How *curious*!" Lord Baydon said once again. "And how did he meet these young ladies?"

"They are the cousins of the lawyer who recently assisted my husband's aunt. Their father, I gather, is an invalid, and Mr. Rafferdy has taken it upon himself to aid them in what small ways he can. It is said they are quite sweet and pretty, but the poor things are horribly disadvantaged, as you can imagine, living as they do in Gauldren's Heights and having no society of any worth."

Rafferdy was about to say that he found the society of Miss Lockwell worth a good deal more than that of anyone he had ever encountered in Lady Marsdel's parlor. However, before he could do so, Mrs. Baydon became suddenly animated and clapped her hands together.

"Lady Marsdel is to have another party, on the eve of the next long night," she said. "You should invite your new friend, Mr. Rafferdy. Not all three of them; that would never do. But the eldest one—I have gathered she presents herself well, for one of her class. You must tell her to come."

"I will do no such thing," he said, and was going to add that he would not inflict such suffering upon an enemy, let alone someone whom he admired. However, Mrs. Baydon spoke more quickly.

"But think of the benefit to her! Think of what connections she might make—connections far above any she could ever have hoped for. You would do her a great service, and by extension a service to her sisters."

Mr. Baydon cleared his throat. "It seems this new compulsion to be charitable is catching."

"You must bring her with you," Mrs. Baydon said.

"I hardly know if I am coming myself," Rafferdy said. "In fact, I rather imagine I won't."

"How unfortunate," Lord Baydon said. "Mr. Bennick will be quite disappointed to miss you." He tipped the sugar bowl into his coffee.

Rafferdy was not certain he had heard correctly. "I'm sorry, Lord Baydon, but did you say Mr. Bennick would miss me?"

"So I did!" Lord Baydon said, clearly happy to have something to speak about that was within his comprehension. "I encountered him the other day on Marmount Street. He inquired specifically about you, Mr. Rafferdy. He said he enjoyed meeting you and was looking forward to speaking with you again."

Rafferdy found this puzzling. Why would Mr. Bennick ask about *him*? "We did not even truly meet," he said aloud without meaning to.

"But of course you have met Mr. Bennick," Lord Baydon said. "I know it for a fact, for I was there when it happened."

This made no sense. Rafferdy was certain he had not been in the same room with Mr. Bennick and Lord Baydon at Lady Marsdel's party. He said as much, and to his astonishment Lord Baydon laughed.

"It was not at the party but years ago," Lord Baydon said. "I suppose it's to be expected you don't remember. You were very small at the time. I was smaller myself, back then!" He laid a hand on the expanse of his waistcoat. "Mr. Bennick and Lord Marsdel were acquaintances. I'm not sure how they met—Mr. Bennick was a good deal younger than Lord Marsdel—but he used to come around to the house on the Promenade often. Your mother and father used to visit often at that time as well, and you with them. You would have met Mr. Bennick then. You must have made quite an impression on him for him to remember you all this time. It's been many years since Mr. Bennick has made an appearance at my sister's house."

This news astonished Rafferdy. That Mr. Bennick would remember meeting him as a child seemed incomprehensible. Rather, it had to be their encounter in the parlor that Mr. Bennick was referring to.

"It's settled, then," Mrs. Baydon said, a bit smugly. "You have no choice but to come, Mr. Rafferdy. And since you are coming, there can be no excuse for not bringing your new acquaintance with you."

"I must be off" was all he said, and with that he called for his hat and coat, gave his thanks for breakfast, and was away.

Strange as Lord Baydon's news had been, Rafferdy put it out of his head and directed his driver to proceed with haste through the city. The moon was at its full, and so it was a day for worship. The Baydons had the benefit of a clergyman who called at their parlor on Brightdays, and Rafferdy had the benefit of no piousness at all, but he knew that those folk who still observed such rituals did so in church.

From certain overheard remarks, Rafferdy knew his object this morning made just such a habit. He directed his driver to Gauldren's Heights, then left the cabriolet to walk along Whitward Street. He stayed as far from the door as he might and still observe it and before long witnessed the expected departure. They went on foot, and their mother did not accompany them.

He followed them at a distance to a modest, even dour church a bit Uphill. Once they were inside, he located a ready boy such as could always be found on a street corner, gave him a message and a coin, and sent him scampering toward the Old City.

An hour later—and none too soon—Eldyn Garritt arrived in a hack cab, looking red-cheeked and flustered.

"What's this all about?" he said after Rafferdy paid the cab. "I was in the midst of something when I got your message."

"So it seems," Rafferdy said, observing his friend's rumpled and ill-adjusted attire and the shadows beneath his eyes.

Garritt's cheeks flushed a deeper shade, and he adjusted his coat and shook out the cuffs. "I was up all night working on business."

"So you mean to say that coins were exchanged?"

That his friend was so obviously not amused only delighted Rafferdy further. From what font sprang his friend's inherent good-ness, he did not know, but he doubted the nearby church contained a more pious or diffident soul than the one that dwelled in Eldyn Garritt's breast. He often wondered why he and Garritt were friends at all. Though he supposed the good were always drawn to the wicked for wanting to save them, and the wicked in turn to the good—not in hopes of being saved or with desires of corrupting but rather like a moth in the dark, fascinated by a light it can never really know but might at least behold.

"I would hardly have expected to find *you* in this part of the city," Garritt said with a frown. "Indeed, I would hardly expect to see you awake on a middle lumenal before the sun's over the Citadel. And what could be so urgent that you felt the need to summon me halfway across Invarel on a moment's notice?"

"If I am to run into her by chance while out for a stroll with a friend, there must be a friend in evidence," Rafferdy said. "Otherwise the tale lacks a certain credibility, wouldn't you agree?"

Before Garritt could voice an answer to this, the doors of the church opened and dispensed its congregation onto the street. Rafferdy took his friend's elbow and nudged him into motion, so that the two were just approaching the soot-streaked portico of the church as Miss Lockwell and her sisters descended the steps.

Garritt just had time to murmur, "I should have known you'd devise yet another means of encountering her." Then Lily had caught sight of them and was tugging on her eldest sister's arm. Such was the look of astonishment and delight on Miss Lockwell's face upon seeing them—an expression accompanied by a noticeable coloring of her cheeks, much to the benefit of her appearance—that Rafferdy felt immediately rewarded for the effort of coming here, and any qualms he might have suffered flew away like the pigeons that sprang from the cornices of the church into the morning sky.

A few more steps on either side brought both parties into close proximity. Expressions of pleasure at the good fortune of this *unlikely* but welcome meeting were exchanged, and a plan was quickly proposed by Lily that they should all walk together back Downhill.

"I am sure Mr. Garritt and Mr. Rafferdy have other matters to attend to rather than to accompany us," Miss Lockwell said.

"On the contrary," Rafferdy said, "we have nothing to do that could be more important than to accompany you home. Isn't that so, Mr. Garritt?"

"I doubt we'll hear you utter truer words today" was Garritt's reply.

After this, any polite resistance that remained was quickly dispensed with, and soon they made a cheerful party walking down the street. Lily had claimed a position on Garritt's right arm, and he had offered Rose his left.

"I fear, Miss Lockwell, that Mr. Garritt has but two arms," Rafferdy said. "You shall have to make do with mine."

There was a hesitation on her part, but one that made it all the more appealing when she did accept his offer, for it showed there was no overzealous desire to attach herself to him but rather a natural affection tempered by a keen awareness of their disparate and unbridgeable situations. He was struck by the fact that the only woman who intrigued him was one who was perfectly aware she could in no way ever possess him. It was paradoxical; he could not contain his good humor.

"May I ask what you find so amusing, Mr. Rafferdy?" she said as they walked.

"Is it not obvious?"

"Not in the least. Nor is this the first time I have observed you to laugh at a jest of which no one else is seemingly aware."

"Those are the most delightful kind."

"Is that so? Yet the humor of the situation cannot be lessened in the sharing of it. Indeed, I should think it must only multiply if it encountered additional subjects upon which to work its mirthful powers."

"You are right, of course. However, if you cannot already see the humor, which is quite plain to me, how can I possibly explain it to you? It would be like trying to describe the color blue to a man who has never seen it. You either know *blue* or you don't."

"So you mean to say one can never know something unless one has experienced it directly?"

"I do."

"Then I could not disagree with you more, Mr. Rafferdy." Her green eyes brightened, and there was a firmness to the set of her fine chin. "For you see, I have gained many valuable experiences in books. Through their pages I have visited places and witnessed events I would otherwise have never known. I have stood on the field where ancient battles were waged. I have wandered through keeps fallen to ruin and have spoken with kings and queens who now lie entombed beneath marble and dust."

"But those experiences are nothing real!" he exclaimed, at once amused and taken aback.

She inquired if he read very much, and he was forced to admit that he had, much to his discredit, read very little.

"Then I forgive you for your statement, Mr. Rafferdy. All the same, you are in error. It is true that, in the strictest sense, I have not been to those places or conversed with those people. Yet the result of reading about them is every bit as affecting as if I had. For all these happenings have entered into my memories and reside there now as if they are mine. Indeed, they *are* my own. I can see in my mind's eye all the legions of Tharos lined up on the field of Seramar. I can feel how the stones of Erenoch trembled just before they came tumbling down. I can hear the defiance in Queen Béanore's voice as she announced her abdication."

Such was the light in her eyes and the look on her face that he believed she *could* see these things. He confessed his ignorance; he begged her forgiveness. It was granted at once, graciously.

"I must say," Rafferdy went on, "you make books sound magickal in a way I had never considered."

"Indeed, it would certainly qualify as magick if you ever cracked the covers of one," Garritt said from behind. He laughed, and Lily joined in.

Rafferdy laughed too, though his cheeks felt warm, and after that he found he desired to speak of something other than books. He inquired of his companion how the church service had gone. She answered that it had gone well enough, though she felt the priest might have spoken the sermon with a bit more ardor in his voice and that his surplice might have been better kept, being rather stained, and also that the church was always very dark inside.

"It seems every month," she said, "there are fewer on the benches at St. Hadlan's than the month before."

"Perhaps if the priest put on clean clothes and opened the windows, attendance might grow."

"You might be right, Mr. Rafferdy. Everything about St. Hadlan's . . ." She appeared to think for a moment. "It feels weary somehow. That the service should be solemn, I grant you. But surely the windows might be scrubbed without removing any of their holy tincture. I fear if things continue as they are, my sisters and I will, some Brightday soon, find ourselves the only three in the pews."

"In which case they will yet be well graced," he said, but her only answer was to shake her head. This bemused him; in his experience, young women were always pleased by idle compliments.

"Where is Mrs. Lockwell today?" he asked, and learned that their mother found the walk Uphill intolerable. An offer of his barouche was made for Brightday next, that they all might attend service as a family. Miss Lockwell attempted to decline, but her sister was quicker at accepting.

"A barouche!" Lily exclaimed. "Think of how elegant we will all look riding to church. Everyone will stare at us. It will be grand. You will ride with us, Mr. Garritt."

"A barouche seats but four, plus the driver," he informed her.

Lily frowned; she appeared to struggle with the idea of refusing the offer. However, the lure of conveyance in a fashionable carriage was too great. "But you and Mr. Rafferdy will meet us afterward, Mr. Garritt," she said finally. "You must say you will."

"Only if they should find it convenient," Miss Lockwell said before Mr. Garritt was forced to respond. "And their coming should not in any way be counted upon. The gesture is already far too much."

They made a detour through Uphill Gardens and walked along

flower-lined paths. As they went, Rafferdy took pleasure in his conversation with Miss Lockwell; her mind was keen and her wit sharp. While in some this might have resulted in a sort of hardness, in her the effect was softened by the delicacy of her speech and by her statements that evinced a completely disinterested mind—one concerned not at all with herself but only with the benefit of her mother, her sisters, and those around her. This fascinated Rafferdy; her lack of vanity was novel to him. And it did not hinder his enjoyment that she made an appealing sight on his arm.

From her expressions, he concluded that Miss Lockwell enjoyed their conversations as well. Though it was also obvious that, with some regularity, her sister's speech caused her discomfort—being often thoughtless and very nearly always silly.

"I *so* wish to attend a play," Lily exclaimed in one such instance. "My mother and sister say I can't go, but they don't understand, not as you and I do, Mr. Garritt. Besides, no one could complain about the suitability of my going to Durrow Street if you were there with me."

Rafferdy felt Miss Lockwell grow stiff upon his arm at this outburst. Garritt said only that he did not know when he might ever go to Durrow Street. Undeterred, Lily continued to propose schemes that involved Mr. Garritt accompanying them somewhere or another. Rafferdy felt some sympathy for his friend; he was certain many men would enjoy the fluttering attentions of a decently pretty, if silly, young girl. However, he was equally certain that Garritt was not one of them.

He must have laughed again, for Miss Lockwell looked up at him. "Do not fear, Mr. Rafferdy," she said with a smile. The others had fallen a bit behind as Lily made a fuss over some flower. "Unlike my sister, I suffer under no misconceptions that you will ever accompany me to masques or plays or to anyplace more extraordinary or notable than these gardens around us. Even if our natures allowed it, our situations never would."

"I must say, Miss Lockwell, that while I have long believed this was your understanding, I am relieved to hear you speak it aloud." However, even as he said these words, he felt something less like relief and more like regret.

"Your encounters with us have been dreadful, then," she said with a laugh. "I imagine you must see it as ill fate rather than good fortune that chance has conspired to bring us into contact on these several occasions."

"On the contrary!" he said with an enthusiasm of which he had hardly known himself capable. "It has been a great while since I have found myself so entertained as I have been in your company. And since you comprehend, given our relative positions, that our meetings can progress only toward friendship, then it means there is no harm in letting them lead us in that direction, nor can there be any danger of impropriety."

"I see you have thought through it all quite logically," she replied. Her words struck him; they were so cool.

The sunlight felt suddenly oppressive. That wasn't at all what he had meant to imply. Reflecting on his words, he found them distasteful, even calculating, as if his only concern in the world was respectability, which in all his five-and-twenty years had never been the case. A sudden recklessness overwhelmed him.

"There is to be a party at the house of Lady Marsdel, who is an acquaintance of mine, three nights hence, at the start of the next long umbral," he said. "I insist you attend as my guest."

This caught her off guard. Her cheeks grew bright, and her breath quickened. He could not help but be pleased at the effect upon her; she looked very pretty just then.

When she recovered her capacity for speech, it was to say she was certain she could not—indeed *must* not—be included in such an affair. For his part, he was adamant that she would be welcome, that Lady Marsdel would be most interested to meet her, and that he would send his cabriolet, which would bear her to Lady Marsdel's house in the New Quarter.

"To her house in the New Quarter!" she exclaimed, though it seemed less an expression of wonder than dismay.

"Do not be concerned with any difference you might perceive between Lady Marsdel's house and your own."

"You mistake me. The grandness of Lady Marsdel's house can hardly be a concern to *me*. I should instead be concerned that my sisters and I might one day have no house at all."

She looked away, and he perceived that, in her sudden passion, she had uttered more than she wished.

"I understand your meaning," he said in a low tone. "I have it from your cousin that your house is entailed to him. While I have not yet met your father, from our conversations I can only suppose his health is not good. You must fear your removal from Whitward Street."

"You know much, Mr. Rafferdy," she said. "However, while your facts are correct, your understanding is imperfect. Our house is entailed, as you say, but it is on my mother's side, not my father's. She was the eldest of only sisters, you see, and there was no son, nor any male heir, when her father passed. Thus the house went to my mother for the duration of her life. But at the time of his death, the next eldest daughter was with child and not a few months later bore a son. That is our dear cousin Mr. Wyble, to whom the house will one day go."

Rafferdy could not help but wince at the name. "Ah, Mr. Wyble. I hadn't realized your relation to him was by your mother. I had assumed it was through your father."

"It matters not," she said with a laugh. "I think, as far as Mr. Wyble is concerned, we are no relation at all!"

That the law should one day permit an insipid man like Mr. Wyble to deprive three young women of their home was abominable. However, the day this would transpire was many years off—Mrs. Lockwell was in no way old—and no doubt her daughters would be comfortably married by then. Still, it rankled.

"It seems unfair you cannot keep your house as long as you wish to reside in it," he said.

"Indeed, it is unfair." Her cheeks shone from exertion, and the wind had stolen several locks of gold hair from her bonnet. "That is, it is precisely unfair by design. For we are merely women, you see, and all laws conspire to keep us dependent. Though upon what or who we will depend, I cannot say. That we might have any sort of power over our own fortunes is a thing society forbids. Why this is so, I am at a loss. Perhaps over the ages men have found us to be incapable of making such choices. Or rather, perhaps they did not like or trust the choices we made. Either way, the result is the same. A man might make his own way in the world, Mr. Rafferdy, but a woman must transfer all her hopes to others, however ill she might thereafter be treated."

Rafferdy wished to make a response, but none came to him. Then the others had caught up, and a few more minutes saw them to the gate of the house on Whitward Street. Farewells were exchanged, the sisters retired indoors, and Rafferdy found himself walking along the street back to where his cabriolet waited.

"I would ask you what you're doing," Garritt said, "but you always have your own reasons for things. Still, I'm hard-pressed to know what your intentions are this time around."

So lost had he been in his thoughts that Rafferdy had forgotten his friend was walking alongside him. "To know my intentions regarding what?"

Garritt shook his head. "It is cruel to fortify her expectations and to give her cause to anticipate an event that can never come to pass.

Hope is no good thing to have when all hopes must necessarily prove false."

"So you think I should inspire despair instead?"

Garritt's expression was serious. "You are many things, Rafferdy, but not a fool. You know there can never be any real connection between you."

"No doubt that's why I like her," Rafferdy replied.

"That might suit your fancies, but I can hardly believe it matches *hers*. This can only end in one fashion, when it becomes clear she depends upon your offering a thing you can never grant her. You shouldn't have invited her to Lady Marsdel's."

Rafferdy was suddenly vexed with his friend. "You are wrong. She expects nothing of me. And what is there to fear from inviting her to Lady Marsdel's, save that a dull party might be made interesting?" They had reached the cabriolet. "I do not go in your direction. Here is a coin. Hire yourself a hack cab." He climbed in.

Garritt laid a hand on the edge of the door. "I was never certain if concern for another was something you were capable of, Rafferdy, but I do believe you have an affection for her. If that is the case, you will let her alone. Better to do so now than later, when she has developed a true attachment. This is no game. You can not simply open your purse to pay your debts when you are done and be on your way, not if you use her ill."

Now it was Rafferdy's turn to be serious. "I have known you for many years now. You are my friend, Garritt—indeed, for all the various people with whom I am acquainted, you are perhaps in truth my only one. Yet if ever again you imply that I would willingly cause harm to Miss Lockwell, it will be the last thing you ever say to me. Walk on!"

Those final words were directed to the driver. The cabriolet started along the street, and Rafferdy did not look back.

The brief day was half over by the time he arrived at Warwent Square, and clouds had cast a pall over the city. He changed into a robe and told his man to bring him tea in the parlor, for he intended to spend the rest of the day there by the fire, answering letters.

Upon sitting at his desk, he found that day's post lying atop the heap of notes and invitations. At once his eye caught a rather bulky letter, addressed to him in a bold, even garish hand. There was no return address. He sipped his tea, then opened the envelope with a small knife.

Something fell to the table with a clatter.

Rafferdy stared for a moment, then reached down and picked up the ring. It was silver, set with a blue stone and etched with spidery runes. The ring felt cold to the touch, as if the letter had been waiting outside on a chill day rather than here in the warmth of his parlor.

He hesitated, then slipped the ring onto his right hand. It nestled snugly around the base of his fourth finger. A shiver crept along his spine, and he wondered why Mr. Mundy would go to the trouble of sending him the ring. Rafferdy had made it perfectly clear that he had no intention of buying it. While his affectations were many, a pretension to magick was not among them. He would leave that for university men and puffed up young lords in Assembly.

"If that little toad thinks I am paying for this ring, he is quite mistaken," Rafferdy said. He took up the envelope, searching it for any sort of note or letter. There was none. He set the envelope back down. The gem winked at him like a blue eye. The ring was every bit as ugly as he recalled. A feeling of revulsion came over him, and he grasped the ring to take it off.

It did not budge.

Rafferdy tried again, gripping the ring and giving it a tug, but the thing would not go past his knuckle. It made no sense; the ring turned freely around his finger. Yet no matter how hard he pulled at the damnable object, the ring would not come off his finger. Soon he was sweating and his hand was raw, but for naught. At last he was forced to give up, panting for breath.

He took a shaky sip of tea, then studied the loathsome ring. Had Mundy put some enchantment upon it? Was this some sort of ploy to extort Rafferdy into paying for the thing? Perhaps. Yet Mundy had not seemed like the sort of man who would part with something without being paid first. If that was the case, it meant that someone else had bought him the ring—someone who knew Rafferdy had looked at it.

Again he stared at the ring.

"Mr. Bennick," he said.

The magician knew that Rafferdy had followed him that day. Mundy must have told him everything. So Bennick had bought the ring, and had placed the spell upon it, and had sent it to Rafferdy. It was the only possibility. And it would explain why Bennick had inquired about Rafferdy when he encountered Lord Baydon.

What game was Bennick playing? Why would the magician do such a thing? To punish him for daring to follow that day?

Rafferdy had no idea. However, there was one thing he knew for certain. Mr. Bennick was going to be at Lady Marsdel's upcoming party—and that meant Rafferdy could not be. Such an encounter could only cause the most extreme discomfort. Whatever game Mr. Bennick was playing, Rafferdy would have no part of it.

His determination to avoid Lady Marsdel's party wavered for a moment when he thought of Miss Lockwell. He had asked her to attend; the invitation could not be rescinded. Yet he could not just abandon her to Lady Marsdel and her guests.

But there was no way around it. If he had to endure an evening in the presence of Mr. Bennick, Rafferdy would be so agitated that his company would be far harder to bear than his absence. Besides, he had no doubt Mrs. Baydon would take excellent care of Miss Lockwell.

His mind settled, he called for his man and told him to take a message to Vallant Street, informing Mrs. Baydon that he would be unable to attend Lady Marsdel's upcoming affair, that he was ill, that he did not expect to be recovered for many days, and that she must give his regards to her aunt.

"Shall I call for the doctor, sir?" his man inquired.

"No, but do call for the cabriolet."

"Very well, sir. And where shall I tell the driver to take you?"

"To Greenly Circle, and with haste."

Rafferdy went to his room, stripped off his robe, and donned his clothes. Minutes later he was out the door and into the damp afternoon. It was time to pay Mr. Mundy another visit.

And to have him remove this blasted ring.

# CHAPTER TEN

OVER HALF A month had passed since she first conceived her plan, and still Ivy had not ventured to the old house on Durrow Street.

It would not be a simple thing. First, it would have to be a long lumenal. Even days of middling length were out of the question, being already overfilled with all the usual requirements of living. By her calculations she would need at least four hours to make the trek to the Old City, discover the house (whose location she recalled only vaguely), perform her investigations, and return home with a bolt of lace from Albring's.

Purchasing the lace would be her reason for being away from Whitward Street for such a prolonged period. For one thing, Albring's shop was on the edge of Gauldren's Heights nearest the Old City. What was more, it had a reputation for excellent lace but inferior service, and so she might credibly make an excuse that she had been forced to wait for the order. In fact, the lace was already bought and paid for, and the order needed only to be picked up. Mrs. Lockwell had wanted for some lace from this shop for a long time, and it was Ivy's hope that her mother, in her excitement, would not think to question why Ivy was away for so long.

After thorough consideration she deemed the plan sound; however, putting it into action had proved difficult. There was a profusion of short lumenals, and each time the almanac promised a longer day, something conspired to distract her: either Cassity had misplaced something that had to be found at once, or Lily was in a desolate mood over the ending to one of her romances and required the consolation of her sisters, or Mr. Lockwell was having another one of his spells and shouted at people who were not there and pounded at the window glass, so that Mrs. Lockwell wrung her hands and begged Ivy to go to him. Ivy would sit with him for hours, murmuring such things as she thought might soothe him, until at last he grew still and his eyes emptied of fear.

All the while she longed to ask him about the message he had left for her years ago in the book of Tharosian myths, to ask him who the twelve wanderers were and what door was to open. Instead, she would draw the curtains against the dusk, kiss his brow, and call for Wilbern to put him to bed.

Nor was it true that every event that conspired to keep her from Durrow Street was entirely unwelcome. More than once, while out on various errands, she chanced upon Mr. Rafferdy just strolling around a corner or driving past in his cabriolet. It was improbable that she should meet him in this way even a single time, let alone on several occasions. Indeed, she was beginning to wonder how she had gone so many years *without* meeting him, given that she now came upon him with such regularity.

Not that she could claim she was sorry for the fact. Each of their meetings was as enjoyable as it was unexpected. Time always passed pleasantly as they walked or, when wanting a rest, sat on a bench in some favorite cloister or arched nook.

Ivy did not know what she hoped to gain from her encounters with

Mr. Rafferdy. She supposed she hoped to gain nothing at all, other than a moment's diversion from worrying about the state of their finances, or her father, or Mr. Wyble's next visit. When she was with Mr. Rafferdy, she had the feeling she laughed more than she spoke. The observations he made about others in his circle of acquaintance, the little stories he told, were wry yet never truly cruel, and if there was anyone he ever really deprecated, it was only himself. She could not say what it was she felt when she was with him, save that the shadows around her retreated and her heart lightened—until such time as she returned to Whitward Street, and dusk fell, and the dark seemed to press in once more.

While Ivy expected nothing from her encounters with Mr. Rafferdy, the same could not be said for her mother. Mrs. Lockwell never failed to ask if she had seen Mr. Rafferdy if she was away even a minute longer than expected, and, thus confronted, Ivy could do nothing but confess the truth. Her mother's opinions were only further reinforced by Ivy's invitation to Lady Marsdel's house. It was Lily who divulged the news upon their return from church.

"He favors you, Ivy!" Mrs. Lockwell exclaimed after Ivy was forced to describe the particulars of the invitation. "Oh, don't give me that look, for it's true. A gentleman does not go out of his way to walk with a young lady if he does not particularly like her. When he saw you he might have said he had business and gone on his way with a tip of his hat. Politeness would require no more of him. But it is more than being polite that he intends. To be invited to a party in the New Quarter—that is high praise! I do hope there is dancing. If there is dancing, he will dance with you all night, I am sure of it."

"Mr. Garritt walked with us after church as well," Lily said. "He looked very well. Poor Mr. Rafferdy was quite plain next to him. You should have seen how charming he was, Mother."

However, she paid Lily no attention, for Mrs. Lockwell's enthusiasm was always so wholly given that it could be bestowed upon but a single thing at a time. Only then her elation turned into a panic (the two sensations being often interconnected for her), because she did not know what Ivy could possibly wear to a party at the house of a noble lady. They must head for the finest dress shops Uphill at once, and cost could not be—no, *must* not be—of any sort of concern.

Despite Ivy's protests, Mrs. Lockwell might have swept them out the door that moment, but there came a crash from upstairs. Either Cassity was cleaning or Mr. Lockwell was agitated. Ivy went up to investigate.

It was her father. He had knocked over a stack of books. Once the books were picked up, Ivy sat with him until the full moon lofted above the rooftops of Gauldren's Heights. As its cool light bathed him, Mr. Lockwell grew placid, and Ivy was at last able to steal back downstairs. There she discovered that Mrs. Lockwell, having succumbed to a headache, had retired to her room. Ivy took supper with her sisters. It was a quiet affair, for Rose rarely had much to say, and Lily was unusually subdued.

Ivy was preoccupied herself as she took a candle into the parlor to consult the almanac and see how long the umbral would be. She was certain her mother was wrong, that Mr. Rafferdy in no way intended to make her an object of peculiar favor. On the contrary, his statements demonstrated that, for all his lively wit, he was a man of sense. To her this was a relief. She could never claim friendship with a man so frivolous as to think that two people of such widely disparate circumstance could ever hope to be united in any way other than by mere acquaintance.

She shut the almanac and turned from the secretary. As she did, the light of the candle illuminated her reflection in the window, facing her like a partner lined up at a ball.

"Why, yes, Mr. Rafferdy," she said, "I would like very much to dance."

Ivy gave a courteous bow, and her reflection bowed in return. She picked up the hem of her dress and danced several steps as her mirrored partner did the same, shining against the dark outside, a smile upon her face.

"What are you doing, Ivy?"

She stopped and turned to see Lily standing in the doorway.

"Nothing," she said. "I was just checking the almanac. The umbral is not to be long at all. We had better hurry to bed or it will be light before we fall asleep."

Before Lily could say anything more, Ivy blew out the candle and left the darkened parlor.

OPPORTUNITY CAME AT last on the third lumenal after Brightday. According to the almanac, the day was to be twenty hours, and given its length most people would be taking a long rest in the afternoon. As her mother and sisters went upstairs to retire, Ivy excused herself on the pretext that she was not at all tired and that she thought she would venture out for a stroll.

"Of course you are too distracted to rest!" Mrs. Lockwell said. "If I were going to an affair at Lady Marsdel's, I am sure I should be even more excited than you are and should be able to rest even less. But you do not want to look worn tonight. You must promise to sit quietly for a few hours when you come home, or else you will look ragged. And take your bonnet! You already have far too many freckles."

Ivy made all the required promises, then was out the door. The long afternoon had grown hot, and those few people in evidence on Whitward Street moved as if through water rather than air. Ivy shut the gate behind her and walked as quickly as she could Downhill.

Her gold hair clung to her cheeks by the time she reached Albring's shop. She had decided it best to retrieve the lace right away, in order to give her as much time as possible for her investigations.

It took several knocks on the door to summon a girl who did not look pleased at being roused from her afternoon rest. She fetched Ivy the parcel of lace wrapped in paper and handed it over without a word. Ivy had no time to utter even a hasty thank-you before the door was shut again. She put the parcel under her arm and searched for a hack cab.

She was forced to walk several streets over to Hinsdon Street but at last managed to find a cab to hire, though first she had to wake the driver, who sat nodding in his seat.

The cab was an exorbitant expense but one she had resolved to bear, for she did not know the streets of the Old City and could not navigate them unassisted.

"To Durrow Street, please," she told the driver.

The man gave her an odd look, but she handed him the fare before he could speak—a quarter regal, enough to buy a whole box of candles.

He took the coins. "What cross, miss?"

"I'm afraid I don't know," she confessed.

"Durrow Street is more than a mile long, miss, and one fare ain't enough for me to spend all day driving up and down it."

Ivy's cheeks glowed, and not from the heat. Already her plan had gone awry! She did not know the address of the old house, and asking her mother about such things had been out of the question. She had thought simply to direct the cab to Durrow Street, that she would recognize the house upon passing by it. However, the illogic of this plan now struck her.

The driver glowered at her. Sweat trickled down beside the crimson bulb of his nose.

"Take me to Béanore's Fountain," she said, remembering how once her father had walked with her to the monument from the house. He had sat her on the edge of the fountain and told her stories about the ancient queen. It was one of Ivy's few and earliest memories of their time on Durrow Street. She had been small; it could not have been far from the house. The driver flicked the reins, and the cab rattled down Hinsdon Street and through the Hillgate.

It had been many years since Ivy had been to the Old City—not since she had come here with Mr. Lockwell in the days just before his affliction struck him. There were a variety of bookshops in this part of Invarel he had liked to frequent, and he had brought her with him on two or three occasions.

To Ivy the shops had been marvels, crowded with shelves of books, and stacks of books, and chests overflowing with more old books. She remembered the smell inside: musty-sweet with paper and leather and turpentine. So thick was the atmosphere of mystery in one such shop, she fancied that over the years some measure of the ink had sublimated from the pages, suffusing the very air with knowledge, so that one could gain wisdom merely by drawing a breath. She had shut her eyes and inhaled deeply, but a dizziness came upon her before any sort of enlightenment, and next she knew she was standing in the street with her father pinching her cheeks.

The cab rattled past a storefront, and Ivy glimpsed rows of books beyond dim windows. Was that one of the places her father had visited? One shop had hung a sign above the door painted with an eye; she remembered how it seemed to stare at her. However, this shop had no sign at all. Still, Ivy was tempted to stop the driver, to look in the shop and see what books they might have concerning magick.

She dismissed the notion; there was no time for delay. Besides, it was clear after her failed attempt to work an enchantment that she would not progress in the study of magick without help. It was just such help she was seeking now. There was something at the house on Durrow Street *they* wanted, the two magicians who had come to the door that night. And if she could promise it to them, they would help her. She was sure of it.

The cab maneuvered through the labyrinth of narrow lanes. Around a corner the fountain came into view, its marble etched and gray, and Béanore in her chariot with a bronze crown and a cape of pigeons, all just as Ivy remembered it. The cab stopped, and Ivy was ushered out.

Despite her need for haste, she could not help lingering a moment at the fountain. As a girl Ivy had loved stories of Queen Béanore, and her father had often indulged her with tales of the oldest days of Altania. Béanore was the daughter of the king of one of Altania's southern realms. This was over sixteen centuries ago, when the island had not a single monarch as it did today but rather a collection of thains and petty kings who ruled and fought over twenty little chiefdoms.

When the armies of Tharos sailed across the sea and attacked, Béanore's father was one of the first to fall in battle. The other realms would have succumbed quickly to the Tharosian legions commanded by the young emperor Veradian. However, Béanore fashioned a bow from a willow switch and with a single shot was able to inflict a great wound upon Veradian. Then she called the other chieftains to unite with her to drive the Tharosians back, and against the common enemy they set aside their squabbling. They swore allegiance to Béanore, and so the first monarch to rule all of Altania was not a king but rather a queen, and under her banner—with its silver branch and golden leaves—they drove the Tharosians back across the sea.

Veradian never returned to Altania himself; the wound from the arrow had weakened him, and after a few years he died. But in time his son sailed across the sea with more ships, and while Béanore held them back for many years, in the end the forces of Tharos were too much. She was captured and forced to abdicate her crown, relinquishing it to Veradian's son. However, before she could be dragged in chains back to Tharos, she escaped, riding into the deep green forest that covered most of the island in that time. She was never seen again.

Some said Béanore was the last true Altanian monarch, for all of the island's rulers after that time were descended of the line of Tharos, or more lately of the Mabingorian houses out of the north. And in all the centuries since, Altania had been ruled only once more by a queen.

A man walked past Ivy and gave her a look. His clothes were as drab as the pigeons. His eyes were weathered like the stone of the monument. She became aware that there were others like him lingering about the fountain in small groups. Despite the afternoon swelter, a chill came upon her. She gripped the packet of lace, then moved down the street—not too quickly, yet quickly enough.

✺

IVY RECOGNIZED THE house the moment she laid eyes upon it.

Indeed, so familiar did its shape seem to her that she wondered how she could have had difficulty picturing it. The ruddy stone, the tall windows, the peaks of the gables, even the gargoyles grimacing from the cornices—she remembered everything as she saw it.

The house was farther from the fountain than she had thought; she could only suppose her father had carried her part of the way that day long ago, or else they had driven and she had forgotten it. She had begun to despair as she walked by countless unfamiliar houses and shops, past nameless closes and ancient little graveyards.

Then the street bent a little, and there it was, set in its own yard and bordered by an iron fence. The other houses pressed in close, but with that fence, and the aloofness granted by the yard, and its reddish stone so unlike the gray of the buildings all around, the house gave the impression that it had been there long before the rest.

By the time Ivy reached the gate, her heart was pounding, but she could not claim it was from exertion. She glanced over her shoulder. The street was growing more crowded as people started to rouse from their afternoon torpor and ventured out to take advantage of the last hours of the long lumenal. However, no one looked at her as they went about their business.

Assured she was not an object of attention, Ivy moved to the gate. There was a heavy lock, but this was no surprise. She drew a key from her pocket, which she had taken from one of the drawers of the secretary in the parlor. While her mother had never told her what the key was for, Ivy had long known it was the key to the house on Durrow Street. It was overlarge and heavy. She put it to the lock.

Before she could turn the key, the gate swung open. It had been shut but in no way latched.

Ivy frowned. How strange that the gate was not locked! Had it been so all these years? She withdrew the key, and as she did she noticed several marks around the keyhole. They looked like scratches in the iron, or rather like scorch marks, being silvery and radiating out from the lock in sharp lines. Perhaps at some point thieves had shot the lock with a gun in order to break in and rob the house.

Except that could not be, for the lock wasn't broken. She turned the key and was able to lock the mechanism easily, then unlock it again. She withdrew the key and touched one of the scorch marks. A bit of the silver residue stained her finger.

A thrill passed through her. There was another explanation she could imagine. The gate *had* been locked, but it had been opened without breaking it and without the benefit of a key. Logic left but a single alternative. It was magick that had opened the gate. And that meant . . .

"They've been here," she said, taking the key from the lock.

Now her excitement became dread. If the magicians had been here, perhaps they already had what they wanted!

She willed herself to be calm. Reason dictated that if they had already gained the thing, then they would not have come to the door at

Whitward Street that night. Which meant that, whatever they sought, it must still be here. Ivy hurried up the walk.

The house was larger than their dwelling on Whitward Street. The front part alone was broader and just as tall, and there were a pair of wings off either side. Nothing grew in the yard save thistles and a few hawthorn trees that clung with little resolve to shriveled leaves. A pair of stone lions reclined to either side of the door, baring their teeth in mossy yawns. Ivy remembered that she used to talk to them and had even given them names, though what they were she could not remember. She reached out to stroke a stony mane.

Ivy snatched her hand back. A feeling that she was being watched came over her, but of course it was nonsense. The iron fence was coiled thick with tendrils of her namesake, screening her from the street. As for the house, no one could be watching her from *that* direction. The windows were all shuttered and barred.

She approached the front door. It was carved from a massive slab of oak and bound by iron. It might have done for a door in an old fortress on a hill, a thing to keep barbarians at bay. As a girl she had barely been able to push it open on her own. She took out the key and set it to the lock.

It didn't fit.

Ivy could only stare. This was something she had not foreseen. However, after several failed attempts, there could be no doubt. The key was too large and not shaped right, and no direction she turned it made a difference. It would not fit in the lock. All these years she had assumed this was the key to both the gate and door at Durrow Street, but she had only been half right. And where the key to the house might be, she hadn't the faintest idea.

Ivy pushed on the door, but unlike the gate it did not open. She tried the handle, but it, too, resisted her will. No one had passed this way.

They had tried, however. Ivy examined the iron plate; a circle of silver marks was arrayed around the lock. The lines were finer, fainter, as if this metal had been less easily scored than that of the gate. Her disappointment was tempered: she could not get in, but neither could *they*. And the key to the door had to be in her father's possession. She had only to find it. Hope was thwarted, yes, but far from lost.

There was nothing more she could do here. While her visit to Durrow Street had not given her the result she had hoped for, Ivy could not say it had been useless, for she had seen evidence that confirmed her theory: the magicians had sought something here.

"And I will discover what it is," she told the lions. She patted their muzzles, then headed back into the yard.

Slowly but surely the sun was making its way westward toward a bank of gathering thunderheads. However, she took a few minutes to walk around the house to make a survey of the rest of the yard and also to be sure none of the bars over any of the windows had been prized loose.

Nothing had been disturbed, as far as she could see, and as she finished her circuit she let out a sigh. There was something affecting about the silent house, about the shabby gardens and the twisted little trees. It was forlorn, but there was a sort of peace about it as well. Though the city lay just beyond the ivy-twined fence, for all she could hear it might as well have been miles away and this place a house on a far-off moor in the country.

Ivy had never been out of the city in all her life, and the fancy was so captivating that she let herself half-believe it for a moment. She plucked a twig from a stunted chestnut, twirling it in her hand as she shut her eyes. She listened to the murmur of the leaves and pictured herself in the country near some little patch of wood—not a copse of New Forest, tall and evergreen, but an ancient stand of twisted trees: a remnant of primeval forest, like the deep woods into which Queen Béanore had vanished a long age ago.

Somewhere pigeons warbled, breaking the power of the spell. Ivy let the twig drop from her fingers and opened her eyes.

A man stood in the gate.

Such was her astonishment that she could not move. That she should run occurred to her, yet that action—indeed, any action—was beyond her. A paralysis had seized her.

The man wore black—that it was a man she did not doubt, for he was tall, if unusually slender—and her heart fluttered as she wondered if it was one of *them,* if they had known she would come here and had watched for her. Only he did not wear a cape as they had. His attire was strange: a collection of frills and ruffles and ribbons, of gored sleeves and pantaloons and a broad-brimmed hat. She had seen drawings of men in such garb in books of plays. It was like a dandy's attire from another century, or like a harlequin's costume. Only black, all black, from head to toe—even his face, which was covered by a black mask. It was a smooth and lacquered thing, neither laughing nor smiling, devoid of any expression or feeling. A death mask.

*Who are you?* she tried to call out. However, he made a slight motion with a black-gloved hand, and the words cleaved to her tongue.

Still, Ivy could not move. She could only follow with her gaze as he entered the yard, as he walked among the trees with a capering step and up to the front door of the house. He patted the lions. They stretched and licked his fingers with gray tongues.

Ivy felt herself swooning, only she did not collapse; she was a rod planted in the ground. A shadow fell upon the yard as the clouds thickened overhead. The man reached toward the door, then withdrew his hand. He turned, and now the mask was wrought in a black grin.

"The way must not be opened," he said.

At least, she believed he said this. For she could not see his lips move behind the mask, and she was not certain she *heard* the words so much as she felt them impinge upon her mind, like something read in a book.

*Why?* she wanted to ask him. But her mouth would not open.

He moved from the door and descended the steps.

"They have forgotten," he said, drawing near. "Or they choose not to remember." He snapped a bit of branch from a hawthorn and twirled it in his hand, just as she had done. "In their arrogance and their desire they will try to open it. You must not let them."

*Who will try to open it?* she strained to ask, and could not.

All the same he answered her. "They call themselves the Vigilant Order of the Silver Eye. They have been watching you. One day they will come, and when they do—"

He hissed and dropped the twig. A red drop fell from his hand; a thorn had bitten him through the glove. In that instant, Ivy found her tongue.

"What will they do?" she cried. "Who are you? And why should I listen to you?"

He curled his fingers into a fist. "You should listen to me," he said in a low voice, "because that is what your father did."

The mouth of the mask was shaped in a grimace now.

Ivy tried to ask him how he knew her father, when they had spoken, and what had been said, but at that moment a clap of thunder sounded and a wind sprang up. Dust and dried leaves filled the air, and she was forced to turn her back to the gale. At last the wind subsided. She turned back and blinked to clear her eyes.

There was no one else in the yard. The iron gate swung on its hinges, then creaked to a halt. The lions grinned at her, things of motionless stone.

IT WAS LATE in the afternoon by the time Ivy walked through the door at Whitward Street. The driver had let her off Downhill, for her funds had been scant (the fare being more than she had expected) and he refused to go the entire way. As a result she had been forced to walk the last mile through a downpour as the clouds let loose in a violent torrent.

Though it was Ivy who was shivering and wet, it was Mrs. Lockwell who was in a state of distress upon her arrival. Where had Ivy been for so long? Did she not know Mr. Rafferdy's carriage would be here in only two hours? What could she possibly have been doing all this time?

Ivy gripped the packet of lace and started into the story she had formulated. She needn't have bothered. The future was of far too great a concern to Mrs. Lockwell for her to consider the past.

"What a state you are in!" she despaired. "How will you be made to look presentable in so short a time? Your hair will need five hundred strokes if it needs one. And if you do not have a scalding bath at once, you will catch your death. Now, up the stairs with you!"

Thus was disposed any notion of Ivy resting quietly for a few hours before the party.

The bath was taken—gratefully, for she felt chilled after her dash through the rain—and thereafter ensued an hour's worth of tugging, pulling, fussing, and arranging. At last Mrs. Lockwell pronounced she could do no more, and as she surveyed herself in the looking glass, Ivy could not deny that her appearance was good. Rather than marring her complexion, the exertion of the day had heightened her color and brought out a vividness in her eyes, which made them a match for the gown she wore.

The dress had been Mrs. Lockwell's in her youth. It was a rich thing, made from Murghese silk that glittered like sun on leaves. Over the last few days Rose had carefully brought it in to match Ivy's size, and Lily had taken off the sleeves and retied the ribbons to give it a more fashionable appearance.

"Look at you, Ivy!" Mrs. Lockwell exclaimed, her despair quite forgotten. "I was no older than you when I last wore that dress. It was at the ball where I met your father. How I loved to dance! I could dance all night in those days and still beg the musicians to play. If I had known I would never have the occasion to wear it again, I might have refused your father's proposal. But it came so quickly, as did your brother. After that my figure was never the same, and then there were so few balls to attend. So few."

Her mother's voice faltered. Ivy looked at her with concern. Mrs. Lockwell seldom mentioned their brother, who had died soon after a difficult birth and nearly took his mother with him. For many years after that it was thought Mrs. Lockwell would never bear another child. But then came Ivy, and a few years later Rose and Lily all in a hurry, and so their little garden flourished after all.

The moment passed. Mrs. Lockwell gripped Ivy's hands and pronounced that all eyes would be upon Ivy the moment she stepped through the door. Ivy, in contrast, hoped it was the case that no one would notice she was there. Though if she were to win a glance from *him,* she supposed she would not mind.

After that there was nothing to do but sit in the parlor and try not to wrinkle her dress. It was difficult to stay still. Despite how long she had been awake that day, Ivy was anything but tired. After her encounter at the house on Durrow Street, her mind was abuzz with thoughts. Only she did not know what to think—except perhaps that she should be in terror. Yet she was not. She had gone there hoping to meet someone who knew her father, and she had.

But who was the man? And why did he affect such a peculiar costume? She was certain he was not one of the two magicians who came to the front door that night, though he had spoken as if he knew them—rather, as if he was at odds with them.

An urge came upon her to run upstairs, to go to Mr. Lockwell, to ask him about the man in the dark mask. But he could not answer her questions, and at that moment Lily, who had been sitting by the window, cried out, "The carriage is here!"

Rose gasped at the sight of the cabriolet drawn by a handsome gray, and Lily was at once exultant for her sister and anguished that she was not going herself. She demanded that Ivy catalog a whole host of details—everything that was worn, and said, and eaten, and danced, and whether Mr. Garritt was there, and how he looked, and if he asked about her. Then Ivy was kissing her sisters, and gripping her mother's hands, and hurrying out into the purple evening.

The driver helped her into the cabriolet. While she could not help feeling a note of disappointment to find the seat beside her empty, she could not say she was surprised. He had said he would send the carriage for her, not that he would come himself.

Besides, she could claim no imperfection in the situation, for to drive through the New Quarter on a warm evening was such a novelty that Ivy found, like her mother, she could not think of what had happened to her that day, or of what might happen that night. Instead, she watched the lamplighters move along the avenues even as their celestial counterparts set the stars alight in the sky. The rain had washed the city clean, and the air was a confection of clematis and violets and peony. Music and light spilled out of so many grand houses that the two seemed at once ubiquitous and united, as if to play a note was to send forth a ray of illumination, and a quartet was enough to set the grandest halls aglitter.

Too soon the carriage stopped, and Ivy found herself walking up the steps of a great house of white stone toward that music, and that light, and the bright sound of laughter.

A terror seized her at entering the parlor, in which her own familiar sitting room would have barely served for a nook. Just as her mother had predicted, all eyes turned toward her, though it was in no way a cause for delight. Fortunately, though severe, her discomfort was brief, for almost at once she found herself greeting Mrs. Baydon, who was, she knew, a friend of Mr. Rafferdy's. Given their mutual acquaintance, and this being the house of her husband's aunt, Mrs. Baydon felt free without any fear of impertinence to make the introduction herself.

"Besides, I feel as if I know you already," Mrs. Baydon said, taking Ivy's arm and leading her into the parlor. "We have heard such a great deal about the three Miss Lockwells. You will discover you are quite famous here. Our dear Mr. Rafferdy hardly speaks of anything else."

"Then I imagine you must make every effort to talk instead of the weather or the doings of Assembly," Ivy said, genuinely startled.

"But it is not so at all!" Mrs. Baydon replied. "We ply him for every detail of his encounters with you and your sisters. We have not had such amusement in a long while."

Ivy could not believe that was the case, but her companion was all kindness, and of an age with her, and she was grateful for the security of Mrs. Baydon's arm as they made their way about the parlor. Her companion was light-haired, like Ivy, but taller, and her pink gown was of the latest mode. Ivy could not help but notice how old-fashioned her own gown was in comparison, but the brilliance of Mrs. Baydon's charm was enough to illuminate them both, and more than one older fellow remarked that he had never seen a pair of more handsome women.

A moment of dread came upon Ivy when she was presented to their patroness. Lady Marsdel asked where she lived, and what the situation of her sisters was, and why Mr. Rafferdy had taken such a fancy to her family. Ivy answered Lady Marsdel's questions as plainly as she could, in no way attempting to inflate her situation, though neither did she try to demean it. As for the last question, she said she could not speak to another's feelings, but she did not think that she or her sisters were the object of any sort of special regard. She thought only that Mr. Rafferdy, possessed as he was of so agreeable a manner, had simply made the best out of the chance events that had precipitated their several recent encounters.

"I am pleased to see you are a young lady of good sense," Lady Marsdel said with a snap of her fan. "Yet you are also very pretty, Miss Lockwell, if not very tall. I think the reports of your charm have been understated. And while I believe you are correct that Mr. Rafferdy has made the best out of his meetings with you and your sisters, I am not inclined to assign chance much credit for their frequent occurrence. I should say instead that you would do well to be on your guard against them in the future. You understand, don't you?"

"Yes, ma'am," Ivy said, though in fact she could not say she did understand, and she felt quite rattled. Thankfully, with that they were dismissed; she curtsied again and was led away.

"Do forgive Mr. Baydon's aunt," Mrs. Baydon said. "But you see, she takes a great interest in Mr. Rafferdy. He is the child of her cousin, and very much a favorite of hers, for she has no sons of her own."

"And where is Mr. Rafferdy?" Ivy said, looking around and thinking that they had gone all around the room by now.

"But did he not tell you? Oh, I can see by your expression he did not. How awful of him! Yet I cannot be surprised, given his general want of character. The dreadful man has abandoned us."

Ivy came to a halt. "Abandoned us?"

"He is not coming. He sent me a note claiming he is ill."

"Ill? Is it very serious?"

"But you must not worry!" Mrs. Baydon said with laughter. "You do not know our Mr. Rafferdy well, or else you would not. I have never seen him afflicted by a physical ailment. I am certain his complaint is of a far different sort, and I suppose there was someone he feared he would meet if he attended tonight, someone disagreeable to him. However, it will be his loss, and I cannot say I am sorry, for I have you all to myself this evening. Come, we shall have a grand time." She led Ivy onward through the warm and noisy room.

They spoke as they took several more turns about the parlor, though most of the energy in the conversation was on Mrs. Baydon's part, for which Ivy was grateful, as for her own part she was distracted. She could not keep her thoughts from Mr. Rafferdy.

It was strange that he was not here. She could not help but consider Mrs. Baydon's suggestion that he had not come because there was someone he wished to avoid. And who could that someone be but Ivy herself? After all, Mr. Wyble was not in attendance tonight. Yet if that was the case, why invite her in the first place?

It was a thing done on a whim, she decided, after they stopped to sit and a glass of wine and a bit of cake had steadied her. The impulse to invite her had come out of his benign nature, and his understanding of her limited situation, and a kind wish to expand it. However, he had soon after realized his mistake; it had been inappropriate, just as she had said at the time. But once extended, the invitation could not be rescinded. The only solution was to not attend the party himself, to avoid any appearance of impropriety or indiscretion—on his part or on hers.

Good. She applauded his sense. She was grateful he had not placed either of them in an awkward position; she was utterly relieved. She could not be more glad that he was not here.

Still, as she looked about the room, she could not help thinking how pleasant it would have been to see him, if only to catch his eye for a moment and win one of his smiles.

However, he was not here, and with the matter resolved, Ivy was able to properly enjoy herself. They were invited to play cards with Lady Marsdel's brother, Lord Baydon, and her nephew, Mr. Harclint. Ivy was paired with Lord Baydon, and in that she was lucky, for Lord Baydon was corpulent and jocular and an excellent player, while Mr. Harclint—inclined to be thin, serious, and to forget which suit was trump—caused Mrs. Baydon to at last surrender her cards with a sigh. She rose and begged her leave of the two gentlemen, claiming she needed some air.

"Will you come with me, Miss Lockwell? I think another turn about the room would do me good."

"I imagine a turn away from Mr. Harclint's playing is more what is needed," Ivy murmured as they strolled.

"I hope my motivation for leaving was not *that* obvious."

"It was perhaps to Lord Baydon," Ivy said. "As for Mr. Harclint, I fear such a thing is no more obvious to him than when to put down his queen." For a time after that, if anyone they passed inquired as to the cause of their mirth, the two young women could only lean upon each other and laugh.

At last they ended up at a table where Mr. Baydon sat reading an issue of *The Comet*. He gave Ivy's hand a firm shake upon their introduction, though that hand was the only portion she was able to see of him aside from a crop of curly hair, as the balance remained hidden behind his broadsheet. Mrs. Baydon brought out a puzzle, and as they fit together the wooden pieces, a little group gathered around them.

Before long they had completed enough of the puzzle to see it was a painting of a country scene. Mossy trunks slanted beyond a field-stone wall, and twisted branches disheveled with old leaves wove together against a stormy sky. Red tinged the clouds, but whether from a sun that was rising or setting, Ivy could not say.

More than once Sir Earnsley remarked upon their skill in fitting the puzzle. "The speed with which you work is most impressive," the old baronet proclaimed. "By Loerus, I could no sooner piece together a picture than I could paint one."

"If I could paint a picture, I am sure I should not like for it to be cut up into small pieces," said Mr. Harclint, who had wandered their way and plopped into an empty chair. "I am sure Lord Farrolbrook has never turned any of his pictures into puzzles. It is said he's a painter of extraordinary skill."

Ivy mentioned that she was not familiar with Lord Farrolbrook, and they were treated to a rather long discourse on the man who was "surely the most illustrious member of the upper hall of our Assembly." Ivy thanked Mr. Harclint for the education. Her words seemed to encourage him to continue, but at that moment a fit of coughing on Mrs. Baydon's part prompted him to go fetch a cup of water. Ivy noted that Mrs. Baydon's affliction was well-timed, but she could not complain.

"For all his descriptions, Mr. Harclint has failed to tell you the most important fact about Lord Farrolbrook—that he is purported to be a skilled magician."

Ivy looked up at the speaker, a tall man with dark eyes standing beside the table. She was not certain when he had joined their little group; she had not made his introduction.

"A magician!" Sir Earnsley shifted in his chair and blew a breath through his mustache, looking very much like an old walrus on his rocky throne. "Do spare us that topic again, sir. I'm sure Lord Farrolbrook is no more a magician than anyone else you might meet in this room."

"It is true," the tall man replied, "that many who claim to be skilled in the occult arts do so out of a wish to appear important and a desire to impress others who are easily misled." His dark eyes flicked in the direction Mr. Harclint had gone.

"Yet for some few at least it must be true," Ivy said, and only when the others looked at her did she realize she had spoken the thought aloud. Her cheeks grew warm, yet with everyone gazing at her she had no choice but to raise her voice. "I mean only to say that the existence of magicians is well documented in our histories. While some accounts must be treated with skepticism, logic alone would argue that not *all* who claim to practice can be false."

Ivy lifted her gaze toward the tall man. She found him fascinating to look at. He was at least twenty-five years her elder and in no way handsome; his features were all angles, his nose aquiline, and his eyes so dark they seemed only to catch light and reflect none back.

He nodded to her. "Your argument is persuasive, Miss . . ."

Mrs. Baydon, upon realizing an introduction was necessary, made the required exchange. His name was Bennick, and he was an old friend of the late Lord Marsdel.

"You ask magicians to identify themselves," he went on, "when by its very nature magick is a secret art. I would say it is an axiom that the more likely one is to speak of it, the less likely one is to practice it."

"Then I imagine you practice it not at all!" Sir Earnsley said.

Mr. Bennick bowed toward the baronet. "In that, sir, you cannot be more correct."

"I wonder," Mrs. Baydon said as she laid another piece in the puzzle, "given that magicians all go about it so secretly, if we haven't all met one and don't even know it."

"I cannot say if you have met a practicing magician," Mr. Bennick replied—though it was Ivy he looked at. "But I know for a fact you are acquainted with a young gentleman who is often a guest at this house and who is a scion of one of the seven Old Houses from which all magicians can trace their descent. That some among his forefathers were enchanters is a fact. I have read many histories of the arcane in which their names appear."

Mrs. Baydon looked up from her puzzle. "Indeed! And who is this remarkable individual? Do point him out!"

"I cannot. He is not here tonight."

"Well, I suppose that wouldn't be mysterious enough if he were." She resumed fitting the puzzle.

Ivy, however, could not let the topic go so easily. What young gentleman could Mr. Bennick speak of who was so often at this house but not tonight? There was only one such person she could think of—and it was not her cousin Mr. Wyble.

For a time she did not know what to say. Even if she wished for some confirmation from Mr. Bennick, she dared not mention Mr. Rafferdy's name. So she labored vigorously at the puzzle. At last, perceiving his dark eyes still on her, she looked up and said, "You seem learned in ancient lore, Mr. Bennick. May I ask you a question?"

His only answer was a nod.

Now that she had his attention her question seemed outlandish, but there was nothing to do but speak it. "Tell me, sir, do you know of any legends or myths that speak about twelve wanderers coming together in one place?"

"You say *twelve* wanderers, Miss Lockwell?"

"Yes, that's correct."

"Then I cannot help you. I know of no myths of ancient Tharos or the northern counties that speak of such an event. However, twelve is a number of significance in the study of magick. There are, for instance, twelve houses of the moon, each with its own occult properties, and the number twelve comes into play in many spells and enchantments. May I inquire as to the reason for your question?"

Ivy shrank under the force of his dark stare. "It's nothing," she murmured. "Only something I read and did not understand, that's all. Please don't think of it further." She bent back over her work.

They had made good progress on the puzzle. More of the trees were complete now, their branches drooping over the top of the wall, while leaves scudded before the clouds. A pair of travelers had appeared beside the wall. The gentleman gazed out of the picture, as if looking back the way they had come, but the lady's head was tilted up toward the trees.

Ivy supposed the particular stand of forest depicted in the painting was the Evengrove. While there were few patches of Wyrdwood left in the heartlands of Altania—and those that remained were small, whittled down by ax and plow over the centuries—the Evengrove was a notable exception. Not thirty miles from Invarel, a great tract of primeval forest was preserved behind high stone walls first erected by the Tharosian emperor Madiger and later improved during the reigns of numerous kings.

Folk seldom ventured into the Evengrove, for no roads had ever been hewn into the preserve. However, travelers made a common practice of walking along Madiger's Wall, and it was a popular subject for artists. Ivy set another piece in the puzzle.

"Oh, well done!" Mrs. Baydon exclaimed, clapping her hands. "I have looked at that piece a dozen times and couldn't see where it fit. What a clever thing you are, Miss Lockwell!"

Ivy merely bowed her head. The room had suddenly become too warm. She longed for a breath of wind, like that which the travelers in the painting must have felt.

"Do set down your news for a moment, Mr. Baydon. Tell us, what do you think of our work?"

He peered over the edge of his broadsheet, revealing a face not unhandsome but cast in frown. "I think it's perfectly ghastly, what with those hoary old trees. And those two people look like they've just come from a funeral. You'd find more jolly-looking folk in a workhouse."

Ivy tilted her head, studying the picture. "I don't think it's ghastly at all. The wood is sad, perhaps, and very old. But it's appealing in its way. It makes me think of . . ."

"Of what does it make you think?" Mr. Bennick said.

Ivy's cheeks glowed from the attention, but she sat up straight in her chair and spoke in a clear voice. "I don't know exactly. It makes me think of something ancient, I suppose. Ancient and strange and forgotten. Like a story no one tells anymore, or a song whose tune no one quite remembers. I've always wanted to see the Evengrove, only I never have, and here it's so close to the city." She touched the picture.

"But that's a marvelous idea!" Mrs. Baydon said. "After this night it is to be another long lumenal. What a fine traveling party we would make if we can convince Mr. Rafferdy to come! What do you say, Mr. Baydon? I'm sure we can use Lord Baydon's four-in-hand. We'll stay at an inn—there must be one near Madiger's Wall, what with all the travelers—and have them pack a dinner for us to take when we venture out to the Evengrove."

"A patch of old Wyrdwood is not a place for picnics," Sir Earnsley said.

"I couldn't disagree more. Surely it's a beautiful place."

"Beautiful, you call it?" The old baronet shook his head. "Perilous, I say. Full of whispers and shadows. Where I come from, a man gives a stand of Wyrdwood a wide berth when he's out walking. There's a reason walls were built around them."

"Well, of course there's a reason," Mr. Baydon said, setting down his copy of *The Comet*. "The walls were meant to preserve a few groves of Altania's aboriginal wood from any sort of modern progress. Though I can't see the bother. What good is a shabby bit of forest anyway? Those old trees are always losing their leaves—not like the fine New Trees we have here in the city, which have the good sense to hold on to their greenery all year round. Still, I am sure it's harmless enough."

"Harmless!" Sir Earnsley let out a snort. "You would not say that if you had lived your life in the country."

"Indeed, if I had lived my life in the country, I am sure I would be as bound to superstition and codswallop as any Outlander."

"But you must know of the Risings, Mr. Baydon. Have you not read the accounts in the histories?"

"The histories? I'm afraid the *Lex Altania* is no more historically accurate than a book of nursery stories. Such works might still be studied in country schools, Sir Earnsley, but here in the city we prefer to get our knowledge from more reliable sources." Mr. Baydon tapped a finger against his issue of *The Comet.*

The men continued their argument, but the voices faded to a drone in Ivy's ears, like the noises of cicadas on the endless afternoon of a greatday. She stared at the puzzle on the table, and again she noticed the way the dark clouds above the trees were tinged with crimson. Maybe some in this city still believed the histories, after all. Maybe the red light was not the light of sunrise or sunset, but rather the glow of fire.

Mr. Baydon had likened the *Lex Altania* to a book of nursery stories, and it was true her father had read to her from it when she was a child. Written over twelve hundred years ago by an obscure Tharosian captain, the *Lex* told the history of the earliest days of Altania. Modern scholars considered the accounts in the book to be fanciful and largely invented. Yet Ivy remembered how Mr. Lockwell had always handled the book reverently each time he took it from the shelf to read to her.

*All good tales bear a truth,* he had told her once when she asked if the stories in the book had really happened. *Though sometimes you have to look beyond the surface to see it.*

He had never read the parts of the *Lex Altania* about the Risings to her, but she had studied all three volumes from cover to cover in the years since. She had to concede, the idea that patches of primeval forest had ever risen up and lashed out against mankind was fantastic.

Yet she felt her father was right, that there was a truth behind the story of the Risings. The deep forests that covered the island had been mysterious and full of peril to the men who first landed their ships on these shores, and they had struggled to subdue it with ax and fire. Was it really so strange for them to believe the forest had fought back?

Ivy set another piece in the puzzle, then let out a gasp. In the picture, the trees swayed back and forth as if under the force of a wind. However, the clouds remained motionless in the painted sky. A chill passed through Ivy, but her skin was afire. The trees bent and stretched toward the two travelers. The black lines of branches reached out . . .

"Tell us, Miss Lockwell," Mr. Baydon said, "what do you think of those ridiculous old histories Sir Earnsley is so fond of?"

It was only with the greatest force that she pulled her gaze away from the puzzle. Spheres of light glowed at the tips of all the candles in the room, expanding and shrinking in time to the beating of her heart.

"I think . . ." she said.

"Yes, Miss Lockwell?" Mr. Bennick said, his dark gaze on her.

She lifted a hand to her brow. "The lights," she said. "They're too bright."

The room spun around her. All was a flurry of dazzling sparks. She heard the scraping of chairs, expressions of shock, and one deep voice that cut through the others.

"Fetch a doctor at once, Mr. Baydon. Miss Lockwell is not well."

---

# CHAPTER ELEVEN

ELDYN LIMPED THROUGH the Lowgate just as a greasy sunrise, rank from the exhalations of all the tanneries in Waterside, slicked the surface of the Anbyrn.

The umbral had been swift, no more than five hours from dusk to dawn, but by all rights he should have been back from his night's work in Hayrick Cross an hour ago. However, a mile south of the village he had spied a band of four of the king's redcrests riding along the road, and he had been forced to dive into a hedgerow to keep from being seen. The moon was bright that night, and even his trick with the shadows could not have preserved him from their notice.

After that, fearing other soldiers would be on the road, he had made his way south by muddy back lanes and bridle paths. More than once he had gotten lost when some track dead-ended, and upon jumping a stile to go overland across a field he was spied by the farmer, who fired his musket and loosed his dogs. The gun was easily dodged, but not so the hounds. One of them got a chunk of Elydn's boot, and a piece of his leg with it, before he scrambled up a wall and lost them that way.

As he entered the Golden Loom, he kept up his guard against an encounter with Miss Walpert, which he feared nearly as much as a run-in with soldiers. Despite his rebuff of her proposal a half month back, she had not lost any interest in him. Not that he should complain, for her father had lately reduced his rent, and Eldyn knew it was due to her goodly words about him. He ought to be thankful. He *was* thankful. All the same, he had no wish to come upon her—especially now.

Fortunately, the inn was quiet, and he was able to slip upstairs unseen. That was well, as he was certain he looked a sore sight, with the nettles in his coat and the blood on his leg. It would not do to have anyone ask questions or to wonder where he was at night, in case the king's men (or, worse yet, one of the Black Dog's own agents) ever came to the inn looking for news of suspicious doings.

*And if they did, all you would have to do is point them to Westen,* Eldyn told himself as he filled a basin and poured water over the back of his neck. However, that was an absurd idea. Who would the magistrate believe when they went before the court? Westen struck a fine figure in his rich clothes, gold as the day. Then there was Eldyn, long-haired, ragged, and far too thin—a pale night thing.

Sashie had not risen, or at least she had not yet emerged from her room. As far as she knew, he had been out at tavern all night with Rafferdy. In truth he had not seen Rafferdy since the full moon, not since they quarreled about his intentions toward Miss Lockwell. Since then, none of Rafferdy's usual notes had arrived at the inn. Not that Eldyn's night work left him time for hanging about taverns.

Yet he missed his friend. Eldyn would have liked to talk to him, to hear his laughter and his prattle about clothes and parties and dice. Only what could Eldyn himself say in return? How he was carrying messages that surely were intended for spies and traitors? He took off the yeoman's garb he had donned for the night's mischief and stuffed it in a bag. He made what bath he could with the basin of yesterday's water, then donned his second best shirt and his best breeches.

As for his boots, they were done for; the one was torn, and the other half gone above the ankle. He took a knife and cut off the tops, making them into something like the moccasins the aboriginals of the New Lands wore. He had no choice but to get fitted for a new pair of boots that day. Luckily, the men who gave him the messages to carry usually gave him a little money as well, slapping him on the back and calling him *brother* as they pressed the coins into his hand. Eldyn felt no fraternal kinship for these men. Their faces were rough, their eyes sly and full of murder. But he would nod and pocket the coins just the same.

As a result, he had enough funds to keep him and his sister at the inn for the present. He had hoped to use what remained of the money from his mother's jewels to buy a coat, but boots it would be instead. He carefully brushed his old coat one more time and set it over a chair, then laid down on the bench to try to doze for a little while.

He was awakened by the sound of the door to Sashie's chamber opening. She would come out of her room and sit with him these days and would even accompany him to the public room for meals. Her manner was civil, and she would answer any question he asked—though coolly, and she would volunteer no conversation on her own. She had made no attempt to approach Westen or in any way to break the command Eldyn had given her forbidding that relationship. Yet it was equally clear that she had not forgiven him.

"Good morning, dearest," he said, sitting up on the bench as she exited her little chamber. He rubbed his neck; the bench was bare wood with only a blanket thrown over it.

"Good morning, brother," she said, without a glance his way.

She wore her plainest dress and no ribbons in her hair, but her sadness made her look fragile and so all the more lovely, like a porcelain treasure from a Murghese palace. A fierce desire to do right by her came over him. He would give her all she deserved, all their father had promised and never given her, and then she would know that he loved her, that he wanted only the best for her. Despite his weariness, he stood.

"What would you like to do today?" he asked merrily. "Come, we can do anything you wish." He suggested several things that he thought might lift her spirits: a walk through a garden, or a boat ride on the river, or even a visit to the countryside. He had some coin; he could afford it. And such an expense would be worth the cost if it brought a little color to her cheeks and a smile to her lips.

Only she could not be compelled to leave their chambers, let alone the inn or the city. "I will stay here today," she said. "If I sit by the window, I can just see the little pear tree in the courtyard. A lark comes there sometimes, and if I open the window I can hear its song. It's the prettiest thing. Nothing could give me more joy than to hear it."

With that she sat by the window and gazed through the glass. His sister made no complaint about her situation, but as usual when he tried to engage her in conversation she responded with few words. If the lark came, he did not see it, and he heard no birdsong save for the inane cooing of the pigeons.

At last he could bear the confines of the room no longer. He had intended to stay with her all the day—a middle lumenal—so that she would not be alone so much, but the walls pressed closer with every hour, and each clatter of hooves he heard through the window belonged, in his imagination, to an agent of the Black Dog, come to question folk at the inn about traitors to the Crown.

"Perhaps you can be content here, but I must go out!" he cried at last, leaping up from the bench.

She said nothing, and only looked at him with languid eyes.

"I will be at Mrs. Haddon's," he said. "Tell Mr. Walpert if you need me for anything. He can send a boy to fetch me. I will bring you something sweet to eat when I return."

She had already turned her gaze back out the window. Eldyn donned his coat, took his hat, and shut the door quietly behind him.

❦

I T HAD BEEN some time since he had been to Mrs. Haddon's coffee-house, and her business had not suffered in the interim. The place was, if anything, more crowded than ever.

"Yes, things are always mad after such a short night," Mrs. Haddon said when he commented on her business. "A brief umbral leaves little time for mischief, let alone sleep, and what can't be got in bed must be got in a cup instead if one is to stay awake through the day." She gave his cheek a quick pinch, then hurried off.

Eldyn gaped after her. What did she mean by those words? *A brief umbral leaves little time for mischief* . . . Did Mrs. Haddon know something of what he had been doing at night? Only that was mad. She was the proprietor of a coffeehouse. What did she know of spies and rebels?

Perhaps more than he thought. He surveyed the room and saw plenty of young men reading *The Fox* and *The Swift Arrow*. In this place, criticism of the king and the magnates was consumed as eagerly as the contents of the cups Mrs. Haddon brought, and it similarly fueled the spirits of those who partook of it. He wondered if it was wise for him to be here. However, even as he considered this he saw Orris Jaimsley waving at him. His old classmates from St. Berndyn's College sat around their usual table. He went over to them.

They clapped Eldyn on the back as he sat down, got him a hot cup, and passed him a flask under the table. "By God, we've missed you, Garritt," Jaimsley said. "I haven't heard one bit of sense since you were last here. You're the only serious and sober one among us."

"I warrant I'm as liable as any of you to lose my sobriety," he said with a grin, and tipped the flask over his cup. They laughed, and Eldyn laughed with them, glad for the coffee, glad for the whiskey, glad for the company of familiar friends. It had been too long since he had done this.

He passed the flask back and asked how they had been faring at tavern without him. Jaimsley treated him to a long description of Talinger's spectacular successes with the ladies, and of Warrett's equally spectacular failures, and his own amusement over it all. Then Eldyn asked how their studies for the term were progressing.

"But haven't you heard, Garritt?" Curren Talinger said. "No one's been to classes in a quarter month. Well, no one save those mealy-mouthed prigs at Gauldren's College. Precious little pets they are—they do anything the deans tell them to do. But not the rest of us. We came to university to learn how to think, not to think what they tell us to."

Eldyn stared. "You mean you're not attending lectures by choice?"

"No one is," Dalby Warrett replied. The laconic young man was unusually animated, and his color high. "Well, except at Gauldren's, as Jaimsley mentioned, and some of the men at Bishop's and Highhall. But the rest of us walked out, and we're not going back or paying our tuition. Not until they let Baddingdon go free."

Eldyn listened as they spoke of the events that had transpired at the university over the last half month. It seemed that Professor Baddingdon, a popular lecturer in rhetoric, had become increasingly critical of the king. The dean of his college had cautioned him to cease such talk, but Baddingdon, a Torlander, had a reputation for being as quarrelsome as he was clever. In response to the warning, he delivered a lecture in which he likened the king to a sparrow charged with guarding a field rich with grain, while the members of Assembly were cast as crows, pecking at the corn. And he said what Altania needed was a hawk with keen eyes and strong talons, one that would fly across the sea and send the crows scattering. Of course, it was plain to all that he spoke of the Usurper Huntley Morden, the hawk being the symbol of that house, and the verdant field was Altania itself.

"He said that during his lecture?" Eldyn said, astonished that a man of learning could be such a fool.

Jaimsley nodded. "I suppose so many fawning freshmen have regarded him in awe for so long that he thought he was above any reproach. But no one is above *their* notice. They must have gotten wind of what he was intending to speak about, because they didn't even wait for him to finish his lecture but rather took him right there and then, in front of his students. He was put in chains and led out like a common criminal."

"By agents of Lord Valhaine?"

"Not just any agents. Everyone said it was the White Lady herself who took him. She had been in the back of the hall with a hood pulled up, and as soon as he uttered the words about the hawk she put back her hood and stepped forward, and that was that. Baddingdon was done for. He started to rail against the king, but one look from her and his tongue froze in his mouth, and no one lifted a finger to help him."

Talinger made a warding sign. "It's said no one can bear her gaze, not even the king's Black Dog, and it's him that she serves."

"Well, I should not have given way so easily had I been there," Warrett proclaimed, making a fist and striking the table. "I wouldn't have let anyone treat old Baddingdon like that."

"You would have pissed your pants when she glanced your way, is what you mean," Jaimsley said, and though Warrett gave him a hot look, he did not argue the point.

"There's been talk, you know," Talinger said then. The Torlander spoke in a low voice, so that the others had to lean in close to hear him.

"Talk of what?" Jaimsley said, a frown on his homely face.

"Surely *you* have heard it, Jaimsley. Some of the men—no, I would say a great many of them—say we should go fetch him from Barrowgate."

Eldyn nearly laughed, but it was out of horror, not humor. "You cannot be serious, Talinger. You cannot!"

"Why can't I? There's more than a thousand of us, even if you leave off them prigs from Gauldren's and Bishop's and Highhall. It's wrong that they've thrown him in the pits with murderers and whores. Baddingdon is old. He'll not last long in that prison. What should stop us from marching on Barrowgate, breaking down the gates, and setting him free?"

*Because they'll cut you down,* Eldyn wanted to say.

Only, Warrett spoke first. A hungry look had come over his face, erasing what had been soft and vaguely handsome and replacing it with a hard mask. "Now you're talking sense, Talinger. Nothing can stop us. Not if we all stand together."

Eldyn's stomach had gone sour, and Jaimsley was shaking his head.

"Why do you look at us like that, Jaimsley?" Talinger said, his accent reverting to a rolling Westland growl. "Aren't you always telling us that it's the people who should rule?"

"Yes, and I still believe it. But talking of rebellion is one thing. Doing it . . . Well, that's another matter altogether."

"Aye, it is at that," Talinger said. "You like to talk of it, but you're afraid to do anything about it. But not me. I'm not like you, Jaimsley. I'm not afraid."

"Aren't you? Tell me, which one of you at this table has ever so much as broken one of those rules in a voice above a whisper?" He nodded toward the Rules of Citizenship posted on the wall nearby. Their sheepish expressions answered his question. "And you speak of making rebellion."

Eldyn started to let out a breath, thinking they were going to let the subject drop. But then Talinger leaped to his feet, his chair falling back with a clatter that suspended conversation in the shop.

"I'll show you what I think of those rules," he said. He did not rush or go furtively. Rather, with deliberate motions, he walked to the wall, pulled down the Rules of Citizenship, and tore the paper they were printed on into halves, quarters, eighths. He let the pieces fall to the floor. "That's what I think of someone else telling me what to do," Talinger said in a loud voice. "I don't care if it's pale ladies or black curs or kings giving the order. An unjust law is no law at all."

All was silence. No one made a move. Talk of disobedience to the Crown was one thing, but action—everyone had seen what action got you when one of the king's men or an agent of the Gray Conclave was about. Eyes glanced back and forth. All waited for someone to stand up, point a finger, and call for soldiers to carry the young Torlander to Barrowgate.

Instead, after a terrible moment, it was Mrs. Haddon who bustled toward him, huffing, her frizzy wig aflutter. "Well, well, a fine joke that was, young Mr. Talinger. A fine joke indeed. You know you could have simply told me that printing of the rules was out of date. You needn't have made such a silly little play of it. Here—this is the new one de-livered just yesterday. I meant to put it up, but I quite forgot. Though I'm sure they won't throw a daft old woman in prison for being ab-sentminded. I would hardly remember my own name these days if you boys weren't always calling it out to me: a cup, Mrs. Haddon, bring another cup!"

She unrolled a sheaf of paper and stuck it on the nail on the wall, then took Talinger's elbow and led him back to the table. Gradually, the sound of talk filled the coffeehouse again, though lower than be-fore.

". . . and it's not yet here, my boy," Eldyn heard Mrs. Haddon whispering to Talinger as they drew near. "But the time will come. Sooner than we all think, I wouldn't doubt. And when it does we'll wonder why we wished for it at all. A terrible thing it will be, a terri-ble thing. But that's to worry about then. For now we must watch and wait. Do you see?"

Talinger gave her a mute nod. His face, bright with passion a mo-ment ago, was now white behind his red beard.

She pinched his cheek, bringing a bit of color back. "There, that's a good lad. You'll be fine if you don't lose your wits. You can take him from here, boys." She gathered up their half-drunk cups.

The message was not lost upon them. They hurriedly rose.

"You fool, you damn Westland fool," Jaimsley hissed as he led Talinger toward the door. "And you're a fool as well, Warrett, for encouraging him like that. Do you know what could have happened—what could still happen to us? Just because no one did anything doesn't mean that no one was watching, that they haven't already gotten our names and put them down on a list."

Talinger hung his head and Warrett looked away, and while the words were not directed at Eldyn, they struck him like a blow to the gut. What if someone *had* watched? What if *his* name was on a list?

"What is it, Garritt?" Jaimsley said to him once they were outside the shop. "You've gone white as whey. You needn't worry, you know." He nodded toward Warrett and Talinger, who stood a bit apart, looking chastened now. "I was just trying to give them a bit of a scare. There are enough true traitors and spies about these days for the king's agents to concern themselves with. Even if they did see what just happened, the most these two are liable to get is a bit of hard questioning from a captain. And it's not like they have any secrets to spill. Can you imagine either one of them as rebels?"

Jaimsley laughed, and Eldyn made an attempt to follow suit, but a sickness was spreading inside him. Perhaps Talinger and Warrett had no secrets to spill, but Eldyn could not say the same. It was a cruel bit of fate that had made him—the one in their group who had never spoken a word of rebellion—into the one who was now engaged in what was surely traitorous activity. What if the White Lady came and turned her unnatural gaze upon him and the truth of his night work spilled from his lips against his will?

"Are you certain you're well?" Jaimsley asked, laying a hand on his shoulder. "To tell the truth, I've been worried about you, Garritt. You don't seem yourself of late."

"I'm thirsty, that's all," Eldyn said. "God, I need a drink."

"Yes, and not coffee," Jaimsley said with a crooked grin. He clapped Eldyn's shoulder, then called to the others. "Come on, gents. There will be no lectures at university today. We might as well go to tavern, if you two will promise to behave yourselves."

The promise was solemnly given. They walked down narrow streets and soon became a merry band, for laughter must always follow a close call with danger. However, more than once Eldyn could not help glancing over his shoulder, looking for a pale face behind him.

ON THE NEXT day's edition of *The Fox,* there was another advertisement for pewter candlesticks, silver snuffboxes, and gold thimbles.

As before, deciphering the code led Eldyn to an address in the Old City. It was always a different house and different men, but their eyes were the same: hard and crafty, glancing up and down the street to make sure he was alone. Sometimes the message tube they gave him felt strangely warm, as if it was not ink that sloshed inside the chamber at one end but rather blood. He made his way to Hayrick in the middle of a hard rain and was grateful for the long lumenal that followed, and the chance to get some sleep.

Two editions of *The Fox* went by with no advertisements, and as it was published thrice a week he began to let himself hope his ungodly work was finished. He went for a walk in Gauldren's Heights and fancied which house he would let for himself and Sashie once his returns from the trading company came in. Something more Uphill than Down, he thought: a solid, respectable house.

Except on his way back to the Golden Loom, he bought the newest edition of *The Fox* from a boy on a corner, still damp off the press. At once he saw the advertisement that was, among all the many eyes that read the broadsheet, for his eyes alone. He read the address, then tossed the paper in the gutter. The print had stained his fingers black.

That night was the first night he was forced to release the ink in the tube. He was early to the well, as he always was, for he dreaded to think what they might do to him were he late. The mask he always wore for these meetings chafed against his face. Eldyn had no way to mark the exact time, but at last he became certain that the appointed hour had come and gone, and there was no sign of the red-haired man. As a sliver of moon rose, so, too, a fear rose in him, and he retreated from the well, making for a small thicket of New Forest beech and elm.

And not a moment too soon. A pair of men stepped from the mouth of the lane and into the moonlight by the well. Neither was the red-haired man. They looked around, but Eldyn wrapped the shadows around himself and slunk back into the wood. The two finished their circuit, then went back to stand by the well. One of them carried a club.

The message would not be delivered this umbral. Eldyn forced his way through the thicket, ran across a field where a single cow lowed, and leaped over a stone wall.

"By God, so the devil comes to me!" a voice hissed, hardly a dozen feet away from him.

Eldyn staggered back against the wall. A man with broad shoulders and bandy legs stood on the road. He wore a blacksmith's apron. There was a hammer in his hand.

"Give me that," he said, gesturing to the leather tube.

Terror gripped Eldyn's heart even as he gripped the tube.

"Here, here!" the man cried out. "To me! I've got him!"

He started forward, hammer raised. His hands were big, the backs of them covered with black hair.

"I said give that up, devil. I know it's to him you were bringing it, but *he* won't be coming to get it, I can tell you that. Come now, hand it over without any trouble, and I won't have to crack your skull."

The way he tightened his grip on the hammer belied that promise. Eldyn did not wait; what the nature of the message in the tube was, he did not know, only that he was sure it would be his undoing if read before any court of law. He turned the end of the tube, and dark liquid flooded out. In the moonlight it looked indeed like black blood.

The man let out a shout and sprang forward, but Eldyn flung the leather tube at him, striking him in the face. The man dropped his hammer, howling and pawing at his eyes, for the ink had splattered them. Eldyn scrambled back over the wall and ran past the cow to the south edge of the field, which was bordered by another thicket.

This he dashed through headlong. Branches scratched at his face and ripped his clothes, but the sound of shouts behind him and to his right propelled him onward without heed. On one occasion the voices rang out not twenty feet to his right, but then he splashed across a brook, through a hedge, and down a footpath, all the way weaving the shadows around himself and praying to the saints for a cloud to cover the moon.

The next time he heard the voices, they were behind him again and farther away. He kept moving, not south along the main road to the city but east, skirting around sleeping hamlets and farmsteads and slinking along the lines of walls. At last he staggered through the Morrowgate, having gone halfway around Invarel, and found a hack cab. When the driver eyed his torn attire and bleeding cheek, Eldyn made some weak mention of a tavern fight. Coins passed hands; no questions were asked. Eldyn made it into the inn and upstairs, unseen.

He was safe. By St. Andelthy, he was safe. Yet no matter how many times he told himself that the message was destroyed by the ink, that he was not caught, he could not stop shaking. When Sashie came from the room, she found him in only his dressing gown, shivering, his hair still wet from a hasty bath. He told her he was ill with a cold.

It was not until two days later that he learned the red-haired man had been taken to Barrowgate.

He read it in *The Messenger* as he sat in the public room at the Golden Loom drinking a cup of beer. The story described how a villainous rebel had been caught in the village of Hayrick Cross, north of Invarel. His name was Wayt Howburn, and he had been a journeyman at the blacksmith's there: a walleyed man with red hair. It was the master of the shop, a devoted subject of the Crown, who had turned him in, for having grown suspicious he had searched Howburn's room and discovered a bundle of letters.

The letters were written in a code of some sort and had not yet been deciphered, but they could only be the work of spies and traitors to Altania, for who else would compose messages in such an unholy manner? Howburn was in Barrowgate, awaiting trial. That he would hang was all but certain.

Trembling, Eldyn set down the broadsheet and reached for his beer. His hand groped thin air; the cup was not where he had left it. He looked up, and the breath went out of him.

Westen raised the missing cup in a toast and took a swallow. He was dressed in rich clothes, as usual, and wore a look of amusement upon his face.

Anger burned away some of Eldyn's fear. "I should think you would not be so gleeful," he said in a low voice, glancing to make sure the few others in the room were not listening. "Your man has been caught, and all the messages with him."

The highwayman set the cup down next to Eldyn's hand. "So the king's men believe. Those who serve the Crown are necessarily idiots."

"But they found the papers."

"They found *some* papers," Westen said.

A pain stabbed at Eldyn's temples. He wanted to take a swig of his beer but did not. "I don't understand."

The highwayman stroked the line of his smooth-shaven jaw with a knuckle. That he was so good-looking and so finely dressed made the gesture all the more mocking.

Eldyn cast another glance out of the corner of his eye, then leaned in closer. "What were those papers they found?"

"Not the letters you carried, Garritt, if that's what you're thinking. I can only imagine Lord Valhaine will waste days trying to decode them. Of course, when he finally does, he'll find they contain nothing but a rather rude verse concerning the bedroom habits of the king."

"But then Howburn—"

"Howburn was no patriot. He thought he could sell what he knew to the king's men for a goodly sum. But the blacksmith beat him to it and delivered him up to the soldiers for a grand total of a dozen regals. There's a 'devoted subject of the Crown' for you. The only crown he cares about is one stamped on a coin."

Eldyn pressed a hand to his head. "But then the letters—"

"Are safe. They were never in Howburn's possession for long. It was his job to pass them along."

"And the papers the blacksmith found were fakes," Eldyn said, "planted there to mislead the agents of the king."

Westen grinned, a flash of lightning. "You're far better at this than you give yourself credit for, Garritt."

"But he will hang," Eldyn said. "Whether the letters are false or not, no matter what they contain, in the end he will surely hang." A terrible thought came to him. "What if he accuses us to save himself?"

"And whom will he accuse? He has never seen me in his life, and you wore a mask when you went to meet him, as did the others. Howburn will go to the gallows alone."

Eldyn succumbed to thirst and took the cup, taking a draft. He set it down. "Either way, it is over."

Westen laughed; the sound gave Eldyn a shudder.

"Over? No, it is far from over, Garritt." He laid a copy of *The Fox* on the table and tapped a bit of print on the last page. It was an advertisement for pewter candlesticks, silver snuffboxes, and gold thimbles.

Eldyn stared at the paper. The beer he had drunk curdled in his stomach.

"It will not be over," the highwayman said, "until the old stag is dead and the people of Altania roast its flesh on a spit."

A dread came over Eldyn. He thought of his near miss with the king's men, of the dog that had attacked him, of the blacksmith and his hammer. He could not do this anymore.

"I am finished." He took a breath, then looked up and made himself meet Westen's gaze. "I have done what you wanted of me. I am finished with this wretched business."

"But I am not finished with you," the highwayman said. He reached for the cup, though Eldyn still held on to it, and their fingers brushed. Eldyn snatched both his hands back and put them in his lap.

"I say again, I have done enough," he muttered. "I am through with this devil's work."

"That was not our agreement, Garritt. I know you are a gentleman of your word. Or do you mean to tell me you are giving me my hundred regals back?"

Eldyn only looked at his hands.

"Then it is as I thought, and our agreement stands." Westen drained the cup and set it on the table.

Eldyn wanted to weep, but he forced himself to stay steady. By God, to act so unmanly in front of the highwayman would be unbearable. Eldyn, not *he,* was the lord's grandson.

"I was nearly caught twice. I cannot hope to escape a third time. I have my sister to think of. I cannot do this."

"Not for the sake of your country?"

"I am sure it is better for my country's sake that I not do this."

"You say that, Garritt, but you do not believe it. You see as well as I how ill the magnates use Altania, how ill they use its land, its people, and how the king totters upon his throne and does nothing. A storm gathers. Fly with it, or it will beat you down."

Eldyn made no reply. The highwayman leaned in closer. "I told you that Howburn never saw me in his life, but I wear no mask with you, Garritt. Because what I said before was true. We are alike, you and I. We both want something better for ourselves and for our country. Yet unlike you, I am man enough to do something about it."

"I *am* doing something about it!" Eldyn said, but the words sounded weak. He hung his head, ashamed of the way his cheeks stung. The bench opposite him scraped against the floor. Boots thumped behind him, and a hand fell upon his shoulder.

"You must choose whether or not to be a man, Garritt." The highwayman's breath was warm against his ear. "Do this for your sake, for your country's sake. And if not for that . . ." He squeezed Eldyn's shoulder. "If not for that, then do it for the sake of your precious sister. For I know you would never do anything, anything at all, that might cause her to come to harm. Would you, Mr. Garritt?"

The sound of boots retreated. Eldyn sat at the table, staring at his empty cup, and it was many minutes before his legs felt solid enough to stand upon.

EVENING WAS FALLING, a violet curtain that dropped by inches before a long night, as Eldyn raced through the streets of the Old City.

Westen's speech had indeed filled him with resolve, but not the sort the highwayman had intended. Eldyn would choose to be a man, but he would choose in his own way. He was not his father. He was not a highwayman.

And he would not carry more messages for traitors, or for dogs who threatened his sister.

He hurried along a darker part of Durrow Street, past the grog houses, past the beggars and the whores, past the men who huddled around the fires that burned in the street, drinking gin.

"Hello there, love!" called out one of the women who sat on the filthy steps of a church. "You're a fine thing to look at. Come on over, and we'll show you something the priests never did." She raised her bottle toward him and hiked up her skirts over her knees.

Eldyn ran past without looking, and their laughter followed him.

"I bet the priests *did* show him a thing or two. What they got under their cassocks, that's what. And I bet he liked it. Well, you keep on going, love. The theaters are that way, and they know what to do with a thing like you!"

He ignored their catcalls and pressed on, through the worst section of Durrow Street: a quarter-mile length known as High Holy by its denizens—and by those who ventured there seeking its dark and violent pleasures. For though the old chapel on its little hill had been abandoned years ago, the Church still owned it, as well as the buildings around it.

As he left High Holy behind, Eldyn could only admit that some of what Westen had said was true. Altania and its people had been wronged by men of wealth. Nor had the king or the Church done anything about it. Yet that men like Westen could do any better was absurd.

Westen fancied himself a kind of hero, but he was nothing more than a robber and a thief. He stole from the rich because it suited him. However, if men like him ever ruled the country, then they would steal from the poor just as easily. If Altania was to be made a better place, it would not be by the hands of criminals but through honest men.

And Eldyn Garritt was an honest man. He would not go back on his agreement with Westen, however foolishly and in a weak moment it had been entered into. He would pay the highwayman back, and with interest.

It would be simple enough, he was sure of it. His last meeting with Mr. Sarvinge and Mr. Grealing had gone exceedingly well. Any awkward or uncomfortable feelings had dissipated at once. The two had accepted his investment of a hundred regals gratefully, even humbly. They had apologized for being so sharp with him, but he understood they had only acted as business required; it was in no way personal. They had in fact always held the deepest belief that he would make good on his word. So he had, and they could not have been more pleased. The trading company was set to depart for the New Lands; his investment had come just in time. His profit of twenty times his investment was assured.

Eldyn looked at the signs on the buildings as he went, searching for Inslip Lane. He had never been to their place of business before, but he knew the address. He would speak with Mr. Sarvinge and Mr. Grealing. They were reasonable men. The trading ships were on their way to the New Lands—indeed, were likely there by now. He would ask them for an advance against his returns. In exchange, he would be more than willing to take a smaller profit, perhaps fifteen times his investment; the remainder of the profit would be theirs as payment for the advance. He was certain there was no way men of such good business sense could fault an arrangement that would cost them so little and that would bring them such benefit.

True, Eldyn would be reducing his own profit. But fifteen hundred regals would still be a large sum of money. And the cost would be worth it to be free of that scoundrel Westen.

Music and laughter spilled onto the street ahead, accompanied by flickering lights of many hues. Eldyn passed a row of theaters, their doors flung open to the twilight. Men with powdered faces and powdered wigs and red smiles stood along the street, conjuring flower-laden trees, tiny suns, and miniature dancers who whirled in midair, all in an effort to entice people into the various theaters.

There seemed no lack of patrons. Many entered the theaters with their hats pulled low, while others had no fear of the lights and kept their heads uncovered, laughing boldly if they thought anyone was looking. There were even some women holding on to the arms of men, dressed in silk and glitter and so made up with powders and rouges that they were hardly less things of illusion than what the Siltheri conjured from light and air. One young woman smiled at Eldyn and dipped a finger into the cleft of her ample bosom. He turned away, letting the evening air cool his face.

He found himself near one of the illusionists: a young man nearly as made up as some of the women. He wove slender hands back and forth, and all at once a small unicorn pranced around him, white as milk, a trail of stars cascading from its pearlescent horn.

"You should buy a ticket and come in," the young Siltheri said. "You are sure to find a performance that pleases you at the Theater of the Unicorn." He made a circle with his fingers, stroking the shaft of the unicorn's horn.

Eldyn kept walking, leaving the light and music behind. He reached into his pocket and touched the disk of silver there: the coin that bore the faces of the sun and moon on its two sides. A compulsion came over him to go back to the theaters, to step inside their doors.

There was no time for diversions; he had business of the greatest importance to attend to. Eldyn squinted at signs in the failing light. He could only hope they were still there, that they had not yet gone out for the evening.

At last he found Inslip Lane, nearly at the very end of Durrow Street where it met the wall of the Old City. The odor of the river spilled over the wall; mosses flourished on the stones. He turned down the lane, which soon reached a dead end. He peered at the houses in the sputtering light of a streetlamp. At last he found the numbers painted on a door. A breath of relief escaped him—a light glowed through the panes of the window.

Eldyn rapped on the door, hoping he was not disturbing them. There was no response, so he knocked again. As he did, the door swung open.

The scene he beheld astonished him so greatly that for a moment he could not move. A woman of considerable girth, her frowsy hair spilling out of her goodwife's bonnet, was rummaging through the drawers of a cabinet. Such was her muttering and the racket she was making with the drawers that she must not have heard his knocking. However, a gust of air rushed through the open door, causing the candle on the table to flicker and flare, and she turned around with a gasp.

Taking her for a thief, Eldyn sprang forward and seized her by the wrist, intending to hold her while he called out for a constable. However, she howled and railed as if he were murdering her and jerked her hand with such surprising force that he was obliged to release her, upon which she snatched up an andiron from the hearth and brandished it at him.

"Off with you!" the woman shouted. "Saints mark me, I'll not let another steal from me this day!"

These words so baffled Eldyn that he was forced to consider that he had misread the situation, that perhaps this was not the right house. So he raised his hands, as seemed prudent given her weapon and her apparent willingness to use it, and explained his situation. He had come looking for two respectable men, Mr. Sarvinge and Mr. Grealing, on a matter of business; he had thought this was their house.

"No, this is *my* house," she answered him. Her face had been marred by pox, but he was forced to admit it did not have an evil look to it. "I am the landlady here."

He asked if she had ever seen Mr. Sarvinge and Mr. Grealing; he described their general appearance.

"Oh, aye, I know them well enough. The one skinny as a stick, and the other as round as a puddle of oil. And if I saw either of them, I would dash their heads in." The andiron drooped in her grip. "But I don't doubt I'll never see either of them again. And I warrant you will neither, if that was your hope."

An ill feeling came over him. Forgetting the length of iron she held in her hand, he stepped off the threshold. "You're mistaken. I have business with them."

"Aye, and so do I! They owe me ten regals in rent, they do. Kept promising me they'd have it for me. 'Just another day, missus. Just give us one more day.' They swore to Eternum and back they'd pay me. Now swearing is all I have." She let out a curse, then dropped the andiron, reached into the drawer, and pulled out a fistful of papers. "A fine pair of talkers they were. But words is all they had to trade. I'll never get my coin out of them. And neither will you, if they owed you anything. Sure as a long umbral is dark, they're halfway to Torland by now."

She threw the papers at Eldyn. They swarmed to the floor, and one landed on the table before him. It was a printed certificate of investment for a trading company to the New Lands. He sagged against the table.

"But we had business . . ."

The landlady snorted. "The only business those two had was swindling folk. If you gave them anything, you'd have as soon given it to the illusionists down the street for all you'll get in return."

With that she snatched up the candle, set her bonnet straight, and marched through the door, leaving Eldyn alone in the gloom.

# CHAPTER TWELVE

T FIRST THERE had been good reason to hope the situation was not in any way serious.

Miss Lockwell was hardly the first young lady to have fainted at a party. It was agreed by all that the evening had offered more stimulation than she could have been accustomed to. The wine, the presence of so many important personages, the general grandness of everything had all worked to overwhelm her. She was carried to a bed upstairs and the doctor summoned.

"It is the fault of fashion," Lady Marsdel proclaimed to those who remained in the parlor. "To be considered stylish, a young woman's gown must squeeze the breath out of her and not leave room for two bites of food. Soon ladies everywhere will be so beautiful that they'll never be seen at all, swooning before they can leave their rooms for want of air and nourishment."

A message was dispatched to Whitward Street, so that Mrs. Lockwell might not wonder at her daughter's failure to return. The note expressed the conviction that it was the most minor of conditions; Mrs. Lockwell could certainly expect her daughter's return tomorrow.

Mrs. Baydon, feeling a keen distress for her new friend, sat with her for many hours, as did the doctor, who held all manner of salts and acrid-smelling potions under her nose. However, all such efforts failed to induce consciousness, and by the end of the umbral a fever had come upon her. The doctor called for cool cloths; he bled her arm into a silver bowl. Dawn found her pallid, her eyes shut, her breathing swift and shallow.

At breakfast the doctor spoke with Lady Marsdel. The situation was dire; the mother must be called for at once. After writing the unhappy letter on behalf of her husband's aunt, Mrs. Baydon dashed off another missive—a note to Mr. Rafferdy.

He had just been rising after what he indulged himself in thinking had been a wretched night. However, upon reading Mrs. Baydon's note, all thought of the previous dozen hours vanished, and he was dressed and out the door before his carriage was ready—a fact that gave both his man and his driver some cause for wonderment. He arrived at Fairhall Street nearly simultaneously with Mrs. Lockwell, and he could hear her voice ringing out even as he set foot in the door.

"My poor daughter!" came the mother's cries. "She was out in that dreadful rain yesterday, I hardly know why. A horrible storm it was, stirring up all sorts of vile mists and humors, I am sure. I told her she must rest, that she would catch something dreadful if she didn't keep to her bed. But she was all aflutter about the party. Coming here meant the world to her, though I dread to say it might cost her the world in the end!"

Rafferdy entered the front hall to witness the end of this speech. "Oh, Mr. Rafferdy!" Mrs. Lockwell exclaimed at the sight of him, but after that she was overcome by her distress.

Lord Baydon took her arm and led her to a chair. "There, there, madam," he said. And, unable to think of anything else that might help, he attempted to lend his words all the greater efficacy by repeating them. "I say, there, there."

Water was fetched, and one of Lady Marsdel's fans for air, and the two elements revived Mrs. Lockwell enough that she was able to follow Mrs. Baydon upstairs. The doctor started up after, but Rafferdy touched his arm, speaking quietly with him at the foot of the staircase.

"How serious is it?" he asked.

"It is very serious, Mr. Rafferdy. I cannot make light of the young lady's condition. The fever came upon her with great speed and force."

"What will you do to treat it?"

"I fear I can do no more than I already have. Now the thing must run its course. It lies only in her power to break the fever now, and in God's."

"But how long will it be before she recovers?"

The doctor gave him a stern look. "Mr. Rafferdy, it is not a matter of when she will recover. Rather, it is a matter of whether she will recover at all. As for the answer to that, we can do nothing but wait."

At that moment Rafferdy felt a sort of fear he had never in his life known before. So strong was the feeling, and so entirely novel to him, that he was forced to sit, put a hand to his brow, and try to fathom what it was that had come over him.

Of course he had felt fear before. He had experienced all the usual childish horrors: of the dark, of strangers, of being lost. There had been one terrifying experience when he had been chased by one of his father's hounds that had turned feral.

As a man he had known the fear of losing, the fear of discovery, and the fear of not getting everything he wished. But this new dread that owned him now was different from all those. There was no threat of any harm to himself, yet his hands trembled as they had on the day he had shrunk against the stable wall as the slavering hound prowled toward him. His father's stablemaster had brought the dog down with a rifle shot. It had collapsed at his feet, dead. Only this time there was nothing to shoot at, and it was not for himself that he was afraid.

And that was what was so different about it. Even as he realized this, his shaking ceased. An urgency rose in him, a desire to make himself useful.

"Are you well, Mr. Rafferdy?" Mrs. Baydon said, for she had returned from upstairs. "Your color is very high."

"I must see if I can be of aid," he said, leaping to his feet.

He made as if for the stairs, but she held him back. "Only her mother and Dr. Mercham can be with her now. If you wish to be a help, then stay here and give us the benefit of your conversation, so that we do not all sit here and stare and become morose. There is nothing *we* can do except wait, and the more lively we can make the hours, the more swiftly *they* will pass."

He gripped his hat in his hands. "I should have been here last night."

"I agree. You are awful for not having come. Yet you can hardly think what happened is *your* fault. While I have no doubt your presence has at times caused some to feel discomfort, I am equally certain it has never been the case that your absence has caused anyone to fall ill. Besides, I can assure you that she had a wonderful time."

Rafferdy looked at her. "Did she really?" The thought of her there, moving about Lady Marsdel's parlor, brightening it with her presence in a way mere candles could not, gave him cause to smile. "I am certain she was the prettiest creature in the room."

Mrs. Baydon arched an eyebrow. "Well, *one* of the prettiest, I might presume to think. Though I begin to think that some glances, had they been in attendance, would have been only for her."

Despite Mrs. Baydon's hopes that Rafferdy would entertain them, they made for a dreary party. Lady Marsdel continued to expound upon the evils of current fashion, while her brother offered every belief that it was no more than a trifle of a cold and that Miss Lockwell would be down at any moment, wanting a ball to dance at, for that was all any young woman ever wanted.

"My father-in-law can always be counted upon for optimism," Mrs. Baydon whispered to Rafferdy.

"Indeed," he said, flipping the pages of a book he was not reading, "Lord Baydon is remarkable in that quality. If confronted with the loss of all his worldly fortune, he would profess his belief that he would surely stumble upon a halfpenny in the street before long, so there could be no cause for worry."

Mrs. Baydon began to laugh but stifled the sound at a snap of Lady Marsdel's fan.

At last, as the middle of that middling but interminable-seeming lumenal approached, the doctor and Mrs. Lockwell came down. She leaned upon his arm and, despite her plumpness, appeared somehow thin, or rather, faded.

Rafferdy was the first to his feet. "How is she?"

"There is little change," Mercham said. "The fever has not broken."

"I dread I must impose upon your hospitality further, your ladyship," Mrs. Lockwell said to Lady Marsdel in a faint tone. "It is terrible that I must ask such a thing of you, but she must be allowed to stay."

The doctor agreed. "Her situation is precarious. She cannot be moved. However, for the present I would suggest everyone keep from that part of the house to avoid any risk of contagion."

This advice was readily agreed upon.

"Lily and Rose!" Mrs. Lockwell exclaimed, becoming suddenly animated. "What if they are not well? I must go to them. Only I dare not leave my poor Ivy."

Rafferdy tossed down his book. "I will fetch them here, madam. My carriage is outside. That is, if that is acceptable to you, your ladyship." He added this last belatedly, with a nod toward Lady Marsdel.

"Far be it from me to decree to you how things should go in my own house, Mr. Rafferdy. It seems doctors and sons of cousins can do quite well at ordering my affairs." She fed a bit of cake to the puff of dog beside her, a thing as fringed and frilled as the pillow on which it sat. "But of course you must go. We cannot expect Mrs. Lockwell's motherly attentions to endure being so divided for long." She hesitated. "There are only the two of them, didn't you say?"

"Indeed, your ladyship, only two," Mrs. Lockwell said, brightening. "And each as sweet and pretty as their eldest sister, I am sure you will agree!"

"I will reserve my judgment of their sweetness and prettiness until I meet them." She looked at Rafferdy. "Go, then, and be back within an hour, or I shall be vexed. We will suffer all manner of tedium while you are gone."

Rafferdy was certain he had added little if any amusement to the proceedings; however, he was forced to revise his appraisal of this. For upon his return an hour later, the two younger Miss Lockwells in tow, he found the party in the sitting room even more dour than when he left it.

Lily and Rose were presented to Lady Marsdel. It was an experience that left Rose bereft of the capacity for any sort of expression, while Lily bestowed a theatrical curtsy upon her ladyship.

"Well, you are neither of you so pretty as your sister," Lady Marsdel pronounced after examining them both, "but your height is good, and your complexions. You are both tolerably pretty girls."

Rose at last managed a curtsy and hurried to a corner of the room, but Lily appeared aghast as she slouched off. Rafferdy could not help trading a smile with Mrs. Baydon.

"I suspect," he murmured to her, "that being merely tolerably pretty is something the youngest Miss Lockwell finds quite intolerable."

Mrs. Baydon agreed. "However, while my aunt's words might be unwelcome, they aren't untrue. Both are handsome girls, in that plain, solid way of the gentry. No doubt they will each do fine, in their own way. But they do not compare to Miss Ivoleyn Lockwell."

"You have my agreement on that!" Rafferdy said.

Mrs. Baydon regarded him. "Yes, I suspected I would."

DUSK CAME, AND still there was no change in the patient's condition. Lord Baydon had returned to Vallant Street with Mr. Baydon, and Lady Marsdel had retired to her chambers. Lily had occupied the afternoon by playing the pianoforte, and the dreary airs she pounded out had done little to lift the atmosphere of gloom. At some point Rafferdy heard the doctor and Mrs. Baydon whispering; Mercham had asked if she knew a priest who might be summoned if there was need.

These words brought a kind of madness over Rafferdy. He could not stop pacing; he felt if he ceased moving, the darkness that nipped at his heels would overtake him, like the hound that had chased him so long ago. As he paced, he twisted the ring on his right hand. His visit yesterday to Mr. Mundy's shop off Greenly Circle had been pointless. The little toad of a man had only cackled with glee when Rafferdy demanded that he remove the ring.

It was not within any power of *his* to remove it, the wretched fellow had said. If the ring had no present owner, it might be tried on and removed at will, but once the thing was bought and claimed—or in this case, once it was bestowed and accepted—it could be removed only by the most powerful enchantments. Or by the death of the owner. And, Mr. Mundy assured him, the former often resulted in the latter.

When Rafferdy demanded to know who had bought the ring, Mundy repeated that his customers received the utmost discretion. Not that Rafferdy needed confirmation; that Mr. Bennick had bought it and sent it to him he could not have been more certain.

But why? That was a mystery that was not as easily answered. Had Bennick really done it to punish him for following that day? It seemed an elaborate and expensive way to torment someone so little known to him, and for so small a slight.

He had stayed up all night, drinking whiskey until his head ached, tormented. Each time he looked at the ring, the blue gem seemed to stare back at him like a hideous, mocking eye.

A commotion on the stairs brought him out of this miserable reverie. It was the doctor; he had come down and was speaking to Mrs. Baydon. Rafferdy hurried toward them.

"It has passed," Mrs. Baydon said with a smile. "Her fever has broken."

"The worst is over now," Mercham said, "but she is still very weak. I must return to her."

The doctor left them, and Rafferdy sagged against the newel post.

"But what is wrong, Mr. Rafferdy?" Mrs. Baydon said as the doctor left them. "By your expression, I would hardly think you glad at the news."

Rafferdy could only shake his head. Sometimes relief was more unbearable than worry.

"Come, let us tell the others," Mrs. Baydon said. She took his hand, then frowned as she lifted it. "But what's this awful ring you're wearing? I can hardly bear to look at it."

"It's the latest fashion," he said, and before she could inquire more, he led her to the parlor to deliver the glad news.

MISS LOCKWELL REMAINED at the house on Fairhall Street for the next quarter month. While her fever had passed, Dr. Mercham would not permit her removal until her strength was sufficiently restored.

Mrs. Baydon spent many hours with Miss Lockwell, amusing her with talk and bringing flowers from the garden, for her charge wanted greatly for being out of doors. For his part, Rafferdy visited her every day—twice on long lumenals—and read to her from a book of Tharosian epics during one particularly long umbral.

"For a man who reads so little, you read very well," she told him as he turned a page. She sat in a chair by the fireplace, wrapped in a shawl. "I don't know why you don't read more often."

"What use is there in doing something one is already good at? The practice can bring no possible improvement."

"It is said there is pleasure in doing something one excels at."

"Which is precisely why you will so often find me doing nothing at all."

She laughed, the action bringing color to her cheeks. By then she was spending much of her time in an upstairs parlor that was favored with afternoon sun; it was there he paid her his visits. He liked to imagine her condition always improved in those first few minutes after he entered the room. It was a vanity, perhaps, though hardly his only one.

"You are very dutiful in your charge, Mr. Rafferdy," Lady Marsdel told him one evening at supper. "It is admirable of you. But you seem to think we are incapable of seeing to the needs of one rather smallish young woman."

It took him a moment to formulate a reply. It was just that he felt a responsibility, he said, having been the one to invite her. What sort of proper gentleman would he be if he abandoned her?

"But she is in no way abandoned!" Mrs. Baydon protested. "That she could be looked after with more concern is not possible were she in her own home. Besides, I think I have earned a claim to Miss Lockwell myself. She is *my* friend, you know. I am sure I have spent more time with her than you. And," she added with an arch look, "since when was it a very particular concern of yours to be a proper gentleman?"

That was a question, Rafferdy was forced to admit, for which he had no answer.

THE NEXT DAY Miss Lockwell was deemed fit enough to come downstairs for a few hours and engage in the society of the household.

"But I cannot possibly," she said when Mrs. Baydon brought her the news. "I have already imposed upon the hospitality of her ladyship in the most unimaginable way."

"It is my aunt herself who said you should come down," Mrs.

Baydon said. "So there can be no imposition, and you can have no reason not to come. If your spirits allow, that is."

"Of course they do," Rafferdy said, taking her arm and leading her to the stairs before she could mount any further protest.

It was soon clear the change in scenery was just what she needed. Her eyes were clear, and she smiled often. Despite this improvement, she seemed determined to do no more than sit quietly and listen to the conversation of the others. Rafferdy made several attempts to provoke her participation, but she resisted all such efforts.

"I've heard that Viscount Argendy is to give another masque," Mrs. Baydon said. "Though I cannot imagine I shall be allowed to attend."

"You cannot imagine it, yet you have brought it up," Mr. Baydon said over his broadsheet. "What a curious situation. I would have thought it impossible to speak of something one cannot even imagine. How about you, Rafferdy? Can you perform such a singular feat?"

"I cannot imagine you will ever smile while reading an issue of *The Comet*," he said, at which Mrs. Baydon clapped her hands.

"You see, Mr. Baydon?" she said to her husband. "It is not so impossible a thing, after all. Though I suppose it *is* impossible I will ever go to a masque. And by all reports the last was such a success! It was said they made the interior of his house to look like a garden, with fountains and trees and fauns running about. Next time he promises to have twice the number of illusionists."

This news sent Lady Marsdel's fan into a fit of fluttering. "It is bad enough that those with no sense of propriety or shame slink down to Durrow Street to view the work of those indecent illusionists. But to invite them into the very homes of superior society to work their mischief—it is intolerable!"

"But it's *not* indecent," Mrs. Baydon protested. "How can it be, when it's the fashion? Wouldn't you agree, Miss Lockwell?"

Ivy looked up from the book in her lap, her expression startled. With everyone looking to her, she was at last forced to speak. "I am sure my opinion on the subject cannot matter."

"You seem a sensible girl, Miss Lockwell," Lady Marsdel said. "Why should your thoughts not be heard? I demand you speak them aloud!"

Ivy hesitated, then shut her book. "I do not disagree there might be pleasure in seeing something so novel as a performance by illusionists." She smiled at Mrs. Baydon. "I cannot believe exposure to such things, for a mind that is truly good, could really cause lasting harm.

However, for me, any enjoyment that might be derived from such a spectacle would be outweighed by the knowledge that my actions have brought discredit to myself and thereby to those to whom I am most intimately attached—that is, my father, mother, and sisters, whom I admire and love. So I could not go. Any wish I might have for myself, however enticing, cannot be indulged if it brings about something I would not wish for *them*."

"Very well spoken, Miss Lockwell!" Lord Baydon proclaimed. "I could not have said it better myself."

Indeed, it was difficult for Rafferdy to imagine Lord Baydon could have said it at all.

"Really, Miss Lockwell," Mrs. Baydon said, "had I known that you would so eloquently remove all chances of my gambit succeeding, I would have thought twice before seeking your opinion."

Ivy's expression was one of dismay. "It was in no way my intention to cause you any distress, Mrs. Baydon. If I have done so, please forgive me. My opinion was asked, and I gave it as truthfully as I could. In no way did I mean it as any sort of comparison with yourself."

"Now, Mrs. Baydon, you've given her a fright," Rafferdy said, keeping his voice light but feeling a note of real concern. Ivy's color had gone pale again. "She cannot know what a teasing thing you are, not as I do."

"But of course I'm teasing!" Mrs. Baydon said, and hurried over to Miss Lockwell, taking her hand and assuring her that she was in no way upset or affronted. At last Miss Lockwell was forced to concede that she was as sincere now as she had been satirical before.

"You have to know that we say outrageous things sometimes, but you mustn't think anything of it." Mrs. Baydon smiled. "Besides, no one could ever think it *your* intention to cause harm. I am sure you are incapable of it."

"Now you will make a saint of me!" Miss Lockwell protested. "I am not sure this is in any way less teasing. Indeed, I think it more so. I would rather be wrongly accused of doing ill than be thought to never do ill at all. For when I topple from that high pedestal, as I inevitably must, it will make the fall all that much further."

"Nonsense, Miss Lockwell," Rafferdy said seriously, "for in that case you have only to spread your wings and fly like any angel."

"Here, here!" Lord Baydon said, and clapped his hands.

Mrs. Baydon returned to the initial subject. "Well, I will do what is right. I won't attend Viscount Argendy's masque. I wish I could feel so virtuous a resignation as you display, Miss Lockwell. However, I warrant I am bound to be peevish. I allow that it would bring discredit for me to go, and so I must not. Yet I cannot help but think that going should not bring discredit at all."

"On that point I can offer no disagreement," Miss Lockwell said. "However, one cannot alter the world, so I suppose one is left with no choice but to alter oneself."

"We must give up our wishes, you mean."

"That may be so. Or perhaps . . ." She seemed to think about this. "Perhaps it simply means we must seek them in a different manner, or in another place. If one door is closed to you, then look among all that are open. It may be that what you seek is through one."

"I doubt any of *them* will lead to a masque."

Miss Lockwell smiled. "No, I suppose not. But ask yourself: what is it that made you wish to attend the affair at the viscount's? Was it the performance itself? Or was it something else—the newness of it, or the chance to see something beautiful? Surely there are sights of beauty and novelty that *are* within your power to witness."

Once again Mrs. Baydon sighed, only this time it was an expression of amazement. "Miss Lockwell, I believe you are right. I *will* seek out such things—beautiful things. I feel hopeful of a sudden. You have quite deprived me of my peevishness and want for complaining."

"And for that, Miss Lockwell," Mr. Baydon said, folding down his broadsheet, "you have my gratitude."

A peculiar feeling came over Rafferdy, a kind of agreeable agitation. He wanted to speak, but he didn't know what to say. He wanted to move, but he didn't know where. What she had said fascinated him, but he had no idea if it gave him hope or a kind of irresistible dread. *One cannot alter the world, so one is left with no choice but to alter oneself.* A compulsion came over him to make himself anew. But into what?

He turned to address her. However, before he could think of something to say, Lady Marsdel gave her fan a beckoning flutter.

"Do come over here, Miss Lockwell. You have positioned yourself too far away. I would have you sit closer so my old ears need not strain."

The object of this speech dutifully rose. Rafferdy hurried forward to lend his arm.

"Is there something you wished to say to me, Mr. Rafferdy?" Miss Lockwell said softly as he led her across the parlor.

"Why do you ask?"

"You were treating me to a rather odd look just now."

"You are a rather odd creature, Miss Lockwell. You claim you are not utterly good by nature, yet everything you do demonstrates otherwise. Your actions are at odds with your words."

"I can only say that it is not my intention to confound. But I will also say that you equally confound *me*."

"How can that be? I am sure I am the simplest thing in existence."

"On the contrary. While you claim to be utterly thoughtless, everything you do indicates that the opposite is true. In fact, I doubt there is a man alive who thinks more than you, Mr. Rafferdy."

She sat down beside Lady Marsdel, and for the next hour he could only watch her and wonder what she had meant by *that*.

OVER THE NEXT several days, Miss Lockwell's recovery continued apace. Indeed, her convalescence soon seemed a forgotten thing, and she was rarely given time to sit quietly in her room.

Her presence was needed at breakfast, for after listening just once to the specific proportions of lemon, milk, and honey, she was able to prepare Lady Marsdel's tea perfectly—something the servants had never been able to do properly despite repeated instruction. She was needed after breakfast as well to keep her ladyship company, because Mrs. Baydon could seldom be counted upon to offer interesting companionship at so early an hour. Mrs. Baydon in turn wanted Miss Lockwell on long afternoons to play cards, and on shorter lumenals there was increased competition for her presence, as Lady Marsdel liked to have her read to her for an hour or two before they dined, her ladyship's eyes no longer being up to the task.

"You do read nicely, Miss Lockwell," Lady Marsdel said one evening. "You have no impulse to insert your own comments or observations. You are content to defer to the wisdom of the author at choosing the best words. Quite unlike Mr. Rafferdy, who turns everything into a comedy. You cannot trust him at all when he reads. He once tried to convince me that a book of famous members of Assembly contained an entire chapter pertaining to monkeys."

"Well, if it didn't, it should have," Mr. Rafferdy said to Miss Lockwell in a conspiratorial tone.

"In fact, your ladyship," she said when she no longer appeared in danger of laughing, "I have found Mr. Rafferdy to be an excellent reader."

A flock of peacocks quivered in her ladyship's hand. "Indeed! I find your words incredible, Miss Lockwell. But I know that, unlike some, what *you* say is to be trusted. Yet it is very curious."

Evenings were the busiest time for Miss Lockwell; after dinner, in the parlor, everyone seemed to want her company and conversation—though the latter usually had to be coaxed from her, at least when she was the center of attention. However, Rafferdy found that if he could lead her aside to a secluded corner, she became talkative, even animated. He would spend as much time as he could conversing with her, until Lady Marsdel's complaints that she could not hear what they were saying became too forceful to ignore.

It was during one of these times, when they sat together at the far end of the parlor as a protracted twilight hung suspended outside the window, that she noticed the ring he wore. He grimaced, twisting the hideous thing on his finger, pulling at it out of habit; but of course it did not come off.

Rafferdy thought he would make up some story about it—how he had lost a bet with Eldyn Garritt, perhaps, and was forced to wear the ugly thing as a sort of punishment. Instead, he found the truth spilling out of him: how he had followed Mr. Bennick that day; how it was a magician's ring; how he could not remove it from his hand.

All the while he spoke, her eyes grew brighter, and finally she said, "Then you *are* a magician, Mr. Rafferdy!"

He winced as if she had struck him or had called his coat very handsome for one of *last* year's styles. "On the contrary, I deny it utterly. I have no wish to put on airs. Well, not *that* sort of air."

"But it is not an air, Mr. Rafferdy. This cannot lie." She gestured to the ring. "I have read many—that is, I have read something about magicians, and they are always described as wearing rings that denote their House of descent. And at the party, Mr. Bennick told us that he knew you to be descended of one of the seven Old Houses."

If Rafferdy had needed any further proof of who had sent him the ring, now he had it.

"Mr. Bennick, you say?" He looked at the ring. The blue gem caught the light, winking and leering at him. "Well, I do not know his motives, but power is nothing I crave or seek. I have no wish to be any sort of magician."

"My father was a magician," she said.

He regarded her with a new understanding. That explained *her* interest in magick.

"I do not think it was power he sought. I believe, rather, that it was knowledge. He used to have a ring like that."

"Used to, you say. But Mr. Mundy told me that, without a powerful enchantment, a ring like this does not come off while the magician lives."

"My father is no longer a magician. He has not worn the ring since he became ill years ago." She looked out the window, and he could see the rapid flutter of her pulse in her throat.

They sat quietly for several minutes. Again he regarded the thing on his hand, and it occurred to him that Mr. Bennick did not wear any sort of ring. But he had been a magician; Mundy had said so. Surely he had once worn a ring like this, which meant they could be gotten off. Which also meant an unpleasant task lay before Rafferdy, but one he could not avoid. He must speak to Mr. Bennick as soon as possible.

"I always wished I could do magick," she said, still gazing out the window. She smiled, though it was a rueful expression. "I've even tried to work spells, but to no effect. The practice of magick is for men, as are so many things in this world. Whether it is right or fair is beside the point; I could no sooner be a magician than Mrs. Baydon or my sister Lily could attend a masque without garnering discredit."

Now she turned to him, and color rose in her cheeks as an excitement came over her. "But you, Mr. Rafferdy. You *are* a magician. Or, that is, you could be if you chose to make a study of it. And how I wish you would become a master of it! For if you did, then you could be the one to bring him some relief, to help him at last."

It was only after she spoke these last words that she appeared to notice what he had become aware of the moment it happened: she had placed her left hand over his right. He did not move; he dared not.

"Forgive me," she said, pulling her hand back and casting her eyes downward. "It is not my place to tell you how you should occupy your time."

He could still feel the warmth of her hand. "Of whom do you speak, Miss Lockwell?" he said at last. "Who would you have me help?"

He detected a quivering about her countenance. Nor could it be ascribed to her recent illness; she was all but recovered. It was something else that caused her distress, or rather caused her to hope. She started to speak, but at that moment Lady Marsdel called out to Rafferdy, complaining that he was being quite selfish with Miss Lockwell's company.

This pronouncement could not be ignored. They rose; he gave her his arm. Her hand alighted on it as light as a bird, and they joined the others.

❧

AT LAST THE doctor pronounced Miss Lockwell well enough to return home.

"I will tell her the news at once," Mrs. Baydon said. "I am sure it will be a great relief to her."

"A relief?" Lady Marsdel said. "What cause can Miss Lockwell have to be relieved? Surely it has been no hardship for *her* to stay here. Nor can I imagine her mother has suffered in any way with her gone, what with two other daughters to attend her. It is *we* who shall suffer. Our society has been altered to accommodate her unexpected presence, but now it shall be altered again with her removal. It is all most inconvenient.

"I do say, Miss Lockwell," Lady Marsdel said, when the subject of this speech was brought into the room and given the news, "will you not stay awhile longer? Your mother cannot possibly need you."

Miss Lockwell gave many thanks for all the kindness that had been showed her. However, she could not be prevailed upon to stay. Rafferdy offered to deliver her to Whitward Street, but Mrs. Baydon interjected that she had already arranged for her father-in-law's coach.

"The seats are larger, and it's very warm inside," Mrs. Baydon said. "The lumenals have been so short lately, and there is a chill in the air."

It was just as well, Rafferdy decided. Better to make his good-byes here, where she was not yet distracted by the attentions of her mother and sisters. Only, Mrs. Baydon and Lady Marsdel and Lord Baydon all hovered about. In the end there was no chance to do anything but press her hand, a gesture from which she quickly withdrew. But her glance did not so swiftly leave him, and he liked to imagine it was his face to which her last look was directed before the coach moved away down Fairhall Street.

"I shall miss her company very much," Mrs. Baydon said. "She is such a sweet thing. And, as I have noted, she presents herself exceptionally well for one of her class. I would go so far as to say, if given a proper dress, she would not stand out at any party we might throw here."

"You are mistaken, Mrs. Baydon," Rafferdy said. "I am certain Miss Lockwell would indeed stand out at such an affair. There can be no doubting, if she were properly attired, that everyone in attendance would think her the prettiest thing they had ever laid eyes upon."

He spoke these words with unusual feeling. Had he been of less distracted mind, he might have thought twice upon noticing the startled look Mrs. Baydon gave him.

RAFFERDY WAS IN a fine mood all the way back to Warwent Square. His humor was so good that he chose to go on foot, and every little garden that he passed, every splash of color that he knew would be pleasing to *her* eye, pleased his as well.

However, upon arriving home, his spirits reversed. His rooms were small and dim. He meant to catch up on correspondence and other business, but he had no sooner picked up his pen than a compulsion came upon him to leave, and he quit his apartments after being there hardly an hour.

He thought it was his intention to go to his club, to enjoy some brandy and conversation with other young gentlemen who, while worth a great deal of money, had little of any worth to say—that is, to have a drink with his peers. However, when he opened his mouth, it was a different direction he gave his driver, and soon the cabriolet passed through the Lowgate, jouncing along the grim streets of Waterside.

When he exited the cabriolet, he found himself on a drab but not entirely unwholesome lane, in front of a shabby inn. The sign over the door advertised *The Golden Loom*.

It had occurred to him as he left Warwent Square that he had not seen Eldyn Garritt in half a month. It had not been by any intention that this was the case. Rafferdy had been cross with him at their last meeting, he recalled; however, it had been mere noise and air, like everything Rafferdy ever said. Garritt had to have known *that*.

Only no letters had come from Garritt. Perhaps he had been upset after all, the silly man. And Rafferdy had been preoccupied, first with the wretched affair of the ring, and then with Miss Lockwell's situation. Well, he was here now, and if Garritt was still fool enough to be angry with him, Rafferdy would keep buying the punch until he won forgiveness, or at least until the both of them fell into a stupor. He spoke to the innkeeper, who led him upstairs. He rapped upon the door.

It was not Garritt who answered but rather his sister. Rafferdy had never met her, but her identity could not be doubted, as her resemblance to her brother was strong. She was a rather lovely thing, he thought at first, a young woman of about eighteen. She said that her brother was not in, then shuffled to the window and sat, staring outside at some beleaguered stick of a tree. It was only through great effort that he prized a few more words out of her. She did not know where her brother was. When did she expect him? But she never expected him anymore; he was ever out until odd hours, and she cared to know nothing about what he did.

What a sullen creature! Any beauty she possessed was marred by her listless air and pouting expression.

"When he returns, you will tell him I came," he said, but she only shrugged, so he went to the table in the corner, rummaged until he found a scrap of paper, and scratched out a note for Garritt. He started to give it to the sister, then thought better of it and left it on the table.

By the time he returned home, a letter had come from Vallant Street, inviting him to dine with the Baydons. He wrote back, declining. They could imagine he had much business to catch up on.

However, the correspondence of the last several days remained unopened on the desk. His affairs were neglected. Over the next several days he did not go out. He did not even bother to dress, instead wandering around in his gown, eating hardly anything but drinking a great deal of whiskey.

A cloud of misery settled over him, such as he had never known before. Everything that usually held amusement for him now seemed dull and pointless. It was impossible to imagine how he had ever derived pleasure out of shopping for clothes, or gambling, or attempting to win applause from stupid people at stupid parties, as if such recognition was something to be admired rather than scorned. At any given moment he had no idea whether it was night or day; the umbrals and lumenals flickered by.

Each time a note arrived he checked the address to see if it was from Garritt; none of them was. Vallant Street invited him twice again, and Fairhall Street did not ask for but rather *required* his presence. He ignored these summonses. What pleasure could he bring to or derive from such affairs when the only thing he wished to behold would not be there? Why go to a dinner where he could not whisper behind his napkin and make her laugh? Why go to a party when he could not walk about the room and marvel at the sight of her upon his arm? He could see no purpose in going anywhere where Miss Lockwell was not.

So instead, he must go to her.

The shroud of fog lifted, and everything was bright and sharp-edged. How was it he had not thought of it before? Never in his life had he denied himself anything he had wished for, so why had he denied himself *this*?

There could be only one logical answer to that question. He had not known until that moment what it was that he wanted. Perhaps he never really had known. The clothes, the gambling, the parties—perhaps all of it had been a substitute for this one unknown thing.

Only it was unknown no longer. Rafferdy stood, filled with a sensation more intoxicating than drink had ever imparted him. He felt positively *eager*. He found his man and discovered it was the afternoon of a middling lumenal. Good, he thought, as he dressed and put on his best coat; it would be a perfect time, and they could have no other engagements. He told his man to summon the driver. He would go to Whitward Street; he would see Miss Lockwell. And he would confess how profoundly he both admired and loved her.

He started to examine his appearance in the looking glass, then turned away. *Her* eyes were the only mirror that mattered to him now. He hurried down the stairs and into the front hall. A clatter of hooves sounded outside; the carriage had been brought around. Whistling a cheery tune, he took his hat, then threw open the door.

A carriage was indeed parked in the street before his house, but it was not his cabriolet. It was a four-in-hand: a large and grand conveyance, black with gilt trim, led by a handsome brace of chestnut horses.

Rafferdy's momentum carried him to the base of the steps, and there he stuttered to a halt. His manservant had opened the carriage door and was helping a gray-haired man disembark. The older fellow limped, leaning on a cane, his left foot wrapped in a bandage. All the same, he carried himself in an upright manner. His progress was slow up the walk, but Rafferdy could only stand and watch him come.

"Were you going somewhere, Dashton?" the gray-haired man asked as he drew near. "You have a look as if you were just leaving."

Rafferdy could not help glancing off down the street, and he fingered the hat in his hands.

"You need not answer. I see it is indeed the case. I suppose my arrival must keep you from some pressing engagement or lively affair. However, I trust you will not begrudge me this interruption in deference to the distance I have come." The gray-haired man had come to a halt before him. "Well, aren't you going to greet me?"

For a wild moment Rafferdy's compulsion was to dash down the street like a madman. Then the light went out of the world, as if a cloud had passed before the sun. Only the sky was a clear, cold blue. He turned to the older gentleman and gave a bow.

"Greetings, sir," he spoke. "You are very welcome here."

"Am I indeed?" Lord Rafferdy said. "I imagine you will feel differently once we have talked, for it is time we addressed your future. It can wait no longer. Nor can I. For hours I sat in the coach, yet after even this brief walk to the step I must sit again. Let us go in."

MINUTES LATER FOUND them in the parlor. Rafferdy's man had brought them brandy and the tobacco box, as well as a stool on which Lord Rafferdy had settled his bandaged foot.

"The door will still be there when we are done speaking, I quite assure you," Lord Rafferdy said.

Abashedly, Rafferdy realized he had indeed been hovering at the door, one foot in the parlor and one foot out. He crossed the room and slouched into a chair—then leaped back out of it as if the seat had scalded him. He could not bear to be still.

"I prefer to stand," he said.

"A standing man sees the dawn sooner, as the Murghese say." Lord Rafferdy took a sip of brandy. "I was not much one for sitting myself when I was your age. I liked nothing more than to be on the move. I suppose that was why I decided to serve as an officer in the royal army. I wanted to travel, to see the Northern Realms, the Principalities—even the deserts of the southern empire. But that was years ago. These days, the only traveling I do is sitting in a chair like this, with a book open before me."

"You traveled here," Rafferdy said.

"So I did."

"Can I ask what brought you to the city despite the great discomfort and trouble I know it can only cause? Why have you come, sir?"

"For the very same reason, I imagine, that you wish to leave."

Rafferdy frowned at his father. "I don't understand."

Lord Rafferdy's gaze went to the door. "I am told she is very pretty."

Rafferdy's legs no longer seemed capable of bearing him. He sank back into the chair.

"And I am given to understand her manner is excellent for one of her station," Lord Rafferdy went on.

*For one of any station!* Rafferdy wanted to say, but words were beyond him. How did his father know these things?

"From everything I have heard from my cousin, it is easy to understand how a young man might be charmed."

So his question was answered. Lady Marsdel must have written to him, urging him to the city. Rafferdy gripped the arms of his chair. "What is it you are trying to tell me, sir?"

Lord Rafferdy set down his glass, directing his solemn gaze toward his son. "Only what I have always told you—that your position in life confers many advantages, but also demands certain requirements. However, I did not come here to make a reprimand, if that's what you fear. That a young man's attentions should be captivated by a charming young woman is in no way out of the ordinary. And if her station is not exalted and her associations simple, that can serve only to make her own charms shine the brighter. Yet there comes a time when indulgence must be left behind and more-permanent commitments made. Nor is charm alone enough when considering such commitments. There are other ideas that must be considered, among them suitability, advantage, and duty to one's family."

Rafferdy hardly knew how to act. His own feelings had been revealed to himself just minutes ago, and now he was being told to abandon them. "And what of duty to myself, to my own wishes? What if I say I am ready to make a commitment, however *unsuitable* and of little *advantage* to my family. Am I to suppose, then, you will disown me—that if I do not do as I am told, you will deprive me of my name and my fortune and make of me a pauper?"

Lord Rafferdy shifted in his chair. "My own father made such threats to me once, the day I put on my regimental coat. He forbade me to serve in the army and told me if I did not remove the coat that he would remove me instead, that I would be a son to him no longer. His wrath was a terrible thing to behold. I saluted him and left Asterlane to lead my regiment."

Rafferdy was astonished. "*You* defied an order from your father?"

"So I did."

"Then he did not do what he said he would?"

"To whom would he have passed his estate, if not to me? I was his only son. As you are mine. All the same—even if you were not my only child—my hopes, my thoughts, my intentions still could not be so easily transferred to another. And if your behavior displeases me, is it not I who should be blamed? To punish you would prove nothing, save that I am not only a poor parent but also a smallish and spiteful man."

Rafferdy could not conceal his disbelief. "Then no matter what I choose, even if I should make a commitment to one whom you deem beneath me, you will not disown me?"

"No, I will not. You will always be my son, and any wife you take my daughter." His expression grew more somber yet. "However, just because I do not disown you does not mean that no one will. Others in society will not look favorably on such a match."

"I don't care what they think," Rafferdy said, and downed his brandy.

"That is a thing that is easy to say, I think, but not so easy to bear. I see a rather large heap of letters and invitations on the desk there, but you could expect that stack to dwindle until it was gone. Be assured that most, if not all, of the society you have enjoyed will turn its back upon you."

"It doesn't matter," he said, though a bit less certainly now. "I was going to decline those invitations anyway. I find those affairs boring."

"Then perhaps it will not be so ill for you. But remember that it is not only you who will be divided from society. Even as she is beneath the circles you moved in, she will be above those that were once her own. Every day she will be forced to suffer that isolation. Or, when in public, to bear the looks, the whispers, the coldness that others, out of disdain, are so able to project. Would you have her endure that for your own satisfaction?"

Rafferdy slumped back into the chair. A moment ago he had felt a kind of jubilant defiance. He had thought himself brave to flirt with the idea of defying his father. Yet his only consideration had been what he wanted for himself and what he feared his father would do. Never for a moment had he thought about what *she* might want, or what would be best for *her*. No, it had not been out of bravery he had thought to defy his father.

He set down his glass and held his hand to his brow.

"I think you understand," Lord Rafferdy said.

"Perfectly," Rafferdy said with a grimace. "You need deprive me of nothing, for society will do your work for you. How excellent it must be to take nothing yet receive everything you wish."

He had flung the words at his father, intending them to induce anger. Instead, his father's expression was one of sorrow.

"If you think I take pleasure in this, you are mistaken. Why should I not want to see you happily situated? It is yet my hope you will be, with one who is both charming *and* suitable. Regardless, it is not merely for society's sake that society's approval must be sought. There are other reasons why one should not draw unwanted attention to oneself."

These words struck through the grim fog that clouded Rafferdy's brain. He looked up at his father. "What do you mean?"

Lord Rafferdy glanced toward the window. "I was surprised you never asked me at Asterlane," he said at last.

"Asked you what?"

He turned his gaze back toward his son. "Why I have decided to enclose my lands."

"I thought you were . . ." Rafferdy shook his head. "But it doesn't matter. Now you are putting up walls, and you are like every other lord."

"Just so. For were I to follow my own wishes—as you would follow yours—and not enclose my lands, I must necessarily bear the scrutiny and attention of others. They would wonder why I chose not to do as they did; indeed, they would see it as a criticism of their own decisions. Their only choice would be to repudiate their actions or repudiate me—and the latter is far easier done than the former. However, even as you must not be separated from your society, I must not be separated from mine. A man who is like his peers can move freely among them, and there is work to be done—work that cannot be performed under the watchful eye of suspicion."

Rafferdy sat up in his chair. "What sort of work do you mean?" A strange feeling came over him, at once curious and dreading. "What business is it you do for the Crown?"

"How often in the past I have wished you would ask me that question!" Lord Rafferdy said with regret. "Yet now that you have shown interest, I find I cannot be forthcoming with you. But I will, when the time is right. Until then, I will say only that there is much to do, that serious matters lie before us—indeed, before all of Altania. All the more reason why it is better not to distance ourselves from society by our actions, not to separate us from those who might help us—or those who might . . ." He shook his head.

"Who might what?" Rafferdy said, his sense of dread sharpening.

But Lord Rafferdy said only, "Fashion and the expectations of others are not the only reasons I have chosen to enclose my lands around Asterlane. Soon there may be other needs for the safety of walls."

"I don't understand. What other needs?"

His father glanced again at the heap of letters and invitations on the table. "You have dwelled all your life in a world populated with light and music and the pleasurable company of others. Nor have I been so anxious as you perhaps think to remove you from such an existence. Yet have you never asked yourself what lies beyond the circle of illumination in which you dwell, out in the coldness, in the silence?"

"Never," Rafferdy said. "What can there be beyond what we know? For if we do not know it, it cannot exist. And if I want to hear stories of better worlds than this one, I'll go to a church and listen to the prattle of priests."

"It is not of better worlds that I speak," Lord Rafferdy said, looking at him now. "And the darkness is not so empty as you imagine. Think of attending a party at night, in a house brightly lit with candles. If we happen to glance out the window, we cannot see into the darkness or know what lies outside. Yet any out there in the dark can see inside to us."

Rafferdy could not fathom what these words meant. All the same, the hair on the back of his neck prickled, and once again he found he could not bear to sit still. He rose from the chair.

"Are you leaving, then?" his father asked.

Without even thinking of it, Rafferdy had moved to the door. Once again the urge came over him to rush out, to go as fast as possible to Whitward Street and present himself at her door. All his life he had indulged his every desire, but without any real satisfaction. It had all been whim, a craving for diversion no different than a hungering for food or a thirst for drink: base instincts, and meaningless. But to be with her—it was the first thing in his life he had ever truly *wanted*.

For a long moment Rafferdy gazed through the door. He breathed out, and could not help thinking it was some better part of him that was expelled with the air from his lungs. Then he turned around and crossed the room to his father.

"You said it is time to address my future, sir."

Lord Rafferdy looked up at him and nodded.

## CHAPTER THIRTEEN

IVY'S HOMECOMING WAS a joyful occasion. Her mother and sisters had quit Fairhall Street after that first night, once it was certain Ivy was out of danger. While notes had been frequently sent back and forth, they had not seen one another since that parting, and so there was much to tell on both sides. For Mrs. Lockwell's part, a quarter month's worth of exclamations had to be compressed into a short space. Ivy bore it all lightly, with many smiles; she could not remember a time when she had been so happy.

Rose was unusually talkative upon Ivy's arrival home. The wisteria was blooming, she said; she must show Ivy the queerest insect she had discovered in the garden, if it could be found again. There was a crack in the window on the second landing that caught the light in the most amazing way when the sun was setting. She had counted all the steps in the house again and was certain there was exactly one more than before.

"Do you think the house is growing taller?" Rose asked, her eyes going wide.

"Well, it *is* a magician's house," Ivy said.

Upon which Rose immediately began climbing the staircase to make her count again.

Lily forwent the melancholy air she had been affecting of late, Ivy was grateful to notice, and even played several songs on the pianoforte that did not require a minor key. After that she modeled an array of new ribbons and bonnets. Ivy gave each one dutiful appreciation and decided to worry later about the damage any purchases made in her absence had done to the household ledger.

"We must make a party," Lily proclaimed. "Even if it's just us, it will be a jolly affair. Mrs. Murch will make cakes. You can read from a play if you like—something dramatic. Rose can wear one of my new ribbons, while I will do a dance for us." She whirled around, ribbons fluttering.

Lily's idea was met with enthusiasm by all the denizens of the house. Even Mr. Lockwell seemed to come more to life with Ivy's homecoming. According to Mrs. Lockwell, he had refused to leave the attic since Ivy's departure. However, he allowed Ivy to lead him to his room, where Wilbern dressed him; and when she took his hand and guided him down to the parlor, he did not resist, though it had been years since he had descended from the uppermost floors.

Mrs. Lockwell came into the parlor, and when she saw him sitting there she stopped, tears springing to her eyes. Ivy thought she had made a mistake, that she should return Mr. Lockwell to his room; only then her mother brushed her cheeks and brought her husband a cake. She sat by him, feeding him little morsels and telling him all manner of foolish things—how she wanted to change the drapery, and put paper on the walls, and bring in more light—such as he used to listen to indulgently.

Lily danced, while Rose sat on the edge of the sofa, hardly daring to move for fear of disturbing the ribbons in her hair. Ivy, finding she had quite an appetite, ate several of the cakes herself. She thought to bring another to her father, but as she turned she saw that, while the rest of them were engaged, Mrs. Lockwell had taken his hand. She stroked it as she spoke to him in soft tones, the opposite of her normal utterances. Perhaps it was just the fading light catching his eyes, but it seemed he watched her, his face serene.

At last Lily wilted into a chair, while Ivy and Rose applauded with vigor; Mrs. Lockwell did the same, coming over to join them. On impulse Ivy took her mother's hands, then gazed at her sisters and at Mr. Lockwell, and her heart swelled inside her.

"I missed you all," she said. "I missed you all so much while I was gone. I never want to leave again. I can't bear the thought of it. I have spent more time away than should be allowed in a lifetime."

Mrs. Lockwell patted Ivy's cheek. "There, you are a good daughter,

Ivoleyn. I am sure you believe you speak the truth. But I don't doubt you will be of a different mind soon when a handsome man comes to take you away from us. It is we who shall miss you then."

"But I cannot imagine what you speak of," Ivy said with a laugh. "I can expect no such occurrence, I am sure."

"Well, you should expect it," Mrs. Lockwell said. "For I am a good judge of such things, and I am certain I am not mistaken when I say that Mr. Rafferdy means to propose to you."

Ivy was astonished. "I am sure you can have no direct knowledge of such a thing," she said, a bit breathless of a sudden. "Do not mistake a kindly manner and a genuine concern at the well-being of an acquaintance—of a friend, I might even go so far as to say—for something more than it is."

However, Mrs. Lockwell would not hear any argument on the subject. "Think what you wish, Ivoleyn, but you will see I am right soon enough. There is no gulf too great for true affection to bridge. One day—before this month is out, I should think—a carriage will arrive at our house, and Mr. Rafferdy inside it. And when that day comes, you will see that you are not, after all, so very sorry to leave us. Now," she exclaimed, "let us continue our party!"

They did, eating more, and dancing more, and playing a game of blindman's bluff, which gave them much amusement until Rose, unable to catch them despite the small size of the parlor, began to weep behind the blindfold. But her tears were mingled with laughter as Ivy and Lily went to her and took the scarf from her eyes, and she said, "There, I have found you both, after all." For which they embraced her.

It grew late. Mrs. Lockwell was nodding in her chair. Cassity had gone home, and Mrs. Murch and Wilbern had retired downstairs.

"See to your mother," she told her sisters, "and I will take Father to his room."

Ivy clasped Mr. Lockwell's hand and led him up the stairs. However, it was dark, and Ivy was forced to leave her father on the third landing and retreat downstairs for a candle.

"So, you have returned at last from your wanderings," he said as she came back up the stairs. His voice was solemn but with a keen note of interest to it. She had not heard him speak so clearly since he fell ill.

"I wasn't wandering," she said at last, thinking he had been addressing her. "I only went to get a candle."

He did not respond to her words, and as she drew near she saw he was not facing her but rather stood at the window looking out, his face tilted upward. She stood beside him and followed his gaze. Between two gables was a wedge of night sky. There, amid a handful of familiar stars, shone an interloper: a dull, ruddy spark. She had never seen it before yet knew it all the same; it could only be the new celestial body she had read about, the one that had been detected recently.

According to the reports, the new object in the sky had grown steadily brighter, but Ivy had not known it had become visible without the aid of ocular lenses. What its nature was, men of science were still debating, but most supposed it to be some kind of comet, despite its lack of a tail. While the stars around it danced and glittered, the new object in the sky emitted a dim but unwavering glow.

"What do you see, Father?" she asked, but he did not answer her. Instead, his hands moved before him, tracing circles and twisting about in an intricate dance whose purpose—if indeed it had one—was beyond her fathoming.

She set down the candle and put her hands over his, stilling them. "Come, Father," she said, and he followed her to his room. Outside, the red stranger watched from the sky.

⁂

THAT HER MOTHER could be right concerning Mr. Rafferdy's intentions was impossible. Each time Ivy considered it over those next days, the idea appeared only more absurd.

That he had seemed to enjoy their conversations, she conceded. That he was altogether agreeable and had gone out of his way to make himself amiable to her and her mother and sisters, she would not impugn. However, the significance of these things must not be overstated. When placed opposite all the weighty evidence of position and fortune, they could not cause the scale of possibility to so much as budge.

The more she studied these facts, the more Ivy convinced herself of the soundness of her reasoning. Indeed, she concluded one afternoon as she worked on her poor basket, there was no use in wasting another moment's thought on it; the matter was resolved; she could expect—*would* expect—nothing from Mr. Rafferdy.

"I see a black carriage coming down the street!" Lily said from her perch by the parlor window.

Ivy winced, then sucked her finger; she had pricked it with the needle. Her heart pounded. But it was only from the start that Lily had given her, she told herself. All the same, she did not draw a breath as Lily described the progress of the carriage.

"Oh, it's not stopping," Lily said, and turned from the window with a frown. "I do wonder when Mr. Rafferdy will come. And when he does, he had better bring Mr. Garritt with him, or I shall be very cross."

"You must not expect such an event," Ivy said, resuming both her breathing and her sewing. "And I wish to hear no more about Mr. Rafferdy. I assure you I will speak no more about him this day!"

Lily sulked from the window and sat at the pianoforte, though she did not play anything. In the time Rose finished one shirt and began another, Ivy succeeded only in tearing out the seam along a sleeve.

"There!" she announced with grim satisfaction. "How horrified Mr. Rafferdy would be to witness such a poor display of sewing. It is best he is not here. He would cease any association with me at once."

And a short while later, when the clatter of a passing carriage sounded outside, she exclaimed, "There is no need to look, I am quite certain by the squeaking of the wheels *that* is not Mr. Rafferdy. His cabriolet is very quiet, as I remember. Do not even bother going to the window, Lily."

That night was an unusually short umbral, a mere four hours according to the almanac. While it was light when they sat down to supper, it was already full dark by the time they finished their soup.

"We must hurry to bed!" Mrs. Lockwell said, rushing them from the table, "or it will be light before we get a wink of sleep."

Despite the brief night, Ivy rose early. Dawn found her in the kitchen, heating a kettle for tea. Though the sky warmed from gray to pink to blue while she drank her cup, the rest of the household had not stirred, having gone to bed only a few hours ago. Even Mrs. Murch, who was usually very early, had not made an appearance; so when the bell rang for the post, Ivy ventured out to retrieve it herself. She waved to the postman across the street, and he cracked a great yawn in reply.

The day was already sultry, having had little chance to give up yesterday's heat. She took a bundle of letters from the box, dismayed to note that the topmost was a bill from a fashionable Uphill clothier. She returned inside and without further examination set the stack of letters on the table in the front hall; her mother always insisted on going through them before anyone else and would be upset if she perceived this was not the case.

The stack slid to one side as she let go, revealing a letter addressed in a cramped, formal hand.

Ivy stared. She reached for the post, determined only to straighten the stack, then found the letter in her hand. It was addressed to Mr. Lockwell and sealed with red wax, just like the one that had come some months ago.

It was not *hers* to open. All the same, her fingers slipped beneath the wax seal, prying it from the paper without cracking it. She trembled and was forced to hold the letter with both hands in order to read it in the morning sun that streamed through the front window.

*Dear Mr. and Mrs. Lockwell,*

*I address this to you both, though it is my belief that only one of you will read it, for if things had altered for the better I am sure I would have heard such news. It is my hope they have not altered for the worse. It is also my hope that this missive will win a reply, though my previous letters have gone unanswered. That I have only the best wishes for you and your family, I cannot make more plain than I did when last we met, and the intervening years have not altered my intentions.*

*My little cousins, which I previously described to you, are now come to my house at Heathcrest, and I still have great need of someone to see to their care and education. I have only a small staff, and they have little time or ability to see to the shepherding of young souls and young minds. The children need a governess, and I am sure I could do no better than to have one of your three daughters.*

*If she is not otherwise occupied, I think the eldest would do the best, being of an age (if I recollect rightly) to carry some weight of authority with my two charges. This would be beneficial. While they are kind children, and clever, since the passing of their mother they have wanted for the benefit of a regular household and the influence of solid governance. I fear this is something I can little provide myself, being so occupied with the duties of my work, which often require me to be away.*

*I trust you will present this opportunity to your eldest. While I can offer nothing that compares to the brightness and busy society of the city, there are goodly folk in this part of the country, and it is possible she might make some acquaintances that are both fitting and pleasing to her. I fear there is nothing else I can promise her, save my gratitude and fifty regals a month she may put to her future.*

*It is long since I have seen you both, but I hope in honor of our past acquaintance you will treat me to a reply as soon as possible.*

*Yours with Respect,*
*Alasdare Quent, Esquire*
*Heathcrest Hall, Cairnbridge, County Westmorain*

Ivy folded the letter and creased it. She went to the kitchen, warmed a knife on the stove, and held it against the circle of wax. Once softened, she pressed the letter shut and let the seal cool.

Though she performed these motions calmly, her mind raced. Fifty regals a month! How such a sum would alter their lot. They would have enough to buy all that was needed, as well as a few things that were merely wanted, and still have a good amount to save toward the future.

Why her mother had not presented her with the proposition expressed in this letter—and the letters prior to it—Ivy could not imagine. There was no reason keeping *her* in the city, unless it was the reason that her mother imagined, and that was no reason at all. She did not know this Mr. Quent; Mrs. Lockwell had never mentioned him. However, it was clear he had been a friend of the family, or at least a friend of Mr. Lockwell's.

So why had Mrs. Lockwell kept these missives a secret?

Ivy heard heavy footfalls coming down the stairs. She rushed back into the hall and slipped the letter into the stack, turning just in time to see her mother coming down the steps.

"You are up very early," Mrs. Lockwell said. "And you have a bright look about you. Have you already been out for a walk? By the saints, I can hardly imagine such a thing! I feel as if I could sleep through a greatnight. What have you been doing?"

"Nothing," Ivy said. "The post just came. I will put on water for tea. Mrs. Murch is not yet risen."

As her mother took up the letters, Ivy moved down the hall toward the kitchen door.

"Ivoleyn, wait. This letter here—"

Ivy halted, her hand on the doorknob, then turned around, a coldness descending in her stomach. Mrs. Lockwell frowned at one of the letters, then held it out toward Ivy.

"This note is addressed to you. I can see no sign of who sent it. Were you expecting anything?"

Ivy murmured that she had not. So relieved was she that her mother had not noticed her handiwork with the wax seal that she took the note without looking at it. She tucked it into the pocket of her skirt and went to the kitchen.

It was not until after breakfast, when she sat at the secretary in the parlor to look at the ledger, that she recalled the note in her pocket. She glanced over her shoulder. Rose was sewing contentedly, and Lily stared at the window with a rather less contented air while Miss Mew made a nest in her poor basket. Ivy returned her attention to the note, which had been folded so as to make its own envelope. *Miss Ivoleyn Lockwell* was written in an elongated hand on the front, but there was nothing to indicate the identity of the sender. Ivy opened the note.

*I believe you will find this of interest* was the message in its entirety. It was signed simply *Bennick*.

Before she could wonder at the exceeding brevity of the letter—or the fact that Mr. Bennick had sent her a letter of any length at all—a scrap of newsprint fell to the secretary. Ivy unfolded it, seeing that it was an article clipped from one of the broadsheets—*The Messenger,* perhaps, by its stodgy typeface. She read it but with more confusion than interest.

The article concerned the new celestial object, the one she had seen the other night. Some men of science were now suggesting it was not a comet after all but rather a planet. This idea seemed remarkable, given that the object had not been observed in the heavens during all the course of recorded history; not even the ancient Tharosians had ever noted it. However, according to some astrographers, it was not beyond the realm of possibility.

The eleven known planets moved in the heavens as the spheres of aether, on whose surfaces they resided, turned about their axes. Ivy had observed this motion herself when she turned the knobs of her father's celestial globe. The furthest planets resided on the surfaces of the largest spheres, and these spheres were so great, and turned so slowly, that some of the planets did not complete their grand circuits for a generation. Indeed, it took Loerus a full forty years to make its rounds.

It was theorized by some, the article went on, that if the celestial sphere that contained the planet was sufficiently large, and its axis was offset from the other spheres to an extreme degree, it might take many thousands of years to complete its circuit. Therefore it was possible that it had been eons since the last time this planet had drawn close enough to be seen, before the ancient precursors of the Tharosians first put stylus to clay.

Ivy set down the article and could not help frowning. It was fascinating, to be sure. That there could be a thing so great and important as an entire planet that had heretofore remained undiscovered was remarkable. However, that there was much left in creation to discover Ivy did not doubt; after all, it was only a few centuries ago that the New Lands were found across the eastern sea.

What Ivy found equally—if not more—remarkable was the fact

that Mr. Bennick had thought to send her the article. They were acquainted in only the slightest way. At Lady Marsdel's he had told her about Mr. Rafferdy's descent from one of the Old Houses, that was all.

No, that was not all she and Mr. Bennick had spoken of. Ivy reached again for the note. *I believe you will find this of interest.*

She set down the note and opened a drawer, taking out the riddle she had found in the old book, the one her father had left for her. Ivy had concealed it under a stack of demands and receipts, confident it would not be disturbed in that location. Again she read the cryptic lines.

> *When twelve who wander stand as one*
> *Through the door the dark will come.*
> *The key will be revealed in turn—*
> *Unlock the way and you shall learn.*

Upon reading the riddle, her first thought had been of the planets; her father had been something of an astrographer himself, and he had taught her long ago that the Tharosian word for planet meant *wanderer.* However, she had dismissed that line of reasoning, for the planets were eleven in number.

"No," she murmured, picking up the article Mr. Bennick had sent her and holding it alongside the riddle. "Not eleven anymore."

All this time her first guess had been right; the riddle *did* concern the planets. Mr. Bennick had said he knew of no myths that spoke of twelve wanderers, but what if this planet was more ancient than myth itself? What if it had last appeared before men first looked up at the sky—or before there were men at all? If that was the case, it was no wonder it was unknown in story and legend.

Yet Mr. Lockwell *had* known of it, or at least he had seemed to. *So, you have returned at last from your wanderings,* he had said two nights ago, when she first saw the red glint in the sky.

How her father had come to be aware of a celestial object whose existence had never been noted in all of recorded history, she could not guess. However, she owed Mr. Bennick thanks for remembering her odd question.

Again she studied the riddle. She had to believe she was capable of solving it; her father would never have left it for her if he didn't think it was within her abilities to fathom. But why use a riddle at all? Why not just tell her?

*Because he wanted you to be ready,* she thought. And, more darkly, *Because he did not want others to know.*

She read the first line, and now that she knew it referred to planets, its meaning was clear. *When twelve who wander stand as one.* It had to refer to some sort of conjunction—a grand conjunction of all the planets, appearing together in the sky.

The next line described what would happen when this celestial event took place. It spoke of a door and the dark coming through. Ivy could not help but shudder; the line reminded her of how she felt sometimes when night fell, how the darkness seemed to creep into the house, eating the light. And it also reminded her of the man she had encountered at the old house on Durrow Street.

*The way must not be opened,* the man in the mask had said.

Ivy closed her eyes, recalling that strange meeting. She had thought back to it several times since then, trying to remember everything that had happened, everything he had said. Only it was vague to her, as if from a dream. The fever she had succumbed to that night had dimmed her memories of the day. And it had all been so peculiar: the outlandish and outmoded clothes he wore, the dark mask, the way she had been unable to speak. He had spoken about a door and about a group of people: the Vigilant Order of the Silver Eye. None of it made sense to her. But could it be a coincidence that both Mr. Lockwell and the stranger had spoken of a door?

*You should listen to me,* he had said from behind the mask, *because that is what your father did.*

She *had* listened to her father. He had taught her how the planets Vaelus and Cyrenth never stood in conjunction, just as their namesakes were doomed never to meet. Which meant the first line of the riddle made no sense after all. Even if there were twelve planets, they still could never stand as one. She was missing something in the riddle. Her father would not have gone to such trouble to leave her a piece of nonsense. There had to be an answer.

Her head ached from staring at the papers. With a sigh, she returned the riddle to the drawer, and the article from Mr. Bennick with it.

🜚

THE MONTH DREW on, and still no carriage stopped at their front door.

Mr. Rafferdy was merely waiting for the right moment, Mrs. Lockwell made a point of declaring every day.

"It must be that he is making certain all his affairs are in proper order," Mrs. Lockwell said as they took an early breakfast after a long umbral, "so that when he makes his proposal it will appear as attractive as possible."

"No doubt," Ivy replied solemnly, "for a woman of my position can be compelled by only the strongest of persuasions to accept the proposal of a young, wealthy, and charming man."

"I should think not!" Mrs. Lockwell exclaimed. "But I would begin to think you are not interested at all in him, Miss Ivoleyn Lockwell, for the way you talk. You had best not act like that when he comes. You will be sorry if you cause him to take his proposal to some other woman. Don't think there aren't plenty who would accept in your stead!"

Of that, Ivy had no doubt. In fact, she thought as she went into the parlor, she was certain there were any number of young women who would receive such a proposal long before she would. She had not her mother's unfounded hopes nor her sister's romantic notions. The sound of horses and wheels clattering came from the street. A cart, no doubt. She paid the noise no heed and moved instead to the secretary to look over the ledger.

"Ivy!" came a cry from downstairs. "Ivy, come down here at once!"

It was her mother, and such was the shrill sound of her voice that Ivy thought at first some terrible thing must have occurred. She set down her pen and started for the stairs.

"Ivy, where are you? Come down here this instant! He's here, oh, bless us, he's here!"

Ivy halted, gripping the top of the banister, then hurried to the window and glanced out. A black four-in-hand decorated with gold trim had pulled up in front of their house.

In that moment, with one gasp of breath, all her arguments and assumptions that this could never be—that it was impossible, that it defied logic in every way—were dismissed. Instead, reason lost out, as it always must no matter how strongly founded, to wonder and delight.

For so long she had not let herself so much as entertain a hope that, when proven false as it surely must, would cause a pain that could not be borne. To not hope, to expect nothing, to dismiss at every turn—these had been her only protections against certain devastation. Disappointment could not ensue when one failed to gain what one had never wished for.

But now . . . She lifted a hand to her mouth but could not contain her smile. Now there was no *reason* to refuse hope any longer. Her logic had not been wrong; it *was* impossible. All the same, he was here; he had come. And now that a joy she had previously forbidden from her mind and heart was at last allowed to enter, it could only expand rapidly and quickly filled her. Speech was quite beyond her, but it felt as if a light streamed outward from her, radiating all around.

"Wonderful," she managed to murmur at last. And it was so. This would make her life—all of their lives—wonderful indeed.

There was another cry from below. Ivy descended the stairs, moving with deliberation despite the frantic wavings of her mother's hand. She regretted the plain dress she had put on that day, and she had done nothing with her hair, but there was no use in worrying about that now. If all the obstacles of position and wealth could not deter him, she could not imagine a plain frock would. She began to open the door, but Mrs. Lockwell held her back.

"This is a moment you will remember as long as you live, Ivy. You are a very lucky girl." She smiled, smoothing Ivy's hair with a touch. "And a very pretty one. No wonder he is so attached to you. Now go." She opened the door, and when Lily started to follow, Mrs. Lockwell shooed her inside. "Back in with you, Liliauda. Go be a bother to your other sister. This is something Ivoleyn can do only by herself. Don't give me that frown—I said go!"

Then the door shut, and Ivy stood alone on the front step. Her pulse fluttered in her throat. She could hardly draw a breath. All those thoughts, all those feelings so long held in check by sense, now given their freedom, welled up. Her eyes strained to behold him. She wanted nothing but to be near him. Yes, she would say when he asked her; with all her heart, yes. She gripped the railing as the driver came round and opened the door of the four-in-hand.

A woman stepped out.

Ivy blinked the sun-dazzle from her eyes. So unexpected was the sight that she could hardly comprehend it. But, no, she was not mistaken; for there was Mrs. Baydon passing through the gate and walking up to the steps, looking smart in blue silk. She reached the steps and greeted Ivy. The words were polite, but even in her confusion Ivy could not help but notice that they were spoken coolly; she did not reach for Ivy's hand.

Ivy willed herself not to look past Mrs. Baydon toward the carriage, to search for the one she craved to see but who was not there. Instead, she gave Mrs. Baydon her full attention as well as a greeting that was every bit as welcoming as the other woman's had been distant. At this, Mrs. Baydon's cheeks colored. Ivy asked if she would come in, but Mrs. Baydon asked if they might sit in the garden instead.

"It is so pretty here. There is not a garden along the Promenade that blooms as wonderfully as your little yard here does. And there is that inviting bench under the wisteria. May we sit there?"

They went to the bench and sat. For a minute or more they did not speak. The wind made whispers in the ceiling of leaves above them.

"You have perhaps been given the wrong idea, Miss Lockwell," Mrs. Baydon said at last. The words were stiff and practiced.

Ivy shook her head. "The wrong idea, Mrs. Baydon? About what?"

"It is not *his* fault," she went on. "I do not blame him. Nor do I blame you, Miss Lockwell. You can hardly be faulted for wishing to better yourself. Rather, I blame myself and my husband's aunt. We went too far in welcoming you into our circle, I think. We thought only of ourselves, of our own amusement, and gave no thought to how it must seem to *him* as well as to *you*—how it must appear as if some form of approval had been granted, some degree of favor, when in fact none was intentioned or even possible."

Ivy did not know what to make of these words; she was at a loss. "Lady Marsdel's kindness in allowing me to stay at her home is something for which I will always be grateful. However, I can think of no special favor I sought while I was there. Indeed, it was always my wish to be as out of the way, to be as little trouble to anyone, as possible. If there is some particular thing I did that made it seem I desired such attention or approval as you've mentioned, I hope you will let me know it so I can make an apology. For I confess, I cannot remember any such occasion myself."

Mrs. Baydon's expression softened, and now she looked at Ivy. "Please forgive me, Miss Lockwell. In your absence I was persuaded to . . . that is, I am ashamed to say I allowed myself to believe something unkind about you. Only now that I am here with you and see you once again, I know it was awful of me. Of course you went out of your way to have as little effect as possible upon my aunt's house. Even so, be assured that you did have an effect—a most profound effect—upon our household and acquaintances.

"Nor was *he* the only one. We were all of us taken with you. Your charms are many and were much in evidence during your stay at my aunt's. So you cannot think it so wrong of us, so terribly absurd, that we thought it was intentional on your part, that you wished to make yourself as agreeable to all of us as possible and that you had designs on him. Of course, a connection between two of such disparate positions can only be unthinkable. I felt it was my duty to tell my aunt, and she wrote to his father at once."

The garden air went cold, or at least so it felt to Ivy. It took her a long moment to find the ability to speak. "I am all astonishment, Mrs. Baydon. I have been accused of something that I am sure I have never done. Who is this you speak of? Upon whom did you think I had designs?"

"Why, Mr. Rafferdy, of course," Mrs. Baydon said with a puzzled look. "You mean to say you did not—you *do* not—seek to marry him?"

This was too much. To have restrained herself from engaging in any act, even any thought, that might have been deemed the least infraction against propriety, only to be accused of such a great crime— it was too awful to suffer. "I assure you, I have never sought after such a thing in any way! And if there was ever any sort of intention on his part, it was never something I looked for or encouraged. And I cannot imagine there *is* any such intention on his part. He considers me an acquaintance, a friend perhaps, nothing more."

"I believe in that you might be mistaken, Miss Lockwell, or at least might once have been. But you mean to tell me he has never spoken to you of a proposal?"

"Never!" she said, and after that she could speak no further. Her voice fled her.

However, Mrs. Baydon brightened and took her hands. "I am relieved, Miss Lockwell. I am so relieved. Not only for *him,* but for myself. Of course such a thing would never have occurred to our dear, sensible Miss Lockwell. How could I have thought otherwise? And it was in no way Miss Everaud's fault. She has never met you; she cannot know your goodness as we do. But for the rest of us—it was awful of us to believe as we did. We deserve in every way to be chastised for such foolish thoughts as we engaged in.

"But more importantly, I am relieved for *you*. I should have hated for you to have to suffer a disappointment. Yet now that I know the truth—that you never had such thoughts for him—I am assured you will be as happy as I am to hear the news that I came here to tell you today."

"News?" Ivy said, certain she was beyond any further astonishment. "What news, Mrs. Baydon?"

She squeezed Ivy's hands. "News of the grandest sort. Perhaps you remember me discussing my friend Miss Everaud? If so, then you know how dear she is to me, just as you know how much affection I have for our Mr. Rafferdy. How could I not find joy in something that gives happiness to two for whom I care so much? And he could not possibly do better. Not only is Miss Everaud the most beautiful thing you will ever see, she is the daughter of one of the finest families. It is an excellent match, I am sure you will agree."

The heavy perfume of the wisteria blossoms dulled Ivy's mind. "Match?" she said. "What match do you speak of?"

"Why, Mr. Rafferdy's, of course," Mrs. Baydon said, laughing. "And I know you will rejoice in it even as I do. He and Miss Everaud are engaged. It is all done and arranged. They are to be married in two months' time!"

🌿

IVY HARDLY REMEMBERED saying farewell to Mrs. Baydon or going into the house. She found herself in the front hall, the door shutting behind her. Her mind could hold on to no thought other than a single one.

Married! Mr. Rafferdy was to be married.

She could not be shocked. A little bit, perhaps. It was hard to believe he was ready to be settled in such a manner. But given his age, and the importance of his family and that of his betrothed, it was not truly surprising. A match would have been wanted on all sides.

"I will be happy for him," she said aloud. She would hope Miss Everaud was half so pretty as Mrs. Baydon said, and half so sweet. She had no doubt she was every bit as rich. She should suit Mr. Rafferdy well—very well indeed. Yes, she *would* be happy for him.

A sob came out of her, and her cheeks were wet with tears.

There came the sound of shuffling steps. Wilbern was coming into the hall. Wiping her cheeks, Ivy dashed up the stairs. Lily and Rose were in the parlor, but Lily was pounding away upon the pianoforte, and the music did not halt as Ivy ran past the door.

She did not stop on the third floor, afraid Mrs. Lockwell might be in her room. Instead, she went around to the back stairs and up to the attic. Sunlight poured through the window, turning the dust on the air into sparks of gold, like some illusionist's phantasm. Ivy went to a chair in a corner next to one of the bookshelves and sat there and wept.

It was only when she felt a touch on her shoulder that she realized she was not alone. She looked up and saw Mr. Lockwell standing above her. His hair flew in a white cloud around his head. His blue eyes, usually focused on some distant place, were instead intent upon her. She tried to speak, to tell him there was no cause for worry, but she could not voice the words.

He patted her shoulder. "Do not cry, little one," he said. "This is your house now."

Despite her tears, a wonder came over her. She took his hand, holding it against her cheek. "I love you, Father."

He smiled at her. Then he pulled his hand away, moved to the bookshelf, and muttered as he ran his fingers over various tomes.

Ivy wiped her cheeks and stood. She drew a breath. There, it was done. There was no more need for crying. She had never really had a hope, after all. That Mr. Rafferdy was to marry in a way that suited his position was hardly something she could fault him for. She would never think ill of him, not after all the kindness he had shown her and her family. And she hoped that one day she would be able to meet him again, to give him all her wishes for happiness, as a friend who had only the warmest regard for him.

She would be well. *They* would be well. Their life here on Whitward Street was everything she could ask for. Any such small concerns she had about finances were nothing to detract from their contentment. It would all be worked out. She had no need to hope for a better situation.

"Besides, why would I ever wish for anything that would take me away from you?" she said to Mr. Lockwell, taming his hair with a touch.

"It was here," he said, frowning. "But I can't find it." He pulled out a book and let it fall.

Ivy retrieved it, put it back on the shelf, and kissed his cheek.

"I'll go see how dinner is coming along," she said, and went to find her mother.

Mrs. Lockwell was not in her room, so Ivy went downstairs. She found Rose in the parlor, petting Miss Mew.

"Where is our mother?" Ivy asked. "I thought I would see if she needs help with supper."

However, Rose didn't know where Mrs. Lockwell was, so Ivy went in search of Lily.

"There you are," Ivy said as she stepped into the dining room. Lily stood near the sideboard. "I asked Rose where Mother was, but she didn't know. Have you seen her?"

Lily did not answer. She gripped the back of a chair and stared at the far end of the table.

"Lily?"

Ivy drew closer and saw that two of the chairs were askew. Cassity must have disarranged them. Ivy walked around the table to straighten the chairs.

"Oh," she said.

A fly buzzed in a lazy arc across the room. Mrs. Lockwell lay on the floor in a patch of sunlight. Her eyes were shut, her mouth open, and her arms at her sides.

"Lily," Ivy said, "go tell Cassity to fetch a doctor."

Lily did not move. Ivy knelt on the floor, took her mother's hand, and held it in her own. The fly struck against the windowpane; it bounced back, then tapped the window with its body again, again.

"I said, fetch the doctor," Ivy repeated, sternly this time. Lily let out a sobbing noise and ran out the door.

However, there was no need for doctors. Ivy had only wanted to get Lily away. Mrs. Lockwell's hand was icy in her own. She gripped it tight.

"We will be well," she said to her mother, and again to herself. "We *will* be well."

The buzzing of the fly ceased. Outside, the sun fell behind a cloud, and darkness took the room.

## BOOK TWO

Heathcrest

I T IS NIGHT as I write these words, and as is so often the case here at Heathcrest Hall, I am alone.

My little room, which I have to myself, is situated on the uppermost floor at one end of the house. A larger chamber was offered to me on my arrival. Its furnishings were rich: an old Murghese carpet, a fortress of a bed, and a desk roomy enough, I am sure, to have borne King Atheld and his squire from the shores of Altania to the Isle of Night in some degree of comfort.

I expressed to the housekeeper, Mrs. Darendal, that I did not feel my position warrented such appointments. While the words came from politeness, I can only think they caused insult, for the room I was shown to next—this room—was in every way the opposite of the other. But having made a point of finding the first chamber too grand, I could not in turn complain that this one was too austere.

Nor do I regret it. Here I have but a wrought-iron bed and a table not much larger than this sheet of paper on which I write. Yet this room suits me. I like the way it is tucked into the corner of a gable, so I can hear the rain drum against the roof. I like the chair someone left here long ago, crafted from willow branches woven together in the most subtle pattern, so that it seems it was not made at all but rather sprouted into being. I like that the window looks east toward Invarel.

In daylight, I have a picturesque view of the heath and downs surrounding the house. On a clear day (of which we have few), I like to pretend that the ragged shapes I can just make out atop the next ridge are the roofs of the houses in Gauldren's Heights and the towers of the Citadel. However, what I see, I am told, is a stand of old Wyrdwood several furlongs distant. Imagine—a stand of primeval forest within view of the house!

How I wish it were closer. To see the Old Forest rowans and hawthorns would be like seeing an ancient tale come to life. I should, quite easily, be able to picture Queen Béanore slipping among them. Besides, it would give my eyes something green to behold. Currently I am deprived of any such sight. There is no garden at the house, and there is little that grows naturally close by, save for heather and gorse. There is not a single tree, Old or New, within a half mile of the house.

It is more than twice that distance to Cairnbridge, the closest village, and as a result we are seldom disturbed here at Heathcrest. At present it is the eighth hour of the fourth night since the new month. It is a longish umbral, and the house is quiet. I can hear the hiss of the candle and all the small scratchings of pen against the paper. I can almost fancy that I am an inhabitant of one of Lily's romances, penning a secret letter in the deep of a greatnight. Only I do not know to whom I write this. It is not to some young duke or dashing soldier who I hope will come rescue me; I am here by my own choice.

All the same, this letter *is* secret. For it is my intention, I think, to write a bit each day (or night) as time allows and to set down all those things that concern my thoughts but that I can tell to no one. Not to my employer, for the master of Heathcrest is a serious man—stern, I might say—and does not take well to being disturbed. Nor can I tell them to the woman who keeps his house. Mrs. Darendal, whom I have mentioned, though efficient in her business, seems little disposed toward talk of any sort.

As for the children, they must not be troubled by such things. It is my duty to be a steady influence upon them, a source of dependable comfort. And while my heart craves nothing more than to tell my sisters of all that weighs on my mind, I must resist.

After all, it is easier for me than for *them.* I have gone to a new place, with new duties that occupy me. Rose and Lily have remained behind in a dwelling whose very familiarity must, rather than console, serve to remind them at every turn of the beloved mother they have lost. Even worse, they must see the home they have known all their lives ruled by another and themselves relegated to the periphery of it, turned into objects that cannot be wanted even as they are told they are welcome to stay.

No, my letters to them must be filled with hope and cheer. And what do my concerns matter compared to theirs? My time is well occupied. My charges, while they are awake, require all of my attention and energy. If at times, in the dark of a long umbral like tonight, when the children are asleep and I am wishing for company, then I have only to take out my pen and write, and I am close to you, Father.

For I realize now it is to *you* that I write this letter. You are the only one I can bother with these odd little thoughts, these small worries that occur to me. Even if these words never reach you or can have little chance of being read in the event they are placed in your hands— even so, you help me more than you can know. For I have only to think of you, of all that you have borne, and I know that I will overcome any difficulties my current situation presents.

But this is all turned around! I am not telling things in their proper order. *To understand a tree, one must study its roots,* wrote Telarus in the *Lex Altania.* I must explain how I came to be here, Father. That my situation can have changed in so short a time, and that it can have been altered so completely by the simple act of answering a letter, is a thing I can scarcely comprehend. Yet so it has; and if I can endeavor to explain it to you, perhaps in the effort I will grasp it myself.

🌿

 THE FIRST THING I knew was that we could not long depend upon the charity of our cousin Mr. Wyble.

It was plain to me, from the moment he arrived to offer us his condolences, that he intended to suffer no delay in establishing the house on Whitward Street as his own in habitation as well as in title.

"I have always felt I was coming home every time I paid you a visit," he told us as we took tea in the parlor. "And now it is true not only in feeling but also in fact. Is that not remarkable, Cousin Ivoleyn?"

"I agree, it *is* remarkable," I said to him. Remarkable that the man would arrive so quickly. Surely, in the wake of a tragedy that had cost us so greatly and that had benefited him so much, a small delay on his part could not have resulted in much trouble for him. But the law has no compassion, Mr. Wyble often told us, and in that regard the lawyer seemed much the same. It had been only a quarter month since that terrible day.

"Of course you are welcome to stay, dear cousins, until you are situated elsewhere," he said, making a magnanimous gesture with a biscuit.

"You are very kind," I said when it was clear he waited on a reply.

"Do not think there must be any sort of hurry on your part," he went on. "I am aware, after such a drastic change of situation, that it will take some time to make arrangements for yourselves and your father. You must not worry. You will find me exceedingly patient on the matter. More tea?"

He directed his gaze at Rose. She gave a startled look, then stood to pour him another cup. I took it from her gently and delivered it myself. Rose has a tendency to spill things, and the tea was very hot.

I thanked him on behalf of my sisters and my father, though he had granted us nothing the law had not already. The terms of the entailment gave us half a year to quit the house. And I had no doubt that, however great its initial surplus might be, by then Mr. Wyble's patience with us would be exhausted. That we must remove to the house on Durrow Street as soon as possible was my only thought.

"I am sure we will all get along most agreeably," Mr. Wyble said. "We shall dine together, of course; we are family. And I have formulated a plan for the arrangement of the house. I have concluded that you should take the fourth floor for yourselves. True, it has the largest room in the house, which I know to be exceedingly comfortable and pleasant. However, logic must supersede any little want or desire I might feel. For that floor is closest to the attic, which I know is your father's place. The new servants will have the first floor, and I shall make the second and third floors my apartments."

Lily looked up from her empty cup. "But what of the parlor?" She turned to me, her eyes widened in fear. "How shall I play the pianoforte? You know I have to play! Mother told me to keep practicing."

I spoke before Lily could become more agitated. "Your arrangement sounds very impartial, Mr. Wyble. But you do not mean, I am sure, that we are not to have any use of the parlor."

"Of course I mean no such thing! I would never deprive you of such a comfort. On the contrary, I was thinking you could have the parlor for a full two hours once each quarter month. What do you think of that, cousin?" he said with a smile toward Lily.

She clapped a hand to her mouth, stood, and fled the room.

Mr. Wyble looked to me. "Is the poor child ill?"

"No, I am sure she is well," I said. "But you must know how—that is, it has been a difficult time for her."

He affected a solemn look. "Difficulties are the trials in which God judges us, cousin. We must be strong when faced with adversity so as to better represent our own case before Him. Do you not agree?"

I gave him a smile in answer. "Rose," I said, "I see Mr. Wyble's cup is empty again. Would you take him another cup of tea?"

$\clubsuit$

SEVERAL NIGHTS LATER I sat at the dresser in what had been Mother's room, going over the household ledger. I sought to draw up a budget, and though it would not be easy, it seemed to me we would be able to use the sum I had managed to accumulate over the years to pay for the expense of opening the house on Durrow Street. After that, your small income, Father, would be enough to keep us—but only if we lived in the most frugal manner.

My eyes ached from reading in the candlelight. Indulging in a sigh, I shut the ledger.

"I know where Mother kept the letters, you know," Lily said.

I looked up. Rose sat on the edge of the bed while Lily braided her fine brown hair.

"What letters, dear?" I said.

Lily did not look up from her work. "They're in the dresser, in the bottom drawer, under her wedding lace. I saw her put them there."

*It is not right to spy on others!* I wanted to chastise Lily. Instead, I hesitated, then knelt and opened the drawer. I removed the bits of lace that had been carefully folded away, and there, just as Lily said, was a cache of papers. I recognized the letters on top at once. All were addressed to you in that same cramped, formal hand. None of them was opened.

It seemed wrong. Yet what had been hers was *ours* now. She had not been able to pass on the house, but this wedding lace had been her own, and these letters. I took out all the papers and laid them on the dresser. I opened the first letter, then the next, and the next. There were more than I had thought. All of them were from the same Mr. Quent.

The one I had read that day before replacing the wax seal was among them. The others were similar in tone and nature. All were polite but also implied a past friendship, as well as what seemed a genuine interest in helping the Lockwell family. The most recent letters all bore the same hope, that one of the daughters—myself, in particular—would consider serving as a governess to the gentleman's two young wards, who would be coming to live with him soon, or, indeed, now were doing so.

"Who are those letters from?" Rose asked. I looked up to see her standing above me, pretty in her new braids.

"They are from a friend of Father's in the country," I said. "He wrote to inquire about our father's health. I believe they were friends once."

"Maybe Father was his friend," Lily said from the bed. "But Mother must not have thought very much of him. That drawer was where she always hid things she disliked. Things like bills and—" She clapped her hand to her mouth. "By Loerus, I promised I wouldn't tell you!"

A note of alarm sounded within me, one that made me disregard her swearing. "You promised you wouldn't tell me what?"

Lily only chewed her lip. I removed the letters from the stack and examined the papers beneath. At once my heart grew heavy. Each paper I unfolded bore similar words: *Sum Yet Due* or *Notice of Debit*. Some of them bore the names of Uphill shops, but most appeared to regard a series of loans. Strangely, each loan was for the exact amount as the monthly sum of your income, Father.

A dread came over me. "There is no income," I said. "Or at least there has not been for nearly a year." The papers made it clear. Your investments had finished paying out last year, and since then Mother had taken out loans to make up the difference.

The night pressed in around the candle, causing its light to contract. These debts would consume all of our small savings. There would be nothing to pay for the expense of opening the house on Durrow Street. And even if we were able to move there, we would have no income to live on.

"Oh, Mother," I murmured over the papers. "Dearest Mother. I know this was never your intention. But we are ruined. We have nothing."

Too late I realized that I had said these words aloud. Lily stared at me with a fearful look. "We have nothing? Do you mean we will have to go to the workhouse?"

At this utterance, Rose burst into tears.

I stood and held Rose close. "Hush, dearest. Do not cry. Everything will be well, you will see."

"I'm afraid to go to the workhouse," Rose said. "What if they won't let me sew shirts? I don't know how to do anything else. I don't know how to do anything at all."

With that her tears were renewed. Neither was I far from them myself, nor was Lily, by the shining of her eyes.

No, this would not do. I had told my mother that awful day that we would be well, and so we would. Even as I looked over Rose's shoulder at the hated papers that assured our paupery, I saw also the letters that would provide our salvation.

With the gentlest motions I pushed Rose away. I took her hand, and Lily's. I told them I knew what to do, that everything would be well. I do not know if it was the authority I carried as the eldest or if it was all my past efforts at practicality that reassured them, but they grew calm. Rose smiled at me, and Lily even kissed my cheek, a gift I received with some chagrin. For I had no doubt that what I intended to do would distress them both even as it assured our future. I told them to go to Rose's room. I waited for the door to shut, then I sat at the dresser, took out pen and paper, and commenced writing a letter.

*Dear Mr. Quent,* I began.

$\mathcal{I}$ KNEW THE MAIL kept to its timetables whether it was day or night, be it a short lumenal or a long umbral. All the same, I was astonished when after less than a quarter month a letter came written in that same precise, small-set hand. Only this time it was addressed not to you but instead to *Miss Ivoleyn Lockwell*.

So anxious was I that I could not wait to go up to our rooms; I opened the letter there in the garden and read it on the bench where I had spoken with Mrs. Baydon that day that now seemed so long ago. This time the news I received in that place was far more welcome. He expressed his sorrow and condolences at our loss. His words were well intentioned, if labored in their construction. I read on, and my heart leaped.

He still had need of a governess! He had not been able to secure anyone of worth to watch over his little cousins, who had lately arrived at his house. My presence was needed at the soonest possible time, but he could no longer see paying me fifty regals a month. Given how difficult it was to secure someone of quality for this position, my own worth had necessarily increased, and the sum should instead be sixty regals monthly!

For several moments I was overwhelmed. Our current savings would remove the debts our mother had accrued, and with the income I would receive from Mr. Quent, I would be able to save enough to move my family to the house on Durrow Street. How long I could expect the arrangement with Mr. Quent to last I could not know, but this would grant us time—more than a year, at the least—to determine a course for the future.

However, after a moment my elation faltered. Between now and that happy future lay harder things. It would be some months before

I had saved enough to effect our move from Whitward Street. During that period I would be far from my sisters, and they and you, Father, would be forced to suffer Mr. Wyble as your landlord.

There was no other way. Again I read the letter, and I saw that Mr. Quent had made arrangements for me to travel with the mail on the lumenal after next. The fare was already paid. There was no need to write Mr. Quent a reply; I would be arriving as quickly as any letter could.

That night—as we readied ourselves for bed after a day that had felt short no matter that the almanac claimed it to be of middling length—I told Lily and Rose what I was to do. I rued the timing of my speech. Our spirits, I confess, were low. Supper that evening had been a disheartening affair. We had been forced to let Mrs. Murch, Wilbern, and Cassity go. It was a sadness on top of a sorrow, but Mr. Wyble had insisted on hiring his own servants.

The new housekeeper was a sullen woman and a poor cook. However, the first time Mr. Wyble complained that something was not to his satisfaction, she replied by saying that she would not tell *him* how a lawyer should act if he would not tell *her* how a housekeeper should act.

He proclaimed she was correct to chastise him, that of course he would not hear her opinion on matters of law, so her opinions on the keeping of the household could only be right. After this, despite her dismal efforts at any sort of cleaning and at the table, everything she produced was lavished with the highest praise on his part, no matter how unkempt or wanting for salt.

Her husband, who saw to the grounds and was supposed to perform any repairs about the house, was no better, being inclined to do little more than smoke his pipe on the back step. He treated me to a walleyed glare the one time I found him out back and suggested he might see to the window in the front hall, which was stuck.

"You're not the lady here, young miss. You'll not tell me what to do." He spat on the step and proceeded to chew on his pipe.

That Lily and Rose would be under their own care could not be avoided, and when I told them I was leaving the day after next to take employment with Mr. Quent in the country, their shock was exceeded only by their despair.

"But you cannot leave us here!" Lily cried. "What are we to do without you? How can we endure Mr. Wyble? I can't stand the sight of him. It's only you that has kept me civil at all."

I did not mention that Lily had been anything but civil. "You are very strong," I said, endeavoring to sound cheerful. "Both of you. I know you will do very well without me. But I believe you must not count on our cousin for anything. Nor can you look to his servants for any aid. You would do better to avoid them, I think. And do not let them up into the attic. Their presence can only cause our father distress, and it will be up to both of you to care for him."

Lily shook her head. "But what if he—if one of his spells should—you know only you can calm him, Ivy."

I cannot lie; I did feel some concern about leaving you, Father. But even as I felt a flutter of doubt, Rose gave me cause for new resolve.

"I will care for our father," she said. "I think he will listen to me. He talks to me at night sometimes."

I could only feel wonder. In many ways Rose lived in a different world than the rest of us. What she did in her nocturnal wanderings I did not know, but at that moment, while I could not say my worries were erased, I knew that you would be cared for and loved.

Not to be outdone by her sister, Lily pronounced that *she* would care for you as well and that no one would do more than her. I embraced them both and gave them what advice I could. (That is, I explained how you could dress yourself if clothes were laid out, but how you might need to be encouraged to eat, and how best to soothe you if an agitation did come upon you.) They listened closely, and Lily repeated back all of my instructions. My relief was great; I felt I could in good conscience go.

However, I cannot say I was glad. Now that all was determined, a gloom had come over me. The next day was another middle lumenal and rushed by. Mr. Wyble expressed no regret at my leaving when I gave him the news. I am sure he could not have expected to be rid of one of us so soon, and now had every hope that the rest would be disposed of as easily.

The next morning my sisters helped me carry my two little satchels Downhill to the mail post. I had wanted nothing more that morning than to bid you farewell, Father, but I did not wish you to see my departure, for fear it might alarm you. So I kissed you good night the evening before, just as I always did, and smoothed your hair, knowing it would soon be wild again.

"Be good," I told Lily as the driver loaded my satchels on the coach. There was so much I wanted to tell her—how she must set a good example for Rose and keep her spirits up, and how she must not torment Mr. Wyble, for whatever she thought of him they must all dwell under one roof—but it was more than I could put into a few words, and the other passengers were already climbing into the coach. "Do be good," I said again, and kissed her.

Then it was Rose's turn. "Be brave, dearest," I told her, and held her tight. "You must keep watch over Lily and our father."

"It will be darker in the house without you," she said. "I won't have light to sew during long nights."

I wanted to tell her to light candles—to light as many as she wanted—but at that moment the driver called out. The other passengers were aboard. The horses stamped at the cobblestones.

I kissed Rose again, and Lily, and before they could see my own trembling I hurried to the coach. A gray-haired gentleman reached down from inside and helped me up the step. The door was closed. I found myself on the seat by the window, looking out. Lily waved her handkerchief—in a slow and overly artful manner, I thought—as a whip cracked and the coach made a great lurch forward. It hurtled Downhill. The gray stones of the Hillgate flashed by. My sisters were lost to sight.

OF MY JOURNEY I need say only a few things. It was long, for one, and consisted of a monotony of creaks and rattles and jolts broken only by those brief respites as the mail was delivered according to its schedule at each stop, keeping always to its timetables whether it was light out or dark.

Each time we halted, I would creep from the coach with the other travelers, all of us moving like crippled things from being folded up and tossed about for so long. If the schedule allowed, we would venture inside whichever crossroads inn or public house we found ourselves at for a bit to eat or drink. However, the fare was generally as burnt or awful as something Mr. Wyble's housekeeper might have prepared; they were bare and cheerless places.

Hardly would any of our aches have abated before the horses were changed and all of us crowded once again into the hard, dark interior of the coach. That the various letters and parcels in their trunks could be packed any less tightly than we passengers was something I could not imagine.

At Morrowset, the others I had journeyed with from Invarel disembarked. I was the only one of the group traveling onward. As the driver lit the lanterns that hung from the pole beside his bench, I climbed back into the coach along with a new set of travelers.

They were a plainer and grimmer lot than those I had traveled with from the city. They were country folk, I suppose, and were less inclined toward talk; indeed, they seemed disposed not to speak at all and instead were intent only on sleep. As if rest were somehow a possibility! The coach hurtled over roads that grew coarser by the mile. All the same, the other travelers folded their arms and bowed their heads, appearing as if they had fallen into the deepest repose. Though more than once, on the edge of my vision, I noticed one of them stealing a glance at me through cracked eyelids, only to clamp his eyes shut if I looked at him directly.

Hoping to find at least one other willing to pass the time in conversation, I made an effort to speak to the man who sat on the bench beside me. Unlike the others, he did not seem to sleep, and I thought perhaps he was from the city like myself. His coat was fashionably cut, and on his right hand was a gold ring carved like a lion's head.

I got the impression he was young, but I could not see if he was handsome or not, for there was little light inside the coach and he kept his hat on. Nor did it matter. My attempts at conversation were futile, my questions unanswered. I gave up and resigned myself to silence.

Nearly all of that leg of the journey was conducted in the night, so there was no scenery for me to look at out the windows. My head began to ache incessantly, as did my shoulders and spine, and I could feel the force of the night pressing inward, as if the coach were an egg being crushed in a dark hand. It was difficult to breathe.

I must have fallen into a kind of stupor—not sleep, for it had none of sleep's wholesomeness or recuperative properties—for when the coach came to a stop, my head went up and my eyes opened. Red light flickered in through the windows as the coach's lanterns swung without, and the illumination cast sharp shadows across the faces of my fellow travelers. The young man sitting next to me reached a hand inside his coat.

Outside, voices spoke—the deep voices of men. What words they uttered I could not tell, but by their tone they seemed to want something. We all sat motionless, straining to listen.

"Well, I've not time for any sort of inspection," we heard the driver say. "I'm pushing my timetable as it is."

There was a silence, then again the voices spoke. There were at least three of them. They were pressing for something.

"By God, the night is too short for this, Captain," the driver said, his voice rising so we heard it clearly. "I've shown you my papers. I've got nothing aboard save the mail and seven travelers. I thought it was the business of brigands to be interfering with the post, not the king's own soldiers. If you want to detain someone on the road, why don't you make it the highwaymen? A good evening to you, Captain!"

The reins snapped, and the coach lurched forward. We all remained frozen, waiting for the sound of hooves pounding after us in pursuit. But there was only the rattle of the wheels and another crack of the reins. After half a mile the man beside me removed his hand from his coat. I glanced at the other travelers, and they glanced at me, and I could see that all of us were making a count, though there was no need.

Our number was eight, as it had been ever since the stop at Morrowset.

After that no one pretended to sleep, and we all sat rigid as the coach rattled onward. What sort of land we traveled through now I could not tell, for the lanterns' illumination reached no more than a few paces from the coach. We were a tiny island of light adrift in a dark sea.

A few more times we stopped at some silent post to deliver the mail. On such occasions we would get out and stretch our legs, and once we took a bit of cold tea and toast that had been set out for us on a table in the deserted public room of an inn, as if left there by ghosts.

It was after one of these stops that we returned to the coach to find our number had been reduced by one. The young man in the fashionable coat who had been sitting next to me was nowhere to be seen. When the driver asked if all were aboard, we told him our number. He nodded, then climbed into his seat and whistled to the horses.

We spoke no more of it. But after that, we slept.

❦

FOR SOME HOURS I must have been unconscious, for when I opened my eyes again, the light of a pale dawn gleamed through the windows of the coach.

It seemed we had passed through a door to another world sometime during the night. Gone was the cultivated countryside that surrounded Invarel, with its picturesque villages, broad green fields, and manor houses and well-tended groves nestled behind high walls.

Instead, the land I saw was a wild, half-formed place: all heather hills and ridges of gorse speckled with bog and marsh. The practice of enclosure had not reached out so far into the hinterlands (County Westmorain being closer to Torland than Invarel), and the only walls I saw were rough lines of fieldstone drawn upon the landscape, not to exclude people but merely to prevent cattle and sheep from wandering. A series of low fells glowered in the distance, shreds of mist catching on their tops.

The road dropped into a dell and followed alongside a small river for a mile. Then we crossed a bridge and so came into the village of Cairnbridge: a small collection of solid stone houses with slate roofs. We made our stop at the lone inn, which stood across from the village green. The coach did not linger; its timetable left no time to spare. I was the only one to disembark, and the other passengers did not bid me farewell.

I looked around, but at this early hour the village was silent. A gray cat eyed me but ignored my little clucks and coaxings and instead slunk down the alley next to the inn. Mr. Quent had written that I would be met at the station, but I could not detect a living soul in view.

There was nothing to do but wait. However, anxious to move after so many hours of confinement in the coach, I left my bags on the step of the inn and walked across the village's one cobbled street to the common green. I let myself through a gate in the low wall and stepped into the field beyond.

I found myself in the company of a pair of red cows, but they paid me no heed as they chewed a meal of grass. I walked along the wall, and as I went, I, too, derived sustenance from the little field. The air murmured through the grass, and a crow let out throaty calls, watching me with bright black eyes from its perch on the wall.

As I walked, I felt a kind of peace such as I had not felt in many days, indeed, not since that terrible day of my mother's passing. It was strange that in a place that was in every way alien to me I should feel so comforted. Even the heathland that I glimpsed beyond the village, forlorn as it was, did not dim my spirits. Rather, I felt a sort of muted wonder at its starkness, and in the morning light my eyes attempted to discern all the subtle shadings of russet and gold, of gray-green and loamy brown.

My wandering had taken me around the perimeter of the commons to the far side, and it occurred to me that I was now a good distance from the inn and that someone looking for me might not easily notice where I had gone. I started directly across the field, picking up the hem of my dress as I went, for the grass was wet with dew.

As I approached the center of the field, I came upon a stump. Its size was remarkable, and I paced around the edge. Given its circumference, the tree for which it had served as a foundation must have been of an enormous size—indeed, must have dominated the entire field. I attempted to count the rings in the stump, but there were far too many.

As I examined the stump, I noticed the outer bark was blackened and cracked, and the hard soil around it was devoid of grass. My gaze caught a rusty edge that jutted from the ground. I bent closer; it was the head of an ax, broken in two.

A wind sprang up, and the grass hissed and tossed. The crow spread sooty wings and sprang off the wall, letting out several harsh calls as it rose into the sky. I clutched my bonnet against the wind and stood.

A hand touched my arm.

I let out a gasp and turned around. A man stood before me. He was short and bandy-legged, dressed in a brown jacket, his head crowned by a shapeless hat. He peered at me with a leathern face.

"I'm supposing ye must be Miss Lockwell," he said, the words so thick and slurred I wondered if he suffered from some impediment.

It took me a moment to find the power to speak. "Are you Mr. Quent?"

"Mr. Quent, she thinks I am! Saints and stones guard me." He shook his head. "Nay, I keep the grounds up at Heathcrest. I was told to come fetch ye. I would've been here sooner, but the mare threw a shoe, and I had to heel it on back an' fetch the old gelding."

I was, I confess, relieved to discover that this was not my employer, though for this feeling I chided myself. What did it matter if Mr. Quent was handsome or homely? Besides, I had no reason to think ill of this fellow. His manner of speech was not a defect, I had determined, but merely a thick west-county accent.

Having recovered my manners, I thanked him for coming and learned that his name was Jance.

"This tree must have been magnificent when it was alive," I said, looking again at the stump. "Do you know what happened to it?"

"Mrs. Darendal will be wondering after us," he said. "I warrant we'd best get going. The carriage is at the inn."

"I just need to retrieve my bags from the steps, and I will be ready to go, Mr. Jance."

"No mister," he said. "It's only Jance."

"Of course," I said, and I followed him across the commons. Above, the crow floated in circles like a bit of ash on the breeze.

❧

T HE CARRIAGE TURNED out to be an old-style surrey, with a seat for two suspended between four large wheels, and the gelding attached to it was far more than old, being an ancient thing I was sure was older than me.

We made our way at a pace I could have easily beaten afoot. Not that I had a wish to proceed faster, feeling some trepidation now that I was so close to meeting my new employer. What if he did not think I had the right look or the proper manner about me?

Only that was foolish. He had not been able to arrange for any other governess, and beggars could not be choosers. No matter what he thought upon our meeting, he would simply have to make do with me.

This thought cheered me, and after that I enjoyed the ride, gazing with interest at all the sights around me. We passed several crofts and farms and the ruins of an ancient-looking stone chapel. At last we made a slow ascent up and around the shoulder of a broad hill, and as we neared the top I caught my first view of Heathcrest Hall. As its name suggested, it stood upon the high point, all alone save for a nearby tumble of stones.

I cannot say I found the house welcoming at first sight. It was too stern for that, all broad plinths and thick columns and brooding lintels—features constructed not for grace but rather for strength to withstand fierce elements. It was nothing like the airy houses of the New Quarter. All the same, after some study, I thought it handsome in its way. Old-fashioned, to be sure, even a bit dull. But comforting too. I could imagine that, no matter how the winds might howl, within those walls one would always be protected.

Gamely giving up what seemed its final breaths, the horse pulled the surrey up the hill, and we halted before the house. Jance unloaded my bags and without further words freed the horse from its harness and led the poor creature away. With nothing else to do, I picked up my satchels and went to find Mrs. Darendal.

When several knocks on the front door yielded no response, I let myself in. The front hall was everything I would have expected of a country manor: a room that ran the full length of the house, heavy-beamed and paneled with wood. There were as many heads of stag and boar on the walls as there were ancestral portraits, so that one got the impression all were held in equal regard. I could have made a bedchamber of the fireplace that dominated one end of the hall. Seeing no one about, I started that way to make a closer examination of it.

"You shouldn't have come here," said a low voice.

I turned and saw no one else in the room, though to my left a large stuffed wolf, mounted upon a pedestal, gazed at me with glassy eyes.

"This is a perilous place," came the gruff voice again. The sound was emanating from the wolf.

"I have no doubt that it is," I said. I made sure to appear properly alarmed, as one should when addressed by such a creature.

"You should go back to the city at once," the wolf said.

"You seem a very clever wolf. How do you know I'm from the city?"

"You smell like government."

"I am sure my nose is not so discerning as yours," I said to the wolf. "All the same, I've traveled very far to reach this place. Why should I leave when I've only just arrived?"

"Because we'll eat you if you don't!" cried a badger that stood on a nearby end table. It proceeded to roar in a manner that was distinctly unbadgerlike.

"Chambley, I told you not to say anything!" the wolf complained, its voice rising several octaves.

"I can say anything I want," the badger replied crossly. "If you're a wolf, then you can't be my sister, and that means you can't tell me what to do." There came another fierce roar.

"*Chambley!*"

I had played this little game long enough. I stepped around the stuffed wolf and gazed down at the girl crouched behind it.

"Good morning, Clarette," I said.

She frowned and looked up at me. I guessed her to be nine or ten. "You're not supposed to know my name."

"Why is that?"

She scowled, stroking the wolf's fur. It was worn and patchy. "We haven't met. You're not supposed to say my name if we haven't met. Mother says—she said it isn't proper."

I nodded and took a step back. "I am Miss Lockwell," I said, and held out my hand.

She stood and solemnly shook my hand. "I'm Clarette Davish."

"I'm very pleased to meet you, Clarette," I said, but she had already released my hand and was stroking the wolf again.

"What about me?" growled the badger. A small hand stuck out from beside the table on which it perched, waving.

"I'm very pleased to meet you, Sir Badger," I said, giving the hand a firm shake.

A boy suddenly appeared on the other end, standing up from behind the table. His eyes were very large in a small face. "My name is Chambley Davish. I'm not really a badger, you know."

"I see. Thank you for telling me. I confess, I feel some relief at this revelation."

"You shouldn't pretend like that," he said. "I know you didn't really think I was a badger." He climbed onto a horsehair chair and slouched backward. His feet did not touch the floor.

"She was only being nice," Clarette said. "Adults say all sorts of things that aren't true just to be nice. Don't they?"

Her eyes were dark, like her hair, and very sharp. I could not deny the truth of her words. "I suppose they do."

"Mother said we shouldn't ever lie. But how is saying something that's not true just to be polite any different than lying?"

I considered her words. "It's different because it's not intended to harm or do any sort of wrong. Sometimes one says something that's false in order to avoid saying something that's hurtful. But a lie . . ." I nodded. "A lie is something you say when you know you *should* say the truth, only you don't."

Chambley looked at his sister, but she only petted the wolf and said nothing more.

"Well," I said at last, "I have had a long trip, and I believe I'm ready for some tea. Would you two like to join me?"

"Oh, but we can't," Clarette said.

"Why not?"

"Mrs. Darendal says we're not allowed to have tea. She says it's bad for children, that it will make our bones grow crooked and rot out our teeth."

"Does she indeed?" It appeared I was going to have to have another conversation about saying things that weren't true, only this time with Mrs. Darendal. "Well, I'm in grave want of a cup, and it would be rude of me to take tea while you had nothing at all. So we'll just have to not worry about your bones and your teeth this once."

The two children exchanged startled looks.

"Well, then," I said, holding out both hands, "who would like to show me to the kitchen?"

Upon which my hands were seized from either side, and I was tugged across the hall.

❧

THE KITCHEN WAS a low, rambling room with a fireplace nearly as cavernous as that in the front hall. There was no sign of the housekeeper, though there was a woman—somewhat older than me—scrubbing the table, her face all but lost beneath a large bonnet.

I introduced myself as the new governess and asked if she might fix a kettle for tea for myself and the children. However, my words received no response. Instead, she ceased her work, took up a bucket, and without looking up departed through the kitchen door.

"Her name is Lanna," Clarette said. "She won't speak. She never does. Lanna used to talk and talk, but Mrs. Darendal told her Mr.

Quent won't put up with servants who chatter. She said Lanna would be dismissed if she spoke even one more word, and Lanna's family is terrible poor. She hasn't said a thing since that day."

"But that's remarkable!" I said, taken aback. "To never say a word—what sort of person could order such a thing?"

Chambley folded his arms and leaned on a sideboard, staring at a loaf of bread. "Do you think we could have toast with our tea?"

"We're very hungry," Clarette said.

Their faces *were* thin, and Chambley seemed as much a bird as a boy as he alighted on one of the large chairs at the table. His hair was dark like his sister's, which made his small face look all the paler. I wondered if they were ever fed.

"Yes, you may have toast," I said, and with that I rolled up my sleeves, put on the kettle, and found a knife for the bread.

Though I was tired, our little tea revived me greatly, and I found I was able to use the opportunity to gain some knowledge of my charges before I was officially installed as their governess. It was difficult for me to fathom why Mr. Quent had thought them in such dire need of guidance. True, the little game they had played with me upon my arrival indicated some lack of restraint in their behavior, a bit of willfulness even, and suggested a prior indulgence.

However, given what I knew of their situation—how their mother had died after a long illness, how over a year later their father was still not in any state to be able to care for them, and how they had been transferred among a succession of distant relatives—I could only think they were surprisingly good.

I quickly saw that Clarette was the leader of the pair and that her brother, who was two years her junior, would follow her in anything. She was a clever girl, always thinking up games for them, like their little play in the front hall. Hers was a vivid imagination, if occasionally morose. However, given her experiences over the last year, this could only be understandable. As was Chambley's nature, which was oversensitive. He seemed aware of every little sound or flicker of light and often started in his seat if a creak was heard or the shadow of a bird passed outside the window.

In all, I was not displeased. Here were two young minds that I was confident could be engaged if interesting material was presented to them with proper attention and zeal. I poured another cup of tea as the children made a game with the spoons and bread crusts. What its rules were I was not immediately able to grasp, but they played it very intently, and occasionally crusts or spoons were removed or returned to play.

There was a groaning of wood. Chambley jumped in his chair.

"It is only the house settling," I said.

But Clarette had set down her spoon and was staring at something behind me. I turned and could not help a small gasp. A woman stood in the door of the kitchen. Her hair was pulled back in a knot the color—and indeed, by its look, the hardness—of iron. Her dress was the same hue, and without any adornment. Her mouth was a flat line.

The children slouched in their seats and gave the teacups guilty looks. At that moment I felt like slouching as well, as if I were a child myself, caught in an illicit act. But that was absurd! I stood up, willed my shoulders back, and gave a smile as I introduced myself.

"You must be Mrs. Darendal," I said.

She looked at the things on the table, as if cataloging each item. Her eyes were deeply set above high cheeks. She must have been striking in her youth, but age had shown little kindness. What might once have been beautiful had gone sharp. Her glances cut the air.

However, if she thought ill of what I had done, she did not speak of it and instead said only, "I will show you to your room, Miss Lockwell. You must take some rest after your journey. The master says you will begin with the children tomorrow."

I cast a smile back at them. "Really, I need only a little rest. I am sure we can begin our lessons today."

"Mr. Quent said you would begin tomorrow. I am certain if that is his recommendation you will follow it. That is, unless you feel it is your place to correct him, Miss Lockwell."

I could not help wincing. "Of course not."

We went first to the room I described earlier, which was far too grand, as I remarked, then came to the little room beneath the gable. I expressed my belief that it would do very well.

"Jance will bring up your bags," Mrs. Darendal said from the door. "Dinner will be served promptly at two o'clock. Do not expect anything more than a simple meal. Nor should you plan on there being anything more later. I am sure you are used to dining as late as you please in the city, but here in the country we do not fix supper on short lumenals."

At these words a bit of impertinence came over me. That her manner was stiff I might almost forgive, as I did not know her. But that she should presume, after such a brief acquaintance, to know *me* was something I could not accept.

"I assure you, I expect nothing of the kind," I said. "I am quite used to dining but twice on short lumenals, for they are, you can be certain, every bit as brief in the city as they are in the country."

The housekeeper made no reply. She turned and reached to pull the door shut behind her.

"Did you tell the children they are not allowed to have tea?" I said, taking a step forward.

She halted, then looked back at me over her shoulder. "Is that what little miss told you?"

This reply startled me, but I did not let it deter me from continuing. "Yes, just as she told me how Lanna was ordered never to speak a word. I know I am new to this house. Yet I can only wonder when I hear such things."

"Indeed, I can only wonder as well," Mrs. Darendal said. "For the children have tea and toast every breakfast, though often they turn their noses up at it. And I have known Lanna all her life, and she has not spoken a word since she was a girl. The doctor says she has lost the capacity for speech. She is mute. Is there anything else you wish to tell me, Miss Lockwell?"

However, at that moment I was incapable of speech myself.

The housekeeper nodded. "Then I suggest you take your rest until dinner." And she shut the door behind her.

❦

MR. QUENT WAS not at dinner that day or at the breakfast we took in the middle of the long umbral that followed.

"The master sends his welcome and asks that you begin your work," Mrs. Darendal said as she entered the small parlor on the first floor, at the back of the house.

"So you have spoken to Mr. Quent," I said, surprised. "Then he must be in residence. But where is he? I should think he would like to meet the person he has taken into his employment."

Mrs. Darendal's face was all lines and angles in the light of the sole candle that lit our meal. "The master's business often takes him away at a moment's notice. He arrived well into the umbral but then set off again over an hour ago. Nor should you expect to see him often even when he is here. He is a busy man and cannot be concerned with domestic affairs. That is why you were hired, Miss Lockwell."

"Of course" was my reply.

However, I was beginning to wonder if what had seemed formality in Mr. Quent's letters had instead been the product of coolness and distance. A man who hired the likes of Mrs. Darendal to keep his house could not be concerned with matters like kindness, comfort, or warmth. From what I had seen so far, Heathcrest Hall was well organized and scrupulously clean, but the fireplaces were all barren, and the few candles could do little to keep it warm or drive away the shadows.

Well, if Mr. Quent could not concern himself to see what the children were doing, then I could look after them as I saw fit. This parlor, I had been told, was to be used for our studies as well as for taking meals. I moved about the room and lit several more candles.

"We aren't supposed to do that," Chambley said. "Mrs. Darendal says if there's one candle, then there's enough."

I knew from yesterday's experiences that I could not, as a matter of course, believe what the children told me about the housekeeper— though this particular statement did seem credible.

"One candle might be enough to eat by," I said, "but it is not enough to learn by. Sometimes it takes more than one light to show the way."

Clarette scowled. "What does that mean?"

"It means," I said as I examined the bookcase near the windows, "that real illumination comes not from one source but from many."

Chambley heaved his small shoulders in a sigh. "I know what she's saying. She means we're going to read lots of books." He put his hands to his forehead. "Books make my head feel like it's filled with jelly."

"Perhaps you've not been reading the right ones," I said, and pulled a volume from the shelf. "This should provide a good start. Have you read any of the histories of Telarus?"

Clarette crossed her arms and slouched in her chair. "I've never heard of him. Is he someone you know from Invarel?"

I could not help a smile. "No, he does not live in Invarel. And while I cannot say I have ever met him, I do feel that I know him from his writings. That is the mystery of books. When I read one of his histories, I imagine I am having a conversation with Telarus himself, yet he lived over twelve hundred years ago."

"You mean he's dead?" Clarette said eagerly, sitting up in her chair.

"Yes," I said, a bit reluctantly given her reaction, but I could hardly deny the fact. "He died many centuries ago, but his wisdom and learning are still with us today."

"So reading is like talking to a ghost," Clarette said, her dark eyes agleam in the candlelight.

"Primitive peoples believed in ghosts, Clarette. We live in a scientific age. We have no use for ghosts anymore." I sat at the table and opened the book. "Now, which of you would like to begin reading?"

WE STAYED IN the parlor for several hours, reading. I drew the curtains shut so we might more easily believe it was morning rather than the middle of a long night, and we went through one of the early volumes of the *Lex Tharosia,* which concerned the time before the founding of the republic.

At first the children eyed the door often and seemed on the verge of bolting. Determined to engage them, I chose a chapter that described a siege when barbarians from the western steppes attacked the city of Tharos, and I read it with vigor. The legions of Tharos fought bravely, but they were outnumbered. Then, just when the barbarians were battering the gate, I set down the book.

"What are you doing?" Chambley said. His eyes were large in his face. "We have to find out how the legions drive off the Murgonoths."

Clarette leaned across the table toward him. "But they don't drive them off. After all, it's not Tharos anymore. It's the Murgh Empire. The Murgonoths march in and kill the soldiers and burn all of Tharos to the ground."

"No, they don't!"

"Well, I bet you they do."

"We do not make wagers, Clarette," I said. "And you might be surprised what happens. If you wish to find out, you have only to read on. I've read quite enough myself, I think."

The idea that reading might grant them something they actually wanted seemed to astonish them, but after a moment Clarette took up the book, and then Chambley took a turn. Both demonstrated some degree of halting and stumbling; all the same, I was given sufficient cause to hope that, with a good deal more practice, both would become accomplished readers.

At last the Murgonoths broke down the gates. They flooded into the city, but the Tharosians were nowhere to be found. Then, to their surprise, arrows flew over the city walls. They looked out to see that the legions of Tharos now surrounded the city. They had escaped through secret tunnels, which they had collapsed behind them, and had taken all the food with them. The Murgonoths were trapped within the very city they had attempted to conquer. The barbarians soon succumbed to starvation, and the Tharosians were able to re-enter their own city without unsheathing their swords.

"You mean that the Murgonoths were all dead," Clarette said with a bit too much glee.

Chambley stared at the table. "I don't want to think about them all there in the city. I wouldn't go in. The city would be full of gho—" He looked up at me and shut his mouth.

I decided it was time for another subject, and after that we spent
an hour on ciphering. Chambley surprised and pleased me with his
ability; he could total large sums quickly. Clarette, however, could
hardly be made to look at her paper; her gaze kept flickering to the
curtained window. At last I could no longer tolerate this behavior.

"What is it you hope to see outside, Clarette?"

Both of the children looked up at me.

"I've noticed how you keep looking at the window. However, I
don't know what you can possibly hope to see. The almanac says it will
be night for over twelve more hours. Tell me, what were you looking
for?"

She gazed at me with her dark eyes but said nothing. Chambley
gripped his pencil and looked at his paper.

"Well, then, if you will not tell me, perhaps I will open the curtain
and see for myself what is outside."

I rose and moved to the window, but as my hand touched the curtain, Chambley leaped up from his chair.

"No, don't open it!"

I turned to regard him. "Why not?"

He was looking at Clarette. "What if *she's* out there?"

"What if who is out there, Chambley?" I said. "Direct your attention to me, not to your sister. Do you mean Mrs. Darendal? I'm quite
sure she is inside the house."

The two of them exchanged a long glance. I almost thought
Clarette moved her lips slightly. Chambley's face was pale.

At last Clarette looked at me, and in the candlelight her face
seemed older than its ten years. "He doesn't mean Mrs. Darendal."

"Then who, Clarette? Who does he mean?"

They did not answer me, and I could not suppress a shiver. But it
was only a draft of air slipping between the curtains, and now I was
growing cross at their behavior. I gripped the curtains and threw them
to either side. Chambley clamped his hands over his eyes.

"There," I said. "There's nothing."

It was pitch-black outside the window. There were no stars. The
window looked eastward, away from the village, and not a light was to
be seen out on the heathland. I suffered again that feeling I sometimes
do in the midst of a long night, the sensation of the darkness pressing
inward, like the Murgonoths pressing inward on the city of Tharos,
wanting to vanquish it. Only there were no secret passages by which
we might escape. We were trapped inside, with only our feeble candles to push back the darkness.

"Miss Lockwell?"

I realized I had been staring at the dark. I turned around. Clarette was smiling. It was, I thought, a smug expression. I did not care for it.

"We have studied enough for now," I said. "Go play quietly in your room. I will call you down when it is time for your dinner."

❧

𝓘 WILL NOT DENY it: as I went to bed for the second time during that long night, my spirits were low.

Other than the children, I had not seen a living soul since breakfast, and I could easily understand how Chambley's imagination tended toward thoughts of ghosts, for as devoid as it was of living beings, this house was well populated with shadows, whispering drafts, and far-off groans. Even our supper appeared as if by the work of specters, laid out for us in the parlor while we walked up and down the front hall for some exercise.

I laid in my sleigh bed for a long time before sleep came; I longed to see you, Father, and my sisters; I missed my mother. I felt very alone. However, the voice of the wind outside was not sinister, merely mournful, so it seemed to me I was not alone after all, and at last I slept.

The next day, and for many days after that, my spirits were greatly improved. There were several longer lumenals in a row and one very short umbral that was over almost before we shut our eyes. While I cannot say the increase in light transformed Heathcrest Hall into a cheerful place, it did serve to soften the somber atmosphere, so that it did not seem such a startling thing to laugh or to suddenly speak in a raised voice.

As much as possible, and whenever the weather allowed, I took the children outdoors. That air and exercise would benefit them both, I had no doubt. A fair complexion might be fashionable, but their skin was so pale as to be nearly translucent. The first time I took them out, they blinked and rubbed their eyes, though the sun was half lost in a misty haze.

"Mother says—she said the damp air is bad for me," Chambley said. He took shallow breaths through his teeth.

"His lungs aren't strong, that's what Mother told us," Clarette said.

He shook his head. "Not strong."

"Well, there's only one way to improve them," I said, "and that's by putting them to use." Clasping their hands lest they attempt to retreat inside, I led them down the front lane.

Our walk was not long that day. We made it only to an old stone that stood along the lane not far from the house. It was black and pitted, unlike the gray outcrops on the distant fells, and nearly as tall as me. Clarette discovered that, when viewed from a certain angle, the stone bore what looked like the profile of a grotesque face looking toward the house. Someone had carved the word *Heathcrest* into its dark surface long ago.

I wanted to press on, but the mist began to descend quickly, and we hurried back to the house. However, over those next days our ramblings took us farther down the lane and along footpaths that crossed the summit of the ridge.

"We're awfully far from the house," Chambley said as we started down one of the side paths. He was breathing rapidly, as he often did on our walks; however, I had come to the conclusion that it was not exertion that caused this effect but rather apprehension.

"On the contrary," I said in a cheerful tone, "I am sure we're not two furlongs away. If Mrs. Darendal were to stand on the front step and call to us, we should hear her clearly. Now, come."

He did, though as we walked I noticed that he glanced often over his shoulder.

The day was clearer than any since I had come to Heathcrest, the air clean with the scent of juniper. So encouraged, I led the children on until we came to a prospect surmounted by a scatter of stones. The stones were long and flat. Some were worn by wind and spotted with lichen, but others were paler and sharper-edged.

The view was excellent. I could make out the roofs of the village to the west and, closer to Heathcrest, the gray bones of the ruined chapel. Then I noticed the roof of a building standing alone to the south. I could not see what it was, as it was settled into a low place in the land, so I went to one of the stones, which leaned at an angle upon another, and climbed up it.

"What are you doing, Miss Lockwell?" Clarette called out.

"Getting a better view," I replied.

This time it was Chambley's voice that rang out. "But you'll fall and dash your head!"

"Only if I am very careless or very foolish," I replied. "In which case I will have deserved my fate."

I reached the top of the stone. My view was much improved, and I saw that the building was a house. It was a fine country cottage or lodge by the look of it, and I wondered who lived there. I let my gaze rove into the distance, and a serene feeling came over me. It was strange that a landscape so forlorn could be so appealing to me—indeed, even *familiar*.

The children were calling out. Their voices were high and sharp, though I could not make out what they said. I cast one more look at the scenery, then climbed back down the stones to them.

"There, I am perfectly well," I said. "Do you see?"

It was not at me they were looking. Instead, their faces were turned toward the east, and both had gone quiet.

"What is it?" I asked.

Chambley started to speak, but Clarette grasped his hand—hard, by the cry he let out. "It's time to get back," she said. "That's why we were calling for you." She pulled her brother, and they started back along the path.

I looked to the east, but I saw nothing save empty heath all the way to the scraggly line of the old Wyrdwood atop its own ridge a half mile off.

WHEN WE RETURNED to the house, I directed the children to play quietly in their room. I had thought this might elicit protests. However, Clarette only smiled, took Chambley's hand, and led him up the stairs.

I removed my bonnet and, deciding a cup of tea was in order, turned to make my way to the kitchen.

"You take them outdoors a great deal," Mrs. Darendal said. "Should they not be spending that time studying instead?"

I gasped, for I had not seen her there in the shadow beneath the staircase. Her sudden speech had startled me, nor could I help but think that had been her intent.

"Vigorous exercise clears one's thoughts, and a fresh mind learns more quickly," I said.

"But the little master's lungs are—"

"Are quite capable of drawing in air and will only get better at the task the more they are given the opportunity to do so." It was rude to interrupt, but I would not allow such talk when he could be in earshot. "I observe him closely, and I would halt our walks at the first sign of any distress, but he does very well."

Mrs. Darendal said nothing. Her face was as motionless as one of the portraits on the wall. At last she nodded and started up the stairs, and I continued to the kitchen.

However, I could only imagine that Mrs. Darendal was pleased when it rained all the next day, forcing us to stay indoors, and after that there were several short lumenals in a row. With little sun to burn it off, a fog settled in around the house, so that even by day we had to resort to candlelight to read.

The children grew cross, and Chambley jumped at every noise. Nor did Clarette help in this regard, for I caught her more than once telling her brother fanciful stories: how quickly greatwolves could gobble a person up; how the eyes of the trophy animals in the front hall watched you no matter where you went; how there was something awful in one of the rooms upstairs, and that was why they were forbidden to go in there.

I did my best to counteract such stories when I was a witness to them. However, given the sly looks Clarette gave me—and how apprehensive Chambley appeared—I could only believe he was audience to many more such tales when I was not present.

My only hope was to fill his mind with other, better thoughts, and as we could not go outside we spent most of our time together reading in our parlor. Sensing their natural interest in things ancient and legendary, and hoping to direct that interest away from Clarette's macabre imaginings toward something more worthwhile, I took from the shelf a book of old Altanian epic poems.

At first the children could hardly be made to look at the book; to them, poetry was a punishment. However, I told them not to think of these as poems but rather as stories intended to be sung. I instructed them to picture a bard in a thatch-roofed hall, thick with the smoke of braziers onto which honeyed herbs had been thrown, strumming his lute while he sang of legends that were ancient even in those ancient days.

"We aren't going to have to sing, are we?" Chambley asked with an alarmed look.

"No," I said with a laugh. "You would find my singing to be very ill, I am sure. But let us imagine we are bards of old, telling tales to a chieftain in his hall, or perhaps to Queen Béanore herself."

This thought seemed to engage them, particularly Clarette, and after that they read with interest. We were thus kept occupied over several days as we read some of the oldest true Altanian literature.

Chambley particularly liked the story of King Atheld. He was lord of one of the petty kingdoms in southern Altania, in the time before the Tharosians sailed to these shores. In the first year of his reign, a greatnight came, longer than any that had ever been known before. On and on the umbral went. The world grew cold. Crops withered in the fields, and cattle froze to death.

Atheld knew his people would perish as well. So, alone except for his loyal squire, he sailed westward in a small coracle looking for the Isle of Night. At last he found it and there took back the coal of the sun from the magician who had stolen it. The greatnight ended; light and life returned to the world.

"But that's just a myth," Clarette said, crossing her arms. "It didn't really happen. The sun isn't a hot coal."

I smiled at her. "No, but astrographers have made the calculations, and they determined that an unusually long umbral—one lasting over two hundred hours—did indeed occur during the time of King Atheld. So you see, behind a myth can lie a greater truth." Then my smile faded, for I thought of the similar words you had written to me, Father.

"Is something wrong, Miss Lockwell?" Chambley was looking at me, his head tilted to one side.

I drew a breath. "Not at all. I was only thinking how to reply to Clarette. It *is* true that myths are stories. But for people who lived long ago, myths were also truth—and a way to explain and make sense of the world around them."

Clarette leaned over toward her brother. "Do you hear that, Chambley? Myths can be true. You know what *that* means, don't you?"

Chambley sat up straight in his chair. "That means there can be ghosts."

"On the contrary," I said in as cheerful a voice as I could manage. "While scientists have studied the heavens and can predict when a greatnight will end, they haven't found one whit of evidence that indicates there are ghosts."

"But if there aren't ghosts, then who's the Pale Lady?"

Clarette let out a hiss and seized her brother's wrist. "Chambley!"

"Clarette, let go of your brother," I said. And to him, more gently, "What lady do you speak of?"

"The lady out in the fields. The one who waves to us."

Clarette squeezed his wrist. "Stop it, Chambley."

"Clarette," I said, making my voice sharp. "Release your brother at once."

"She wants to make us into ghosts, doesn't she? That's why she keeps waving to us. She wants us to come to her."

"Stop it," Clarette said, his flesh turning white beneath her fingers. "Stop it now."

"Clarette, release him this instant!"

I started toward them, but at that moment Chambley's eyes went wide, staring at the window behind me.

A scream rang out. It was Clarette. She snatched her hand back and covered her eyes. She screamed again, and Chambley cried out as well, and then both of them together screamed again and again, making a shrill racket. I tried to move, but I was a thing formed of cold clay; I could not bring myself to look at the window, for a dread of what I would see there had come over me. Only by great will did I finally manage to turn my head, to move to the window, to gaze through the glass.

I saw only fog and my own white reflection.

Still the children screamed. I went to them, trying to pull their hands from their eyes, but they were rigid, their limbs filled with uncanny strength. Their hands were making red marks on their faces.

"Stop it!" I said, but my voice could not be heard over their cries. "There's nothing out there. Stop it at once!" But they were hysterical, rocking in their chairs. Chambley's breath came in gasps. I went to him, grasping his shoulders. I fear I would have shaken him, except for at that moment a deep voice spoke behind me.

"What is going on in here?"

At once the children fell silent, slumping in their chairs like cast-off dolls. Their faces were white beneath scarlet splotches. Their eyes were wide, only this time they looked not at the window but at the door of the parlor.

I turned around. A man stood in the door. He was not particularly tall, but there was a substance to him that made him seem larger than he was, so that when he stepped into the parlor his presence was felt as a heavy weight. I laid a hand on the back of a nearby chair, as if, without this grip, I might otherwise have fallen toward him.

His eyes were dark beneath scowling brows, his mouth a line set deep in a curling beard. His hair was wet against his forehead, as if he had just come in from outside. Indeed, his brown coat, which was cut for riding, and the mud spattered on his boots left no question to the matter. Nor could there be any question as to who he was.

"Mr. Quent, it is good to meet you," I said, having recovered the ability to think. I took a step from the chair and held out my hand to him.

He did not take my hand. Instead, he turned his gaze on the children. "Leave us," he said. "I must speak with Miss Lockwell alone."

Clarette and Chambley said nothing. They did not look at him. They rose from their chairs. Clarette took Chambley's hand and led him from the parlor.

"Go play in your room," I called after them, but I received no answer; they were gone, and I was alone with Mr. Quent. He said nothing, but I could not feel it was *my* place to speak first. Nor did I have any idea what I would say. I was still trying to understand myself what had happened. I went to the window and drew the curtains shut, then gathered up the books on the table, which had been scattered in the commotion.

He cleared his throat. "Is everything well, then?"

"Yes, very well."

A silence. Then, "The children seemed very excited just now."

I could not bring myself to look at him. "They were so, I confess. I was trying to calm them. They have very strong imaginations."

"Those books—what were you reading to them?"

"We were reading from the old Altanian epics."

I could feel him glowering.

"And you feel such topics are appropriate for young children?"

"I read the same stories myself when I was their age. A knowledge of the classics can only form a solid foundation upon which to base a study of more-modern works. Though I admit, it is possible the story today encouraged their minds more than I intended."

I carried the books to the shelf and returned them to their places.

At last he spoke. His voice was so deep I could feel it as a vibration on the air. "You were brought here to keep order and quiet, Miss Lockwell, not to encourage their minds."

It was foolish. He was my employer and I had only just met him, but an indignation rose within me at these words. The way he had been so short with the children—had not even greeted them after so many days away—how could he not expect them to disobey him? I turned and looked at him directly.

"Is that the case, Mr. Quent? Then I must be in error. You see, I was under the impression that I was brought here to teach them. How that can be accomplished without encouragement is, I confess, beyond me. Perhaps you can instruct me in the matter, for it seems you have very particular thoughts on the topic. Indeed, so particular that I can only wonder how you ever wanted for a governess at all."

I thought he would raise his voice with me or express his displeasure. Instead, he regarded me in silence, and I could only regard him in turn.

He was not so old as I had thought he would be, though he was over forty, I was certain, despite his dark hair. His figure was athletic rather than fine, being somewhat barrel-chested. As for his face, it was stern and squarish, with a high forehead: not handsome, though it might have been described as strong, even well-crafted. However, fashionable observers would also have pronounced his visage utterly ruined by weather, for it was deeply tanned, with lines incised across his brow and around his eyes. To me his face seemed as wind-hewn as the landscape around Heathcrest Hall. I could no more imagine a smile blossoming upon it than flowers upon the moor.

At last I could endure the force of his dark eyes no longer. If he was not going to speak, I could not imagine a need to remain in the room with him. I started toward the door.

"You are very sure of yourself, Miss Lockwell."

I halted at the door, gripping the molding so he could not see my hand tremble. How could he have been more wrong? At that moment I wished I was back on Whitward Street, back with my sisters, and with all my familiar things. I felt a child myself.

All the same, I stood straight and looked back at him. "Will you be joining us for supper tonight, Mr. Quent?"

"I seldom know what my business will allow. It is most unpredictable. That I might be called away in a moment is all I can say. I fear I can tell you nothing more about it."

Despite myself, I smiled. "I did not ask you about your business, Mr. Quent. Only about supper. I hope you will be able to join us."

Without waiting for his reply—indeed, if my patience would ever have rewarded me with one—I left him in the parlor.

❧

HE DID JOIN us for supper that night, in body if not in spirit. For he entered the dining room, sat down, and picked up his soup spoon without giving us so much as a glance. He appeared startled when I greeted him, as if he had forgotten anyone else would be there.

After that he made only the sparest replies to any of my attempts at conversation and for his part made no inquiry regarding the progress of our studies. Nor did he inquire about my sisters—or even about you, Father, though I knew you had once been acquaintances. He ate his soup as if it were the gravest of tasks.

The children were sullen and slouched in their chairs; the clock consumed each bite of time with a tick. Lanna came in, bringing a plate of beef and cabbages but no hope for conversation.

At last I grew peeved at the silence. "Would you like the children to demonstrate their reading after supper, Mr. Quent?" I said in as lively a voice as I could manage. "I believe you will find they are improved, even in just these last few days."

He had already risen before I finished speaking. "I must attend to my work. Good night." He gave a stiff bow, turned on a heel, and was gone.

"He doesn't like us," Clarette said. "He wishes we weren't here."

"You know that isn't so," I said, but it was an automatic utterance, like the clock chiming the hour. I affected a smile for their sake. "Mr. Quent is a busy man, that's all. That's why he brought me here."

Chambley hung his head. "But *you* don't want to be here either."

"Now you're speaking nonsense," I said. "I would not have come all this way if that were the case. Let's go upstairs. It's time for bed."

I do not know if it was their cherubic faces or the way they slipped their hands into mine, but all the vexation I had felt toward them after their outburst in the parlor vanished, and I held their little hands tightly in my own as I led them up the stairs.

"You should not have frightened me like that today, you know," I said as we reached their room. "I'm afraid I did not make a good first impression on Mr. Quent because of it."

"We didn't *want* to frighten you," Chambley said.

"On the contrary, I think you had every intention of frightening me." I looked down at Clarette. "It was a game, wasn't it?"

She smiled up at me. "Yes, that was it," she said. "A game."

"There, that wasn't so hard, was it?" I brushed her dark hair. It was fine as silk. Chambley started to say something, but I shook my head. "No more talk. It's time to sleep." With that I sent them into their room.

I took a candle and went up to my own room. I tried to read, but as always the candlelight was too dim, and my thoughts kept turning back to that afternoon's commotion. I rued the way my introduction to my employer had gone. However, that the children should be prone to bursting out in an improper manner could only be expected given the oppressive atmosphere in this house. I had felt it myself ever since coming here and especially since Mr. Quent's arrival—the dreadful need to always go about like a mouse, creeping along without making a noise.

No doubt that was why today's outburst in the parlor had disturbed me so, for in no way did I believe the children had seen any sort of apparition. They had wanted to frighten me, that was all. And for a moment, suffering under all the gloomy weight of the silence that possessed this house, I had almost believed in ghosts.

However, the only presence that haunted Heathcrest Hall had sat at the head of the table earlier this evening, eating beef and cabbage. While I would grant the spirit the respect it was due, I was determined that I would not exist in fear of it.

🍂

THE MASTER OF the house was in residence for the next several days, though if Mrs. Darendal had not repeatedly reminded me of this fact,

I would have been hard-pressed to know it. He did not come to observe the children's progress, nor did he take any more meals with us. If he was seen at all, it was from a distance, and at such time he was always moving away, his shaggy head bowed and his broad shoulders slumped.

I confess, I could not find cause to complain about the arrangement. The farther *he* was from our parlor, the less *we* had to fear making some unwanted noise. While it was my intention that our studies should be ordered and not boisterous or unruly, it was not my belief that the children should never be allowed to laugh or to make such cheerful or even silly noises as were a natural part of childhood.

Mrs. Darendal was not of a similar mind, and on more than one occasion her stiff gray figure appeared in the door of the parlor.

"Hush!" she would say. "The master is at work, and your voices carry like a flock of crows."

Whether it was our voices she thought of as crows or if it was we who bore the comparison, I did not know. But one time, after she had left, the children paraded around the table, flapping their arms and letting out caws and cackles. I ordered them to cease—but not so quickly as I might have done, for it took me a moment to be sure I would not cackle with laughter myself.

Since the incident in the parlor, I had not taken the children on any more walks outside the manor; I was reluctant to give them any opportunity that might allow them to claim they had seen apparitions. However, the lack of exercise had an ill effect on them as well as me, until none of us could keep our eyes on a book. After that, we resumed our walks. A series of longer days had burned away the mist, so that the weather was clear and not at all conducive to the viewing of ghosts. All the same, we did not wander so far from the house as before.

Yet often I was tempted. On fair days I longed to venture to the edge of the rise that Heathcrest commanded, to gaze at the straggled line of the Wyrdwood to the east, to see something green. However, I did not want to take the children so far, and I never had enough time during daylight hours to go there on my own, for the children required all my attention.

What little time I did have to myself came in the afternoons of longer lumenals—days that contained too many hours for all of them to be spent in walking or reading or studying. At such times I would send the children to play as they wished in their room, and I in turn would retreat to the kitchen to sit and take a cup of tea.

On those occasions Lanna often joined me. Through gentle and persistent effort I had won first a look from her and eventually a smile. She could not talk to me, but I was grateful for her company; Heathcrest was not an easy place to be alone. I found that if I spoke about whatever thoughts came to my mind, she would find something to work on nearby.

Thus, while she polished plates or sliced radishes, I would speak of Invarel; of all the little gardens and cloisters I had loved; of the Citadel on its crag; of the grand carriages I saw driving up to the New Quarter; and of the boys hawking broadsheets on corners. I knew that she listened, for sometimes she ceased her work and stood with her head tilted and eyes shut. So I would keep speaking—until Mrs. Darendal entered, as she always did before long, and Lanna scurried away. Mrs. Darendal would treat me to a sharp look. I, in turn, would reply with a smile and ask if she wanted a cup of tea.

"You leave the children to themselves often," she said one afternoon. "I heard them in their room. Should you not be looking in on them?"

I sipped my tea. "I'm sure they are very well."

The housekeeper started toward the door, then paused. "But I cannot think it is good for them to spend so much time alone."

"On the contrary, being on their own is exactly what they need. One should never feel they are being observed at every moment. If one does not feel trusted, one will never learn to be trustworthy."

"But you cannot know what they are doing."

I set down my cup and stood, feeling a warmth in my cheeks—from the tea, of course. "Mrs. Darendal, I was hired by Mr. Quent to care for the children. I trust you will not question his judgment by instructing me how to do my job." Without waiting for a reply, I left the kitchen.

After that, much as I enjoyed Lanna's company, I found myself avoiding the kitchen. Instead, during such time I had to myself, I took to making a tour of the house. It was quickly apparent that making a thorough exploration of Heathcrest Hall would take some time; it was larger than I had thought at first, for there were many parts of it the current occupants never went into. However, while the doors to these rooms and wings were shut, they were not locked, so I spent several afternoons wandering through chambers filled with claw-footed chairs, yellowed Murghese vases, and scientific instruments of greenish copper whose purpose I could not fathom.

Portraits hung on many of the walls, their subjects clad in the attire of another age, their faces proud, even haughty. I wondered if these were Mr. Quent's forebears. Only they did not look like him. Some of the men wore large rings with a crest upon them. I had seen no rings of any kind on Mr. Quent's hands. Nor did he seem to have a title other than *Esquire,* which any well-to-do gentleman might append to his name. I could not help thinking this seemed a grand house for a mere gentleman.

At the head of the main stairs was a portrait of what I supposed was, given its prominent location and the more modern attire of its subjects, the last family to dwell in the house prior to Mr. Quent. A lordly-looking man of late-middle years sat in a chair, a similarly aged but still-handsome woman resting her hand on his shoulder. Beside them stood a young man, his good looks marred by the hint of a smirk the artist's brush had lent him.

Only after passing the painting several times did I notice that there was one more figure in the portrait. A girl of perhaps nine or ten stood apart from the others, her dark dress and dark hair melding with the shadows cast by a curtain. Only her face stood out, as pale as that of the porcelain doll she held in her hands. As I explored the house, I saw the lordly man, the woman, and the younger man who was surely their son in other paintings, but in no other portraits did the dark-haired girl appear. Who she was, what had become of her, was something I did not discover in my explorations.

However, there was something I did learn one afternoon as I wandered the house: Clarette had not been making up a story when she told Chambley there was a locked room upstairs. It was on the second floor, in the west wing, though none of the other rooms in that part of the house was locked.

There was nothing remarkable about the locked door; it looked like all the others. Nor was there any reason to think it was different on the inside, and I assumed the room beyond was similarly filled with furniture, or murky paintings, or empty trunks. I would have forgotten about the room had it not been for the fact that, as I started down the stairs, I heard the sound of a door opening behind me.

Peering between the banister posts, I saw a door open and shut down the hall. A quick count assured me it was the very door I had found locked a minute ago. A pair of heavy black shoes and the hem of a gray dress appeared in view. There was a jingling noise and the sound of a lock turning.

I bit my lip and hurried down the stairs, lest Mrs. Darendal catch me.

The next afternoon I again sent the children upstairs to play. Once they were in their room, I went directly to the west wing, to the second floor, and counted the doors until I came to the one. It was still locked. I hesitated, then pressed an ear to the wood.

Silence.

I knew it was foolish. What was beyond the door was none of my business. Nor was it likely of any interest. But that this one door of all the doors in this wing was locked made it a thing of curiosity, and the fact that I had seen Mrs. Darendal coming from it even more so.

Hoping to learn something by another avenue, I went downstairs and outside. The day was growing blustery; clouds ebbed and surged overhead, and the wind tangled my hair. I walked around the west side of the house and counted the windows on the second floor, making sure I had picked out the right one. However, it was all but covered in ivy, and so my efforts were thwarted by my own namesake.

I went back into the house. It was time to retrieve the children. We had a whole chapter yet to read before supper, and the afternoon was blowing away with the storm clouds. I climbed the stairs. However, when I came to a stop, it was not at the door to the children's room, but rather at the locked door.

It was wrong. All the same, I knelt and put an eye to the keyhole. Squinting, I tried to make sense of what I glimpsed beyond. I saw green light and tall, shadowy shapes.

"Is there something you're looking for, miss?"

I leaped to my feet. I suppose I gasped; at any rate, it took me a long moment to find my breath, and then all I could utter was, "Mrs. Darendal!"

The housekeeper walked toward me down the corridor. I heard a faint jingling as she did. The corners of her mouth were drawn in a frown more severe than usual.

"I discover the children in their room," she said. "Alone. And then I find you here."

I tried to think of some excuse for my presence but could devise none under her scrutiny. "I only wondered," I said. "This door—none of the others is locked, but this one is. Do you know why?"

"You have been trying doors, then?"

My cheeks colored, but I stood straight. "Heathcrest Hall is very grand. I've been enjoying making an exploration."

"There is nothing in there," Mrs. Darendal said.

"Of course," I murmured. I started past her toward the stairs. "But . . ." I gripped the banister and turned to look at her. "But if there's nothing in the room, then there can be no need to keep the door locked, can there?"

The housekeeper moved to the stairs. She laid her hand on the banister near to mine. She smelled of dry things: wool and ash.

"You asked me not to tell you how to manage the children, Miss Lockwell. And I will ask you not to tell me how to manage the house. No one is to go in that room, save for Mr. Quent alone."

"Of course," I said, and hurrying past her so she would not see the way my cheeks glowed, I went to find the children.

WE WOKE THE next day to discover Mr. Quent gone. Not that this affected me or the children in any way; we continued our lessons and walks as before. Nor did our habits alter when Mr. Quent returned at the end of a short, blustery lumenal, for it was hardly more difficult to avoid him when he was there than when he was not.

As my second month at Heathcrest passed, he was gone as often as he was in residence—or even more, perhaps, for I seldom knew when he had left. One time I had assumed him to be at the manor, only to look out and see him ride up, boots and coat and horse all mud-spattered, his hair wild from wind.

*He should wear a hat!* I thought. *His face shall become even more ruined by the weather than it already is.*

We were generally able to avoid encountering the master of the house. However, there were occasions when it was too dark to venture outside, yet the almanac and our weariness of sleep forced us to make a day of it. At such time the children grew restless, even unruly. I did my best to control them, but I could not be with them at every moment.

Once, after rising in the midst of a long night, I went to fetch our tea and upon returning found my charges not in the parlor where I had left them. At that moment I heard a crash from the front hall, followed by the shrill sounds of argument.

Upon entering the hall, I saw that one of the mounted animals— a fox—had been knocked from its stand. Lanna knelt beside it, attempting to put the stuffing back in its middle, while Clarette and Chambley pointed and shouted at each other.

I felt a chill draft and saw that a nearby window was ajar. The night flowed in, unimpeded. I hurried to the window and latched it, then asked the children what had happened. Their voices were so high-pitched I was forced to shout in an attempt to gain their attention. However, before my efforts had any effect, Mr. Quent appeared at the foot of the stairs.

He did not say anything. All the same, the weight of his presence was felt at once. The children fell silent and looked up, their faces going pale. I did the same. Lanna ceased her work, clutching a handful of fluff.

At last I managed to speak. "Clarette, Chambley, go to the parlor. Take up the chapbook and read Chapter Fourteen. I will expect you to provide me with a summary when I return."

The two slunk away without a sound. Mr. Quent said nothing further, so I knelt beside Lanna and examined the fox. It was old, getting bare of fur in places, and after its fall was coming apart at every seam.

"I am no doctor," I said, "but the prognosis does not seem good." I looked up at him with an attempt at a smile.

His expression did not alter. "What took place here?"

"I did not witness it myself. I was coming back from the kitchen. I suppose the children were playing and knocked it over, and they were arguing over who was to blame." I stood, smoothing the pleats of my dress. "It has been rainy and dark these several days, you see, and we have not been able to get any exercise or go—"

"Lanna, did you see what occurred here?" He looked down at the young woman.

She stared up at him, rigid lines in her neck.

"Answer me, child." His voice was gruff, even hard. "I heard you working in the hall. Tell me what took place. If it is not as Miss Lockwell thinks, then I must know."

She opened her mouth. It seemed, in her dread of him, the poor creature even attempted to speak, only no sound came out; she hung her head. The stuffing slipped from her fingers, falling like snow.

I could not speak myself; I was astonished. No, I was appalled. That *I* did not know of Lanna's condition upon first meeting her was understandable. But that *he,* after having her in his house for so long, could still be insensible to her state was confounding.

"Miss Lockwell," he said, addressing me in his low voice, "I thought I had made myself clear in our prior conversation. It is a requirement that we live quietly in this house. Because of—that is, it is necessary that Heathcrest be a solemn and thoughtful place. Commotion and loud disturbances cannot be tolerated."

"Of course, Mr. Quent," I murmured. But inwardly I cried out, *Oh, grim and dour man! You do not know poor Lanna cannot speak, because you expect muteness of everyone around you! You would buy silence at the price of any sort of contact with a fellow human creature.*

"Go fetch Jance," Mr. Quent said to Lanna. "I will have him take the fox out to the coach house. I imagine Miss Lockwell's diagnosis is correct. Her father was a doctor, and no doubt she has inherited something of his ability."

I hardly heard his words, so consumed was I with my outrage. Lanna hurried from the hall. I started to go myself, but I halted as he knelt and picked up the stuffed fox. He stroked it with a hand—a tender gesture such as I had never seen him give the children.

"I shot this one myself, many years ago," he said, his voice low.

He touched the fur of its head, and it was only as he did this that I noticed, for the first time, that his left hand was missing the last two digits. A thick scar covered the place where the ring finger and littlest finger should have attached to his hand. I marveled that, in all our prior interactions, I had never noticed.

I think he became aware of my attention, for he stood and slipped his left hand into his coat pocket. I realized then that I had often seen him that way.

He fixed me with his dark gaze. "You must give me your word, Miss Lockwell, that you will not allow the children to engage in another outburst like today's."

His gaze was so intent, his presence so heavy and brooding, that my every instinct was to demur. However, I forced myself to look at him directly. "I cannot make a promise for myself based on the actions of others, Mr. Quent. But I will promise to redouble my efforts to engage the children's minds and energies, especially on days when we cannot go out. Toward that end, I must see how their reading is progressing." Without waiting for his reply, I hurried from the hall.

I did not press the children for an explanation of what had happened; to be seen as their accuser would not help my cause with them. Nor did they offer any account on their own. All the same I could only believe that something *had* happened, for after that day, the openness they had shown me since my arrival was reduced.

I more often observed them whispering to each other, only to cease when I drew near. They often stared out the window, when a glance confirmed there was nothing outside. To make them pay attention to a book was a feat. Clarette was all sighs, and Chambley jumped at every sound. I started to despair that I would ever be able to occupy their attentions—in which case another incident like what had happened in the hall was inevitable. I began to really fear that Mr. Quent might dismiss me.

That would be a disaster. I had received letters from home. They were few and too short for my taste. However, Rose was no more voluble when writing than speaking; as for Lily, writing was like sewing: a chore done for the benefit of others.

Still, I had written many times to encourage their replies and so in bits and pieces had managed to gather some news of the situation on

Whitward Street. Even allowing that Lily's dislike for our cousin colored her descriptions, it was clear that Mr. Wyble intended them all to be gone from the house the moment the law allowed, now but four months in the future.

Nor could it be too soon for Lily. She had not been able to play the pianoforte, as Mr. Wyble declared the sound adverse to his concentration. The garden out front was all withered and brown, and there was never any chocolate or oranges to be had.

*But what of our father?* I wrote several times. At last I got an answer from her, though it was hardly better than no answer at all.

*He does not speak but makes noises,* Lily wrote. *He is dreadfully ill without you. Rose cares for him.*

My heart ached to read these lines. I wanted nothing more than to run to the village, to ride with the mail back to the city, to see my sisters and to see you, Father. But I could not. That our only hope was to remove ourselves to the house on Durrow Street was clearer than ever. To do that would be impossible without my income from Mr. Quent. Thus I renewed my efforts to govern the children and my own spirits as well.

For our lessons, I chose those subjects I thought would be of most interest to them. When the weather at all allowed, I bundled them against the damp air and took them on a walk outside. The exercise seemed to benefit them, but I did not like the way their gazes ranged to and fro, as if seeking some particular thing.

I tried to keep our walks close to the familiar grounds of the manor so that the children might find nothing in our excursions to excite their imaginations. But one day, after telling myself we should turn back, I found myself continuing onward, toward the eastern edge of the ridge—then even a little bit past, going down the slope, following a bridle path through the gorse.

I felt a growing resistance on either side; the children's hands sought to wrest themselves free from my own. I tightened my grip and moved down the slope, toward the uneven dark line that clung to the downs to the east. A little nearer, that was all; then I would have a better view of it.

A few shreds of mist had crept into the hollow at the foot of the ridge. Dew pearled on the heather, and the air had a greenness to it. The ground began to rise up again. Above, I made out wispy crowns above knotted trunks.

One of the children—Chambley, it had to be—made a small sound, like a moan. I felt them try to pull away from me, but I clamped my fingers around their little hands. Disheveled branches reached over a high stone wall. Just a little farther . . .

A pounding rang out behind us. The children cried out, and I turned, not knowing whether to be relieved or alarmed when I saw a horseman riding down the path from the house. In a moment he was upon us. He did not dismount but rather glared at us from the saddle.

"What are you doing out here?"

I felt that Clarette was going to say something; I squeezed her hand so that she let out a soft gasp instead.

"We are out for some exercise, Mr. Quent," I said. "This is the first day in several that it has been dry enough to venture much from the house."

The horse—a massive beast—pranced and snorted; Mr. Quent controlled it with a flick of his right hand. "I have just returned to Heathcrest. Do you know where you go? Had I not looked down as I rode up to the house, had I not happened to see you—"

"Then we would have turned back in a few moments ourselves."

"You have already come too close."

"Too close to what?" Chambley said, then swallowed. "Too close to what, *sir*?"

"To that." Mr. Quent pointed to the line of shabby trees behind the stone wall. The mist had melted away. The wall was, I realized with a start, closer than I had thought—no more than a furlong.

"It's just an old patch of forest," Clarette said.

His cheeks darkened above his beard. "Your education is lacking. It is a stand of Wyrdwood, and you can have no cause to go near it. In fact, it is best that you stay as far from it as possible."

Chambley looked up at him, his eyes large. "Is it dangerous?"

"Dangerous? Yes, it is dangerous, but only to those who are careless and who do not heed its warnings."

"But it's only a lot of trees," Clarette said.

"Only trees?" His left hand was in his pocket, but I could see motion beneath the black cloth, as if he clenched and unclenched those fingers that remained. "Yes, as you say, they are only trees. But they are older than you—older than any of us. They were here in Altania before the first men were, and you'll not find a house or croft in this county that stands within three furlongs of such a grove. It isn't for no reason that we build walls around them."

A shudder passed through Chambley's thin body. Clarette looked over her shoulder, eyes narrowed, back toward the wood.

Mr. Quent seemed about to add to his speech, but he had already said more than enough, in my opinion. "Come, children, let us go back. It's almost time for our tea."

I said no words to my employer but instead led the children back up the hill, keeping to a stiff pace, so that by the time we reached the house all of us, not just Chambley, were panting. I sent the children to the parlor and told them I would be in with their tea directly. While I had not looked, I had been aware that Mr. Quent rode behind us all the way and had heard his boots follow us into the hall. Once the children were out of sight, I took off my bonnet and turned to him.

"That sort of talk is not acceptable, Mr. Quent," I said. "I will not have it around the children."

His expression could not have been more astonished if I had struck him. He took a step backward.

"You may be as stern as you wish with me, Mr. Quent. I can bear it, I assure you." My cheeks glowed with heat after stepping from the cool outdoors into the hall, but I held my chin high. "Reproach me in the strongest terms. Speak to me in the most alarming manner you choose. I can and will endure it. But I will not allow the children to be witness to such a talk as you gave us out on the moor."

At last he found his voice. "I only warned them of the wood."

"Warned them, yes. And terrified them as well! And gave them new tinder to fuel every little shadow and phantasm that creeps into their minds. I felt their hands—they were cold as ice. They could not stop shaking all the way back to the house. You say you wish them to refrain from making another commotion, to be quiet and studious. Yet with one speech you have undone, I am sure, every effort I have made these last days to engage them and direct their thoughts in proper directions."

Furrows creased his brow. "What would you have me do? Would you have me deceive them and say that all of you were not in peril today?"

"I would have you not frighten them any more than they already are, Mr. Quent! They have lost that which was dearest to them and are far from all they have known. Their state is already one of agitation. Any more speeches such as you gave today will serve only to make the task you have given me impossible. It will put them beyond my or any control." I dared to take another step toward him. "And I assure you, we were not in any sort of danger today."

He made no effort to defend himself against these words. Instead, he stood with his hat in his hand, an expression on his face I found peculiar. It was not anger or rebuke but something else. A thoughtfulness, or rather a kind of resignation.

"You are right, Miss Lockwell," he said in his low voice. "I should have spoken to you alone, and not in front of the children. For that, you have my apology. All the same, I will ask you to not venture near the Wyrdwood again, with or without the children. Do I have your word on this?"

I could only give it to him. "Of course."

He made a stiff bow and, as he rose, seemed about to say something more. But then he turned on a heel and departed the hall. I managed to wait until he was gone, then sank into one of the horsehair chairs, clutching both of its arms.

That I had dared to scold my employer, a man nearly twice my age—a man who could, with little effort, I was sure, toss me away with a single arm—came crashing down upon me. The weight of the thought pressed me into the chair. Had I doomed myself? Had I assured my dismissal?

No, I thought. He had agreed to my terms, and I to his. Slowly, by degrees, my heart slowed its beating. I found I could move again and rose from the chair to fetch the children their tea.

❦

Two NIGHTS LATER, deep in a long umbral, I woke to the clatter of horses outside. I snatched a shawl around my shoulders and crossed the cold floorboards to the window. Brightday had just gone, and outside all was lit by a gibbous moon, its light tinged just the faintest red by the new planet.

I could see nothing and so left my room and went to the landing at the top of the stairs. From there I could look down into the front courtyard. I watched as two figures dismounted from their horses. They wore regimental coats, and though the crests on their hats looked black in the moonlight, I knew by day they would be red. Sabers hung at their sides.

They strode toward the house with purpose, but before they reached the steps, Jance came hurrying down to them, wild shadows scattering before the lantern in his hand. He sketched a bow, and the men followed him up the steps, disappearing from view. I heard a distant echo as the front door opened and shut far below. I gathered the shawl around myself and hurried back to my room.

When I went downstairs in the gray before dawn, I asked Mrs. Darendal about Mr. Quent and learned he was gone again. The housekeeper did not say where, yet that he had left with the soldiers was certain. I wondered what could have called him away with such haste in the middle of a long night.

"What is your intention with the children today?" Mrs. Darendal asked as I prepared a tray for their breakfast.

I paused, tray in hand. "It is the same as any day."

She nodded. However, as I neared the door she said, "But you will not take them toward the Wyrdwood."

Had she been listening to Mr. Quent and me in the front hall that day? It could only be so. That anything in this house could be private from *her* was impossible. It seemed she was always around every corner or just on the other side of every door.

"Why would we go to the Wyrdwood?" I said in a light tone. She did not answer. I left the kitchen with the tray.

We did not go outside that day, or the next, or the next after that, which was a very long day, though it may as well have been a great-night, for a fog had settled in around Heathcrest once more, turning all to gloom.

It was late on that long, dreary day when, for want of exercise, I took to exploring the manor again. Since the dawn twenty-two hours ago, we had risen, had a day's worth of activity, eaten supper, retired to our beds, and awakened again, and still true night was ten hours off. The children had not been able to stop yawning during our second breakfast of the lumenal, and I knew there was little point in resuming our studies. I sent them back to their room to amuse themselves in what quiet way they wished. And I wandered through dim halls and silent chambers, running my fingers over dusty tables, leaving behind marks like secret runes.

I soon found myself in the corridor with the locked door. I had passed this way several times in my wanderings, and each time I had resisted trying the handle. Mrs. Darendal had said the room was forbidden to anyone but Mr. Quent. All the same, *she* had been in there. I wondered if he knew.

Perhaps it was a result of my recent disagreement with him, or perhaps it was the restiveness I felt, but this time I could not withstand the temptation of curiosity. I tried the handle. As before it was locked. After looking around to make sure I was alone, I knelt and peered through the keyhole. All I saw was dim green light.

Resigned that so great a curiosity could never be satisfied through so small an aperture, I rose. It was time to see to the children. However, as I started toward the stairs, a jingling drifted up from below. I was in no mood for another encounter with *her*. Quickly, I ducked into a room I knew to be empty and, closing the door all but a crack, peered out.

Mrs. Darendal appeared at the top of the stairs. Her hair and face

were drawn up as tightly as usual; her grimness, then, was not just for
the benefit of others. As I watched through the crack, the housekeeper
went to the locked door. Despite all her talk of obeying the master's
will, she seemed to defy it with great frequency. She glanced both ways
down the corridor, then took a ring of keys from her pocket, fit one in
the lock, and opened the door.

A crash sounded from below.

I winced, for I was certain I knew the source of the noise. Just before coming upstairs, I had observed Lanna in the front hall, dusting
near the fireplace. As I recalled, the mantel bore several porcelain
vases. Mrs. Darendal looked up, her mouth a thin line. She shut the
door, twisted the key in the lock, and marched downstairs. I waited
until she was gone, then stepped into the corridor.

My thought was to go to the front hall. I did not think Mrs.
Darendal would scold Lanna *too* harshly if I was present. However, as
I passed the door where the housekeeper had stood moments before,
I halted. The door was not square against the frame. I tried the handle; it was locked, but even as I touched it, the door creaked open an
inch. In her haste, Mrs. Darendal had not latched the door properly
before turning the key.

Not only did she transgress upon Mr. Quent's rules, she was careless with his secrets! I gripped the handle, meaning to pull the door
shut, to go downstairs, and to see that Lanna was well.

The door swung open before me.

That I had pushed it rather than pulling it shut was the only possibility, but I could not recall doing it. My heart quickened. I knew I
must leave, that I should close the door and go downstairs.

I stood amid wavering green light, and the door shut behind me.

It took my eyes several moments to adjust to the dimness of the
room. The light filtering through the ivy-covered window was dappled
and shaded, like the light in a forest.

Gradually, shapes came into focus around me. While the other
rooms on this floor were filled with the flotsam and jetsam of forgotten years, all shrouded in white, the furnishings in this room were uncovered and neatly arranged. There were several handsome chairs and
a table that bore an assortment of books, old coins, magnifying lenses,
and polished stones. On one side of the room was a pianoforte,
trimmed with gilded wood, which Lily would have given her best ribbons to be allowed to play.

I told myself sternly that I should go. However, the crime had already been committed; leaving now would not alter that, and Lanna's
mishap would occupy Mrs. Darendal for several minutes. Knowing I

would never have another opportunity, I made a quick survey of the room.

It was wrong of me; I will not try to defend myself. But my employer was so silent and such a cipher to me. If by examining the objects in the room I might come to understand him a little better, it might help to make our relationship not warmer, I thought, but perhaps less strained.

I moved through the flickering green light. A pair of portraits hung on one wall above a credenza. At once I recognized the man on the right.

It had to have been done years ago, for he appeared young in the painting. Indeed, he looked little older than I did. I could not say he was any handsomer then than now. He had the same thick, curling brown hair and the same deep-set eyes and overhanging brow. Yet he was clean shaven in the painting, and his expression, while serious, was not grim. It was, if not a comely or cheerful face, then at least a goodly one. I wondered what had altered him so over the years.

My gaze went to the hands. He had posed with his right hand resting on a book and his left hand tucked in his coat pocket. So *that* could not be the cause of his change.

I turned my attention to the other portrait. In the painting, a young woman stood in a garden. Her hair was gold, and her eyes were the same color as her leaf-green dress. It struck me at once that she looked akin to me. The likeness was far from perfect, of course; our faces bore a very different character. I knew mine tended to be fine and pointed. *As sharp and pretty as the stroke of a pen,* you once said of my looks, Father—and coming from anyone else I should have been mortified.

*Her* face—indeed, the whole of her—was softer and rounder than mine. Her smile was mild, I thought, and very sweet. All the same, no one would have thought twice if the two of us had stood together and presented ourselves as cousins. I wondered who she was. Her portrait hung next to Mr. Quent's, but there seemed little order to the paintings in the house. For all I knew they had lived centuries apart.

Propped up on the credenza was a smaller painting in an ebony frame. Only it wasn't a painting at all. It was too crisp, too perfectly clear for that. It was an impression, created by an illusionist by willing the image in his mind onto an engraving plate. In it, three young men posed in their regimentals, rifles in their hands and Murghese turbans on their heads. Palm fronds drooped from above. Their pale Altanian faces were peeling from sunburn, and they grinned as if they had just gotten away with something grand and improbable, arms draped around one another's shoulders. A small plaque mounted on the frame read *THE THREE LORDS OF AM-ANARU*.

Fascinating as the impression was, I felt my time growing short and so hastened on through the room. There were shelves of books, some of them very old, given their worn spines. I would have liked to stop and peruse them, but I had not yet explored the end of the room near the window. I glanced back at the door—still shut—and hurried to the far side of the chamber. Here I found a wooden cabinet as well as the only object in the room that was draped with a cloth. By its shape and size I supposed it to be another painting, large in size, on an easel. I dismissed it—I had seen enough dim old paintings in this house!—and directed my attention at the cabinet instead.

As I did, a queer sensation came over me. I had the feeling I had seen a similar thing before. The cabinet was narrow, about four feet high, and contained several drawers. Its spindly legs were bent, and the sides bore deep scrollwork that looked like nothing so much as shaggy hair. The grooved trim at the top suggested a pair of swept-back horns, and the front of each of the drawers was carved with a single closed eye.

Though the cabinet was quite hideous, I found myself drawn to it. I tried the drawers, but none of them would open; nor was there a lock or latch on any of them. I examined the cabinet more closely. As I did, I again felt sure I had seen something like it before.

No—not *like* it. Rather, I was certain I had seen this very object at some prior time. Yet how could that be? I touched the top of the cabinet, brushing away a patina of dust. Three letters were carved into the top, surrounded by swirling lines and moons and stars.

How long I stood there frozen, I do not know. I stared at the letters until the lines around them seemed to writhe and the moons and stars revolved in orbit. That those three initials should appear here, in the house of one who had been his friend, was beyond what chance would allow.

*G.O.L.*

Gaustien Orandus Lockwell.

I *had* seen this cabinet before. My memories of that time were dim, like the paintings that hung on the walls of Heathcrest Hall. However, if I thought back, I could picture it in one of the rooms at the top of the stairs, beyond a door carved like the drawers with a single shut eye. It had been at the old house on Durrow Street, and the cabinet was yours, Father.

A memory came to me—an unusually vivid and clear recollection. I saw you, Father, in that upstairs room at Durrow Street. I must have been very small, for you seemed to tower above my vantage point. You stood in front of a cabinet—*this* cabinet—and I do not think you knew I was there, standing just outside the door. I watched as you touched the drawers, pressing the eye on each one—

A distant *boom* jolted me from my recollection. It took me a moment to understand that what I had heard was the sound of the door shutting in the front hall below. I looked out the window, peering between the screen of leaves, and a coldness gripped me. Through the ivy I could just make out Jance in the courtyard, leading a massive chestnut gelding toward the stables.

He had returned! That I must fly was my only thought. Yet even as I turned from the window, I hesitated, looking again at the cabinet. Before I could even think what I was doing, I reached out and pressed the eye carved into one of the drawers.

There was an audible *click*. When I withdrew my hand, the eye was open, staring outward.

Again I looked out the window, but the courtyard was empty. I listened but heard no sounds coming from outside the room. Now holding my breath, I pressed another eye, and another, my hand moving in the same order I had observed your own doing all those years ago.

As I pressed the last eye, there was a louder noise, as of some mechanism within the cabinet turning. I hesitated, then tried the topmost drawer. It slid open.

The drawer was empty. In quick succession I opened the others, only to find they were similarly devoid of contents—all except for the bottommost drawer. In it I discovered a single object: a small box of black wood that fit easily in my palm when I picked it up. Despite its small size, it was heavy. A thin line suggested a lid that could be removed, but there was no sign of a hinge or latch. A silver symbol was inlaid in the surface: an eye inscribed within a triangle.

A noise emanated from below me: a thudding, as of heavy boots. My dread was redoubled. I could not be seen coming from this room! I pushed the drawers of the cabinet shut, and as I did, the eye on each one closed with a *snick.* It was only when all were closed that I realized I still held the small box in my hand.

There was no time to replace it. I tucked the box into the pocket of my dress, then turned to dash across the room. However, in my haste my foot caught the end of the cloth that draped the easel. I stumbled, tugging the cloth, and with a whisper it slipped to the floor.

Dismay filled me. I could not leave it cast down like that; my presence here would be revealed. I turned to take up the cloth and throw it back over the easel.

A forest stood before me.

The painting was so large, I could have walked through it as if it were a door. And it seemed like a kind of door to me. Perhaps it was how vividly the trees had been rendered by the artist's brush—from the moss on their rough bark to the smallest crooked twig—or perhaps it was how the green light in the room seemed not so much to fall upon the painting as fall *into* it, flickering among the bent trunks and mottled leaves, suffusing the image with a lurid glow that mere paint could never have produced.

The trees seemed to sway back and forth in the painting of the Wyrdwood, but it was only an illusion caused by the wavering light. I took a step closer, and a certainty came over me that the painting depicted not just any stand of the ancient forest but rather the very patch that stood to the east of Heathcrest. The trees looked just the same, as did the mossy stone wall.

It occurred to me that I should go. I wanted to, but I could not turn away from the painting. The air deepened, as if a premature twilight fell, and I let out a gasp. Now that I was closer, there was no mistaking it—the trees *did* sway back and forth in the painting, as if tossed by a wind. It was no illusion, nor was it a hallucination brought on by fever, like that night at Lady Marsdel's. The shabby leaves trembled; the branches bent and dipped, reaching over the stone wall that bound the trees and held them back.

I heard the footsteps again, just outside the room now. The sound of a deep, muffled voice passed through the door. Still, I could not turn away from the painting. There was something caught among the branches of the trees. It was pale and fluttering, like a piece of gauze that had been carried upward by a wind and had caught in the twisted branches. I leaned closer.

My breathing ceased. A rushing noise filled my head. It was not a piece of cloth in the trees.

She wore a white dress. Dark branches wove a cocoon around the woman, cradling her high above the ground, coiling around her arms and legs, caressing her white skin. Leaves tangled in her fair hair. I bent so close that my face nearly touched the painting. But would it indeed encounter canvas if I moved forward another inch? Or would I find myself in the wood, like her, caught among the branches of the trees?

In the painting, the woman turned her head toward me. I caught the edge of a black smile and the glint of green eyes.

Pain stabbed at my head. The rushing noise was my own blood surging violently through my brain. The emerald light pressed in all around, filling my eyes, my nose, my mouth, suffocating me. Through the roaring I heard the sound of a door being thrown open and a stern voice calling out.

There was a distant noise, and I knew it was the sound of my own body striking the floor. For a moment all was a haze of green light.

Then, darkness.

✦

WHEN I OPENED my eyes again, the green light was gone. The only illumination came from a single candle. I sat up and found myself on a sofa in the front hall. A dark shape hulked nearby: one of the hunting trophies, I supposed—a shaggy brown bear.

The shape moved toward me.

I had little time to feel fear, for as the figure stepped into the circle of light I saw that it was not a bear. Still, the comparison was not unfitting, for there was an ursine quality to his curling brown mane and to his heavy, rounded shoulders and the weight of his step.

"Mr. Quent," I said. My voice was faint.

"Miss Lockwell," came his rumbling reply.

Now fear did come over me, nor was it a fanciful dread of shadows. I remembered the secret room, and the painting, and the suffocating green light. I remembered falling and then, just as the darkness came, a pair of strong arms bearing me up off the floor.

"Mr. Quent," I said again. *It was wrong of me to go into the room. I do not know what possessed me. I can offer no defense. I can say only that I promise to never return there.*

But I could not draw in the breath these words required. My heart fluttered in my chest like a bird in a cage.

"Perhaps you should lie back down, Miss Lockwell. I do not believe you are fit to rise yet."

His voice was low and measured, and I wondered at it. Why did he not berate me for my transgression? I knew him to be capable of the harshest words of reproof. Why did he not use them upon me now? Certainly this time I deserved them!

Astonished, I could only do as he suggested and lie back down on the sofa. The light of the candle grew and shrank by turns.

For several minutes I lay there, motionless. Stunned, really. All the while he stood just on the edge of the light. He might have made for a foreboding figure, only somehow he wasn't. It was as if his form was a solid column, a buttress that held the darkness back. At last the throbbing in my head receded and the candle's flame burned more steadily.

Alarm cut through the dullness in my brain, and I sat back up. "The children! I left them alone. I must see to them at once."

"There is no need for that," he said. "Mrs. Darendal gave them their supper, and I have put them in their beds."

"You!" I gasped.

"You seem very surprised. I do not know why. They are quite easy to carry. Easier than yourself, Miss Lockwell. You seem small enough, yet you are something of a burden to bear."

I shrank back against the sofa, mortified. Of course he had carried me. How else could I have gotten down here?

"How poorly you must regard me," I said at last. I looked down at my hands in my lap. "But know it is no more poorly than I regard myself. I cannot explain. I don't know what I was thinking. But I *wasn't* thinking. I had been exploring the house, as I sometimes do." I realized belatedly that admitting to snooping was not likely to help my cause. "It's what I do for exercise, you see, when I cannot take the children outside. Perhaps the long confinement indoors has had an effect upon my nerves. It *must* have been so. And the light in the room was so strange! It was all green, coming through the leaves. When I saw the painting of the wood, it seemed to—"

I halted. There was no need for him to think me weak of mind as well as weak of character.

I sat that way for a minute or more, and he said nothing. At last I forced myself to look up at him. I knew my cause was lost—that when it was day again I must take my bags and leave. So what more harm could it cause to ask the one question on my mind?

"The woman in the painting," I said to him. "The portrait that hung next to yours. Who is she?"

I saw his left hand stir in his coat pocket. "It is Mrs. Quent in that picture. My wife, that is."

I should have felt fear at my imminent dismissal. Instead, I felt sorrow. I would go, but he would still be here, alone in this echoing house. Nor could there be any hope *she* would join him; now that I knew she had existed, the evidence of her absence was everywhere around us, in all the shadows, in all the empty silences.

I made myself look at his face. "When did she pass?"

"Years ago," he said, and that was all.

For a time we were silent. At last, feeling stronger, I pushed myself up from the sofa and found I could stand, if just.

"Miss Lockwell," he addressed me in a somber tone. "I think—"

There was no need for him to speak the words. "I understand perfectly, Mr. Quent. You will not get any argument from me." I gave a rueful smile. "Nor from Mrs. Darendal, I would think. And though you owe me nothing, all the same I will ask you for something—that you allow me to be the one to tell the children."

The lines in his brow deepened. "To tell them what?"

My mind was indeed dull! Had I muttered the words instead of spoken clearly? "To tell them that I have been dismissed from your service. Is that not what you intend?"

"What I intend, Miss Lockwell," he said with a serious look, "is to find you a better source of exercise."

And I sat back down on the sofa.

THREE DAYS LATER, when I was recovered from the incident in the upstairs room, Mr. Quent went to the village with Jance. When they returned two hours later, Jance was leading a gray mare.

Mr. Quent called me outside; I went eagerly, leaving the children with instructions to continue their reading. The mare was a pretty little thing, with a muzzle like twilight velvet.

"Mr. Quent," I said at last, trying to contain my delight. "This is too much."

"Do you know how to ride, Miss Lockwell?"

I could only confess that I did not.

"You need not fear," he said. "She is a gentle creature."

Before I could say anything more, he had lifted me into the saddle. This seemed barely an effort for him. Despite his words that day, it could only have been an easy thing for him to carry me downstairs. My cheeks burned, and I felt fresh shame at what I had done, but I bent my head under the guise of stroking the mare's silvery mane.

"Hold them like this," he said, putting the reins in my hands—an action that required both of his own. His fingers were rough but not ungentle, and the dexterity of his left hand appeared little reduced by the lack of the fourth and fifth fingers. Once he was done showing me how to hold the reins, that hand was quickly returned to his coat pocket.

Those first few times I rode, I went at a slow walk, with Jance leading the mare by the bridle. However, she was such a docile creature there could be no chance of my falling. It was not long before I was able to ride on my own and even urge her into a trot if I felt brave.

Soon I looked forward to those rare hours when I could send the children to play or rest quietly in their room. Jance always seemed to know when I would need her saddled, and within moments of leaving the house I would be riding out from Heathcrest, over moor and down, reveling in the feel of the wind against my face. Sometimes I felt I could ride all the way to Invarel. It was a foolish notion, but when I was riding I forgot the confining dimness, the stifling silence that dwelled within Heathcrest.

"You are getting very freckled," Mrs. Darendal said to me one night as she brought a plate of parsnips into the dining room. Since my collapse she had been all but silent in my presence, but it seemed the urge to direct me had overcome her reticence. "You should not go riding so much."

I smiled, determined to be pleasant. "I wear my bonnet."

"A bonnet cannot protect you from the wind. It will ruin your complexion. It is already hardened, I can see."

"I see no such thing," Mr. Quent said. Whatever his business was, it had not called him away of late, and he had dined with us more frequently. "In fact, I would say I have never seen her look so well."

The housekeeper treated him to a look I was glad not to have received myself. Mr. Quent, however, seemed not to notice, and Mrs. Darendal retreated.

I could not speak for my complexion, but that the exercise and fresh air had done *me* good, I was certain. My mood had improved; the malaise I had suffered under—without really knowing it—had lifted. I was sure the fit I had experienced in the room upstairs would not happen if I were to enter there today. It had been an effect of melancholy and a weakened spirit.

"Tell me, Clarette, Chambley, how do your studies go?"

I looked up. Mr. Quent had addressed the children. However, Clarette was not looking at him but rather at me, her mouth open. Chambley clutched a piece of bread.

I set down my fork. "Tell Mr. Quent what you have been reading, Clarette." My voice was encouraging, but I could hardly have been more surprised than the children. However, once I prompted them to discuss what we had been learning of Tharosian history—their favorite topic—they chatted and chirped, and Mr. Quent listened for a quarter of an hour to accounts of ancient battles and the treachery of emperors.

At last I gently urged the children to finish their meal. Then I sent them upstairs with the promise I would follow.

"Thank you, Miss Lockwell."

I turned in the doorway. I could not read his expression or the look in his brown eyes. "For what, Mr. Quent?"

"For your work with the children. They are much improved since you came. I fear my instinct was always to be stern with them, but a gentle word from you achieves more than all my most serious lectures."

These words took me aback. That he should be thanking me after what I had done was hardly comprehensible—that after I had violated his will and trespassed upon his most private sanctum he could express gratitude was almost unbearable.

"I must see to the children," I said, and hurried from the dining room.

As I climbed the stairs, I could not feel so certain as the master of the house that my charges were improved. It was true they had been quiet since the day of their argument in the front hall, even subdued, but I did not take that as a sign of their well-being.

Riding had improved *my* condition, but I could not think what could be done for *them*. They seemed to grow more wan by the day, and Chambley's breathing had become a constant labor. However, I could rarely convince them to go out of doors. Clarette, I felt, might have been coaxed, but she would not let herself be parted from her brother, and he was reluctant to leave the house except for the briefest intervals.

"Please, let's stay inside," I overheard him whisper to Clarette one day as I returned to our parlor with their coats. "It can't be a good thing to go out. Not if *she* wants us to do it." For some reason I did not think it was me he was speaking about.

Now I opened the door to their room. As I did, Clarette turned suddenly from the window. Outside, a lingering twilight draped the moor. Chambley sat on his bed. He was shivering, though the room was warm. I hurried to sit next to him and put my hand to his forehead. It was clammy with sweat.

"Clarette," I said, "what happened? You brother was very well when I sent you upstairs."

She did not move from the window. Her eyes appeared black in the fading light.

Chambley let out a whimper and leaned against me. "Did something happen just now, Clarette? Answer me at once."

"But I can't answer you!" she burst out.

"On the contrary, you can and will."

"You said I was never to say again that I saw things outside."

"No, I said you were not to tell a falsehood, Clarette."

"But you'll say it's a lie, even when it isn't. So I can't tell you what happened. You'll scold me!" Her back had gone rigid. I could not tell if she was frightened or angry. Chambley threw his arms around my neck.

"Clarette," I said, making my voice low but firm, "I will never scold you for speaking the truth. Now tell me what happened."

She turned and pointed to the window. "We saw her. Standing out there below our window."

"Whom did you see, Clarette? Was it Mrs. Darendal? Or was it Lanna?"

"No, it wasn't them. It was *her*."

Now *I* was growing angry. I had had enough of this behavior. Chambley could not stop shaking. "Who do you mean, Clarette? It was not myself. And if it was not Mrs. Darendal or Lanna, then who could it be?"

Her eyes narrowed. "I told you that you wouldn't believe me."

"I *will* believe you, Clarette, if you tell the truth."

She only shook her head, taking a backward step toward the window.

My voice rose. Such open disobedience could not be tolerated. "Clarette, answer me at once. Who did you see out the window?"

Chambley pushed away from me. "It was *her*," he cried out. "It was the Pale Lady. She was standing outside the window and looking up at us. Clarette said she wanted us to come down, but I said I wouldn't go." He leaped off the bed and glared at his sister, his small hands clenched into fists. "I don't care what she says to you. I won't go out to her. *I won't!*"

At last I understood. Clarette had been telling him stories again, frightening him. I stood and advanced toward Clarette.

"Is this true?" I said. "Is this what you told your brother?"

She looked up at me. "Yes. It *is* true. We saw the lady in white outside the window. We watched her run from the old wood. She came from the trees on the other side of the wall."

Now I went cold. For a moment I was back in the forbidden room. I saw again the painting of the trees, and the woman in a pale, tattered dress caught among the branches . . .

I took a breath to clear my head. Clarette must have seen into the room after my collapse; the door would have been open. She had seen the painting. She was being cruel, that was all, teasing me as she had her brother.

I fixed her with my gaze. "You will take back your words, Clarette. Tell your brother you are sorry for what you said."

"But I'm *not* sorry!"

She started to turn away, but I caught her wrist.

"Tell your brother you are sorry for frightening him."

She said nothing. I tightened my grip around her wrist. I saw her face go white; I knew I was hurting her.

"Tell him, Clarette!"

Her jaw was set, her mouth a thin line. Behind me I heard Chambley sniffling. A haze descended over my vision. I do not know what I might have done in that moment; I fear it might have been something terrible, something I would have regretted ever afterward. However, before I could act, something moved outside the window. It was pale in the gloaming below.

Like a flutter of white cloth.

I let go of Clarette's wrist and was dimly aware that she rushed away from me, to her brother. The window drew me forward. I leaned on the sill and bent close to the glass.

I had not imagined it! Something moved in the gloaming, away from the house and toward the east. Was it a sheep strayed from its field? No, it went upright, threading over the ground, white tatters streaming behind it. Then, in the time it took to blink my eyes, it was gone. Full dark fell. I saw nothing in the window save my own startled expression.

I turned around. Clarette and Chambley sat on the bed, their arms circled around each other, their eyes wide as if they beheld some horrific sight. Only they were not staring at the window. They were staring at me.

I drew the curtain over the window with a trembling hand. "It is time for bed," I managed to say. Unable to utter anything more, I left them alone in the room.

THE NEXT MORNING I carried a breakfast tray up to their chamber. It was early; the night had been short, and the sky bore just the faintest blush of dawn. However, I had not been able to sleep all night.

I knocked gently and entered. They lay without moving in their beds. Chambley was fast asleep, his small face at peace, his breathing deep and steady. Clarette, I felt, was not sleeping, though her eyes were shut. I set the tray down on the table in the corner, opened the curtain, and sat on the bed beside her. With a hand I smoothed her hair; it was soft and dark, as if spun from shadows.

"I know what it is like to be on one's own," I said in a quiet voice. "My father is very ill. He does not know who anyone around him is, not even me. And my mother passed away not long ago."

There was a rustling across the room as Chambley sat up in bed, his face bleary. "But it's not the same for you," he said. "You're very old."

I could not help a smile. "I'm not so much older than you, really. Besides, it is hard to be left by one's parent at any age."

He rubbed his eyes with a fist. "I want Mother to come back."

"You know she can't, Chambley. But she's watching over you and waiting for you. One day—a long time from now, but one day—you'll see her again."

"You mean in Eternum."

"Yes, in Eternum."

He shook his head. "But I don't want to go there. It's full of ghosts."

Clarette sat up and looked at her brother. "You'll be a ghost too, silly, so what will it matter? They can't scare you if you're one of them."

While I could not argue with Clarette's logic, I did not entirely appreciate her encouraging discourse on the topic of ghosts. However, Chambley laughed.

"Yes, I shall be a ghost too!" He wrapped the bedclothes around himself and made groaning noises while Clarette giggled.

I indulged them for a minute in this play, then held out a hand and urged Chambley to come to me. I put my arm around him as he sat on the bed.

"I owe you both an apology," I said. "I am very sorry for being so cross with you last night. It was wrong of me. I know you were doing your best to tell me what had happened."

Clarette looked up at me, frowning. "Do you believe me, then?"

Before I could answer, Chambley was on his knees, bouncing on the bed. "You saw her, didn't you? You saw *her* out the window."

I chose my words carefully. I did not want to excite their emotions unduly. "I confess, I did see something—though I could not tell exactly what it was or even if it was a person. Yet it was white and moving east away from the house."

"I told you," Clarette said. Her expression was, I thought, a trifle smug.

I did not correct her. "You *did* tell me you had seen something, and I should have taken your words seriously. I promise to do so in the future. But I need you to promise me you will always tell me exactly what you see, no more and no less. Do you promise?"

"I swear it," Chambley said, crossing his heart.

I looked at Clarette. For a moment she did not move. Then she gave a mute nod. If that was all I was going to get, I would take it.

"You do not need to be afraid," I said. "You are not alone. If you ever see something that frightens you, you have only to let me know. Do you see? We will keep one another safe."

I drew them in close on either side of me, though I cannot say whether it was my intention to give comfort or to receive it. Chambley threw his arms around me, embracing me with fierce affection. However, while Clarette did not attempt to pull away from me, neither did she return my embrace. She was stiff beside me.

At last I let them go. I poured them their tea at the table in the corner and told them we would begin our lessons after breakfast.

"I will speak to Mr. Quent," I said as I prepared to leave them. "I will let him know we've seen something outside the house."

"No, you can't!" Clarette said, setting down her cup and jumping up from her chair. "You can't tell him!"

These words shocked me. "But don't you want him to make sure all is safe around the house?"

She licked her lips and glanced at Chambley, then looked again at me. "It's only . . . Mrs. Darendal said we're not to bother him."

"I am quite certain he would not find the matter of intruders on his property to be a bother," I said.

However, the children appeared genuinely distressed at the thought of telling Mr. Quent. As I thought about it, I decided it would be better to know exactly what I had witnessed before concerning him with it. I still did not know what it was I had seen, and it would make the claim that there was a trespasser more credible if I could provide more specific details.

"Very well," I said. "I will not tell Mr. Quent—yet. But I will be keeping watch, and I want you both to be vigilant. If you see anything unusual, tell me at once. And by no means respond to anything someone you do not know might say to you. If someone asks you to do something—someone other than Mr. Quent, or myself, or Mrs. Darendal—you must come to me at once."

I smiled at them to dispel the solemn tone; I wanted to reassure them, not frighten them. "In the meantime, I cannot see that we have any cause for worry, or to alter our habits in any way. We will go for a walk this afternoon." Chambley started to protest, but I quieted him with a look. "We must have exercise if we wish to remain in good health. Come downstairs when you finish your breakfast, and we will continue our work with Tharosian grammar."

AFTER THAT DAY the behavior of the children was greatly improved; in truth, they were better mannered, more studious, more eager to do what was asked of them than at any time since my coming to Heathcrest. They recited their lessons dutifully, moved quietly through the house, and did not once disturb the master with their activities when he was in residence.

Mr. Quent again remarked at their improved demeanor. Even Mrs. Darendal, while not evincing any sort of kindness toward me, had at least ceased her frequent criticisms and seemed resigned to my presence. I had every cause to be happy, yet I could not claim that I was. For as the lumenals passed, long and short, an unease crept into my mind, just as the mist crept into the hollow places on the moor and pooled there.

I could not pass a window that looked eastward without either resisting or giving in to the urge to gaze at the tangled shapes atop the far downs. Nor could I walk along the corridor on the second floor without feeling a pressure close in around me, as if the shadows were pushing me along, trying to direct me toward that forbidden room.

The children, too, for all their good behavior, had begun to cause me unease. Not Chambley to any degree. *He,* I thought, had truly warmed to me; he often held my hand as we walked, and he would kiss my cheek after supper and, in the most endearing manner, say to me, "Good night, Miss Lockwell."

Clarette, though her manner was always obedient, never showed me such little affections. I often had the sense that she was watching me, and I would glance up from the book I had been reading aloud just in time to see her turn her gaze from the window. Often, as I approached our parlor, I caught the sound of whispering, and always I was certain it was Clarette who spoke in a sibilant voice. However, by the time I stepped through the door, they would be smiling, their hands clasped before them, attention directed at me.

At such times I wanted nothing more than to question them, to demand to know what they were speaking about; however, I refrained. I wanted them to trust in me. Only then could I be assured they would come to me if they saw something again. Thus I did not question them regarding anything outside our lessons, nor did I speak to Mr. Quent about the intruder I had glimpsed.

While I could not ask questions of Mr. Quent, or the children, or Mrs. Darendal, there was still one person I could speak to—though her ability to respond was limited.

"Did you know the mistress of the house?" I asked Lanna one

afternoon as I sat in the kitchen, taking a quiet cup of tea. The children were in their room, and though I would have liked to go out for a ride, the short day had succumbed to a dreary rain.

Lanna looked up from the loaf she was kneading and gave me a puzzled look.

"I'm sorry," I said, setting down the cup. "I mean Mrs. Quent. Did you know her when she was mistress here?"

Lanna hesitated, then nodded.

"You must have been young when you came to work here. I imagine it has been long since . . . that is, I wonder how long it has been."

"It has been twelve years," answered a voice behind me, "since Mrs. Quent dwelled in this house."

I was thankful I had set down my cup, for otherwise I would surely have spilled it. Mrs. Darendal came into the kitchen and set down a bowl of potatoes. Lanna bent over her loaf, kneading the dough with renewed energy.

"So long ago," I said. I looked at her directly, determined not to let her think she had caught me gossiping. "They must not have had long together."

"No, they did not." The housekeeper took up a knife and began peeling potatoes. "It was just four years to the day after they were married when she left us."

I could not help a gasp of dismay. "To the day? How dreadful to happen on *that* day, and after so short a time."

Mrs. Darendal's face, usually so hard, seemed to soften a degree. "It was a sorrow, to be sure. Everyone had such high hopes for this house—that it would be occupied by a great family again, as in the old days, and that it would bring life to the county. For a time we still held hope the master would take another wife. But he is forty-three now, and his work engrosses him completely."

I hardly knew what to make of this speech; it was more than Mrs. Darendal had said to me at one time since my arrival.

"You are very curious about business that does not concern you, Miss Lockwell." Her eyes flicked toward me, gray as the knife in her hand.

"Forgive me," I said, and leaving my cup I hurried from the kitchen.

I went upstairs to my room, shut the door, and sat on the bed. I was agitated, but I was not certain why. It was not because of Mrs. Darendal's harsh words; I was used to *those*.

"You are sorry for Mr. Quent, that's all," I said aloud.

Yes, that was the case. How sad for him to have lost Mrs. Quent after only four years of marriage. I wished that he could find another to fill this house with light and life, rather than shadows and silence.

But he was so old! Who could be expected to marry him at forty-three?

True, he was vigorous from all his exercise; there was every reason to expect his life to be a long one. And in his favor he had good teeth, and his hair was untouched by gray. But take away the shaggy beard and the weathered lines of his brow, and his face would still not be handsome.

Besides, with whom could he form an acquaintance in this forlorn part of Altania? Who would dwell with him in a remote place such as this, without the benefit of any society? No, I feared Mr. Quent's only companion would be his work; that, and the shadows that dwelled in this house.

These thoughts led my mind to my family in Invarel. I took out Lily's most recent letters and read them again for comfort, though they afforded little enough, being brief as usual and curtly written. I was sure from her tone that Lily imagined me off on some grand adventure while she and Rose remained trapped in a tower by an awful master.

"If only I could show you what it is really like here!" I said aloud. "I cannot think you would envy me then, dearest. It is certainly no adventure, not like in one of your romances."

I would have given much at that moment to be back at Whitward Street with her, and Rose, and with you, Father. Had I seen him at that moment, I think I might have embraced even Mr. Wyble with real warmth. And there was another I would have liked to see, if it was even possible now that he was married (as he surely must be).

But I was not there, and I could not tell Lily these things. I put the letters back in the stand by the bed. Another object inhabited the drawer. I picked up the small box of dark wood and set it on my palm. Again I was struck by how heavy it was for so small a thing. The silvery eye stared up at me.

I had been surprised when I found it in the pocket of my skirt several days ago. Until that moment I had forgotten taking it from the cabinet, for it had happened just before my collapse.

Returning the box was an impossibility—I dared not attempt to enter that room again. I could only hope its disappearance had gone unnoticed. So far no mention had been made of it. I began to wonder if Mr. Quent had even known the box was there; perhaps he had never opened the cabinet himself, not knowing the secret of how it was unlocked.

While it speaks ill of me, I must admit that on several occasions I tried to open the box. I justified these acts with the knowledge that the box belonged to you, Father, and that I might serve as your proxy in your absence—a weak premise, I concede.

However, circumstance ensured my character when conscience could not, for my efforts to open it were fruitless. There was no hinge, nor even a groove to slide a knife in and pry it open. All the same, I was certain there was something within. As I turned the box in my hands, I could feel the weight inside shifting, though what it might contain was beyond my ability to guess.

*He* would know, I thought.

*The way must not be opened,* the man in the dark mask had said, in that voice that seemed to me as my own thoughts. *In their arrogance and their desire they will try to open it. . . . They call themselves the Vigilant Order of the Silver Eye. . . .*

I touched the silver eye and triangle etched into the surface of the box. It could not be chance. Not when I knew this box had belonged to you, Father. Not after what he had said.

*You should listen to me because that is what your father did. . . .*

He would know how to open this, I was sure of it. I remembered the way he had moved his hand, how speech had fled me, how the stone lions had licked at his fingers. Only I had not seen him since that day. I could not know if I would ever encounter him again. Besides, perhaps it was as he had said: perhaps some things should not be opened.

$\mathcal{T}$OWARD THE END of my third month at Heathcrest, there came a welcome series of longer days and excellent weather. I had never seen it so clear since coming to Heathcrest; the extended periods of sunlight warmed the air and dried the sodden ground, and the landscape around the house was brightened by the blooms of red campion and laurel.

On long lumenals, it was the custom in the country (even more than in the city, where diversions could be found at any hour of day or night) to take an extended rest in the middle of the day. However, it was to be outdoors that I needed, not to sleep; with all the mist and gloom, I felt I had not been really awake for months.

So, while the children slept during the languorous afternoons, I had Jance saddle the gray mare and I took her out, ranging farther and longer in my rides than I ever had before.

Aware that Mrs. Darendal might find ample cause for criticism in these lengthy excursions, I made a habit of asking before I left what items might be needed for the kitchen. Jance did not go into Cairnbridge every day, and it was common for there to be some item or another wanting when it came time to fix supper. It was simple enough for me to stop at the village on my way back to the house and to return with whatever thing was required. Thus productively employed, and being always sure to don my bonnet, I was able to fend off overt disapproval on the part of Mrs. Darendal.

On my first few visits to Cairnbridge, I found the local people to be courteous if not quite friendly. That they evinced some surprise at seeing me could not be hidden. Still, they knew who I was and that I was employed up at Heathcrest Hall.

I soon began to see that Mr. Quent's serious demeanor was not entirely out of character for this region of Altania. While I would not call the people I met grim, there was all the same a general want of cheer wherever I went. People spoke, but in lowered voices. They smiled, but fleetingly. The folk I saw looked prosperous enough, yet they went about in a furtive way.

Often, when I went into the inn to make a purchase, there were several country squires talking around one of the tables. While I made no effort to eavesdrop, it was generally impossible not to overhear their conversation. When men gathered over a cup, it was either to make merry or to complain, and these men seemed to have little cause for celebration. On several occasions I heard them talk about how the roads had grown thick with brigands. These days the mail had to go with a rifleman on the bench next to the driver, and each of them knew someone who had sent a wagonload of wool or grain to Abbendon (the nearest large town) only to learn it had never arrived.

Nor, given what I overheard one day, was the king doing enough about it.

"The only soldiers we ever see are those passing through," one of the men grumbled over his cup. "They're leaving the outland garrisons and heading back to the city. I suppose the king is more worried about the rebels in Assembly than the ones on the Torland border. But I say there'll be rebels everywhere before long if they don't do something about the roads. The king won't find it very easy to defend his crown against Huntley Morden's men, not if he finds all his own men have left him."

These words were quickly hushed. The cup was pulled from the speaker's hand and glances cast my way. I hurried from the inn, package in hand.

The next time I went for a ride, my mare had the bad luck to throw a shoe. However, I could not count my misfortune very great, for I was close to Cairnbridge when the mishap occurred, and almost immediately a boy came upon me on the road. He was about twelve, towheaded, and introduced himself as the son of one of the local landed families. He offered to walk the horse to the farrier a mile south, and if I would wait at the village, he would return her to me there in two hours.

I could not refuse such a kind offer—especially when I was not likely to get any other. My return to Heathcrest would be delayed, but there could be no helping it. Besides, the children would not rise for several hours yet. I enjoyed my walk to the village, observing the many wildflowers along the road and listening to the birdsong.

In Cairnbridge I hoped to sit at the inn and have a cup of tea. However, I found the dining room empty that day; all were taking a rest in the middle of the long lumenal. I realized I had been lucky to encounter the boy, and I wondered if he would have to rouse the farrier from his bed.

To pass the time, I walked around the stone wall that bordered the common green. However, there was no shade, and after making a circuit I was hot and went back to the inn to stand in the shadow of its eaves.

I gazed at the field beyond the low stone wall and saw the stump of the tree that had once stood there. It would have been cool had that grand old tree still stood; it would have shaded the entire center of the village. Why had no one thought to plant a replacement for it?

I let my gaze wander farther afield, seeing if I could spot any type of shade. But there were no trees within view. There was a dark smudge atop a hill several furlongs to the north, but it was ash gray, not cool green. I retreated back inside the inn and sat in the silence alone.

"Miss Lockwell?" said a voice.

I started in my seat. Away from the sun in the dim and quiet of the inn, I had begun to doze; it appeared sleep was something I needed after all. I saw a man I did not recognize standing above me. He was only a bit more than my age, though his face was tanned and already somewhat weathered, and his hand, when I accepted it in introduction, was very rough. His speech and manner, in contrast, were gentle—even soft, I would say. I learned that he was none other than the farrier and that his name was Mr. Samonds.

"Thank you!" I said when I discovered he had brought my horse with him and that she had been reshod. "But surely you did not need to come all this way yourself. What happened to . . . ?"

"Young Mr. Graydon went home," he said. "But do not think ill of him. He was intent upon keeping his promise to you. However, I knew he had been sent on an errand for his father—who is also my cousin, you see—and so I released him from his duty."

"I certainly do not think ill of him!" I said. "I am much in his debt, and in yours."

He gave a short bow, then offered me his arm. I was not aware that country farriers were usually so gallant as Mr. Samonds. However, being still a bit dazed from my unexpected nap, I gratefully accepted his assistance and walked with him outside to where my mare stood placidly before the inn.

"Oh, but you must be paid!" I said aloud, realizing I had no money. I had not planned to come to the village, so I had taken nothing from the household fund. As for my own wages, at my request Mr. Quent had been sending them by note to an account he had arranged for me at his bank in Invarel.

"You must send a bill to Heathcrest Hall," I said to Mr. Samonds. "That is where I am employed. Do you know where it is?"

"Yes, I know it very well. I used to go there often when I was a boy."

"You used to go there?" I could not conceal my surprise.

"Yes," he said with a smile. "You are shocked at the idea of a tradesman's son being invited to such a fine house."

He had misread the source of my astonishment. "Not at all, Mr. Samonds. It is only that . . . we do not ever receive guests at Heathcrest. It is a very quiet place."

"Is that so? I suppose it must be. But it was different then."

"I am sure" was all I could say.

He helped me into the saddle. However, as I arranged myself, an idea occurred to me. "If you don't mind, Mr. Samonds, how long ago did you used to go to Heathcrest?"

"A long time ago, Miss Lockwell. I was younger than Mr. Graydon is now. It was thirteen or fourteen years ago."

"Was Mr. Quent the master of the house then?"

"He was."

"So you knew him?"

He grinned up at me. "Everyone in the county knew him. The house had been empty for several years, you see; but when Mr. Quent came back and took a wife, it became a bright and happy place. Such parties and balls were thrown there—I wish you could have seen them! I am sure they rivaled anything in the Grand City."

Now I was astonished anew. "Parties and balls? At Heathcrest?"

"Yes, and there were always guests there. Gentlemen friends of Mr. Quent's mostly. They came often from the city—for hunting parties, I suppose. Though, come to think of it, I don't remember seeing them out on the moors much. Well, it's often the case that hunting parties involve more parties and fewer hunts. Nor were the local folk forgotten, for we were invited up to the house on occasion. My mother was often called to dine there, for Mrs. Quent was her cousin, and that is how I came to visit there myself."

"You knew Mrs. Quent?"

"I did," he said, only then his smile faded.

He looked away, and I knew the conversation had turned to a topic that troubled him. Nor could I wonder why. Mrs. Quent had passed, and with her had passed the balls and parties and guests.

"It's been a long time since I've been to Heathcrest," he said at last, looking back at me.

I did not know how to reply; I was sorry my words had saddened him. However, he shook his head and asked me then if I wanted company for my ride back to the house. I thanked him but assured him I knew the way very well.

"I'm sure you do," he said. "I've seen you out riding before. I helped Mr. Quent pick this mare and shod her myself. She's a pretty thing, and you sit her well. Have you been enjoying riding?"

"Very much," I said.

"Good. I'm glad she is being put to such good use." His expression grew serious again. "But Miss Lockwell—forgive me for being so forward—you do not ride out late in the day, do you? And you do not stray far from either Heathcrest or Cairnbridge, do you?"

I assured him that I always went out in daylight and that no matter where I went I could always see either Heathcrest's gables or the roofs of the village. This answer seemed to please him, and he stroked the mare's nose. I thanked him again for all his assistance and reminded him to send his bill to Heathcrest.

I took the reins of the mare. However, just as I was about to urge her into a walk, I turned in the saddle. He had been raised here; it occurred to me he might know. "The tree in the common field over there," I said. "It must have been very beautiful once. I was curious how it perished. Do you know what happened to it?"

"It burned," he said, and the words, so unlike everything else he had uttered, were hard. He took a step back. "Ride directly to the house, Miss Lockwell. I am sure you are wanted."

I nodded, and as there was nothing more I could say, I urged the gray mare onward.

WHEN I REACHED Heathcrest, I found Mr. Quent just mounting his horse in front of the house. I assumed that his business had called him away once again. In my surprise, I forgot myself and asked where he was going.

"To look for you, Miss Lockwell," he said with a glower as he helped me down from the gray mare.

A horror spread through me. I had not thought my absence would cause the master himself to put aside his usual occupations and come looking for me.

"Mr. Quent, I am so sorry to have troubled you!" I said, and quickly explained what had happened.

He appeared visibly relieved at my explanation—indeed, so relieved that I could only wonder at what he had imagined had happened to me. I did not ask him; instead, I apologized once more for causing concern.

He gave a curt nod and mounted his horse.

"But you are still going somewhere?" I asked in surprise. He wore a broad-brimmed hat and a wool coat with a short cape about his shoulders.

"I am called away by my work. I should have been away an hour ago."

Shame and horror filled me anew. Had I known my actions would in any way affect his duties, I would have run back to Heathcrest on foot! I wanted to tell him these things, but he looked so imposing upon the massive horse that I could not speak.

The gelding pranced, eager to be off. He controlled it with a flick of a gloved hand. It seemed he wanted to say something, for he opened his mouth; only then he shut it again.

"When will you be back?" I said at last, breathless.

But at the same moment he tipped his hat and said, "Remember our agreement, Miss Lockwell."

He whirled the beast around and in a clatter of hooves was gone. Jance came to take the mare to the stable. Feeling very weary of a sudden, I entered the house.

I went to the kitchen to fix the cup of tea I had not gotten in the village and made some for the children as well, as it was nearly time to rouse them for their second breakfast of the long lumenal. Mrs. Darendal was there.

"I met Mr. Samonds, the farrier, in the village," I said as I fixed a tray for the children.

Mrs. Darendal kept peeling apples.

"He was very kind to assist me," I said, determined to be cheerful. "He told me how he used to come to Heathcrest as a boy."

"Many people used to come here," she said.

"His mother and Mrs. Quent were cousins, I understand."

This received no disagreement, so I could only assume it to be true.

"I wonder," I said, then paused, choosing my words carefully. "That is, it is regretful that those who enjoyed this house once are no longer able to do so. And it is such a remarkable place. I wonder if it might be possible—if sometime we might invite someone to supper. Mr. Samonds perhaps, and his wife if he is married."

"I am sure *he* will never marry," Mrs. Darendal said. She spoke this with what I thought was a hard little smile. She sliced another apple into a bowl. "You should wake the children."

I said nothing more and took my tray upstairs. The children were already awake when I entered. Chambley threw his arms around me in an embrace, which I gladly returned.

"Good morning," I told him.

"It's the middle of the day," he said, rubbing bleary eyes.

"I know," I said. "But we must pretend it's morning, mustn't we? For it's twelve more hours until dusk. Now drink your tea. Here's a cup for you, Clarette."

She did not move from the window. As always I wanted to ask what she was looking at and if she had seen the figure in white again; instead, I went to her with a cup.

"Drink it before it gets cold," I told her.

Clarette set it down without taking a sip, then turned back to the window.

"What are we going to study today?" Chambley asked.

"We should work on our reading. We can read anything we want."

"Can we read about dragons?"

"There are no such things as dragons," Clarette said, turning from the window.

He scowled at her. "There are in books."

"That's very true," I told him. I smiled at Clarette. "Isn't that so?"

She turned her dark eyes on me. "Mr. Quent is gone again, isn't he?"

"Yes, his business has called him away. Did you see him ride off?"

Even as I said this, I remembered that the window of their room was on the opposite side of the house from the front courtyard, where

I had encountered Mr. Quent. The window looked east, out over the empty moor. Toward the Wyrdwood.

Clarette turned again to the window, leaning on the sill and gazing out. Despite the sultry afternoon I felt a chill creep up my arms. I folded them over my chest. "Drink your tea," I said, "and come downstairs when you are dressed."

AFTER THAT DAY, despite the continued fine weather, my spirits fell—further, in truth, than they had since my arrival at Heathcrest. Since Mr. Quent's departure the house seemed more silent than ever. It should have been impossible—he spoke so little—yet it *was* quieter. The silence was a palpable thing, like dust or cobwebs. It smothered everything.

I began to wish I had not promised the children I would keep their secret; I regretted not telling Mr. Quent about the white figure I had glimpsed running toward the Wyrdwood in the gloaming. I determined I *would* tell him as soon as he returned. Only there was no way to know when that would be. It could be a few days, or it could be a half month. Until then, I could only be vigilant. I kept watch out the windows, and when we ventured outside I never released the children's hands.

Despite all my observations, I saw nothing unusual as the days passed. Yet I was growing increasingly certain—indeed, I was by now utterly convinced—that Clarette *had* seen something, that even now, though she did not speak of it, she continued to see the being in white.

Several times I came close to asking Clarette if she had seen the intruder—or (as I feared was the case) if the intruder had spoken to her. Always I refrained. Clarette must *want* to tell me. If I attempted to force the knowledge from her, any hope I had of winning her over was ruined.

My only respite were those long afternoons when I was able to leave the children secured in the house and venture out for a ride. I never felt fear at such times. *I* was not likely to encounter the intruder; it was clear it had no wish to show itself to *me*. And I believed that it most likely made itself known to the children during hours of gloom or twilight.

"You will be back before nightfall, won't ye, miss?" Jance would sometimes ask as he helped me into the saddle, even though the umbral was many hours off. By the third or fourth time he said this, I laughed.

"I can only think I look very foolish when I sit on a horse," I said, "for in the village, Mr. Samonds said much the same thing to me. I assured him he had no cause for worry, and now I say the same to you. I've brought my good sense with me as well as my bonnet."

The groundskeeper squinted up at me. "You ought not make a jest at Mr. Samonds, miss. He has a right to worry about a young lady riding close to dark. That was when his sister went missing."

My mirth perished. What had caused me to laugh like that? I seemed to mock Mr. Samonds when he had been only kind to me.

"His sister!" I said, shocked.

"Aye. It's been over a year now. She went out walking late one day before the fall of a greatnight, and she never came back. They took lanterns with them and covered half the county, staying out all through that long, shivering umbral. But they didn't find her, nor have they since. She were about your age, miss. Looked a bit like you too, fair-headed and all. Halley, that were her name."

How horrible I had been. The sight of me on a horse must have made Mr. Samonds think of his sister, while I had only considered my own pride! I assured Jance I would be back long before sunset and that I would ride only between the house and Cairnbridge.

"That's good to hear, miss," he said, and handed me the reins.

As I rode, I thought of the farrier and of his sister, Halley Samonds. How selfish I had been to think only of myself. Yet it was strange. The heathland was so open; all one had to do was climb up any of the ridges or hills and one could see for miles. It seemed impossible that she could have gotten lost.

❧

A FTER A MIDDLING night came another long lumenal, and once the children were in their room, I again took the gray out for a ride.

"Didn't you go out yesterday?" Mrs. Darendal said as I put on my bonnet.

"We're nearly out of butter," I said with a smile. Without waiting for her answer (for I knew she tended to worry less about what was missing from the larder when the master was not in residence), I took a napkin in which to wrap my intended purchase and hurried out the door.

The day was not so fine as those that had preceded it; clouds lingered over the ridgetops, as if caught on the stones. All the same, I felt relief as I always did once free of the oppressive quiet of Heathcrest, and I let the mare trot as fast as she wished down the road.

At that pace I reached the inn after no more than half an hour. However, once there I discovered there was no butter to be had; the woman who usually brought it had brought none that morning. One of her cows was dead.

I asked the innkeeper if it had gotten sick, but he told me no, the animal had not fallen ill; rather, it had been killed, and the other cows were so frightened their udders had gone dry.

"But who would do such a thing?" I thought of the reports of highwaymen I had overheard. "Was it brigands?"

"It weren't no kind of man," the innkeeper said. "By the look of it, some beast took the cow down. That's what she told me, at least."

"A pack of dogs, you mean?" I asked, for I could think of nothing else that would attack so large a creature.

The innkeeper shook his head. Not beasts, he told me, but *a* beast, and he said if I wanted butter I would have to go to Low Sorrell to get it.

As I climbed into the saddle again, my first thought was that I should return to Heathcrest. But I had been gone less than an hour; I was not yet ready to return to the confines of the house. Besides, while I had told Jance I was riding to the village for butter, I had not specified Cairnbridge. If Low Sorrell was the village where the butter was to be found, then that was where I should be expected to go—or so I reasoned.

I had never been to Low Sorrell, but I knew it was only three miles down the road. It would take little more than an hour to ride there and back, and the mare seemed ready to trot as quickly as I wished.

The road wended among several hills and then down into a quaint valley. Ancient stone walls stitched across a patchwork of tilled fields, meadows, and bracken. I passed a stand of aspen trees—a copse of New Forest, not bounded by any wall—and lingered for a few minutes beneath their trembling shade. By the time I reached the cluster of stone houses near a small bridge, my mood was greatly improved.

I halted before a building I took to be a public house. The village was not, I was forced to admit despite my good cheer, as charming as Cairnbridge. The grass in the commons was yellowed, and the houses were stained with soot and patches of moss that gave them a scabrous look.

It was only the damp air that made everything look shabby, I supposed, for the village was close to the bogs. However, the people who went about had the same dilapidated look as the buildings. Nor did any of them greet me, though a few treated me to sidelong glances. These people were not country squires and well-to-do tradesmen, I reminded myself; rather, it was the tenants who dwelled down in the lowlands.

As no one stopped to greet me, I took it upon myself to speak to a gray-haired man passing by, inquiring if he knew where I might buy butter. He muttered several harsh-sounding words and made an odd motion with his hand, then turned his back to me.

I had no idea what to make of this reaction, but I decided it best to seek out someone who was used to speaking with a customer. With that in mind, I ventured into the public house. A haze of smoke hung on the air, along with a sour smell. The rumble of conversation filled the room but fell to a hush as I entered. A dozen rough faces turned in my direction. I could only wonder what I looked like. Was I such a fright after my ride?

No, that was not why they stared. My dress, though very simple to me, was of fine black linen, not coarse gray homespun. I saw there was not another woman in the place. However, if I had intruded or broken some rule, then the infraction was already committed. I might as well make my inquiry.

"Good day," I said to the bald man who stood at the plank of wood that served as a counter. "I wonder if you might tell me where in the village I could purchase butter."

"There's none you can buy here," he said.

I was taken aback—though at this point not entirely surprised—by his harsh tone. "I was told in Cairnbridge I might do so."

He scowled, as if I had accused him of lying. "There's none here in Sorrell, but cross the bridge and keep going until ye reach the third croft. Ye can talk to them there."

That I could trust these directions I was far from certain; however, I thanked the man. He gave a curt nod without meeting my eyes. At the same time his hand dropped behind the counter, but not before I saw him touch his thumb and middle finger together three times. It was, I thought, the same motion the man outside had made.

"Good day," I said again, and, keeping my chin up, I walked to the door and into the sunlight. I heard a burst of talk behind me, but I kept moving, returning to my horse.

My hands trembled as I took the reins. I did not know what I had done to earn such strange consideration from the men in the public house. Perhaps it was only to be expected that men who were obedient in their landlords' presence might turn surly in their own village with a cup of ale at hand. All the same, their looks, their behavior, had left me unsettled. The day had lost any luster it had held. The air was damp, the clouds dreary. I wanted only to ride as quickly as I could back to Heathcrest.

No, I should not be so easily deterred by a few rude looks. I had come on an errand, and I would see it done. I rode along the muddy street, crossed the bridge, and followed the track.

I soon came to a row of small farms or crofts in the meadows along the stream, and in front of the third I saw several cows grazing, which I took for a hopeful sign. I tied the mare at a post, then followed the footpath up to the croft. It was less a country cottage and more a hovel of gray stones with a wattle-and-daub chimney, but there were nasturtiums blooming in the yard and violets beside the front step; these encouraged me onward when my steps might otherwise have faltered.

As I neared the house, a young man—taller than I, but very thin—came around the corner. When he saw me he stopped short, and his eyes went wide. The bucket he had been carrying slipped from his hand. White liquid flowed over the ground.

"Oh!" I exclaimed, taking a step toward him. "I'm so sorry."

He retreated, and his left hand curled in as he tapped thumb and middle finger together. My cheeks burned, and my eyes stung. To receive another such reaction was more than I could bear that day. I started to turn, to head back down the path.

"I suppose she's come for butter," said a reedy voice from the direction of the house. "Don't just stand there like a lump of peat, Corren. Pick up the bucket and go fill it again. The red cow has been complaining all morning—I've told you she needs milking twice a day."

The young man snatched up the bucket and ran back around the house. A woman stood on the steps of the house. She was wrapped in a gray shawl and leaned on a crooked stick that served for a cane. She gestured to me with a hand that was every bit as bent as the cane.

To leave was still my instinct. But the woman motioned to me again, and as it was the first encouraging gesture I had seen since coming to Low Sorrell, I could not resist.

"There's a girl," the woman said as I approached the steps. "Come in, come in. I'll get you the butter. It's ten pennies a pot. That's robbery, I know; but when robbers roam the roads, even honest folk must resort to thievery to make a living. What times, these are! Come in, my dear, I said come in. And you'll have a cup of tea, of course."

"Tea?" I said, surprised by her words.

She squinted at me. "You aren't simple, are you, dear?"

"Yes," I managed to say. "I mean, yes, I'd like tea very much, thank you."

I followed her into the house. The front room was spare and dim, but it was neatly kept, and there was a bowl of yellow nasturtiums on the table. I felt no fear as I accepted a seat and a cup. The tea was warming—fragrant with rose hips—and I felt myself restored as I sipped it. My host was not, I saw now, so old as I had thought. Her crooked limbs must have been the result of a malady of the bones, not the product of age.

"This chair," I said, noticing the seat I had taken. "It's very like the one in my room at—in the house where I live."

"At Heathcrest Hall, you mean."

So there was no hiding who I was. "Yes, at Heathcrest." I touched the arms of the chair, which had been bent and braided of willow branches.

"My nephew fashioned it. I imagine he made the one you have up at Heathcrest as well."

"It's beautiful," I said, and then realized I had yet to introduce myself, so I set down my cup and did so.

"I am Cathlen Samonds," she said in reply.

"Samonds!" I said. "But your nephew—it isn't Mr. Samonds, is it? The farrier in Cairnbridge, I mean."

"Aye, he's the very one. My brother is his father. Or he was, that is, when he still dwelled with us in this world."

"I'm sorry," I said, but she only shook her head and drank her tea. "I suppose that's how the chair came to be at the house," I went on. "Mr. Samonds—that is, your nephew—said he went there often as a boy. He must have brought the chair there."

"Aye, he made several things for the house—chests, stools, and other things. The chair would have been a gift for Mrs. Quent."

"She was his mother's cousin, I understand."

She nodded, then took a nasturtium from the bowl and ate it, flower, leaf, and stem.

"The young man out there," I said. "Is he your son? I'm sorry I startled him. I will pay for the milk."

"That's my neighbor's son. I've never married. Besides, I like to believe any son of mine would have been a bit less thick." She laughed, and her teeth were as crooked as the rest of her. "But he's a good lad in his way. And you need not worry over the milk. It's good to spill a little now and then, to give back to the ground what we take from it." She took another flower and ate it.

"Thank you," I said, and didn't know what to say after that. I sipped my tea as Miss Samonds ate flowers.

"I imagine they were right wary of you in the village," she said. "To tell the truth, I'm surprised they spoke to you enough to tell you how to find me. You must have had to draw it out of them."

"Indeed, they were very strange to me," I said, setting down my cup. Now that the subject was broached, my curiosity had to be satisfied. "Such looks they gave me—just as the boy out there did—as if I were the most frightful thing, and they would make this peculiar gesture. Why would they do such a thing?"

"Because you have Addysen eyes."

"My eyes? What do you mean?"

"Your eyes are green. It isn't a common color, at least not around here. There's only one family in this county as ever had green eyes in it, and even then it was just the daughters. Not that there were ever many sons of *that* family."

"The Addysens, you mean."

"Aye, the Addysens. And I'm guessing by your look you want to hear all about them. You'd better take more tea, then."

I hesitated, for I knew I should hasten back to Heathcrest before the children rose. However, by then my curiosity could not be denied. I accepted another cup of tea.

"There's no older family in the county than the Addysens," Miss Samonds said, "though there were the Rylends, who were every bit as old. Earl Rylend dwelled up at Heathcrest Hall, as you must know. Your own Mr. Quent was raised in his household like a son. But the earl had no child of his own who lived to inherit his name. When he was gone, the house, but not the Rylend name, went to Mr. Quent.

"I cannot imagine that he sought it!" I was not certain why I felt it necessary to make so vehement a defense of my employer, but that Mr. Quent was someone who aspired to a title out of vanity I could not imagine.

Miss Samonds shrugged, then went on as bees droned in the yard outside the window. The Addysens, she said, had long made their home at their lodge at Willowbridge, some miles to the north. The last Addysen squire to dwell there had been Marwen Addysen. For a time he had served as a captain at a garrison in Torland, but he had been called back when his elder brother was thrown from a horse and broke his neck. This all happened nearly a hundred years ago.

Much to the dismay of his family, Marwen brought a wife back with him, a young woman from one of the Torland clans. However, the deed was accomplished; there was nothing to be done. By then Marwen's father was near to death and indeed soon passed. So Marwen became squire at the lodge at Willowbridge, and his wife the lady of the house.

"What was she like, the woman he brought from Torland?" I asked, and took another sip of tea.

Miss Samonds laughed. "Oh, she was a wild thing, Rowan Addysen was! Or at least so the stories say. It was said if there was a ball she would dance every song, and when the musicians stopped playing she would run outside and dash off her shoes and dance in the grass by the light of the moon. She was lovely too, and generous. All the accounts say she was much liked by all who met her."

"And she had green eyes?"

"Aye, that she did. So did each of her three daughters, and so did all of *their* daughters. So it was that to have green eyes was to have Addysen eyes. But she never had any son, and she raised her daughters mostly by herself, for Marwen died when Willowbridge Lodge burned to the ground one night when Rowan and her girls were off at a ball."

It seemed the daughters themselves were peculiar in their way. For one thing, none of them took their husband's name when they were married. Not that their husbands liked the idea much, but that was the price of getting Rowan Addysen's approval—and more importantly, a part of her fortune, which was enough to rival that of the Rylends. So it was that her daughters were able to find men who would agree to that peculiar condition and Rowan's daughters kept the name Addysen, and gave it to their own daughters as well.

"But not to the sons?" I asked.

Miss Samonds shrugged. "As I said, there were never many sons that came out of that lineage. My nephew is one of the few. But Rowan Addysen only said her daughters had to keep the name. And maybe that was why the men agreed so quickly when they accepted their portion. For a daughter doesn't have much chance to carry on a man's name, does she? And by the time her granddaughters married, Rowan Addysen was in the grave, and none of them who took a husband kept the Addysen name for their own."

What a strange story! But that Rowan Addysen was a fascinating character could not be denied. "Are there many of them, then? Rowan's granddaughters, I mean."

"Aye, there were near to a dozen. Not all stayed in the county, of course. Some went back west to Torland to take husbands there, and some met an early death, as some do. Yet a number of them stayed here."

"And they all had green eyes."

Miss Samonds set down her cup. "Some less green, some more. But, aye, every one of them."

But Mr. Samonds's eyes were brown, I recalled. This was peculiar and made me think of Miss Mew. Only female cats were ever tortoiseshells, and only Addysen women ever had green eyes. How was it such a trait could be passed only to daughters, not sons? I did not know. However, interesting as this was, it did not explain the reaction I had gotten in the village.

I started to ask this question, but it appeared Miss Samonds had anticipated it.

"They're not thought of as a good thing these days," she said. "Eyes of green, that is."

"Why is that?"

Up to this point, Miss Samonds had been talkative and open, but now her expression grew closed, even canny. She seemed to be thinking.

"The great oak tree on the commons in Cairnbridge," she said at last. "Do you know what happened to it?"

"It burned some years ago. That was what your nephew Mr. Samonds told me."

"Aye, it did burn. Nearly twenty years ago now."

"How strange that they have not planted another in its place."

"You think it strange? And did you know there was an old stand of Wyrdwood near the village that burned that same night? Would you think that strange as well?"

I recalled the dark smudge I had seen atop the hill just north of Cairnbridge. "I don't know what you mean, Miss Samonds." All the same my breathing quickened, as if I *did* know something, and my hands felt damp. I pressed them against my dress.

"No, you don't know, do you? I wonder if it is good or ill." She shook her head. "Well, you should ask Mrs. Darendal about it, all the same."

"Mrs. Darendal?"

"That's right. She's still the housekeeper up at Heathcrest, isn't she?"

I nodded.

"Ask Mrs. Darendal, then," Miss Samonds said. "She can tell you what happened better than I can. Ask her what happened to the oak tree on the commons in Cairnbridge nineteen years ago."

Before I could say anything more, she had risen and fetched me a pot of butter. I paid her, then found myself at the door. A mist was falling outside. I pulled up my bonnet and ventured out into the damp. However, as I reached the bottom of the steps, I remembered and turned around.

"Miss Samonds, you still haven't told me. The gesture the men made with their hands—what does it mean?"

She did not look at me but rather into the mist. "It's a sign," she said. "A sign against poison and bad luck." She tightened bent fingers around her cane. "A sign against curses."

The door shut, and the violets beside the step lowered their heads as the mist turned into rain.

By THE TIME I returned to Heathcrest, Jance was waiting for me. He hurried out of the stables as I rode up, took the reins, and helped me down. It was an act for which I was glad, for I was drenched through, and my fingers were so numb I could hardly pry them from the reins.

"Are ye well, miss?" He held me steady. "Are ye hurt?"

My mind was as numb as my fingers. "Hurt?"

"I went to Cairnbridge, but ye weren't there. An' then I heard word about Deelie Moorbrook's cow, an' my mind can only get to thinking. So I ride back here, an' ye weren't back yet. I was just going to ride out to try to find ye, only then I see ye coming up the hill. Are ye sure ye aren't hurt, miss?"

I assured him I was just cold and explained that I had gone to Low Sorrell to buy butter. He gave me a startled look, but he said nothing as he led me to the house.

Inside, he called for Lanna, and when she saw me her eyes went wide. She led me up to my room and helped me out of my sodden clothes. Soon I sat before the fire, wrapped in a shawl, drinking hot tea.

"Thank you, Lanna," I said when at last my shivering subsided.

She appeared quite relieved. I supposed I had given everyone a fright.

"Well, I know it was foolish of me to ride so far," I said. "But at least we shall have butter on the table tonight."

Lanna treated me to one of her rare smiles.

"The children—they haven't risen already, have they?"

She hesitated, then nodded.

So I had been gone too long after all.

"I will see to them at once," I said. Despite Lanna's looks, I set down my cup and rose. "There, I'm quite well, thanks to you," I assured her, and though my legs were not so certain as my words, I went downstairs.

I found Clarette and Chambley in our parlor. They sat at the table, books open before them. They had not seemed to notice my approach, and I paused in the doorway. Their heads were bent together. Clarette's hand was cupped between her mouth and Chambley's ear.

I made a sound at the door. Chambley seemed not to hear it, but Clarette's look shifted in my direction. A chill came over me. There was a hardness to her gaze that seemed unnatural in the eyes of a child. She continued to whisper in his ear.

"Good day, children," I said.

Chambley sucked in a breath and looked up, his eyes large and dark in his round face. Clarette folded her hands on the table. I entered the room, though as I did my shivering resumed.

"It's chilly in here," I said. "You must be cold."

"We're very well," Clarette said.

And Chambley said, "Where were you?"

"I was delayed." I stooped to light the kindling on the hearth. The hairs on my neck prickled. I could feel her eyes on me. "I went to Low Sorrell to buy some things we needed. I'm sorry I was gone so long." I rose and smiled at them. "I see you've been keeping yourself well occupied in my absence. Let's see what you've been reading." I sat and took up one of the books.

"You go out riding when we're in our room," Clarette said. "You go every time it's a long afternoon."

I set the book back down. How could she know that? The window in their room faced east, and I always left from the west side of the house.

"You're going to be leaving us," she said.

These words astonished me. "What a strange thing to say! Nothing could be further from the truth."

"And Mr. Quent is always gone," Clarette went on in a low voice. "We'll be here all alone."

"All alone?" Chambley said, looking at his sister with worried eyes.

"No, not alone," I said to him. "I have absolutely no intention of leaving Heathcrest."

"But you *will* leave," Clarette said.

"That is nonsense." My voice was sharper than I intended, but I was tired—tired from the cold, tired of being treated so strangely that day. "Surely I know my own intentions better than anyone."

"It doesn't matter what you intend to do," Clarette said. "You're going to be leaving."

This was too much. I struck a hand against the table. "How can you possibly know such a thing, Clarette?"

Her dark eyes flicked toward the window. The curtains moved outward, then sank back. Despite the fire the air turned cold. In a swift motion, I rose and crossed to the curtains, throwing them back. The window was ajar.

A gasp escaped me. With a shaking hand I pulled the window closed, latching it, then turned around.

"Go to your room!"

Chambley shook his head. "But we haven't finished our reading."

I pointed to the door. "I said go!"

Chambley's lips trembled, but Clarette seemed almost to smile. She clasped her brother's hand, then led him to the door. As they went, she bent her head toward his.

"I told you," I heard her murmur.

I wanted to shout at her, but a heaviness came over me. As they left I sank into a chair and laid my head against the smooth wood of the table. She was right. I *did* want to go. I wanted to go back to Invarel, to Whitward Street, to my sisters and to you, Father. I wanted to go home.

The candle sputtered as it burned low. I rose and cast a look at the window, but I saw only gray outside. Then I went to see if Mrs. Darendal needed any help with supper.

❧

NO, THAT CANNOT be." I heard Mrs. Darendal's voice as I neared the kitchen. The words were spoken in a hush, but such was the effect of the slate floor and the high ceiling of the hallway that I could hear as if I were standing beside her.

"Aye? An' if that ain't the case, then what else can it be?" I recognized Jance's thick country accent. I halted outside the doorway.

Mrs. Darendal's voice rose over the noise of chopping. "Perhaps there were dogs on the loose."

"It weren't dogs. Ranuff Brint went to Deelie's place and saw the prints. He said its paws were as big as his hand all splayed out. There aren't no dog *that* big."

"And had Mr. Brint come from the inn when he observed this? I know he is often there."

I could hear Jance's scowl in his voice. "Maybe he did and maybe he didn't, but he weren't the only one who saw those prints. They're saying it was a greatwolf."

The sound of chopping increased in volume and rapidity. "There hasn't been a greatwolf out of Torland in two hundred years. It was something else that took that cow."

"Aye, and what would that be, then?"

The sound of the knife ceased.

"What is it?" came Jance's voice.

"I thought I heard something. I was mistaken." The sound of chopping resumed.

I waited in the corridor, counting my heartbeats until I reached a hundred, and then entered the kitchen. Jance was just in the act of putting on a coat of oiled canvas. He nodded to me, then passed through the back door. Outside, the gloom had darkened further.

"Did you find the butter?" I asked. "I left the pot in the larder."

"Low Sorrell is a long way to go for butter." Mrs. Darendal picked up another onion and wielded her knife against it. "Where are the children?"

"In their room." I expected her to ask why we were not at study. She only kept working.

I went to the stove and heated the kettle for tea. As I watched, waiting for it to hiss, I thought of what Miss Samonds had told me. *Ask Mrs. Darendal. . . . She can tell you what happened better than I can. . . .*

But tell me what? Why the tree had burned? Or why the folk in Low Sorrell had made a sign against ill luck and curses when they saw a woman with eyes of green?

A thought occurred to me, something I had been too cold and dull to realize before. Miss Samonds had said that her nephew, the farrier, was one of the few sons born to a granddaughter of Rowan Addysen. That meant his mother had to have been an Addysen. And her cousin had been . . .

"Mrs. Quent," I said.

Behind me, the knife clattered to the table. I turned around.

"She was an Addysen, wasn't she? Mrs. Quent."

Mrs. Darendal picked up the knife. It gleamed in her hand. For a moment I half fancied she would brandish it against me. Then she resumed chopping vegetables.

"Her name was Gennivel Addysen before she became Mrs. Quent."

I took a step closer. "And she was a granddaughter of Rowan Addysen."

"I suppose she must have been."

"The folk in Low Sorrell acted very queer when they saw me. Do you have any idea why?"

"I imagine they thought it was odd that someone had ridden all the way to their village on a day such as this."

"No, that wasn't it. They made a sign with their hand when they saw me. A sign against curses. Do you know why they'd do that?"

Still Mrs. Darendal said nothing; the knife flashed as she worked. Ever since I came to Heathcrest, the housekeeper had been reticent, hardly willing to speak to me. I had always thought she simply disapproved of my intrusion, but it was more than that.

"Miss Samonds said you could tell me what happened to the tree on the Cairnbridge common."

Mrs. Darendal set down the knife. "You want to know about the tree on the green, do you?"

"I do."

"You *think* you want to know, Miss Lockwell. Do you really?"

I didn't know what these words meant. I *did* want to know. "It has to do with my eyes. That's why they acted so strangely in Low Sorrell."

"They're simple folk there," Mrs. Darendal said. "They don't put on airs, and they don't pretend not to see what's before them. They're country folk, and they don't forget things quickly."

"You seem to know the people of Low Sorrel well."

"I was born and raised there. And I never thought I'd leave. I never wished to, but when Mr. Darendal made me an offer, I could hardly refuse it. He had just come into his father's land outside Cairnbridge." She looked out the gray window. "Who was I to refuse that? And I thought him kind and more than handsome enough."

I watched her, fascinated. The words were soft, even tender. "You loved him," I said.

She glared at me, and her words were hard again. "What does it matter if I did? He's been gone near twenty years. He was a fool, and what do handsome looks and a kindly way matter then? Why he thought he had to go there that day, why he couldn't leave it to others—to *her* own people—I don't know. But he took up an ax, and he—"

Her lips pressed together in a tight line. I should have gone, should have left her alone with her memories. Instead, I moved another step closer. "He took an ax—to the tree, you mean. The tree on the green."

For so many months I had lived in dread of Mrs. Darendal and her ire; I had sought always to stay out of her way. Yet at that moment it was her eyes that were alight with dread. She retreated a step.

"Aye," she said in a low voice. "To the tree."

"And others went there." A peculiar energy came over me, like the lightning that precedes a storm. "They brought axes with them, like Mr. Darendal. I saw the ax heads there, rusting in the grass. They brought torches as well. But why?"

Mrs. Darendal took another step back, but the table was behind her; she could go no farther.

"What happened to Mr. Darendal that day?"

The housekeeper shook her head, leaning back against the table.

"Why did they go to the green in Cairnbridge?" I made my voice sharp. "Why did they burn down the tree?"

The housekeeper struck the table behind her with her palms. "Because the witch had gotten to it!"

A piercing scream rang out. For a moment I thought it a woman's scream. Then Mrs. Darendal glanced at the stove behind me, and I remembered the kettle.

Now it was I who retreated. I snatched up a cloth and used it to pull the kettle from the stove. As its noise dwindled, I lifted a hand to my brow; my head throbbed. At last I dared to look at her. Her expression was hard once more; the knife was back in her hand.

"The witch?" I said. "I don't understand."

"Don't you, Miss Lockwell? You are from the city, but you have read the histories, I am sure. Have you never heard of a Rising?"

"A Rising," I said faintly. Suddenly it was difficult to draw a breath.

She gave a grim nod, then went back to her work. I thought she would say nothing more to me, that our conversation was over. I started to leave the kitchen.

"She was an Addysen as well," Mrs. Darendal said.

I stopped at the door and turned around. "The witch?"

"Aye. Now get your tea, Miss Lockwell, and sit down."

I did, and then I listened as the housekeeper spoke of what had happened on the green in Cairnbridge nineteen years ago.

✦

LOW THUNDER RUMBLED as I entered the front hall. According to the almanac, night would not fall for two more hours, yet I could hardly see to find my way. The only illumination came from the occasional flashes of lightning, which sent shadows scurrying and made the heads of stag and boar on the walls shift and move as things again alive.

I sank into one of the horsehair chairs. Another flash of lightning cut through the gloom, as sharp as the knife Mrs. Darendal had wielded as she spoke of what happened to the tree in Cairnbridge— the gallows tree, she had called it.

Long ago, the tree on the common green would never have been allowed to grow. That was the first thing she had told me. In the country, it was the custom to plant no tree within four furlongs of a stand of Wyrdwood, and it was less than that from Cairnbridge to the patch of ancient forest that had stood on the hill to the north of the village.

But it was only a little less than four furlongs, people had said—surely very near to four—and the patch of Wyrdwood was small, no more than three hundred paces all around the wall that enclosed it.

Even so, had it not already been a great tree by the time people settled again in Cairnbridge, it would have been cut down. However, the county had been all but devoid of population after the Plague Years. For over a century the village had been empty of people, its fields fallow, and in that time a seed had taken root on the common green.

By the time people returned to Cairnbridge, the tree was already a great thing, spreading its branches across the common field, providing shade on long afternoons and acorns to roast in the cold depths of a greatnight. Nor did people entirely recall the reasons for the old customs. So it was that the proud oak had been allowed to grow until its branches reached over the entire green, and no one ever thought of the little stand of straggled trees that stood on the hill to the north.

Yet the ancient trees of the Wyrdwood sink their roots deep, and over long years the slender fibers might travel far beneath the ground. A few of them must have finally reached the New Oak on the commons nearly half a mile below, twining with its roots, merging with them. All the same, nothing might ever have come of it. Only then . . .

Where the two men came from, no one knew for certain.

They were drifters. Some who spoke to them at the inn said they had been driven off the land they had occupied when it was enclosed by an earl for his private hunting ground, in one of the counties nearer to Invarel. With nowhere to go, they had gone westward, to places enclosure had not yet reached, and with no good work to do, they had taken to drinking. They had come to the inn at Cairnbridge early on a short day, and by that evening they had been thrown out and told to be on their way.

What happened then no one witnessed, but it could be guessed well enough. As they stumbled from the village in the dusk before a greatnight, they had come upon a young woman riding home. Being rough, and drunk, and full of hatred, they had accosted her. The woman fled, but the men overtook her, dragging her from her horse and away from the village, up a hill to the north. Until they came to an old stone wall.

Again lightning cut through the gloom, and I shuddered. Had the men used her ill? Perhaps they had, or perhaps they had only tried.

Either way, the result was the same. The young woman had cried out for help.

And the Wyrdwood had answered.

Perhaps she had not known she was a witch. Or perhaps she had fled toward the wood with purpose. It did not matter, at least not for the two men. By the time people from the village came up the hill with torches, they found the pair swinging among the branches, hung by lithe green switches braided around their necks.

By then the great oak on the commons was burning. However, the tree was not destroyed without terrible cost. In contact with the trees of the Wyrdwood, the oak on the green had heard her call just as they had. It had lashed out with no warning, taking two men as they stepped from the inn and strayed near the green. It had taken three more who had tried to free the first two from its branches. For, in the witch's blind fury, they were no different from the men who had accosted her.

The folk of Cairnbridge might have forgotten the old ways before then, but they remembered them quickly enough that night. The bell on the village church rang out; men answered the call with ax and fire. They hewed at the hard wood of the oak, threw oil against it, and set its branches alight, until it became a column of flame a hundred feet high. Thus the great old tree was brought down—but not before it took two more men and hung them high in the gallows of its branches.

One of those men was Mr. Darendal. Seven men in all were killed in the Rising that night, in addition to the two drifters who met their end in the Wyrdwood on the hill.

*And what of her?* I had said when Mrs. Darendal fell silent.

*What of Merriel Addysen, you mean?* She looked at me with hard gray eyes. *The witch was still hiding in the Wyrdwood when they burned it from wall to wall. I am certain her spirit now dwells in the darkest pits of the Abyss. For God knows the doors of Eternum are shut to such a thing of sin.*

With that Mrs. Darendal had set down her knife and left the kitchen.

Thunder rattled the windows again, and I rose and staggered up the stairs. There had not been a Rising in centuries, if there had ever really been one at all—so I had always thought. Yet if Mrs. Darendal was to be believed, there had been one in this very county not twenty years ago.

And I *did* believe her. How could I not? I had seen the burnt patch on the hill north of Cairnbridge. I had seen the looks they gave me in

Low Sorrell. Had Merriel Addysen possessed green eyes? I could not doubt that she had, not when I had seen the way they regarded *me*.

Yet if this had happened here, if there had indeed been a Rising just as in the ancient accounts, why was it never spoken of? Why was it not taught in schools and written about in books? Surely the king would want such a thing widely known, so people might be warned and take precautions.

I could not think; my mind was aflutter. Another peal of thunder shook the foundations of the house. My only thought was that I must go to the children, that they would be frightened of the storm. I hurried down the corridor and opened the door to their room.

It was empty and silent.

"Come out this instant!" I said, certain they were playing a trick on me—some ruse of Clarette's devising.

I peered through the murk. The covers were thrown back on their beds. The door of the wardrobe hung ajar. So they were hiding elsewhere. I was on the verge of turning to go in search of them when I felt a chill draft. The curtains to either side of the window billowed outward. I went to the window to close the sash against the gale. Just then lightning flared again outside. As it did, motion below caught my eye.

Two small figures ran across the grounds behind the house.

I could not move. Dread was a cold metal cage enclosing me. The two little shadows flitted away from the house and vanished into the mist.

The curtain brushed my face like a damp hand. I lurched back. Then, my paralysis broken, I dashed from the room. Stumbling down the stairs, I made for a servants' entrance at the back of the house. The latch was stiff. I pried it open with my fingers, pushed the door open, and ran outside into the dreary air of late afternoon.

"Chambley!" I cried out. "Clarette!"

The fog stifled my voice. I ran in the direction I had seen them go, calling for them until my voice was ragged. There was no reply. The wind snatched at my hair, and the mist dampened my face and slicked the stones beneath my feet so that I nearly fell a dozen times as I ran. Still I did not see them. What had possessed them to go out into the storm?

But I knew. Chambley dreaded to leave the house; only Clarette could have compelled him to leave. And why would Clarette go—unless she had been called?

"Chambley!" I shouted again, suddenly certain that, even if she heard my voice, Clarette would not answer me.

I had reached the edge of the ridge. I turned around, wiping damp hair from my eyes. All I could make out were indistinct shapes. The house was a hazy patch behind me. I saw no sign of them.

Just as the weight of despair threatened to press me to the ground, a gust of wind rushed over the ridge. The clouds broke apart, and a low shaft of heavy gold light fell through, illuminating the moors. In an instant I saw them: two small shapes below, picking their way east across the fields and bracken. Beyond them rose another slope, and the sun caught upon the twisted shapes that crowned the hill, tingeing them red, so that they looked for all the world as if they were afire.

"No," I tried to cry out, but my voice was a hoarse whisper. "No, not there!"

I ran down the slope, over clumps of heather and patches of scree, so that it was a wonder I did not go tumbling and break my neck. By the time I reached the bottom, the gap in the clouds had closed again.

The land turned upward, rising in a steep slope. In a flash of lightning I made out black shapes twisting above me, and below them a gray line. I used my fingers as much as my feet to propel me up the face of the hill, so that soon my hands were raw and bleeding.

Another bolt of lightning rent the clouds, and in that brief moment I saw them: two little figures standing hand in hand. They had reached the old stone wall not thirty feet above me. The lightning faded; I was blinded by the darkness. Then came another flash. A figure all in white fluttered above the children, as if floating among the branches that drooped over the mossy wall.

"No, get away!" I shouted, but the words were lost as thunder shook the air. I ran toward the wall, but my sodden dress pulled me down, tangling around my legs. I clawed my way upward on all fours.

Again lightning flashed. I did not know how it could be possible, but I was sure the branches that hung over the wall reached lower than they had a moment ago. I could no longer see the figure in white. Despite her ghostly appearance, she had not been floating, I knew, but rather had stood atop the wall. Only she was no longer there. The gloom closed in again, only to burst apart a heartbeat later in another flash of light. Now the branches reached so far that they nearly brushed the ground. The children looked upward, their mouths open in fear.

A grimness came over me. I was no longer afraid or weary. I sprang up the slope, covering the last few feet in an instant.

"Get away from the wall!" I called out, and this time they heard me, for they turned around, their faces white as moons. Chambley flung small hands out toward me, and a moment later, to my surprise—

and fierce delight—Clarette did as well. I gripped their chilled hands and pulled them toward me. They were shivering.

"Hurry!" I said. "We must go."

However, as we turned from the stone wall we found a curtain of branches hanging before us. They wove in a tangle, barring the way. I tried to move along the wall, but more branches drooped down to either side of us. A creaking rose on the air, and the wall shuddered at our backs. Wet leaves fell in a black snow. Clarette screamed.

Another tremor shook the wall. Clarette twisted away from me. I tried to tighten my hold on her, but our hands were both slick. Her fingers were wrested from mine, and she stumbled into the web of branches.

"Clarette, come back!" Chambley cried.

His hand slipped free of my own, and he dashed after his sister. I tried to grab for him, but a wind rose up, whipping the branches, and I was forced to use my hands to thrust them away from my face.

Lightning flared. I saw that he had managed to wriggle under the boughs to his sister. However, Clarette was not as small; she could not similarly escape the cage of branches. They huddled together. I tried to go to them, but the branches tossed back and forth under the force of the gale, thrusting me back against the wall.

Or was it really the storm that propelled the limbs of the trees? For they seemed to strain and bend as would best hinder our movement, without any regard to the direction of the wind. Again the stones shuddered at my back, violently, as if they would split wide open.

Clarette and Chambley screamed. Then I saw it too. Something pale fluttered beyond the black web of branches.

"No," I murmured. "No, this will not be."

I had said I would keep them safe. I had promised them. I had promised *him*. An anger rose in me such as I had never felt before in my life. I thrust my hands at the boughs before me.

"Let us go!"

A crack of thunder rent open the sky, and cold rain pelted down as a wind rushed among the trees. The branches heaved and shook, groaning as they bent under the gale.

I twisted myself free. The branches tossed back and forth, then lifted, and I was able to rush forward. I grabbed the children by their hands and pulled them with me as I ran down the hill. I do not know if it was dread or if something was really there, but I thought I saw a glimmer of white out of the corner of my eye. I gripped the small hands in my own, so hard I was sure I was hurting them, but they did not resist. The children were weeping, their faces bruised and marked by red lines. I was weeping as well.

Together we careened down the slope as the fury of the storm was unleashed upon us. Just as we reached the bottom of the hill, there was a clattering noise, and a dark form reared above us. Red light flared. The children cried out, and we went tumbling to the ground in a heap.

A strong hand clasped around my wrist. I gasped, raising my head, and blinked against the red light. It was a lantern, I realized, and as my eyes adjusted I saw a familiar, bearded face above me.

"Miss Lockwell," said a deep voice. It was not angry, as I might have imagined, but low, even regretful.

I could only gaze up in wonder.

"I've found them!" he called out now, and I heard the sound of a horse as another red light bobbed toward us in the gloom.

"Mr. Quent," I said. I wanted to say more, to tell him to see to the children, to take them to Heathcrest at once, but I could do no more than repeat the words. "Mr. Quent."

He pulled me to my feet, and I had to throw my arms around his shoulders to keep from sinking back to the ground. The children clung to him at either side.

"What has happened, Miss Lockwell?"

I looked back over my shoulder, at the dark shapes on the hill above us. A bit of white fluttered among them, then it was gone.

"She's in the wood," I murmured. But I do not think he heard me above the storm.

"By God, you're freezing," he said. "All three of you are freezing. You'll catch your death."

The other lantern drew near. It was Jance on horseback. "Take the children," Mr. Quent said to him, and he handed them up as easily as if they were sacks of flour.

"I can walk," I said, or tried to say, recalling the way he had been forced to carry me once before, not wanting him to have to do so again. It was no use. Mr. Quent lifted me up and set me on his horse, then climbed up behind me. I leaned back against him. He was warm and solid, and despite all that had happened, all dread and worry left me.

For a moment he went rigid. Then I felt him breathe out, and his arm encircled me. With his other hand he flicked the reins, urging his horse into a canter. I shut my eyes and pressed my cheek against his chest, and all the way back to the house I felt not rain, or wind, or any tremor of fear.

𝒯HAT NIGHT WE took ill, the children and myself.

My recollection of what happened after we returned to the house is dim: visions glimpsed through a fogged window. I remember I could not stop shivering, though I was set before a roaring fire, and that I trembled too much to drink the tea Lanna brought me. I remember how the children's faces were like marble as Mr. Quent carried them upstairs, Mrs. Darendal following. Their eyes were shut. They looked like little angels carved of stone.

When he returned, I had presence of mind enough to tell him what had happened; I do remember that much. I did not hold anything back or attempt to deflect any blame from myself. He paced in front of the fire as I told him how I had been cross with the children, how I had found them gone from their room and had seen them out the window running toward the Wyrdwood.

I told him also what I should have told him long ago, about the figure in white. I explained how it was my belief that this being had been in communication with the children, or at least with Clarette, and that I feared it was due to the urging of this trespasser that the children ventured out into the storm.

I described then what took place at the wall by the Wyrdwood. Or I attempted to, for by then my head was already filling with a haze and my teeth clattered so violently I could barely speak. I tried to describe how the wind had tossed the branches of the trees so that they bent down further than seemed possible, trapping us among them, then how the wind had changed and we had been able to escape.

Except that wasn't what had happened, was it? The wind hadn't changed; indeed, the gale had blown more fiercely every moment. I had thought us lost. Only then I had shouted, *Let us go!* And the branches had lifted.

Yet how? I wanted to explain these things to him—perhaps he would understand—but by then my shuddering had grown so forceful I could not speak.

His face was grim; in truth, it was more stern than I had ever seen it. He gripped his left hand—the maimed one—inside his right. That he must be furious I was certain. I had failed to tell him of the trespasser, had failed in my most fundamental duty to keep the children safe. However, when he spoke, it was only to say that I looked very ill and that I should go to my room.

To my credit, I was able to ascend the stairs on my own, but I would not have been able to undress myself without Lanna's help. She stripped me of my sodden dress. After that I could do no more than fall into my bed, for by then the fever had come upon me.

What can I tell you of what followed, Father? I fear you know better than I the labyrinths in which an ill mind can be lost. In a fever, nothing seems as it really is. One gets tangled up in the tatters of thoughts and phantasms even as in the bedclothes. The shadows were a cage, coiling around me like black branches.

Here and there were lucid moments. I remember once I rose from the bed and stumbled to the window. Outside, a red light bobbed along the ground, and for a moment in my delirium I wondered if the new red planet had fallen to earth. Then I saw a second light, and I knew it to be Jance and Mr. Quent, that they were walking around the grounds of the house with lanterns.

I crawled back into the bed. My bones ached, and in my dreams I imagined them bending and twisting into new shapes like willow branches in Mr. Samonds's hands.

WHEN I OPENED my eyes again, gold light slanted into my room. For many minutes I lay in bed, watching the light move upon the ceiling, until I realized it was not morning but evening.

I turned my head and saw that I was not alone. A figure sat in the bent-willow chair. It was not Lanna.

"Well, there you are," Mr. Quent said, sitting up straight. His coat hung on the back of the chair. He wore only a white shirt, open at the throat and turned up at the wrists, and his same riding breeches from the night before. Dried mud still caked his boots.

I sat up, but as I did a dizziness swept over me. I would have fallen back but in one swift move he was beside me, and eased me down, and set pillows behind me. Whether it was illness or wonder that had rendered me speechless, I could not say.

"The doctor told me you would not wake until tomorrow at the soonest," he said in his gruff voice. "However, I said to him, 'No, you do not know our resourceful Miss Lockwell. She would never stay away so long, not when she is needed.'"

He did something then I could scarcely have imagined, let alone comprehend. He smiled at me.

I was so astonished I could only stare. Was this the Mr. Quent I knew? His curly hair was wild, falling over his brow; his teeth were a fierce white crescent amid his beard; and all I could think was that I had never seen him look so well.

"I'm so sorry," I started to say, but at once his expression grew somber.

"No," he said. "No, please believe it is I who am sorry, Miss Lockwell." For a moment there was a look of such regret in his brown eyes, a look that rendered them so soft that I could not bear it—not in one so stolid as he. Feigning a recurrence of my weakness (which was hardly far from the case), I leaned back against the pillows and turned my head toward the window and the fading day.

I heard his boots leave, and when the door opened again a little while later it was Lanna. With her help I rose and bathed myself and dressed, and was infinitely better for it. True, I felt a bit hollow and light, but that was all. That I should be perfectly well in a day I was certain. I could only hope the same was true of the children.

After Lanna left, I took a moment to use the little mirror above the chest of drawers to arrange my hair, and I pinched my cheeks to bring color into them. Why I did these things I was not certain. All I can say is that when a knock came at the door, I was not surprised, though my heart gave a leap in my chest all the same.

"Come in," I called out, and he did.

Like myself, Mr. Quent had changed. He no longer wore his riding gear. Instead, he had put on gray breeches and a dark blue coat I had never seen before. The coat was a close fit, as if it had been cut for him in younger days, though I cannot say the effect was ill.

He told me that he expected I was in want of supper, and since I might not be ready yet to venture downstairs, he had taken the liberty of bringing up a tray. I could not have been more shocked or my expression of thanks more sincere, for I was suddenly very hungry.

He brought the writing table into the center of the room, arranged the willow chair for me, and sat himself on the edge of the bed, and we had our supper that way. There was soup, hard-cooked eggs, and roast pheasant from a bird he had shot that day, and every sort of thing that was suitable for an invalid. I confess, I was not dainty; I ate ravenously, though I could only think he had already supped, for he touched almost nothing.

We spoke little, and he seemed content mostly to watch me, though he did inform me that the children were resting. They, too, had succumbed to a fever, and the illness had gripped them more strongly that it had me. However, the doctor had assured him they would recover, perhaps more slowly than I had but just as fully. I was greatly relieved.

"I want to thank you, Miss Lockwell," he said at last.

I set down my cup of wine for fear of spilling it. "For what?" I finally managed to say.

It seemed difficult for him to formulate his words. He rose, moved to the window, and peered at the night. At last he turned to look at me. "There are few who could have endured what you have endured here at Heathcrest, Miss Lockwell. This is not, I know, an easy place to dwell, and the task you were given was not a simple one. That it was too much to ask of you, I knew. That to invite you here could only be an act of selfishness such as I had always scorned in others, I knew as well. Yet I invited you all the same, and when others would have been driven off by what they found here, you stayed. For that, I thank you."

I was struck dumb. That after all that had happened, after the way I had failed him, he could thank *me*—it was too much to comprehend.

"You must know now why I was reluctant to bring them here," he went on. "This is . . . it is not a place for children. However, the aunt and uncle who I had hoped would take them had at that very moment lost a daughter of their own, and the sight of a small girl was something their aunt could not bear. So I was forced to take them instead. Knowing how often I must be away, my one hope was that I could arrange for someone who could properly care for them under the most difficult, the most trying of circumstances."

"But I have failed!" I said, unable to endure such misplaced praise any longer. "The children nearly caught their death of a fever last night. Don't you see? I nearly lost them!"

He regarded me with a serious expression. "No, Miss Lockwell, you saved them. Had it been any other person I had hired, had it been anyone else who had followed them when they ventured out—as they were eventually bound to do—then truly they would both have been lost."

I sat back in the chair, gripping the braided wood beneath my hands. Once again I saw the children huddled before the wall, their faces pale and scratched, the branches whipping in the wind. And the figure in white fluttering in the trees above.

"It's Halley Samonds, isn't it?" I looked up at him. "They said she was lost. But she's there, in the Wyrdwood."

He nodded.

"The children have seen her more than once. She showed herself to them. I think she's been speaking to Clarette. They believe she's a ghost. But she's no wraith, is she? She's alive."

"So I believe."

"Of course," I said, more to myself than to him. Halley Samonds.

The daughter of Miss Samonds's brother. The sister of Mr. Samonds the farrier.

The great-granddaughter of Rowan Addysen.

"I should have told you sooner," I said to him. "I knew they had seen someone, but I wanted them to feel I trusted them, so that they would trust me in turn. It was wrong; I should have told you." I shook my head. "Except you already knew."

He moved back to the table, though he did not sit. "Knew? Perhaps I did know. I certainly suspected it after her disappearance. And I knew if ever she had a wish to reach me, the children would present a way."

"Reach you? But why would she—"

"Please, Miss Lockwell, let us save that question. You fear you did wrong by not telling me what you knew. If that is the case, then any offense you have committed is far outweighed by my own wrongdoing. There is more I have not told you. And I will. However, the start of a long night is not the time for such conversations."

Though these words filled me with great curiosity, I nodded. Despite my whirling mind, a heaviness had come upon me, and I felt an overpowering desire for sleep. I was not yet well. It was by then all I could do to rise to bid him good night.

He bowed, seemed to hesitate, then bowed again and departed. With my last strength I readied myself for bed and climbed beneath the covers. It occurred to me that I should be afraid, yet the darkness did not trouble me as it so often did, not that night. I knew *he* was below and that while he was there no harm could come to me. I slept, and did not dream.

I WROTE THOSE LAST pages some time after those events took place, Father. Much more has happened in the days since then—so much I hardly know if I can explain it. How can such thoughts, such feelings be composed in ink on paper? They are too brilliant to be rendered in black and white, yet somehow I must explain for you to understand what is to happen next.

I can say only that I have seen what I had not before. Sometimes illness can strike a person blind, but I think sometimes it can grant one new sight as well. Heathcrest Hall had not changed, but the eyes with which I beheld it had. Before, I had thought the house stolid and old-fashioned, with its heavy columns and brooding eaves: well-constructed, perhaps even imposing, but not a thing to be admired.

How my impression of it has changed! Now everywhere I turn I find something to appreciate: handsome panels of old wood, windows as tall as doors, the scents of smoke and sage, and walls that have with silent strength withstood long years of wind and rain. It is not a grand dwelling like the marble edifices in the New Quarter; it is in no way fashionable. But how could I not have thought it the finest, most admirable house in all of Altania?

There! That must be explanation enough for you, Father. Except I have gotten ahead of myself. Let me tell you first about what took place shortly after that night I last described.

When I woke the following morning, I found that, aside from being somewhat weak, I was very well. The children were also improved, I learned. However, in them the fever had burned more strongly, and its effects still lingered, so they were yet confined to their room.

I paid them a visit and embraced them both. We did not speak of what had happened at the Wyrdwood. In fact, their recollection of the prior two days seemed vague. The doctor had said they might never entirely recall all that had happened just before and after they took ill, and if they indeed were never able to fully remember that night, I could not be sorry.

My health continued to improve so rapidly that, when the doctor saw me next, he pronounced that I wanted for nothing but exercise to recover my strength completely.

"Then she shall have exercise every day," Mr. Quent said.

I was not quite ready to ride, and he did not think it good for me to be out on my own. So it was that the two of us went for walks at least once a day, and more on longer lumenals. At first our rambles took us only around the house, but the more I walked the stronger I felt, and soon we ranged so far as the old heap of tumbled-down stones. These, he told me, had once been what country folk called an elf circle. The stones had not been arranged by fairies, of course, but rather by the ancient people who had dwelled in Altania long before the coming of the first Tharosian ships.

"I have seen the remains of such circles all over the island of Altania," Mr. Quent said. "How they lifted such massive things we do not know, nor why they did so. They raised the circles as places to gather, the historians suppose, or to hold ceremonies in dread of their heathen deities."

"No, to honor them, I think," I said, making an examination of one of the time-pitted stones. It bore faint traces of spirals and angular shapes. "One does not build things up or bring things forth in the name of what one fears. Rather, one tears things down and ruins them in an effort to appease."

He laughed, a deep, bell-like sound that was all the more engaging for its novelty. "I had never thought of it so. But you are right, of course. Your good sense guides you where the learning of wise men fails. You are remarkable, Miss Lockwell."

However, I did not feel remarkable at that moment, for I still tired more easily than before. I meant to ask him why some of the stones were paler and sharper-edged than the others, but I found I had only breath enough for walking as we made our way back to Heathcrest.

My walks continued, and that my companion continued to accompany me on them was something remarkable to *me*. Never in these last months had his business allowed him to remain at Heathcrest for so long a period of time. Each day we went farther, until finally we ventured past the remains of the stone circle to the very southern edge of the ridge.

This was, perhaps, a bit farther than I should have gone. However, the day was fine, and I knew from the almanac the coming night was to be very long, so it would be some time before I could go out again. I did not mention any distress I felt, but he must have observed I was tired, for he suggested we sit on a piece of a broken wall.

Below us, I saw the house I had glimpsed once before, nestled in a cleft on the side of the ridge, and I asked him about it. It was called Burndale Lodge, he said, and had from time out of mind been the home of the Quents, who had always served as stewards to the Rylend earls.

Or, at least, always in the past. Burndale Lodge had been shut when Mr. Quent moved up to Heathcrest. No one dwelled there now.

Our conversation dwindled, but in the pleasantest way, as speaking gave way to listening: to the song of the thrushes and the sigh of the grass.

"I told you I had done you wrong, Miss Lockwell," he said at last. The wind tugged at his brown hair and brown coat. "And so I have, by not telling you what I should have."

I turned to regard him, startled. "I am certain you had good reasons."

"Reasons? Oh, yes, I have devised many reasons for silence over the years. Reasons to keep a house with little light and no laughter. Reasons to be ever sober and to suffer no amusement or diversion that might distract me for even a moment." He laughed again, but this time the sound was rueful. "That is the thing about quietness—it feeds upon itself. For as my household grew more quiet, only the very quietest of people could endure it. Mrs. Darendal has all but used up her allotment of words in this life, and Jance never had many to begin with. And Lanna is mute despite all my efforts to induce her to speak. I confess, sometimes I have tried the most vigorous encouragements, but to no avail. I suppose I have always known such efforts were doomed. She was very small when the—when she ceased speaking."

Inwardly, I cringed at this speech. How quick I had been to judge him! I had thought him so callous that he was oblivious to Lanna's condition. Instead, he had hoped to cure her of it. However, my chagrin was forgotten as another thought quickly consumed me. I knew she was not so much older than I. She would have been nine at the time, or ten perhaps.

"The Rising that happened nineteen years ago," I said. "Lanna was there, wasn't she? She saw it take place."

His left hand was tucked inside his coat pocket, but I saw it clench. "I suppose Mrs. Darendal must have told you of that. Indeed, I wonder why she did not sooner, given what befell her that day."

"So it is true!" I rose to my feet. "There really was a Rising of the Wyrdwood, just as in the histories."

He regarded me with the gravest of expressions. "There have been many Risings since ancient times, Miss Lockwell."

"You mean even in recent years?"

"Especially in recent years."

A shiver came over me, but it was more from thrill than cold. "And there was one right here." I gazed in the direction of the village, as if somehow I might see the oak tree rising above the slate roofs, its branches reaching over the commons, summoning green shadows.

I looked at him again. "But how can it be we have never heard of them? Surely we should have been told in the city, and Assembly should have been warned of the danger."

"Warned?" he said, and now there was a hard note to his voice. "People in the city *have* been warned. They were warned years ago. It is all there in the *Lex Altania*. They had only to open a book and read."

I sat back down on the bench. "No, they would not have believed you if you told them. They would have said such things were only stories."

"Or the superstitions of country folk."

I winced. However, as I thought of the people I had met at Lady Marsdel's, all so intelligent and witty and assuredly modern—men like Mr. Baydon—I knew the accusation was not unfounded.

"But surely *some* people must know," I said at last.

"There are those who are aware of the recent Risings and who keep watch for signs of others. Not every lord in the Hall of Magnates is more concerned with powdering his wig and inhaling snuff than he is with the welfare of Altania. There is one in particular who knows what must be done. Though his physical strength may be failing, the strength of his mind and his will have not. With the authority of the king, he has commissioned some few inquirers to make such investigations as are necessary."

In an instant it came to me. The soldiers who came at odd hours of the night, his frequent and sudden departures on unknown business. "You," I said. "You yourself are one of these inquirers!"

He was still for a moment, then nodded.

My mind labored to draw in this knowledge. It was not that I did not believe him. I *did* believe. If the Wyrdwood had been capable of rising up in ancient times, why not now? That such Risings were not well known was only due to the fact that so little of the primeval wood was left in Altania and that for so long after the Plague Years much of the countryside where the Old Trees did remain was abandoned.

"But it is strange," I said, and looked at him. "It is so strange you should dwell here within sight of a stand of Wyrdwood."

"Strange, you think it? Despite your fine intellect, on that account I would not agree with you, Miss Lockwell. It is my work to keep watch over the wood and to note its stirrings. There can be no better place for me to dwell. In this place, I will never forget of what it is capable."

I thought again of the things Mrs. Darendal had told me, about the Addysen witch and the gallows tree. It was no wonder Lanna had been struck dumb that day. No one should have seen such a thing, let alone a child.

"To think I had wanted to see a stand of Wyrdwood," I said, shaking my head. "I had thought it would be quaint and picturesque."

"And it is. So is a mountain, or a chalk cliff by the sea, but both are perilous if one is not properly cautious."

Only a mountain never strained to move itself; a cliff did not willingly throw people from its edge. Nor could either thing be easily destroyed. But a grove of shabby old forest, with its leaf mold dry as tinder . . .

"Why have they not burned it all?" I asked. "They burned the stand closest to Cairnbridge. Why not this grove, and the others? If it is dangerous, if there are those who know this to be true, why was all the Wyrdwood in Altania not destroyed long ago?"

"Because we dare not destroy it all."

"I don't understand."

"Don't you? The answer is there in the histories, Miss Lockwell.

Men were only lost to the wood when they burned it, cut it down, drove it back."

"But the magician Gauldren worked the Quelling," I said. Despite my own interest in magick, I had always believed that the Quelling was a legend—an allegory for the clearing of the primeval forest at the hands of men, by which the land was changed from a dense, mysterious wilderness to our familiar, civilized countryside. Knowing what I did now, I could only concede that the spell must have been real.

"As great as Gauldren's spell was, it did not destroy the power of the Wyrdwood. That was not its intent. Rather, it cast the wood into a slumber—a rest from which it can still wake if it is provoked."

"Yet they burned the stand north of Cairnbridge."

His shoulders heaved in a sigh. "So they did, even though once the tree on the commons was burned there was nothing more to fear from the stand. It was well guarded behind its walls. But they had fire in their hearts that night. They went to the Wyrdwood with torches and burned it. And we have since seen the consequences of that act."

"What do you mean?"

"I mean that Halley Samonds was not the first young woman to be called to the Wyrdwood. And I fear for her. It is . . . treacherous to those who are lost to it." A spasm passed through him, and he turned away.

I wanted to go to him, to offer words of comfort. But what comfort could *I* grant him? A despair had come over me as well. For I knew! I knew the truth when I wished I did not. They had never said that she died, only that she had been lost. Where else on this bleak landscape could it have been? It had called to her, just like it had called to Halley Samonds.

"Mrs. Quent," I said before I could will myself to suppress the words.

"It was my doing," he said, his back to me. "At least, so I have told myself all these years. Had *he* not warned me, the vicar of the church in Cairnbridge, of the peril of marrying one of her line? 'You must know what she is,' he told me. As if she was anything other than a pretty young woman. She was only twenty!"

"But he was awful to say that!" I exclaimed, unable to stop myself.

He turned to regard me. "I never set foot in that church again, or any other church. However, though the vicar spoke those words out of prejudice, there was yet truth to them. Why else would they have angered me so?"

I could not speak. For what could I say to him? I could only listen, held captive, as he told me what had happened.

There had been a ball at Heathcrest, for Mrs. Quent had been fond of dancing, and in this as in all things Mr. Quent had indulged her. It was the middle of a greatnight. The entire house was alight with candles and alive with music and breathless laughter. Everyone who was anyone in the county was in attendance, and a good number of nobodies were there as well.

No one minded; there was room for all. The musicians played without stopping, and Mrs. Quent danced every reel and round, while Mr. Quent—who admitted he had no talent for dancing—took his joy by watching her from the side of the hall.

Then a headache came upon her, as they had with increasing frequency ever since he had brought her to Heathcrest. She was quite well, she assured him; she only wanted for some air. She had gone outside, and he had intended to follow her in a few minutes, to be sure she was well. Only then his opinion was wanted for what should be the next dance. Then he was pulled into the parlor where the younger people were staging a play, and after that another hand was needed for a round of cards. He was handed a drink and put in a chair, and amid the light, amid the laughter, he forgot—forgot to check on his pretty young wife. Forgot until someone asked where Mrs. Quent was.

Had she not come inside? Was she not dancing? No, no one had seen her in an hour or more. He had gone outside and there had seen a sight that froze his blood: her lace shawl, which she had donned against the coolness of the greatnight, cast on the front steps.

He ran inside, bellowing at the musicians to stop, calling for men and lanterns. At once the party ceased, and there has never been another in Heathcrest Hall since that night. Men went out in the dark, searching first around the house, then ranging farther afield. Mr. Quent shouted her name over and over, until his throat was raw and bleeding—indeed, so that his voice was ever low and gruff afterward—but there was no answer.

A mist settled over the moor, hindering their work. It was not until the light of dawn burned away the fog that at last they discovered her. She was lying among the leaves and mold by the stand of Wyrdwood on the hill to the east. Frost had powdered her face, so that it was as white as marble. Her yellow dress was torn, and a scrap of the same yellow cloth fluttered in a crack at the top of the wall.

What had happened was plain to all who saw her. She had been attempting to climb the high wall, but its stones were slick with dew and moss. Even as she reached the top, she lost her grip and fell. In an instant, her neck was broken.

"I think you see now," he said, "why I did not want you and the children to venture to the Wyrdwood. It was there that she—" He shook his head.

Though he said nothing more, the rest of the story was clear to me, just as what had happened to Gennivel Quent was clear to all who had seen her there, pale and cold among the fallen leaves. He had blamed himself for not going out to her sooner. He had been distracted by merriment and revelry, and for that he could not forgive himself. As punishment he had made his house a grim and quiet place, even as he made himself a grim and quiet man.

"You cannot blame yourself still," I said at last.

"Can I not, Miss Lockwell? I brought her here to live with me, so near to the thing from which I knew she must be kept. I even knew it fascinated her. The painting in the room upstairs, which I know you saw, was done by her own hand. I thought I could watch over her, that I could keep her safe." His left hand clenched again inside his coat pocket. "Instead, I laughed and played at cards while she walked out into the night and fog."

He turned away. I should have felt horror or sorrow at what I had heard. Instead, a kind of resolve came over me. I stood and took a step toward him.

"It was not your fault."

"You should not pity me," he said. "If you think me blameless, Miss Lockwell, you are mistaken."

"I do not pity you, Mr. Quent!"

He turned back to look at me, as if to see for himself. At last he said, "It was a long time ago. I told you only because I thought, after what happened, you should know."

I nodded.

"She is buried there." He pointed toward the ruins of the old chapel beyond Burndale Lodge.

I told him I should like to visit there, and he said I would, but not that day. By then the sun was low, and he gave me his arm as we started back for Heathcrest, walking in silence.

SOLDIERS CAME DURING the night and called Mr. Quent away. However, he returned after the passage of two middling lumenals and a brief umbral. Over those next several days, we ventured out on more walks. Or, when the weather was inclement, we strolled in the front hall as he told me stories of the people in the various portraits: members of the Rylend family, whose last earl he had served, and whose house this had been.

While before I had wished to avoid him whenever possible, now I looked forward to his company. Our meals were no longer wordless affairs but rather lively with conversation. He had seen much of Altania in his travels—he had even been over the sea to the Principalities once—and I had so many questions about other lands and peoples, things I had read about only in books, all of which he obligingly detailed.

In my first months at Heathcrest, I had hardly noticed when he was gone; now, when his work called him away, I felt the weight of the shadows pressing in, and the silence rang in my ears. Often I sought solace in writing to my sisters. I had been four months at Heathcrest now, and I had saved nearly enough to arrange the opening of the house on Durrow Street. I assured Lily that she would have to endure Mr. Wyble only a little while longer.

I had yet to resume my studies with the children. They had relapsed when the fever settled in their lungs, and though it had been a half month since that night at the Wyrdwood, they remained convalescents upon the doctor's orders. I would often read to them, but they tired quickly, so when Mr. Quent was gone I spent most of my time alone.

While my opinion of Heathcrest had changed, I could not say the same was true of Mrs. Darendal. The housekeeper seemed more reticent around me than ever. I received barely a word from her, only sharp looks, and she would quickly depart a room if I was to enter it, no matter if she had been in the midst of some task.

The next time Mr. Quent returned (again from a trip that was briefer than usual), he invited me into his study on the second floor. I confess, I was both surprised and hesitant. I recalled the way I had transgressed upon his privacy the last time I was in the room, and I could not forget how I had been overcome upon looking at the painting of the Wyrdwood. But I had hardly been myself then. I had been so lonely, my head filled with phantasms and thoughts of ghosts. This time I was invited, and I knew my mind to be sound.

All the same, I could not help but feel some relief when, upon entering, I saw the painting had been removed.

"I thought you might wish to play, Miss Lockwell," he said, gesturing to the pianoforte. He wore the blue coat again, with its old-fashioned but handsome cut. His brown hair had tumbled over his brow despite his best efforts to comb it. "I have been told that all young women are accomplished at music these days."

I laughed. "Not all, I'm afraid. It is my sister Lily who received the musical talent. She is very skilled. I wish you could hear her play!

Though she does have a proclivity for ominous pieces. My mother always asks her to play brighter things. Asked her, I mean."

I felt a sudden ache in my heart, and I turned, making a pretense of examining the pianoforte.

"I confess, I do not know if she had ability or not," he said behind me. "I have little ear for music. I know only that I could have watched her for hours as she played."

I turned to see him gazing at the pianoforte, and then the ache I felt was no longer just for myself. I sat at the pianoforte, and while my skill was no more than rudimentary, he listened intently, and when I was finished he applauded my efforts with what seemed such genuine appreciation that I could only turn away to hide the warmth in my cheeks.

"Are you all right, Miss Lockwell?"

I looked at him. "Yes, I am quite recovered from my illness."

His brown eyes were grave. "That is not what I meant. I mean are you all right *here*, at Heathcrest? I know you want for your family, that you were parted from your father and sisters so soon after all of you were parted from Mrs. Lockwell."

So addressed, I could only speak the truth. "I do miss them, very much. And I will not deny that, at first, I felt terribly lonely here. I wanted nothing more than to go back to the city."

"At first, you say." He hesitated, then moved closer, standing on the other side of the pianoforte. "Do you mean that you have a different opinion now? That is, do you think differently about Heathcrest Hall?"

"I do."

"And is your opinion of it lessened or improved?"

"Oh, improved! It is, I see now, the noblest and strongest of houses, and the landscape is anything but forlorn. It is beautiful in the most elemental manner. It has no need of adornment or decoration to make it handsome. Rather, it is so in its very simplicity."

"I see."

He was silent for a time. I did not know what to say. I thought maybe I should play more, but my fingers had forgotten what little art they knew and lay motionless upon the keys.

"You say your opinion of the house has changed," he said at last. "And what of its master, I might ask? I know you must have thought him grim and stern—that he could only be regarded, by one of sound judgment, as silent and removed, even hard. How could you not think him such? I know better than anyone that he was all those things. What a repulsive being you must have thought him! One to be pitied no less than avoided." He was more animated than I had ever seen him; as he spoke, he placed his hands—both hands—on the pianoforte. "Has your opinion changed in *that* regard? Or is it unwavering, grounded in impressions that cannot be altered by the passage of time or by any change of circumstance?"

I looked at his hands, the right whole and strong, the left maimed. However, the one was no more repellent or pitiable to me; it was as much his as was the other.

"No," I said. "My opinion in that regard is much changed as well."

I looked up and saw an expression on his face that I could only think was pleased. However, his look suddenly changed to a grimace as he glanced down and saw his left hand as naked and exposed as the right. He snatched it up, tucking it into his coat pocket, and retreated from the pianoforte.

I rose from the bench. "It happened a long time ago, didn't it?"

He frowned. "How can you know?"

"From this." I moved to the portrait that hung on the wall, next to the portrait of Gennivel Quent. In the painting his face was not so solemn, his brow not yet furrowed, but even then his left hand was tucked in his pocket.

"I was a boy," he said behind me, the words low. "It was the year I turned twelve."

"How did it happen?" Perhaps it was rude of me; it was certainly forward, but I could not help wanting to know.

"I told you, Miss Lockwell—the more you fight against it, the more it fights back."

"You mean the Wyrdwood?"

"The only way to win against it is to lose something to it. That's what my father told me, and I learned it for myself when a foolish act led me to spend a night alone within the walls of a stand of Old Trees." Slowly, he drew his left hand out of his pocket. "This is what I was forced to lose in order to survive through that greatnight."

I could only stare at him. A night alone in the Wyrdwood! What had compelled him to do such a thing? He did not say, and I did not ask. I recalled my own near encounter with the ancient trees, and I shivered. No, there was nothing that could ever compel *me* to step beyond those walls.

He returned his hand to his coat pocket. "So you can understand, Miss Lockwell, why I am grateful to you for keeping the children from going into the Wyrdwood. I rode there again a few days ago, and there is a new crack opened in the wall—one just large enough for a boy or girl to slip through. I have already arranged for the wall's repair, but had you not followed them that night, they might well have been lured inside."

"I don't understand. Why would *she* have wanted to bring them there at all?"

"I have told you, Miss Lockwell, there are those who do not care for the work I have been commissioned to do."

"You speak of the . . ." I do not know why, but it was hard to speak the word *witch.* "Of Halley Samonds, I mean." If Mr. Quent's business was to investigate and prevent Risings, surely a witch would seek to work against him.

"Not just her," he replied. "There are others. In recent years, some who plot against the Crown have sought to use the ancient groves as a place to hide and plan their treachery."

"But is it not perilous to enter the wood?"

"Yes, it is. But it is possible . . ." His gaze went to the window. ". . . Possible, if one has the benefit of a witch."

"And you think Halley Samonds is in league with such persons."

He looked back at me. "You have heard, perhaps, that the roads have suffered an increase in the number of brigands of late. Thieves steal for a reason, and the highway through Westmorain County leads right to the Torland border."

I believed I understood his meaning. Torland had been part of Altania for centuries, but long ago it had been its own country, and old allegiances and ancient oaths were not forgotten there. When the Old Usurper attempted to seize the crown seventy years ago, it was with an army of Torlanders behind him. It was not difficult to believe there were still men in Torland who wished to see the Arringhart stag torn down in favor of the Morden hawk.

However, it was another thing to think that such rebels prowled the roads here in Altania, waylaying travelers and taking their gold to fund their treasonous efforts. And it was yet another thing to think they were in league with witches who helped them to hide in the Wyrdwood. Still, I could only concede there was a kind of sense to it. After all, the Wyrdwood was the one place where no one else would ever go.

I took a step toward my employer. "Do you know who these rebels are, the men who might be using Halley Samonds?"

"No, but I would give much to know. I think, by luring the children to the wood, they hoped to lure me there as well. They cannot have any love for the inquirers. Any investigations into the Wyrdwood can only serve to uncover their own doings. But who they might be—if they are foreigners or local men—I cannot say. I have never seen them."

A shudder passed through me. "But I *have* seen one!" I realized aloud.

In answer to his questioning look, I explained about my journey to Cairnbridge with the mail. I recounted how we were stopped by soldiers, and how the driver had convinced them to let us go on our way, only after the next stop the man who had been sitting next to me—the eighth traveler—was gone, and no mention was ever made of him.

"I cannot know it, of course," I said, now feeling a bit foolish. Perhaps I had merely allowed my imagination to get away from me, like Lily after reading one of her romances. "Yet I cannot think of any good reason why the man would have left so unexpectedly. He had his hand inside his coat the entire time we were stopped by the soldiers. I recall it was very odd—especially that the driver made no mention of his absence."

"I fear the driver was likely in league with the fellow," Mr. Quent said with a dark look. "Such instances are not unknown. The presence of the soldiers on the road must have convinced them not to go through with whatever mischief they intended. You are fortunate, Miss Lockwell."

I could only nod. To think I had ridden for hours beside a man who was likely a highwayman, perhaps even a rebel against the Crown!

He must have noticed my distress, for after that he asked me to play again on the pianoforte. I complied, glad for something to which I could direct my attention. My brain felt oddly light and fluttering, like a moth that could not decide upon what thing to alight. He listened in polite silence, and at last I confessed I could play no more, and being tired I begged my leave. This was granted with a stiff bow. He said nothing, only watching me with his brown eyes as I went.

However, as I reached the door, he said, "That night with the children, you said the branches seemed to grasp at you, Miss Lockwell."

I turned in the doorway. "Yes, they did."

He took a step toward me. "I wondered . . . that is, you have never told me how you and the children were able to get away from them."

"There was a gust of wind," I said. "The branches were raised up by its force, and we ran as fast as we could."

However, even as I said this, I tried to remember exactly what had happened. *Had* there been a gust of wind at that moment? And if there had, shouldn't the branches have bent down under its force? I found myself gazing, not at Mr. Quent, but rather at the portrait of the green-eyed young woman that hung on the wall behind him.

"You ran," he said. "That's all. Are you sure?"

"Yes, quite sure." I returned my gaze to him, and I smiled. "Good night, Mr. Quent."

With that I took my leave of the master of Heathcrest Hall.

𝒯HE NEXT MORNING I rose to find Mr. Quent gone. His work had called him away during the night. When I found Mrs. Darendal in the front hall, dusting the hunting trophies, I asked her if she knew when he would be back.

"What business is it of *yours* when the master returns?" she said without looking at me.

I was startled by the scorn in her voice. "I cannot claim it to be my business in any way," I said. "For whatever business he is on, it is entirely his own. Rather, I wished only to know."

"It seems you wish to know a great many things, Miss Lockwell." A rabbit became the recipient of a vigorous dusting that removed as many hairs as specks of dust. "Do not think I have not seen the way you creep about the house. You have skulked and spied about since the first day you came here. No secret is safe from you, not even behind locked doors!"

Her accusation was anything but fair. However, I could not defend myself, as the housekeeper well knew.

"Be careful what you seek to know, Miss Lockwell. If you pry too much, you may uncover things you wish you hadn't. There are yet secrets in this house that would make your blood go cold—things *he* will never tell you."

The housekeeper turned her back and took her work to the other end of the hall. Her words left me agitated, and I retreated into the kitchen to take a cup of tea.

What could she mean? What secrets did she speak of? My mind was filled with vague shadows. However, after some consideration, I banished such thoughts. That Mrs. Darendal did not care for me had long been clear. True, I had never known her to speak anything other than truth. However, she had implied that Mr. Quent was keeping something of a terrible nature from me, and that I could not believe. He had told me all about the awful night he had lost Mrs. Quent. When he had revealed such intimate and painful recollections, why should he keep anything else from me?

Mrs. Darendal could not have known that he had granted me such confidences, and I had no reason to tell her. She could think of me what she would. It was not *her* opinion of me that mattered.

My mind soothed by such thoughts, I finished my tea and went upstairs to see if the children wished for a story. However, when I opened the door to their room a crack, I saw them making a game with a collection of tin soldiers and peg dolls. They were playing in the most charming manner, fashioning such innocent little stories with their toys as only children can conceive, and so much like angels did they appear, still clad as they were in their night robes, that I was loath to disturb them. I shut the door without a sound and left them.

My smile soon vanished. What a dreary day that was! The lumenal was not long; still it seemed to pass slowly. I went outside, but the weather was ill and drove me in. The children had no need of me, and I did not wish to wander the house for fear of being further accused of lurking. With nowhere else I could go, I retreated to my room and, as the wind lashed at the gables, wrote a great many of the preceding pages, Father.

The day had long since expired when I set down my pen, my hand stiff from writing. I realized I had never had any supper, and I decided to go down to the kitchen to see if anything might be left on the board.

Upon leaving my room I found all dark and silent. However, as I reached the second floor, I saw a glimmer of light, and following it I came to the door of Mr. Quent's study. There was a smell of rain on the air, and I saw the door was open. The light of a lamp spilled out, so that the illumination of the candle I held could not have been detected within the room.

I peered through the door, and at once my heart leaped. Mr. Quent was within; he had returned to Heathcrest. I thought to make myself known to him—I realized it was not food that I hungered for at all but rather conversation. However, even as I opened my mouth, I comprehended that he was already speaking, and I detected the utterance of my name. Had he seen me? No—his broad back was to the door, and he stood beside the pianoforte, touching but not pressing the keys.

"You tell me your opinion of Heathcrest and its master has changed." His words were low but carried on the still air. "You cannot know how pleased I was to hear that speech from your lips! Surely there could be no higher praise than to earn the good opinion of the sensible Miss Lockwell."

His shoulders heaved, and at first I thought him to be laughing; only then he spoke again, and there was a tightness to his voice that brought to mind a grimace rather than a grin.

"Yet your opinion might yet change again. Indeed, how can it not? And when it does, you might not find it to be improved—not if you knew how selfish I had been. Not if you knew what peril I have placed you in by bringing you here to suit my own purposes."

I retreated from the door, for I did not want to hear anything more. Thoughts of supper and companionship had fled me. My mind fluttered and wavered like the shadows cast by my candle. All I could think was that once again Mrs. Darendal had spoken the truth. There *was* some secret he had kept from me.

But what could it be? My brain was filled with all manner of lurid thoughts and phantasms, conjured half from shadows and half from recalling Lily's descriptions of the books she had read, with their villainous dukes and duplicitous barons. I hurried up the stairs to my room, and in a fit of wild dread I thrust the bent-willow chair against the door.

I huddled in my wrought-iron bed, watching the candle burn as the wind growled over the eaves, and it was long before I slept.

❦

IT WAS AN hour after dawn when I ventured downstairs (though I had some trouble dislodging the chair from the door, for it had gotten wedged somehow). Outside was clear and cool: the perfect morning of what was to be a middle lumenal. However, I thought not of riding my horse, or going for walks, or seeing if the children were well enough to be taken out to sun themselves on the steps. Instead, my legs felt weak as I descended the stairs, and my stomach was hollow as I tried to take in a bit of tea and dry toast.

I had consumed little of either when Mrs. Darendal came to tell me I was wanted by the master in the front hall.

At this I felt no surprise. After what I overheard last night, I had expected a summons. All the same, the dread I had felt last night grew in me again as I walked with slow steps to the hall. Of what would he speak to me? Was he going to reveal what peril he had placed me in? Would that I could tell him not to, for I did not wish to know! That he had concealed something from me was terrible enough. That such knowledge should be worsened with the particulars was something I could not bear.

I perceived that Mrs. Darendal followed me as I went. I said nothing; it was all I could do to place one foot before the other. At last I stepped into the front hall. He turned from a window and bowed to me. As he straightened, his beard parted in what seemed a wolfish grin. He wore a black coat.

"Miss Lockwell, I am glad you are here, for there is something I must tell you." I could do no more than nod and grip the back of a chair.

He closed the distance between us and said, "As you know, this part of the country is not what it was. There are all manner of brigands, as well as—that is, it is no longer safe here for the children."

*And am I safe here?* I wished to say. He paced back and forth—or prowled, rather, it seemed to me.

"As recent events have demonstrated," he went on, "it is in their best interest that Clarette and Chambley not remain here at Heathcrest. That is why I am happy to report I have at last been able to make arrangements with their aunt and uncle in Highward."

Understanding came to me, and now my dread was no longer for myself. I stepped away from the chair. "The children are going to Highward? But when?"

"The carriage comes to take them to their aunt and uncle this very day."

I thought I might fall back into the chair. "So soon!" I said.

"It is too dangerous for them to stay here a moment longer. You know that as well as I, Miss Lockwell."

"Of course," I said. But all I could think was that they would not be the only ones leaving Heathcrest. I thought also of you, Father, and my sisters. I had planned to save five months of wages before removing you all to Durrow Street, but I had been here only a little more than four months; and even if the amount I had accumulated was enough to open the old house, how should we all live there afterward without any regular source of income?

Yet there could be no changing it. I had heard the firmness of his tone. Mr. Quent was not one to alter a decision once it had been made. The children would be leaving; nor could they be the only ones. What purpose did a governess serve with no children to govern? I could not help but notice Mrs. Darendal's expression. It was triumphant, I thought.

"Do you understand, Miss Lockwell?" he said to me.

"I understand very well, Mr. Quent." I did my best to keep my back straight and my voice steady. "I will gather my things at once. I do not know when the mail is set to depart, but if Jance will take me to the village, I will be glad to wait for the next coach there."

"I will tell Jance," Mrs. Darendal said. She made no effort to disguise the gloating in her voice.

"That will not be necessary, Mrs. Darendal," Mr. Quent said.

"Please leave me with Miss Lockwell, if you would. I have something else to speak to her about."

The housekeeper stared at the master of the house, her mouth open.

"I said, please leave us."

Her mouth snapped shut, and after one last glare at me she turned with a swish of gray and departed the hall.

I thought almost to follow her. I could not imagine what was to come next and so could think of nothing to say. Mr. Quent approached me, his expression very serious, but not, I thought, grim. Rather, there was a light in his brown eyes as he looked at me.

"Mr. Quent!" I was induced by his attention to exclaim at last, and bowed my head under the force of his gaze.

"You know it is for the best that the children go," he said.

I nodded; I could not deny it.

"However, though it grows perilous in this part of the country, especially for those in my household, all the same I would ask you to consider staying, Miss Lockwell."

I looked up at him, astonished. "But why?"

"Do you not know?" He hesitated, then reached out to take my left hand and enfolded it within his right. "Can you truly not know the reason?"

He ran his thumb over the back of my hand and looked at me with the most solemn expression. I realized I *did* know, that I had perhaps known for some time now. Thus it was, as he spoke those next words, I could not feign surprise. All the same, I felt a shock go through me at his speech, and I felt it again at the words that tumbled from my own lips in reply, seemingly spoken by another than myself.

In two minutes, it was done. What little trouble it was, it turned out, to completely alter one's life forever! It was no more than the smallest thing, reduced to a few scant words, like the buying of a loaf of bread. He bowed to me. I know not if he smiled as he rose; I could hardly see him. Then he took his leave, and I was alone in the hall.

I sank into a chair under the watchful eye of other quarry he had conquered over the years. I could not tell if they pitied or mocked me. One or the other surely, for I was now to join them.

Those thoughts were absurd. My head was aflutter and my nerves abuzz, that was all. Gradually, the full comprehension of what he had asked, and of what I had said in return, came over me. As it did, a laughter welled up within me, one that could only be given release and that rang off the beams above. To think, those beams, this hall, this entire house was soon to be mine. For I was to be his. I was to be Mrs. Quent!

What must you think of me, Father? Not many pages prior to this, I was writing about how awful I thought him, how stern and silent and unforgiving. You must think I consented to this for one reason only—for the benefit of you and my sisters.

I would be deceiving you if I did not admit the thought at once occurred to me. The moment he made his proposition, all fears I had at the thought of losing my employment were banished. By becoming Mrs. Quent, I would assure the well-being of my family forever. While the full extent of Mr. Quent's wealth is unknown to me, I understand from Mrs. Darendal that it is considerable. I will not want for any funds needed to open the house on Durrow Street and to place you all there in the most comfortable manner.

Only I will not be with you! Yet, while that thought causes me sorrow, I confess I already feel growing in me another happiness, one that must supersede any sorrow or regret. It was not only because I knew it would assure the future of my family that I accepted Mr. Quent's proposal.

I will not deny that my heart has long occupied itself with the most tender feelings for another. So strong were these impulses that I indulged myself by thinking that if I could not have him whom I admired—whom, I will admit it now when I would not before, I loved—then I would never want another. However, those are sentiments best saved for one of Lily's romances. The heart is a far more practical thing and in its life is happily capable of more than a single attachment.

To this day, my regard and affection for Mr. Rafferdy are unwavering; my feelings for him have not changed. I hope—no, I utterly demand—that Fate allows us to meet again and be friends. However, the possibility of any deeper connection between us was never more than a fancy. No doubt, at this very moment, he is already married and utterly content.

And soon I will be as well. You must forget everything I wrote earlier, Father. While my feelings for him are different than what I felt prior with Mr. Rafferdy, you must not think them in any way inferior. Cannot a rugged and misty landscape be adored by the eyes as much as a sunlit garden? Perhaps it is adored even more for not seeking to make itself adorable.

I had thought him dull and somber. Only it was I who had been dull! Yet now I was able to think with a clarity I had never known before, and my heart argued as strongly as any logic. So it is I can tell you, Father, that even if I had not known this marriage would assure your security and that of my sisters, still I would have said yes. Know that I respect him, and admire him, and hold him in the highest esteem; that I love him. Then you shall be as content as I and see how it is that I now consider myself to be the luckiest woman alive in all of Altania.

WELL, IT IS done.

I had thought we would go to the church at Cairnbridge. Instead, the priest came here at Mr. Quent's bidding, and we walked down the road to the ruin of the ancient chapel past Burndale Lodge. The only ceiling above us was the sky, for the roof had fallen in ages ago, and the floor was clover and green grass. The windows were gone as well, but ivy had grown up between the stone buttresses, and sunlight mingled through the leaves in emeralds and golds more vivid than any hues produced by stained glass.

I confess, I think Mr. Quent would have forgone the village priest altogether had it been possible, but it was not, and he was very civil to the man and paid him for his trouble.

It was a small party. Only myself, Mr. Quent, and Jance came from the house. Mrs. Darendal remained behind. "Someone must prepare the meal," she said. Happily, Mr. Samonds came. He brought his aunt with him in a surrey, and they stood as witnesses.

I was very glad to see Miss Samonds, and was grateful beyond words that she had been able to come in response to the wish I relayed to Mr. Quent. She handed me a bundle of wildflowers.

"They're lovely!" I exclaimed.

"No more lovely than you," she said. I squeezed her small, bent hand, and then went to Mr. Quent by the entrance of the chapel, whose doors had long ago fallen to dust. We stood together not twenty feet from Mrs. Quent's grave. However, this did not trouble me in the least. I felt only a benevolence when I thought of her, and I believe she would have been happy. My only regret was that my sisters could not be with me on this day.

It took little enough time, and when it was finished Mr. Samonds drove his aunt back to Heathcrest while the rest of us walked up the road. We ate dinner, though I could not recall the taste of anything or how many glasses of wine I drank. I could hardly bring myself to look at Mr. Quent.

After we ate, Mr. Samonds had a wish to look around the house, for he had many fond memories of it.

"Then you shall see it again," Mr. Quent said. He proceeded to take Mr. Samonds on a tour, and the priest went with them.

"I find I prefer chairs to stairs," Miss Samonds said, and so I sat with her in the front hall, and she found great amusement in admiring all the various mounted creatures from her seat.

"Sometimes," I said, "as twilight falls, it feels a very wild place, with all the beasts around me. It's like I'm in the middle of some great forest."

Miss Samonds gave me a sharp look. "Like a forest, you say?"

I do not know why, but this question made me shift in my seat. I pointed to her cane, which leaned against her chair. "That's very pretty," I said. "The way several branches are twisted together—it makes me think of the chair in my room, the one your nephew made long ago."

"As well it should, for he made this as well."

"He has a gift with wood. Though I would think a farrier would prefer to work in iron."

"Prefer it? No, I cannot think he does, but iron is better for him. Safer."

I laughed. "I can hardly believe *that*. Certainly the metal he works with is very hot, and sparks must fly all about. It must be quite hazardous. What harm can wood cause?"

Even as I said this, my mirth ceased. Miss Samonds touched the cane. "He gathered these sticks by the Wyrdwood. They had dropped from over the wall. He soaked them in water, and braided them together, and let them dry this way. So he made your chair as well, but that was long ago. He has not been to a stand of Wyrdwood in many years."

We were silent for a time. Then I said, "Do you think Mr. Samonds will ever marry?" I do not know precisely why I asked. Perhaps it was simply the cool weight of the new ring on my finger that made me wonder it, and that he was a kind and handsome man.

Miss Samonds shook her head. "There are few sons of Addysen women, and none of them has ever married that I've known of. I fear no woman will ever catch *his* eye, no matter how young or pretty she is."

I believed I understood her; my heart ached for him.

"He would do better in the city, I think," Miss Samonds said.

"Then why does he not go there?"

"He would never say it, but he could not bear to be far from the trees for long. No child of an Addysen can, not once they've held Old Wood in their hands and bent it to their will. Or, rather, found it willing to bend for them when it would not for another. There's a life in it, even when it's fallen from the tree, and it knows the touch of one who can feel that in it."

I wanted to ask her what she meant, but then the men returned from their tour, and Mr. Samonds helped his aunt from her chair. They departed in their surrey and took the priest with them.

Mr. Quent and I were alone then, for Mrs. Darendal was nowhere to be found. He came to me. I found at last I could bear to look up at his face and meet his dark eyes. He took me by the hand and led me on my own tour of the house. The things we spoke of as we walked can be of no consequence to anyone else. I can say only that I have never in my life been happier than I was in those hours. No matter what the almanac said, it was the longest of lumenals, and the umbral that followed could only have been a greatnight for how changed I was before it was through.

At last the morning did come, as it must. He rose with the sun and put on his boots and riding coat.

"I will be back the night after next," he said.

"Let me go with you," I said, though I knew it was foolish.

He took my hand, stroked it, and kissed it in the gentlest manner. "I promise I will take you on a journey soon. To anywhere you say."

"To the city?"

"If you wish it."

With that he was gone. And so began my first full day as mistress of Heathcrest Hall.

THAT DAY WAS lonely, I confess, but I knew it would be and had prepared myself. The house was quiet without Chambley and Clarette. How I longed to hear their voices! I went into our parlor. The curtains were thrown back, and a book lay open on the table, bathed in a beam of sunlight. I picked it up. It was the *Lex Altania*.

They had been gone a quarter month now, and still I missed them. I had thought saying good-bye would be more bitter for me than for them. However, it was not so, and the pain of my tears was lessened only by the force of their own. I could only gasp in wonder as not only Chambley threw his arms around me at our parting, but Clarette also. At last I was forced to release them, for the carriage their uncle had sent stood waiting.

"Were we very bad children, then?" Chambley said, sniffling. "I don't remember. I think we were."

"No," I said in a solemn tone. "You were not so very bad at all." I smiled and touched his chin. "Indeed, I can truthfully say you're one of the finest badgers I've ever met."

"I'm not a real badger, you know."

I leaned down to whisper in his ear. "I know."

I helped them into the carriage and closed the door. However, before I could step away, Clarette reached through the window and grasped my hand.

"You didn't," she said. Her dark eyes were full of anguish.

"I didn't what, Clarette?"

"You didn't leave us."

"No," I managed to say. "No, I didn't. I made a promise, you see."

"And do you promise that we'll see you again? Will you swear to me that you will?"

My heart stilled. For a moment I wondered—was it better to make a promise I knew I could never keep, if it soothed her fears at this moment?

I smiled and squeezed her hand. "Take care of your brother."

She nodded and pulled her hand inside the carriage.

I stepped back, and the driver cracked his whip. The carriage rolled down the track. As it did, I saw Clarette's round face peering out the back window. Only she was not looking at me, or at the house, but rather at the straggled silhouettes atop the ridge to the east. Then the carriage dropped down over the shoulder of the hill and was gone from sight.

Now, in our little parlor, I sat and read a few pages of Telarus for comfort. Then I shut the book and placed it back on the shelf with the others.

That day, and those that followed, all seemed very long. I filled them as I could, by setting down these words and writing to my sisters. I confess, I cannot wait to see the look on Lily's face when we come to the city. I imagine she will think Mr. Quent extremely ancient and dreadfully out of fashion, but she will come to see him as I do, and Rose can only love him.

Such thoughts lifted my spirits, as did making plans for my family's removal to Durrow Street. Feeling brighter inside, I did what I could to brighten up the house, much to the perturbation of Mrs. Darendal. It had come to the point where she would refuse to be in the same room with me and gave me the coldest of looks should we even come within view. I could not say I minded. The silence and the sunlight were better companions, and I spent my days rearranging the rooms and bringing in flowers from the heath.

Now, Father, I fear I must set down my pen for some time. He will be returning soon, and after that we will be coming to the city. Then I shall see you and Lily and Rose. It has been far too long. I promise I will never be away so long again. I have heard very little news of late from Lily; she has been remiss in writing letters. Well, I will learn everything myself soon enough. Look for me in no more than a quarter month.

ᖴATHER, WHAT THINGS I have to tell you now!

I can hardly think it possible to explain all that has happened, but I must try—if only to help make myself believe that it is done, that it is in the past now, that we are both of us safe.

But neither are we together! Mr. Quent has gone west to Torland with a company of the soldiers on business of the Crown, and it will be a month at least before I am to see him again. Nor am I at Heathcrest Hall, and whether I shall ever lay eyes upon it again, I do not know. At this moment I sit in a room at the inn at Morrowset, waiting for the next coach to come, as the mail was already booked from this point onward and I was forced to give up the seat I had occupied since Cairnbridge.

Yet it is just as well I must wait for the coach, for I need more time to compose myself before I see my sisters. I do not want to alarm them. Even as I write these words, my hand seems to shake a bit less. I suppose it will take me the rest of the umbral to describe all that has happened since last I set pen to paper. That suits me; I have not yet the capacity for sleep.

As I mentioned when last I wrote, Mr. Quent had previously been called away by his business for the lord inquirer. Where he had gone, I did not know. I could only guess he must be investigating some rumor of a Rising.

The days were lonely with the children gone. My only company came from Jance and Lanna, and the former was hardly more talkative than the latter. As for Mrs. Darendal—I had thought it impossible she could be more grim, but I was wrong. I learned from Jance that she was expecting a visit from her grown son, who had not come to see her for some time. One might have expected this news to cheer her. However, on those rare occasions I saw her, she wore a look as dour as that of any gargoyle that ever frowned down from the cornices of a church—though I suppose such looks were for *my* benefit.

At last came the day we expected Mr. Quent's return. I knew his business often kept him away longer than anticipated. All the same, the moment I rose after a short umbral's rest, I looked out the window, searching the lane that led up to the house for any trace of him.

There was none, but every time I passed a window I looked out, and what the significance was of the pang I felt each time I saw the empty lane, I could not say. At times it seemed disappointment, at others relief. I wanted more than anything to see him. Or did I?

*There are yet secrets in this house that would make your blood go cold . . .*

In the time that followed his proposal, I had forgotten Mrs. Darendal's words. However, over the last several, silent days they had come back to me repeatedly, as had his own whispered words.

*If you knew what peril I have placed you in by bringing you here to suit my own purposes . . .*

I became agitated and took to pacing the house, moving from window to window, looking out each one: waiting, wondering, dreading. At last I could bear it no longer. I did not want to be near another window!

I went into the kitchen, and, finding it empty, I went to the door to the cellar. I opened the wooden door and with a candle in hand descended into the cool gloom beneath the house. Only on rare occasions had I ever been down here, and then just to fetch a bottle of wine. The darkness here seemed a palpable thing, like a remnant of the void from before the world was made, caught in a hollow beneath the crust of the land. Always I had dashed up the stairs as quickly as I could.

However, that day the darkness suited me. Better the nameless fear it contained than the fear I could all too easily call by name and whose name was now my own. The candle sent the shadows scurrying as I reached the bottom of the stairs.

I made my way to the wine cabinet, which was hardly five steps from the stairs, then moved past, farther into the cellars than I had ever gone. Ten feet I went, twenty. Still the light of the candle did not reach the far wall. Hoary beams arched overhead, suggesting the ribs of some great leviathan. For a moment I felt a fleeting warmth. Then I moved onward, and a chill took the air.

At last a ghostly shape became apparent before me. Indeed, for a sharp moment I feared it truly was some sort of apparition, that there was after all a ghost that haunted Heathcrest Hall. Then, as my eyes adjusted further to the gloom, I saw it for what it was: something tall and squarish draped by a white sheet. It stood against a stone wall; I had reached the end of the cellar.

As I approached, the candlelight skittered across the floor as if it were wet; only it wasn't. Instead, the gray slate had given way to a smooth black stone that reflected the light. The chill deepened.

Shivering, I drew close to the draped object. I meant only to lift the sheet, to peek beneath it, but even as I touched the cloth, it fell away with a whisper. The gold light of the candle went green.

So this was where the painting had gone.

I brought the candle closer. In the flickering light, the trees seemed to sway back and forth, and the roots writhed in the cracks in the stone wall as if trying to pry them apart. Above, a pale thing gleamed among the twisting branches: a figure all in white.

The painting of the Wyrdwood did not fill me with dread as it did the first time I glimpsed it. How could a thing of canvas and pigment have the power to distress me when I had seen the true scene with my own eyes? I bent closer with the candle, examining the painting, admiring the fine brushwork, the care that had gone into rendering each leaf, each mossy stone of the wall.

Gennivel Quent had been a skilled artist. However, I could not believe she had painted this simply from imagination. The depiction was too detailed. Had someone else described the scene to her? Or had this come from things she had seen herself?

I moved the candle, and the flame wavered as a breath passed my lips. The first time I saw the painting, I had been captivated by the trees and the figure tangled among them; I had not noticed the smaller form that stood below and to one side, in the shadows beside the wall. Her little dress was wet and torn, her feet bare and muddy, her hair a sheaf of wheat. She gazed out of the painting with large green eyes set in a small face: a child of no more than three or four.

A creaking echoed behind me.

I turned around with a gasp and lifted my candle higher. Its light did not reach across the cellar, but I caught a dark shape slinking toward me.

"Who's there?" I called out, my voice overloud in the cavernous room.

The shadow drifted closer.

"Is that you, Mrs. Darendal?" I called again. "Or is that Jance?"

Footsteps made cold echoes against the slate floor. I tried to back away, but the wall and painting were behind me. I could not retreat.

"Show yourself!" I cried out, and thrust the candle before me.

The figure stopped, and I sagged against a stack of boxes to keep from falling. "Lanna, you gave me such a fright. What is it? Were you looking for me?"

The young woman made no answer. Of course she could not; despite all Mr. Quent's encouragements over the years, she remained mute. I saw she was not looking at me but rather beyond me. Her face had gone slack; she looked very pale in the dark.

My fear was altered to concern. "Lanna, what's wrong?"

She did not move, and I realized it was the painting she stared at. The poor thing—she had witnessed the Rising on the green in Cairnbridge all those years ago. She had seen the work of the gallows tree. It was that terrible sight that had struck her dumb. I could hardly imagine what memories the scene in the painting must conjure for her. I set the candle on the boxes and bent to pick up the sheet, intending to throw it over the painting.

"You," spoke a small voice.

The word whispered away into the dark. I rose and looked around. Was there someone else there? I could see nobody in the gloom, and I had not recognized the voice. It had been high and thin, like the voice of a girl. But Clarette was gone.

The sheet slipped from my hands. "Lanna, you spoke!"

She did not look at me. "You," she said again. This time I saw her lips move, saw her speak the word. Her voice was stronger now, no longer a whisper. She reached her hand out, finger extended. However, it was not at me she pointed but rather at the painting.

I shook my head. "I don't understand."

Still she pointed at the painting—not at the figure in the trees but at the small form that stood by the wall. A trembling came over me, because I *did* understand. Lanna was several years older than me. She would have been a girl of nine or so. Old enough to know what was happening. Old enough to be struck dumb by the horror of it. Old enough to remember.

Yet I would have been no more than three years old—a tiny child with green eyes. . . .

"It wasn't the gallows tree you saw," I whispered, more to myself than to Lanna. "You were there at the wood. You and Gennivel both."

The candle guttered in a stray draft, and the darkness closed in. I could not breathe. The entire weight of the house above pressed down, as if the old stones would crush us and seal us there in this black tomb. I ran past Lanna and toward the stairs.

I stumbled in the dark, knocking my shins against trunks and stray barrels. I gained the stairs and flung myself up them to the kitchen. Gray light seeped through the windows. I smelled rain. At once the feeling of oppression lifted, and I gulped in breaths of air. Tea. I needed a cup of tea to steady my nerves, that was all.

Yet a cup of tea would not change what I had just seen.

*You,* Lanna had said. She had not spoken in nearly twenty years, but she had said those words to me, had spoken them as she pointed at the painting.

"She is wrong," I said aloud. "She is making up stories." I tried to put a kettle on to boil, but my hands would not stop shaking.

Lanna had been there at the Wyrdwood nineteen years ago, along with Merriel Addysen's cousin, Gennival. How else could the detail contained in Mrs. Quent's painting, and Lanna's reaction to it, be explained?

I heard footsteps coming up the stairs, but I could not bear to face Lanna, not then. I fled the kitchen, running into the front hall. Thunder rattled the windowpanes. A storm was coming. I walked up and down the hall under the watchful eyes of stag and boar. I could not help but think their gazes jeering, as if they had known all along. What other awful secrets of this house did they know that I did not?

Again thunder sounded. Only this time it did not fade, instead becoming a rhythmic pounding. My heart leaped. I knew that sound. I ran to a window and looked out into the courtyard. A moment later the mist swirled and parted, and a horse and rider appeared.

He had come! I hardly knew what I felt. My trembling was renewed, but from relief or dread I could not say. Either way, it would not do. I could not greet him like this. I took a minute to shake the dust from my dress and brush cobwebs from my hair. I drew several breaths, and only when some sense of steadiness returned did I go to the front entry.

I found Jance in the open doorway, stamping mud from his boots. I looked past him but saw only fog and rain.

"Is Mr. Quent not come?"

Jance shook his head. "Nay, it is Mrs. Darendal's son. He's in the carriage house seeing to his horse. I came in to tell her, but this mud ought as well be pitch, and she'll have my hide if I track it in."

I felt a keen disappointment, though that did not mean I did not suffer apprehension at his return. When one dwells in dread anticipation of an event, it is almost more awful when it does *not* occur. All the same, I forced myself to stand straight. Kin of Mrs. Darendal's could mean nothing to me, but I was the lady of the house now, and it was my duty to receive him.

"I will inform Mrs. Darendal," I said to Jance. "Tell Mr. Darendal to come in when he is done with his horse."

"Aye," Jance said with a relieved look, and went back out into the rain, shutting the door behind him.

I went to the kitchen, but Mrs. Darendal was not there. The cellar door was closed; Lanna must have come up, but there was no sign of her. I went to the parlor, back into the front hall, and then up to the second floor. Still I saw no trace of the housekeeper. I looked in every room, even daring to crack the door to his study and peer in. I went to the servants' stair and up to the attic, all in vain. It was possible she had gotten around me by way of the main stair. The house was so large, so dim, I might go in circles for hours and never find Mrs. Darendal.

By then I was quite perturbed. What right had she to conceal herself from me like this, when it was because of *her* son that I sought her? I went back downstairs and through the front hall with the intention of returning to the kitchen to start my search again.

A blast of damp air struck me as I neared the entry. The door stood open, and rain lashed in. Jance must not have latched it behind him. I pushed it shut against the gale, then started again toward the kitchen. As I did, I heard a sound through the opening that led back to the front hall. So she had circled around me—as was her intention, for all I knew! I turned and marched back into the front hall just as another peal of thunder shook the windows. A figure stood not ten steps away, back turned to me.

It was not Mrs. Darendal.

He was tall and wore a knee-length coat of wine-colored velvet. His boots were spotless, as if he had not just ridden through miles of inclement weather. Gold hair fell loosely over his broad shoulders.

The man stood before a stuffed wolf. He must not have heard me over the thunder. After a moment I recovered from my surprise.

"Mr. Darendal, I did not know you had come in," I said, moving closer. "I have been unable to find your mother. I will keep looking, of course."

"That won't be necessary, Mrs. Quent," he said in a low voice as he stroked the wolf. A ring glinted on his hand: it was wrought of thick gold and carved into the shape of a lion's head.

"Oh," I said. I tried to say something else, but speech was beyond me.

He turned around and grinned, an expression not unlike that worn by the wolf. I recalled how I had thought on the mail coach that he was likely handsome. I saw now that he was. He closed half the distance to me with a long, easy stride.

"You need not look for my mother," he said. "I told her it would be best not to be at Heathcrest when I arrived."

"It was you," I managed to say. I wanted to retreat, but my legs would not move. "It was you the soldiers were looking for. Only you vanished from the coach when we stopped."

He pressed a hand to his chest. The lion's head ring flashed like his tawny eyes. "By God, I've been discovered! Whatever will I do?"

My fingers searched blindly for the door frame, discovered it, gripped it hard. "What do you want, Mr. Darendal?"

"Nobody calls me Mr. Darendal." He gave an elegant bow. "You must call me Westen, Mrs. Quent."

"Westen," I murmured, as if it had been a command. I managed to move a step back. At the same moment he took a fluid stride forward, maintaining the distance between us as perfectly as if we were dancers at a ball.

"The soldiers," I said. "Why were they looking for you that night?"

"What makes you think they were looking for *me*, Mrs. Quent?"

I thought of the things I had heard in the village and what Mr. Quent had told me. "You had something they wanted. It was in your coat—a letter, or money. Something to help those who plot against the Crown. You are one of the common thieves who stalk the highway and aid them."

"On the contrary," he said with another grin, "I am a most uncommon thief. Indeed, I can guarantee you, Mrs. Quent, that you could ride all across this county and the next and not encounter a highwayman like myself."

I gasped and tried to retreat, but he reached out and caught my hand in his own. He bowed and touched his lips against it.

A shudder passed through me. His grip was gentle, yet I knew it could tighten cruelly in an instant. "Why have you come?" I whispered.

"You know why I've come." He stroked the back of my hand with his thumb. "Tell me, has Mr. Quent returned from his journey yet? No? Perfect—I did not think so. But he is due to return very soon, is he not? In which case we must be ready for him. We cannot let him arrive before we have made our . . . preparations."

I shook my head. I could utter no sound but a moan of dread.

He placed his free hand against my cheek. "Hush, now. Do not fret. It will be quick as a wink. He will make no struggle. Indeed, I am sure he will give himself up freely. What man would not do the same for the sake of his lovely new bride?" He bent close, so that his lips brushed my ear. "And you are indeed lovely, Mrs. Quent."

His breath was warm against my cheek. His hand slipped from my cheek, down my throat—

There was a bang in the entryway behind me. The door had flown open, striking the wall. I tried to turn my head. Had the wind thrown it open, or was it a figure I saw amid the lashing rain?

"Jance!" I cried out. "Don't come in! He is a brigand and a rebel! You must tell—"

He let out a hiss and thrust me down to the floor. My words ceased as the breath rushed out of me. I heard him go by; then came the sound of the door slamming. I had but a moment. Clenching my teeth against the ache in my chest, I rose up and ran across the front hall.

I heard his shout behind me, followed by the gunshot sound of his boots against the floor. However, I did not look back. I ran up the stairs and along the corridor on the second floor. I could hear him behind me. I had only time to dart through the nearest door and shut it. Even as I turned the lock, the door shuddered from a great blow.

"That was very clever of you, Mrs. Quent," he called out. "But you cannot think you are safe in there."

Again the door shook.

No, I was not safe. However, there was a side door in the room that led to a sitting room. I went through, again latching the door behind me, crossed the sitting room, and passed through another side door, which I also latched. I found myself in a dim chamber filled with furniture draped in sheets, like a silent chorus of ghosts.

I went to the door that led back to the second-floor corridor and pressed my ear against it, listening. I had to wait for the right moment. I heard another blow strike the door of the room into which I had first fled, and another. With this last blow came the sound of wood cracking and hinges crying out.

I did not hesitate. Even as that other door burst inward, I opened my door and dashed out into the corridor. I risked a glance to my right and saw the broken door hanging ajar. He had gone through, but he would discover my trick in a moment. There was no time to head for the main staircase; that would lead me past the broken door. Instead, I made for the servants' stairs and dashed up them.

At the top of the staircase I halted, waiting for his shout of anger and the sound of his boots coming up the stairs. A minute passed; two minutes, three. I heard only my own ragged breathing.

He must have thought I fled downstairs. Soon enough I must. I could not stay here; I had to go to the village, to find Mr. Quent before he returned. My best hope, I decided, was to take the servants' stairs down to the kitchen and go out that way. Only, what would I do outside? It was raining, and night drew near. I would perish of the chill before I reached the village if I went out unprotected.

My room beneath the eaves, which I had continued to inhabit in Mr. Quent's absence, was near the top of the stairs. I went there quickly, without sound. I took my cape from its hook and threw it around my shoulders, then retrieved my bonnet. Both were gray. The fog was thick outside the window; I would fade into the mist. I turned to make my escape.

He stood in the open doorway, a smile on his handsome face.

"She told me your room was up here."

The bonnet dropped from my hands. I stumbled back against the bed and sat down. Mrs. Darendal had told him—she had told him everything about the house. Then she had gone, leaving him to his dark work. She had betrayed us. She had betrayed Mr. Quent.

Now that all chance of flight was gone, I felt a strange calm descend over me. "Does your mother know what you intend?"

His only answer was a sly look. He made an examination of the room, walking slowly around, even stopping at the table to read some of the pages I had written to you, Father. All the while I looked at the open door, but I knew there was no hope. The room was small. If I moved, he would have me in an instant.

"A modest chamber," he said. "But charming. Like yourself, Mrs. Quent. I can see why you chose it over the grander rooms below. The view to the east must be excellent in fine weather. True, it's a bit chilly up here, but you have your cape on. How fortunate! This strikes me as a good place for us to wait." With that he sat in the bent-willow chair, leaned back, and put his boots up on the table.

I lifted my chin and looked at him directly. "What of the preparations you said we must make?"

"They are already under way." He laughed at what must have been my look of astonishment. "What? Did you think I had come alone? There—look out the window. You can see them now."

The calmness I had felt drained away, leaving a cold hollow inside me. With great effort I moved to the window and looked out.

"Do you see them?"

I saw nothing but shadows flitting below. I started to say this, then gasped. The shadows did not move with the swirls of fog but rather stalked and prowled around the house. The mist parted before them and closed behind. Never could I see them in full—it was too dim, the fog too thick—but here and there I saw crooked limbs, sinuous backs. At times they seemed to walk upright, and at others they bent low, as if going about on all fours.

"What are they?" I said, falling back from the window.

"They are Altania."

I turned to look at him. "Altania? What do you mean?"

"The land is rising up."

"The Wyrdwood, you mean. It is the Wyrdwood that rises."

"No, not just the Wyrdwood. The entire land of Altania. The Wyrdwood is just one part—the oldest part. It will suffer those who wall it in, who rob and ravish it for their own profit, to tread upon it no longer. And they—" He nodded to the window. "They are its willing soldiers."

"You mean they are rebels and traitors. They are men!"

He shrugged. "They went to the Wyrdwood, and they gave themselves to her there. They are the defenders of Altania now."

The mist seemed to have crept into my mind. His words made no sense. All the same, I could only think of Deelie Moorbrook's cow, torn apart by a beast. A greatwolf, Jance had said. Only there were no greatwolves anymore. There hadn't been in two hundred years.

"You said they gave themselves to her. You mean Halley Samonds." *The witch,* I wanted to say but could not. "What did she do to them?"

"She opened the way so they could pass, that was all." His gaze went to the window. "And the Wyrdwood made them into what was needed."

"But you . . . you are not like them."

Again he gave me that sly smile. His hair seemed longer than I remembered, wilder, but it was only from the chase he had given me through the house. He leaned back in the chair, lacing his hands behind his head, even shutting his eyes. However, I did not think for a moment that I could get past him. His head was cocked; his nostrils flared with each breath.

I sat on the bed again and watched him. As I did, my fear gave way to a new sensation: anger. What right had he to do this? He said his compatriots were soldiers of Altania. I did not know what had happened to them in the Wyrdwood, but they were still criminals. He spoke of those who robbed for their own profit, but had he not done the same? What authority did he have to speak for Altania, to say what was best for it? What audacity, to think that *he* spoke for the land!

I felt my cheeks glowing. He said the witch had opened the way for them. And so? Had I not once made the ancient trees do *my* bidding? I had told myself it was a gust of wind that freed the children that night when the branches entangled them by the Wyrdwood. That was not true. I knew it then, and I knew it when Mr. Quent asked me how we escaped that night. Only I had not dared to admit it, not to him, not even to myself.

There was no use in such ruses now, not after what I had seen. Halley Samonds had been called to the Wyrdwood, and so had the first Mrs. Quent, but they were not the only ones. I thought of the painting in the cellar, and the tiny girl with green eyes. Eyes like those of the woman in the trees, like those of Mrs. Quent in her portrait.

Eyes like my own.

I looked at Westen and then at the willow chair he sat in, fashioned from fallen branches Mr. Samonds had gathered at the edge of the Wyrdwood. The branches had been woven together into the form of the chair. What if they were woven into another shape?

I did no more than envision it in my mind, yet such was the force of my fury that it was enough. Westen's eyes flew open. He let out a cry and tried to leap up from the chair.

It was no use. Some of the branches that formed the legs had already coiled around his ankles. Twigs rose from the arms like brown snakes, encircling his wrists, binding them. Several stems looped around his chest, twining themselves together as they went, forming a strong band.

He let out a shout, followed by a slew of curses as he strained against the chair. Such was the force of his rage that I leaped up, afraid he would break free. His face grew red. His hands were fists, and the cords of his neck stood out in sharp relief.

The bonds held. Tendrils thrust down between the floorboards, rooting the chair in place. He slumped back, panting. I thought it would be good if the cords pulled tighter. Even as I considered this, they did. He let out a hiss, and a grimace twisted his face. However, a moment later he laughed—though the sound was shallow for want of breath.

"Now that," he said in a hoarse voice, "I had not expected." His grin broadened, though pain still registered on his face. "But then, I don't think you expected it either, did you, Mrs. Quent?"

The switches were still moving, wrapping around him. One slid around his throat.

He sucked in a tight breath. "Careful, Mrs. Quent. You don't want to overdo it. I don't know that Mr. Quent would be willing to remain married to a murderess *and* a witch."

I hardly heard him. In books, I had read that people saw red when they were angry. To my eyes, everything was tinged green.

"I'm going," I said, and picked up my bonnet.

He laughed, though it came out as a choking sound. "I wouldn't go down there if I were you, Mrs. Quent. Do remember—the front door wasn't locked."

I went to the door, then turned to look at him. His breaths were quick and shallow. His face had gone from red to purple.

"This spell . . ." he said. "It will . . . not hold me for long once . . . you are gone."

I did not need long. I had only to get outside, to get my horse, to ride to the village.

His grin had become a rictus, his lips curling back from this teeth. "You cannot stop it," he said. "Even if you . . . warn him. No matter what . . . you do, the land . . . will rise."

"You do not speak for Altania," I said.

Before he could answer me, several tendrils wove across his mouth. His eyes bulged from their sockets. I turned and left the room.

I RETURNED TO THE servants' stairs and went down to the second floor. As I was about to descend to the kitchen, I heard a sound below like men talking, except the speech was low and growling and I could make out no words. Then came a noise like knives being dragged across the slate floor. I turned and ran down the second-floor corridor, past Mr. Quent's study, then slowed my pace, creeping toward the main staircase.

Whuffling breaths rose up from below, and shadows undulated on the walls.

*They are men,* I told myself. *Rebels, to be sure, and dangerous, but they are only men. It is the queer light that makes them appear strange, and the fog that mutes their speech, that is all.*

All the same, I turned and fled down the corridor, back toward the servants' stairs, but even as I set foot on the top step, the sound of baying echoed up from the kitchen.

I could not think. There was nowhere in the house to go except up. But *he* was still there in the attic. Then I thought of Mr. Quent's study and the ivy that obscured the window. A wild plan formed in my mind to open the window and climb down the vines.

I turned and ran back down the corridor. However, I had gone only halfway when I heard a scrabbling on the main staircase. Behind me echoed more howls, closer now. They were coming up from the kitchen as well. I turned around again, and again, but there was nowhere left to go.

Something hard caught my arm from behind, digging into my flesh, pulling me back. I opened my mouth to scream.

"Quiet, you foolish girl!" whispered a harsh voice.

I shut my mouth and the hand released me. Trembling, I staggered around. Mrs. Darendal stood in an opening in the side of the corridor, in a door I was certain I had never seen before.

"Mrs. Darendal," I said stupidly.

The door was low, and I saw that its edges were cleverly aligned with the paneling. Once shut, it would look like any other part of the wall. So that was how she had always avoided me.

"You stand there and stare like a dolt! To think he believes you clever. Come!"

The housekeeper made a motion with her hand, and I stepped through the opening. She pressed it shut behind me; it closed with a *click*. We were in a narrow passage, lit by the candle she held.

We did not move. I hardly dared to breathe. As we listened, something moved outside the door. There was a snuffling just on the other side of the panel. I bit my lip for fear I would scream. Then the sound ceased, and the padding footsteps moved away.

"Follow me," the housekeeper whispered, and she started down the passage. I hurried after, afraid of being left outside the circle of candlelight.

The passage twisted left and right and went up and down little half flights of steps. In some places it was so narrow we had to turn sideways to pass through. I tried to keep track of the twists and turns, but the dark deprived me of all sense of direction. Were Mrs. Darendal to abandon me, I should be lost, trapped in the walls of Heathcrest Hall like a spirit.

At last we came to a halt. The passage dead-ended, and a lump formed in my throat; I feared we were indeed lost. Then Mrs. Darendal did something to the blank panel before us, and a pinpoint of light appeared. The housekeeper put her eye to it, then hissed between her teeth. She retreated down the passage and around a bend, taking me with her.

"We must wait."

I did not need more explanation. Whatever room it was she had looked out on, *they* were there.

At last I could stand the silence no longer. "What are they?" I dared to murmur. "Are they . . . are they men?"

"Lower your voice! You have already caused enough trouble."

I could not have been more stunned if she had struck me. "*I* have caused trouble?"

"It is your fault it has come to this."

A fraction of my dread was replaced by astonishment.

Her face was a hard mask in the candlelight, all edges and shadows. "Do not pretend such innocence, *Miss* Lockwell. It is wasted on me. I know what you are. I have known it since the moment you set foot in this house, and every fear I had, every concern I tried to relate to him, has come to pass. I told him not to bring you here, and when you came I encouraged him to dismiss you at once. Would that he had listened to me."

Now I *did* feel as if I had been slapped. "I thought you merely disliked me. Yet you say you tried, with conscious effort, to drive me away!"

Her expression showed no shame. "It is not only my duty to care for this house but for its master as well. I did everything in my power to prevent him from bringing the children here. Their presence could not be tolerated. All the more because I knew that once they came, *your* presence would become all the more likely. Almost from the first moment his cousins prevailed upon him to take the children, he spoke of you as their governess."

"But why me? Surely there were other choices, ones you would have not considered so poor."

Her face seemed to soften a fraction. "Do not think I speak ill of him. His only fault is kindness. He wanted to see again a person whose fate had once been his concern. There can be no impugning *his* motives." Now her expression hardened again. "The same cannot be said for others, Miss Lockwell. Forgive me, I mean *Mrs. Quent.*" She spoke these last words as if she had swallowed a mouthful of vinegar.

"You cannot think I came here with that intention!"

"I would not presume to know with what intention you came here. All the same, it is *your* coming that has brought us to this."

It was too much. Tears stung my eyes. "How can that be?"

"You cannot see? Then you do not merely look a dolt. *They* know the work he does, and long have they wanted to put a stop to it."

"The rebels," I said. "Those who plot treason against the Crown. Mr. Quent said they have been using the Wyrdwood to meet and gather, to conceal their plottings. And his work is to seek—"

"I have served him for nearly twenty years," she snapped. "I know what he does."

The housekeeper looked away. Her gray dress melded with the gloom, and her face seemed to float: a pale cameo, shaped by years of worry that had long ago become regret. "I wanted only to protect him. That is why we endured a silent life here, in this forlorn place. If we were alone, then we were safe; never would they attack him openly, not in his demesne. Yet if they could find a way to draw him into theirs . . ."

"But the children are gone," I said. "They have failed to lure him to the Wyrdwood."

She raised a sharp eyebrow. "Have they, Mrs. Quent?"

A weakness passed over me. I wished to sit, but there was no room in the passage. The children were gone. The witch had been stopped from drawing them into the wood; *I* had stopped her. Yet in their stead, I had given the plotters even better hope for compelling Mr. Quent to enter the Wyrdwood. For what man would not come to the aid of his new wife?

Yet something had happened they had not expected, just as it had that night at the Wyrdwood. Westen had thought to capture me, but it was he who had been captured instead. A curious feeling rose in me: a sensation of triumph. I even smiled, I think.

A howl echoed from somewhere above in the darkness, and any feeling I had was replaced by dread. I looked upward, into the dark. "What is happening to them?"

"The wood is changing them."

"But how can that be?"

She gave me a look of disgust. "What do I know of the affairs of witches?"

The housekeeper turned away, and her gray hair and gray dress faded into the gloom, so that I could see her only as a woman-shaped void where the candlelight did not reach.

"I told him," she whispered to the dark. "I told him not to go in there."

"Westen," I said. "Your son. Is he—"

"He is a fool. If only his father had . . ." The candlelight wavered. "*He* knew the peril of the wood, but they toy with it. They laugh and believe they can put it to their own uses. All they can think of are their schemes and plans. 'You shall see, Mother,' he tells me. 'We will be free of this tyranny. We will have a king who protects the folk in the country.' As if it matters who sits in the Citadel! What king has ever cared for folk like us? It is not worth giving up your . . . It is not worth dealing with such as *her*."

Now she did turn to look at me. "I hate it. I hate the wood. I hate those women who go to it and work their craft there. I hate its trees. I hate that it took my husband. And I hate that it is taking my son!"

I was struck dumb. No breath would enter my lungs. Her face hung in the darkness before me, and for the first time since my coming to Heathcrest Hall, there were feelings upon it I recognized: anger, and love, and despair. Something glinted on her cheek.

She seemed to see me staring. Her lip curled up. "Now," she said, pushing past me. "I hear them no longer. We must go."

She moved back to the end of the passage. By the time I reached her she had already pushed it open. I saw a wedge of silver light, and though it could only be dim I squinted as if it were a brilliant glare.

"Come, you fool!" she said, seizing my arm and dragging me forward as the opening grew wider.

"Why?" I said as I stumbled after her. After all she had said, I could not understand. "Why are you helping me?"

"I keep this house, and all that is in it, for him, that is why." She pulled me through the door.

I blinked and saw we were in the front hall. We had emerged from behind another panel, this one beneath the stairs. Not ten steps away was the arch that led to the front entry to the house. We both looked around, but the hall was empty save for ourselves and its usual mounted denizens.

"To the door," the housekeeper said.

I hurried toward the arch, but when I reached it I realized the housekeeper was not behind me. Turning, I saw her start up the stairs.

Dread seized me. "Mrs. Darendal, what are you doing?"

"It is none of *your* concern," she said with a glare over her shoulder. She ascended several more steps.

"You cannot go upstairs. They are up there!"

"So is my son. I will not leave him to them." She continued climbing.

"But he is like them!"

The look she sent me across the hall was filled with such loathing, such contempt, that I could only stagger back against it. The housekeeper vanished up the stairs.

For a mad moment I thought of dashing after her. No—she did not want me. Whatever she had done to help me, it had not been for *my* sake. I turned and ran to the front door. It was still open.

I ran through. Mist coiled around my ankles, pooled on the stones, slithered down the steps. I hesitated, thinking of Lanna and Jance. Were they still in the house? I could not know, but if I had any hope of aiding them, it was to escape this place, to ride to the village, to seek help. I started down the steps.

A dark form moved in the mist before me, and I halted. There was a sound like a blade being drawn over a whetting stone. The shape stalked up the steps.

"No," I said, or tried to. The mist filled my mouth; I could not speak.

The shadow prowled closer.

I fled back up the front steps, but as I reached the top a growling sounded on the air, so low it was a thing felt as much as heard. A dark form loped through the open door. I turned; the other shadow was halfway up the steps.

There is a point where dread becomes so great the mind can no longer endure it and so gives it up completely. In my fear, a kind of madness came upon me. My heart did not slow, but I no longer felt any desire to run. Terror had made a crystal of my mind: sharp-faceted and clear. They were not here to murder me but for another purpose.

Let them, I thought with a sudden elation. Let them try to make use of me for their own ends! I spread my arms wide and held my chin high.

"Come, then, take me," I spoke into the fog. "Take me to the Wyrdwood—if you dare it."

There was a snarl, and the shadow leaped up.

Lightning flashed, a clap of thunder rent the air. There was a pitiful whine. The thing crumpled in a heap on the steps below me and did not move again. There was a clattering sound. More shapes moved up the steps. Only these were tall and upright.

"By God, hold your fire! There is a woman there!"

At the same moment another snarl sounded behind me, and again light and sound tore the mist asunder.

"Damn you, I said hold your fire!"

The mist swirled and parted. A man stood before me, a rifle in his hands. He wore the blue regimental coat of a captain.

"Madam, are you well?" His eyes were wide. "Tell me, are you hurt?"

I tried to answer him, but my ears rang from the rifle shots, and the sound had struck me dumb.

Other soldiers appeared from the gloom behind the captain. "Where is the inquirer? Get him now!"

"I am here," spoke a deep, familiar voice.

So filled with relief was I at the sound that my legs could no longer support me. I would have dashed my head against the steps if the captain had not caught me. Then another pair of hands took me, holding me aloft with easy strength, though they had but eight fingers between them.

"You are well, aren't you?" His brown eyes were intent upon me. "Tell me you are well."

I reached up and laid a hand against his bearded cheek. "Mr. Quent."

"It looks as if we got two more of the dogs, sir," one of the men said.

Dogs. Yes, that was what they had seemed like: great, shaggy dogs. I turned my head. The mist had lifted a bit, and in the failing light I saw two figures sprawled on the front steps of the house, dark pools forming beneath them. Their jackets and breeches were shabby, their hair long and tangled, their faces pale.

Men. They were men.

"Search the house!" the captain called out. "Find any more of the rebels that might be left inside."

Gently, Mr. Quent turned me away.

"Do not look at them," he said. "You are safe now. It is over."

I rested my cheek against his chest. Yet I had seen enough to know that neither of the dead men was Westen. Nor did I believe they would find him inside the house. I remembered the last words he spoke to me.

*No matter what you do, the land will rise. . . .*

A shiver passed through me. Though I admired Mr. Quent more than any man in the world, all the same I knew he was wrong. It was not over.

Night descended. As it did, a gale sprang up, tearing apart the fog, and I thought I could almost hear it: the sound of wind through bent branches and the whispering of leaves.

No, it had only just begun.

❧

𝔗HEY HAVE TOLD me the mail coach will arrive at the inn soon, and its stop here will be brief. I have time for only a few more lines, Father. Then, in mere hours, I will see you and my sisters! Perhaps then my heart will remember how to be glad, for at present it has forgotten that ability. When I close my eyes, I cannot picture him. I have already forgotten what he looks like!

But such thoughts are natural for a new wife, who goes into a silly panic when she cannot envision the face of her husband when he is away—and through such anxiety further assures she will not be able to do so.

There is no cause for worry. He will join us in the city soon, and I am certain you will admire him as much as I do—or rather, that you *would*. But of course that must be the case, for you and he were friends once, and now I understand why. That there is a man who is kinder, more judicious, or possessed of a greater sense of duty cannot be.

Yet it is that very obligation to duty that separates us. The day following the awful events I last described to you, an agent of that lord whom he serves arrived at Heathcrest. Their meeting was not long, but even as the man rode away, Mr. Quent called for Jance and told him to begin making preparations for a journey.

"But you have only just returned!" I told him after Jance was gone, clinging to him like some brainless thing. "You cannot go away so soon."

"You know I must," he said, gravely but gently, and he told me what he could of what the messenger had told him: that there was a report from the far west of Torland, that it spoke of not just a single Rising but of several, and that each had been more alarming in effect than the last. However, the area was remote and sparsely populated. The reports might be in error, but he must go investigate.

His calmness, his even temper, shamed me; I composed myself. However, while I could accept this parting, there was one thing I could not bear. "I cannot remain here at Heathcrest," I told him.

"No!" He took my hand and held it tight. "No, you cannot. I have told Jance to book you passage on the mail. It leaves tomorrow. You will return to the city and stay with your family."

Excitement filled me, but dread as well. How I wanted to see you, Father, and Lily and Rose. And I could not stay in the house, not after what had taken place there. But Invarel was even farther away from Torland than Heathcrest.

"If Mr. Wyble will allow it," I said at last.

"I will write to him and assure him that as soon as I return to the city I will remove you, as well as your father and sisters, from his house."

I nodded. Mr. Wyble would be satisfied by such a letter, for it would assure our ejection from the house on Whitward Street a full half month sooner than might otherwise have been achieved under the law.

"What of Heathcrest?" I said. "Who will care for it, now that . . ."

I could not continue, and he was silent. There were things that were still too terrible to speak of, though I had overheard enough the day before to know what had happened. Upon entering the house, the soldiers had found and shot a third rebel. It was not Westen. They discovered Lanna in the basement. She had had the presence of mind to lock herself in. Now she had returned to Low Sorrel to be with her family. Her mother had already written to Mr. Quent to say she was not coming back.

While I had feared for Jance, he had been able to slip away in the fog to the village and there had met Mr. Quent the moment he arrived. That a band of soldiers had accompanied Mr. Quent on his return was a stroke of fortune; they had intended to continue on their way to In-varel. Instead, all of them had ridden to the house and had arrived in time to aid me.

However, they were too late for another.

I was not allowed to see her. That it had been a gruesome scene I knew from the look on Mr. Quent's face when he told me they had found Mrs. Darendal in his study on the second floor. I heard one of the soldiers say it looked like the work of animals.

"That's what they are—animals," another answered him. "Bloody rebels. They should all be—" But I did not hear what he thought, for the two ceased their talk when they saw me.

"The house will be closed," Mr. Quent said in answer to my question. "There is no use keeping it open when there is no one to dwell here."

So the shadows and silence would at last be left to rule here. "What of others who might have been in league with . . . with the men who came here?"

"A watch has been set around all stands of Wyrdwood in the county. The rebels will not be able to pass. Should anyone try to enter or leave, they will be apprehended."

"Anyone?" I thought of the figure in white, who had seemed to float among the trees.

His voice was low—not angry or hard, but stern as when I first met him. "It is my duty as an inquirer to seek out any person who might have knowledge of a past or future Rising. No one can remain in the wood forever. When she comes, we will take her."

I nodded. Yet I wondered—would Halley Samonds truly need to leave the Wyrdwood? Or could she remain there, drawing sustenance from the land as the ancient trees did? It was a foolish idea; no matter what else she was, she was a woman. All the same, I did not think they would ever find her, unless it was her bones sinking into the mold among a tangle of roots.

I ceased my questions. That he had questions for *me* I could see in his eyes, but preparations for his trip consumed him.

I made my own preparations and went up to my room in the attic to gather these papers and a few other things. I thought fondly of the hours I had lain in the wrought-iron bed, listening to the wind murmur over the eaves. The bent-willow chair Mr. Samonds had made years ago had been reduced to a pile of broken sticks. I did not touch them.

When Mr. Quent had finished his work, we had some few hours left, and we spent them together, forgetting what had happened and what was to come and finding solace in each other's company. All too soon dawn approached, and we rose in the gray light to ready ourselves for our respective journeys. When we were done, we still had an hour before the soldiers were to come for him and before Jance would drive me to the village.

"Would you walk with me outside?" he asked, and I took his arm.

The sun had still not risen, but the fog was lifting, and we walked along the top of the ridge under a coral sky. We spoke of small things as we walked, remarking on the song sung by some bird or a flower that caught our eyes. At last we halted by the fallen elf circle.

"Are you well?" he said, his voice low.

I tried to make sense of this question. "How can I be well when we are to travel in opposite directions?"

"It will not be for long. Not more than a half month, I hope."

"I would have counted a minute not long, even an hour. But half of a month! You subscribe to an entirely different definition of *not long* than I do."

I smiled at him, to let him know I was teasing. He smiled as well, but I could not stop trembling.

"Are you cold?" he asked. "You shake so!"

The morning was balmy, and as the eastern horizon turned crimson, I saw the twisted shapes that crowned the rise to the east. No, it was not from cold that I trembled.

I could not bring myself to look at him. "There is something I must tell you. I do not want to, but I must."

Though I was not looking at him, I could hear the frown in his voice. "Your dread is misplaced. You must know you can tell me anything."

"What if it is something so terrible that, once heard, it must harden your heart to me forever?"

"There can be no such thing."

Would it were so! My gaze was drawn again to the east, and after a moment I became aware that I was speaking. The words that fell from my lips seemed hardly my own. I listened to them with an astonishment that could only have matched his.

I spoke of finding the painting in the cellar and what Lanna had said to me there. I spoke also of my encounter with Westen Darendal in my room in the attic and how I had escaped him. Then I spoke once again of the night the children went to the Wyrdwood and how I was certain that the branches that caged them had lifted not because of any wind that blew but because—and only because—I had wished them to do so.

My words ceased. He said nothing in reply. A minute passed, then two. Still he made no answer. At last I could bear the silence no longer. I turned, willing myself to look up at his face and behold the disappointment, the disdain, the anger that must reside there.

The dawn light revealed none of these things. Rather, he wore a look of such sorrow, such regret, and—impossible though it seemed—such tenderness that I could only gasp.

"No," I said, lifting a hand to my throat. "How can you look at me so?"

He took my hand, turned it over, and showered kisses upon my wrist.

"But you despise me now," I said, shaking my head. "You must! Do you not know what I am?" *I am like her!* I wanted to say. *Like Halley Samonds in the wood!* Only my throat tightened around the words.

"I do know," he said, his gaze on me. "I have always known."

I staggered back from him a step. My wonder gave way to dread. "What do you mean you have always known?"

His heavy shoulders, always rounded, slumped even further. "Now I must say something to you, and when I am done it will be you who will turn from me."

I could not look at him. Instead, I watched the brightening horizon as he spoke in low words behind me. It took but the littlest time, no more than the time it took for the sky to go from saffron to crimson at the start of a middling lumenal, for him to alter forever my perception of myself and my history upon the face of this world.

It was not only because of her habit of walking around the Wyrdwood that Merriel Addysen had been labeled a witch. She had had a child but no husband: a girl with wheaten hair and eyes as green as her own.

"I was the child," I said, looking at the silhouettes of the trees. "I was the child in the painting."

"You were," he said behind me.

I looked at him. "Mrs. Quent painted it. She was there, wasn't she? She and Lanna—they found me."

To my surprise, he shook his head. "No, Gennivel was not there that day. We were not married yet. It was Lanna who came upon the scene first, on her way home with the family cow, I can only suppose. I had gone to the wood as soon as the tree on the green began to burn, knowing the others would go there before long. I heard Lanna's cries as I drew near, though by the time I reached the Wyrdwood she had fallen silent. She has never spoken to anyone since."

I thought of the painting, of the details captured by the skilled brush strokes. "No, you're wrong. Lanna *did* speak to someone. She spoke to Mrs. Quent. She must have done so at some point after you took her into service at Heathcrest. How else could Mrs. Quent have known exactly how to paint it—every leaf, every stone?"

His expression was startled for a moment, but slowly he nodded. "I had always thought she simply heard stories in the village. Such tales fascinated her; she was ever eager to hear any accounts of the Rising. Only too late did I understand why! But I wonder . . . No, I believe you must be right."

"So it was you who found me," I said.

Again he nodded. "It was not hard to take you from the scene unnoticed. So fixed were the others on their intention to burn the wood that they never saw you. And had they . . ."

"Had they noticed me, they would have granted me the same fate they did her." I spoke the words coolly. He did not deny them.

"I took you, and brought you back to Heathcrest, and gave you to Mrs. Darendal. However, we both knew you could not stay there, not after what had happened. That you were an innocent child, only three years old, would have meant nothing to some, so great was their rage and their fear. I knew I must find someone else to take you. That is when I thought of—"

"Of my father," I finished for him. "Of your friend, I mean, for he is not my father after all." A coldness wreathed my heart. I felt as I had that day I found my mother lying on the dining-room floor, a sensation that something vital had been excised from me, leaving a hollow inside. Yet she had not been my mother—I had not even had that much to lose!

"I mean your father," he said, taking my shoulders. "For he is your father. Just as Mrs. Lockwell was ever your mother. Do not for a moment think otherwise. They raised you as their own. You *were* their own."

Despite the chill inside me, I nodded. I knew it was true; I had never felt any lack of love from either of you, Father. It was always the contrary. Still, that neither of you had ever told me—no matter all the attention and love I had received—was a bitter truth to learn.

"She lost our brother so soon after he was born," I said, things I knew of my family now altered by this new understanding. "They feared she would never be able to have another child. So you gave them me."

"I had become intimate with your father during the time he spent at Heathcrest as a guest of Earl Rylend's son," he said. "In the time that followed, I had the pleasure of meeting Mrs. Lockwell. I knew they would care for you. And I thought it best that you go to the city, that you be raised away from . . ."

He did not speak the words, but I saw his eyes move to the east, to the old stand of trees.

"Then why?" I said. "Why did you bring me here? Mrs. Darendal tried to discourage you. She told me she did."

He lifted my hand and touched the ring he had placed on my finger. "I did not expect this to happen, if that is what you mean."

"But only to care for the children, then? Surely you could have found another to do *that*!"

"Could I? Could I have found one who would guard them as you would, from all the dangers I knew to be present in this place?" He shook his head. "No, I knew there could be no other, that only *you* would do. And you did not fail me. It is I who have failed you. That I could be worthy of you is impossible—especially now that you know how I have most selfishly used and deceived you."

This time it was he who turned away, and I gazed at the broad expanse of his back.

I will not lie, Father. For a moment I let anger command me. I tremble to even think it now! Had we not been out on the heath but rather in my little room in the attic—had the chair of bent willow been there, I can only think Mr. Quent's fate at that moment would not have been so different from Westen's. I had been a pawn to him, a thing to be used in securing the welfare of the children, with no thought given to my own. I was forever altered. What had been done to me in my time at Heathcrest Hall could never be undone.

Yet I did not wish it to be. For all that had taken place, for all the terrible knowledge I had gained, I did not wish to go back. It was, in the end, better to know the truth than to dwell in ignorance, however blissful.

He stood stiffly, resolutely, like a statue expecting the blow of a hammer. I crossed the distance to him, reached up, and placed a hand on the slope of his shoulder.

"Come to the city as soon as you can," I said. "I will be waiting for you at Whitward Street."

I felt a shudder pass through him. At last he turned around. "I will," he said. "You have my word."

We made our good-byes there on the ridge. I need not recount them to you, Father. While brief and not uttered without regret on both our parts, they were sweet, and I smile even now as I recall them.

Then it was time to go. We did not speak as we returned to the house. There was nothing more to say until such a time when we would be together again, but he caught my hand in his, and we walked that way. As we went, the rising sun transmuted the eastern sky from gold to crimson, and in the dawn light it looked as if the Wyrdwood was on fire.

𝕿HE MAIL COACH is arrived. The innkeeper has taken my satchel downstairs. The ink is not yet dry on these last pages, but I must fold them, no matter how badly they might be smudged, and go down myself, or I will be left to wait for the next coach.

That is something I could not endure! It has been too long since I have seen you all—another twelve hours cannot be suffered. To set eyes upon you, Father, and my sisters is all I crave. It has been weeks since I have gotten a letter from Lily. Sometimes I fear something dreadful has happened. Only that is foolish; I am certain you are quite well. That is, as well as one can be while dwelling under one roof with Mr. Wyble.

In a few hours, I shall see for myself how all of you are faring. Expect to be kissed more than you will probably care for. There! This is the last sentence I will write—I come.

BOOK THREE

# Durrow Street

# CHAPTER FOURTEEN

RAFFERDY HAD BEEN in the city only an hour after returning from his latest trip to Asterlane when a letter arrived for him from Fairhall Street. He had been away far longer than promised; he would present himself for tea that afternoon. This was in no way to be construed as an invitation.

All the way from County Engeldon, Rafferdy had ridden in the coach alone, the curtains drawn to shut out the passing countryside. It had been his intention to do the same upon arriving at his house in Warwent Square, to sit in the darkened parlor with nothing for company save silence and a bottle of whiskey.

However, even as he picked up a pen to decline, his eyes fell upon the parcel of papers he had tossed on the writing desk. One of his father's lawyers had given them to him just before his departure. Rafferdy had yet to untie the black ribbon that bound them—as if that color was not enough for him to know what business they pertained to. His father had been shut up with his lawyers much of late.

*Fashion and the expectations of others are not the only reasons I have chosen to enclose my lands around Asterlane,* Lord Rafferdy had told him. *Soon there may be other needs for the safety of walls. . . .*

Suddenly the dimness of the room became an enemy rather than an ally. He went to the window, threw back the curtains, and let the light of the middle lumenal pour in. Beyond the garden fence, people passed by on the street. He studied them, trying to detect any deviations from the usual scene—any sign, however subtle, that the changes had already begun.

Boys ran with stacks of broadsheets. Ladies in fashionable dresses twirled parasols; young men tipped their hats and smiled.

Rafferdy stepped back from the window. "Lady Marsdel is right," he said aloud. "You *have* been away too long."

He returned to the table and scribbled a note in reply to her ladyship's letter. Then he called for his man.

🍂

THE PASSAGE OF another hour found him leaving his cabriolet on the Promenade and walking up the steps of Lady Marsdel's residence in the New Quarter. His arrival did not go unnoticed; Mrs. Baydon met him before he could reach the door.

"It's been nearly a month, Mr. Rafferdy. I hardly know whether to scold or praise you!"

"I believe I'd prefer the latter, if given a choice."

"The choice is mine to make." She threaded her arm through the crook of his own. "However, I suppose it must be praise, for I'm glad you've come. You are our only hope. None of us is lively, interesting, or articulate enough to suit her ladyship, nor have we been for the past half month. We have been found totally wanting for any engaging qualities, as she often tells us, and she requires real entertainment."

"Does she? How unfortunate that I left my hurdy-gurdy and monkey in Asterlane."

"Please, Mr. Rafferdy. I'm being serious."

He treated her to his most solemn look. "As am I, Mrs. Baydon."

This won a laugh from her; it was the loveliest sound he had heard in a month. He had spent so much time lately with men for whom all words carried weight and value, he had forgotten the pleasure of spending them foolishly.

Less enchanting was the sound of Lady Marsdel calling out his name as they entered the front hall. Amplified by lofty ceilings and marble floors, her voice was an omnipresent thing.

"It seems my husband's aunt has detected your presence."

"Just as any spider detects a fly the moment it enters her web. Come, let's see what's being served for tea."

"You are, of course," Mrs. Baydon said, and took him to the parlor.

For the next quarter hour he was treated to a discourse on his thoughtlessness and negligence of his obligations. He could not simply come and go as he pleased, Lady Marsdel informed him. He was attached to this household, and such an association carried benefits as well as duties; he could not enjoy the one without performing the other. He had been very lax in this regard. She did not want to hear that others required him; no one could possibly require him any more than she did.

Rafferdy bore this all indulgently, even fondly. Would that Lady Marsdel did have a higher claim! At least then he would know what was expected of him and that he was capable of it.

"Well, then, sit down," she said when she had finished. "Tell us of your trip to Asterlane. You must have much to relate for how long you were gone. What amusing things did you do? Spare us no details."

"I'm afraid I did nothing amusing whatsoever." He sat at the table with Mr. and Mrs. Baydon and took a cup of tea.

Lord Baydon laughed, manufacturing another chin in the process. "Nothing amusing? You'll not make us believe *that,* Mr. Rafferdy."

"It's impossible to make someone believe anything, Lord Baydon. Rather, they must *want* to believe it. Yet it's the truth. I have spent the last month helping my father with his business."

Lady Marsdel flicked her fan. "How is my cousin of late? He does not write to me often enough, and he says little of substance when he does. I cannot imagine what could possibly occupy him so."

Nor could Rafferdy. His father's illness had all but made a cripple of him, yet he shut himself in his study every day, working endlessly on papers and letters, often receiving visitors—and not only his lawyers. Other men came at all hours to call on him, even in the depths of a greatnight. Some were agents of the king, Rafferdy knew, and some soldiers. However, there were others whose allegiance he could not guess.

Lord Rafferdy never said who the men were or what their business was, and Rafferdy never asked—not for fear that his father would once again refuse to tell him but rather for fear that this time he would, that he would speak again of what lay beyond the light. Their conversations instead pertained to the affairs of the estate and the building of the walls around it.

For most of the month, Rafferdy had helped oversee the construction of the walls and had managed the removal of those tenants (legal and otherwise) from the lands that were to be enclosed. There were many days he rode back to Asterlane after his duties were finished and drank himself into blindness.

Not that it mattered. Even when his eyes were shut he could see their faces, could recall their expressions as they looked a final time on the crofts and cottages they were being made to abandon.

*Stop looking at them like that!* he sometimes wanted to shout. *Can't you see that they're hovels, not palaces?*

He had thought it would be a difficult job. Instead, it was easy. The notices were drawn up and delivered; the evictions preceded in an orderly manner and without protest. He bested his father's estimates of how long the proceedings would take by over a quarter month. It was terrible work.

"I asked you a question, Mr. Rafferdy. Is it your manners or your hearing that you've lost? I said, how is my cousin?"

Rafferdy looked up from his tea. "He is well. He cannot get about so well as he used to, of course, but he is well."

*Endures,* he might have said, rather than *is well*. It was as if he was holding on for something. However, this little amount of news appeared to satisfy her. She traded the fan for her puff of a dog, fussed with the ribbons atop its head, and expounded on the awful weather in the city and how there was no telling what sort of wretched humors were rising off the river.

"But it must be worse for those closest to the Anbyrn, I am sure," Mrs. Baydon said.

"No, I am sure that cannot be," Lady Marsdel said. "It is the very nature of the most noxious vapors to rise upward. Which means we are at the greatest risk of breathing them here in the New Quarter."

"I agree with her ladyship," Rafferdy said, standing and moving to the window. He looked toward the Citadel and the twin spires that surmounted the Halls of Assembly. "Indeed, I am quite sure the atmosphere grows more poisonous the higher up one goes in Invarel."

"I am sure you are right!" Lady Marsdel said. "Yet I can only suppose you are making some sort of joke, Mr. Rafferdy, as you always do."

He turned from the window. "No, not in the least. I agree, it is unusually hot in the city, and if you feel you are suffering any ill effects from the weather, I urge you to depart for your house at Farland Park. Your health is not something to put at risk, your ladyship."

She could not argue with this. All the same, she regarded him down the length of her nose. "I say, you've grown very serious in your absence, Mr. Rafferdy."

"If so, can you claim you are disappointed? I was previously given the impression that everyone wished me to be more serious."

"What I wish, Mr. Rafferdy, is to be provided with engaging company, and you have provided very little so far."

"Then perhaps it was a mistake to invite me. I shall go at once."

The dog was removed, the fan returned and snapped open. "I shan't let you off that easily, Mr. Rafferdy. Return to your seat, and I do not care if it is the latest fashion to be grim—make yourself lively!"

Rafferdy bowed and returned to the table; her first command at least he could obey.

"It seems everyone is serious these days," Lord Baydon said, his hands clasped over the expanse of his waistcoat. "I suppose it's only natural. Young people always do the opposite of what I expect them to do. I imagine they must want only to frolic and go to balls, and so necessarily they slouch about and speak in glum detail about diseases and politics."

Mr. Baydon set down his copy of *The Comet*. "I suppose that statement is directed at me."

"Being my only child, you are chief among the young people I know. But I have observed this same seriousness in others."

"And why should we not be serious?" Mr. Baydon said, tapping a finger against the broadsheet. PLOT TO SET FIRE TO ASSEMBLY SENDS THREE TO GALLOWS, read the headline. "When some are serious in their desire to harm the very foundations of our civilization, the rest of us must be serious in our resolve to stop them. What else can we do to alleviate this situation?"

"Stop reading the broadsheets, for one," Rafferdy said.

This won a frown from Mr. Baydon, but Lady Marsdel cried, "Hear, hear, Mr. Rafferdy. It's the fault of those awful newspapers that we have all these bandits and rebels running this way and that. If the broadsheets stopped publishing so many articles telling people what they don't have, they might find themselves content with what they *do* have and not seize upon this foolish desire to stir things up."

Rafferdy nodded in her direction. "Ignorance is bliss, you mean to say. You may well be right. However, I would also say that it is natural for a man to wish to improve his lot."

"Rubbish. There is nothing natural about it. True contentment comes from knowing one's place in the world, Mr. Rafferdy. Mark my words—wanting something different can lead only to misery."

He thought of the people he had driven from the grounds of

Asterlane, of their dull, silent faces and their bawling children. "What if one's place *is* a miserable one?"

"What misery could *your* place possibly cause you, Mr. Rafferdy? I am sure there are many who would readily trade with you."

Of that he had no doubt.

After this, Lord Baydon began an exposition on his firm belief that everyone was worried about the current state of affairs for no reason at all and that everything should work out pleasantly for everyone in the end. As he spoke, Rafferdy rose and returned to the window, gazing outside. A minute later, Mrs. Baydon came to join him.

"Well, that certainly enlivened things," she murmured. "Though I'm not sure that's the sort of entertainment my aunt was hoping for."

"It was not my intention to entertain," he replied in a low voice.

"On the contrary, Mr. Rafferdy, it's always your intention to entertain. Though I will say my aunt is right—you do have a more sober air about you. You still make jests, but they are not so light as before. Not that I would say this new demeanor doesn't become you. I used to think you only really good-looking when you smiled, but your face has changed. I've never seen you look so well. Seriousness suits you." She leaned against the windowsill and gazed out. "Still, it couldn't harm you to laugh a bit. Why don't you go to a party? I'm sure you have a mountain of invitations waiting."

"What reason is there for me to go to a party?"

"What reason do you think? To have a pleasant time, to enjoy yourself. Besides, you never know when you might meet someone."

"I am quite certain that the only person I would wish to meet will never be at any of the parties for which I've received invitations."

She bit her lip and glanced at him. Across the room, Lord Baydon rambled on. These were the best of times, he declared; they should all laugh next year to think they had complained when they looked back to see how grand everything really was.

"So you no longer attempt to disguise it, then," Mrs. Baydon said to him. "You cared for Miss Lockwell."

He returned her gaze. What need had he to dissemble when circumstance had removed any possibility of impropriety—indeed, any chance at all of ever seeing her again? "I do care for her. I will make no apology for it—save if I were to ever make it to her."

"But you cannot really mean that. Her family is so low!"

"And what of Miss Everaud's family, which was purported to be so high?"

She flinched at these words, and he could not say that had not been his intention. It had been over two months since his engagement to Miss Everaud, entered into at the encouragement of his father, had been broken off at the urging of the same.

The particulars were still unknown to Rafferdy. There had been intimations about Lord Everaud, soon echoed by rumor, and finally given form in an article in *The Messenger*. Even then, exactly what had happened was not clear. There was talk of money being sent to the Principalities, not as part of any legal kind of trade, and of communications delivered by Murghese couriers bearing a seal in the shape of a hawk.

While no charges were filed, opinion convicted more certainly than any evidence that could be presented in a court. Immediately upon publication of the article, the Everauds retreated from society in Invarel and returned to their home in the south of Altania. Now they were gone from there, to where no one could say for certain, though most believed they had fled across the sea. It was whispered that Miss Everaud was already married to a Murghese prince and now went about clad head to toe in veils.

There was real anguish on her face. "Mr. Rafferdy, you must know that I . . . that is, if I had known, if I had even suspected, I never would have—"

"I know, Mrs. Baydon," he said, softening his tone. "You are and ever have been my friend. But I have your aunt to judge me, and she does so quite well on her own. I do not think she requires your assistance."

She smiled, as he had intended, but then a sigh escaped her. She looked again out the window, touching the gold locket at her throat. "I will not deny that *she* is worthy of you, if not her relations. And liking someone can never be wrong, not when the object is so deserving in every way of being liked. I truly enjoyed Miss Lockwell's company. I think we might have been—no, I will say that we *were*—friends." She looked at him again. "Yet surely you know . . . for you two to ever be together . . . it would have to be a very different world than this one. You must concede it is true, Mr. Rafferdy."

He glanced back at the table, where Mr. Baydon had resumed reading his broadsheet, and saw the large words printed beneath the headline. *'A New Altania Comes,' Traitor Warns From Gallows.*

"Yes, on that point I agree with you," he said.

He led Mrs. Baydon back to the table, and after that he spent the rest of the afternoon attempting to entertain her ladyship.

# CHAPTER FIFTEEN

OF ALL THE large and influential trading companies in the Grand City of Invarel, there was none so hulking in its largeness, so overwhelming in its influencing effects, as Sadent, Mornden, & Bayle. Just as all water in the city flowed into the River Anbyrn before it was allowed to pass down to the sea, there was not a segment of commerce in Altania, from the least business to the most lucrative investments, that did not flow at least in part through the halls of Sadent, Mornden, & Bayle. However, it was not upon a tide of water that this commerce was carried, like ships upon the river, but rather on a steady and ceaseless flow of ink.

On any given day inside the main hall of the trading company, the sound of pens scratching against paper far exceeded the buzzing in any hive of bees, and while it was not honey being extracted by their activity, it was something even more sweet to the tastes of men.

Two long tables stretched the entire length of the hall, a row of clerks seated on stools on each side. So closely were the clerks arranged that the slightest movement to the right or left might cause one's arm to come in contact with his neighbor's. This would elicit a complaint from the one jostled, especially if by the action his pen had been made to jump or skitter.

At Sadent, Mornden, & Bayle, clerks were paid by the page, and mistakes were not tolerated. If one smudged the last row of figures at the bottom of the sheet, it must be thrown away and a fresh one started, and the clerk's pay would be docked for the cost of the wasted paper and ink. Thus they worked with shoulders hunched in, spines curved, and heads bent, pens scratching as they recorded transactions, documented trades, and tallied rows of figures that, if placed end to end, would stretch longer than the River Anbyrn itself.

As the clerks around him labored, Eldyn Garritt set down his pen and flexed his stiff fingers. Holding the quill for hours on end had formed them into a permanent curl, and the tips were stained black—just as they had been that night at the village of Hayrick Cross, when he broke the message tube he had been carrying for Westen and threw it in the blacksmith's face.

Eldyn grimaced at the memory. Sometimes, as he worked, he wished there was a way that mistakes could be blotted from his life, like the way the ink from the broken vial had blotted out the treasonous missive inside the tube. However, while a mistake might be crossed out, it could never really be removed. Even if the parchment was scoured with sand, traces of incriminating pigment would remain. The sheet could only be thrown away—and Eldyn had no wish to be disposed of just yet.

Besides, perhaps time could do what ink could not. *I am not finished with you,* Westen had said that night when Eldyn told him he would carry no more messages for him. However, in the half year since, Eldyn had not seen the highwayman. He had come to collect neither his hundred regals nor Eldyn himself. It was as if he had faded from the world, like words on a sheet of paper left too long in the sun, which became more ghostly with each passing day, until all trace of them was gone.

Then again, tincture of gall might be applied to faded ink to darken it, and Eldyn could not help but wonder if turning a page might bring some new, unpleasant chapter into view. Sighing, he rubbed his aching right hand with his left, trying to force the blood back into it.

"What are you doing, Garritt?" said the clerk who sat across the table from him. He was about Eldyn's age, and his name was Tems Chumsferd, though everyone called him Chubbs for his thick neck and thick fingers.

"I have a cramp in my hand," Eldyn said. His fingers were tingling now with a thousand pinpricks as blood seeped back into them.

"Well, you'll have a cramp in your head soon if you don't get back to work. Whackskuller's coming this way."

Eldyn winced. Mr. Waxler was the head clerk at Sadent, Mornden, & Bayle. He spent the days patrolling up and down the tables, examining the work of each clerk over their shoulders. He carried a wooden baton—about two feet long, slender but sturdy—with which he would reach and tap against a page to point out an error or smudge. However, if a clerk made too many errors, it was not the paper that would receive a tap but rather the back of the clerk's head—and none too gently. Eldyn had received such correction more than once in his first weeks on the job.

"Here he comes," Chubbs muttered. He dipped his pen in the inkwell the two shared between them and bent back over his sheet of figures.

Eldyn picked up his own pen and continued his work, forming precise columns of numbers. The sound of Mr. Waxler's footsteps approached; these were distinguished by a case of dropfoot on the right side. The footsteps drew closer: *clump*-CLOMP, *clump*-CLOMP. Eldyn dipped his pen and wrote as swiftly as he could, not lifting his eyes from the paper before him.

The footsteps ceased.

"Mr. Garritt," said a thin voice behind him, "were you not working on this very same page the last time I passed by?"

Eldyn craned his head to look at the hawk-nosed man standing behind him. The clerks around him scribbled furiously.

"I believe I had just started it, sir," he said. "And I am now very near to the end. Nor are there any mistakes."

Mr. Waxler's eyes narrowed as he made an examination of the paper. His face was flat and dotted with moles, like a piece of gray paper speckled with ink. "No, I see no mistakes, and your writing is very pretty, Mr. Garritt. However, I would prefer that it were swifter and more economical. Why the long ascender here, or the needless flourish there?" The tip of his baton rapped against the page. "Ink is the lifeblood of Altania, Mr. Garritt. It should not be squandered. I am docking your wages ten pennies today for waste. Now continue your work."

The head clerk moved on—*clump*-CLOMP—and Eldyn bent his head back over the page, letting out a sigh as he did.

"Be glad, Garritt," Chubbs whispered. "You got off easy."

"So you say," Garritt whispered back. "It does not seem so easy to me." Ten pennies was a fifth of his daily wages. He had hoped to go home at a decent hour today, but he would have to work an extra half shift to make up for the lost pay. A normal shift was ten hours, but those who wished for it could work an additional five. However, not many clerks chose to do so, for as one grew tired, one made more mistakes, and an unlucky clerk could end up owing more in docked wages for spoiled paper and wasted ink than he earned in the second shift. However, these days Eldyn rarely made mistakes, and he usually took the extra work to earn another twenty-five pennies—though he hated to leave Sashie alone for so long.

Chubbs tapped his pen against the edge of the well, then started a new sheet. "Well, just be glad you still have a job."

Eldyn did not reply. Despite its size, the hall was stuffy and rank with the fumes of ink and of clerks who did not bathe as regularly as they should. Only a dim light leaked from the oil lamps above, but if one wanted more illumination, one had to purchase a candle from the head clerk at an exorbitant price. Eldyn always made do with what light there was, even though his eyes often ached and by the end of a second shift were so blurred and sore he could hardly see. Sometimes, if the day was very dark, Chubbs bought a candle; at such times, Eldyn was grateful for what little extra light fell upon his own page.

Despite all this, Eldyn *was* glad for the job. After weeks of going to every trading and banking house in the city in search of a clerking position, he had found nothing. Everywhere he went, the tables were already filled. As the last of his funds dwindled, he had feared he would have to take work as a common laborer. Even then, how would he earn enough to sustain him and Sashie?

Desperate, he had gone again to Sadent, Mornden, & Bayle, which he had visited twice before. His luck would have been no better than on those first two tries; however, just as Mr. Waxler was telling him there were no open positions, a small gray-haired clerk nearby let out a moan and toppled backward from his stool. By the time they picked him up off the floor, he was stone dead.

Mr. Waxler had said nothing, only nodding to the empty stool. The pen was prized from the dead clerk's hand and given to Eldyn. Eldyn sat in the empty place at the table, dipped the pen, and set it against the page, continuing exactly where the old clerk had left off. And that was how he gained his position at Sadent, Mornden, & Bayle.

At last the primary shift ended. Most of the clerks rose and shuffled toward the doors to collect their wages from the paymaster. Eldyn dipped his pen again and kept writing.

"Staying for the second shift again, are you?" Chubbs said, his round face puckering in a frown. "I don't know how you do it, Garritt. My hand is numb as stone, and my eyes feel like they've been bathed in ink and jabbed with a quill. Take care you don't ruin yourself. If you lose your hands or your eyes, Whackskuller will give your place to someone else."

"I'm fine," Eldyn said. "Good night, Chubbs."

The other man sighed. "Good night, Garritt. Next lumenal, then." He went with the large portion of the clerks out the door while Eldyn, along with a few others, remained at the tables.

For a moment Eldyn paused. He was tempted to rise and follow Chubbs outside; his hand hurt, and he wanted to leave this dismal place. However, he had already been docked part of his pay today, and his salary barely covered his expenses as it was. He needed the extra work if he wanted to save anything for his and Sashie's future.

Eldyn dipped his pen again, tapping it carefully to remove the excess ink, then continued working as the sky turned to gray outside the high windows.

❧

ƁY THE TIME he left the trading house, the brief twilight had given way to the start of an umbral that, according to the table printed on the front page of *The Fox,* was to be thirteen hours. The day had failed more quickly than he had expected, and toward the end of the shift he had been forced to buy a candle for five pennies. He rued the expense, but it was worth it to finish the half shift.

At this hour, the streets of the Old City were still well populated, and he walked without fear to the tiny apartment he had rented for Sashie and himself. The apartment was not far past Duskfellow's graveyard, down a drab lane, tucked in the rafters above a shoe-maker's shop. It was the third place they had dwelled since the night they had fled from Westen.

He still could not recall that terrible umbral without a shudder. After discovering that Mr. Sarvinge and Mr. Grealing were swindlers and had made off with his money, he had run all the way from Inslip Lane back to the Golden Loom. There he stuffed their few possessions in a sack, tossed a few coins on the table to cover the last week of rent, then—without stopping to offer a word of explanation to Mr. Walpert or a farewell to his daughter—he dragged his sister into the night. Sashie had protested, complaining she did not want to go. However, he promised her he was taking her somewhere better, some-where with softer beds and finer chairs—somewhere more fitting her station—and at last she acquiesced.

Having made such a promise, he had no choice but to take her to an establishment in Gauldren's Heights, and perhaps it was just as well. Being a respectable inn, it had a man always on duty at the door, and as long as they did not go outside he was fairly certain Westen could not molest them there.

All the same, soft as the beds were, he found little sleep at that inn and spent many wakeful hours gazing out through a gap in the cur-tains, watching the street below, dreading to see a tall, golden-maned form prowling up to the inn. That Westen meant to collect his hun-dred regals, Eldyn was certain. Just as he was certain that money alone would not be enough to satisfy him.

Despite Eldyn's fears, he saw nothing. Still, after only three days he had no choice but to move them again, or else the exorbitant rent would quickly make paupers of them. They spent the next three weeks at a boardinghouse in a dilapidated corner of the Old City. By then he had been down to his last regals, and it was all he could afford.

The place was frightening. Their room was a dank cell with no glazing over the window, only iron bars and a rotted shutter. There was a bed, but the thing was so infested with vermin that they leaned it in a corner and slept on a pair of wooden benches instead. He used one of the tattered blankets he had scrounged as a curtain to close off half of the room for Sashie's privacy, but it was hardly needed; they slept in their clothes, for the place was damp and cold.

The only advantage of the boardinghouse was that there was little chance of Sashie venturing out while he was gone and encountering Westen; she was terrified to leave the room. Especially at night, the boardinghouse was filled with moans, hard laughter, and often the distant sound of screaming. They kept the door bolted at all times, and Sashie would admit him only upon seeing his face through a crack in the door.

The other advantage was that he doubted Westen would think to look for them in such a wretched place. Whether that was the case or not, he saw no sign of the highwayman during the three awful weeks they spent there. At last, when they were down to their final pennies, Eldyn had obtained the position at Sadent, Mornden, & Bayle. He had removed Sashie from the boardinghouse at once and had let the small apartment over the shoemaker's shop.

Nor was it a moment too soon. The next week, in one of the broadsheets, he read how a fire had swept through that very same boardinghouse, killing more than a dozen of its residents who could not escape their rooms. He had not told Sashie.

In the months since, he had sometimes wondered if he should move them again. Westen might find them if they remained in one place for too long. However, as the weeks went by and he saw no sign of the highwayman, his dread lessened. He began to think it likely that Westen was no longer in the city. Perhaps he had even been shot and killed by soldiers or one of his would-be victims, though Eldyn was fairly certain he would have read about such an incident in the broadsheets.

Besides, Eldyn did not want to make Sashie move again. Nor did he think he could find them a better place given his current salary. As the weeks became months, he had even begun to think Westen had forgotten about them. Surely the highwayman had other schemes and concerns to occupy his attention. And what was a hundred regals to *him*? He had only to rob another coach to earn thrice that.

Leaving the busier thoroughfares behind, Eldyn walked among the shadows of Cowper's Lane, climbed the back stairs to their apartment, and unlocked the door.

"There you are!" Sashie gasped as he entered, rising from her seat by the little window that looked out over the street. "I didn't see you come up the street. Though I don't know how I didn't see you. I've sat here for hours and hours staring out."

He grimaced. Out of habit, he must have unwittingly woven the shadows around himself as he walked along the lane.

"I expected you hours ago," she said, without giving him a moment to speak. "I was on the verge of going out to look for you."

Alarm filled him. "You know you aren't to go out alone. Not in this part of the city. It isn't—"

"I don't care what it is. You can't keep me shut up in here. The sound of hammering comes right through the floor. You don't hear it—the shop is closed by the time you come home—but I hear it all day, every day, for hours and hours. They pound on the shoes, pound, *pound*." She lifted her hands to her temples. "It's driving me mad."

He moved to her. "I'm sorry, dearest. I know it's hard to be here alone. But my free day is soon; I'll take you out. We can go for a walk along the Promenade. Or I'll take you to Gauldren's Heights. We'll go to one of the shops Uphill and buy you a new dress."

"I don't need another dress," she said, pawing at the pale blue frock she wore, which he had bought her with a full three days' wages. She looked very pretty in it despite her anguish. "What need have I of dresses in *here* where no one can see me?"

He winced as she flung these words at him. It had distressed him at the Golden Loom when she refused to speak to him, but he was not certain her new manner was an improvement. For a time, after they moved here, she had been so grateful to leave the boardinghouse that she had been a meek, even docile thing, showering him with kisses each time he returned home. However, that appreciation had not lasted, and over the last months her tongue had grown increasingly sharp.

"I need to go out," she cried, then her anger became pleading. "Please, dear brother, please take me out. I'm so lonely here, I cannot bear it!"

Sobbing, she flung herself into his arms, and he could not say this did not please him. He held her close, petted her, and murmured little things to soothe her: how one day soon she would put on her prettiest dress, and he would take her out to the grandest street for all the world to see, and they would sit in the window of the most fashionable shop and have cakes and tea.

"Why can I not go out tomorrow?" she sobbed against his gray coat. He tried not to worry that her tears might ruin it, for he had only recently bought it.

"You know it is not proper for a young lady of worth to go out alone," he said, gently chiding.

Yet it was more than that, for how could she be trusted? Sashie was a sweet and impressionable creature. Despite all of Eldyn's admonitions, what would happen if she were to encounter *him* on the street? A few pretty words from *him,* and all Eldyn's warnings might be forgotten in an instant.

"Soon," he promised her again. "I will take you out soon."

She nodded but said nothing, and pushed away from him. He noted that her face was not at all wet with tears, and his coat was unspoiled. She returned again to her seat by the window, listless now that her outburst had subsided, and gazed out into the night.

Eldyn went to the nook behind a curtain that served for his bedchamber and carefully hung his new coat on a chair. He poured water into a bowl, splashed some on his face, then regarded himself in the scrap of mirror. He had gotten very pale for lack of sun, and these days his shoulders, like his fingers, were habitually curled. He made an effort to force them back, then stepped around the curtain.

"Is there anything to eat?" he asked softly.

Her eyes still on the window, Sashie made a vague gesture toward the table. There, beneath a cloth, he found a cold pork pie and a plate of stewed apples. A woman came in regularly to do the cooking and cleaning, for Sashie could not be compelled to do anything. While Eldyn sometimes fretted at the cost, he did not regret it at that moment, for he was fiercely hungry. He sat, poured himself a cup of thin red wine, then ate until there was not a speck of food left. Belatedly, he wondered if Sashie had supped.

"You have already eaten, haven't you, dearest?"

"I have no appetite," she replied. "I am going to bed."

She rose, crossed to him, and brushed her cool lips across his cheek; then she went to the door of the little antechamber that served for her private room.

"Would you mind, then?" Eldyn said, swallowing. "That is, if you are retiring, would you be disappointed if I went out?"

His sister shrugged, then went into her room. The sound of the latch being drawn was loud amid the silence.

Eldyn winced, but if she was going to shut herself in her room, what use was there in staying here? He retrieved his coat, made certain his hair was arranged, then left the apartment, locking the door behind him.

&

ELDYN HAD NOT meant to come here.

He had thought to go to the old church of St. Adaris, to gaze at the statue of the martyr St. Andelthy, and then perhaps venture to the Sword and Leaf. If the sight of an angel did not lift his spirits, perhaps a cup of the devil's brew would. However, the route from Cowper's Lane to the corner of the Old City where St. Adaris stood took him across Durrow Street. The theaters were just opening for the night, and light and chiming music filled the air.

Eldyn meant to cross the street and continue on. Only then he passed a young man in a powdered wig and a red coat standing on a corner. Tiny birds the color of jewels flitted about the other's head and alighted on his hands. Sometimes they vanished in a flash, then reappeared moments later, opening their throats to emit a sweet trilling music.

"Do you want to come in?" the young man said, his lips, as red as his coat, parting in a smile. One of the birds flew from his hand and into the open door of the theater. Eldyn realized he had been staring. "It's only a quarter regal to enter."

Eldyn shook his head. "I don't have that much money with me." He had brought ten pennies—just enough to buy a pot of punch. A quarter regal was half a day's wages! He started to move away.

"Are you certain you don't have enough?" the young man said. "Why don't you check your pockets?"

Eldyn gaped, not understanding.

The other laughed. "Would you like me to check them for you?"

Now Eldyn did understand, and he blushed. He reached into his coat pockets, thinking to turn them out so the young man would leave him alone.

His left hand came out with a silver coin.

Eldyn turned the coin over in his fingers. The two sides caught the shimmering light in alternation: first the sun, then the moon, then the sun again. He had forgotten about the coin; he must have put it in his pocket when he traded the old coat for this new and had not thought of it since. Now he recalled that night at the Sword and Leaf and how the pretty young woman had given it to him. Only she hadn't been a woman at all.

Eldyn looked up at the other, startled. The young illusionist smiled.

"You need no other token than that," he said, taking the coin from Eldyn's hand. "Why did you not show it to me sooner? You are an honored guest here at the Theater of the Doves! Come inside, come inside."

And before Eldyn could think to resist, the young man led him through the doors of the theater, into the dimness beyond.

# CHAPTER SIXTEEN

$\mathcal{I}$T WAS EARLY, and the gates were not yet open.

Ivy paced on the street, pausing every few moments to look through the iron bars to see if anyone was coming. The narrow yard was empty, the building beyond silent.

She had left Whitward Street in the dark, but the lumenal was to be brief, and the air had already gone gray by the time the hack cab dropped her off at the end of a shabby lane in Lowpark. Elsewhere in the city, the buildings crowded against one another, jostling and vying to occupy a sliver of the high ground above the river. However, here the various structures shrank away from the gray edifice at the end of the lane, leaving a void around its walls.

Again Ivy peered through the bars, but she saw no one. It had been five days since her return to the city, and waiting this long to see her father had been unbearable. However, she had been given no choice; these gates opened to visitors only once each quarter month. All the same, she would wait not a moment longer than she had to and so had come early, to be here as the gates were unlocked.

Not far beyond the city's edge, a rooster called out. A ray of sunlight sidled down the lane, and though it seemed to shun the colorless stones, it set ablaze a bronze plaque on the wall. In contrast to the rust-specked bars, the plaque was polished to a sheen. The words inscribed on it read: *THE MADDERLY-STONEWORTH HOSTEL FOR THE DERANGED*. Not that anyone in Invarel called the building by that name. If one ever had the misfortune to come to this place, it was said of them only, "They're up at Madstone's now."

A groan of metal startled Ivy. Dazzled by the sunlight off the plaque, she had not seen as a man approached the gate. Or perhaps she had not seen him because he wore a suit the same color (or, rather, similarly lacking in color) as the walls of the building. The man withdrew a large key from the lock, then pushed the gate partway open.

Ivy managed to draw a breath. "I'm here to see my—"

"I can deduce who you're here to see."

She shook her head, too puzzled to reply.

"Only the newest ones get visitors," he said, fitting the large key back onto the ring at his belt. "That's how I knew. Come this way, Miss . . . ?"

"Mrs. Quent," she said, and followed him through the gate.

Ivy did not discover the man's name, but as they entered the building she learned that he was the day warden at the hostel and that he had been in the position for twenty years. His face was neither cheerful nor sorrowful, weary nor curious; indeed, it bore little expression at all.

They reached a door. A pair of large men in gray smocks stood to either side; their necks were brutish, the backs of their hands thick with coarse hair.

"It is best if you do not look into the cells," the day warden said, pulling another large key from the ring and fitting it into the door. "Walk directly behind me, and keep to the center of the corridor. Do not stray toward the bars. Above all, do not respond to anything you might hear. Do not nod, do not glance, do not speak in reply no matter what is directed toward you. Do you understand, Miss . . . ?"

"Mrs. Quent," she gasped, but the day warden had already opened the door and passed through. She hurried after. He shut and locked the door behind them, then started down a corridor.

It was dim, as she had imagined it would be, and the air was oppressive with foul scents, as she had also imagined and for which she had prepared herself. It was the noise she had not expected.

The sound assaulted her at once: a tumult of shouts, of keening, of laughter, of howls and groans, moans and grunts, and wordless jabberings whose purpose or cause—or even the very mechanism by which they were formed and uttered—she could not begin to guess. The clamor echoed and reechoed off the arched ceiling, doubling, trebling, cementing itself into a wall of sound as solid, as imprisoning, as any structure of stone.

Ivy halted, stunned for a moment by the din, but the day warden had kept moving. He was already several paces ahead, and she started after him. As she did, arms snaked out between the bars to either side.

So narrow was the corridor that only by walking in the very middle could she avoid their reach.

Remembering the day warden's admonitions, she kept her gaze fixed on his back. All the same, out of the corners of her eyes, she was aware of forms huddling or writhing in the dimness beyond the bars. Nor could she prevent herself from hearing the things that were screamed or wailed or hissed as she passed—terrible things, the imploring no less so than the violent. They would give her anything if she would help; they would slit her throat if she would not. They could see through her skin; she was gray as ash inside. She should strike the warden down and take his keys; she was an angel and must do the work God had sent her here to do—she must set fire to this place.

At last the day warden turned down a side passage. This was narrower and lined not by open cells but rather by shut doors, each with a small iron plate set into it. The cacophony did not fade, but it lessened a bit, such that Ivy could hear the day warden when he said, "Here it is—Number Twenty-Nine-Thirty-Seven. Violent fits and hallucinations alternating with periods of profound catatonia."

Ivy stared at him. "Do you not know his name?"

"We find it is better to catalog our patients according to the order of their arrival, as well as the nature of their affliction."

"But how can you help a person if you do not know who he is?"

"It is not people we are here to help but rather their conditions. It is not the patient that is important but rather the symptoms he or she manifests." The warden's face, previously impassive, became animated. "By setting aside consideration of the person and reserving all attention for the affliction, we can reach a purer understanding of the essence of the malady and can examine it impartially, without any distraction. It is the latest medical technique. We are a very modern facility, as I'm sure you will agree, Miss . . . ?"

"Mrs. Quent," she whispered, her throat tight.

But he had already turned his back to her. He slid the iron plate in the door to one side, revealing a window—or a hole, rather, too small to put even a hand through.

"You're in luck," he said, peering inside. "The subject appears to be awake." He stepped away from the door and motioned for her to approach.

"Can I not enter?"

"That's quite impossible. We can't allow anything that could interfere with the subject while he is in the initial stages of observation. It might contaminate his behavior and thus lead to a misunderstanding of the nature of his affliction."

These words were a blow. Ivy could not believe it was observation he needed. All the same, observe him she must, to see for herself that he was, if not well, at least alive. She drew a breath and peered through the opening in the door.

Shock struck her anew. "He is bound! But why?"

"It is for his own well-being that he is restrained. He was very agitated when he was brought to us."

*Of course he was agitated,* Ivy wanted to cry out. He had been removed from his home, separated from his family, forced beyond the door through which he had not set foot in over ten years. If he had struggled, then it had been only as anyone struggles when subjected against their will to pain and terror. However, she did not say these things; they would be wasted upon the day warden. She made herself become calm. If he saw her face in the opening, then she wanted it to be the familiar and reassuring thing he knew. Again, she approached the door.

"Hello, Father!" she called out softly. "It is your daughter—it's Ivy."

If Mr. Lockwell heard her, he did not show it. He sat slumped in a chair, which was the only object in the room and to which he was bound by strips of cloth around the chest, the wrists, the ankles. His hair was matted against his skull, and he had not been shaven. His face was slack and drooping; his eyes stared without focus.

Ivy wanted to weep; instead, she affected a cheerful tone. "I've come back to the city, and I won't be leaving again. You needn't worry about Lily and Rose. They are well, though they miss you very much. We all miss you. And I have news to tell you—such wonderful news." It seemed he lifted his head a bit, and this heartened her. "I'm Mrs. Quent now. Are you surprised? No more than I am, Father. He will be coming to the city soon, and when he does we will all dwell together and be happier than you can imagine. So do not worry. In no time at all you will leave this place and come to live with—"

The day warden slid the iron plate shut so quickly she barely had time to step back to avoid losing part of her nose.

"Telling the subject lies is not to be tolerated," he said. "It can only reinforce his delusions."

"Lies?" she gasped. "What lies have I told him?"

"That he will leave here anytime soon is impossible. His derangement is of the severest nature. You must not give him hope."

"How can it harm him to have hope? Why should he not believe that he is leaving here, that he is going home?"

He shook his head. "I can see your cousin was right to have your father consigned to us. I only hope it is not too late. He told me that he suspected the subject's delusions had been reinforced by his family for years—an intelligent man, your cousin. It is a sad fact that often, in the desire to aid, the subject's intimate relations only inflict more harm. You do not seem to understand that your father is a very ill man, Miss—what was it?"

This time it was *her* voice that rang off the hard ceiling. "My name is Mrs. Quent!"

The day warden's eyes narrowed as he regarded her, then he nodded. However, all he said was, "You may come back next quarter month if you wish." Then he turned and started back down the corridor.

Ivy cast one last glance at the shut door, then followed after the warden, back toward the screams and the laughter.

🍂

SHE RETURNED TO Whitward Street to find it as silent as the hostel had been cacophonous, and in its way as oppressive. Fearing the housekeeper or her husband would be lurking in the kitchen, she hurried up the stairs. As she passed the parlor she heard Mr. Wyble call out to her in greeting. Her every instinct was to keep climbing, but as they were required to dwell with him for a short while longer, she knew she must be civil with him. She stopped in the door of the parlor but did not go in.

"I know why you were going upstairs so quickly," he said. He sat in a chair by the window, a book open on his lap.

"You do?" she said, wondering if he had at last come to apprehend the grievous blow he had struck to them all.

"Indeed," he said cheerfully. "It is my job as a lawyer to understand the motivations of others. You are aware it is not your day to have the parlor, and so you were concerned that entering to greet me might make it appear as if you had a wish to spend time in here. Out of propriety, so there could be no misconstruing, you thought to hurry past. You are very conscientious, cousin, but we are family. You need not be *so* formal. If you would like to come in and sit for a quarter hour, I should hardly mind it at all."

Ivy gripped the door frame to steady herself. "Thank you for your offer, but I must see to my sisters." Without waiting for a reply, she turned and dashed up the stairs.

She found them in Rose's room. Lily was tearing off the ribbons from one of her gowns, while Rose sat by the window, Miss Mew on her lap.

Ivy took off her bonnet. "I saw Father," she said. "He is very—" She thought of the day warden, of what he had said about telling lies to appease. But, no—she would not hold anything *he* had said in regard. "He is very well. You must not worry for him, and remember what I said: Mr. Quent will be coming to the city soon. When he does, he will bring Father to us, and we will all live together."

Rose said nothing, only continuing to pet the tortoiseshell cat, while Lily swore an oath.

"I can't undo this knot. It's ruined, the whole frock is ruined. Not that it matters. No one will ever see me in it anyway!" She crumpled up the dress, then stood and brushed past Ivy. "I'm going to my room."

A moment later came the sound of a door slamming. Ivy sighed, then went over to Rose. She scratched Miss Mew behind the ears, and the cat purred in response.

"Is he angry at me?"

Rose was looking up at her, her expression troubled.

Ivy shook her head. "Who do you mean, dearest?"

"Father. Is he angry at me? I wanted to stop them. I knew I should, but my arms wouldn't work, and they took him away!"

Ivy knelt by the chair and put her own arms around Rose. "No, dearest, he is not angry at you. He knows this was not your doing. He loves you very much, as we all do. Even Miss Mew."

Hearing her name, the little cat gave a *mew* in answer. This won a small smile from Rose. Then she turned her gaze back out the window.

Ivy quietly departed the room. Deciding it was best to leave both of her sisters alone for the time being, she went up to the attic, which since her return to Whitward Street had been her room. Over the last five days, she had put the attic back in order. On her arrival she had found it in great disarray. Books had been strewn everywhere, and nothing appeared as if it had been cleaned in the months since she had left.

She did not know if the chaos of the attic had contributed to the incident, but it could not have helped his frame of mind. He had been growing more agitated, Lily had told her. He had taken to throwing books, and striking the windowpanes, and shouting out unintelligible words. Mr. Wyble had complained about the noise, saying it could not be tolerated. Lily and Rose had tried to quiet Mr. Lockwell, but with less and less success. Then, one day when the two had thought him calm and had taken the chance to sit out in the front garden to get some sun, another episode had come upon him.

Even so, no harm would have come to Mr. Wyble. Their father never hurt anything besides books when in such a state. However, their cousin, disturbed from his reading, had taken it upon himself to venture upstairs and enter the attic unannounced.

Ivy still had not learned all the details of what happened next. He claimed Mr. Lockwell was hysterical and had attacked him in the most violent and terrifying manner. More likely it was Mr. Lockwell who was terrified by the intrusion of a stranger into his sanctum. Lily said she was sure Mr. Lockwell had done nothing more than fling a book at Mr. Wyble. However, it had had the poor luck to strike him in the nose, causing a great amount of blood to burst out and their cousin to scream that he was being murdered.

By then Lily and Rose had become aware of the commotion and had rushed inside. Rose had managed to calm their father, and Lily had assured their cousin that Mr. Lockwell would never leave the attic, so Mr. Wyble could never come to any harm if he did not go up there.

However, Mr. Wyble had proclaimed that he would not dwell in fear of entering any part of *his* house and that their father was a danger to all of them. The next day men from Madstone's came and took Mr. Lockwell away. Whether Mr. Wyble had the legal authority to have him so consigned no longer mattered. Once placed in the hostel, their father could not be removed unless he was deemed well enough by the doctors there.

Or unless an officer of the government commanded it.

Within hours of her arrival, Ivy had written a letter to Mr. Quent. She had not yet received his reply—the post to and from Torland would take over a quarter month—but she knew he would not allow this. Mr. Lockwell was not only his father-in-law but his friend. As an agent of the lord inquirer, who in turn served the king, he would surely be able to effect Mr. Lockwell's release—if not with a letter then at least in person upon his return. This present situation was awful; *that* could not be denied. However, they would not have to endure it for much longer.

She spent the rest of the afternoon in the attic, then accompanied her sisters to the dining room as a swift dusk fell. The supper the housekeeper brought them was as burned and flavorless as ever, though Mr. Wyble praised everything that was put before him as if it were a feast.

"I am so looking forward to meeting your husband, cousin," Mr. Wyble said, attempting with little success to cut his cake with his fork.

"What a fortuitous match it is for you. He inherited an earl's house, did you say? It is not the same as an earl's title, of course—but still, an earl's house! Think of how your sisters will benefit from such a connection! And I was wondering—that is, given his position—it cannot be unthinkable that with such means as he has that he must have need of a skilled lawyer. You will promise to introduce me to him as soon as he is in town, won't you, cousin?"

"Of course I will introduce you to him," Ivy said. *And he will detest you the moment he meets you!* she added to herself.

That evening she had thought to spend some time with her sisters, but Lily had fallen into a sullen mood, and Rose wanted only to sit at the window in her room, so Ivy returned to the attic.

She spent a while looking through books, but the candlelight was too dim and her eyes ached, so instead she went to the celestial globe. For several minutes she worked its knobs and handles, watching the various orbs spin and revolve, but she could not see the patterns in their movements; to her, it was all chaos. She readied herself for bed.

The night was long, so it was still dark when they went downstairs to take breakfast with Mr. Wyble. He greeted them cheerfully, even warmly, though it seemed to Ivy there was something peculiar about the smile he gave her. That he was pleased about something was clear.

Not caring to look at him, she kept her eyes on her plate as she ate cold toast and drank cold tea. The dismal meal was soon over, and Ivy rose to follow her sisters from the dining room, to spend the rest of the long umbral in their rooms.

"Wait a moment, Cousin Ivoleyn," Mr. Wyble said as she reached the door. "I almost forgot—a letter came for you in the post."

"Thank you," she said, and tried not to appear too eager as she took it from him. However, by the time she reached the landing on the stairs she was shaking with excitement. There was a lamp there, and she opened the letter to read it in that light. It was from him, as she had known the moment she saw the familiar writing. To her dismay the letter was not long, and it was clear he had not yet received her own missive. As she read the scant words, the darkness pressed in around her, collapsing the sphere of gold light into a point.

His return to the city was delayed. The situation in Torland was worse than had been feared. He could offer no details, in the event this letter was intercepted, but she knew his work, and she knew *him;* thus she must understand that only the most dire situation would keep him away. He expected he would be gone at least a month. It could not be helped.

His letter went on:

*I know law requires Mr. Wyble to allow you to remain at Whitward Street only through month's end. However, I have offered to pay your cousin to allow you and your sisters to remain longer. My offer was generous, and I have no doubt it will be accepted. I know you would prefer to be elsewhere, but it is best if you remain under the roof of a relative. Remember that it is only for a little while longer and that I will return as swiftly to you as I can.*

*Until then, there is one thing I must ask of you. The lord whom I serve will soon be in the city. Would you take the enclosed note to him? That it must remain sealed, I am certain you know! I know not where in the city he will be staying when he arrives and so could not send this directly, but I instructed him in my last missive to contact you upon his arrival. If the post makes its timetables, he should arrive the lumenal after you receive this.*

*The sky is brightening. I must go. Night is their time, but now it is nearly day. Time will not allow me to describe the full extent of what is in my heart, my dearest, but know that I am now and ever will be—*

*Yours,*
*A. Quent*

Again she read the letter, then examined the small, folded note that had been contained within. It was sealed with red wax. At last, slowly, she folded the note inside the letter.

"Is something wrong, cousin?"

She turned on the landing. Mr. Wyble stood a half flight below, looking up at her.

"I trust everything is well," he said with a smile. Again, the expression struck her as smug.

"Yes," she said, willing her voice to hold steady. "Yes, everything is very well, thank you."

Before he could say anything more, she turned and ran up the stairs. She waited until she had reached the attic before she let the tears come, and then she wept bitterly.

❦

THAT NIGHT IVY dreamed she was in the Wyrdwood.

She slipped through a gap in the mossy wall, then made her way deep into the stand of ancient forest. The air was moist, fragrant with yarrow and hazel, and the leaf mold made a carpet beneath her bare feet as she wove among the crooked trees. Her white gown fluttered behind her as she went, like tatters of mist.

A wind sprang up. The trees tossed, and their branches bent down toward her, but she was not afraid. She caught them as they tangled around her, setting her feet into crooks, and when the wind subsided and they bent upward again, the branches bore her to the crowns of the trees.

As the trees swayed back and forth, she swayed with them, rising and falling in a languorous dance. Leaves murmured with a kind of speech, and the more she listened the more she understood it. *Look,* the voices told her. *Look out at our land.*

She did, and from this new vantage it seemed she could see all of the island of Altania. Gray-green downs rolled away in every direction, all the way to the silver line of the sea. She saw roads as well, and towns like dull blotches, and a great city with many spires straddling a river, choking it. Then, on the farthest horizon, beyond the edges of the land, she saw a darkness. It was like the shadow of night approaching. Only it came not just from the west but crept from all directions, surrounding Altania. In the midst of the shadow glowed a red spark like a hungry eye.

The wind rose again, and the branches tossed—not gently this time but violently, creaking and groaning, so that she was forced to hold on with all her might. The air had gone the color of ashes.

"Ivy!" called a stern voice.

She looked down. Mr. Quent stood below, and he held a torch in his maimed hand. It blazed with hot light.

She tried to call out to him, but the wind snatched her voice away. His face was drawn in a glower of anger and disappointment. Again she tried to shout, but it was no use; he could not hear her voice over that of the wind and leaves. He thrust the torch into the tinder-dry mold beneath the trees. Flames sprang up, blackening the trees as they writhed.

# CHAPTER SEVENTEEN

DESPITE THE POOR quality of the company he had provided on his visit to Lady Marsdel's house, Rafferdy received another invitation from Fairhall Street before the passage of two shortish lumenals. After an afternoon in the parlor that was hardly more lively than on the prior occasion, he was commanded by Lady Marsdel to stay for supper, because, "at least with one more being in the room, the sound of our forks and knives shall not echo so loudly."

He bowed and said he was glad to be of service, though he pointed out a sack of flour propped in a chair would have as beneficial an effect on the acoustics, and would cost less in wine. When the bell rang, he lent his arm to Mrs. Baydon and escorted her to the dining room.

"I see you still wear that awful ring," she said as they walked. "Is it part of your new affectation of being somber? I will say, to look upon it certainly inspires grimness!"

He glanced at the ring, almost startled to notice it, for he had grown rather used to it. Its leering blue gem did not seem to bother him so much anymore, and even if it did, it would not matter; the ring still would not budge from his finger. Nor, despite his earlier resolve to do so, had he made any attempt to contact Mr. Bennick regarding its removal. No doubt that was the very reaction Bennick had hoped to elicit, and Rafferdy had no intention of granting him any sort of satisfaction. If it meant wearing the dreadful thing for the rest of his life, so be it.

Just as they were sitting at the table, there came the echo of the front door opening. Someone else had arrived, and when the guest was shown into the dining room, Rafferdy could only surmise that the old saying *Think of an evil, and there it stands* was correct. Either that, or the other yet retained some unholy powers despite his lack of a ring and had plucked Rafferdy's thoughts from the air—for the newcomer was none other than Mr. Bennick.

The tall man handed his black hat to the servant, then gave a bow to her ladyship.

"I'm awfully glad you've come, Mr. Bennick," she said. "Perhaps now we'll hear some real conversation. Once again, we've had the most dull day! I have not heard one interesting thing since breakfast."

"Is that so, your ladyship?" he said, straightening his lean form. "And here I was thinking that I had heard a thousand."

"Do tell!" she exclaimed. "I so crave to hear something fascinating. Who have you spoken to today?"

"No one at all," he replied. "I have been silent all day until speaking to you this very moment."

Mrs. Baydon laughed. "That makes no sense at all! How can you have heard a thousand interesting things if you haven't talked to anybody?"

He turned his gaze toward her. "By listening, that is how."

"By listening to what?"

"To any number of things. For example, on the way here, I listened to the sound of storks snapping their bills among the rooftops in the Old City, to a candlemaker scolding his apprentice for spilling tallow, and to the rattling of a loose cobble on the street."

Lord Baydon shook his head, jowls waggling. "But none of those can tell you anything of interest. I have heard all those things myself and have gained no particular enlightenment."

"On the contrary, your lordship," Mr. Bennick said, "they were all very enlightening. By the sound of the storks I knew that many of the birds nested along the street down which I passed—a street where I had been considering buying a property as an investment. However, storks prefer to nest atop abandoned buildings, and the seller had told me that his property was the only one available on the street. Thus I know him to be untrustworthy and not one to do business with. At the same time, the candlemaker's lecture to his careless apprentice told me that tallow is particularly short right now, and so instead of investing in the property I had considered, I shall instead send a note to my banker telling him to purchase shares in a rendering firm. As for the cobble, by the sound it made when I trod upon it, I could discern something was wedged beneath. I pried it up, and this is what I found."

He took a small object from his pocket and flipped it toward Rafferdy. On instinct Rafferdy reached out and caught the thing. It was a coin, corroded and dull, but here and there he saw the glint of gold.

"I haven't had time to examine it properly, but I believe it's quite old," Mr. Bennick said. "The writing on it appears to be in Tharosian, and while I do not think it *that* ancient, it was fashionable during the reigns of some of the middle Mabingorian kings to mint coins in a Tharosian style. I'd say it's five hundred years old, at the least."

Rafferdy ran a thumb over the coin, fascinated despite himself. "To think it's been there all this time, a secret mere inches from where everyone walks."

"There are many secrets just out of our view," Mr. Bennick said. "You should clean it and keep it for a souvenir."

A sudden distaste filled Rafferdy. The coin felt cold in his hand. "No, I could not possibly accept such a gift." He flipped it back toward its finder. As he did, the ring on his finger glinted blue.

Mr. Bennick snatched the coin out of the air. He made no reply but regarded Rafferdy with his dark eyes as he fingered the coin and tucked it back in his pocket.

"There, *that* is what I meant when I said we'd have some real conversation," Lady Marsdel declaimed as Mr. Bennick took a place at the table across from Rafferdy. "I'm so glad you've returned to the city, Mr. Bennick. You have been sorely missed all these years. I wish only that you'd come in time to see Lord Marsdel again. It would have given him great pleasure to see you. Why you exiled yourself for so long in Torland, I can't imagine, though I'm sure you had your reasons."

"I imagine Mr. Bennick was seeing to the business of the Vordigan estate," Rafferdy said. "It is in Torland, I believe."

At this Mr. Bennick raised an eyebrow. "I did not realize you knew so much about me, Mr. Rafferdy."

"As you said, Mr. Bennick, one can learn very interesting things by listening." Rafferdy smiled and ate his soup.

"Tell me, Mr. Bennick," Lady Marsdel said, "what do you think of the loathsome atmosphere in the city at present? Do you not find it unspeakably foul of late?"

"I confess, it has not troubled me," he replied.

"Of course it doesn't trouble *you*," Lord Baydon said. He waggled a capon leg in Mr. Bennick's direction. "You magicians are always meddling about with vile potions and chemicals. Awful stuff. I'm sure your nose is ruined from all the beastly smells. What have you been brewing of late, Mr. Bennick? Things with arsenic and hemlock and whatnot?"

"Nothing stronger than tea, your lordship. As you know, I have not practiced magick in many years." He picked up his wineglass, which the steward had just filled. Holding it beneath his prominent nose, he inhaled deeply of it. "This comes from the northern Principalities, doesn't it?" he said. "From Abanizzo, I believe. It is the vintage of four years ago, when the weather was wetter than usual."

When the steward's nod confirmed this information, Mrs. Baydon clapped her hands. "Well done, Mr. Bennick. Well done indeed."

"How do you know it was his nose that gave him the answer rather than some spell?" Rafferdy said, giving her a look of mischief. "For can a magician who claims he no longer practices magick ever really be trusted to tell the truth? Would it not, in fact, aid him in keeping his studies secret—a desire, you know, of all magicians—if everyone thought he had lost his interest in the arcane?"

This won laughter from around the table.

As the sound of mirth faded, Mr. Bennick turned toward Rafferdy. "Magick cannot be used for such a trivial purpose as detecting the vintage of a wine. And I never said I had lost my interest in the arcane, Mr. Rafferdy—only that I no longer practiced it."

Rafferdy's smile went flat. He did not care for the look on Mr. Bennick's sallow face. It was openly sharp: a blade drawn in plain sight rather than concealed behind one's back.

"Is it true what I hear, Mr. Bennick?" Mr. Baydon said. Given that Lady Marsdel had forbidden broadsheets at the dining table, he was forced to interact with the rest of them instead. "Is it a fact that you believe our own Mr. Rafferdy could make himself into something of a magician? Mrs. Baydon tells me this is the case."

"One cannot be made into a magician," Mr. Bennick answered, swirling his glass, gazing at the red liquid as it moved in a spiral. "One either is or is not." He raised the glass and took a sip.

"Then he *is* a magician!" Mrs. Baydon said. She turned to Rafferdy and touched his arm. "Come, Rafferdy, do an enchantment for us. Please! We so long for some amusement."

Rafferdy shifted in his chair. Mrs. Baydon's words vexed him; he did not appreciate them in the least.

"I shall do no such thing," he said, not caring that he sounded petulant. "Even if I could work an enchantment, I would not. In fact, I am sure Mr. Bennick would agree magick should not be used for such a *trivial* thing as entertainment. That's for the illusionists in their theaters. And even if I cared to indulge you—which I do not—I would fail in the task, for I have not the least idea how to work an enchantment."

"I can show you," Mr. Bennick said, setting down his glass.

Now Rafferdy was truly perturbed. He had thought his speech would put an end to this nonsense. Instead, everyone around the table was gazing at him.

"Oh, do, Mr. Bennick, do show him!" Mrs. Baydon exclaimed.

Mr. Bennick rose from his chair and moved around the table. Rafferdy renewed his protests, stating that he had no intention of making a fool of himself for their enjoyment, but the others would not relent. They wished to see him do magick; Lady Marsdel commanded it. Like the crowd in some ancient Tharosian arena watching gladiators battle, the guests at the dinner table would not be denied their spectacle.

"This is pointless," he said in a low voice as Mr. Bennick stood over him. "I have no idea what to do."

"You need only do what I tell you. Promise me only that you will do your best to follow my instructions."

Rafferdy raised his hands in defeat. If a pain must be endured, better to be done with it as swiftly as possible.

"Mrs. Baydon, I noticed you wear a locket," Mr. Bennick said, turning toward her. "Would you be willing to part with it for a few moments?"

Her eyes shone. "Of course." She undid the chain and handed the locket to him. It was made of gold: oval-shaped with a tiny hinge. "But there's nothing at all of value inside it. Just a snip of Mr. Baydon's hair."

Mr. Baydon gave her a dry look from across the table. "You seemed quite delighted to receive it at the time, as I recall."

"You weren't married then," Lord Baydon said. "She didn't know you very well. However, now that she has a good idea of your entire value, she knows what a small piece of you is worth!"

Mr. Bennick took the locket, then gave it to Rafferdy.

"Open it," Mr. Bennick instructed.

Rafferdy did so, using a fingernail to prize it open. As Mrs. Baydon had said, there was a curl of brown hair within, tied by a ribbon.

"Now shut it again, and close it inside your fist. Yes, like that. Hold your other hand above, and repeat the words I say to you. They are in an ancient and unfamiliar tongue, a language older than all of history, so listen carefully—you must be sure to repeat them exactly as I say them."

Rafferdy frowned up at the taller man. "What if I make a mistake?"

"It would be best if you did not."

Rafferdy swallowed. He didn't like the sound of that. "Don't I need to draw some strange symbols or odd runes?"

"Not for such a small enchantment as this. Your hand will contain and direct the magickal energies. Now clear your mind of other thoughts."

Before Rafferdy could ask anything more, Bennick uttered several strange words. They were harsh and guttural and in no language Rafferdy had ever heard. Indeed, he supposed they were in no language at all but were pure gibberish. However, when it was seen that this "enchantment" had failed to have any effect, Rafferdy would refuse to let the blame be placed on him; he would make no mistake in his recitation, and all would see it was Mr. Bennick who was the real fool.

The words, however, were oddly difficult to speak. His tongue, usually quick and glib, seemed to labor to form the sounds. His brow furrowed, and he had to force his lips to shape the words, as if they were alien things—sounds his faculties had never been designed to utter.

By the time he finished, sweat had beaded on his forehead, though the incantation had consisted of no more than half a dozen words. Nothing happened as the last syllable faded to silence. The candles did not gutter; there was no charge on the air.

"Well, that was entirely without purpose," Rafferdy said, leaning back.

Mr. Bennick regarded him. "Was it? In that case, hand the locket back to Mrs. Baydon."

Rafferdy did so, and gladly. His jaw ached, and his throat was sore; he took a sip of wine.

"Oh!" Mrs. Baydon exclaimed. "Something is wrong—I can't open it." She turned the locket around and around but to no avail.

"Well, it was quite easy for me," Rafferdy said. However, when she handed it back to him, he found he could no longer open the locket. At first he took care not to damage it, but he soon gave that up and tried with all his might. However, the tiny hinge would not budge.

"You cannot open it that way," Mr. Bennick said. There was a pleased look on his aquiline face. "No one at the table can. It's been sealed with magick, and only magick can open it again."

"Nonsense," Rafferdy said, and kept trying to open the locket, though without success. "There must be some trick."

"What trick can there be?" Lord Baydon said. "It was in your hand the entire time."

"It's true, Mr. Rafferdy," Mrs. Baydon said, clapping her hands and laughing. "It had to have been magick that locked it shut."

He scowled at her. "Magick, yes, but we already know who in this room was the real magician. You spoke the incantation even as I did, Mr. Bennick, and with more proper inflection, I am sure. It was you who locked it, not I."

"I can prove to you quite easily that was not the case," Mr. Bennick said.

"How so?"

"Do you recall the words of the incantation? Yes? Then hold the locket in your hand and speak them again."

"I will not. I am finished with this ridiculous farce."

"But *we* are not," Lady Marsdel declared. "If you are so certain you cannot work magick, Mr. Rafferdy, what have you to fear? Now, speak the words! You are very clever—I have no doubt you can recall them."

Calls of "Hear, hear," went around the table.

Rafferdy glared up at Mr. Bennick. *You have gotten your revenge against me again, sir,* he wanted to say. *First you cursed me with the wretched ring, and now you're making a mockery of me.*

However, he tightened his hand around the locket, then spoke the six words of the incantation. He did not know if it was from his prior experience or from the energy of anger, but this time the words were easier to utter.

"There," he said, and thrust the locket at Mrs. Baydon.

She accepted it and put a fingernail to the thin crack where the two halves met. It opened easily under her touch.

"Marvelous!" Lord Baydon exclaimed.

Mrs. Baydon laughed, and Lady Marsdel applauded by striking a spoon against a dish. Even Mr. Baydon seemed amused.

Rafferdy, however, was not. *It's a trick,* he wanted to say. Yet it wasn't. He had handled the locket himself; there could be no other explanation. Somehow, Bennick had made him to do magick. But how? And moreover, for what purpose? The former magician returned to his seat. His expression seemed neither surprised nor leering. His dark eyes were as unreadable as ever as he picked up a fork and ate his supper.

"You really did it, Mr. Rafferdy," Mrs. Baydon said, smiling at him. "You performed an enchantment. You cannot deny it."

"I must concede it appears so," Rafferdy said grudgingly. "You've bested me, Mr. Bennick, though I have no idea how. Nor can I see what opening and shutting a locket has to do with real magick."

"That is the very foundation of magick," Mr. Bennick said. "It is the opening of things that are shut and the shutting of things that are open. It is also about the binding and unbinding of things. You should come speak with me sometime if you wish to learn more."

"I don't wish it, thank you very much."

"Come now, Rafferdy," Mr. Baydon said, scowling across the table.

"Clearly you have a talent for this stuff. There are men who pay hundreds of regals a year to go to university in hopes of learning the smallest amount of magick, and here Mr. Bennick's given you a lesson for free and offered you more. Surely you must want to know how to wield such power."

"What I want is another glass of wine," he said, and handed his empty glass to a servant.

"My offer remains open if you change your mind," Mr. Bennick said.

Mrs. Baydon laughed. "You're wasting your time, I'm afraid, Mr. Bennick. I fear magick seems too worthwhile. Our dear Mr. Rafferdy has never had an interest in anything that might be remotely useful."

"Or perhaps he simply has yet to find the right use for it," Mr. Bennick said. His glance went to Rafferdy's hand and the ring there.

"Well, since you all want so badly for me to perform another trick, I will oblige you," Rafferdy said.

"And what trick is that?" Lady Marsdel demanded.

He rose from his seat. "I shall make myself disappear." And bowing to her ladyship and the other guests, he took his leave, retrieved his hat, and went out into the night.

# CHAPTER EIGHTEEN

𝒯HE BELLS OF St. Galmuth's were tolling as Eldyn walked past Duskfellow's graveyard and deeper into the Old City. He kept the shadows close around him as he skirted the ragged fringes of High Holy. It would have been safer to take a hack cab, but he would be spending too much as it was that night. He went swiftly, a wraith in the dark.

All at once the night air brightened, and Eldyn turned a corner onto the west end of Durrow Street. Despite the late hour, crowds of people moved up and down the street. Some went boldly, others furtively, all of them searching for the theater most likely to cater to their tastes. Music and laughter spilled out of the open doors, along with colored light that shimmered on the air like a glamour. Eldyn moved down the street, forgetting his stiff fingers and aching back, forgetting the dim apartment over the shoemaker's shop and Sashie's reproachful looks.

Over the last quarter month, since attending the performance at the Theater of the Doves, he had returned to Durrow Street several times. However, with no special coin to grant him admission, he had been forced to pay for his ticket like everyone else.

He knew that it was wrong, that it was frivolous, that he should save the money for his and Sashie's future. Each time he walked home, he vowed he would not return. Only then would come a particularly awful day at Sadent, Mornden, & Bayle, or a quarrel with Sashie, and he would find himself here once again.

Like tonight. Eldyn walked past the theaters. A performer or two stood before each one, crafting illusions and conjuring phantasms. These were small things, meant to intrigue and entice and also to indicate the nature of the performance that would take place inside. The true wonders would be revealed only to those who entered.

In front of one of the theaters, a pair of illusionists tossed balls of blue and green fire back and forth. Beyond, a man, his face powdered, danced with a lithe figure swathed in a white cloth, then pulled away the sheet to reveal nothing but air. Across the street, a lady—or what *seemed* to be a lady—in a silver gown used a wand to draw glittering squares in midair, then pushed them open as if they were windows, revealing seascapes and mountains and sun-drenched fields beyond.

Eldyn watched each performer for a few moments, then moved on, trying to decide where to go. The second time he had come to Durrow Street, he had gone to the Theater of the Doves again. Since then he had gone to the Theater of Dreams, the Theater of the Veils, and the Theater of Mirrors. In each he had seen wonders and visions: confections of light and sound that, like sweets, only left one hungrier the more one consumed.

A man in a black suit beckoned to him. As Eldyn drew near, he saw that the other was unusually thin, and though his face was carefully powdered and rouged, it did not hide the hollowness of his cheeks.

"Look," the man said, and with a palsied hand he gestured to a gilded cage that hung from a stand.

Eldyn looked into the cage, expecting to see a jewel-colored bird like those from the Theater of the Doves. Instead, on the perch inside the cage sat a creature the length of his hand. It was naked and looked like a tiny woman except for its gossamer wings, green hair, and curling tail. The creature let out a trilling laugh as Eldyn gasped. Its tail coiled around its body, caressing, probing; the creature writhed on the perch, eyes glowing red.

The man in the black suit gave a grin as skeletal as any adorning a tombstone at Duskfellow's. "You'll see the full-size ones inside, and more. Come, enter the Theater of Emeralds."

Eldyn shook his head, then hurried down the street. There were many theaters that offered sights such as those at the Theater of Emeralds, and they did not lack for patrons. However, *that* was not the sort of performance Eldyn sought. It was the fantasias, the idylls, and the reenactments of myths of ancient Tharos that entranced him. As the illusionists worked their craft, the stage became like a door to another world. For a little while at least, Eldyn could be somewhere far away from Invarel.

"Don't wish to be seen, do we?"

Eldyn turned around, startled. He had reached the last theater on that side of the street: a narrow edifice, rather plain and dilapidated compared to the others, being without gilt trim or lacquered doors. The columns along its facade listed a bit, and the only ornamentation was a sign above the doorway, a silver circle with black lettering. It read: *Theater of the Moon*.

"See?" the voice said again. "You're not the only one who can do that trick."

Eldyn looked around but saw no one. "Who's there?" he said.

Laughter sounded next to him. "So you can be fooled by your own trick." The air rippled like a dark cloth, and the figure of a man Eldyn's age, or a bit younger, appeared as if stepping from behind a curtain. His features were finely wrought and pale, and his gold hair was tied back with a red ribbon, but the rest of him was clad in black.

"Now it's *your* turn to show yourself."

Eldyn belatedly realized that, as he fled from the Theater of Emeralds, he had gathered the shadows around himself. With a thought, he let them fall away.

The young man's smile was a white crescent in the gloom. "There you are. You shouldn't bother with shadows, you know. They won't hide you from *our* eyes. Is this your first time to Durrow Street? But, no, that can't be it. I believe I've seen you before. Which house do you work for?"

Eldyn shook his head. "Which house?"

"You must be even newer than me! Which theater do you perform at?"

Now Eldyn frowned. "I've come to see a performance. I don't work at a theater."

"No? I would have thought . . . that is, are you certain we haven't met before?"

"I don't see how."

The young man gazed at him a moment, then shook his head. "Well, it doesn't matter. If it's a performance you wish to see, come no further. The Theater of the Moon is the finest on Durrow Street."

"It doesn't look like much," Eldyn said, eyeing the slanted columns and the curtain covering the door, which even in the dim light looked shabby.

"It's not how it looks outside but what's within that matters."

"I haven't even seen you work an illusion. Why don't you show something of your play like at the other theaters?"

"Because I can't. Even the smallest glimpse would spoil the wonder of what you'll see inside. You cannot experience just a shard of it. You must behold it in the fullness of its splendor."

Now it was Eldyn's turn to laugh, and he crossed his arms. "How do I even know you're really illusionists? You probably just have a few actors in ratty costumes hanging about on wires and pulleys." Except the other *was* an illusionist. How else could he have so easily mimicked Eldyn's talent with shadows?

The young man's expression grew solemn. "You can't know. That's how illusion works. You can never really know anything; you can only believe." He made a sweeping gesture toward the door.

Eldyn hesitated. Perhaps it was the other's kindly face. Or perhaps it was that, somehow, he *did* look familiar. Whatever the reason, Eldyn reached into his pocket, drew out a quarter regal, and counted the coins into the illusionist's hand. Then he stepped past the curtain.

WHEN ELDYN AGAIN stepped past the curtain, this time leaving the theater and heading out onto Durrow Street, he knew he was not the same person who had entered two hours before but someone—something—different. It was as if all he had been before, all he thought he had known, had poured out of him, leaving him an empty vessel ready to be filled with something new. Yet with what? He could not say, only that it had to be something *better*.

And to think he had nearly left the theater before the performance began! At first, upon taking a seat in the balcony, he had thought his fears had proven true. The chairs were rickety, the walls cracked and flaking, the cloth draped across the proscenium half-patched. A scant collection of people made up the audience, slumping in their chairs, loudly consuming nuts or tipping back bottles. Thinking the joke was on him—that the real illusion here was the way his money had been made to vanish—Eldyn had started to rise from his chair.

At that moment the lights went out. For a minute, the darkness was unbroken. It was so black he could not see his hand move before his face. He began to grow alarmed. Was some harm going to come to those fools who had been convinced to enter? Were they to be robbed of whatever funds they had left? Then, just as he was about to get up and try to feel his way toward the door, a face appeared in the darkness.

The face was silver, set inside a silver circle that hovered in the blackness, eyes shut. Whether it was the face of a man or woman, he could not say. Then, just when he realized what the face must represent (for this *was* the Theater of the Moon), the eyes opened, and the face began to sing.

Eldyn sank back into his chair.

When the song was finished, the circle of silver light expanded, revealing the moon as a beautiful, silver-clad youth who charmed all he encountered. Only then he made the mistake of letting his shadow fall upon the figure of a proud and jealous king who, clad in a coat of gold flame, could only be the sun. The king condemned the silvery youth to death for this transgression. However, the youth fled, while forces of the king pursued him across a fantastical landscape, beneath a deep ocean, and finally into the starry heavens themselves.

From time to time, it occurred to Eldyn that the illusions were not so elaborate as what he had seen at the other theaters; they were simple, even austere. The ocean was conjured by nothing more than flickering blue light; the stars were but a flurry of white sparks. However, it was the story itself that enchanted Eldyn. With the rest of the audience, he cheered the youth each time he escaped his pursuers, and he hissed and booed each time the king strutted onstage.

Despite all his efforts, the king could never capture the silver youth. At last their journey came full circle, back to where it began, and once again the youth's shadow fell upon the king, dimming his glory. Except this time—almost willingly, it seemed to Eldyn—the youth came too close to the flames, and in a flash of light and puff of smoke he was consumed.

The audience gasped and fell silent. The king threw his head back and laughed, his red hair crackling and throwing off sparks. But his laughter ceased as his own fiery aura began to dwindle and fade, then with one last sputter went out. He fell to the stage in a heap of cinders, and the theater went black. For a long, lightless minute, all was silent.

Then, in the darkness, a silver face appeared and began to sing.

Now, as Eldyn walked through the darkened city, he could not stop thinking of the play. He thought maybe he understood. The king and the youth were like the sun and moon—no, they *were* the sun and moon. Did not the moon sometimes move before the sun, casting its shadow on it as the youth had done to the king? The king had pursued the youth, but he had never been able to catch him, just as the sun could never pass in front of the moon in the sky. All the same, when the sun shone forth, the moon vanished under the force of its light.

Yet when darkness fell and the month turned, as it always must, the moon would shine forth anew.

Yes, Eldyn understood what had happened onstage, but he didn't understand what it meant or why it made him feel as he did—as if he himself had been running all his life but had now come full circle and was ready to begin again. Yet begin what? He glanced up at the sky, seeking illumination, but there was no moon that night.

He walked onward through the Old City, and as he did the feeling of exhilaration, of *possibility,* receded. It seemed the farther he got from Durrow Street, the harder it was to remember just what had happened onstage—how the actors had looked or what visions they had conjured. Soon all he could picture were the rickety chairs, the moldy curtain, the unshaven men drinking gin in the balcony.

An illusion—that's all it had been. There was no truth to any of it. These narrow, grimy streets he walked through—these were real. This was all that mattered.

It was late. He meant to go directly home, but when he saw a familiar sign down a street, a sudden thirst came over him. His boots took him that way, and he passed through the door of the Sword and Leaf.

As he entered the tavern, it seemed a bit of the night tried to follow after him, as if not wanting to let him out of its clutches. Eldyn gave the door a hard push, shutting out the dark. He sat at a table, ordered punch, and did not look up until his first cup was drained.

He had a faint hope that he would see Rafferdy grinning and waving at him from across the tavern, wanting someone to buy him a drink, but the place was mostly empty. The few other patrons did not talk or laugh and drank alone.

Eldyn had seen Rafferdy little these last months. Rafferdy's work for his father kept him busy and often took him away from the city. Even when he was free, his appetite for drink and amusement seemed diminished.

It was just as well. Eldyn's position at the trading house left him little time or money for pleasure. Nor had he told Rafferdy that he was working as a clerk; the last time they met, he had said only that he was still working on his business, and as usual Rafferdy had not pressed for details.

However, that night as they had left the tavern, Rafferdy had given him a fond clap on the back. "Do take care of yourself, Garritt," he had said. "I believe you've been working too hard on your business. You're fading away. At this rate you'll be a phantasm the next time we meet. Then the sun will rise, and you'll be gone."

It had been a joke, but now Eldyn thought of the illusion play and how the silver youth had vanished in a puff of smoke. He put another lump of sugar in his cup and filled it to the brim.

*I will write a note to Rafferdy tomorrow,* he told himself as he drank. Only he wouldn't. When would he have the time? He would need to work a second shift again to make up the cost of this punch he was now drinking. The thought occurred to him that he would go to Mrs. Haddon's on his next free day to see his old university friends. Only he wouldn't do that either. Two months ago he had read in *The Swift Arrow* how an agent of the Black Dog had appeared at Mrs. Haddon's coffeehouse. Nor was it just any of Lord Valhaine's spies, but the White Lady herself.

Lady Shayde had not spoken to anyone; she had merely sat at a table while she slowly drank a coffee. All the same, the effect could not have been more chilling if she had rushed in with a band of guards and arrested ten men for treason. Who would go to Mrs. Haddon's and speak criticisms of the king or Assembly now?

Certainly not Eldyn—not after what he had done for Westen. Eldyn had never seen the White Lady, and he hoped to God he never did. It was said her face was the color of snow, and that one look from her and all your deepest secrets would spill out of you like water from a cracked pot. He did not dare go to Mrs. Haddon's, and he could only hope that Jaimsley, Talinger, and Warrett were keeping away as well.

Eldyn drained his punch and called for more.

❧

TWO HOURS LATER, Eldyn staggered out the door of the Sword and Leaf and onto the street. He had consumed a second round of punch, and a third, but there had been something wrong with the stuff. It had not dulled his mind, allowing him to forget the dismal apartment he shared with his sister, or his position at the trading company, or his poverty. Instead, each drink had only brought these things into clearer focus, making them larger, until he could think of nothing else. It was only the hopes, the wishes and ideas of better things to come, that the drink caused to fade, until his brain was not capable of envisioning a single good thing—not even something so small as a pretty flower in the hand or a ray of warm sun on the face.

In this frame of mind, he stumbled down the street. As he started off, it again seemed to him that a patch of darkness peeled away from the inn and followed after. However, he could not muster the will to worry. He lurched along, and so deep was he under the effects of the punch that he did not bother to wrap the shadows around himself as he went.

It was his intention to go home, to bang on the door and tell Sashie to let him in, for he was in no state to fit a key into a lock. However, when he passed the iron gates of Duskfellow's, a wild desire came upon him to enter the graveyard. He pulled at the bars, but the gate was locked. However, the stones of the walls were rough and thick with vines, and even in his current condition it was little problem to climb up and over the wall.

He lost his grip at the top and fell to the soft turf below, missing the sharp edge of a broken tombstone by inches. Using the stone as a crutch, he pulled himself up, then wove and wheeled among the graves.

It was only when he came upon the small headstone that he realized he had been looking for it, that this was why he had come here. Unlike the timeworn grave markers all around, the writing on this stone was sharp and legible in the faint starlight: *VANDIMEER GARRITT.*

An urge came over Eldyn to kick the headstone, as he himself had been kicked so many times. He tried, but his boot caught the ground, and he fell atop the grave on his hands and knees.

"You bastard," he said. "You sodding bastard, this is all your fault! You stole everything from me. Everything I ever had and ever could have. Even dead, you couldn't leave me alone."

His shoulders heaved, and he vomited on the grave.

At last the clenching of his gut ceased. For a moment Eldyn stayed on his hands and knees, panting, catching his breath. The act of spilling his guts had cleared his head a bit. Finally, he felt steady enough to slowly stand.

"You called me a coward," he said, wiping his mouth as he looked down at the tombstone. "Well, you were the one who took the coward's way out. You killed yourself as sure as if you'd put a bullet in your brain. The whiskey just took a little longer, that's all. So now you're dead, and what do I have?" His hands clenched into fists. "You said I was weak. Well, if you were here now, I would knock out what few teeth you had left. Come, you bastard, let me prove it to you. Show yourself!"

Even as he spoke, it seemed to him a livid mist rose up from the grave. The mist coiled upon itself, thickening as it floated higher, forming wraithlike into a shape. The shape was dim, its edges indistinct, as if seen through a greenish mist, but there was no mistaking it. It was the figure of Vandimeer Garritt, hulking and scowling in death even as in life. The apparition raised a hand, not in greeting but as if to strike.

A gurgling scream sounded behind Eldyn.

Eldyn staggered around. Not five paces behind him stood a man in patched clothes and a ragged cloak, a small knife bared in his hand. The whites of the man's eyes shone in the starlight, and his mouth was a dark, toothless circle amid a scraggly beard.

"Who are you?" Eldyn said, astonished.

The other gazed not at Eldyn but past him. The knife dropped from his hand, and with another cry he turned and fled, vanishing in the gloom among the gravestones.

Shock sobered Eldyn. He stared after the man, then he bent and picked up the knife. The hilt was worn, but the short blade had been honed to a wicked point. Eldyn had no doubt it had been intended for him, only something had frightened off the would-be robber.

He turned back toward his father's grave, but the dark air was empty. The specter of his father was gone—a hallucination brought on by anger and memory and too much drink.

Yet if that was the case, why had the robber fled? He recalled how the man's eyes had widened, gazing past him toward the grave, as if he had seen something there. . . .

"But that's impossible," Eldyn murmured. "Another man can't see a figment of my *own* imagination."

His skull throbbed; he could not think. He needed to rest his head, just for a minute, then he would go back to the apartment. Eldyn sat on a marble bench in front of a crypt, then lay down on it, pressing his cheek to the cool, mossy stone.

HE WOKE TO the tolling of the bells of St. Galmuth's.

Eldyn sat up, then groaned as he held a hand to his aching temples. Gradually the pain subsided, though it did not disappear. He brushed his cheek, and bits of moss came off. Above, the sky was a honey color.

The umbral was over. He must have been lying on the bench for hours. That no one had molested him during the time seemed inconceivable. Duskfellow's after dark was a known refuge for thieves and murderers. Yet, aside from the aftereffects of too much punch, he was well, and a quick check confirmed that his wallet (and its scant contents) was still in his coat pocket.

Not wishing to press his luck, Eldyn hurried from the graveyard. By the time he reached the street, sun slanted among the buildings. At first he started back toward the shoemaker's shop, then he realized there was no time. After a middle umbral, all clerks were expected at the trading company a half hour after dawn. The bells had already stopped tolling. Eldyn changed direction, then broke into a run.

He stopped for only a minute to wet his handkerchief at a public well and bathe his face. He brushed off his coat with a hand and made a mirror of a window to arrange his hair. It would have to do.

By the time he turned a corner onto Marble Street, he saw the line of clerks already filing through the doors of Sadent, Mornden, & Bayle. He reached the trading house just in time to join the tail end of the line and slipped in with the others.

"Cutting it a bit fine this morning, aren't you, Garritt?" Tems Chumsferd whispered as Eldyn took his seat.

He was already scribbling away at the paper before him. Eldyn picked up a quill and did likewise, continuing the row of sums where he had left off the night before.

"You know me, Chubbs," Eldyn whispered back. "I never make a mistake." He gave his pen a flourish.

"I won't deny you've better penmanship than just about anybody, but if Whackskuller ever catches you late . . ."

"He won't," Eldyn said. "Because I won't be."

Chubbs started to respond, but hisses sounded to either side. A moment later came the *clump*-CLOMP of Mr. Waxler approaching. Both Eldyn and Chubbs bent their heads over their work.

The shift crept by. The only noise was the scratching of pens and the buzz of flies. The hall grew stuffy, and Eldyn sweated in his coat. As the hours passed, he never had another opportunity to speak with Chubbs, for Mr. Waxler seemed particularly interested in him that day. Often he heard the head clerk pause behind him. Eldyn ignored the throbbing in his head and wrote in precise, economical strokes. Despite Whackskuller's attentions, the shift ended without the head clerk's baton striking either Eldyn's work or his head.

Most of the clerks rose from their stools. Uncharacteristically, Chubbs was staying for the extra half shift, but Eldyn knew he was far too weary after last night. He would have to make up the money another time. He stood and stretched, forcing his shoulders out of their hunch.

"Good night, Chubbs." He gave the other clerk a wink. "Remember, ink is the lifeblood of Altania. Don't waste it."

Chubbs scowled at him. Eldyn grinned back, then was out the door and into the warmth of a long afternoon.

There were still a few pennies in his pocket, so he stopped by a bakery to pick out something for Sashie. He imagined she would be vexed at him for his long absence, and hopefully a sweet would appease her.

Soon he was walking home, a sack of almond and anise biscuits in hand. He fell into a jaunty cadence, enjoying the feel of the sun on his face. Free from the trading house and bathed in the warm light, his weariness was forgotten, as were the shadows and specters of last night. His free day was coming soon; he would take Sashie to Gauldren's Heights and then see if Rafferdy would meet him for a drink. In the meantime, he could work an extra shift or two and save up enough to attend another play on Durrow Street. Perhaps he would go to the Theater of the Moon again. Only this time he would avoid Duskfellow's on the way home!

Whistling a bright tune, he turned onto the little lane where the shoemaker's shop stood. The shop was quiet; the city had paused in the midst of the drowsy afternoon, waiting for the coolness of twilight to wake it again. He walked up the steps and entered the apartment, bracing himself for the full brunt of Sashie's displeasure.

She turned from the window and smiled at him. "Hello, dear brother!"

He was so astonished he could only stare. She tucked something into her dress pocket, then came over to kiss his cheek. He received no rebuke for not coming back last night, no spiteful glance. She returned to her seat by the window. Gold light bathed her face, coloring her pale skin and catching in her eyelashes. She looked very pretty.

Bemused, he set the sack on the table. "I brought you biscuits. The almond ones are your favorites, aren't they?"

"Yes, how lovely," she said. "Thank you." She did not rise from her seat but kept gazing out the window, humming a gentle song.

To that agreeable accompaniment, Eldyn took off his coat, brushed it, and hung it on a chair, then sat at the table. He had discovered a copy of yesterday's edition of *The Swift Arrow* abandoned on the street and now spread it out and read as he nibbled an anise bis-cuit (which was *his* favorite). All the while Sashie hummed her little song, and a pleasant breeze wafted through the open window.

"You seem very happy," he said at last, looking up.

"I'm happy you're home." She turned in her seat to smile again at him. "Do you think we could go shopping soon? I would very much like a new hat. That is . . . if it isn't too awfully expensive."

"Of course you shall have a new hat!" he said, delighted at once by her eagerness and concern. "You deserve it. We shall go as soon as the best shops open on my free day."

She treated him again to a smile—a fond reward he had won rarely of late—and turned again to gaze out the window. Eldyn read a bit more. Then, motivated by his affection, he picked out the nicest-looking almond biscuit and—stealthily, so as to surprise her—crossed the room and leaned over her shoulder to present it to her.

"Oh!" she gasped, and something fell from her hands onto the windowsill.

Hastily she snatched it up, then hid it in her lap.

Eldyn sucked in a breath. "What's that you were holding, Sashie?"

"Nothing important." Her hand started to move to her pocket, but he was swifter. He reached out and snatched it from her. The al-mond sweet fell to the floor.

The sunlight went thin. A putrid smell wafted in through the win-dow. With a thumb he stroked the rich silk handkerchief in his hand.

"Where did you get this, dearest?"

She gave a little laugh, but the sound was tight and false. "Our fa-ther gave it to me years ago. I had forgotten I had it. I only just found it again."

"Don't lie to me, Sashie."

"It's no lie, sweet brother, I found—"

"I said don't lie to me!"

He grabbed her wrist, pulling her up and out of the chair. A gasp escaped her, though whether from surprise or pain he did not know. He did not lessen his grip on her.

"When did he give it to you?"

Her face had gone white. She said nothing.

"I know this thing. I've taken it from you once before. He was here, wasn't he? Westen. How long ago? Tell me!"

She shook her head, tears springing into her eyes.

A heat rose in him; a rushing noise filled his head. His fingers dug into the flesh of her wrist. "By God, you will tell me, or—"

She threw her head back and looked up at him. "Or what? You'll strike me? You should see yourself. How like our father you look!"

It was as if she was the one who had struck *him*. He reeled away, holding his hand to his head. The handkerchief fluttered to the floor. She darted forward and snatched it up.

Eldyn had gone cold. His stomach churned. "Sashie—"

"You're wrong," she said quietly, folding the handkerchief and tucking it in her sleeve. "He didn't give it to me. I found it this morning when I looked out to see if I could see you coming. It was on the doorstep." Now she glared at him. "Though I wish he would come."

"You don't mean that."

"I do mean it! I hate being alone all day long. I hate staring out the window and seeing other people talking and laughing and going places. I hate this place. I want to leave!"

"Then pack your things."

Her mouth opened, and she gaped at him.

Eldyn could not be angry with Sashie. She didn't understand, but he did. The handkerchief was a message. Or rather, a warning.

"I said pack your things. Anything we can't carry, we leave behind. We leave here at once."

Now it was she who was afraid. "But where are we going?"

"Somewhere safe. Somewhere he can't find us." Except where that was, he did not know. He said only, "Now, get your things."

A quarter hour later, the door to the little apartment over the shoemaker's shop swung back and forth on its hinges. The dim rooms inside were empty of life—until a rat crept from a corner and up onto the table to claim the feast of biscuits that had been forgotten there.

# CHAPTER NINETEEN

*I*VY!" ROSE CALLED again.

With a gasping breath, Ivy sat up in bed. Rose stood nearby, her face illuminated by a single candle. The eaves of the house shuddered as another gale struck them. A storm had blown in during the night.

"Are you all right?" Rose said, her face worried. "You were crying out for Mr. Quent."

Ivy held a hand to her head. She had dreamed of the Wyrdwood again, just as she had several days ago. It was the same as before: the swaying trees, and Mr. Quent, and the flames.

"I'm fine," she said. She managed a smile for her sister's sake. "It was just a dream. I can't even recall it now."

Rose put down the candle and sat on the edge of the bed. "You must miss him very much."

"I do," Ivy said, and now her smile was stronger. "I cannot wait for you to meet him, dearest. Lily will think him old and awfully serious, I have no doubt, but I think you will like him very much."

"Do *you* like him?"

Ivy drew her knees up beneath the bedcovers and circled her arms around them. "I love him with all my heart."

"Then I will love him too," Rose said, smiling. "I won't be able to help it."

Ivy smiled too, all thoughts of the dream vanishing.

An hour later they took breakfast in the dining room as rain lashed against the windowpanes. It was too wet to go out, so Ivy resigned herself to a long day shut upstairs with her sisters. It would have been more comfortable to sit in the parlor, but it was not their day to use it, and she would not ask Mr. Wyble to make an exception—even though she suspected her request would be granted. He seemed very pleased again this morning and even remarked that the Miss Lockwells should stay as long as they liked at Whitward Street. The sum Mr. Quent was paying her cousin must have been generous indeed.

They had just finished breakfast when a pounding came at the front door. None of them could imagine who would come to call on such an awful day—or indeed, who would come at all. Moments later the housekeeper arrived in the dining room. While usually disinclined to any sort of hurry, it was clear from her huffing she had run up the stairs.

"I have a message," she said. "It is from a magnate!"

Mr. Wyble leaped from his seat. "Excellent news! Lady Marsdel must require my services again. Give it here."

"But it is for the eldest miss."

Mr. Wyble frowned, but before he could speak, Ivy hurried forward and took the letter. "Thank you," she said.

The housekeeper regarded her through squinted eyes, then gave a shrug and departed. Mr. Wyble's looks were all curiosity (colored with some degree of disappointment). However, before he could ask any questions, Ivy took her leave. She waited until she reached the attic to open the letter; she was not surprised by its contents. It was a brief message from one of his servants, requesting only that she meet the lord inquirer later that day at a respectable inn located near the Halls of Assembly. It did not mention the note she had received from Mr. Quent but did state: *Please bring anything you might think of interest to his lordship.*

Ivy could not help feeling a small bit of pride and pleasure at that last part. How like a spy she felt! She could imagine she was a character in one of Lily's books, carrying secret messages for the king. However, it was not to serve the king that she did this task but rather to serve Mr. Quent, and that thought gave her real pleasure.

She arrived at the inn just before the appointed hour. The inn was called the Silver Branch, and given its proximity to Assembly, it was frequented by many members of the Hall of Citizens and not a few members of the Hall of Magnates. It was sometimes said that laws were voted on in Assembly but they were made at the Silver Branch. Spirited debates about the best way to govern could be heard there at all hours, and it was not unheard of that, when the beer flowed as freely as the rhetoric, words were traded for fisticuffs.

Fortunately, Assembly was not in session at the moment, and the inn was quiet as Ivy entered. A man took her coat, and when she spoke her name she was shown to a private parlor. Entering, she saw not the elderly lord she expected but rather the back of a young man who stood by the window, gazing out through rain-speckled glass.

"I'm sorry," she said. "I must have been shown to the wrong room. I'll go ask if—oh!"

The young man turned around, and his brown eyes went wide. His expression was shocked, but it could not have been more so than her own. For several seconds each could do no more than stare at the other.

"Miss Lockwell," he said at last, at the same moment she blurted out, "Mr. Rafferdy!"

He stepped away from the window. "What are you—that is, it has been so long, and I had heard you were gone from the city."

"I am gone," she said, then shook her head. "Or rather, I was. But I'm back now."

"So I see," he said, and suddenly his expression was not so much shocked as it was amused.

She winced. What a dolt she must seem! He must wonder why he had ever willingly spent time engaged in conversation with her. No doubt he had been relieved to escape his association with her.

Except she did not believe that. The smile he wore now was not a polite mask but an expression of genuine warmth, and as she looked at him it was as if no time at all had passed since their last meeting. All her affections, all her hopes and disappointments, long ago set aside, now returned to her in a torrent. She had not confessed it to anyone, not even to herself, but she had wanted her mother to be right, had wanted more than anything to see his carriage appear before the house on Whitward Street, to see him walk up the front steps.

No, this would not do! To hope for such a thing *then* had been foolish, and to regret it *now* even more so. To wish for Mr. Rafferdy in her past was to preclude Mr. Quent from both her present and future, and that was a thing she could not bear.

Even if it were possible things could have transpired differently, still Ivy would not have wished it. Not that, confronted with them again, she could deny Mr. Rafferdy's charms. No doubt, as his wife, he would have indulged her every whim and desire. With laughter, wit, and good looks he would have begged her affections. How willingly, just a matter of months ago, she would have given them!

Yet not now. She was sure no one would ever accuse Mr. Quent of being charming or indulgent. However, it was not because of what he did for *her* that she loved him. It was not for hope of recognition or any attention that Mr. Quent labored. Rather, he did his work alone and in the shadows for the sole reason that he knew it must be done—not for himself or any other, but for the well-being of Altania. Given a choice between two such loves, two such men, Ivy knew she could only choose the latter.

Besides, so much had happened since that time. It was foolish to recall feelings from over half a year ago: for however strong they were, they had been felt by another person. She was not who she was then.

And neither was he, she was sure. He looked more serious than she remembered, though he looked well. His suit was well cut and fashionable, but it was a subdued gray, and there were fine lines around his eyes she had never seen before, though they were not displeasing.

Ivy drew a breath to steady herself. While this meeting had come more quickly than she could have imagined, and quite unexpectedly, it had always been her wish she would see Mr. Rafferdy again. Now here he was, and she would be glad for it. She *was* glad.

"But still, it is strange you are here," she said, not intending to speak the thought aloud but doing so.

He shook his head. "Strange? How so? I have only come to meet my father. He is in town on business, and I promised to meet him here before accompanying him to Lady Marsdel's house."

She took a step toward him. "No, I mean only that it is curious you are here, at this same moment. I've come to meet someone as well, but they must have shown me to the wrong room."

"Who are you meeting?"

She didn't know how to answer. However, before she was forced to think of something to say, the door opened. She wondered if it would be her appointment or his.

"There you are, Father," Mr. Rafferdy said to the older gentleman who appeared in the doorway.

*His* appointment, then. Which meant this could only be Lord Rafferdy. Ivy supposed he had been a tall man once, like his son, but age had eroded his stature and expanded his girth. He leaned heavily on a cane, limping into the room, his face red beneath a white wig. Mr. Rafferdy hurried forward and, with awkward but kind movements, helped his father to a chair.

Ivy regarded Mr. Rafferdy fondly. She wanted to talk to him, to learn how he had been these last months and how Miss Everaud—that is, how Mrs. Rafferdy was faring. However, she would have to hope to see him another time. And now that they were both in the city, and their situations were so altered, why could she not hope for that? That she would introduce him to Mr. Quent was a thought that gave her a pleasant anticipation. For now, though, she must leave him with his father.

However, as she started to retreat, Mr. Rafferdy said, "Father, this is an acquaintance of mine, Miss Lockwell."

Lord Rafferdy shook his head. "Miss Lockwell? By her presence here at this time, I was given to believe that this is Mrs. Quent."

Now it was the son's turn to frown. "Mrs. Quent?"

Ivy experienced shock anew. On those few occasions Mr. Quent had spoken of the man he served, he only ever called him the lord inquirer. She had not known his name. Yet that it should be *his* father— it was strange providence indeed.

Mr. Rafferdy's brow furrowed. "Who in the world is Mrs. Quent?"

She cleared her throat. "I am."

He looked to her, blinking. "But then . . . you are married?"

"I had always understood the title *Mrs.* implied such a fact," Lord Rafferdy said. "However, I am an old-fashioned man and out of date with the latest modes. Regardless, do you mean to say you know Mrs. Quent?"

"I do. Or, that is, I did."

Despite her astonishment at the situation, Ivy found herself smiling. "I assure you, I am quite the same person, Mr. Rafferdy. My name has changed, nothing else."

For a moment his look was blank. Then all at once he smiled and, despite the gray suit, he was the Mr. Rafferdy she remembered.

"I doubt that very much, Miss—Mrs. Quent," he said. "I am certain just from looking at you that much has changed."

For a moment it seemed his smile contained the slightest tincture of regret. However, she could not imagine that he was any less satisfied than she at how their fortunes in marriage had worked out, and his smile was renewed as he explained to his father how he had come to be acquainted to Ivy by means of her cousin and Lady Marsdel.

"I see," Lord Rafferdy said. He appeared thoughtful for a moment, then nodded. "Well, while my son might presume fate has conspired to deliver you here for the benefit of his amusement, I believe in fact you have brought me something, Mrs. Quent."

"Of course!" she said, having quite forgotten the note. She took it from her pocket and gave it to the lord inquirer. He tucked it into his coat without looking at it.

"And what news have you from Mr. Quent?" he asked.

"Only that his return is delayed for as long as a month."

He regarded her with gray eyes. "I know it must be a hardship for you, madam, to have him so far away. Nor am I at liberty to tell you precisely why it is important that he be where he is at present. Yet I will say this: the hardship will be worth his while, and yours. You have my promise on that."

Ivy did not know what to say. That Lord Rafferdy spent his words as judiciously as his son spent them freely, she had no doubt. She murmured only "Thank you, my lord," and bowed her head.

When she lifted her eyes, she saw that Mr. Rafferdy was gazing at her. Now his expression was one of neither shock nor amusement; rather, it was with curiosity that he regarded her.

Leaning on his cane, Lord Rafferdy slowly gained his feet. "Must I be the one to invite her to tea, then?"

In a flash, Mr. Rafferdy's smile returned. "Of course—you must come with us back to Lady Marsdel's."

For the third time in a quarter hour, Ivy was astonished. "You are very . . . It is kind of you, but I told my sisters I would not be long."

"Do not worry, Mrs. Quent," Lord Rafferdy said. "We will force you to endure our hospitality for only a short while. I am sure, given what I now know, that my cousin would welcome your presence at her house."

"Lady Marsdel would be glad to know you have returned and that you are well," Mr. Rafferdy said. "They all would be glad. You must come."

Presented with such an invitation, Ivy could not refuse, and she soon found herself in a four-in-hand riding through the rain-slicked streets of the Old City and up the grand arc of the Promenade. Lord Rafferdy directed the conversation as they went, prompting Ivy for her opinion on all manner of topics, from history to science to politics, for Mr. Quent had told him she was the daughter of a doctor and had inherited a keen intellect.

Ivy did not feel particularly keen at the moment. His manner was solicitous, but all the same there was an imposing air about Lord Rafferdy. She answered as best she could and was grateful when the carriage halted before Lady Marsdel's house. The rain had ceased, and Lord Rafferdy told the two younger people that he would take the steps at his own pace and that they should go ahead.

"You've impressed him, you know," Mr. Rafferdy said in a low voice as they ascended to the house.

"Yes," she said, "I'm sure I've impressed upon him the notion that I'm as brainless as a stick of wood. I do not know what test I was being given, but I am very certain I failed it."

"No, I know what failing one of his tests is like, so you must trust me when I say you passed the exam in a most excellent fashion. You would be at the head of the class." His smile became a grimace. "While I would be the one lurking in the corner with an odd-shaped hat on his head."

"You are making a poor joke. You know perfectly well you are an exceedingly clever man."

"A poor joke, you say? So now my sense of humor is to be disparaged along with my intellect?"

"If so, then it is only by yourself. For *I* think very highly of your faculties. As does your father."

He laughed at this. "Now it is you who makes the ill joke."

"No, I do not. You are very like him, you know."

"Like him? Yes, I am quite like him, the same way a cloud is like a rock or a bird like a bulldog."

Now it was Ivy's turn to laugh. "You are like him," she said, "in that you are both rocks and bulldogs, neither of which is very willing to be budged."

Before he could answer, they had reached the front door.

$\mathcal{I}$F SHE HAD feared her reunion with the members of Lady Marsdel's household would be awkward, then those fears were unfounded. She was welcomed immediately and with warmth. Mrs. Baydon embraced her, and Mr. Baydon set down his paper to shake her hand. Lord Baydon pronounced he was not at all surprised to see her, for it had stormed all morning, and some delightful thing must always follow rain.

For her part, any awkwardness Ivy might have felt vanished at once. Everyone in the parlor was seated in their familiar place, and it seemed as if she had seen them just yesterday. And why should she not feel comfortable? The only problem that might have once caused discord between them had been resolved, to utter contentment on all sides. She accepted tea and submitted to all their questions happily, though she kept her answers away from any topics that might reveal the nature of Mr. Quent's work for the lord inquirer.

It did feel strange, even unfitting, to be surrounded by such good cheer when her sisters were forced to endure Mr. Wyble's company, and their father far worse. But if her own spirits were strengthened, it would only serve to help her lend strength to those she loved. Besides, an idea had already begun to form in her mind. She had written to Mr. Quent, urging him to ask the lord for whom he worked to petition for her father's release from Madstone's. And had she not just ridden in a carriage with that very lord?

"You look well, Mrs. Quent," Lady Marsdel pronounced. "A bit freckled, perhaps, though I suppose that is to be expected from dwelling so long in the country. I am pleased to learn you have done well for yourself. A country gentleman with a sizable fortune is the best sort of match you might have made. A good arrangement should lift one up but not cause one to strain in an effort to reach too high. Is that not your thinking, cousin?" She looked over her fan at Lord Rafferdy, who had only lately entered the parlor.

"It has been," he said. He glanced at his son, but Mr. Rafferdy gazed out the window, seemingly oblivious to their conversation.

"We shall have to meet Mr. Quent when he returns to the city," Lady Marsdel went on. "I gather he has some business with you, cousin. Is that not so?"

"I long had an association with Earl Rylend, whom Mr. Quent served previously," Lord Rafferdy said, and eased himself into a chair. He offered no more explanation of his relationship with Mr. Quent, and Lady Marsdel did not inquire further. Instead, she proceeded to expound on the wretched weather, how every day seemed to bring something worse, and how fortunate her cousin was that he came to town so seldom.

Mrs. Baydon left temporarily in search of another puzzle to fit together, and Mr. Baydon retreated behind his broadsheet. While the others spoke, Ivy moved to the window where Mr. Rafferdy stood.

"Her ladyship is right," he said quietly as she drew near. "You do look well, Miss—forgive me, Mrs. Quent."

She smiled at him. "You need not beg forgiveness. It is all so new, even I forget what to call myself sometimes."

"I would simply call you remarkable. I trust this Mr. Quent of yours does the same. He is very lucky to have you."

"No more than Mrs. Rafferdy is to have you," she replied. "I hope very much to meet her one day."

Even as she spoke these words, she saw his expression darken, and she knew something terrible had happened.

"That will be impossible," he said, "for there is no Mrs. Rafferdy."

He spoke in a lowered voice, and in a minute she knew the whole terrible story, or at least as much as she needed to know. Her heart ached for him. To think she had been considering only her own worries.

"Mr. Rafferdy, I am truly sorry."

"You have no need to be sorry. I was saved from an unlucky match, one that would surely have led to disaster for my family. No, I am grateful."

"What you say is true. It is better that her father's actions were not revealed after she and you . . . but all the same, to endure such a dreadful happening—"

He shook his head. "It is long past, as far as I am concerned. I have had little time to think about it. Besides, it is nothing compared to what you have endured. I never had a chance to tell you how saddened I was to learn about Mrs. Lockwell. All of us were."

Such was the concern in his expression that her feelings on that matter were suddenly renewed, coming back to her all in a rush, and, compounded by thoughts of her father, they rendered her incapable of speech for a moment.

"Forgive me," he said. "Let me take you to a chair."

"No, I am quite well."

He studied her with that new, serious look of his. Then he gave her a wry smile. "So you are married, and I am not. I confess, when I saw you last, I was presumptuous enough to think our positions would be reversed when next we met."

She smiled in turn. "As had I. But either way, the result is the same. We are now free in every way to be acquaintances, Mr. Rafferdy. Or rather, I would hope, to be friends."

His smile wavered, but then it returned stronger than before. "It is my hope as well. And since both of us are in agreement, it is already done."

Mrs. Baydon returned then and set a wooden box on the table. "Mr. Baydon, could you put down your paper? I'm trying to choose a puzzle to fit together, and I need your help."

"I have you, Mrs. Baydon, and that is all I require to puzzle me." He turned a page.

She frowned at him. "No, I need your help opening the box. The lid is quite stuck."

"Why don't you have Mr. Rafferdy open it? As we all know, he's very good at opening things."

Mrs. Baydon's eyes shone. "Yes, you're very right. Come, Mr. Rafferdy, work that spell of yours and open up this box."

Ivy might have thought these words a jest, except for the way Mr. Rafferdy's face reddened. "Spell?" she said to him. "What spell is that?"

Mrs. Baydon answered for him. "The spell Mr. Bennick taught him. It turns out our Mr. Rafferdy is a magician after all, despite all his protests."

Ivy looked at him in wonder. "Is this true?"

He gave Mrs. Baydon a look of displeasure, but she only laughed, and at last he sighed. "It is true that I worked a spell," he said to Ivy. He twisted the ring on his right hand as he spoke, its blue gem winking. "But only with Mr. Bennick's aid. I am sure I could not recreate it."

"Nonsense," Mr. Baydon said, setting down his broadsheet. "If you would apply yourself to the study of magick, I am sure you would do very well."

"What reason would I have to do such a thing?"

"Reason? What reason do you need? Who should not want to discover for themselves a new power if they could?"

"I find I have quite enough power as it is," Mr. Rafferdy said. "I in no way crave more." The words were uttered so sharply that the room fell silent.

It was Lord Rafferdy who finally spoke. "Well, the day is short, and I am sure you are wanting to return to your sisters, Mrs. Quent. We have kept you long enough. I will have my driver take you home. I am glad to have met you and look forward to seeing you again."

Ivy expressed her thanks to him, to all of them, and was made to promise many times over that she would return soon, especially the moment Mr. Quent was in town.

"I do trust you will live up to your promise," Mr. Rafferdy said as he helped her into the carriage; he had accompanied her outside into the gray afternoon. "You must come back soon, Mrs. Quent. My father and I will be in the city for another half month before returning to Asterlane."

"You have my word," she said with a smile. "And that, Mr. Rafferdy, holds a power as sure as any spell."

$\mathcal{I}$VY HAD THE driver drop her a bit Downhill from the house. She knew her sisters would be wanting her, but the afternoon had been so pleasant; she did not want it to end just yet. Besides, all her worries would still be waiting for her when she arrived home.

As she walked, she thought about how she would compose a letter to Lord Rafferdy. There had been no opportunity to speak to him privately at Lady Marsdel's, and her father's condition was not something that could be easily discussed before so many people. However, she would write to him that night and ask for his assistance. While it might be somewhat presumptuous to do so, having only just reencountered him, any impropriety was surely outweighed by the grave nature of the situation.

Her hopes lifted, she walked past gardens and fountains, then struck out across the marble expanse of Moorwent's Square, which the rain had emptied of people. She was alone in the square save for the statue of General Moorwent upon his stallion, his sword pointing to the west. Breathing the cool air, she strolled past the statue.

"You have been gone too long."

Ivy turned around—then gave a small cry. On its pedestal, the horse tossed its head, muscles rippling along its stone neck. The general's sword no longer pointed west but rather toward the sky.

"They have tried again to open the door," the voice said. It was low, a man's voice. "They failed, but barely. Soon they will try again. It is only a matter of time until the binding breaks and they succeed."

Ivy knew that voice; she had heard it once before, at the old house on Durrow Street. Even as she thought this, the marble stallion stamped its hooves, and *he* appeared from behind the statue. As before, he was clad in clothes that seemed a costume from another era: archaic, even gaudy, but black, all black from head to toe, like the mask that covered his face. It seemed to alter as he approached: now amused, now angry, now something else she could not name. *Longing,* she thought for some reason.

"Who are you?" she said, for this time she had not lost the faculty for motion or speech. He had to know she would not attempt to run. All the same, she trembled. "What do you want?"

"Who are *you*?" he said. Or seemed to say. Whether he spoke the words or they sounded in her mind, she did not know. "What do *you* want?"

She made herself take a step toward him. "I want to know who they are and why they want to open the door."

"I already told you who they are." He shaped black-gloved fingers into an oval before his face. "They are the Vigilant Order of the Silver Eye, and they want to open the door for the same reason *he* wanted to close it."

"*He,* you say. You mean my father."

"He gave everything to close the way. It must not be opened again."

It was absurd that she should listen to anything this strange character said. He belonged in Madstone's far more than her father did. Except he had done magick—*was* doing it. She took a step toward him.

"Why must the door not be opened?"

"Because if it is opened, *they* will come through."

"They? You mean the Order of the Silver Eye?"

Now the mask flowed into an expression of fury. "No, you're not listening! I mean *they* will come. The Ashen." He pointed up at the sky, just as the statue of the general pointed with his sword. The stone horse opened its mouth in a silent cry.

Ivy had no idea what these words meant. All the same, a chill came over her, and the day seemed to darken a shade. "The Ashen." Her throat had gone dry. "Who are they?"

"They are ancient—older than the oldest history of this world. Older than speech itself. As old as the darkness between the stars, and as hungry." Now the black mask was wrought not in anger but revulsion. "They first came long ago, in a time when your forebears still dwelled in caves and hovels of sticks, huddling close to their feeble fires, clad only in filthy skins. The Ashen would have enslaved them all. The entire history of this world—all the civilizations that have ever risen and fallen in the eons since then—would never have been. But the first magicians stood against them and closed the way, so that the Ashen could not enter and their hunger was denied."

The damp air had gone cold. His words were like nothing Ivy had ever read in any of her father's books; they hardly even made sense. All the same, there was something in them that rang true. She thought of how she felt sometimes when night fell, how the darkness seemed to press in from all around, as if wanting to consume all light, all life.

"Why now?" she asked. "Why did these . . . why did the Ashen not try to return long ago?"

"They could not. By the time they were ready to attempt to break the enchantments wrought by the magicians, the distance had grown too far for even them to bridge. But now . . ." Again he cast the mask skyward. "Now the distance shrinks every day. They cannot yet reach by themselves, but if the way was opened for them, then through—"

"*Through the door the dark will come,*" Ivy murmured.

The mask turned toward her. "So you *are* listening. Good."

She shivered. "But the magicians stopped them long ago. You said so yourself. They can do so again."

"What magicians? In the last three hundred years, Altania has had but a single great magician, and he is long dead. Your father knew this. That is why he shut the door. That is why you must keep it shut."

A despair came over her. "My father can't help me now. He—"

"He has already helped you," the stranger said.

Again she thought of the riddle. *The key will be revealed in turn— Unlock the way and you shall learn.* Only it made no sense. Wasn't she supposed to keep the door shut, not unlock it?

"But I don't know the answer!" she cried. "What is it?"

"What is the answer?" He cocked his head, and now the black mouth was curved into a smile. It seemed a mocking expression. "Why, you've already held the answer in the palm of your hand."

She could only stare. It was no spell that had rendered her speechless this time, only astonishment.

He moved his onyx face close to hers. "They seek power, thinking they can use the Ashen for their own ends, but they are wrong. Instead, they will bring destruction upon all of Altania. You must enter the house before they do. It is the only hope." He started to back away.

"Wait!" she cried. "Don't go!"

"I have already placed you in too much danger. If they knew I had spoken to you, they would move even more swiftly."

Before Ivy could say anything more, he turned with a flourish of his black cape and vanished behind the pedestal on which the statue stood. She looked up. The horse stood motionless; the general's sword again pointed west.

Several pigeons flapped past her. A pair of men strolled through the square, talking. When at last she could move, she walked behind the statue. As she had expected, there was no sign of the masked man.

It didn't matter. She knew what she had to do. *You've already held the answer in the palm of your hand. . . .*

Ivy hurried Uphill, and when she reached the house on Whitward Street she did not stop to speak to her cousin or her sisters but instead raced up the stairs to the attic. She went to the shelf where she had hidden it behind a book and took it out.

As always, the small box was curiously heavy in her hand. She ran a finger over the silver symbol inlaid on the lid: an eye inscribed in a triangle. Then she went to her father's desk, sat, and took out pen and paper. She would write to Lord Rafferdy later, but first she had another letter to compose.

*Dear Mr. Rafferdy,* she wrote.

# CHAPTER TWENTY

*I*T WAS A small but comfortable house in the eastern end of the Old City, just past the Citadel. Rafferdy wasn't certain what he had expected—something more dilapidated, perhaps, with gargoyles leering from the eaves. And dimmer, with dusty windows that permitted the trespass of light only grudgingly, and suspicious heaps of books everywhere. Instead, the parlor the servant showed him into, while modest, was bright with sunlight and well-furnished.

True, along with a number of presumably scientific devices, there were many unusual objects of art within—Murghese ossuaries, jade figurines of pagan gods, and primitive idols carved of wood, which must have had their origins among the aboriginals of the New Lands. Still, these only lent the room a touch of the exotic and were things that might be found in the house of any well-traveled gentleman. None looked like the occult artifacts with which a magician might ply his craft.

Rafferdy sat in a chair, and when the servant left he drew out the small wooden box. He turned the box around in his hand, and the silver eye on the top seemed to wink as it caught the light. As when she gave it to him yesterday, he could not discern any sort of hinge or latch, but that something was contained inside he had no doubt. It was heavy in his hand.

He had been delighted at first when he received her note asking to meet with him. However, as he picked up his pen to reply, his spirits fell, and he considered declining the invitation. For what use was being around her? It was like looking at glorious sweets in a shop window but never getting to taste any of them. She was Mrs. Quent now; that could never be altered.

Only that notion was ridiculous. Once, in a kind of delirium brought on by feeling, he had thought to make her into Mrs. Rafferdy. However, that had been no more possible *then* than it was now—as his father had made clear.

All the same, he could not deny he had felt a pang when he saw her at the Silver Branch, and he had experienced a second, more severe spasm when he learned of her situation. Mrs. Quent. He could not unite the name with the picture of her in his mind. She seemed too fresh, too charming to bear such an austere and utilitarian appendage.

But there it was. She was married, and much as the notion bothered him, he knew he should rejoice in the fact. For it meant he could now be allowed to see her, to enjoy her company anytime they wished. Their association was no longer forbidden; indeed, it should even be encouraged now. He would take what portion of Mrs. Quent he could and would be grateful. He had written her a note, accepting her invitation, and had met her at Halworth Gardens yesterday afternoon, expecting a stroll in the sun and lively conversation.

Instead, she had asked him to work magick.

Again he studied the box, turning it in his hand. She did not say where she had obtained it or what she thought was inside, only that she had reason to believe it might contain something that could help her father and that she was certain it was bound shut by an enchantment.

*I have no intention of doing magick,* he had wanted to tell her. *Even if I have a capacity for such power, it is nothing I wish to have anything to do with. The only magick I have ever done was the result of a parlor trick, and even if there was something real to it, I could not hope to repeat it on my own. Nor is there anything in the world that could induce me to go to him willingly to seek his help.*

That is what he meant to say. Instead, he had said, *Give it to me, and I'll see what I can do.*

Such was the look of gratitude in her eyes that he could not bear it, and he made a jest that if she heard a loud noise and saw a large column of sparks rising up from the vicinity of Warwent Square, then it was only him attempting to work a spell.

This had won a laugh, and at the sound all his worries fled. They spent a pleasant hour walking in the garden, comparing the people they saw to flowers—shy Miss Primroses or grandiose Lord Peonies or old ladies in their bonnets, heads drooping like harebells. They parted with a promise to meet again soon, no matter the outcome of his experiment with the box.

He returned to his home and wrote a note. When the reply came back later that same day, he was hardly surprised at its contents. Rafferdy was welcome to call at his earliest convenience.

Footsteps echoed into the parlor. Rafferdy stood, tucking the box inside his coat. A moment later, Mr. Bennick entered the room, and the two men shook hands. As always, Mr. Bennick was dressed in black; the color emphasized the sharp lines of his face and the shadows around his eyes.

"I imagine you were surprised to get my letter," Rafferdy said.

"Not in the least," Mr. Bennick replied. "I knew it was only a matter of time until you came to visit with me."

Rafferdy was taken aback by the cool surety with which these words were uttered. "Indeed? Then I must presume you possess an enchanted mirror that shows you the future. In which case, I would very much like to see how I should bet at cards tonight."

"Magick cannot reveal things that have not come to pass—though there are some who hold it can open windows to the past. It was not a spell that told me you would come. It was that." He gestured toward Rafferdy's right hand.

"The ring, you mean?" Rafferdy said.

The taller man nodded. "I knew eventually you must come either wanting to know how to get it off or wanting to know why you were able to put it on in the first place. I confess, it was the latter result that I hoped for when I sent it to you. Would you care for a sherry?" He moved to a cabinet and took out a decanter.

Rafferdy's outrage was redoubled, and so agitated was he that it took him a moment to find his voice. "So you admit it, then! You admit you sent me this wretched thing." He clenched his right hand into a fist. The gem on the ring winked like a blue eye.

"Of course I sent it to you," Mr. Bennick said as he filled a pair of glasses. "A fact I was certain you'd quickly deduce. Didn't you?"

Rafferdy stepped toward him. "Yes, I did. But why? Was it a

punishment for that day I followed you? I was curious, that was all. It was a silly game, nothing more."

"It was not my intention to punish your curiosity, Mr. Rafferdy, but rather to reward it."

"Reward it? With a hideous piece of jewelry I can never remove in my life? You have a strange notion of a reward!"

"It can be removed," Mr. Bennick said, and handed him a glass.

Rafferdy could only stare as the other man sat in a chair by the window. He motioned to the chair opposite him. Rafferdy drew in a breath, quaffed half his sherry in one swallow, then sat.

"What did Mr. Mundy tell you about the ring?"

"That a magician could remove it only with powerful enchantments, spells that would likely cost the magician—" Rafferdy drew in a breath. "Cost him his mind or his life."

Mr. Bennick smiled, but it was an unwholesome expression to Rafferdy's eye, like the leer of a salacious faun in some ancient Tharosian comedy.

"That sounds like our good Mr. Mundy."

"So it's not true, then?"

"On the contrary, it's perfectly true. That is, it is true that a *magician* cannot remove a House ring without grave peril. But one who is not a magician—such a person can remove it easily."

"That makes no sense," Rafferdy said, exasperated by this talk. "If one isn't a magician, how can one put it on in the first place? Besides, I'm not a magician. I can't do magick."

"But you have done magick, as you well know. Even if you had not, you would still be a magician, Mr. Rafferdy, for you were born one." Mr. Bennick took a sip of his sherry. "You were a small child when I first met you at Lord and Lady Marsdel's—four or five years old, no more. All the same, I thought I saw a glimmer of it in you, so I researched the Rafferdy lineage and discovered I was right. You are directly descended from one of the seven Old Houses—the House of Gauldren, to be exact."

None of this was truly new to Rafferdy, yet it disturbed him all the same. "Then that means my father is a magician as well. Why didn't you give him a ring?"

"Because he would not be able to wear it. All magicians are descended from one of the Old Houses, Mr. Rafferdy, but not all who can claim such ancestry are born magicians. Only in a few does the Old Blood run true."

Rafferdy slouched in his chair. "Lucky me."

"Some would say you are lucky, but that is for you to decide."

"What if I decide to remove the ring?"

"That is your decision as well."

Rafferdy sat up. "How can it be done? You said it yourself—a magician can't take it off without grave risk."

"It's simple," Mr. Bennick said. "You must make it so you are no longer a magician."

This was absurd. He was being toyed with. "You said I was born one. How can I make myself into something I'm not?"

Mr. Bennick's dark gaze went to the window. "There are spells," he said at length. "Spells that, if performed carefully and worked by enough magicians acting in concert, can forever extinguish the spark of magickal talent within a man. He can remember what it is like to do magick, how it feels, can even speak the incantations and draw the runes of power, but the ancient words are ash on his tongue, the runes dead pebbles in his hands. Once the spell has been worked upon him, he is a magician no longer. Nor, once it has been done, can it ever be reversed. He is cut off from magick forever." Mr. Bennick turned his gaze back. "Is that what you want, Mr. Rafferdy?"

Rafferdy licked his lips. It made no sense; he had no desire to be a magician. All the same, Mr. Bennick's words had set his stomach to churning, and a clammy sweat had broken out on his brow. It was as if someone had asked him to consider severing one of his limbs with a knife. He found himself looking at the hand with which Mr. Bennick held his glass. It was the right hand and was unadorned by any ring. But everyone said he had been a magician once. . . .

Mr. Bennick set down his glass and stood. "So which is it, Mr. Rafferdy? I wonder which reason has brought you here today. Do you wish to have the ring removed, or do you wish to know what it means to wear it?"

Rafferdy looked at him through narrowed eyes. "Either way, why are you so keen to help me?"

"It is as I said that night at Lady Marsdel's house, Mr. Rafferdy— already the clouds gather on the horizon. A time will come again, perhaps sooner than we think, when Altania has need of great magicians."

"You think I can be one?"

"That is entirely up to you, Mr. Rafferdy."

Rafferdy glanced out the window. Above the rooftops, the sky was a flawless blue. However, he saw a boy on a corner hawking broadsheets, and he knew Mr. Bennick was right. Clouds were gathering— clouds of ink, and paper that crackled like lightning. But it was only a storm of words that brewed. Besides, it was not for Altania's sake he had come here, but for the sake of one person only. He drained his sherry glass and stood.

"I want to know more about magick," he said. "I want to learn more about the opening and closing of things."

For a long moment Mr. Bennick regarded him, eyes half hooded. At last he nodded. "Then let us begin."

## CHAPTER TWENTY-ONE

ELDYN SET DOWN the broadsheet—the latest issue of *The Messenger*—and knew that, for the moment, they were safe.

"I want to go out," Sashie said.

She paced before the door, turning every few steps, for the room was cramped. Eldyn had not chosen this inn for its comforts but rather for its paucity of windows and their narrow breadth—insufficient for even a slender young woman to pass through.

"Come and have an orange," he said, taking a pair of fruits from his coat pocket. "I bought them for you. I know how much you like them. They came all the way from across the sea." He held out one of the oranges.

"I can't breathe in here!" she cried, twisting her hair around a finger. "There's no air. I'll go mad if I can't go out, I swear it!"

She grabbed the door handle and tried to open it, but the door did not budge. Eldyn had locked it from within, and he kept the key on a chain around his neck. At first he had kept it in his pocket, until he woke one night to discover her trying to pilfer it.

Now she came to him and flung herself on her knees by his chair. "Please, dear brother. Please, you must let me go out. I can't bear it in here any longer. I'm suffocating." She turned large, pleading eyes up to him. "I only want to see the sun, to feel the wind on my face. Just for a moment, that's all. I'll perish if I don't."

She *did* look wan and faded. All the same, he shook his head. "You know that's impossible, dearest. You can't leave. Not until I am certain you understand—not until I can trust you to do what's right."

"You can trust me, dear brother." She rested her cheek against his leg. "I will do what you say. You must believe me."

He set down the orange and stroked her head. "I want to believe you, Sashie. I truly do. And I know you want to do what's best."

"Then you'll let me go outside?" She raised her head, her eyes wide and unblinking.

Eldyn sighed, then shook his head. "No, dearest."

At once her eyes narrowed, and her fingers dug into his leg. "I hate you!" she hissed, and leaped to her feet. "I hate you more than I ever hated Father! At least *he* didn't hold me prisoner."

She snatched up one of the oranges, then sulked to the little alcove that served as her bedchamber and jerked the curtain shut. Eldyn did not go to her; it was better she stayed in there, away from the one grimy window. Again he picked up the broadsheet, and for the first time in the days since they had fled the apartment over the shoe-maker's shop, he smiled.

"Even *he* can't be in two places at once," he said.

Earlier, he had dared to venture out to buy the oranges, hoping to cheer Sashie with them. On his way back to the inn he had passed a boy selling broadsheets, and a notice on the front page had caught his eye: HIGHWAYMAN MAKES OFF WITH MURGHESE GOLD. Eldyn had read the first lines of the story, and when the boy complained that only the large print was free, he paid his penny and took the broad-sheet back to the inn.

According to the article, the gold—a thousand crescents marked with the seven stars of the empire—had been on its way to a magnate in one of the western counties and represented the handsome profits from a trading venture. The shipment was heavily guarded, but one of the guards had been in a conspiracy with the highwayman. When the thief accosted the shipment, the guard turned on his fellows. One of the guards was shot dead, and the others were bound with rope while the highwayman and his accomplice made off with the Murghese gold.

In the fray, a bullet grazed the highwayman's head, knocking off his hat and sending his mask askew. While none of the guards got a good look at his face, enough was seen to be able to offer a general de-scription of the highwayman: he was youngish, tall, and broad-shouldered, with hair as gold as the coins he stole. The thieves were last seen riding west and were certainly on their way to Torland with their ill-gotten fortune. That the gold would find its way into the hands of would-be rebels was a certainty.

The incident had happened only two days ago. Again Eldyn calcu-lated the possibilities. Even if Westen (and there was no doubt in his mind that he was the highwayman in the story) rode as hard as possible to Torland, handed off the stolen gold, and came back by the swiftest coach, it would still be eighty hours at the earliest before he could return to Invarel. Which meant it did not matter if Sashie showed herself in front of the window. And which also meant they had time to make their escape.

They would book passage on a ship down the river, to County Caerdun in the very south of Altania. They could begin their life anew, far from Invarel—far from anyone that knew who they were. True, he did not quite know how they would live when they arrived in Caerdun. He had little more than the money to pay for their passage and no time to earn more before they left.

Not that he would still have a job if he were to return to Sadent, Mornden, & Bayle. There was no point in going back to the trading company. When he did not show up several days ago, his chair would have been given to the next man waiting in line for a job. He hoped Chubbs was well and avoiding Whackskuller's baton.

He felt a momentary pang when he thought that he would never again see Chubbs, or his old college companions, or (with an even greater pang) the theaters on Durrow Street, but it was the only way they could be safe from Westen. It was the only way they could be free.

Hardest to bear was the thought of not seeing Rafferdy again. While they had seen each other little of late, the thought of being so far away from his only true friend was painful. However, there was no choice. He would write to Rafferdy and tell him only that he was going away; he would not say where, for fear Westen might try to extort such information out of him. And perhaps someday, when Eldyn knew it was safe at last, he would be able to return to Invarel and tell Rafferdy all about it over a cup of punch.

He picked up his orange, turning it over in his hand, marveling that it had come so far from the place it grew, on a ship all the way from some sun-drenched orchard in the Principalities across the sea, on the eastern edge of the empire. He peeled the orange and ate it, savoring its sweetness. Then he left the chamber, locking the door behind him, and went to book passage for himself and his sister on a ship of their own.

*❧*

THE DOCKYARDS WERE down in Waterside, and since the weather was fair (and since he wasn't certain exactly how much passage on a ship down the river would cost), Eldyn forwent a hack cab and walked instead. The night had been short, the lumenal was to be longish, and the air was already growing sultry. As he walked in the sunlight, he could imagine he was already basking in the gentle climes of southern Altania, beginning his new life there.

Perhaps it was thinking of the future that made him nostalgic for the past. Besides, he was walking through Waterside already, and it was hardly out of his way. He turned down a narrow lane and walked past the fuller's and the brewery. Then he rounded a corner, and the Golden Loom came into view.

The inn looked drabber than he remembered. Had Mr. Walpert's health taken a turn for the worse so he could no longer keep the place up? No—it was only that Eldyn's memories of the place were overly kind. For a time, he and Sashie had been happy there. After what they had endured of late, it was no wonder seeing the Golden Loom filled him with fond thoughts. But far gladder times lay ahead of them, in Caerdun in the south. Besides, his thoughts would not be nearly so fond if Miss Delina Walpert were to come out the door and see him there! Eldyn hurried on, giving the inn a wide berth.

Just ahead, on the other side of the street, a tall figure appeared from around a corner.

The capacity to move, to breathe, fled Eldyn. The soles of his boots adhered to the cobblestones of the street. It could not be that he was here. He was in Torland, gloating over his ill-gotten gold. That was what the story in *The Messenger* had said.

Westen walked toward the Golden Loom on long legs, his boots and the brass buttons on his coat gleaming in the sun, his gold hair loose about his shoulders. He moved not furtively like a criminal but like a lord in his own land. A few more strides and he would be even with Eldyn. All he had to do was turn his head just a little to the left. The street was neither wide nor crowded, and nothing would hide Eldyn from the highwayman's gaze.

Even if he could have moved, Eldyn dared not for fear the motion would attract attention. Westen reached the door of the inn. He started to open it—he was going to go inside.

The highwayman paused. Perhaps it was some feral, robber's instinct that let him know he was being observed. He stepped back from the door, then turned around.

Night fell.

The sun was extinguished in an instant, but there was no moon, no stars, no streetlamps or glowing candlelit windows. All was black as the Abyss. Eldyn staggered, hands groping before him. Had fear struck him blind?

A hand fell on his shoulder. "This way," spoke a voice in his ear.
He was aware of a slender silvery shape beside him.

"Quickly now, follow me," the voice said.

Who or what the silvery figure was, Eldyn did not know, only that
it was not Westen. The shimmering form held out a hand. He grasped
it in his own, then lurched after the other as he was led through darkness.

Eldyn felt them turn left and right, and several times his boots
caught on something rough and hard, but each time the silvery figure
kept a grip on him and pulled him onward. At last he could run no
further. He staggered to a halt, his sweating hand slipping from the
other that grasped it.

"It's all right," the voice said. "I think we've gone far enough."

A silvery hand moved, and the sun appeared, burning the darkness away in an instant. The light dazzled Eldyn's eyes so that for a
minute he was as blinded as he had been in the preternatural dark. At
last he blinked the tears away, and he saw the Lowgate just ahead up
the street. They had come farther than he thought, to the edge of the
Old City.

"Are you well?" said the voice beside him.

He turned and saw that his companion was not some shimmering
wraith but rather a young man in a black coat. He was of a height and
age with Eldyn, but light where Eldyn was dark. His eyes were sea-
colored, and his hair was bound with a red ribbon behind his neck.
His features were fine, but a squared-off jaw, pronounced brows, and
a short blond beard lent him a manly look.

"So that's who you've been running away from," he said.

Eldyn shook his head, still trying to understand what had just happened. "What did you say?"

"I know you've been on the sly. Moving out of your apartment so
quickly, the way you're always casting glances over your shoulder. By
the look on your face when that tall fellow came into view, I can only
guess he's the one you've been trying to avoid. Bad luck to run right
into him, wasn't it?"

Eldyn frowned. "How do you know all that?"

The young man gave a sheepish grin, then chewed his lip.

"Have you been following me?" A fresh dread came over Eldyn.
"By God, are you in league with him?"

The other laughed. "Would I have helped you escape from him if
that were the case?"

Eldyn was forced to admit he had a point. But if the other had
helped him to escape, how had it been done? It was as if the shadows

that usually cowered from the sun by day, in corners and beneath grates, had crept out to cloak them. . . .

The bright light burned the last of the gloom from Eldyn's brain. It had been an illusion, of course. He looked again at the young man and realized it was not the first time he had seen him. The beard was a new affectation, but otherwise he looked just as he had that night on Durrow Street, outside the Theater of the Moon.

Only it wasn't just outside the theater Eldyn had seen him, was it? He thought of the silvery form he had glimpsed in the darkness.

"The moon in the play," Eldyn said. "That was you."

The young man grinned and bowed with a flourish. "I trust you enjoyed the performance."

Eldyn had, but the illusions had not ended when he left the theater that night. "You followed me. I saw a shadow behind me when I entered the Sword and Leaf, and then again when I left. I thought it was my imagination, only it was you."

"You saw that? You weren't as drunk as you appeared. Don't look so offended—if someone was watching over you, perhaps you should be glad of it. Duskfellow's is not exactly a safe place to take a nap at night. You frightened that one robber off with your trick, conjuring that ghost, but others would have found you soon enough if—"

"If you hadn't covered me with shadows," Eldyn said, understanding at last. "Fair enough. I am glad you were there. But that doesn't explain why you were following me then. Or today."

The young man shrugged. "Our theater is always looking for new talent, and I saw what you could do with shadows. Working light is the same, really, the other side of the coin. Besides, you seem . . ." He shook his head. "Well, it doesn't matter. We know each other now. Or we should, at any rate. My name is Dercent Argray Fanewerthy. It's an awful name, I know. From the moment of my birth, my dear parents were evidently trying to make it a certainty that I would run away and join the theater at the earliest possible moment. Everyone calls me Dercy. Everyone I don't despise, that is."

Despite all that had happened, Eldyn couldn't help returning the other's grin as well as his handshake. He introduced himself. Then a new wonder struck him.

"Dercy?" he said. He thought back to that night half a year ago, when he went to see the angel, and the old priest shouted at him.

*What are you doing, Brother Dercent?* the older priest had said to the younger. *Are you talking to someone out there?*

"The old church at St. Adaris," Eldyn realized aloud.

Now it was the other's turn to appear surprised. "How did you know that I . . . ? Wait a minute, I know why you look familiar. Brother Garus thought it was an illusionist that night, come to the church to taunt us, but it was you there in the shadows."

Eldyn could only nod.

"I took you for an illusionist as well," Dercy said. "Not that I was as outraged as Brother Garus at the notion. On the contrary, I left St. Adaris not a month after. Much to the disappointment of my parents, I'm sure. Not that I've spoken to them since they gave me over to the deacon at St. Adaris. I suppose they thought it would keep me out of trouble. Shows how little they knew about priests."

These words struck Eldyn like a blow. To think that Dercy had tossed away what Eldyn had always dreamed of. "You left the Church?"

"Yes! And you are partly to blame, Mr. Garritt. After seeing you that night, I knew I could not stay there, that there were better things waiting for me beyond those iron fences. Brother Garus said you were wicked, a devil, but I knew he was wrong. Scripture says that evil can come under the guise of beauty, and perhaps that's so, but beauty that is true—there can never be ill in that. Though I glimpsed you for only a moment that night, I knew fat old Garus was wrong about you. For, I thought, how could one be wicked when he looked so much like an angel?"

He suddenly fell silent and glanced away. Eldyn was grateful, for he could not suppress a grimace. He was no illusionist, but he thought of the things he had done, and he wondered if Brother Garus wasn't right, if he wasn't a wicked thing. He had always told himself it was his father who had kept him from entering the Church, but what if that wasn't the reason at all? What if he was simply afraid God wouldn't have him?

Dercy turned back, and his expression became one of worry. He reached a hand toward Eldyn—

—then pulled back, his eyes growing large. "Behind you," he said.

Eldyn looked over his shoulder, and his heart lurched up into his throat. A tall figure in a rich coat of russet velvet walked up the street. Eldyn turned back to tell Dercy to run.

The street in front of him was empty. He looked in either direction, but there was no sign of the other young man anywhere. Dercy was gone. He had woven his illusions and had abandoned Eldyn. Nor was there any time for Eldyn to work his own trick with shadows. He started to dash up the street, but his boot caught on a stone and he went sprawling to the cobbles, knocking his chin so hard he saw stars.

A strong hand gripped his arm, pulled him to his feet, and dragged him into the dimness of an alleyway.

"Hello, Mr. Garritt," Westen said.

Eldyn let out a strangled sound and tried to flee, but the other's grip was too strong. The highwayman pressed him against the wall.

"I am displeased with you, Mr. Garritt. I am sure I made myself very clear when last we spoke, and though it was many months ago, I am certain you can recall what we discussed."

Eldyn shook his head. "But I thought that—"

"You thought I had forgotten, that I had other matters to concern me, and that I was far away." He smiled. "Well, as you can see, I am very much here. And I have not forgotten our agreement."

Words burst out of Eldyn in a babble. "I can get you the money. . . . I can give you some of it today . . . if you would just let me . . . I can earn the rest." He was ashamed of the fear in his voice, ashamed of the way he trembled. "I'll pay you back, I swear it."

"Do you honestly think it's the regals I care about?" Westen said in a good-natured tone. "Trust me, I have far more gold than that little sum I gave you. Or haven't you been reading the broadsheets of late?" He brushed his coat aside, revealing a fat purse at his belt. He let the coat fall back, and his tone became more serious. "No, it is not gold you have robbed me of, Mr. Garritt. Rather, it is my reputation. You see, men know that I always honor my promises. That is why they trust me. But that trust must go both ways, and so the men I do business with must see that if one does not honor his promises to me, there are consequences for that breach of trust."

He put a hand beneath Eldyn's chin, lifting Eldyn's gaze to meet his own.

"Do you understand me?"

Eldyn nodded, then winced, for his chin still smarted.

"Are you well, Mr. Garritt? You took quite a tumble there." The highwayman ran a thumb along his jaw, stroking it. Somehow that gentle touch was worse than any blow.

"Please," Eldyn said, his words hoarse. "Do with me what you will, but leave my sister out of this. It is not her fault."

Westen arched an eyebrow. "Do with you what I will, you say? Indeed, I could think of a thing or two to do with you, Mr. Garritt. I always thought your sister pretty, but you are prettier still." His hand moved down to Eldyn's throat, fingers encircling it, squeezing ever so slightly. "Tell me, Mr. Garritt, is this how I should punish you?"

The highwayman leaned forward and pressed his lips to Eldyn's in a kiss. Eldyn let out a moan, and new shame flooded him.

Westen drew back, a grin on his face. "Pervert. You should be back down at Durrow Street. I know you've been going there. But don't fear—others might frown upon the Siltheri, but I know they have a part to play in what's to come. How can the king's men engage an army that isn't there or predict the motions of a foe they cannot see?"

Eldyn scrubbed his mouth with the back of his hand. "I don't know what you're talking about."

"Don't you? Then understand this. You are mine, Eldyn Garritt. You belong to me. I bought you for a hundred regals. You will carry what messages I say, to whom I say, and when I say. That is the nature of our relationship. Out of generosity—indeed, out of benevolent affection—I am giving you one last chance to behave. But if you choose not to . . ."

His smile did not waver, but it became a feral expression, a display of teeth and hunger.

"If you choose to fail me again, I will have no choice but to approach your sister at some moment you are not with her—and you cannot always be with her. Nor can you hide her from me. I know where she is at this very minute, at the inn on the edge of Lowpark. I will lure her to me with flattering words. I will take her to some secret place under the guise of showing her some delightful thing." He bent his head, lips brushing against Eldyn's ear. "And there I will ravage her in the most brutal fashion, over and over again, until she is utterly ruined, in spirit and in body, fit only to be a Waterside whore—until the time comes, no doubt sooner rather than later, when she drinks herself into her grave."

Where it came from, Eldyn didn't know. Perhaps he had inherited some small part of Vandimeer Garritt after all. Fear burned away as a hot rage flared up within him. He clenched his hand into a fist, then with all his might threw a punch at Westen's face.

The highwayman stepped aside and brought his hand up, deflecting the blow. As Eldyn's arm came down, Westen grasped it and twisted it about the wrist, so that Eldyn let out a gasp. His anger burned to a cinder and was extinguished. No, he was not his father.

"You cannot fight me, Mr. Garritt." Westen's smile returned. "But I think you see that now. You will resume your work at once. I have no doubt you recall what to do. Simply read the advertisements in *The Fox* as you did before. Do you understand?"

Eldyn stared. His eyes stung, and his jaw throbbed. He wanted to lie down in the street and let the people, the horses, pass over him, until he was ground into the stones and was gone.

Westen twisted his wrist another degree. "Answer me, Mr. Garritt. Do we have an agreement?"

No, there was no need to lie in the street; he was already worn down. Eldyn opened his mouth to speak the word he must.

"There he is!" shouted a voice. "In that alley there—the tall one, just like I told you."

Eldyn jerked his head up at the sound of boots against stone. Westen turned around. A pair of the king's redcrests ran into view from up the street. They must have come from their post by the Lowgate. In a moment they were upon Westen, gripping his arms from either side.

"Caught in the very act, it would seem," one of the men said. "Don't you robbers usually wait until nightfall, or have you become so brazen you'll accost a gentleman in broad daylight?"

Eldyn felt a cacophony of emotions: relief, pain, and a kind of aching gratitude at the soldier's words. *A gentleman,* the man had called him. Even as Eldyn thought this, he noticed that Westen's coat, so rich a moment ago, now appeared shabby and patched. Eldyn's own coat, decent but plain, was now richly embroidered with gold. Beyond the soldiers, another figure came into view. It was Dercy, grinning.

"You are mistaken," Westen said smoothly, letting go of Eldyn's hand. Eldyn could only be impressed at his calm. "My friend and I were merely having a friendly disagreement. I am no thief—as I am sure you will agree if you give me a chance to explain."

*Or, rather, if they give him a chance to bribe them,* Eldyn thought. He doubted it would be the first time the highwayman had bought himself freedom with gold.

Eldyn looked up at the soldiers. His gold . . .

"Is this true, sir?" the redcrest asked him. "Do you know this man?"

Eldyn licked his lips. "Yes, it is true," he said, and Westen grinned.

"It is true," Eldyn went on, his voice rising, "that this man is not just a common thief but, I believe, the very worst sort of criminal—a traitor to the Crown."

In a quick motion he reached forward, his hand darting inside Westen's coat, and snatched away the purse. Westen grabbed for it but only succeeded in knocking it from Eldyn's grasp. The purse fell to the cobbles and burst open in a glittering spray.

For a moment all of them stared at the gold coins that tumbled to the street, then one of the soldiers bent to pick up a coin. He held it in front of him, turning it around so that it caught the sunlight. Seven stars glittered on one side and a sickle shape on the other.

"By God, no common thief indeed," the soldier said. "I suppose there are nine hundred ninety-nine more Murghese crescents just like this one." He tightened his grip on Westen's arm. "You should have run to Torland like the broadsheets said."

The other soldier had already whistled and motioned with his hand. Several more redcrests came into view. They grasped Westen and pulled him into the street. The highwayman did not resist. One of the soldiers asked Eldyn if he was well, if he knew this man. Eldyn said he was fine and that he had never seen his assailant before. It was only things the thief had said that had made him think he was a traitor. The soldiers told him he could go and that he had done a service for king and country. That this rebel would hang in Barrowgate was a certainty, they said.

Eldyn moved away, but after a few steps he turned and glanced back over his shoulders. Westen was looking at him. The highwayman grinned and shook his head. Despite the warm sunlight, a shiver coursed through Eldyn. Then the soldiers turned Westen around, not gently, and hauled him toward the Lowgate.

"Are you all right?" Dercy said beside him. "I came as fast as I could. It took a moment to make the soldiers believe me. I had to—" He made a weaving motion with his fingers. "Well, you know. I had no idea about the gold though. Brilliant stroke of luck that was."

The soldiers passed through the Lowgate and were gone. Eldyn let out a breath. "Come on," he said. "Let's go get a drink."

"God be praised!" Dercy said, draping an arm around Eldyn's shoulder as the two went in search of the nearest tavern.

## CHAPTER TWENTY-TWO

𝓑RIGHTDAY CAME, AND again the Madderly–Stoneworth Hostel for the Deranged was open to visitors. However, as before, Ivy was allowed only to observe Mr. Lockwell through the small window in the door of his cell.

She watched her father pace in circles, sometimes pausing to make twisting motions with his hands. His hair and beard were matted, his face slack and grayish. Ivy wanted to call to him through the door, to tell him that she had written to Lord Rafferdy, that soon they would take him out of there, that they would take him home. However, before she could speak, the day warden shut the window.

The subject's behavior was very atypical, the warden said as he led her back to the front gate. They did not yet understand the nature of his malady. Until they did, they could not risk any sort of contamination. He must remain isolated. She could come back next week if she wished. They would in no way be surprised if she did not.

"I will come," she said.

The warden nodded absently and shut the gate behind her.

When she arrived back at Whitward Street, she told Rose and Lily to get ready for church. Lily dragged about. What could God care, she complained, if they sat in a musty old building and listened to some man droning on?

"We do not go because God cares," Ivy said, putting on her bonnet, "but because we care, and because our mother cared. Now get your shawl. It's chilly out."

The church was no more than half full, and Ivy was forced to concede the quality of the sermon was likely to do little to change Lily's opinions. The priest mumbled through it, and his surplice, while thankfully clean, was in need of mending. Pigeons flapped among the rafters, unnerving those in the pews—especially the ones who had worn their best hats.

However, when the time came to kneel in prayer, she forgot the birds and the dull sermon, and the dust on the windows only made the light that fell through them all the more golden. Bathed in that light, she shut her eyes and bowed her head in prayer.

She meant to pray for her mother, and for her father, and for Mr. Quent's safe return. Instead, it was the words of the first prayer she had learned as a girl that came as a murmur to her lips. *Though I stand in darkness, I will fear no shadow. Though I am lost, I will know the way. Though I dwell in sorrow, I will weep no tears. For I am not alone.*

It seemed impossible—nothing in her life had changed, and the old church was as dilapidated as ever—but all the same her heart felt lighter as she walked with her sisters down the steps of the church. When they reached the bottom and saw a tall young gentleman in a gray coat step from a glossy four-in-hand, her spirits rose higher yet.

"Mr. Rafferdy!" Lily shouted before Ivy could say anything. She dashed forward to greet him, Rose barely a step behind her.

Lily held out her hand, demanding that it be kissed. Mr. Rafferdy graciously obliged and would have given Rose the same greeting, but she became shy and bowed her head as he tipped his hat to her.

"I'm very cross with you!" Lily pronounced as Ivy joined them. "We haven't seen you in months, and then Ivy gets to go to a party with you the moment she arrives back in the city."

"I told you it wasn't a party," Ivy said. "We met quite by chance and had tea, that's all."

"You should at least have called on us," Lily went on. "Fifteen minutes would have done. Your manners are dreadful, Mr. Rafferdy."

"Lily!"

Ivy was prepared to say more, but Rafferdy affected a serious look and bowed toward Lily. "You're quite right to chastise me. I am, as our liege above certainly knows, an awful man."

"No, you aren't!" Rose exclaimed, looking up. "You're anything but awful. The priest said God is in the light, and there's light all around you. I can see it even when my eyes are shut. It's blue and silver, not green and gold like Ivy, but every bit as bright. Maybe brighter."

Rafferdy cocked his head and gazed at her. "I'm not quite sure what you mean, Miss Rose."

"She doesn't mean anything," Lily said, rolling her eyes. "Rose says all sorts of silly things. Don't pay it any attention."

"It's not silly," Rose said, and it seemed she wanted to say more, but she grew flustered.

Ivy took her hand. "Come, dearest. We had best walk home before it rains."

"Or better yet," Mr. Rafferdy said, "let me drive you home."

This suggestion was met with great enthusiasm from Lily, and Rose brightened at the idea. Ivy could find no reason to decline the offer, and the four of them drove back Downhill in the carriage.

"Everyone looks so small from in here," Lily said, leaning out the window. "It's marvelous. But it's dreadful that Mr. Garritt is not here. Where is he, Mr. Rafferdy? Have you seen him? You must tell him he's been just as awful as you have for avoiding us."

Mr. Rafferdy confessed it had been some time since he had seen Mr. Garritt, as both had been busy with their respective business, but he assured her he would pass along the message when next they met. As he spoke, he gave Ivy a wink; she turned away to conceal her smile from her sister.

When they reached Whitward Street, Ivy hoped that her sisters would go in and leave her to speak to Mr. Rafferdy alone. However,

Lily insisted that he come in for tea, and he readily consented, though once inside, Ivy realized that they had nowhere to receive him.

"It is not your day or time to go in there," the housekeeper said, appearing from the dining room as Lily bounded up the steps and into the parlor. "I will tell the master when he returns!"

"If Mr. Wyble is not here, then he cannot possibly mind if we use the parlor," Mr. Rafferdy said, coming up the stairs. "Now, can he?"

"It's not their day to use it," the woman said, though she seemed loath to look him in the eyes.

"Dear madam," he said, "it is not my intention to disregard the rules set by the esteemed master of the house, but I am certain an exception can be made. You see, I consider Mr. Wyble to be a very good friend. When he returns, be sure to tell him I said so. I have no doubt he will be in no way displeased."

Ivy was certain that would be the case. It was all Mr. Wyble craved: to be considered the friend of those he thought better than himself.

While the housekeeper did not appear pleased herself, she made no further objections and even consented to bring them a pot of tea, which was nearly hot. They enjoyed an hour in the parlor, talking, laughing, and listening to Lily play her favorite—that is, her most morbid—pieces on the pianoforte. Then, just when Ivy was wondering how to ask her sisters to leave for a while, Rafferdy stood and said that he had something he needed to discuss with Ivy in private. So gentlemanly was he in making the request, again kissing Lily's hand, that even she could make no complaint and departed willingly with Rose, after extracting one last promise from him that he would pass along her greetings to Mr. Garritt.

"Thank you, Mr. Rafferdy," Ivy said when they were alone. "You are very indulgent of my sisters, particularly my youngest. More, perhaps, than is entirely prudent, but I do appreciate it."

"Young ladies should be indulged," he replied. "How else are they to become the silly, pretty things society requires them to be? If they are denied too many indulgences, they are bound to turn to books instead and end up like yourself, Mrs. Quent—strong-minded and full of opinions. Besides, any time I can break one of Mr. Wyble's rules, I cannot pass up the opportunity."

She laughed. "Be careful, Mr. Rafferdy. He *is* a lawyer. It might be unwise to violate too many of his regulations."

"You may be right. I suppose he'd lock me away with glee if I trespass too freely on his domain."

It had been a joke; he could not have known. All the same, Ivy's own mirth ceased, and she turned away.

"What's the matter, Mrs. Quent? You suddenly went pale."

She had not intended to tell him. While she had asked for his help, he did not need to know what had befallen Mr. Lockwell. All the same, before she could stop herself, she told him how Mr. Wyble had consigned her father to Madstone's. As she spoke, his face was possessed by that new seriousness she had first observed at the Silver Branch; again she could only wonder what had happened to him in the months she was away from the city.

When she finished, he offered at once to speak to his father, to see what must be done to extract her father from such intolerable conditions. This moved her, and she thanked him. However, she was forced to confess that she had been presumptuous enough to write to Lord Rafferdy the very lumenal after their encounter at the Silver Branch.

"And has he replied?"

Ivy nodded. "I received a note from him almost at once. He said he would make inquiries to determine the best course of action and that he would contact me again as soon as he had news."

"You can be assured he will. If my father says he will do a thing, then he will, without fail. I am glad you did not wait to write to him." He shook his head. "All the same, it must be terrible to bear. Here I invited you to tea and made you endure the inane chatter of my associates, while all the time you were enduring this hardship! Forgive me, Mrs. Quent."

"No, I was glad to spend time at Lady Marsdel's," she said. "I left with a lighter heart, and that has helped me to do what I must. Besides, we will have my father with us again very soon."

"And you think this can help him somehow?" He drew the small wooden box from his coat pocket.

"I do," she said.

"But how?"

She didn't know how to explain her encounters with the man in the black mask. If she told him, he might decide to commit *her* to Madstone's. Instead, she said, "I'm not entirely sure. I think I'll know more when it is opened. If it can be opened. Have you . . . ?"

A scowl crossed his face, and now he looked more like the old Mr. Rafferdy she remembered. "No, I haven't been able to open it. I don't know why everyone is so keen for me to attempt magick. It's clear I have no aptitude for it. I've been to Mr. Bennick's house three times. I've endured his company, I've listened to every musty word he's uttered, and I've repeated them over and over, but it's no use. The thing is as locked as ever." He slumped into a chair. "There! Now you know I am utterly worthless."

Ivy could not help a small smile. "You are far from worthless, Mr. Rafferdy. But I think perhaps I am right when I say you are accustomed to getting what you want with little effort."

"Avoiding effort is precisely what I have always wanted."

"Yet some things can be gained only through diligence and by applying oneself."

"Have you been talking to my father? You sound very like him."

Her smile faded, and a heaviness came over her. "Please, Mr. Rafferdy. Won't you try again to open it?"

Now the look on his face was one of chagrin, and he sat up straight. "Of course I will."

He held the box in his hands, gazing at it. Then he spoke an incantation in the tongue of magick. He uttered the words easily and smoothly—far more fluently than Ivy had been able to do that time she attempted a spell. However, it was to no avail; the box remained fast shut.

"There, I told you," he said, holding the box toward her. "It's no use."

"Are you certain that is a spell of opening?"

"Yes, I'm certain. It's the same spell he had me say that night when I opened Mrs. Baydon's locket."

"If I understand correctly, it was you who bound it shut. Is a different spell needed for something you did not enchant yourself?"

"I asked Mr. Bennick that. I did not mention the box, of course, only that I wondered what else the spell might be used on. He said it would open any small object locked by magick, as long as the spell was equal in force to that which first bound it. However, it's clear I'm no match for the enchantment that was placed on this thing."

"No, you're wrong!" Ivy said, standing. "Mr. Bennick didn't say you had to have equal ability or talent. Rather, he said that the spell had to be of equal *force*. You spoke the enchantment well, Mr. Rafferdy, but you did not believe it would work. I could tell from your face and the sound of your voice. Magick words and runes don't have power in and of themselves. They are symbols, that's all—tools meant to direct the mind and magickal energies properly. It is the will of the magician that truly matters." She felt herself blush. "At least, that is what I've read in books."

He looked up at her, and she feared she had gone too far, that she had insulted him, and he would leave. Instead, he laughed.

"I think it would have been better if it were you who was descended from the House of Gauldren, Mrs. Quent, and not I."

"It would not matter if I was, Mr. Rafferdy. I am a woman and can never work magick." She spoke the words with regret but with humor as well. "So, as women must always do, I must rely upon another to do what is forbidden to me."

"Indeed, how like a woman!" he exclaimed. "You demur on the account of being powerless, yet I have the feeling I am not the only one who has grown accustomed to easily getting what is desired. With such a lack of power as you so prettily and eloquently display, Mrs. Quent, you are assured of achieving your every end without fail. A truth to which I'm sure your own Mr. Quent can attest. Very well, then, direct me as you will. Any power *I* may possess is at your disposal. I have no doubt *you* would use it far more wisely than I."

Ivy felt her spirits rise with real hope. "Try the spell again, Mr. Rafferdy. However, this time I want you not merely to speak the words, but to envision each word as a thought coming from your own mind, each sound as a breath from deep inside. With each utterance, you must feel your will being exerted upon the box."

A furrow creased his brow as he raised the box and gazed at it. The magician's ring glinted blue on his hand. For a long moment he was silent. Then he drew a breath and spoke in the ancient tongue of magick.

The sunlight coming through the window went thin, and the air in the parlor darkened a shade. Ivy shivered, crossing her arms. As he spoke the final words, it seemed to her there came a sound on the very edge of hearing, like a rumble of thunder that had all but faded away.

Their eyes met. "Go on," she said at last.

He shook his head. "No, you try it."

She took the box from him, running her fingers over it, attempting without success to pry it open. However, as she touched the silver eye inlaid in the wood, the symbol depressed under her fingertip.

The top of the box sprang open with a *click*. So surprised was she that she fumbled the box and something small fell out, striking the parlor floor with a loud noise. Mr. Rafferdy bent forward and retrieved it.

"It's just a ball," he said. "A metal ball."

He held it out to her. It was, as he said, a small sphere forged of some metal. It was reddish in color, as if rusty, but smooth to the touch. The ball was cold in her hand.

He stood. "I'm sorry, Mrs. Quent, but I don't see how that's going to be any help. Perhaps you were mistaken about the box?"

Ivy turned the orb over and saw there was a small hole in it. She thought of her father in his cell at Madstone's, how he had sometimes paused in his pacing to make twisting motions with his hands. No, she had not been wrong about the box.

"Come with me," she said, and without further explanation she hurried from the parlor and up the stairs. It took him a moment to react, so that by the time he came into the attic she had already reached the corner where the celestial globe stood.

"What is this thing?" he said as he drew closer.

"It's my father's. It shows the mechanics and motions of the heavens." She examined it, searching, looking for something she had never seen before but that she was certain was there. It had to be. "The larger, hollow orbs represent the celestial spheres."

He touched one of the balls suspended on the end of a metal arm. "And I suppose these are the eleven planets."

"No, not eleven," she said, gripping the metal orb in her hand.

And there it was. It was on the rear side of the globe, close into the center, and very small—a round nubbin of metal. It was no wonder, given the profusion of gears and levers and arms, that she had never seen it before. She took the reddish metal ball and lined up the hole with the post. Then she pushed it into place.

There was a metallic sound. The ball pushed back against her hand, as if somewhere deep within the globe a spring had been released. She let go of it, and the post extended outward from the globe, telescoping into a thin metal arm with the reddish orb at its end.

Mr. Rafferdy raised an eyebrow. "Well, that did something, all right. But what is it?"

"It's the twelfth planet," Ivy said. "The red wanderer that appeared in the sky a few months ago. It's been gone for millennia, since before recorded history began, but now it's come back."

*So, you have returned at last from your wanderings,* her father had said that night when she first saw the red spark in the sky. Somehow he had known about the planet and had incorporated it into the globe. She put her hands on the knobs and levers and began to work them.

"What are you doing?"

Ivy watched the spheres and arms as they spun and turned. It was all different now. Something must have been altered in the interior workings of the globe. The planets moved in patterns she had never seen before. The two smallest planets, Vaelus and Cyrenth, swung toward each other—then passed by without touching. She kept working the dials and levers.

*"When twelve who wander stand as one,"* she murmured.

"What's that?"

She shook her head. "It's a riddle. Something my father left for me."

He walked around the globe. "I see. They're lining up, aren't they?"

He was right. At first the planets had been scattered in all directions around the globe. However, each time the spheres made a full revolution, they drew nearer and nearer one another. Now they were all on the same side of the globe, now gathered in the same quadrant, now forming a ragged line. She kept turning the knobs, even though her hands had started to ache, simulating the passage of dozens, of hundreds of years.

This time it was not a *click* but a tone like the chiming of a bell. Ivy pried her stiff fingers from the dials. On the far side of the globe, all twelve of the balls—the planets—stood in a perfect line.

"It's a grand conjunction," she said, filled with wonder. "But that's impossible. The planets never all line up." Or at least they never had in the memory of mankind.

He walked again around the globe. "Look here!" he said.

Ivy followed him, looking where he pointed. A small opening had appeared in the centermost sphere. It was too dark to see what it was, but something glinted within.

"Go on," he said. "You're the one who solved the riddle."

Ivy leaned forward, slipping her fingers into the opening. She came away with something small. She opened her hand, and as when Mr. Rafferdy had worked magick, a shiver passed through her.

*"The key will be revealed in turn,"* she said softly. She turned the iron key over in her fingers. It was cool and heavy.

"I think there's something else in there." Mr. Rafferdy leaned in and plucked something out of the niche in the globe. It was a piece of paper, folded several times into a neat square.

"Please, you open it," she said, for her hands were shaking.

"It's a letter," he said. "Addressed to you."

"Would you read it for me?" Her hand was a fist around the key.

"Are you certain?"

She nodded. Mr. Rafferdy took the letter to the window where the light was stronger.

*"My Dearest Ivy,"* he began, *"if you are reading this, it means something has gone awry, and I have been forced to do something I hoped I would not have to do. I cannot say I am entirely surprised; that things might take a bad turn is precisely why I have made these preparations. Since you are reading this, it seems my riddles were not beyond you. Not*

*that I thought they would be; I know you are an exceedingly clever girl.
Or young lady, I suppose by now. How I wish I could see how you have
grown!*

*"But there is no time to wonder about that. The hour grows late,
and I have only a little time left to write this and to conceal the key.
That they will come searching for it, I have no doubt. The binding is
strong and will endure for a long while. However, in time, others will
attempt to undo our work and open the way—and I fear those who do
so will be members of my own circle, the Vigilant Order of the Silver
Eye."*

Ivy could not suppress a gasp. The man in the black mask had told
her of the order, but that her father had been a member of it was
something she had not considered.

Mr. Rafferdy looked up from the letter. "Are you well?"

"Yes, I'm fine. Please, go on."

He returned his gaze to the letter. *"I have discovered that there are
deceivers within the order. They will seek to open the door, thinking
they can use what would come through for their own ends. They are
wrong. To break the binding would open the way for something unspeakable. That I have time on my side is my one comfort, for the enchantment is one of great power, and it will take many years for them to
undo the work we have done.*

*"Yet they will not stop trying. Eventually, they will attempt to open
the door. This must not be allowed. I wish I could have told all of this
to you directly, but you are too young as I write this, and since I do not
know who within the order I can trust, I must resort to these little puzzles, which I am confident only you will be able to solve. It is only you
I can trust, my dearest Ivy. That is why I gave you the book of myths and
my magick cabinet."*

Ivy's heart ached. "But he was never able to give me the book. I
only found it recently because of the carelessness of one of our maids.
And I never received the magick cabinet. My mother must have banished it from the house; she loathed such things. She must have given
it to Mr. Quent."

Mr. Rafferdy met her gaze. "But what is this door he speaks of?
Does that key go to it?"

"Finish the letter," Ivy said. "Then I will tell you what I know."

He read on. *"Clever as you are, my dearest, you will not be able to
protect the doorway on your own. There are enchantments in the house,
defenses that can be renewed. However, you must find another who can
help you—a magician. Who that will be, I do not know. I can tell you*

*only not to trust any of the members of my order. That most are good and conscientious men I believe, but I cannot know who among them is false. You will have to use your own judgment.*

"*I recommend only that he be a magician of considerable skill. It will not be easy, and you will have little time. Once you enter the house, they will be alerted—they will sense that the seal has at last been broken, and they will come. You will find the door in the chamber behind my study. It is there that the magician must work the enchantment. I have set out the words of the spell on the reverse of this page. That the magician succeed in this task is of the greatest imperative. All of Altania depends upon it.*

"*I wish I had time to tell you more. I do not! I will say only that if he should come to you, listen to him. I will not give his name, for I do not know it myself, though I have spoken to him many times over the years. Nor have I seen his face behind the dark mask he wears, but I trust him more than I trust myself. If he should ever speak to you, heed him.*

"*My time is gone. I must go. Give my affection to your mother and sisters, and know that no matter what happens you have, and shall always have, my love.*" Rafferdy turned over the letter. "There is something written in the language of magick here, as he said."

A weakness had come over Ivy. She went to a stool used to retrieve books from the highest shelves and sat. "That's what he meant in the riddle," she murmured. "*Through the door the dark will come.*"

"What will come through the door? And who's this person he described, the one he said might speak to you? It certainly seems like he might be able to help if we could find the fellow."

Ivy looked up at him standing by the celestial globe, the letter in his hands. His velvet coat had gotten dusty, and his expression was at once serious and puzzled, giving him a quizzical look. Despite everything that had happened—that was going to happen—her heart felt suddenly light. Her father had told her she needed to find a magician to help her, someone she could trust utterly. But she already had.

"I have spoken to him," she said, meeting his gaze, "twice now."

Then she told him about the man in the mask.

# CHAPTER TWENTY-THREE

RAFFERDY GAVE HIS hat and ivory-handled cane (his latest affectation) to the servant, who bowed as he accepted them.

"I will tell the master you've arrived," the man said as he rose, though given his expression he might as well have said, *I will tell the master there is a bit of moldy cheese on the table,* or *I will tell the master there are several charity workers at the door.*

"Thank you," Rafferdy said.

The man shut the doors, leaving him alone in the parlor. It was sometimes said that a man's character was reflected in his servants. That adage appeared true enough in this case. Rafferdy could not recall a time he had willingly come to call on someone he found so repulsive.

However, it was not for his own entertainment he had come here, he reminded himself. He paced around the room, wishing he had kept his cane; he enjoyed the feel of it in his hand, and he liked to imagine it lent him an air of gravity.

As always, the room appeared comfortable and mundane, filled with the warm sun of a lingering morning. Yet appearances could deceive. In his previous visits here, he had come to learn more about the objects that decorated the room. He knew now that the soapstone urns contained dust from Tharosian graves; that the rusty knife on the mantel had once been used by chieftains of the remote north to offer up sacrifices to pagan gods; and that the massive book that rested on a wooden stand, retrieved from the vaults beneath a padishah's library, was bound in fine leather that came not from the hide of animals but from a source that set Rafferdy's own skin crawling in sympathetic reaction each time he considered it.

He willed his attention away from these peculiar objects and instead drew a piece of paper from his coat pocket. On it he had made a copy of the spell Mr. Lockwell had included on the back of the letter they had discovered inside the celestial globe.

*You must think I'm the one who should be in Madstone's,* Miss

Lockwell—that is, Mrs. Quent—had said yesterday, after she told him about the man in the black mask who had appeared to her twice now.

In truth, Rafferdy did not know what to think. Mysterious strangers, magickal doors, secret societies—all of it seemed fairly preposterous. And what was this grave danger that the masked fellow had warned would come through the door if it was opened—these Ashen, as he called them? That sounded like something one good sneeze would blow away. Besides, what need had Altania for fantastical threats when it already had magnates, bankers, and rebels aplenty? No, he did not know what to think.

Except he did not think Mrs. Quent was mad. Indeed, he was certain she was at least twice as clever as he was, and far more sensible. Besides, her father had seemed to know this peculiar masked fellow and had warned of similar dangers in his letter. While Rafferdy could not imagine he had the power to do anything to help Altania, if he could help Mrs. Quent gain entry to the house on Durrow Street, he would do so. It was her hope that something inside the house would give her insight into the mishap that had befallen her father years ago and that such knowledge might make it possible to cure his malady. He did not know if that was the case, or even if he could possibly work the spell written on the paper, but for her sake he would try. Besides, it would be a novelty to do something for someone other than himself.

Again he studied the words of the spell. They were stranger than anything Mr. Bennick had so far shown to him. His lips could not shape themselves around the syllables. In his letter, Mr. Lockwell had warned that members of the Vigilant Order of the Silver Eye would be alerted once they entered the house, that he would have to work the spell before they arrived. However, at his present rate, it would take him hours to mumble his way through the spell.

Rafferdy sighed and folded the paper. "I can only hope the wicked magicians are in no particular hurry," he said.

"In a hurry to do what?" asked a deep voice behind him.

In a smooth motion, Rafferdy slipped the paper into his pocket, turned around, and smiled. "To take my soul, of course. Isn't that what all wicked magicians want? To find some young apprentice they can trick into signing away that better, ethereal part of him in exchange for the promise of power? But if it's my soul they're after, they'll have to wait. It will be years before I'm so much as the lowliest acolyte. Not that they'll find my soul of much value when they do get it. I am sure by now it is a bedraggled thing."

Mr. Bennick went to a sideboard. "I do not believe it will be nearly so long as you suggest before you are much more than an apprentice," he said as he poured a pair of sherries. "I have had students, some from the oldest Houses, who after a year of study have not successfully performed a single spell. You performed one within minutes. So by your measure, your soul is very much in peril. Or what is left of it, at any rate." He handed Rafferdy one of the glasses. "To magick," he said, and took a sip of his drink.

Rafferdy was forced to shore up his smile lest it crumble. "Cheers," he said, and downed the contents of his glass.

"I was pleased to receive your note asking to continue your studies," Mr. Bennick said. "As I told you, I believe you have rare ability, but that ability is worth little without application. Was there some particular thing you wished to learn today, something of special interest to you?"

Rafferdy winced. Had the magician seen him reading the paper?

"I had no particular thought," he said. "You're the master, and I am merely the student. I will leave it to you."

"Learning cannot happen if there is not something one wishes to learn, Mr. Rafferdy. You have mastered the binding and opening of small objects; I can teach you no more in that regard. However, as you have seen, that is little more than a parlor trick. To progress deeper in the arcane arts—I will say only that it will not be as simple as what we have done so far. So if it is the case that there is not something particular you desire to know, perhaps it is best if your lessons end now."

His eyes were dark as he took another sip of sherry. That this was his first test, Rafferdy had no doubt. Except if he failed this exam, there was no paying a few regals to get a better score as at university.

"There is something," he said, and drew in a breath. "I was interested in learning how—that is, you mentioned once that enchantments can lose their potency over time, that a box I bind shut will before long lose all traces of magick so that anyone can open it." He took a step toward Mr. Bennick and was surprised to hear a note of what sounded like genuine interest in his voice. "I was wondering what can be done to make such an enchantment endure longer, even for many years—that is, to renew an existing spell."

Mr. Bennick raised an eyebrow. "Usually novices want to learn how to call lightning or some such thing."

Rafferdy shrugged. "I can neither drink lightning nor smoke or wear it, so it's of no use to me."

"Your inquiry pertains to a vital subject," the other man said. "One that weighs upon the mind of many who study the arcane. It is not unusual for a magician to desire to keep some things hidden for years, even long after his own demise. Nothing is more precious to a magician than knowledge—not just gaining it, but protecting it as well. A magician who can master such bindings would be considered powerful indeed."

Rafferdy willed himself to meet the taller man's gaze, to hold it. He had to appear as if he really wished to learn.

Yet he *did* wish to; he was suddenly more curious about it than he had been about anything for ages. Exactly why, he wasn't certain. Maybe it was only because if *she* was interested in it, then it was necessarily interesting to *him*.

"Can you teach me?"

Mr. Bennick crossed the room. Rafferdy followed after, ready to plead his case.

"As I said, you should not think it will be easy," Mr. Bennick said. He stopped before the large tome on its pedestal, the ancient book whose covers were fashioned of human skin. It was bound with brass bands and a padlock shaped like a grotesque head, its mouth forming the keyhole.

"Well, I should hope not," Rafferdy said. "If it were easy, then any sod would be a magician. In which case I wouldn't find it the least bit interesting. For the moment everyone is doing something is the moment it stops being remotely fashionable."

"Is that the reason you wish to study magick, Mr. Rafferdy? Because it has become fashionable of late?"

Rafferdy started to form some flippant answer. *Of course,* he was going to say, *the only reason to do anything at all is because it's fashionable.* Then he thought of the wealthy young men he had known at Gauldren's College, sons of lords like him. He recalled how they had liked going to taverns and coffeehouses and speaking in overloud voices of this arcane rune or that secret word of power they had learned.

A feeling of disdain came over Rafferdy. Fashion was something one necessarily pursued in public in order to better make an impression upon others, but somehow he could not imagine that Mr. Bennick, when he was a magician, had ever gone to a pub or party and spoken loudly of some spell or enchantment he had done.

"No," he said at last. "If I wish to be fashionable, I'll buy a new coat."

"Very well," Mr. Bennick said. "We will begin with the Codex of Horestes. The original was written over three thousand years ago and has been lost. Yet there are a few copies, and this is one of them. It is old in its own right, at least five hundred years."

"That seems like an awfully valuable thing to leave lying about one's parlor," Rafferdy said.

"Hiding a thing is only one way to guard it," Mr. Bennick said. "And this tome has its own protections."

He drew a ring of keys from his coat and used one of them to unlock the book. As he opened it, an odor rose on the air, at once medicinal and dusty. It made Rafferdy think of the mummies he had seen long ago on display at the Royal Museum, dug up from the sands of the far south of the empire.

"Come," Mr. Bennick said. "Read aloud with me."

Breathing in that ancient perfume, Rafferdy did.

HOW LONG THEY stood there with the book, Rafferdy did not know. It seemed a short while, but when Mr. Bennick closed it and Rafferdy looked up, he saw the day had burned to ash outside the window. His legs ached, and his mouth tasted of dust.

He took a step back from the pedestal and would have staggered if the taller man had not caught his arm.

"You should sit for a while," Mr. Bennick said. "I will get you another sherry, if you like."

"Yes," Rafferdy said. "I think that . . . yes, thank you."

He sank into a chair near a bookshelf and held a hand to his head. His temples throbbed, and his stomach heaved to and fro like a ship on a stormy sea. Outside the window, lamplighters moved down the street.

They must have stood there reading for hours. More than once Rafferdy had wanted to turn his head, to move away; however, he had been unable to pull his gaze from the book. The spidery lines of ink had been a dark path that, once embarked upon, could not be turned from; he could only keep following it forward.

All the same, it had not been easy to read the book, and not only because of the archaic language or the queerly slanted script. He knew it had only been his imagination, an impression encouraged by the strange odors that rose from the book and perfused his brain, but the words had seemed to writhe on the parchment, as if unwilling to let themselves be read even as they bound the eye and kept it from looking elsewhere.

Now, as he sat, sweat cooled on Rafferdy's brow, leaving him clammy. Mr. Bennick locked the book, then poured a glass of sherry and handed it to him. Rafferdy gulped it quickly, lest he spill it.

"Do you understand what you read?" Mr. Bennick's sallow face was impassive as always, but there was a glint in his deep-set eyes.

Rafferdy set down his glass and drew out a handkerchief to mop his brow. "I don't know. Yes—that is, I think so. Some of it, at least."

What they had read had been like a diary, a journal written by Horestes of his journeys to far-off places and down shadowed roads. However, where exactly Horestes's travels had taken him, Rafferdy wasn't certain. The author wrote in fractured ramblings, and he called nothing by its proper name. *I followed the gaze of the eye of Sarkos for forty nights,* he wrote, or, *I walked through the shifting fields of the Copper Sea until I saw the two towers of Baelthus thrusting up to stab the sky.*

Rafferdy had seldom paid attention at university. However, he vaguely recalled from a lecture on astrography that Sarkos was a Tharosian deity as well as the name of a constellation of stars that was seldom glimpsed in Altania, and then only on the horizon, but which rose high into the sky in the far south of the empire. As for the towers of Baelthus, they were supposed to be the two mountains that held up one end of the sky, raised by one of the Magnons, godlike beings who existed before the deities of Tharos.

There were countless more such references in the Codex—the author wrote of following the sword of Actheon and digging deep beneath the belly of Ranramarath—but none of these things meant anything to Rafferdy.

He put away his handkerchief. "I don't suppose it would have been magickal enough for him to have just written, *To find the secret cave, go south for a hundred miles and then turn left at the rock that looks like an old man's nose* or some such thing."

Mr. Bennick gave a sharp smile. "That would be easier, wouldn't it? However, to protect their secrets and to make sure they did not fall into the hands of those who might misuse them, ancient magicians often wrote in a kind of code, referring to symbols that only another who had spent long years studying the arcane would understand. Unfortunately, the meaning of many of the references Horestes and others used is lost to us now. It is one of the greatest tasks of a magician, to spend long hours poring through old books, searching for clues to the meaning of these symbols and codes."

"Sounds delightful," Rafferdy said.

Mr. Bennick laughed, though it was a rueful sound. "It is, as you can well imagine, tedious work. Long years can be spent following a line of investigation, pursuing some fragment of knowledge, only to discover in the end it is fruitless. Yet on those rare occasions when you stumble upon some scroll that has not seen light in a thousand years and in its faded words learn something that has long been lost—there is no thing in the world that could give greater satisfaction."

As he spoke, Mr. Bennick's left hand went to his right, stroking the fourth finger. Rafferdy watched with interest.

The other man seemed to notice his gaze. He pulled his hands apart.

"Well, I know one thing that would give me great satisfaction," Rafferdy said. Finding he was steady enough, he went to the sideboard to refill his glass. He took a sip, and the throbbing in his head eased a fraction.

"He was mad, wasn't he?" Rafferdy turned around. "Horestes, I mean. He was positively frothing."

Mr. Bennick shrugged. "Perhaps he was mad. Or perhaps he had simply learned things, seen things, that a man's mind was not crafted to grasp or endure."

"Not crafted to endure? I don't follow you."

"Do you know there are colors beyond the ones we can see?" Mr. Bennick said. "Naturalists have discovered insects that dwell in the deepest caves and that can follow sources of light that are utterly invisible to our eyes. In the same way, there is knowledge that is older than mankind—knowledge that, like that light, is beyond our natural ability to perceive, for never in all the years of our formation have we encountered it. It is the magician's task, like that of the insect, to seek out that strange light, to try to comprehend it."

Rafferdy did not care for this comparison. "On the contrary," he said, "I'm quite sure knowledge was invented by man, like the wheel and spoons and chocolate. In which case, how can there be knowledge older than man himself? Besides, I'm certain the bishop at St. Galmuth's will be happy to inform you that God created man in the beginning, so there can't be anything more ancient."

"Before God there were the gods—the deities of Tharos. Before them came the Magnons, whom the Tharosian gods slew. And there are beings older yet, gods whose names have never been forgotten because they were never known." He returned to the Codex on the pedestal, resting a hand on it. "Names that, if you were to hear them spoken, would be so queer, so alien, so unlike anything you or a thousand ancestors before you had ever heard, that the very sound of them might shock your mind so profoundly as to render you incapable of speech, or motion, or thought. All the same, it is a magician's task to seek out such names, such words, such knowledge, no matter that peril."

Rafferdy felt the flesh on his neck crawl. He thought of what Mrs. Quent had told him about her father, how she believed he had been doing magick when his affliction befell him. Had Mr. Lockwell learned something in his studies—glimpsed something—that his mind could not bear?

He realized that Mr. Bennick had turned from the book and was watching him.

"Are you well, Mr. Rafferdy? We have read only the beginning of the Codex of Horestes, but the chapters that follow address more directly what you said you wished to learn. I trust I haven't frightened you from the idea of continuing your studies."

Rafferdy stood straight. "Not at all. I've always thought it might be entertaining to be mad. Besides, I'm weary of azure and lavender and saffron. I'll look forward to discovering one of those heretofore never-glimpsed colors, and when I do I'll order a new scarf of that hue."

"That I would like to see, Mr. Rafferdy," replied Mr. Bennick.

## CHAPTER TWENTY-FOUR

OU'RE THINKING TOO hard," Dercy said. "Quit trying to force it to change. Because you can't change it, not really. Instead, just look at it and see what you want to see."

Eldyn frowned, staring at the pebble that lay on the table between them. "Easy enough for you to say," he muttered. "I'm sure you could just wave a hand and turn it to gold."

"Why settle for gold?" Dercy pointed at the pebble, and in an instant it was gone, replaced by a gem that caught the dim lamplight inside the tavern and spun it into glittering fire.

Eldyn groaned and leaned back. His head ached, and it felt as if his eyes were irrevocably crossed. "It's hopeless. I'll never be able to do it." He picked up his cup of punch to take a drink, then grimaced. The cup was empty.

Dercy laughed and scratched his short blond beard, his eyes glinting like the diamond. "Oh you'll do it, all right. You'll do it because it's the only way you're going to get another cup of punch."

"Why can't you just . . . ?" Eldyn wiggled his fingers.

"I told you, it's your turn to buy a round. Besides, they've gotten suspicious of me here. The barkeep always bites the coins I give him to see if they're real, and I'm not *that* good an illusionist. At least not yet. Besides, with that angel's face of yours, they'll believe anything you tell them. You hardly need an illusion at all. The barest wisp of a phantasm will do. Here, this will help."

He reached into his pocket and pulled out a copper coin.

Eldyn scowled. "You can't buy a cup for a penny, let alone a whole pitcher."

"No, but you can buy one for a piece of silver. The best lies are the ones closest to the truth, the saying goes. Illusion is the same. It's easiest when it strays only a little from what's true. The eye will see what it wishes to see; all it needs is a little encouragement." He set the coin on the table and pushed it toward Eldyn. "Go on."

It was no use. Over the last several days, Eldyn had tried again and again to work an illusion at Dercy's encouraging, but he had failed utterly. He could still gather shadows to him with a thought, but that was all. How he had conjured the vision of his father in Duskfellow's graveyard, he didn't know. It had been a fluke, an accident brought on by drink and anguish and memory. There was no point in even trying.

Which was a shame. He had no wish to leave the Sword and Leaf. The evening was to be long, and his thirst was far from quenched. However, the last of his funds had gone to purchase another half month of room and board for himself and Sashie at the inn in Lowpark. He would have to look for work again tomorrow and take whatever he got.

It was not a thought he relished. These last days had been grand, and he had no wish for them to end. The day after Eldyn had escaped Westen, Dercy had arrived at the inn, grinning and brandishing a fresh copy of *The Comet*. NOTORIOUS HIGHWAYMAN IN BARROWGATE, trumpeted the headline. And below that, *Thief of the Murghese Gold Sure to Hang.*

Eldyn had read the words again and again, hardly comprehending them. He could not grasp what this news meant.

"It means it is time to celebrate," Dercy had declared.

Eldyn barely had time to put on his coat and tell Sashie he was going out before Dercy grabbed him by the arm and hauled him out into the swift-falling evening. They went to Durrow Street (with a stop to purchase a bottle of whiskey) and that night went to not one but three illusion plays, sneaking the bottle back and forth between them and growing quite merry. They let out hearty applause at the glorious performances and heckled just as enthusiastically as a phantasm wavered and vanished despite all the frantic arm-wavings of some hapless illusionist.

After the last performance, they had not gone home. Instead, Dercy took Eldyn to some unsavory tavern on the fringes of High Holy. Within they discovered a number of Dercy's compatriots from the Theater of the Moon, as well as performers from several other theaters, all still in their costumes from the night's performances.

Eldyn had expressed reluctance to join a party of so many who were strangers to him—indeed, who were strangers of the strangest sort, all glittered and powdered and shimmering like things of air and light themselves. However, before he could retreat, Dercy pulled him forward and introduced him. Calls of welcome rang out, and cup after cup was placed in his hand. Soon the dank interior of the tavern was gone, replaced by a forest of silver trees with gold leaves that fluttered down all around. The rotund bartender seemed resigned to the wings sprouting from his back. Those few derelicts who had wandered in off the street looking for grog became fauns and goblins. Soon Eldyn found himself laughing and singing along with all the marvelous creatures around him.

The next day, Eldyn had not awakened until well into the afternoon. Nor was it long after that when Dercy came to the inn and once again whisked him off for further entertainment. Eldyn had lived through far too many grim times, Dercy declared; he had much to make up for.

So it went. Each evening they went to plays on Durrow Street, and if Dercy was performing at the Theater of the Moon, Eldyn would sit in the balcony with a bottle of wine and watch, enrapt, as once again the fiery king pursued the silvery youth without ever being able to capture him. By day (when they were awake) they walked through the city or sat in coffeehouses, and Dercy would amuse them both with small illusions—often worked at the expense of some hapless victim who was suddenly confused to see a flower sprouting out of his cup or a hat of green leaves crowning some somber old gentleman passing by.

Eldyn could not remember the last time he had felt so light, so at ease and full of good humor. Even his inability to work illusions had been but a fleeting shadow, a cloud that passed before the sun quickly and was gone. Each day brought new wonders, new delights, and never once, as he and Dercy made their way to and fro across the city, did he look over his shoulder or fear to see a tall figure in a russet coat striding his way.

No, he had no cause for fear now. However, seeking employment was the last thing he wished to do. The thought of taking another clerking position was unbearable. He wanted to stay here and drink and talk and laugh with Dercy. If only he had money for another pot . . .

Dercy snapped his fingers. "Now we're in business!"

Eldyn picked up the coin and turned it over and over. Were his eyes playing tricks on him?

Yes, they were—and that was precisely the point. The coin was no longer dull copper but rather bright silver.

"Quick," Dercy said. "Spend it while it lasts."

Eldyn hesitated—how would this be any different than stealing? He may be poor, but he was still a gentleman.

However, he was thirsty as well. As Dercy turned away, hiding his face from view, Eldyn went to the bar. He ordered another pot and acted in every way as natural as possible as he handed the coin to the barkeep. The man did little more than glance at it, then threw it in the drawer beneath the counter.

Moments later Eldyn returned to the table with the punch.

"It worked," Eldyn said, heart pounding, still astonished at how easy it had been.

"Of course it worked," Dercy said, filling their glasses. "I told you—you're an illusionist."

"But what happens when the spell wears off?"

"Nothing at all. I've glimpsed their money drawer here—all the coins are tossed together. By now that coin you handed him looks like any other copper penny in there. They'll never know they were duped, and—oh, don't give me that look. Even an angel needs to sin now and then. No one likes anyone who's too high and mighty. Not even God above."

He handed Eldyn one of the cups. Despite himself, Eldyn grinned.

"To illusion," Dercy said.

They struck their cups and drained them, and any sour remorse Eldyn tasted was washed away by the sweet, strong punch.

❧

THE NIGHT WAS brief, and the middling lumenal was already half over by the time Eldyn woke. Sashie assailed him at once.

"I cannot find any oranges," she said. "I searched all the pockets of your coat. Did you not bring me any? Of course not—you think only of yourself and your new friend. You go out to plays and parties while I sit here in this wretched room. Not that I could go to a party even if I wished. I have nothing good to wear. You have a new coat, but all I have are these same awful rags. I'm not fit to be seen."

She swiped at the skirt of her frock. In fact, she looked quite pretty.

"Please, dear brother. Please let me go out." She knelt and clasped her hands on his knees. "I will perish if I cannot go out. I beg you, let me go."

He began to tell her she could not. Except that was not true, was it? He had been keeping her locked up out of habit, yet there was no reason for it anymore. *He* could not harm Sashie now, not from behind the bars of Barrowgate, and there was no danger of *her* going to Westen; she could not have done so even if she wished.

"Of course you may go out, dearest," he said.

"But I cannot breathe in this awful place, you have to—" Her eyes went wide as his words registered. Her tears were suddenly gone.

"I must look for work today, but take this." He gave her his last silver coin. It didn't matter. He had a number of pennies, which would serve him just as well now. "Buy yourself some pretty thing. You deserve it for all you have endured, and more. Once I have found work again, I will buy you a closet full of dresses—all the latest fashions."

She gaped at him, then all at once threw her arms around his neck and showered him with kisses. He was *dear brother* then, and *sweet brother*. He endured her sudden and violent affections gladly; he had missed them. At last she went to the mirror and arranged herself. With a promise to be back for supper, she was out the door.

Eldyn smiled as he watched her go. It was good to see her glad again. This had been hard for her, perhaps even harder than for him, for she could not truly understand what danger they had been in. He forgave her any cruel things she had said; he knew she had not meant them.

Besides, soon these last dark months would be but a dim memory. The future held only promise; nor would they have to journey to Caerdun in the south to begin a new life.

However, between now and that happy future, he would have to earn a little money. Yet that thought dimmed his smile only a little. Whatever work he took, it would not be forever. Eldyn did not know what the future held for him, but he knew now that there were possibilities he had never before considered.

He washed his face and put on his coat, then drew a penny from his pocket and flipped it in the air. By the time he caught it again, it had turned from copper to silver. Grinning, he slipped the coin back in his pocket and headed out to find work.

*H*E FOUND RAFFERDY instead.

So astonished was Eldyn to see his friend that he barely recognized him at first. Or perhaps it was the uncharacteristically solemn look on Rafferdy's face that made him seem so unfamiliar. He hardly looked like the man Eldyn knew. But, no—it was Rafferdy sure enough, striding across Greenly Circle, dressed in a charcoal-gray coat and carrying an ivory-handled cane.

"Ho, there, Rafferdy!" Eldyn called out. "Wait up!"

Rafferdy stopped and looked up at the sound of his name. When he saw Eldyn hurrying toward him across the circle, a grin split his face, and then he looked like the old Rafferdy indeed.

"Garritt, by God, it's good to see you!" he exclaimed, clasping Eldyn's hand and shaking it long and vigorously. Eldyn returned the gesture with equal energy.

"It's been too long," Eldyn said.

"Far too long," Rafferdy agreed. "Yet now that I see you, I can't imagine why that is. Surely your business can't have been occupying you all this time. What was it you were doing? Something about the New Lands, if I recall. How did that all turn out?"

One day he would tell Rafferdy the whole story, but only when both of them were drunk enough. "It wasn't what I thought it would be," Eldyn said, truthfully enough.

"Nothing ever is," Rafferdy said. "I presume you're on to new endeavors?"

Eldyn slipped a hand into his coat pocket, touching the penny there, and could not help a smile. "I believe I am," he said. "But what of you? You've been busy yourself of late. Has your work for your father still been occupying you, or are you on to other schemes?"

Rafferdy looked away, across Greenly Circle, and a shadow of that seriousness again crossed his face. In that moment he looked older than he ever had before, though Eldyn could not say he looked unwell.

"What's the matter, Rafferdy?" he said, then he laughed. "Why, you look positively lordly. Have you decided to quit worrying about all that power and start enjoying being a magnate?"

Rafferdy turned to fix him with a sharp look. "What I would enjoy is a glass of whiskey."

"Really? You looked like you were walking with great purpose just now. Weren't you going somewhere?"

"It can wait," Rafferdy said. "Besides, a drink can only help, and I see a tavern right there across the circle."

"It's a bit early for liquor."

"Nonsense. The lumenal is to be short. If we do not act with haste, the day will be over. We'd best drink now while we have the chance."

Eldyn couldn't argue with that logic. Besides, it seemed both he and Rafferdy were on errands neither anticipated with pleasure. The lumenal was to be longer tomorrow. He could always look for work then. One more day wouldn't make a difference.

"Well come on, then," he said. "We've already lost another minute just standing here."

They proceeded to the tavern, finding it dim, cavelike, and utterly to their liking. There they passed several pleasant hours smoking, drinking, talking, and laughing. Eldyn had forgotten how much he truly *liked* Rafferdy. He was at once reminded of fond days past and filled with hope at what the future held for both of them.

Their mood became solemn only once, when Eldyn asked if he ever saw Miss Lockwell. Eldyn often thought of her still, and he knew how much Rafferdy had cared for her.

"She is Miss Lockwell no longer," Rafferdy said. He finished his whiskey and poured another.

"She is married?" Eldyn said, shocked by this news. "To whom?"

"To a man who, it turns out, works for my father."

Eldyn could not disguise his horror. "You mean a servant?"

"No, you misunderstand. Mr. Quent is an agent of the king, as is my father. He assists Lord Rafferdy in his work for the Crown—whatever that is. I confess, it is still a mystery to me. I have never met this Mr. Quent, but I gather he has worked for my father for many years. What's more, it turns out he was, in the past, a friend of Mr. Lockwell's. So it seems Miss Lockwell and I were connected before we ever encountered each other. A curious world, isn't it? We think we meet people by chance, when chance has nothing to do with it." He took a long draft from his glass.

Eldyn didn't know what to say, so he took a drink himself. He knew this could only have been hard news to his friend. First his own engagement to Miss Everaud had been broken off under a cloud of scandal, and now this. How unfortunate the subject of marriage must seem to him! All the same, Rafferdy must have known that, no matter what happened, he never would have been able to marry Miss Lockwell.

"I'm glad for her," Rafferdy said, his voice gone smoky from the whiskey. "I am given to understand he is somewhat old for her but that he has a large estate and is a respectable gentleman. So she is pretty, and he is rich. No doubt society will judge it an excellent match. I know my father does; thus a woman he found intolerable for his son is in turn found ideal for his associate. Strange, isn't it, how it's the direction we are viewed from that makes us attractive or abhorrent? But it is well. Yes, I am glad for her."

Despite Rafferdy's grave look, Eldyn believed him.

"To Miss Lockwell," he said, raising his glass.

"To Mrs. Quent," Rafferdy replied.

After that, they drank for a little while in silence.

Gradually their spirits rose again, and their talk resumed. Soon they were laughing again like old times as Rafferdy imitated some lord or lady he had overheard at Lady Marsdel's. At last the whiskey was gone, and with a sigh Rafferdy said that his errand could not wait.

"What is it you must do that you find so disagreeable?" Eldyn asked.

Rafferdy twisted the ring on his right hand. "I am, if you can believe it, on my way to a lesson in magick with Mr. Bennick."

At first he thought Rafferdy was making another jest. But no—he was serious! Eldyn expressed his extreme astonishment and pressed Rafferdy for his motivations. Last Eldyn knew, Rafferdy had mocked those young men at university who studied the arcane arts.

"My reasons will have to wait for when we meet next," Rafferdy said. "I am now very late."

Indeed, it was later than Eldyn thought as they stepped out the tavern door. The sun was already nearly to the Citadel, and boys walked about Greenly Circle, hawking the evening broadsheets.

Eldyn shook Rafferdy's hand and began to ask when they should plan to meet again. However, as he spoke, one of the boys passed by, holding up a copy of *The Messenger*.

Rafferdy frowned. "What is it, Garritt? Did you have too much to drink? You look unwell of a sudden."

Eldyn reached into his pocket, fumbled, and pulled out the penny. It was dull copper again. "Here!" he said, throwing the penny to the boy. "Give me one of those."

He snatched the broadsheet from the boy, then turned it over, reading the headline that had caught his eye: NOTORIOUS HIGHWAYMAN ESCAPES.

"What is it, Garritt? You're pale as if you saw a ghost."

Yes, it was like being haunted by the ghost of one thought dead. Eldyn read the first lines of the article. It had happened that morning, in the gray hour just before dawn. Howls were heard coming from the jail beneath Barrowgate. A guard was found dead, his flesh torn as if by some animal, his mouth stuffed full of Murghese gold. The prisoner was nowhere to be seen. . . .

A hand fell on his arm. Eldyn flinched away, but it was only Rafferdy. He looked at Eldyn, concern on his face.

"What's wrong, Garritt?"

Eldyn shook his head. "It is . . . forgive me. I must go."

Before Rafferdy could say anything more, Eldyn turned and ran across Greenly Circle, clutching the broadsheet in his hands.

***

H̲IS BLOOD DRUMMED in his ears by the time he reached the inn in Lowpark. Despite his dread, he had been forced to walk the last part of the way, for his lungs felt as if he had breathed fire.

The inn was quiet as he entered. Hope rose within him. Perhaps he had not come yet; perhaps he was waiting for dark to fall. Eldyn hurried up the stairs to the chambers he shared with Sashie.

The door opened as he touched the handle. He stepped into the room, and a low sound escaped him. The bedclothes lay in a tattered heap, and the pillows were gutted, their contents strewn about. The curtains had been ripped down, the table overturned. There were lines on one wall—four gouges made close together. Eldyn reached out a shaking hand, tracing the gouges with his fingers. A sickness welled up inside him.

Footsteps sounded behind him. He lurched around, and so strong was his relief, his joy, that it overwhelmed him as much as fear had a moment ago.

"Hello, sweet brother," Sashie said, smiling in the doorway, a basket in her hands. Then she stepped inside, and her smile vanished. The basket slipped from her grasp. Oranges rolled across the floor.

He went to her and took her hand. "Are you all right? Did you see anyone following you?"

"Following me? I don't understand." She gazed around, her eyes large. "What's happened, brother? Who did this?"

"We have to go. Now."

"But my things, my dresses—"

"There's no time for that." Tightening his grip on her hand, he pulled her after him, into the hall and down the stairs.

He halted at the bottom. She began to question him again, but he pressed a finger to her lips. He gathered the dim air around both of them like a cloak, then listened. Usually there was a low murmur of conversation in the public room or clatters from the kitchen. However, the inn was silent. The lamps had not been lit against the coming night.

Eldyn waited. He could not believe Westen was far. He had come looking for Sashie but had not found her. Yet surely he was close and had seen them both enter the inn. In which case, why did he not attack?

Because he did not want to kill them—he wanted something far more than that. He wanted Sashie.

Eldyn tightened his grip on his sister's hand. She let out a gasp of pain, but he ignored it. Their only hope was to make a dash for the door and run down the lane. There would be people on the main thoroughfare below. He could not believe Westen would show himself in front of a crowd—not when he was a wanted man, not when a drawing of his face had appeared in every broadsheet in the city.

"Move quickly," he whispered. "And do as I say."

Keeping the gloom close around them, he started for the door, pulling Sashie after him.

Ahead, something stirred in the dimness of the public room. He glimpsed the silhouette of a tall, upright figure as it passed before the silver square of a window. The figure was lost to sight, but a moment later another shadow appeared, this one nearer to the floor. A low sound, a kind of growling, rose on the air. Sashie screamed.

There was no point in concealment now. He flung the shadows off. "To the door!"

He pulled Sashie after him but hardly needed to, for she was fast on his heels. When they reached the door he dreaded it had been locked, but after fumbling with the latch he was able to thrust it open. They pushed out into the twilight and ran down the deserted lane.

Like a coil of night, a dark shape burst out of the door of the inn behind them. Again Sashie screamed, and fear renewed Eldyn's strength. He careened down the lane, pulling his sister after him. The sound of sharp things against stone followed behind, drawing closer with each step they took. They were a quarter of the way down the lane, now half. He could see light and people ahead.

Something nipped at Eldyn's heels, and he nearly went tumbling to the cobbles. He caught himself and ran on, but it was no use. Their pursuer would have them before they reached the end of the lane. His only hope was to give Sashie time to escape.

It was, like all the bravest things, an act born out of fear and foolishness. He pulled hard on Sashie's arm—so hard she cried out—and flung her ahead of him. She went staggering down the lane. At the same time he turned around and thrust his arms before him, as if his bare hands held any sort of power.

"Back, devil!" he shouted, as the priest had once shouted at him. "Back to the Abyss from which you came!"

He caught a glimpse of a crouching shadow—sinuous, hump-backed. Two amber sparks winked to life, and the last faint glow of daylight caught on a jagged curve of teeth.

The shadow leaped.

"Get back!" cried a voice that was not Eldyn's.

At the same moment a flash of silver light and a clap of thunder shattered the gloom. Eldyn was blinded, stunned. Something gripped his arm, pulling him down the lane. Unable to see, he stumbled after.

Noise surrounded him—the comforting sounds of people and horses and carriages. He blinked, and his vision cleared. Sashie stood beside him, a dazed look on her face. They had reached the avenue, still thronging with people after the brief day. Lamplighters went about their work. He glanced back at the mouth of the lane that led up to the inn. It was dark and empty.

"Are you all right, Eldyn?"

He blinked again and saw Dercy standing before him. As always the young man was dressed in black. His face was pale.

"Dercy, how did you . . . What are you doing here?"

"Getting you out of trouble again, it seems. I came to see if you were going to join me at the theater tonight. I almost didn't. I was thinking you'd just show up on your own, but I'm glad I did. Is this your sister?"

Eldyn nodded. It was hard to speak. "This is Sashie."

Dercy touched her chin. "Are you all right? Are you hurt in any way?"

She stared up at him for a moment, then shook her head, her lips pressed tight together.

Dercy looked at Eldyn. "What was that thing back there?"

"I don't know." Except that wasn't true. He *did* know. The story in the broadsheet had said the guard had been ripped apart by some animal, and his mouth stuffed with Murghese gold. "It was him, I think."

"You mean the highwayman?" Dercy said with a startled look.

Eldyn swallowed; his mouth tasted like blood. "Yes."

Dercy scratched his blond beard. "Angels above. I don't know how it's . . . Well, whatever or whoever that was, he won't come after you here, not with all these people around."

"But it doesn't—" Eldyn glanced at Sashie. She had moved a few paces off, slumping against a wall. He lowered his voice. "It doesn't matter. Don't you see? Nothing will keep him away. He'll never stop pursuing us. I can't watch her, not every moment. Sooner or later he will find her alone, and he will get to her. There's nowhere in this city that is safe for us."

Dercy laid a hand on Eldyn's arm, his eyes worried. He opened his mouth to say something. At that moment, music rang out over the city: the bright tolling of evening bells. Suddenly he grinned.

"You're wrong," Dercy said. "There is one place in this city where you'll be safe."

Eldyn could only stare. He was beyond wondering.

"Come on, we'd better hurry. The doors close after dark."

Taking Eldyn's hand on the left and Sashie's on the right, Dercy led them through the city toward the sound of the bells.

# CHAPTER TWENTY-FIVE

WITH A PEN, Ivy pointed to each word of the spell on the paper as Mr. Rafferdy spoke them aloud. From what she had read in one of her father's books of magick, a certain fluidity and cadence was required for a spell to be effective. If uttered too haltingly or in a stuttering fashion, it could fail—or worse, it might function but with unexpected consequences.

The intent was not for him to speak the entire spell at once—they did not want to work it here in the parlor at the house on Whitward Street!—but rather to go through it in parts, to verify Mr. Rafferdy could pronounce all the words correctly. Alone, Ivy had tried to speak some of it herself and had found it all but impossible; her lips could not form the sounds. It was as if she lacked some innate capacity necessary to speak the language of magick. However, like a person who could not play an instrument but who could recognize every note of a symphony, she knew the words as well as Mr. Rafferdy did—perhaps even better—and could discern if he was speaking them correctly or not.

She moved her pen at a steady pace, forcing him to speak more quickly than he might otherwise have done. The words of magick fell from his lips in a drone. There was a tension on the air like that before a storm. She moved the pen to the next line. Yes, that was it, just a few more words to—

Ivy winced. The tension on the air cracked like the pane of a window slammed shut. Rafferdy leaned back in his chair, a hand to his forehead.

Concern filled her. "Are you all right?"

"I'm quite well. Though if you wanted to pick up one of the andirons over there and strike me on the crown of my head, I imagine it could only improve things. Please, feel free."

Ivy set the pen on the table. "You're getting better every time you read it, you know."

"That's a very pretty way of saying I'm terrible. You think me a wretched excuse for a magician. Even now you are deciding how to tell me you intend to find someone else to help you. Do not worry. You need spare me no hurt. I will hardly feel it over the aching in my skull."

"I am thinking no such thing!" she said, rising. "You have done what I could never do—you nearly reached the end that time. I know that if you only keep . . ."

She halted. He was looking up at her, his brown eyes alight.

"You know perfectly well you've nearly mastered the spell," she said, suddenly perturbed. She paced before the window. "You've known the whole while we've been sitting here!"

"Well, I didn't want you to think it was too easy for me. I'd rather you thought I was suffering. It makes me seem nobler, don't you think?"

She stopped and regarded him. "I hardly know what to make of you sometimes, Mr. Rafferdy. You disparage admiration even as you secretly encourage it. You are an exasperating man."

"You've only just now discovered this?"

"Apparently I am not so clever as you. But since, as you have now revealed, you do not need the benefit of my tutelage, I will go upstairs and see to my sisters. I know that if *they* ask my help in something, it is because it is truly needed."

She started toward the parlor door, and at once he was on his feet, imploring her to stay, assuring her that her help was indeed needed, more than she could know. That new seriousness came to his face as he spoke, and she could only believe he was sincere.

At last, Ivy agreed to stay. However, as she sat back down, she thought with some satisfaction that Mr. Rafferdy was not the only one who could gain a compliment when it was desired.

"I really believe I'm beginning to master it," he said. "Each time I meet with Mr. Bennick, I encounter more of the words of the spell in the Codex of Horestes. At first I thought it was only chance that I was encountering some of the same words of your father's spell in the book."

"Isn't it?"

He shook his head. "I don't think so. Old Horestes used a word or phrase from the spell to name each of the places he went on his journey or the things he saw there. I didn't realize it at first, but the words in the tale of his travels appear in the same order as they do in the spell."

"You mean the journey *is* the spell."

"It must be so. Mr. Bennick said magicians never tell anything in a straightforward manner."

Wonder filled her. "So instead of writing down the spell, he wove the words of it into a tale of a journey to mysterious lands."

"Just so, and we're nearly to the end of the chapter. There were only a few pages left when last Mr. Bennick and I met. I'm sure to encounter the final words of the spell this next lesson. When I hear Mr. Bennick read them, I'll know how they're pronounced."

"Which means you'll be able to speak the entire spell."

"I believe so. Only it's odd, wouldn't you say? That the book Mr. Bennick is having me read just happens to contain the spell your father set down in the letter he left you—it's rather a brilliant stroke of luck."

"Perhaps not," Ivy said after considering this for a moment. "After all, you asked Mr. Bennick to teach you how to do the very thing that the spell my father left for us does: renew an existing binding. It does not seem so unlikely that two magicians would think of the same spell for the same task. Indeed, it may be the only spell there is to accomplish such a thing."

"Well, if you're going to be sensible about it, then I suppose you must be right," Rafferdy said. He stood and went to the window. Outside, the light had gone gray. "His magick was taken from him, you know. I've thought about it, and it's the only explanation. How else could it be that he no longer wears a House ring? And it's more than that. I see the look in his eyes when I utter a spell. He can still speak the words, but there's no power in them—even I can feel that. I wonder if he gave it up willingly."

Ivy stared, shocked by these words. "You think his magick might have been taken from him by force? Is that possible?"

He shrugged. "I don't know. Either way, it must have happened a long time ago. By his own admission, he hasn't performed magick in years, and I'm certain he couldn't if he wanted to."

Ivy folded her arms. She hardly knew Mr. Bennick, but the thought of losing by force something so essential to one's self, so much a part of one, left her with a chilled feeling. She shivered.

"Is something wrong?"

"No," she said. "It's only that . . ."

"It's only what?"

She shook her head. "It's foolish. You'll mock me if I tell you."

"I only mock those who put on airs or wear awful hats. You do neither, Mrs. Quent."

Ivy gazed out the window. Twilight had settled like ash over the city. Never in her life had she told another how she felt at times when night fell, but she told him then: how sometimes it seemed that the darkness was a living thing, creeping through cracks and beneath doorways, seeking to consume all light, all life. On a moonless umbral, it was only the feeble protection of candles and streetlamps, and the faint aegis of the stars themselves, that kept it from devouring all the world.

As she finished, she looked from the window and saw him staring at her. "There," she said, trying to make her voice bright, "I knew you would laugh at me."

Only he wasn't laughing. His eyes were shadowed in the gloom of the parlor.

"My father said something very much like that to me once," he said quietly. "How we were like people at a party at night, dwelling in a world of light—how we could not see out into the darkness, but that things outside could see in to us."

Again she shivered. "What sort of things?"

"I don't know. But sometimes, when I speak the words of magick, I almost feel as if I'm at that party, looking out that window, and I see something out there, something I'm not sure I was meant to. . . ."

*What do you see?* Ivy wanted to ask him. However, at that moment light flared in the doorway, and the housekeeper entered with a lamp in hand. She set it down and began to move around the parlor, loudly rearranging things in a haphazard fashion. The message was clear: their license to use the room had expired.

Mr. Rafferdy accompanied her downstairs and out into the front garden. There, beneath the shadow of the wisteria, they made a plan for tomorrow. As twilight fell, an urgency had grown in Ivy; the masked man had told her it was not long before members of the order tried to open the door at the house on Durrow Street. She asked that they not delay, and he agreed. After his meeting with Mr. Bennick, he would proceed directly to Durrow Street.

As indicated in her father's letter, the spell called for several materials—certain compounds with which the runes of power must be traced. It had been previously agreed that she would procure these at Mr. Mundy's shop, for they could think of nowhere else to purchase them. Knowing that Mr. Rafferdy found the idea of entering that place again to be abhorrent, she had volunteered to get the things, then meet him at Durrow Street.

"Until then, Mrs. Quent," he said, putting on his hat and tipping it toward her.

She wanted to thank him, to wish him luck, but the words tangled on her tongue like the language of magick. Before she could say anything, he was out the gate and walking away down the street, whistling as he went and swinging his cane.

$\maltese$

$\mathcal{O}$VY WENT INSIDE and climbed the stairs, intending to go to her room. However, as she passed the parlor, Mr. Wyble appeared in the doorway.

"Excuse me, cousin," he said, "but am I right to think that I heard Mr. Rafferdy say he is an acquaintance of Mr. Bennick's?"

She could not disguise her shock. "Yes, you heard correctly, though I must wonder that you heard anything at all."

His hand went to his chest. "How ill you must think of me, cousin! But I had no intention of eavesdropping. I was passing from the dining room, and your voices came to me by chance—indeed, quite against my will."

"Then it seems it is I who must apologize to you, Mr. Wyble, for accosting your ears in so rude a fashion."

He bowed, all solicitude. "No, dear cousin. You need not apologize to *me*. I took no offense at all. However, I take it then that Mr. Rafferdy does know Mr. Bennick?"

Beyond shock, Ivy could only answer. "He does, but why do you ask? I cannot imagine Mr. Bennick is of interest to you."

"Only he is, Mrs. Quent! He is of great interest to me. You see, I previously had the most beneficial conversation with him."

"I don't understand. Do you mean you met him through your acquaintance with Lady Marsdel?"

"No, it is quite the opposite. It was Mr. Bennick who suggested my services to her ladyship. It was very generous of him, and very unexpected. You can imagine my surprise when he approached me! But I gather he knew Mr. Lockwell once, and I'm sure your father must have talked about me and my skills as a lawyer. So that is how Mr. Bennick must have known of me."

Mr. Wyble spoke on, asking if she might persuade Mr. Rafferdy to speak to Mr. Bennick on his behalf, for he was hoping he might have the opportunity to be of further service to Lady Marsdel. Her ladyship must be very busy. It could only be expected she had not thought of one of Mr. Wyble's station. Yet at a mention from Mr. Bennick, perhaps she would be favorably reminded of his previous service to her.

Ivy listened to all this numbly. She gave some vague assurance that she would speak to Mr. Rafferdy, then begged her leave and turned to hurry up the stairs.

"Thank you, cousin." His voice followed her up. "I will be most grateful for any help Mr. Rafferdy could offer in passing along my regards to—"

She shut the door to her room and leaned against it. Lily looked up from her book. She was reading in bed by the light of a single candle. "Is something wrong, Ivy? You look as if you just saw something horrid."

"I was talking to Mr. Wyble."

"Oh," Lily said, "then I was right." She returned her nose to her book.

Ivy sat on the edge of her bed. Thoughts spun through her mind like the spheres of the celestial globe in the attic. How strange, she thought, that Mr. Bennick had introduced Mr. Wyble to Lady Marsdel. True, it was not difficult to conceive that Mr. Bennick had known her father. Mr. Lockwell had been friends with Mr. Quent, who worked for Lord Rafferdy, who in turn was part of Lady Marsdel's circle, just as Mr. Bennick was.

No, it was not the connection that was difficult to believe, but rather that Mr. Bennick had gone to such trouble to secure work for Mr. Wyble. Ivy had no idea why he would do such a thing. What benefit was it to him? Lady Marsdel could afford any lawyer, and surely Mr. Wyble was nothing to Mr. Bennick.

Outside the window, the night thickened. It pressed against the glass like dark water, seeking a way inside. Only it was not the windowpanes that held it back, but rather the scant light of Lily's candle. Ivy rose, took another candle from the table drawer, and another, lighting them.

Lily looked up from her book with a frown. "I thought you said candles were expensive."

Ivy looked out the window. Above the rooftops, the new red planet gazed like an eye from the night.

"They are," she said, then lit another.

☙

𝕿HE NEXT DAY was to be a very short lumenal—little more than seven hours from dawn until dusk. Ivy's intention had been to go on her errand to Mr. Mundy's shop directly after breakfast, so as to leave plenty of time to get to Durrow Street and meet Mr. Rafferdy by noon.

However, Mr. Wyble engaged her at length over the breakfast table, telling her again (and again) how fortunate he had been to have Lady Marsdel's patronage and how he looked forward to further benevolence on her part with Mr. Bennick's help—which was no doubt in Mr. Rafferdy's power to assure, if Ivy would only ask him.

At last she extracted herself from the dining room, only to be forced to intervene in a quarrel between Lily and Rose. The two had been arguing more and more of late. Being confined to the upper floors had made Lily cross and had prevented Rose from having as much solitude and quiet as she was used to, so that she was easily agitated.

At last Ivy was able to resolve the argument, without ever knowing what it was about, and convinced her sisters to retire to their separate rooms. This done, she hurried downstairs and out the door, but by then the sun was already above the rooftops and galloping swiftly, as if Elytheus was indeed whipping the horses that pulled his fiery chariot in the ancient myth. Abandoning any thought of walking, she hired the first hack cab she saw and directed the driver to Greenly Circle. .

It took her some time to locate the shop—Mr. Rafferdy had not recalled precisely which street it was on—but after twice making a circuit around the circle she saw it winking down the dimness of an alley: a faded silver eye painted on a board above a door.

She paused outside the shop and looked up at the sign. The eye was not inscribed inside a triangle but otherwise looked like the eye on the small box she had found in her father's magick cabinet. Had members of the order ever come here to purchase items for their craft? A dread came over her. What if some of them were inside the shop at that moment?

It did not matter. Even if they were, they would not know who she was. Ivy drew a breath and pushed through the door.

Mr. Rafferdy had expressed distaste when he described the shop to Ivy, but she had quite a different reaction as she moved among the shelves and heaps and towers of books. Some of the tomes had gilt writing on their spines, some words in foreign tongues, and some had no writing at all, their covers as black as the depths of a greatnight. What secrets, what marvels, would she discover if she were to open one of them and read? She reached out, touching one of the dark books whose spine bore no title.

"Be careful of that one," said a croaking voice. "It has a rather nasty—oh!"

Ivy turned around. A small man had appeared from behind a shelf, his mouth a circle of surprise. The stack of books he had been holding tumbled to the floor.

Ivy cringed at the noise, then hurried to him. "I'm so sorry. I didn't mean to startle you. Please, let me help."

She knelt to gather up the fallen books. As she rose, she saw him gazing at her. He had recovered from his surprise, and it was a speculative look he wore now on his round face.

"I'm sorry," she said again, holding out the books.

"You can set them there." He pointed to a table. "And do be careful. Some of them have a will. They might well have leaped from my hands on their own, so you needn't worry. No harm done. They've suffered worse than a little fall like that. Yes, much worse over the years. It's a wonder they've survived at all." He moved about the shop as he spoke, picking up books here and setting them down there with little discernible rhyme or reason.

Ivy set the books on the one clear spot she could find on the table, next to a yellowed skull and several murky jars. Mr. Rafferdy was right. The shop's proprietor did indeed give one the impression of a toad, hopping all around.

"The hat shop is the next street over," he said, setting down a handful of books and picking up several more.

"I'm not looking for hats."

"Then what are you looking for? Dresses? Ribbons? You won't find anything like that here, as you can see."

Ivy took a piece of paper from her pocket and held it out. "I need . . . that is, I'm looking for these things."

Frowning, he set down his books, then took the paper.

"Are these things *you* intend to use?"

"They are not," she said, truthfully enough.

He read the list. "No, I shouldn't think so. I suppose you haven't the foggiest notion what any of these items are for. How could you? Someone wiser sent you, of course. What is his name?"

"I don't see how that matters."

He shrugged. "I would know who my customers are, that's all."

"Then you have no need to look further, for she stands before you."

"But you said these are not for yourself."

Ivy felt her cheeks glowing. "I know it is against the laws of nature for a woman to do magick, but I did not know it was against the laws of Altania for a woman to purchase items in a shop."

"There, there! I only meant to help. I know most of the magicians in the city, what they study, and what their needs are. I only wished to make sure these were all the things the one who sent you needed."

Now it was chagrin Ivy felt. This was hardly the time to let her pride come forth! It was not *his* fault women could not work magick. She made her voice calm, even demure. "The list is correct, I am quite sure."

"Very well, these are all things I have. I shall get them for you at once, Miss . . . ?"

"Mrs. Quent," she said. Belatedly she wondered if she should have given him her real name, but what did it matter?

"Pleased to meet you, Mrs. Quent. I am Mundy—Adabrayus Mundy."

"How do you do, Mr. Mundy?"

Ivy held out her hand, but he had already turned his back to her and was rummaging through jars and boxes. She took the opportunity to explore more around the shop, though with the proprietor so close she did not dare to open any of the books, much as she wished to. She settled for breathing in the dusty air and imagined as she had when she was a girl that the very atmosphere might impart her knowledge.

A thought came to her: was this the place her father had brought her that day long ago? It seemed very like it. She tried to remember which way they had come from Durrow Street. . . .

"Here you are, Mrs. Quent."

Ivy turned, and Mr. Mundy held out a parcel wrapped in black cloth. She accepted it and paid the bill.

"It's for a spell to strengthen some sort of enchantment or binding, isn't it?" he said, then shook his head. "But why ask you? There's no way *you* could possibly know."

She should have thanked him and left, but again her pride rose within her, and she drew herself up, so that despite her smallish stature she was as tall as he. "Just because someone cannot do a thing does not mean one cannot have knowledge of it, Mr. Mundy. I would think someone who sold so many books as yourself would understand that fact. My father is . . . He was a magician himself, and I have read extensively from his library. I know quite well what these things are for."

Mr. Mundy's eyes went wide again for a moment. Had she offended him with her speech or shocked him with her confession that she had read from books of magick?

It didn't matter. She had what she needed. "Thank you, Mr. Mundy. Good day."

Behind his spectacles, his pale eyes turned to slits beneath drooping lids. "Good day to you, Mrs. Quent," he said in his croaking voice. "Do come again for anything you need. And . . . good luck with your endeavors."

Ivy could not suppress a shudder. Mr. Rafferdy was right: he was a repugnant little man. She had no intention of ever returning here, no matter how many books of magick he had. Taking her parcel, she left the shop and returned to Greenly Circle.

Obtaining the items had not taken as long as she thought. Despite her earlier delays, if she took a carriage to Durrow Street now, she would get there well before Mr. Rafferdy. However, if she were to return home, she would hardly arrive before it was time to depart again, so she decided to walk to the old house. The morning was bright, and many people were about; it would be safe enough to go on her own.

Keeping to the main avenues, she soon reached Durrow Street, turning onto it just at the square where Queen Béanore's fountain stood. Ivy crossed to the center of the square, smiled up at the statue of the queen upon her chariot, then sat on the edge of the fountain to listen to its bubbling waters and rest for a moment.

A shadow flitted above her. Fearing it might be a pigeon that wished to alight on her head, Ivy glanced up.

Dark tears streamed down Queen Béanore's face. Her cloak rippled in an unseen wind.

Ivy gasped, leaping to her feet. She looked all around, but the square was suddenly empty of all save pigeons. Then a gray flock fluttered up from the cobbles, and in their place stood a figure all in black.

She hesitated, then moved toward him.

"Home," she heard his voice speak, though as before his mask was motionless. "You must go home now."

"You mean to the house on Durrow Street?" she said, finding she could speak. "I'm on my way now. That's why I'm here."

He shook his head. Now the black mask was drawn down in a scowl. "No," came his voice. "*Home.* You must go now!"

She halted, a chill passing through her despite the morning sun. "What is it? What's wrong?"

Another flock of pigeons flew before her. She stepped back, away from the gray flurry of wings. In a moment they were gone.

So was he. People moved through the square again. Water danced and sang in the fountain.

"Home," Ivy murmured.

Then she was running across the square, looking for the nearest cab available for hire.

$\mathcal{J}$T SEEMED TO take an eternity to reach Whitward Street. She clawed at the seat each time the driver halted the horses to let some cart pass by on a narrow street. In truth it was but half an hour. All the same, the carriage had hardly rolled to a stop before she paid the driver and leaped down to the street without his help. She stumbled, caught herself, then ran through the gate, up the steps, and into the house.

"What is it?" she said upon finding the housekeeper in the entry hall. "What's happened?"

The woman looked at her with a sour expression. "What's happened? The master is away, and the young misses have taken over the parlor when it isn't their allotted time, that's what's happened!"

Even as she said this, Ivy heard the rumble of dreary piano music emanating from above.

"Nothing else has happened, then?" It didn't make sense—he had told her to come here. "Are you certain that's all?"

The housekeeper frowned at her. "That's all that's happened that concerns *me.* Though I suppose *you* might want to know that a letter arrived for you while you were out."

She pointed to the sideboard, then disappeared through the kitchen door. Ivy stared after her, not knowing what to think. Then she went to the sideboard and picked up the post.

In an instant she was opening the topmost letter, for it was from Mr. Quent, and she could not break the seal and unfold it quickly enough. How she wished he were here in person! Yet even this part of him was a blessing. She read the first lines eagerly.

Her elation vanished, and she sagged against the sideboard as she read on. The paper trembled in her hand like a pale leaf before a storm.

*My Dearest—*

*You have told me you think me to be a man of good sense and solid judgment. Know that your sentiments, however lovingly intended, are wrong. I have been careless—even reckless. That I should have told you this long ago is now as plain to see as this ink upon the page.*

*Yet it did not occur to me that I had any need to do so! Never did I think that he would return to Invarel—not after what happened years ago. Yet he has done just that, and I have been thoughtless not to warn you. I only hope he has not approached you. Surely it would be brazen of him. He must know what risk he would expose himself to by attempting such a thing.*

*I reassure myself that he has no doubt kept far from you, and your father is nowhere that he might reach him. All the same, I must caution you, for I have just learned in a missive from Lord Rafferdy that Mr. Bennick has indeed returned to Invarel after many years of exile in Torland. Heed these words, dearest: you must have nothing to do with him! He is dangerous—a deceiver and a traitor. While I am to this day not certain of the particulars, I believe—no, I will say I am certain—that it is because of Mr. Bennick's actions that Mr. Lockwell suffered his awful fate.*

*They had both belonged to the same arcane order of magicians, your father once confided in me. Shortly after your father fell ill, I questioned Mr. Bennick, and he was sly and secretive. Nor did he show any sort of remorse at what had befallen Mr. Lockwell, who had purportedly been his friend.*

*Despite his dissembling, I was able to glean a few things from him. He had been working an enchantment that Mr. Lockwell had implored him not to. However, the spell went awry, and as a result something terrible would have taken place (though what, I cannot imagine).*

*Before this awful happening could occur, Mr. Lockwell intervened. He managed to undo whatever it was Mr. Bennick had achieved. However, the effort required was great, and the cost to your father grievous. His mind was broken—irrevocably, or so Mr. Bennick told me. Alas, of all the things he said to me, this was the only one I fully believed as the truth!*

*So you see, you must have nothing to do with Mr. Bennick. He is no longer a magician—his power to do magick was taken from him by his order. Why, I do not know; as a punishment for what he did, I suppose. Regardless, you must not think because his power is gone that he is no longer dangerous. He knows other magicians, and that he might one day seek to convince them to attempt again that thing your father once prevented him from accomplishing is something I suspect.*

*You must do nothing that might offer him any help. If there are books or papers of your father's he ever comes seeking, do not give them to him. My work here has been difficult, but it is at last near to its completion. There is no need to reply—I will return before any letter can reach me. Until then, keep yourself safe, dearest. I shall be with you soon, but know that either near or far, I am ever—*

*Yours,*
*A. Quent*

With shaking hands, Ivy folded the letter. Dread had brought clarity to her like cold rain washing down a fogged window. One by one she fit the events together in her mind, like the pieces of one of Mrs. Baydon's puzzles, until the picture became clear: the ring he had given Mr. Rafferdy, the article about the new planet he had sent to her, his invitation to give Mr. Rafferdy lessons in the art of magick. He was no longer a magician, but he had said himself that just because he no longer practiced magick did not mean he no longer possessed an interest in it.

The Vigilant Order of the Silver Eye had taken his magickal talent from him. Yet in his letter, her father had said he believed there was more than one traitor in the order. What if Mr. Bennick was able to deliver to them something they wanted? Were there not some in the order who might reward him by giving him his magick back?

He had told Rafferdy that, once taken away, a magician's talent could never be restored, but Ivy could not believe that. He had only wished to frighten Mr. Rafferdy into studying with him. He had needed Mr. Rafferdy, just as he needed Ivy. He had used Mr. Wyble as a way to arrange their introduction, then had used them both in turn.

He had known Mr. Lockwell, had known about the riddle, and had sent her the article to help her solve it. Then he had taught Mr. Rafferdy the very spell included with her father's letter—the spell that must have undone what Mr. Bennick had tried to achieve years ago—knowing that understanding it would induce them to use the key and open the door to the house on Durrow Street. Once the door was open, he would bring others from the order there, and deliver to them what they sought. . . .

Upstairs, the music ceased. A moment later a slim figure appeared at the top of the stairs.

"Ivy?" Rose's voice drifted down. "Is that you? Are you coming up to sit with us in the parlor? It was Lily's idea to go in. It's not our proper time, but it's good to be in there again. It makes me think of what it was like before. Won't you come sit with us?"

A pang passed through Ivy, then she cleared her throat and forced her voice to be light. "Not just now, dearest," she called up. "There is . . . I have an errand I must do."

Ivy put the letter in her pocket, and she felt the iron key there. She could only believe Mr. Bennick knew everything they intended. No doubt at that very moment he was on his way to the house on Durrow Street.

And so was Mr. Rafferdy.

She gripped the key in a fist. Then Ivy was out the door and into the swift-passing day.

# CHAPTER TWENTY-SIX

𝒯HE BELLS RANG out with the dawn.

To others in the city they signaled the end of night, the coming again of lighted times, but to Eldyn the music of the bells meant nothing. He had not slept, and the sun—however bright its rays—had no power to dispel the darkness that pursued him. The moment he stepped out the doors of St. Galmuth's, the shadow would be there, waiting for him.

Rosy light spilled through a stained-glass window, illuminating the small side chapel where they had spent the night, off the west transept of the cathedral. Sashie stirred on one of the pews where she lay curled up beneath Eldyn's coat, but she did not open her eyes.

Eldyn wasn't sure to whom the chapel was dedicated. Given the bronze staff in her hands, the figure on the altar might have been St. Alethyn, protector of orphans or cripples. Or it might have been St. Sophella, renowned for smiting infidels with her rod. Eldyn hoped it was the former rather than the latter.

Last night the rector had shown them to the chapel as darkness fell, though not before the priest at the doors of the cathedral had nearly cast them out. It seemed charity was no longer freely given at St. Galmuth's—not when the number who needed it would have filled the catheral many times over. Dread had seized Eldyn, and he had glanced over his shoulder into the gloom behind them, looking for a prowling shadow and twin amber sparks. Sashie had whimpered beside him.

Fortunately, from his days at the church of St. Adaris, Dercy was familiar with the ancient rules. He had demanded to speak to the rector, and as they waited he instructed Eldyn on how to speak the request for sanctuary; when the rector arrived, Eldyn did so. Even so, the priest might still have cast them out, but the rector would not have it.

"I do not know how it is in the parish you came from," the old rector had said in his thin voice, "but the laws are remembered here at St. Galmuth's. The first soul to request sanctuary after the fall of night must be granted it for the remainder of the umbral. They will stay here tonight, and, if he will hear it, they can make their case to the archdeacon tomorrow. He will judge if their plight warrants the protection of the Church."

Eldyn and his sister were let inside, though to Eldyn's dismay Dercy did not come with them. All the same, as the great doors closed with a *boom,* Eldyn's fear receded. In here, no evil could find them.

However, as the light strengthened, so did Eldyn's dread. The old rector might still adhere to the ancient ways, but what of the archdeacon? What if he was not moved by Eldyn's plea? Or worse, what if he would not hear their case at all? He watched the warm light fall upon the altar. Others might have seen it as a sign of hope, but to him the ruddy illumination stained the pale statue of the saint like blood.

The tolling of the bells ceased, and as their music faded he heard footsteps behind him. He turned to see Dercy enter the chapel. The young man held out his hand, but Eldyn gripped him close in an embrace.

"Thank you," he said as they broke apart.

For a moment Eldyn couldn't fathom Dercy's expression—it seemed at once sad and hopeful—but then the young man's blond beard parted in a grin. "It seems the time I spent at St. Adaris counted for something, after all. Brother Garus used to bore me to tears with his stories of how he was once a priest at St. Galmuth's, but I'm glad for them now."

"As am I," Eldyn said. He glanced back at Sashie, then lowered his voice. "But have you heard—do you know if the archdeacon will hear our petition?"

Dercy's smile vanished. "I don't know. He might, but they say he is a very busy man. The good news is that you are allowed to stay until the archdeacon either agrees to hear your request or denies it, and it sounds like that could take days. In the meantime, you'll be safe here."

Eldyn looked again at the statue on the altar. She seemed to be gazing down, as if at someone kneeling before her, and he wondered if it was with benevolence she looked or with retribution. Yes, they were safe here, but for how long? A few days, perhaps. And even if they were granted sanctuary, how long could they dwell here in a cathedral? What sort of life would that be for Sashie, trapped like a bird in the high-vaulted church?

"I'm tired," he said quietly.

A hand touched his shoulder, and he turned around. Dercy gazed at him, worry in his blue-green eyes.

"Maybe you should try to sleep."

Eldyn shook his head. "That's not what I meant. I want to end this. I'm tired of running from him, I'm tired of letting him be the master of this game. I won't play it anymore, not by his rules." Strangely, as he spoke these words, his fear and weariness receded. "I don't care how it ends, but I want this to stop now."

Dercy gripped his arm. "Then you have to stop running. It will never end if you don't. You can't just keep responding to what he does. You have to be the one to take action."

Eldyn understood. It was like the play at the Theater of the Moon. No matter how far the silvery youth ran, he could not escape the sun king. The only way to end it was to confront the king himself, to destroy his pursuer. Even if it led to his own destruction.

*I would do it,* Eldyn thought. *If it would free Sashie from Westen, then I would do it, no matter the cost.*

"Only how?" he said aloud. "He is stronger than I, and he can wield a gun. What power do I have against him?"

Now Dercy was grinning again. "You do have power. I've seen it, and so have you. He may have fists and guns at his disposal, but you have something else. If you're going to defeat him, you have to do it in your own way."

Eldyn looked down at his hands, and as the light turned from red to gold, he thought he knew what Dercy meant. His father had called him weak, and all these years Eldyn had believed him. Only he wasn't weak. He just hadn't understood the nature of his own strength.

"So how do I do it?"

Dercy studied Eldyn for a moment. Then he glanced at Sashie, still sleeping on the bench, and his grin broadened. "You do it by giving him exactly what he wants."

They bent their heads together, whispering like the priests beneath the vaults of the cathedral.

🦇

ℐT WAS AFTERNOON, and sunlight bathed the cathedral of St. Galmuth's as one of the great bronze doors opened a fraction. A moment later a lithe figure slipped out. The young woman had dark hair and fair skin, and if any eyes saw her (and indeed, certain eyes were watching for just such a thing) they would have considered her a very pretty thing.

She cast a furtive glance over her shoulder, then hurried down the steps of the cathedral to the street below. She unfurled a parasol and raised it against the brilliant afternoon sun, shading her face, then looked left and right, as if unsure of which way to go. After a moment she chose left and moved down the street with the crowds, deeper into the Old City.

Again, if eyes had been watching, they would have seen seconds later how a tall form separated itself from the dimness of a doorway and stalked down the street after her.

The figure of the young woman wove among the crooked lanes of the Old City, then passed through the Lowgate into the danker ways of Waterside. Men cast her looks as she went, as if stumbling upon a flower in the midst of a rubbish heap. Coming upon such a thing, what man would not crave to pluck it? However, it was broad daylight, and there were redcrests here and there. No one accosted her.

At last the young woman stopped before an inn on a narrow lane. The sign over the door read *The Golden Loom*. From beneath her parasol, she drew out a silk handkerchief and gave it a flutter.

It was the sign he had been waiting for. He appeared from a shadow and approached on long legs, clad in velvet and leather. His mane of hair fell over broad shoulders, shining like gold in the sunlight. She gasped as he appeared suddenly beside her, then the white curve of a smile appeared in the dimness beneath the parasol.

"I knew it," she said, her voice very soft. "I knew if I came here you would find me."

"So I have, my sweet. I've been waiting for you, and you have not disappointed me. I am pleased with you. Very pleased." He smiled, and bent his face toward hers.

She lowered the parasol further. "Not here!" she whispered.

He withdrew, a bemused expression on his handsome face. "You are right, of course. In my delight to see you, I forget my manners. Besides, there are those who, if they noticed me, would not look so kindly upon me as you do. It is best if we go inside."

He held out his arm, and she accepted it. Inside it was cool and dim, but she traded her parasol for a fan, using it to conceal her face as he spoke to the innkeeper. Coins changed hands. A private dining chamber was reserved. Wine was delivered, and sweet things to eat, then the innkeeper was told not to disturb them.

When they were alone again, he moved to the door and locked it. Then he poured wine for them both and handed her a glass.

"You need fear no prying eyes in here," Westen said. "The innkeeper and I have an . . . arrangement. He can be trusted. Pray set down your fan and let me see your lovely face in full."

"Draw the curtains first."

He laughed. "What a modest thing you are!" But he did as instructed, and then she set down the fan and smiled at him. It was a lovely expression, demure but not too timid. And if her cheeks were powdered and rouged a bit more heavily than usual, and her lips painted a deeper red, he seemed not to notice. He sat beside her, took a long drink of wine, then set his hand atop hers. She started to pull away, but he clasped his fingers about her own, holding her hand in place.

"You need not fear," he said. "No one recognized you here, not with your fan before your face. Nor were you followed from the cathedral. There is no way your brother can know where you are."

"My brother!" she said scornfully. "How I am glad to be away from him. Would that I never saw him again!"

He raised an eyebrow. "You speak ill of him, yet I know he loves you deeply. Do you not love him in return?"

"Do I love him? Nay, I loathe him! He has been my captor and my tormentor all these months. He has imprisoned me in wretched hovels, never letting me see the light or breathe the air. If he professes to love me, then it is as a man loves a pearl he locks away in a musty box where no one can ever see it. It is a wonder I have not wasted away."

Alarm suddenly crossed her face, and now it was she who clasped his hand tightly. "You aren't going to take me back to him, are you? Please, I would rather you take out your gun and end my life. I won't go back to him!"

"Now, now," he said, lifting his other hand to her chin. "You need not speak so wildly. You are free of him forevermore—I promise you that. If ever I would ask you to go back to him, it would be only for a short time, and then only to help me punish him."

"To . . . to punish him?"

"Yes, to punish him for how he has wronged you and how he has wronged me."

For a moment she gazed at him, then her lips curved in a smile. "I like the sound of that." She pushed his glass toward him. It was full again, and he did not seem to notice that her own glass was suddenly empty, though she had taken only the smallest sip. He raised the glass to her and tilted it back, drinking deeply.

✦

WATCHING THE HIGHWAYMAN drink, Eldyn felt not fear but rather a kind of thrill he had never known before. He had dreaded that the trick might be exposed under the harsh light of day, but the parasol and fan had served their purpose, and here in this dim chamber the illusion was less likely to be discovered.

As Dercy had told him, it was easy to make people see what they wanted to see. He had only to powder his face and put on the frock Dercy had brought him—one of Sashie's own, retrieved from their rooms in Lowpark—and he was already much of the way there. People had always said brother and sister were very alike in looks.

There in the cathedral, beneath the watchful gazes of saints, Dercy had taught him a glamour to make him seem smaller, finer, and more pale. It was easier to work the illusion than Eldyn had thought. Yet he had done it with the coin in the tavern, and it was not so different than weaving the shadows—save that it was light he was shaping, not darkness.

The rest of the trick was up to him—to move delicately and speak with a soft voice. At first it was a great effort and required much concentration, but, strangely, the more he did it the easier it became. By the time they had entered the private dining chamber at the inn, he felt like he was on a stage giving a performance.

Eldyn's audience set down his cup.

"By God, I have a great thirst," he said, and he filled both their cups again. Then his gaze fell upon Eldyn, roving up and down. "And I daresay I am hungry as well."

Eldyn pushed the plate of sweets toward him, but the highwayman pushed them back.

"That's not what I meant, as you know well." He leaned over the table. His breath was warm and wine-scented. "Sashie . . . it's a pretty name. I always thought you pretty yourself, but today you seem more than pretty. You're like an angel. The sight of you goes to my head more than the contents of this glass. I confess, I had thought to punish your brother through you. I see now that I can, but not in the way I thought."

Eldyn took the chance to switch their cups again, then smoothed a lock of gold hair back from the highwayman's brow. "Whatever do you mean, my dear? What were you thinking of doing before now?"

"It doesn't matter. All that matters is that I know what we must do. I had thought you a creature in his power, yet you have a will of your own. With you I can accomplish what I have not been able to do on my own. Then, when it is revealed to him that you are mine and that I have made you happy in a way he never could, it will ruin him far more than any hurt I might have delivered to him. He will be utterly defeated."

Eldyn suppressed a shudder. Instead, he let out a trilling laugh and leaned closer. "Tell me more," he crooned.

As Westen spoke, Eldyn continued to weave the wan light around himself. He did not know if it was because of the wine or due to some unforeseen effect of the illusion, but the highwayman indeed seemed intoxicated. His eyes blazed, and he spoke with great animation, sometimes rising from his chair and pacing back and forth across the room.

She must not think him a common thief, he said. He did not rob others for profit but instead for a nobler cause. He belonged to a group of men whose goal was nothing less than to bring down the government of Altania—Crown and Assembly both. For one was as corrupt as the other, and only a new ruler, one who heeded the voice of Altania, could lead the people forward.

"And who would this ruler be?" Eldyn asked. "Prince Huntley the Usurper?"

He shrugged. "If the Morden heir will do as the people will, then why should it not be him? Yet if he seeks to rule only for his own gain, then surely Altania herself will choose another. Altania will no longer tolerate a ruler who rapes her for his own benefit and glory, with no thought to her lands and people. Altania will suffer such men no longer."

Eldyn laughed. "Altania will choose; Altania will not suffer. You make her sound like a living thing!"

"She is alive—very much alive." He leaned over the back of Eldyn's chair, and his voice went low. "There are things you do not know, my sweet. Things you will have to see with your own eyes. But the day comes soon when you *will* see them, when everyone will see them. You will see what I have been shown, by the one who now leads us. Then you'll understand what I mean when I say that Altania will no longer suffer men who use her ill."

This time Eldyn could not help a shiver. He did not know what these words meant, though they filled him with a strange feeling. It was not quite fear; rather, it was a kind of unknown anticipation, a feeling that something was going to happen—something at once dreadful and marvelous.

"Are you well, Sashie? Your color looks poor of a sudden. . . ."

Now fear did strike Eldyn's heart. In his distraction he had begun to let the threads of the illusion unravel. With a hasty thought he wove them together again.

"Your words shock me, that's all," he said, and took a sip of wine. Then he transferred the nearly full glass to Westen's hand. The highwayman drank of it. "But tell me," Eldyn went on, "how can so small a thing as I help you with such grand goals?"

"It is always the smallest who brings down the mighty," he said. "A million little drops can make an ocean great enough to drown any king."

With that he laid out his plan. There was a man who was a servant of the Crown. Exactly what he did for the king was not important for her to know right now. All that mattered was that this man's work interfered with the plans of the revolutionaries—indeed, it posed a dire threat to their very purpose of freeing Altania from tyranny—and so he must be removed.

However, this was more easily said than done. He was a powerful man, a member of the Upper Hall of Assembly, and was always guarded when in the city. Furthermore, like a cowardly dog, he had recently built walls enclosing the lands about his manor in the country, so that none could approach him there without being detected.

Still, there were other ways they might get at this lord. There were some few men who were his agents, men who traveled about Altania performing duties in his name, for the lord himself was infirm. One of these men had been, for some time now, the object of Westen's attentions. He was, the highwayman had determined, chief among the lord's servants. If this man could be removed, it would be a grievous blow to the lord's ability to do his foul work.

"What mysterious figures you make them sound!" Eldyn said. "Who is this man and this lord you speak of?"

"Be careful, Miss Garritt," he said, leaning over the table. "If I divulge these things to you, then you will be privy to secrets that the king's Black Dog would give much to learn. The knowledge will make you beholden to me and to my compatriots. We cannot allow our intentions to become known to those we cannot trust."

Eldyn coiled a hand beneath his chin and smiled. "Trust me as you trust yourself, for I am yours to command."

"As you will, my sweet. The man I speak of is named Mr. Quent, and he is one of the inquirers of a certain Lord Rafferdy."

His shock was too great to be concealed. Eldyn lifted his hands, covering his face, knowing his illusion had wavered. However, the action would look natural enough. Surely Westen had expected such a response, and after a few moments Eldyn was able to steady himself and weave the illusion anew. Once he was sure the glamour was again in place, he lowered his hands.

"Are you astonished?" the highwayman said, his expression amused.

Eldyn nodded. "A little, I confess. It's just that . . . Lord Rafferdy . . . It can only be that he is the father of my brother's friend. It's strange chance that the one you seek to . . . that he is in fact connected to me."

He sat, filling their wine cups again. On the contrary, he told her, it was anything but chance. In hopes of getting close to Lord Rafferdy, he had begun following his son. Upon observing the son's friendship with her brother, Westen had thought to use Eldyn Garritt to gain information that might help get him close to Rafferdy the son, and thereby to Rafferdy the father.

Though these words chilled him to the core, Eldyn worked his face into a petulant expression. "I understand very well now. I don't mean a thing to you at all—you were merely using me to get at my brother."

"No, you misunderstand. You were rather a lovely benefit I had not anticipated. It was never my intention to use you, for I had other ways of bringing your brother under my control."

*You lie!* Eldyn wanted to shout. Instead, he said demurely, "Only he isn't under your control, is he?"

Westen's expression darkened. He gripped his cup, then tossed back the contents. "I confess, your brother has been more difficult to deal with than I thought. Not because of any strength or cunning, mind you—rather, I had not anticipated the depths of cowardice and depravity he would sink to in order to elude me. I had thought him a gentleman, at least."

*A gentleman such as you are?* Eldyn would have sneered. Instead, he said, in a scornful tone, "My brother is not a man like you."

"To be sure, but he has been a bother nonetheless. Nor did things go as I planned recently, when I sought to close with Mr. Quent at his estate in the country. I was . . . I was most grievously deprived in that affair of one who was beloved by me. However, I will be vexed by wives and weaklings no longer. I have learned Mr. Quent is even now on his way to the city and that once here he will meet with Lord Rafferdy. I can bag them both with one shot, as it were. All I need is to get near to them. Your brother is the key to that. And you—"

Eldyn laughed gaily. "And I am the key to my dear, sweet brother. He will do anything for me."

Westen laughed as well and reached for Eldyn's hands, but Eldyn drew back.

"Only how is it to be done?" he said. "You say you have tried to get close to them before. Will they not be expecting men to come for them?"

"Yes, as you say, it is men they will be expecting. Yet what comes for them will be something else, something I am quite sure they will not expect." Again he grinned, and perhaps it was only how they gleamed in the dimness of the chamber, but his teeth seemed longer than before. And it could have been nothing more than the reflection of the lamp's flame, but it seemed his eyes glinted amber.

"What's wrong, Miss Garritt?" His voice was low. "You seem to draw away, but I thought you favored me. Is there something that frightens you?"

Eldyn's trembling was not feigned. "It is only that my brother . . . He told me the shadow we glimpsed last night, that thing that seemed like a beast . . . He said it was you, but surely . . ."

The highwayman's smile broadened.

Eldyn gasped, rose from the table, and hurried to the door. But it was locked, and Westen had the key. He turned around. Westen stalked across the room, and Eldyn saw that it was no trick of the light: the highwayman's eyes shone with yellow light.

"By God, it's true," he whispered. "You *can* become a beast."

"Can't every man?" Westen said with a growling laugh. Then he shook his head, and a look of wonder came over him. "No, it's not the same as for the others. I saw how she did it to them, the witch in the Wyrdwood. I watched her. It was the potions, and the ragged clothes and furs they donned, and a few petty spells. She befuddled them, addled their brains, and tricked them so that they were all scrabbling about in the dirt on all fours, howling and snarling. Others who saw them were tricked as well, but they were still men; I saw it. She knew I did, and I refused her potions. Only she just laughed at me. She told me I didn't need them."

There is little distinction between dread and awe. Eldyn felt them both in that moment. "You don't, do you? You don't need potions or costumes to make you into a beast."

Westen studied his hands, slowly shaking his head.

"What are you?" Eldyn said.

The highwayman looked up. "I am what Altania needs me to be." Now his smile returned. "Just as you will be what I need you to be, Miss Garritt."

In an easy step he closed the distance between them. He spoke in a low voice, explaining what she was to tell her brother. How she had encountered Westen and had learned of some rebel plot; how she was to implore her brother to take a warning to Mr. Rafferdy and to urge him to seek out Mr. Quent, who could best protect his father. She would tell them the attack was to come the next day. All the while, Westen would follow them.

"Then, when the opportunity presents itself, we will—" He shook his head. "There is no need to bother your lovely head with such details as that, my sweet. Suffice it to say they will not be ready for what befalls them. Do you understand what it is you are to do? It may seem small, but know that you will be doing Altania a great service."

"Yes," Eldyn said, looking up and meeting the highwayman's yellow gaze. "Yes, I will be."

"You have a courageous heart, Miss Garritt—unlike that brother of yours. I shall make a revolutionary of you yet." He put his hands on the door to either side, pinning Eldyn in place. "Though there is something else I would make of you first." He bent his head down.

There was no way to resist it. Their lips came together in a kiss. It was not rough, as Eldyn would have thought, but soft, and sweet with wine.

"By God, you make me mad as you never have before," the highwayman said. His hands went to the shoulders of the frock, and he leaned against the door, pressing his body forward.

Terror seized Eldyn. There were some things no illusion could conceal. He slipped a hand into the highwayman's pocket, an action that drew forth a low sound of delight. However, in a swift motion Eldyn ducked beneath Westen's arms. He darted across the room, the key to the door in his hand.

"You're quite resourceful, Miss Garritt," Westen said, prowling in pursuit. "I like that very much. Yet I am resourceful as well, and I will not be denied what I desire."

"There is no time," Eldyn said, circling around the table, keeping it between him and the highwayman. "My brother will wake soon. He'll wonder where I've gone."

"I can be quick about it, if that's your worry."

Eldyn donned his most charming smile. "But I'd rather you be slow."

At this the highwayman roared with laughter. "You're no angel after all," he said. "Go, then. I can wait—a little while. It will all be done soon enough. Then you will get exactly what you desire."

"I am sure I will," Eldyn said.

Westen sat then, thrusting his boots upon the table, and filled his cup again with wine. He leaned back, resting one hand on his thigh while with the other he raised the cup. His eyes were no longer yellow but a tawny brown. He looked handsome and at ease, a gold-haired king on his throne. Eldyn went to the door, unlocked it.

"A storm is coming," Westen said, regarding the cup. "When it arrives, more than a few are going to get washed away by the floods. But when the clouds part, a bright morning will shine through, and you're going to be there to see it. I promise you that." He raised the cup. "For Altania."

"For Altania," Eldyn said.

Then he opened the door, leaving the highwayman to his drink and his thoughts, and went out into the light of day.

## CHAPTER TWENTY-SEVEN

BY THE TIME the hack cab came to a halt before the iron fence, Ivy had already opened the carriage door. She made a leap from the running board and barely caught herself from falling to the cobbles of Durrow Street. Recovering her footing, she ran toward the gate.

"Hey there, miss!" the driver called out. "Do you want me to call the redcrests on you?"

Ivy hesitated—it was past their appointed meeting time—but at another angry shout from the driver she hurried back. Her hands shook, but at last she found enough in her coin purse to pay the fare.

"Everyone's a thief these days," the driver grumbled. "The rich as bad as the poor."

Ivy had already turned her back on him. She ran up the path, then pushed through the iron gate—as before, it was not locked—and into the overgrown yard.

She looked all around but to her great relief saw no one in the yard. The high hedges muted the noises of the city, and the only sound was the murmur of the wind through the hawthorn trees. Dead leaves still clung to their branches along with the new, giving them a disheveled appearance that reminded her of the Wyrdwood. She drew close to one of the trees and ran her fingers over its twisted branches, breathing in the scent of leaves—

"There you are!"

Startled, Ivy looked up. A green mist seemed to clear from her eyes, and she saw Mr. Rafferdy walking to her from the direction of the house. He must have been standing by the door, behind the statues of the lions.

"You arrive late for an important—perhaps even perilous—task, yet you still take time to admire the garden," he said, his expression at once amused and annoyed. "You are either the calmest person in the world, Mrs. Quent, or the most confounding."

At once her urgency returned. She was anything but calm! "We can't go into the house," she said, gripping his arm. "We must leave here at once, Mr. Rafferdy."

"Make that the most confounding then," he said, his look becoming a scowl. "Do you mean to say I spent all those hours enduring the company of Mr. Bennick, mastering the pronunciation of that awful spell—which, by the way, I have done, for we got to the end of it today—do you mean that I have suffered all of this for nothing? Reason must have at last convinced you that your faith in me was foolish. All the same, I can work the spell. In fact, I'll show you that I can do so by speaking it to you this very—"

"Mr. Bennick has betrayed us!" she blurted out.

He stared at her, gripping the handle of his cane. "By God, you're not joking," he said at last. "How can you know this?"

"I'll tell you when we're home. It isn't safe to be here."

"But aren't we supposed to work the spell?"

She pulled on his arm. "We can't—not now. He's been using us, lying to us all this time. Don't you understand? It's because of him that my father went . . . that my father fell ill. It's because of what *he* tried to do—what he's still trying to do even now."

Rafferdy resisted her efforts to move him. "What are you talking about? What is he trying to do?"

"I'm trying to open the door to the house," spoke a deep voice.

Ivy and Mr. Rafferdy stared at each other, then together they turned. A tall figure in a dark coat stood on the path just beyond the open gate.

Mr. Rafferdy shook his head. "Mr. Bennick, you startled us. What are you doing here?"

Ivy dug her fingers into his arm. "He told you—he's trying to get into the house. It's what he's wanted all along!"

He looked back at her. "Are you certain?"

"You should listen to her," Mr. Bennick said. "She has her father's mind. I could never win an argument with Lockwell—his logic could never be assailed. Nor can Mrs. Quent's. Everything she has told you is true. I have been using you to gain entry to the house of my former associate—to *this* house. It has been my intention from the start."

With that, Mr. Bennick started toward the gate.

Before Ivy could move, harsh words sounded on the air. Mr. Rafferdy raised his cane, thrusting it toward the gate, and spoke rapidly in the tongue of magick. The ring on his right hand flared, and tendrils of blue fire coiled down the length of the cane. The gate flew closed, shutting with a *clang*.

Mr. Bennick gripped the iron bars and gave a push. The gate did not budge. He raised an eyebrow. "You exerted your will from a distance, and you've bound an object far larger than any you have before. I'm surprised."

Mr. Rafferdy lowered his cane and glanced at Ivy. "You aren't the only one."

Ivy felt both dread and wonder; indeed, the feelings were one and the same. She looked at the cane. The blue fire had faded, but the ring on his hand still winked brightly. "You really are a magician," she murmured.

"Yes, he is," Mr. Bennick said. "One of considerable talent. If he had not been, I would never have wasted my time with him. All the same, impressive as this display might be, it is for naught. Mr. Mundy told me you purchased items for a spell of binding. That's how I knew you were coming here today. However, *they* don't need anyone to tell them. They will know when you enter the house, and they are far more adept at enchantments than you are, Mr. Rafferdy, no matter your natural ability." He let go of the gate. "Against them, this binding won't hold for long."

"It won't have to," Ivy said. She grasped Mr. Rafferdy's hand and pulled him toward the house. "Come on!"

The two ran across the yard. Mr. Bennick did not call out, though they felt his eyes on them as they went. They halted before the heavy wooden door of the house. Ivy glanced at the stone lions to either side, almost hoping she would see them yawn and stretch. However, they were motionless stone. Whoever the man in the mask was, he was not here.

Ivy took out the key and fitted it in the lock. For one awful moment she feared it would not turn. However, it did so easily. There was a grinding noise. She laid a hand on the door.

"Go on," Mr. Rafferdy said.

Ivy realized she had been standing there, as motionless as the lions. She drew in a breath, then pushed on the door. It swung open with a whisper, like an echo of an ancient word murmured in a forgotten tongue. Beyond was a gray dimness.

"Do not gaze into the eye," a voice called out.

Ivy glanced back over her shoulder. Mr. Bennick still stood at the gate, watching them from the other side of the bars.

"No matter what you do, no matter what you think you see, you must not look into it." Then he retreated from the gate and was gone from sight.

Ivy shivered, then stepped over the threshold. Mr. Rafferdy followed after. They turned to shut the door, and Ivy used the key to lock it again.

"Something happened when you did that." He laid a hand on the door. "I heard it, like the sound of another door closing. Did you hear it?"

Ivy withdrew the heavy key, weighing it in her hand. "No, but I think it's the binding on the door. When I locked it again, the enchantment must have been restored."

"Yes, it's as if there's a sheet of glass over the door. Only . . ." He ran a hand over the wood. "There are cracks in it. I can feel them."

Despite her fear, she could not help but marvel at him. "What you did out there—your cane, the way it shone."

He grimaced. "It was nothing. You heard him—they'll break it soon enough. I can only suppose they'll break through this as well now." He looked at her. "The binding's not strong anymore, not after you used the key. If they're really coming as he said, then it won't take them long to gain entry."

"Then we'd better hurry."

Ivy left the door and moved through the dimness of the entry hall. Sheet-draped furniture stood all around like ghosts. The house was silent except for their own footfalls.

"How long has it—" Mr. Rafferdy winced as his voice echoed; he lowered it to just above a whisper. "How long has it been since you've been here?"

"A long time. I was only four or five when we moved to Whitward Street." She reached the foot of the stairs. The knobs atop the newel posts were carved to look like shut eyes, just as she remembered. She touched one, then put a foot on the first step.

"Where are you going?"

She looked back at him. "Upstairs. He said in his letter the door was in the room behind his study."

He swallowed. "Right, then."

Ivy turned to start up the steps—and gasped. The eyes atop the newel posts were no longer shut. Now they were open and staring, their pupils slits rather than circles.

"One gets the feeling we're being watched," Mr. Rafferdy said.

Ivy steadied herself. What reason did she have to fear an enchantment that her father had surely known of—had perhaps created himself? No, *she* was not the intruder here. She made herself continue up the steps, and Mr. Rafferdy came after. The eyes seemed to follow them as they went.

Ivy did not stop at the second landing, instead leading the way to the uppermost floor. While before her memories of the house on Durrow Street had been dim and murky, now that she was here it was as if a black veil had been lifted. She went directly to the end of the upstairs corridor. They came to a thick door into which was carved a single eye. As she touched the doorknob, the eye opened like those atop the newel posts below.

Mr. Rafferdy gave a nervous cough. "So much for nipping in unseen."

"I think this house sees everything we do," she said.

The door was locked, so she took out the iron key. It turned easily in the lock, and the door swung open. As it did, she braced herself for the wailing of some magickal alarm.

There was only silence. Ivy gathered her courage, then entered the room she had never set foot in before and into which she had seen just once all those years ago. The eye in the door blinked as they passed, and a shower of dust fell from its lid.

The room was very dark. Creeping slowly, not sure what she would run into, Ivy moved to the window and drew the curtains, letting in the light of the swift-passing afternoon through the dusty glass.

"There's nothing here," Mr. Rafferdy said.

Ivy turned around. In her mind she could still picture the crowded, cluttered room she had glimpsed through the crack in the door as a girl—a chamber full of mysterious trunks and unknown artifacts draped in black velvet. However, the room she saw now was utterly bare, save for the cobwebs that hung from the ceiling like gray moss. She had known the magick cabinet would be gone, but where were all his other things?

Somewhere safe, of course, somewhere hidden. She paced the perimeter of the room.

Mr. Rafferdy frowned at her. "What are you doing?"

"My father said it was in the chamber behind his study."

"But there aren't any doors in here—only the one window."

He was right. Ivy left the room, stepping back into the corridor. However, her examinations only confirmed what she already knew. The study was at the very end of the corridor; the only way to reach something behind it was to go *through* it. She returned to the study. There had to be a way.

"Mr. Rafferdy, would you lend me your cane, please?"

He gave her a puzzled look, then shrugged and did as she asked. She took the cane and, walking around the edges of the room, rapped the handle against the wall every few inches. Each time the cane made a solid *thump*—until she reached the center of the wall opposite the door. Here, when she tapped the cane, it made an echoing noise.

He gave her a startled look. "Well done, Mrs. Quent. Yet may I ask how we are to get in if there isn't a door?"

"There must be a way to open it," Ivy said, running her hands over the wall, feeling for a latch or crevice. Except that was foolish; she needed to think like a magician. She stepped back.

"Mr. Rafferdy, can you . . . ?" She handed him the cane.

He gripped the silver handle. "I suppose it can't hurt. That is, unless I misspeak the spell. In which case I imagine it might hurt quite a bit. You see, Mr. Bennick told me of an apprentice who once muddled an enchantment so badly he turned himself inside—"

"Mr. Rafferdy," she said gently. "The spell."

"Right." He gripped his cane and pointed it at the wall. "Though you may want to step back just in case."

He drew a breath, then uttered the same words of magick he had when he bound the front gate shut; however, this time he spoke the words in the reverse order. As before, tendrils of blue light coiled up and down the length of the cane. Ivy had the uncomfortable sense that the air in the room rippled like dark water or, rather, that the very space the room occupied was folding in upon itself, as if it were a picture drawn on paper.

The strange sensation ceased. Mr. Rafferdy lowered his cane. "That didn't seem to do anything at all. Perhaps if I speak the spell again—"

Ivy laid a hand against the wall and pushed. There was a *click,* then a section of the wall swung inward.

"Or not," Mr. Rafferdy said, and cleared his throat.

Ivy stepped through the opening. The chamber beyond was not large. One could have lived in the house for years and never known it was there, tucked behind the other room. There was no window, but daylight spilled in through the study.

A heap draped in heavy black cloth stood in the center of the room. Here were his precious objects, she supposed—at least those Mrs. Lockwell had not disposed of. However, marvelous as the things beneath the cloth might be, it was to the walls that Ivy's attention went.

"Repeating oneself is the sign of a dull wit," Mr. Rafferdy said. "Yet I must confess again that I don't see a door."

Neither did she. All the walls in the chamber were blank wood. "It has to be here," she said. "Mr. Rafferdy, may I have your cane again?"

Ivy took the cane and went around the room, tapping against the walls, searching for another door. However, each time the cane struck, it made a solid noise. After going around the room twice without finding anything, she handed the cane back to Mr. Rafferdy.

A thudding sound echoed up from below. They exchanged a startled look, then went back into the study. Mr. Rafferdy looked out the window.

"It appears our guests have arrived for the party," he said.

Ivy joined him at the window. The study was in one of the wings of the house, and from this vantage she could look down into the yard. A chill gripped her. A pair of figures in black cloaks and black hoods stood in front of the house. As she watched, another figure, also clad in black, descended the front step, then two more moved up the path to join the others.

The five black forms arranged themselves in a half circle before the front steps of the house. It was faint, but Ivy could just hear a low chanting. As one, the figures raised their left arms, pointing.

Again a thudding sound echoed up from below, louder this time.

"They're trying to open the door," Mr. Rafferdy said.

Ivy could not take her eyes from the figures below. Blue light flickered around their outstretched hands.

She looked at Mr. Rafferdy. "How long do you think it will hold?"

"I have absolutely no idea."

She wrested herself from the window. "Come on, then."

"Where are we going?"

"To find the door. It has to be somewhere else in the house. Maybe it was moved after he wrote the letter, like the magick cabinet."

"How can you move a door? Take it out of the wall and put it in another? Or do you move the entire wall along with it?"

The idea did seem absurd, but Ivy didn't know what else to think. "It is a thing of magick," she said.

"I suppose it's possible," Mr. Rafferdy said, though a bit dubiously. "But if so, perhaps it's not in the house at all."

She nodded toward the window. "If that was the case, then *they* wouldn't be here."

"Good point." He gripped his cane. "Lead on, then."

They began their search on the uppermost floor, moving from room to room, opening every door great or small. Some led to side chambers, others to closets or cabinets. They rapped on the walls and peered behind pictures and faded tapestries, making sure they missed nothing. As they went, the air in the house dimmed. Outside the windows, clouds gathered in the sky. At last their search brought them back into the upstairs corridor.

"There's nothing up here," Mr. Rafferdy said. "I'm sure we tried every door, and none of them opened onto anything remotely unusual or magickal, unless you count the stork's nest in the one bedroom."

Again a blow struck the front door of the house, rattling the air.

"Down," Ivy said. "We must go down."

They searched the second floor, going from room to room, past empty shelves and furniture draped in shrouds, making sure no door, no matter how small or inconsequential, escaped their attention. Then they went to the first floor, and even down to the basement, but to no avail. There was nothing about any door that might have suggested it was *the one,* the place where they should work the enchantment.

Mr. Rafferdy brushed cobwebs from his coat as they returned to the first floor, to the foot of the staircase. "I'm beginning to think it would be easier to just speak the spell at every door in the house."

"No, there are dozens of them—you would be exhausted before you could finish. Besides, there isn't time."

As if to punctuate this, another *thud* came from behind them. They turned, gazing down the entry hall in time to see the front door of the house shudder in its frame. Lines of blue light, sharp as knives, stabbed through the cracks all around the door. Then the light faded. As it did, the muffled sound of chanting seeped through the door.

"It has to be here," Ivy said. "We must have missed it somehow."

She started up the stairs, running up the steps back to the third floor, Mr. Rafferdy following. Again she moved through all the rooms, running her hands over every wall.

It was no use; they discovered nothing they had not already seen. They came to the top of the stairs again and Ivy started to descend, only then she halted. The will to keep searching drained from her. What hope was there? They had already looked at everything down there.

Sighing, Ivy sat down on the top step. From below came another crash, along with the whine of metal.

"The hinges are breaking," Mr. Rafferdy said. "It won't be long now."

Ivy could only nod. She was beyond words. Her father had been wrong to trust her; she had failed to solve his puzzle in the end.

Mr. Rafferdy sat down on the step beside her. He leaned forward, elbows on his knees. As he did, a spot of gold appeared on the shoulder of his coat. One last ray of light must have filtered in from somewhere to fall upon him.

Ivy frowned. "But that can't be."

"What can't be?"

"That," she said, pointing to the dot of red-gold light on his coat. "The sun must be setting."

"I'm sure it is, but the last time I looked out a window, a storm was coming. The sky has covered with clouds."

"Perhaps it's cleared off."

Ivy held out her hand, catching the spot of light upon it. "No, I don't think so." She stood, turning around. The ray of light was coming from somewhere down the upstairs corridor.

She moved slowly, careful to keep the beam of light upon her hand as she went, following it down the corridor, through the open door of the study. Dust floated on the gray air, and she could see the thin shaft of red-gold light. Hand outstretched, she followed the light across the study, past the secret door Mr. Rafferdy had opened, into the small chamber beyond.

Ivy drew close to the center of the room, the spot of light still upon her palm. It emanated from a small hole in the cloth draping the heap of objects there. Or was it a stack of boxes and chests after all? The chamber was dim now—sunlight no longer beamed in from the study—but as she examined the cloth, she realized what it concealed was rounded, not flat like the top of a crate or an old cabinet.

"Where is the light coming from?" Mr. Rafferdy said.

Ivy gripped a fold of the black cloth and tugged. It fell to the floor with a hiss, and red-gold light flooded the chamber.

It was a perfect sphere of crystal, a thing so large she could not have encircled it using both arms. The crystal orb was suspended within a frame of intricately braided wood that in turn rested upon a wooden stand fashioned of thick, ornately carved columns. The red light emanated from within the sphere, welling out, suffusing the air of the room with crimson.

"It looks rather like an eye," Mr. Rafferdy said behind her, his voice oddly distant-sounding.

He was right. The braided wood wove together, forming a lid from beneath which the orb peered past them with its red gaze. All this time they had been looking for the wrong thing. The door her father had written about in his letter was not some ordinary portal set into a wall. It was this. And in a way it made sense. Were not eyes often described as doorways to the soul?

Fascinated, Ivy peered closer. It seemed there were things within the orb, though it was difficult to see through the haze of ruddy light. She could make out only indistinct shapes. However, she had the impression of a flat, dark landscape receding into a vast distance. Just above the line of the horizon hung a great, livid ball like some impossibly bloated sun.

Ivy leaned closer yet, and a queer feeling came over her: a sensation that the land she saw was not flat at all. Instead, it surged and writhed, like the surface of a furious black sea. Only the sea was not made up of drops of water but of individual motes of darkness, each one moving and struggling, trying to climb its way over the others. Above, dark shapes flitted and lurched across the face of the alien sun.

"No, don't look," Mr. Rafferdy said, pulling her back. "I know he's with *them,* but I think Mr. Bennick's right about this. I don't think it's a good idea to look through that thing."

Ivy held a hand to her temples. Her head throbbed, and she felt ill. A cold sweat had broken out on her skin.

He regarded her with a worried look. "Are you all right?"

"Yes, I'm fine." However, even as she said this, a moment of dizziness came over her. She reached for the wooden stand that held the orb and its frame, gripping it for support.

The crimson light turned green. At once her headache vanished, as did her fear, her weariness. She felt refreshed, as if she had just drunk a cup of cool water. With a gasp she let go of the wooden stand. The air in the room went red again.

"What is it, Mrs. Quent?" His worried expression had been replaced by curiosity. "Something happened just now, didn't it?"

Ivy shook her head. How could she explain it? It seemed impossible, yet there was no mistaking it—the stand that supported the artifact was fashioned from boughs taken from the Wyrdwood. So was the frame that held the crystal sphere. It was no longer alive, but she had felt the echo of life in it, just as she had in Mr. Samonds's bentwood chair. But why would such unusual wood have been used to hold the orb? Surely any sort of lumber would have supported its weight.

"I'm fine," she said. "Really." It was true. She *did* feel fine. Even now she could sense the soothing presence of the wood taken from a grove of ancient forest. She could tell that it had been cut, not picked up as deadfall, yet she could sense no resentment from it. Indeed, she had the feeling it had let itself be taken willingly. . . .

"Now, that's peculiar," Mr. Rafferdy said as he walked around the artifact.

She looked at him. "What is it?"

"Watch it for a moment. Don't gaze into it, but just look at the edges of the crystal. Do you see it now—the way it's moving?"

A bit of the sick feeling sank back into Ivy's stomach. Mr. Rafferdy was right. The motion was subtle but unmistakable; even as she watched, the surface of the sphere expanded inward and outward, growing and shrinking by turns. She started to draw near, to examine the effect closer.

A shadow passed inside the orb, dimming it, and the whole thing shook. The shadow vanished as whatever had cast it moved by, and the artifact settled again upon its stand—though it continued to grow and shrink.

"The spell," she said, turning toward Mr. Rafferdy. "I think you should speak the spell to renew the binding."

He swallowed. "I believe you're right. Give me the paper, then."

She shook her head. "I'm sorry?"

"I said give me the paper."

"What paper?"

"You know, the paper with the spell—your father's letter."

"I don't have it."

He stared at her. "What do you mean you don't have it? Of course you have it."

"You have your own copy of the spell. Surely you took it to Mr. Bennick's."

"No, I was starting to grow afraid he'd discover me looking at it. I left it because I knew you'd bring your father's letter with you."

"But I didn't bring it! It's still at—"

A loud noise echoed up from below, as of something cracking apart. They exchanged wild looks.

"You'll have to speak it from memory."

He took a step back, alarm on his face. "I can't."

"Yes, you can," she said, advancing toward him. "I know you can."

"You're wrong. I don't dare. If I were to make a mistake—"

"You won't. You've spoken every part of the spell over and over."

"Not the last lines. I don't know them by heart—not like you do." He looked at her. "That's it, Mrs. Quent. You know the last phrases of the spell—you can tell them to me."

"No, I can't," she said, despairing. "I can't speak them at all."

"But you could write them down, couldn't you?"

For a moment she stared at him. Then she was running. Ivy dashed from the room, out the study door, and down the corridor. She went from room to room, ripping the cloths from the furniture until, in the third room, she found a desk. A quick search revealed a few sheaves of paper in one drawer and a pen in another, but that wasn't enough. She opened more drawers, rummaging through their contents.

Her fingers closed around a hard object at the back of one of the drawers, and as she pulled it out she felt a spark of triumph: it was an ink bottle. She opened the bottle, dipped the pen, and set its tip to the paper.

It did not leave a mark. She dipped it again, but it was no use. With growing dread she turned the ink bottle over. Nothing came out. It had dried up long ago.

A sound like thunder rattled the house. Only it did not come from the clouds but rather rose up from the first floor.

"Mrs. Quent!" she heard Mr. Rafferdy's voice call out from the corridor. "Where are you?"

"I'm coming!" she called back. "Just a moment."

There was no time to look for more ink. For a second she held her breath, steeling herself. Then with a quick motion she jabbed the nib of the pen into her fingertip.

She had worried it would be hard to draw blood, but her urgency had made her blow more vigorous than intended, and a steady flow of red oozed from her fingertip. Hissing against the pain, she squeezed her finger, directing the trickle of blood into the bottle. Then she dipped the pen and, at a furious pace, began to write.

"Mrs. Quent!" came Mr. Rafferdy's voice again. She concentrated, writing the last few words, making sure they were correct. Then she ran out into the corridor, sucking her wounded finger as she went.

"There you are," he said, looking relieved. He nodded toward the stairs. "I don't know what's happening down there. I don't hear anything anymore."

The house had fallen silent. Perhaps there was still time.

"Here," she said, handing him the paper.

"But this doesn't look like ink. How did you—"

"It doesn't matter," she said, grabbing his elbow. "Hurry—you have to work the enchantment."

Together they ran back down the corridor, into her father's magick room and the chamber beyond. The crystal orb still seemed to expand and contract, an eye opening wider each time it blinked. The crimson light pulsed on the air. Ivy took out the parcel she had purchased from Mr. Mundy and gave it to Mr. Rafferdy. He poured out the various powders, tracing three concentric circles around the artifact, then with a finger drew the prescribed runes.

"I think it's ready," he said, rising.

Ivy examined the runes; as far as she could tell they looked correct. Holding the paper, Mr. Rafferdy faced the orb. His face looked pale in the lurid illumination.

"Now, Mr. Rafferdy," Ivy said, breathless. "Work the enchantment."

"That won't be necessary," said a low voice behind her.

It felt as if she were moving through water. Slowly, Ivy turned around. As she did, a man in a black robe entered the room. Two more came with him. She could see another pair of dark figures through the doorway.

"Mr. Rafferdy, speak the spell!" she cried.

"I wouldn't advise that, Mr. Rafferdy," the magician said, his voice calm and even. "If you speak one word of magick, I assure you that Mrs. Quent will be dead before you can utter a second."

"No, you can't do that," Mr. Rafferdy said. "Magick is for opening and binding things. Your own Mr. Bennick taught me that."

The dark cowl moved as the magician nodded. "Yes, for binding things." He reached out a hand. "What if I were to bind her lungs so that they could not draw a breath? Or her heart so it could not beat?"

Mr. Rafferdy clenched his jaw but said nothing. Despite her fear, an anger rose in Ivy. Who were these men to threaten her so?

"If you take one step nearer, he'll knock it down," she said. "What magick will there be in the orb when it lies in a heap of broken shards? Do it, Mr. Rafferdy. If they come closer, push the stand over."

Beside her, Mr. Rafferdy hefted his cane.

The magician gestured with a hand. "Please, do break the crystal, Mr. Rafferdy. Strike it with your cane, knock it over, and see what comes through. Except you won't see a thing. For the moment you touch it, you'll be dead. The binding on the eye will see to that."

Mr. Rafferdy tightened his grip on the cane. "You're lying."

The black hood tilted to one side. "Am I? Why do you think we've been waiting all these years for the enchantment to weaken? Only we won't have to wait much longer. Even now it is near to opening. When you unlocked the house, you also weakened the binding. For that we owe you our thanks. So you see, Mr. Rafferdy, there's no need to expend your life. The eye will shatter very soon now. And when it does, they will come through."

Mr. Rafferdy scowled. "Who will come through?"

"The Ashen," Ivy said quietly.

The magician nodded to her. "You know much, Mrs. Quent. Yet you know so much less than you think you do. Nor do I have the time or desire to explain it to you. Now, both of you, please stand aside."

Ivy started to protest, but Mr. Rafferdy took her wrist and pulled her back. "We can't," he murmured. "There are too many of them, and they have magick."

Anguish filled her, but he was right. Together the two retreated deeper into the room, to one side of the artifact. The other two came in, and the first three who had entered approached the sphere. As they did, they pushed back their hoods. All were men. Ivy recognized none of them.

"The Eye of Ran-Yahgren," one of them said, a man with a thin nose and a thin, sharp mouth. "God in Eternum, it's real."

"Of course it's real," the first magician said, a note of disgust in his deep voice. He was dark-haired and his countenance stern, even lordly. "And its existence has nothing to do with God—at least not the God to whom the priests in St. Galmuth's mumble worthless prayers. It is a far older deity who should be thanked for this wonder."

"It's beautiful," said the third magician, a man who looked little older than Mr. Rafferdy. He approached the orb, and the crimson light bathed his face. "I can see something inside!" he exclaimed.

He bent closer, peering into the crystal sphere. Ivy started to say something, but Mr. Rafferdy squeezed her wrist, and she bit her tongue. The dark-haired man exchanged a look with the thin-nosed one, but neither of them said anything.

"It's huge," the young magician said, his face close to the artifact. "The sun looks so huge there, and the land—I can't even see it. It's covered with—but it's them, of course. It has to be. I can see them moving past one another, over one another. There are thousands upon thousands of them. How can they survive? What do they possibly consume for nourishment? Unless it is—wait, there is one nearby. I think one of them can see me. I believe it's moving closer." He lifted a hand. "Yes, it's coming this way. It's almost—"

As once before, a shadow filled the orb, as if something had drawn closer to its inner surface. At the same moment the young magician screamed. It was a shrill sound. His hands curled back from the artifact, clawing at his face, his eyes.

"It saw me!" he shrieked. "No, it saw *inside* me, and there was nothing there!"

He staggered back, his hands still scrabbling at his face. To Ivy's horror, she saw blood oozing from between his fingers. The other magicians reached for him, but he twisted his way past them.

"There was nothing!" he shouted again. Then his cry became a wordless scream. He ran out of the room, through the chamber beyond, and into the corridor. A moment later there came a thudding noise, and the screaming ceased.

Ivy watched as one of the magicians left the chamber. He returned a minute later, leaning his hooded head toward the dark-haired man.

"His neck was broken," the magician said. "He fell down the stairs."

"More likely he threw himself down," the dark-haired man said with what seemed the trace of a smile. "It's just as we were promised. Their power is great indeed."

The other man licked his thin lips. "Are you certain we—that is, surely they would not harm *us*?"

"On the contrary," the dark-haired man said. "They would eat you from the inside out until you were nothing more than a husk, one they could climb inside and do with what they wished—but only if we were to allow it. All we have to do is call the circle of power, and any that come through when the enchantment is broken will be bound to us as slaves. Then we will put a new binding on the eye—one we can open and close as we wish. We will not be denied our servants this time." He cast a sharp look at Ivy. "Not as we were once before."

The magician walked around the artifact. "How good of you to draw the circle of power for us, Mr. Rafferdy. You've made our task easy indeed. I have only to correct a few of the runes you drew improperly . . ." He knelt, tracing a hand through the powder on the floor. "There, it is ready."

"What should we do about them?" the thin-nosed one said, pointing to Ivy and Mr. Rafferdy.

"Bind him. He's a magician."

"Are you fools?" Mr. Rafferdy said, stepping in front of Ivy. "That man was one of your own. You saw what just looking through that thing did to him. It's madness to open it. You have—"

Several of the magicians raised their hands and spoke guttural words. At the same moment Mr. Rafferdy ceased moving, his body going rigid. His eyes stared blindly. Ivy let out a cry and touched his arm. It was as hard as stone. She studied him and after a moment could detect that he was breathing. Only the breaths were so slow, so shallow.

She looked up, glaring at the magicians. To her eyes, the ruby light in the room was tinged with emerald.

"What of her?" the man with the thin nose said.

The dark-haired one shrugged. "What can a woman do against us?"

The other nodded. Then the four remaining magicians arranged themselves in front of the crystal sphere, and washed in its impossible light they began to chant in a language older than mankind itself. The symbol drawn on the floor glowed blue. On the stand the artifact shuddered and swelled—a red eye gazing in a baleful stare.

A green veil seemed to descend over Ivy's vision. She let go of Mr. Rafferdy's motionless arm and stood straight. Fear departed her. Who were these men to presume that they could undo what her father had given so much—the very essence of himself—to achieve? She did not know what the place she could see through the orb was or what the things there were. All she knew was that if these magicians—these *men*—wanted something, then it could not be allowed.

*What can a woman do against us?* their leader had said.

Ivy took a step toward the artifact. Jagged lines of blue light snaked across the surface of the sphere like cracks. Enrapt in their spell, the men did not seem to see her. Her lips curved into a smile, and she took another step closer. Yes, she would show them what a woman could do.

Ivy shut her eyes. *Grow,* she said silently. *Grow wild once more.*

The sound of chanting ceased, replaced by muffled cries and choking sounds. Ivy opened her eyes.

It had happened even more quickly than she had thought. The legs of the wooden stand twisted and thickened, sinking roots into the floorboards. At the same time, green tendrils rose up out of the floor, tangling around the feet of the magicians, coiling up their bodies, around their arms, their necks, into their mouths. The men gagged, struggling and reeling.

"Grow," Ivy spoke the word aloud this time.

The Wyrdwood listened. The tendrils thickened into stout cords, binding the men so they could not move, could not speak. The braided frame holding the sphere rippled like a mass of brown serpents. Ivy could sense the tendrils weaving together, pulling the surface of the orb inward, preventing it from expanding. Inside the crystal, furious shadows writhed.

Ivy moved forward. Branches draped from the ceiling, caressing her gently as she went. She stopped in front of the dark-haired magician. His lips curled back from his teeth in pain and disgust, and his face had gone a dusky color. He spoke a word, and though there was no breath or sound to it, she knew all the same what it was he said.

*Witch.*

She looked up at him. "You seek to know what is beyond the doorway. Why don't you look, then? All of you."

The magicians struggled, but they could not resist as the cords bent and straightened, dragging them toward the artifact. Vines pulled back their hoods and held their heads, forcing their gazes toward the opening. When they tried to shut their eyes, small tendrils forced their lids back open, so that they had no choice but to look as their faces were bent nearer to the orb, and nearer yet.

One of them screamed. Another followed suit, and another, letting out wordless sounds of despair. The last was the dark-haired man. Now that he was forced to look, he seemed to do so eagerly, drinking in the sights through the crimson eye. For a moment an expression of wonder crossed his face.

"By God, they are glorious," he said.

Then his jaw yawned wide, and he was screaming like the others, over and over until red trickled from the corners of his mouth.

At last, one by one, the magicians fell silent. They stared mutely now, their faces slack, their eyes devoid of any thought, any feeling. A weariness came over Ivy, and she staggered back from the artifact. With a whisper the branches fell away from the men, uncoiling, sinking back into the floor, retreating into the ceiling. The wooden stand shrank back upon itself, so that in moments it looked as it had before. On the floor the magickal circle faded, then went dark. At the same time Mr. Rafferdy drew in a shuddering breath. He stood up straight and raised his cane before him.

"—to see that it is folly to open it!" he cried. Then he blinked, taking a staggering step forward.

The magicians continued to stand before the artifact, staring, their faces as pale and blank as masks. However, the surface of the crystal orb was moving again, expanding outward as dark things swarmed within. The red glow pulsed on the air.

He looked at her, astonishment on his face. "I have no idea what just happened."

Ivy leaned against the wall. She was tired, so tired. All the same, a warmth filled her, a feeling of fulfillment such as she had never known. She looked up at him and smiled.

"Mr. Rafferdy," she said. "I believe you should speak the spell now."

## CHAPTER TWENTY-EIGHT

𝕿HE CROWD BEFORE Barrowgate was larger than usual that morning. But then, it was not every day that a notorious highwayman met his fate.

Everyone had read the stories in the broadsheets: how the villain had planned to murder a magnate who was known to be an important servant of the Crown; how an unknown patriot had somehow discovered the plot and informed the magnate of the plans; and how, when the highwayman and his compatriots attempted the crime, they found a troop of the king's redcrests lying in wait for them.

Several of the traitors were shot dead in the battle that ensued, but three were caught and hauled to jail, including the highwayman himself—the very same fellow who last month had brutally murdered a guard while escaping from Barrowgate. The trial had been swift and the judgment final. None would be escaping this time. All three were to hang.

Eldyn moved through the crowd, seeking a clearer view of the gallows that had been erected in the square before the black stones of Barrowgate. He passed jugglers and musicians and men hawking ale and sweets. People danced and laughed. It looked like a festival.

Indeed, it was a sort of celebration, was it not? No matter that, until a few days ago, the exploits of the highwayman in question had been glorified in *The Fox* and other broadsheets favored by simpler folk. However, there was one thing people loved more than raising a hero up for his daring successes, and that was casting him down for his public failures. That the people who once drank to his name were the same people who now clapped and jeered and threw taunts at the gallows, Eldyn had no doubt.

Nor did the thought trouble him as it once had. He had once worried about the wisdom of the common folk—that, if given the chance to choose for their country, the people of Altania could not be trusted to choose well. Yet as he pressed through the throng and felt the glee, the outrage, the desire, he knew he had been wrong.

It was not for their wisdom that crowds were important. The people were not the head of Altania but rather its heart. It was their task to feel in a way that Assembly and the Crown could not: to laugh, to want, to lash out in anger or fear without reason or warning. A man might use logic to try to decide what was best, but without feeling—without craving or dread or revulsion—how was he to truly know what to do or feel pleased when it was done? Tomorrow it might be something else they wanted, but today the crowd wanted death.

And they would have it.

A roar went up in the square. The iron door had opened, and three men were led out, their hands and wrists in shackles. Two of them hung their heads as they went, but the third stood tall, a smile on his handsome face, his gold hair shining in the morning sun. He raised up his bound hands as if in a gesture of victory.

Hisses and cries of *murderer!* sounded all around. Someone threw a rotten cabbage, and it struck the tall man in the face. After that he lowered his arms, and he did not smile as the guards led him and the others up the steps of the scaffold.

Eldyn slipped between two groups of men and reached the front of the crowd, just below the gallows. The last time he saw Westen, the highwayman had looked at ease and assured. Now, despite his earlier display of bravado, he no longer appeared so confident as the hangman slipped the noose over his neck. There was a light of fear in his tawny eyes. All the same, he kept a proud face, his shoulders back and his head up.

After leaving the highwayman that day, Eldyn had written a letter to Rafferdy, explaining the danger to Lord Rafferdy and Mr. Quent and giving all the particulars of the highwayman's plan. He had signed it only, *A friend.* He knew the letter might be greeted with some suspicion but also that it could not be ignored and that Lord Rafferdy would see to it there were soldiers at the ready.

Thus it was that Lord Rafferdy and Mr. Quent were delivered to the exact place, at the precise time, that "Sashie" had promised to Westen. And thus it was, when the highwayman and his compatriots prowled from the shadows (though in some accounts it was dogs who were with Westen, not men), guns fired, and the soldiers fell upon them. According to the stories in the broadsheets, the battle lasted only a few moments, and neither Lord Rafferdy nor Mr. Quent was injured in any way.

An energy moved through the crowd. Atop the platform, the nooses had been tightened around all three necks. The moment had almost come. Nearby, Eldyn saw a cart selling sweets. He went to it and bought a treacle tart. On the gallows, the hangman began putting hoods over the heads of the prisoners.

"Nothing stops today!" the highwayman called out, his voice rising over that of the crowd. "It cannot be stopped. The wind changes, and a storm comes. When it does, Altania will rise! Altania will—"

Catcalls and jeers drowned out his voice. His face went red as he tried to shout over the noise, but it was no use. Then the hangman came and put a black sack over his head.

Yes, a storm did come, Eldyn thought, but right now the sun was warm and the sky a flawless blue. Later he would head to St. Galmuth's and meet Sashie. Since their ordeal, she had taken to going there every day to offer a prayer. She had been very sweet to him of late, plying him with frequent kisses on the cheek and always bringing him a cup of wine when he returned to the inn after a day of work at his new clerking position.

His sister had mentioned Westen only once since the night they fled from Lowpark.

"I thought his words meant more because they were whispered," she said one day as they walked along the Promenade in their finest clothes. "And that his gifts, because they were secret, were all the more precious. However, I know now that real love does not come in shadows. It shows itself every day, in bright light for all to see."

She had taken his hand in her own then, and as they walked through the greatday afternoon, he could not remember a time he had thought her so pretty or himself so blessed as a brother.

Today was his free day, so after going to St. Galmuth's, he would seek out Dercy. There was time for a drink before tonight's performance, and Dercy had promised to teach him some new tricks. However, there was no hurry. It looked as if the hangman had been bribed, for he had tied the ropes short. There would be no quick deaths today; the people would not be denied their entertainment.

Eldyn took a bite of the treacle tart. It was sweet and good. And when the hangman pulled the lever, he cheered along with the rest of the crowd.

⟡

THE PARLOR AT Lady Marsdel's house on Fairhall Street was pleasantly quiet as its usual denizens amused themselves in their customary manner. Mr. Baydon read through the latest issue of *The Comet* while Lord Baydon sat on the sofa, hands resting on the expanse of his waistcoat, snoring softly. Nearby, Lady Marsdel fanned herself along with the bit of white fluff that served as her dog, for the afternoon had grown sultry. At the table, Mr. Rafferdy helped Mrs. Baydon fit together a puzzle.

Not that he was being of much assistance, she informed him at frequent intervals. Why, now that he was a magician, he could not simply work a spell to find the most confounding piece she was missing, she did not know. She could only imagine he enjoyed making it difficult for her.

"Isn't that the point of a puzzle?" he asked her. "I thought it was supposed to be difficult."

"Really, Mr. Rafferdy, for a clever man you seem to have a difficult time grasping the simplest things. One only wants puzzles to be difficult after they're finished. That way one can feel proud of one's accomplishment. However, while we're in the act of doing them, it's preferred that they are easy."

He could not help smiling. "I believe that the most difficult puzzle in the room is yourself, Mrs. Baydon." Then he picked up a piece and set it in place, much to her delight.

"I see you're still wearing that awful ring," she observed. "Though I suppose you have to if you're going to be a magician. Still, it's quite hideous. How unbearable it must be for you to wear so unfashionable a thing! Everyone must stare."

Rafferdy lifted his right hand. The gem set into the ring sparked with blue fire, but it was only the sunlight glinting off the facets of the stone. "To tell you the truth, I don't really care what others think of it," he said. "I've rather grown to like it."

Mrs. Baydon looked at him.

"Now it's you who's staring," he said. "Do I have a bit of jam on my face or something?"

"You really have changed, Mr. Rafferdy," she said. "And it's not just when you're wearing that new solemn look of yours. It's the air about you. I suppose we'll all have to start taking you seriously now."

"Please don't," he said emphatically. "If you do, I'll have to find others who will see me for the silly, worthless son of a lord that I am."

"Every man has worth, Mr. Rafferdy. The only question is, how much?" With that she directed her attention back to the puzzle.

Rafferdy opened his mouth to utter a smart rejoinder; however, none came to him. He picked up a piece of the puzzle and turned it over and over in his fingers. The ring on his right hand shimmered as he did, and the thought came to him: *She would say you have worth.* Nor was it Mrs. Baydon this thought concerned.

The moment was still vivid in his mind: the thrum of the ancient words of magick as he spoke them, the sapphire light that welled up from the circle of power to encapsulate the crystal orb, and the feeling on the air as if lightning were about to strike. He had always believed that power was the last thing in the world he desired. However, as he spoke the spell, he had wanted nothing more than to feel his own will at work.

And it *had* worked. By the time the blue light faded, the sphere no longer expanded like a widening eye. Instead, it had shrunk in on itself and had gone dark. The only light within it was a single dim spark of crimson. The binding had been renewed.

So the spell had worked, but why had he been given the opportunity to speak it at all? The magicians had entered the room, they had bound him so that he could not move, could not see or hear. Then the next thing he knew Ivy was calling to him, and the magicians had stood before the artifact, their eyes, their expressions, empty.

He could not help a shudder as he recalled the looks on their faces. It was clear they had gazed through the eye and that their minds—indeed, their very souls—were gone. But why? They had seen what happened to the one who looked through earlier; surely they had known not to repeat his folly.

Mrs. Quent had said only that they had been forced to gaze into the eye. How, he did not know. Perhaps, as the binding upon it weakened, it was the artifact itself that had drawn their gazes against their will. One thing he did know was that, whatever its origin and nature, the eye was a thing of unsurpassed evil. Mr. Lockwell had understood. That was why he had sacrificed himself to keep other members from the Vigilant Order of the Silver Eye from opening it.

What would *he* have sacrificed to prevent its opening? Rafferdy hadn't been forced to answer that question, a fact for which he was glad. Nor would he have to answer it in the foreseeable future. The binding on the artifact had been restored, and none of the magicians would ever come again to try to open it, for they were all up at Madstone's now.

Yet they were not the only ones who knew about the Eye of Ran-Yahgren.

What had become of Mr. Bennick, they did not know. They had not seen him at the house on Durrow Street after working the spell, and he had not shown himself at Lady Marsdel's since that day. Perhaps he had returned to his manor in Torland. Even if he remained in the city, there was nothing he could do to open the doorway himself. He was not a magician.

Yet whether or not he could do magick, there was no doubt he was still a dangerous man. Mr. Quent's letter had made that clear. And while it was only a feeling, Rafferdy could not dismiss the idea that he would see Mr. Bennick again one day. Indeed, he counted upon it.

*And I'll have learned more by then,* he thought, twisting the ring on his right hand. *Much more . . .*

"You look very determined all of a sudden," Mrs. Baydon said. "Are you scheming something, Mr. Rafferdy?"

"Only whether to buy a new coat before a new hat, or the other way around."

With that he rose, called for his cane, and begged his leave of Lady Marsdel. This was granted, if grudgingly, and he went out into the bright afternoon.

He had promised to dine with his father that night, for Lord Rafferdy was still in the city. Although the lumenal was not long, he still had several hours to waste, so he walked along the Promenade, past gardens of flowers and groups of young women, all similarly clad in color. However, none of them caught his eye.

Lord Rafferdy had not told him why he thought the rebels had been plotting against him. When the anonymous letter arrived at Warwent Square, Rafferdy had thought it some sort of prank, but there was something about the urgency with which it was written that had caused him to show it to his father, and Lord Rafferdy had taken it seriously.

Which was fortunate. As it turned out, there had indeed been an attack planned against Lord Rafferdy upon Mr. Quent's return to Invarel. However, the king's men had been ready, and the rebels had been apprehended. Rafferdy could only believe the threat against his father had passed.

Yet why had those men sought to harm him in the first place? Rafferdy had never wanted to know the nature of his father's business, had studiously avoided it. Since the thwarted attack, however, he could not help wondering exactly what sort of work it was that his father did for the Crown, with which Mr. Quent assisted him.

*The lord inquirer.* That was the person Mrs. Quent had come to the Silver Branch to meet that day—the person who had been none other than Lord Rafferdy himself. Of what sort of things was he an inquirer? Was it for these inquiries that the rebels had wished to do away with him? Perhaps tonight, if his father spoke again of duties and responsibilities, Rafferdy would not be so quick to change the subject.

He looked up as a cart rattled by, and he realized he was no longer in the New Quarter but instead walked through the narrow ways of the Old City. Perhaps he should go to the Sword and Leaf and see if Eldyn Garritt was there. It would be good to meet with his old friend, to have a drink, and to laugh a bit.

However, as he turned a corner onto a broader way, he realized it was not in search of his friend Garritt that his feet had unwittingly brought him here. Just ahead was an iron fence and high hedges of green. It was Durrow Street he walked down now, and not twenty paces away was a wrought-iron gate.

At that moment a black carriage came to a halt before the gate. Rafferdy ducked into the cover of a doorway, then peered back out. A man exited the carriage. He was neither tall nor handsome and wore a brown suit that could only generously be described as old-fashioned. His shoulders were thick and rather slumped, and behind a coarse beard his face was grim—though, Rafferdy thought, not unkind.

Indeed, as he reached into the coach to help another, lither figure exit, that beard parted in a smile, and he looked younger than he had a moment before. The object of his attention smiled in return, a very pretty expression and one that Rafferdy, not so long ago, would have given much to have received for his own.

The young woman stepped into the street, the skirt of her green dress swirling around her like leaves. She started to accompany the bearded man toward the gate, only then she paused, looking over her shoulder in the direction where Rafferdy stood. He shrank back into the alcove, counting twenty heartbeats. Then he peered around the corner again.

The carriage was gone, the street empty.

He stood there for a minute, looking at the closed gate. At last he took a breath and made his way back down the street. It wasn't far to the Sword and Leaf, and he still had several hours before it was time to meet his father. He might as well go to the tavern. And who knew? That rascal Eldyn Garritt might even show up while he was there.

"If he does, it's his turn to buy the punch," he said aloud.

This thought cheered Rafferdy greatly. He gave his cane a toss, caught it in his hand, then went to get himself a drink.

🦋

⨎HE LUMENAL HAD ended long ago, but twilight lingered for hours, and the night was only just begun.

Usually Ivy felt a feeling of oppression when the almanac told her it was to be a long umbral: an irrational but nevertheless persuasive dread that the night would never end, that *day* was only a fantasy she had made up, a notion conjured from imagination and books, and that all there ever had been and ever would be was darkness. However, she did not feel that way tonight. As far as Ivy was concerned, a greatnight could not possibly have hours enough.

Then again, it wouldn't matter how long the night was if he did not cease working at his business.

"So you think me terribly dull, do you, then, Mrs. Quent?"

Ivy blinked, sitting up in her chair. "What in the world do you mean? I think no such thing."

"Is that the case? Then why did you yawn so prodigiously just now?"

She put a hand to her mouth, realizing it was so.

He tapped his pen against the ink bottle and wrote another line on the parchment before him. "Indeed, considering the evidence, you must have concluded I am dull to an exceeding degree. How could you not? For here before you is a man who has not seen his new wife in over a month—and she is a very charming wife, it should be noted. Now night has finally come, yet he continues to sit at his desk writing letters."

"I'm sure they are very important letters."

"They are. But to a young wife they should seem only to be tedious things, pointless and utterly silly."

She laughed. "I am sure nothing *you* do is silly, Mr. Quent."

He looked up, displaying a sudden grin. With his hair and beard being somewhat in need of trimming, he looked suddenly quite wild, like a faun from a Tharosian play, scheming mischief. She had never seen him like this. All her affections, which had filled her upon his return to the city, were renewed even more strongly, and warmly, than before.

"Perhaps I can prove you wrong, Mrs. Quent," he said. "But first—" He sighed. "First I must continue to be dull and finish one last missive."

She rose from her chair. "In that case, I will go say good night to my sisters. If I desire some silliness, I am certain at least one of them will be able to comply."

However, he had already bent back over the desk. Her smile faded, and for a moment she could not help being reminded of how his work had so often taken him away from Heathcrest, leaving her alone. Ivy left the room, quietly shutting the door behind her.

They had taken the uppermost rooms at the Seventh Swan, an inn not far from the Halls of Assembly. It was a fine establishment—perhaps overly fine, Ivy thought, given that some of the other guests were from the families of magnates. Nor did she think Lily and Rose required their own rooms. But Mr. Quent had insisted. He said that since both were ladies grown, they each deserved a private chamber.

Ivy thought Mr. Quent was under the mistaken impression that Lily was older than sixteen (having just had her birthday). However, she reconsidered when this announcement won him a great amount of admiration on Lily's part and even an enthusiastic kiss on his bearded cheek. For her part, Rose was astonished beyond words, but her beaming smile spoke clearly.

"You are not so unfamiliar with the manners of young women as you would have others believe," Ivy told him. "If it was your intention to win their affections, you've certainly succeeded."

"I trust if I gain their affection, it will be through deeds that are more deserving than merely spoiling them with their own rooms."

Yet he had seemed pleased and could not hide his own smile.

Now, leaving the chamber she shared with Mr. Quent, Ivy went first to Lily's room. Upon entering, she found her sister surrounded by candles, a book upon her knees. Lily hardly glanced up from the book when Ivy spoke—for, she said rather breathlessly, the footman had just been revealed as Baron Valandry's long-lost son, which meant the contessa could marry him after all. Ivy told her good night and started to blow out one of the candles, only then she smiled and left it burning instead.

She went to Rose's room next, knocking softly, and when there was no answer she took the liberty of entering. Rose lay on the bed, still in her frock, curled up with Miss Mew. Both of them were fast asleep. The excitement of these last few days must have finally taken its toll.

Quietly, Ivy moved to the bed. She scratched Miss Mew behind the ears, and the cat let out a great yawn. Then Ivy looked down at Rose; her sister's face was soft and peaceful with sleep. Ivy wondered—how many times had she awakened to see Rose gazing down at her? Only this time it was Ivy who kept watch in the night.

"Do not fear, dearest," she said softly. "He will take care of us all. I promise you that."

Rose did not stir, but her lips curved slightly. Ivy laid a blanket over her, then left the room, shutting the door without a sound.

While the inn was a comfortable place—and certainly preferable to dwelling under one roof with Mr. Wyble—she would be glad when the four of them could leave it. They had gone to the old house on Durrow Street earlier that day to make a survey of it. Mr. Quent had said that it looked to be in solid condition, and while some work would be necessary to reopen the house, it would not be long before they were able to move. Ivy looked forward to that day, and the only thing that would make it more joyous was if it was not four of them who went to live on Durrow Street but five.

However, if that would be the case she did not know. It had been more difficult than she had thought for Lord Rafferdy to arrange her father's release from the Madderly–Stoneworth Hostel. It seemed the hostel operated under a charter that gave it considerable autonomy. Only an order with the king's own seal would free Mr. Lockwell.

While she had every confidence the order would come, it would take time. Until then, Lord Rafferdy had been able to assure that her father would be kept in a private room and made comfortable and that Ivy would be able to spend time with him on her weekly visits there.

As for the malady that afflicted him—she had once believed that the magicians who knew him years ago would be able to help him if she could only find them. She knew now that was not the case. Nor had entering the house helped her understand how to cure him. All the same, she *had* learned something in the house, for she knew now the cause of his affliction. Was not comprehending an illness the first step to curing it? That thought gave her a hope that, however slim, was hope nonetheless.

While she still held faith that Mr. Lockwell would one day be cured, she felt no such belief or concern for the other magicians of his order. Who had come to the house on Durrow Street to retrieve them all, she did not know—more from the order, she supposed. Or even Mr. Bennick. Whoever it was, the four of them who yet lived were up at Madstone's now.

Nor did she feel remorse for what had happened to them. They had been given a glimpse of what they desired. Perhaps the result would discourage any other members of the Vigilant Order of the Silver Eye who thought to try to open the doorway.

Not that she feared any of them could do such a thing. Mr. Rafferdy had renewed the enchantment, binding it. He truly was a magician. How her heart soared for him each time she considered it!

Besides, the house was well guarded. She had seen the man in the black mask briefly earlier that day, as she walked among the hawthorn trees in the yard of the house.

*I am watching,* he had said to her.

*My father,* she had replied. *Can you help him?*

But by the time she spoke he was already gone. All the same, she knew she would see him again one day. It was not chance that he had appeared to her.

Just as it had not been chance that the frame that held the Eye of Ran-Yahgren was fashioned of branches from the Wyrdwood. There was a power in the wood—a property that had allowed it to resist the magick of the artifact. What it was, how it worked, she did not know, but it was there; she had seen it, had felt it. And there in the yard, as she touched the twisted hawthorn branches, a thought had occurred to her—if the Wyrdwood could resist the power of the doorway, might it help her father resist his affliction? She had plucked several twigs and put them in her pocket, not sure what she intended to do with them, but it felt good to have them close.

Ivy paused outside the door of the chamber she shared with Mr. Quent, wondering if he had finished his work yet. To her right was a small window that looked out over the street. A flash of red caught her eye, and she gazed out the window. Above the towers of the Citadel, the new planet shone in the sky: a dull crimson spark. As she studied the recently returned wanderer, a strange idea came to her. The light coming through the crystal sphere had been that same ruddy color, hadn't it?

Shivering, she opened the door and entered the room.

He was no longer working. Instead, he sat in a chair, a book open on his lap. However, he was not reading but instead gazed into the shadows in the corner. She watched him for a minute. His face was grim, as on that very first day she had seen him.

Ivy could not deny that, in addition to joy, she had felt some trepidation prior to her new husband's arrival in the city. The distance from the country, and the intervening time, had given her space to wonder just which man would step out of the carriage—her dear, gruff Mr. Quent, or the stern master of Heathcrest Hall?

But they were both one and the same, she knew now. If his work called him away at times, which it surely would, then it was not for herself she would worry. For her task, to await his return, could be nothing compared to what he must face. And if, by being cheerful when he was with her, she could raise his spirits, then it would give him all the more strength to do what he must when it came time.

Again affection welled up inside Ivy, but it was a deeper sensation than any she had felt before, at once more fierce and more determined. As she watched him there, sitting in the dimness, she knew that her only wish in all the world was to be a light by his side.

"You seem thoughtful tonight," she said at last.

He turned his head, then smiled. "I didn't hear you come in." He rose from the chair. "Are your sisters well?"

"Very well," she said, and went to him.

He had taken off his coat and rolled up the sleeves of his shirt. She looped her arm around his and leaned her head on the slope of his shoulder. She heard him—felt him—sigh.

"Is something wrong?" She looked up at him. "I thought you said everything went well in Torland, that it had been more difficult than you thought but that in the end you had succeeded."

"We did succeed," he said. "We did." But the grimness had returned to his expression.

"Will you tell me what happened there?"

"I will, but let us not speak of it in the dark of a long night. Tomorrow will be soon enough." Suddenly he smiled, and he looked a bit like that wild faun again. "I would rather we pour some wine and speak of other things, for I've finished my work for the night."

"On the contrary, Mr. Quent," she said with a laugh, "I believe it's only just begun."

And taking his hands in hers, she proceeded to work a spell as ancient as humanity itself.

THE LONG NIGHT was nearly over.

The inn was quiet as Ivy slipped from the bed and dressed. Mr. Quent slept deeply, and a quick look into the rooms of her sisters revealed they were asleep as well. Outside, the sky blushed with the first hint of dawn. It would be an hour or more before people rose for the day. However, Ivy could not sleep. Her heart was too light to lie down any longer. She wanted to rise, to move.

As mornings after a long night were always cool, she wrapped a shawl around her shoulders and went outside. For the next hour she walked past imposing edifices and dewy gardens. It reminded her of the walks she used to take around Heathcrest Hall, when the misty weather allowed, and she murmured a pleasant, wordless song as she went.

At last, in a blaze of fire, the sun lifted above the rooftops. The others would be rising soon and wonder where she was. She turned and made her way back to the inn.

She was just outside the inn's door when a boy went running by, a stack of broadsheets in his arms.

"News!" he cried. "Get the news from Torland!"

"Excuse me," Ivy said, stopping him. She didn't usually read the broadsheets, but the word *Torland* had caught her ear. "What news is there from the west?"

"A penny, ma'am," the boy said.

She found a coin in her pocket and took one of the papers.

"The old tales are true!" the boy shouted, running on. "Read about it in the news!"

As Ivy lifted the broadsheet, a morning wind sprang up, and it took her a moment to unfold it so she could read the words printed in large letters at the top of the front page.

A thrill passed through her, and whether it was dread or some other feeling, she could not say. RISINGS IN TORLAND, declared the headline in bold type. And below that, *Stands of Wyrdwood Rise Up, First Time in Centuries, Dozens Slain.*

Except the story was wrong. It wasn't the first time in centuries, nor could she believe it would be the last. And this time it wasn't a secret. This time, all of Altania would know.

Another gust of wind snatched the broadsheet from Ivy's hand, and the pages scattered, flapping down the street like a flock of crows.

ABOUT THE AUTHOR

What if there was a fantastical cause underlying the social constraints and limited choices confronting a heroine in a novel by Jane Austen or Charlotte Brontë? GALEN BECKETT began writing *The Magicians and Mrs. Quent* to answer that question. The author lives in Colorado and is currently at work on the next chapter in this fabulous tale of witches, magicians, and revolution, *The House on Durrow Street*.

And be sure not to miss Ivy's continuing adventures in

## THE HOUSE ON DURROW STREET

by

### Galen Beckett

Life is finally looking up for Miss Ivy Lockwell—now Mrs. Quent.
The magicians of the Vigilant Order of the Silver-Eye have all gone
mad or perished. The threat against her world seems to have abated.
And her beloved Mr. Quent has at last received the recognition he deserves for his part in preventing the magickal uprising.

Now Ivy wants only to make a happy life for her family at the house
on Durrow Street once owned by her father. However, as the pretty
young wife of a national hero, she finds herself an object of curiosity
among the fashionable. Befriended by a famous viscountess, Ivy finds
herself whisked up into the highest circles of society. While she never
aspired to such heights, neither is she entirely reluctant to explore
them.

But while the wealthy dance in candlelit ballrooms, something stirs in
the darkness just beyond the edge of light. There are other magicians,
the man in the black mask warns Ivy, and other doors. As the winds of
revolution blow and spy-hunters abound, Ivy must fight to protect the
two men she holds dearest: her husband, fallen under a cloud of suspicion when his methods come into question; and Mr. Rafferdy, member of a banned magickal order and the only one who can help Ivy
unlock the mysteries of her father's house.

For somewhere in the old house on Durrow Street lies the key to de-
feating the ancient, ravenous beings known as the Ashen—or the door
that will allow them to enter the world. . . .

Coming in Fall 2010 from Spectra